PENGUIN BOOKS

LABYRINTH

Taylor Branch is a former Washington columnist for *Esquire* and *Harper's* and the author of three books, the most recent being his best-selling collaboration with Bill Russell, *Second Wind*, and the novel *The Empire Blues*.

Eugene M. Propper, formerly an Assistant U.S. Attorney for the District of Columbia, now is a member of the law firm of Lane and Edson in Washington, D.C.

LABY

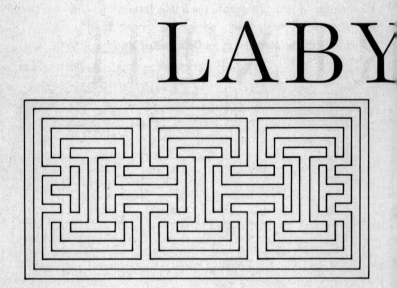

PENGUIN BOOKS

RINTH

TAYLOR BRANCH AND
EUGENE M. PROPPER

Penguin Books Ltd, Harmondsworth,
Middlesex, England
Penguin Books, 625 Madison Avenue,
New York, New York 10022, U.S.A.
Penguin Books Australia Ltd, Ringwood,
Victoria, Australia
Penguin Books Canada Limited, 2801 John Street,
Markham, Ontario, Canada L3R 1B4
Penguin Books (N.Z.) Ltd, 182–190 Wairau Road,
Auckland 10, New Zealand

First published in the United States of America by
The Viking Press 1982
Published in Penguin Books 1983

LIBRARY OF CONGRESS CATALOGING IN PUBLICATION DATA
Branch, Taylor,
Labyrinth.
Includes index.
1. Letelier, Orlando—Assassination. 2. Assassination—Washington (D.C.).
3. Townley, Michael Vernon. 4. Chile—Foreign relations—United States.
5. United States—Foreign relations—Chile.
I. Propper, Eugene M. II. Title.
F3101.L47B73   1983   364.1′524′0924   82-19112
ISBN 0 14 00.6683 7

Printed in the United States of America by
R.R. Donnelley & Sons Company, Harrisonburg, Virginia
Set in Video Century Expanded

For Christy and our daughter Macy

T.B.

For my parents

E.M.P.

AUTHORS' NOTES

During my career as Assistant United States Attorney, I investigated and prosecuted scores of cases, but none was as intriguing or professionally challenging—and none involved me as deeply on a personal basis—as the car-bombing murders of former Chilean Ambassador Orlando Letelier and his American aide Ronni Moffitt.

The brutality of the crime itself would have motivated me or any other prosecutor to go to extraordinary lengths to solve it. But a politically motivated bombing in the nation's capital involves more than the lives of the victims. It is also a crime against the United States and its citizens, because it strikes a blow against our country's commitment to maintain an open and safe capital for people with different values and political beliefs. All the investigators working on the case felt a strong desire to make terrorists aware that the United States will not tolerate such acts.

The Letelier case would not have been solved without the ingenuity and tireless dedication of FBI Special Agents L. Carter Cornick, Robert W. Scherrer, and Larry Wack. They, and I, were also fortunate in having the help of Ambassador George W. Landau, without whose diligence and active participation all other efforts would have gone for nothing. No one cared more about the case or worked more diligently on it than Assistant United States Attorney E. Lawrence Barcella, Jr., and the cause of justice was served by many others whose names appear in the book.

As prosecutor on the case from the day the murders occurred, I had a unique opportunity to work with all these people—to be an active participant in the investigation as well as in the prosecution. I worked on the Letelier investigation for more than two and a half years. When my official duties ended in July of 1979, I realized that I had gained an unusual perspective on the way the United States responds to terrorism. When terrorists are directed by a foreign government and operate on territory where the United States has no authority, their deeds are extremely difficult to investigate—especially if the foreign government is itself a potential suspect.

I believed then, and still believe, that the public interest would be served by telling the story of our investigation so that readers could see in detail how terrorism works and what investigators can and cannot do in such cases. There is no government manual that tells how to proceed. We encountered many obstacles that we did not anticipate, and we invented many of our tactics along the way. We also made mistakes. I believed that other prosecutors and criminal investigators might benefit from our experience. I hoped that the record of the Letelier case would prove instructive to both official and nonofficial readers. At the same time, I wanted to see the story told because I am proud of what we accomplished.

In telling that story, I wanted to work with someone who cared about the case and who would venture into areas even beyond the Letelier-Moffitt murders. Taylor Branch knew and had written about the case, cared about it deeply, and agreed with my view that this book should be based on the recollections and opinions of as many people connected with the investigation as possible. Taylor and I interviewed numerous people, and Taylor spoke to many more on his own: some of what he found was news to me. We spent almost half our working time on the book doing research. Two and a half years later, Taylor and I are more than co-authors; we are friends.

As a former prosecutor, I have special obligations and restraints that do not apply to most authors. Many agencies of the United States government provided information to me as an official of the Justice Department, and I felt a duty to handle that information in a way that would not hamper the operations of those agencies or make it less likely that they would cooperate with future prosecutors. For these reasons, I felt we could not include certain incidents in the book that would reveal classified information or harm intelligence sources. I insisted that we submit six chapters of the completed manuscript to the Central Intelligence Agency for review, to ensure that we had not inadvertently disclosed classified information. Also, several officials of the Justice Department read the entire manuscript to make sure that no security material was compromised.

Though the Letelier assassination was politically motivated, I strove in the investigation to keep the case non-political. We have attempted to write this book the same way.

—E.M.P.

When Gene Propper and I first discussed a literary partnership in 1979, I was leery of the idea. Any joint venture in publishing presents knotty problems of control, and this one presented special difficulties because Gene would be both a co-author and a main character. How could we speak with one voice in the book? At the least, I would have to take extra pains to portray him objectively. Not knowing him well at the time, I thought this might be touchy. Most Washington officials I have known prefer to read that they behaved coolly and rationally in all situations. This offends the good sense of readers and makes for dull characters.

Gene's status as the former Letelier prosecutor was worrisome for another reason. The government's performance in the Letelier investigation was then, and remains today, a controversial subject. Some mysteries and irregularities were unexplained, and various outside observers asserted that the entire case was rigged by the CIA or by the Soviet KGB. Under these circumstances, any writer who works with a government partner is in danger of being taken for a pawn or a collaborator.

I mentioned these drawbacks to Gene, and he voiced an equal number of reservations about me. He was particularly troubled by my Jeffersonian argument that an organization like the CIA is a threat to our form of government.

We sealed our partnership in spite of these obstacles, more or less out of faith that they could be overcome. We certainly wanted to think so. From the beginning, we shared a belief that the Letelier investigation is historically unique and so compelling a subject to writer and government insider alike that the story had to be told. Accordingly, we agreed to divide the responsibilities and to trust that we could agree upon the facts.

As the work progressed, my doubts about its feasibility dissolved. Gene spent countless hours with me, going through his personal notes and records. He introduced me to dozens of sources who might otherwise have been reluctant to talk with me. I visited Chile, Paraguay, three prisons, and numerous American cities to interview my own sources, some of whom would have been reluctant to talk with Gene. They often challenged his account of events; he challenged theirs.

After I learned the bare outlines of the investigation, Gene and I arranged to have some sources meet with others to discuss discrepancies of fact and interpretation. At times we conducted what amounted to round-table debates, during which sources did not hesitate to point out mistakes and foibles that others had glossed over. These sessions were invaluable to me in drawing characters, and I like to think we approached the truth by successive approximation.

The Letelier case combines many of the most topical subjects of recent history: international terrorism, spies, political murders, national security, and the operations of the criminal justice system. Most citizens have access to these weighty matters only through official pronouncements or novels of fantasy. In this book, we have tried to show them as they really were in this one case. The story enters many worlds that were entirely alien to me and that will no doubt be alien to most readers. We see law-enforcement officers struggling with their informants, terrorists maneuvering in fear of betrayal by their own confederates, prosecutors being confounded by petty bureaucracy, killers trying to take care of their families, and the FBI Palm Tree Peekers battling against the Door Kickers.

To preserve for the reader a sense of intimacy with these and other environments, we have chosen a narrative style, using dialogue and direct quotation wherever possible. Naturally, we make no claim that each word was spoken exactly as it is recorded here, but we do stand behind the substantive meaning that is conveyed. We have relied on many contemporary notes and documents, and we have interviewed at least one participant about each conversation that appears. I have tried to be faithful to the individual styles of the various speakers.

Numerous agents and informants play roles in the story, not all of which are glorious ones. Because informants are such pivotal characters in the work of penetrating terrorist conspiracies, we have taken special pains to show exactly how they behaved in the episodes relevant to the Letelier investigation. This effort posed security problems, because some of the informants are likely to suffer violent retribution if identified. Generally, we have managed to protect those who need protecting without altering the record of what they said or did, but we have been obliged to change minor circumstances in two or three passages. We have used no pseudonyms except those explicitly identified as such.

Many tales are presented here, but they all relate to two main stories: how the Letelier murders occurred and how they were investigated. Most of the book is about the investigation—the mystery and the chase. Events are presented as Gene and the other investigators learned of them after September 21, 1976, the day of the bombing. In addition, there is a series of background chapters covering the events that led up to the murders. These chapters are interspersed with the others, but they are clearly recognizable by their early datelines and by the special form in which they are written.

There are many unanswered questions—such as those arising from the performance of the State Department as recorded in Chapter 14—about which we did not possess enough facts to enable ourselves or the readers to reach informed conclusions. In general, we have refrained from offering retrospective opinions about what was good or bad, or what was improperly done. The facts usually speak for themselves, and our chronicle of events is complicated enough without the burden of speculative analysis.

This is not to say that we hold no strong opinions. State terrorism is a beastly, cowardly business that sows many forms of corruption. When those who command armies surreptitiously murder strangers who command little more than their own voices and their own feet, they reveal an especially ugly aspect of human nature. When they get away with such murders, it should provoke lasting outrage.

The Letelier case, for the most part, was solved by a makeshift coalition of mavericks. This is a sad fact, in a way, because it is a sign that many government officials do not love their duty enough to take personal risks or to assume responsibilities, even when a heinous crime requires them to do so. Fortunately, enough officials in this story were willing to risk a ninety percent chance of personal failure and ridicule in return for a ten percent chance of justice. A bad law-enforcement official is much more harmful to society than a bad poet, but a good one is nearly as inspiring. To these particular mavericks, I extend my heartfelt respect as a fellow citizen.

—T.B.

Washington, D.C.
September 5, 1981

ACKNOWLEDGMENTS

More than one hundred people contributed ideas, suggestions, information, and other forms of assistance to this project. Most of them do not wish to be acknowledged publicly by name, because our subject—terrorism and criminal investigation—is one that commands discretion. We want to thank our shy sources, anyway. They contributed many hundreds of hours and a great deal of expert knowledge, without which this book would not have been possible.

We can acknowledge, however, some of the sources for the material in Chapters 2–4, which describe the nonconfidential events at the time of the Letelier-Moffitt assassination. For help in the preparation of those chapters, we thank William Richard ("Skip") Bingham, Jr., of the District of Columbia Fire Department; Dr. James L. Luke, Chief Medical Examiner for the District of Columbia; Thomas A. Gibson, of the Uniformed Division of the United States Secret Service; Carter Cornick, Al Seddon, and Nick Stames, of the Federal Bureau of Investigation; Don Campbell, Charles Roistacher, and Earl J. Silbert of the District of Columbia United States Attorney's Office; and C. A. Hebron, Walter Johnson, Joseph O'Brien, Michael Pickett, and Stanley Wilson, of Washington's Metropolitan Police Department.

We thank Robert Keuch for the benefit of his views, and Assistant United States Attorney Lawrence Barcella, Jr., for generous contributions of time and support. We are also grateful to the FBI's Office of Congressional and Public Affairs for arranging interviews with numerous FBI employees who worked on the Letelier investigation.

Our agent, George Diskant, flawlessly handled the practical arrangements for the project.

Nancy Branch put in countless hours transcribing some of our taped interviews. Lynn Warshow worked rapidly and skillfully to copy-edit a long and difficult manuscript.

Susan Leon and Flavia Potenza always responded kindly and efficiently when we called with messages of distress about our work.

For counsel and assistance we thank Karen De Young, Jim Lobe, Karl Maler, John Rothchild, and Marlise Simons.

Our manuscript was typeset on a Barrister 300 word-processing system. We wish to thank the Washington law firm of Lane and Edson, P.C., of which Eugene Propper is a member, for the use of its facilities. We are grateful to Janet Tudor for her tireless, unselfish labors to computerize the manuscript. And we thank all those who helped us in the Lane and Edson word-processing center, especially Irene Bopp, Ronnie Joliat, Patricia Rosetti, Diane Williams, and Sandy Zier.

Finally, we thank our editor, Amanda Vaill. Her energy, confidence, and support never wavered during the two years we worked together. She never doubted the need for this book or our ability to complete it. Without her, the book would have many more faults than it has.

CONTENTS

PRINCIPAL CHARACTERS

IN WASHINGTON, D.C.

James Adams, *Deputy Associate Director, FBI*
Lawrence Barcella, *Assistant U.S. Attorney*
Griffin Bell, *Attorney General*
Donald Campbell, *Assistant U.S. Attorney*
Warren Christopher, *Deputy Secretary of State*
Benjamin Civiletti, *Assistant Attorney General, later Attorney General*
Carter Cornick, *Special Agent, FBI*
Robert Driscoll, *Desk Officer, State Department*
James Ingram, *Assistant Director, FBI*
Robert Keuch, *Deputy Assistant Attorney General*
Saul Landau, *Institute for Policy Studies*
Anthony Lapham, *General Counsel, CIA*
Isabel Letelier, *Institute for Policy Studies*
Orlando Letelier, *Institute for Policy Studies, formerly Chilean Ambassador to the United States*
Frank McNeil, *Deputy Assistant Secretary of State*
Michael Moffitt, *Institute for Policy Studies*
Ronni Karpen Moffitt, *Institute for Policy Studies*
Joseph O'Brien, *Captain, Metropolitan Police Department Homicide Squad*
Eugene Propper, *Assistant U.S. Attorney*
Robert Satkowski, *Special Agent, FBI*

Al Seddon, *Special Agent, FBI*
Earl Silbert, *U.S. Attorney*
Nick Stames, *Special Agent in Charge, FBI*
Bob Steven, *Desk Officer, State Department*
Frank Willis, *Staff Attorney, State Department*
Stanley Wilson, *Detective, Metropolitan Police Department
      Homicide Squad*

IN NEW YORK

Ricardo Canete, *FBI informant*
Guillermo Novo, *Cuban Nationalist Movement*
Ignacio Novo, *Cuban Nationalist Movement*
Frank O'Brien, *Special Agent, FBI*
Virgilio Paz, *Cuban Nationalist Movement*
Alvin Ross, *Cuban Nationalist Movement*
Joseph Schuman, *Inspector, Immigration and Naturalization Service*
Dionisio Suárez, *Cuban Nationalist Movement*
Larry Wack, *Special Agent, FBI*

IN MIAMI, FLORIDA

Daniel Benítez, *Detective, Dade County Public Safety Department*
Roberto Carballo, *Cuban nationalist, 2506 Bay of Pigs Brigade*
Frank Castro, *Nationalist Front for the Liberation of Cuba*
Ovidio Cervantes, *Special Agent, FBI*
Donald Dumford, *Special Agent, FBI*
Armando López Estrada, *Cuban nationalist, 2506 Bay of Pigs Brigade*
Rolando Otero, *suspected "Miami bomber"*
"Tomboy," *FBI informant*
Bernardo de Torres, *Cuban nationalist, 2506 Bay of Pigs Brigade*

IN CARACAS, VENEZUELA

Orlando Bosch, *head of CORU, an anti-Castro terrorist confederation,
      Cubana Airlines bombing defendant*
Orlando García, *head of DISIP, the Venezuelan intelligence service*
Ricardo Morales, *FBI informant, DISIP agent*
Luis Posada, *Cubana Airlines bombing defendant, DISIP agent*
Viron Vaky, *U.S. Ambassador to Venezuela*
Rafael Rivas Vásquez, *DISIP agent*

IN ASUNCION, PARAGUAY

Pastor Coronel, *Chief of Detectives*
Benito Guanes, *Chief of Military Intelligence*
George Landau, *U.S. Ambassador, 1971–77*
Conrado Pappalardo, *Chief of Protocol*
Robert White, *U.S. Ambassador, 1977–79*

IN SANTIAGO, CHILE

Carlos Altamirano, *Chilean Socialist Party*
Enrique Arrancibia, *member of Patria y Libertad, a right-wing political party, murder suspect*
Ernesto Baeza, *army general, Chief of Investigations*
Mariana Callejas, *agent of DINA (Chilean secret police)*
Manuel Contreras, *army general, Chief of DINA*
Pedro Espinoza, *army colonel, DINA*
Alfredo Etcheberry, *Attorney for the United States*
"Gopher," *FBI informant*
George Landau, *U.S. Ambassador, 1977–81*
Bernardo Leighton, *Senator, Vice President*
Orlando Letelier, *Ambassador to the United States, Defense Minister*
Odlanier Mena, *army general, Chief of CNI (Chilean secret police)*
Enrique Montero, *Deputy Minister of the Interior*
Gerónimo Pantoja, *army colonel, CNI*
Augusto Pinochet, *army general, President*
Carlos Prats, *army general, Defense Minister*
Robert Scherrer, *Legal Attaché, FBI*
René Schneider, *army general*
Miguel Schweitzer, *Counsel to the Government of Chile*
Michael Townley, *DINA agent*

LABYRINTH

1 ▣ AMBASSADOR'S DILEMMA

Ambassador George Landau winces with a hint of cultured distaste, talking on the telephone with Pappalardo. A thin, fastidious man of fifty-six, Landau has a wry appreciation for the shortcomings of people in power, but he does not like it when their exotic desires force their way into his morning. Pappalardo is not a man to be ignored, even by the American ambassador to Paraguay. He is telling Landau that the President, General Stroessner, cannot bring himself to refuse a favor to President Pinochet of Chile. And the President certainly hopes that Landau will cooperate. The false documents need to be processed immediately, that very day, because the agents have urgent orders to move on. Landau says that he wishes Pappalardo had given him more advance notice. Things could have been considered that way and been done properly. Pappalardo replies in his usual all-knowing voice that everything is all right. The CIA is clued in. The agents will report directly to General Vernon Walters, deputy director of the Agency, when they reach the United States. Pappalardo has seen to that. He and the President are informing Landau only as a courtesy, and out of their great respect for the ambassador.

Landau replies with gracious thanks, though he knows that this is no courtesy call. Pappalardo wants his help in shepherding the documents through the consulate downstairs, and the President's all-purpose fixer, factotum, and chief of protocol is pursuing his designs with his usual mixture of flattery and self-inflation. This much is obvious, but what lies behind it?

1

Pappalardo asks whether he should send the false passports directly over to the American consulate. Landau plays for time. Not yet, he says. He will make some arrangements and get back to Pappalardo shortly.

The ambassador calls the CIA office down the hall and summons a technician, from whom he learns that there has been no luck in the telephone search for General Walters. Landau is not pleased. In a manner that underscores the importance of the mission, he tells the technician to keep trying. Then he settles back to ponder his course. For once, he wishes he had the services of a good, professional CIA chief of station (COS) in the embassy, but he knows that there is no chief of station in Paraguay—or any other CIA officer, for that matter, except the communicator and a secretary. And Landau knows better than anyone that this CIA vacancy is his own doing. He has recently fired the chief of station for lying about one of the ongoing scandals in official Asunción, where there are few secrets.

Landau has a clear picture of Pappalardo's proposal from the previous evening's reception, given by the Manufacturers' Association of Paraguay. President Stroessner himself was there in full splendor, surrounded by his aides and his generals, who in turn were surrounded by obsequious hordes of domestic and foreign traders hoping to do business with them. Pappalardo drew the American ambassador aside and said in a low voice that the President had received a call from Chilean President Pinochet, which was most unusual. Pinochet, it seemed, wanted to send two agents to the United States to investigate certain import-export companies dealing in Chilean minerals. Pinochet suspects that the companies were being infiltrated by leftist Allende sympathizers who might be diverting funds from the sale of Chilean minerals into terrorist actions against the Pinochet government. Anyway, said Pappalardo, Pinochet wanted to send his two investigators to the United States under false Paraguayan identities. The agents were in Asunción now. Stroessner, through Pappalardo, has issued them false Paraguayan passports, and now they lacked only American entry visas.

Overnight, Landau hoped nothing would come of this crazy scheme, as often happened with notions from Pappalardo's active imagination. But now Pappalardo is back, pressing hard. Clearly, his story is preposterous. No mission as innocuous as a commercial security investigation would command the attention of two presidents or require such a shuffle of identities. But what is the real story? Landau knows that Pappalardo is capable of making up the entire tale, or any part of it. The only sure thing is that he is asking the American ambassador to issue visas in the full knowledge that they contain not only false names but also false nationalities. This is a crime. The State Department would never approve it.

Pappalardo calls again, with more talk of General Walters and urgency and the President's feelings of obligation. Should he send over the passports now? All right, Landau replies. But have them delivered directly to the ambassador's office, not to the consulate. Landau will take care of it personally. Pappalardo is delighted with the arrangement. His couriers will move at once.

Landau awaits the delivery. He has taken one step, and soon he must take another. It is hard to believe that there is anything too sinister afoot, for if so, Pappalardo would not openly declare the involvement of two presidents to Landau. It could be something financial—perhaps the funds of politicians are moving secretly into the States. Perhaps the Chileans are not involved at all. Or perhaps the idea is simply to corrupt Landau himself, so that the ambassador will no longer be able to play the stickler against the normal flow of Paraguayan commerce. Such a ploy would tie in General Walters and the spy scandal, leading all the way back to the wily Pastor Coronel, Paraguay's chief of detectives. That official, Landau fears, may be setting another trap for him.

Coronel is a man who can exist only in Paraguay, the tiny landlocked nation stuffed like a pineal gland into the huge body of South America. Popularly known as the refuge of ex-Nazis and overthrown dictators, the country has been isolated, a world to itself, ever since its first president closed the border for thirty years early in the nineteenth century, allowing no one to enter or leave—not a trader or a diplomat or a simple traveler. Paraguay's third president combined Napoleonic ambitions with savage tyranny to wage simultaneous, offensive war against Brazil, Argentina, and Uruguay, forcing the only self-inflicted genocide in history. At the end of it, Paraguay was virtually obliterated as a nation or a human stock. Ninety percent of the male population perished in the war.

After that disaster, the remnant of Paraguay alternated between civil war and strongmen dictators for nearly a century until the great Chaco War of the 1930s. Paraguay went to battle against Bolivia over disputed territory in the vast Chaco wasteland, where American oil companies claimed to have discovered rich deposits. The Paraguayans gave no quarter, fighting with the cheerful despera-

tion for which they were renowned. The results were sanguinary—
every fourth Paraguayan male was killed or wounded—and there
was no oil after all, but in Paraguay none of this mattered beside the
stupendous victory.

A Chaco artillerist, Alfredo Stroessner, has ruled longer than any
national leader on the globe except for Tito of Yugoslavia. He has a
ruthless, unsavory image in the world, but most diplomats stationed
in Paraguay still feel a certain charm about Stroessner's country.
Unique in South America, its culture is more Indian than Latin, without the usual layers of Spanish aristocracy. Everyone is Indian and
bilingual. Stroessner himself speaks the native Guaraní, especially
when angry. Paraguay is a land of friendliness, egalitarian simplic-
ity, and, whenever Stroessner is crossed, stark brutality. It is modern jets and barefoot soldiers, the undisputed smuggling capital of
the world. All commerce seems to depend on a complicated system of
concessions and tribute, which elsewhere would be called bribes.
There is the official Stroessner Airport, but there are also four major
contraband airstrips, each controlled by a Stroessner general.

A senator and leader of the Colorado Party, Pastor Coronel has a
devoted political following in his home district, where his photograph
appears on a wall of many homes, separated from the photograph of
Stroessner himself only by a statue of the Virgin. Coronel enjoys
perquisites correspondingly greater than those of an ordinary chief
of detectives. He has acquired, for example, an informal title as the
patron of all heroin and cocaine smugglers moving through Paraguay, and he protects them tenaciously as long as they pay him and
do not allow their products to be consumed in the homeland. In this
capacity, Coronel has run consistently afoul of American efforts to
interdict narcotics traffic. His conduct has been notorious enough for
the Drug Enforcement Administration to classify him as a Class I
narcotics violator. George Landau has gone further: he has forbidden any official of the American embassy to have any contact whatsoever with Coronel.

Coronel has caused trouble ever since Landau's edict. He promptly
arrested an American Peace Corps volunteer out in the hinterland
and charged him with teaching the Paraguayans to smoke marijuana. This was a particularly devilish charge for a Class I narcotics
violator to invent, but the fact remained that the American was in
Coronel's custody and would no doubt stay there until someone from
the embassy came to beg his release. Coronel was taunting Landau
for the edict. Word came that the volunteer was being tortured. Finally, Landau relented and allowed the consul to seek an audience

with the chief of detectives, who produced the prisoner for inspection. Half the volunteer's face was a bloody pulp; he said someone had pulled out the hairs of his beard with pliers. "I cannot control these Indians," Coronel said, with a shrug.

Landau had to bow to Coronel, but his edict remained in effect. Moreover, he approved a subtle campaign against the chief of detectives. The Americans knew that Stroessner was the only one powerful enough to throttle Coronel, and that the way to reach Stroessner was through Pappalardo. Accordingly, Pappalardo kept hearing that the chief of detectives had gone too far and was an affront to the dignity of Paraguay. The conspirators could only wait for the signals to click often enough in the President's mind to make him crash down on Coronel in the night.

But Coronel did not wait. He fought back in the spirit of cornered Paraguayan martyrs by ordering his detectives to scour the nation for Communists. Early in 1976, his detectives caught a Chilean and an Argentine, both underground leaders, on their way to Peru. Coronel let this be known to Stroessner and to foreign intelligence people before sending the famous left-wingers back to their respective homelands. Shortly thereafter, Coronel came up with an even bigger catch—Miguel Angel Soler, underground leader of the tiny, outlawed Paraguayan Communist Party. Coronel had Soler brought directly to his office, where he promptly shot the prisoner twice in the head with his Magnum.* Then Coronel ordered Soler's head cut off and took it to the palace of the President. His message was clear: the Paraguayan military intelligence agency (J-2) may have a huge budget and numerous analysts but it was Pastor Coronel, with his meager resources and his humble detectives, who was protecting the nation from the Communists. To Stroessner's paranoid ear, this more than offset negative reports on the character of the chief of detectives.

A month later, Coronel struck again. His detectives locked up a man who confessed under torture that he worked for the American CIA. He named his contact—the chief of station in Landau's embassy. For Coronel, this was pay dirt. Even the President might not be overly impressed with another confession, especially one unearthed by torture under the broadest Paraguayan standards of guilt, but an

---

*Two diplomatic sources say that Coronel executed Soler in a cell near Coronel's office. An official Paraguayan government source, who was closer to those involved, maintains that the execution took place inside Coronel's office.

American spy was an undeniable treasure. Coronel took the news triumphantly to the palace.

The President could not believe it. The friendly, anti-Communist CIA would never betray him that way. He sent word to Ambassador Landau, asking for an explanation. Landau, in turn, summoned the chief of station, who found himself in the classic spymaster's bind. On one hand, it was against the Agency's most cherished policy ever to acknowledge the identity of an agent; on the other hand, CIA personnel are supposed to work for the ambassador. The chief of station decided to lean toward secrecy. He denied everything to Landau, and the ambassador assured the palace that there was nothing to Coronel's ugly rumor. Then, when the Paraguayans produced an unimpeachable stack of facts and intimate details on the working relationship between the chief of station and the prisoner, both Landau and the chief of station found themselves in trouble. Landau was incensed. CIA people might lie to other people, but not to him. The lie now reflected badly on his control of his own embassy and also on the integrity of his word to the Paraguayan government. He told the station chief that he was through and sent word to that effect to CIA headquarters.

The station chief grumbled as he packed his bags. Perhaps he had made a mistake, given that Stroessner was such a staunch ally of the United States, but the President was, after all, a dictator, and the station chief had thought it was a good idea to place a small bet on other sources of information, if only to keep up with the news. In any case, he supported the Agency position that it was never wise to own up having a captured agent unless you have something to trade for him. Therefore, he thought he should not be fired, especially in an abrupt way that was tantamount to an admission of guilt. He was as angry as Landau and the Paraguayans, and the wretched prisoner was no doubt suffering more tangibly than any of them.

The problems were so bad that General Walters himself, the number-two man in the CIA, laid aside his retirement plans and flew to Asunción. A gifted linguist and a spellbinding raconteur, known for dropping into a country incognito and hopping on a bus so that he could pick up the local dialect before his official arrival, Walters was a rare combination—both a cultural sophisticate and a bareknuckled American soldier. As such, he got on famously with the Paraguayans, telling Pappalardo and other officials countless stories about how he had outwitted the Communists in subterranean battles all over the world. The ugly controversy over the Paraguayan spy seemed to dissolve in the warmth of the camaraderie between Walters and his hosts. At the general's airport farewell, he and Pappalardo exchanged private phone numbers and parted with vigorous *abrazos*. But the designation of a CIA replacement for the embassy was an issue left in abeyance.

Temperamentally, Ambassador Landau was not suited for hugging and back-room tale-swapping with the likes of Pappalardo. His tastes were too formal. Landau was a native of Vienna, Austria, who had adopted the United States as his country and there fought against Hitler as a draftee in the American army. His slight German accent and his World War II background in army intelligence served him well in a country like Paraguay, but Landau was more a diplomat than one of the boys. He was removed from the Walters style of problem-solving, and during the mission he was outside the spirit of the general's negotiations. In fact, it almost seemed as though there never would have been a problem without Landau's interference.

Landau's rectitude got in the way. It was stronger than his dry humor or his sharp wit. In his mind, the ambassador would be obeyed, would tolerate no lies, and would fulfill his obligations. That meant that the station chief had to go, and it also meant that the embassy had to secure the release of the prisoner, who was an American responsibility and also a symbol of Pastor Coronel's defiance. Landau did not want to replace the chief of station until the prisoner was freed. To him, the absence of a CIA officer would not be much of a loss anyway. Station chiefs tended to be pompously incompetent in his experience, going all the way back to his first post in Uruguay, where the station chief was E. Howard Hunt.

To the Paraguayans, on the other hand, the life of the prisoner was insignificant, but it was vitally important to replace the miscreant chief of station. President Stroessner became increasingly disturbed as the weeks went by in July, for he dearly missed his regular CIA briefings. Over the years, he had come to depend on them the way many Americans depend on their morning *New York Times*. The President could not understand the delays that prevented the swift punishment of the guilty. To him, it was inconceivable that the Americans would care so much about one miserable Paraguayan prisoner.

The man in jail is very much on the mind of Ambassador Landau, now that the two false passports have arrived from Pappalardo's office. They are special passports of Paraguay, in the names of Juan

Williams Rose and Alejandro Romeral Jara. Each passport is accompanied by a letter from the Paraguayan Foreign Ministry, signed by Pappalardo, vouching for the bearer as a true Paraguayan on official business. And each letter is accompanied by an application for an American visa. For all Landau knows, any or all of the information might be true. But Pappalardo has said the two men are Chileans. Why would he lie? Does Pappalardo have some sort of private arrangement worked out with General Walters? Is American cooperation in this shady deal the price of getting the prisoner released? Landau doesn't know, but it is obvious that he is being tested under pressure, without time to consult either his superiors in the State Department in Washington or General Walters. To refuse to grant the visas could be a costly act. Pappalardo would surely moan loudly, asking how the Americans could violate the gravest of Paraguayan laws against spying and then deny a minor request from the President himself. Soon thereafter, Landau might hear that the prisoner had been executed. Coronel would grin. Pappalardo would not bother to report such a trifle. And, in Washington, General Walters and his colleagues at the CIA might point to yet another instance in which the regular diplomats botched things by being naïve in the intrigues of a foreign court.

There are dangers in the other course, as well. By granting the visas, Landau would take a giant step into the kind of contraband traffic for which the Paraguayans and Pappalardo were justly famous. Moreover, he would do so blindly, without knowing the real purpose of the false passports, leaving himself open for the Agency people to say later that he had neglected some obvious principle of spycraft. As for the State Department itself, Landau would have to report his action sooner or later to his superiors there, and they would see it as the latest consequence of the "flap" in Landau's embassy. Then they would see that their man in Asunción felt obliged to issue visas to phony people under phony nationalities on the basis of an absurd cover story—all because relations with the President had become strained and delicate. Landau knows that Henry Kissinger prefers ambassadors who keep things running smoothly.

After painful deliberation, the ambassador decides to issue the visas. He sends the papers to the consulate downstairs, knowing they will have an easier passage through the bureaucracy coming from his office rather than from the outside, and then he plans steps to protect himself until he can find out what the Paraguayans, or the Chileans, are up to. Whatever the game is, it appears to be a bit too subtle for the tastes of Pastor Coronel. The chief of detectives may be a factor in someone else's plans, but he is unlikely to be the moving force himself.

As usual, things go wrong. Consul William Finnegan sends a message upstairs to the ambassador. He is sorry to report that he cannot issue the visas because the applications are not complete. Finnegan is nervous. He hates to place difficulties in the way of the ambassador's wishes, but, as Landau knows, the embassy has been plagued lately with visa fraud. Officials of the Paraguayan government have been selling identity documents to Koreans and others for use in entering the United States. It is big business. The consulate in Asunción has been scrutinized intensely by its home office and by immigration and by Ambassador Landau himself. These two Paraguayans have not even bothered to fill in their residence or physical description on the applications. Could the ambassador please send word back through the Paraguayan government to have these two officials come into the consulate to complete the forms?

Landau cannot refuse. He can only sigh and pass the message along to Pappalardo, who is not pleased. The chief of protocol is disappointed that the ambassador holds so little sway over his own bureaucrats. From Landau's point of view, the consular delay has its advantages. While he seeks clarification from General Walters, it would be well to have the visa applications going back and forth in the mail. Pappalardo, however, knows that the Chileans are in a hurry. He tells Landau he will try to have them come into the consulate.

The consul's message soon reaches the Señorial Motel, where Juan Williams and Alejandro Romeral are waiting with frayed nerves. They have been seeking the papers for a week now—seeing far too many people, answering far too many questions. To them, the Paraguayans are slow and primitive, and the idea of presenting themselves at the American embassy is nearly intolerable. But they have orders. They are men who always address their superiors as "my colonel" and "my general," emphasizing a personal, feudal brand of strict vassalage, and they know the harsh penalties for failure. In the end, they will do whatever is necessary to obtain the visas, but the need for haste is now in conflict with the need for care. It is often so in their business. It would be abominably poor tradecraft for them to present their faces inside the American embassy—stupid, sloppy, worthy of punishment. But not to go might seem suspicious, and it would certainly mean more excruciating delay. The two agents decide to go. They do not say so in their telephone report back to Chile, however. They only say that the security of the mission looks increasingly bad. They have been forced to see Paraguayan civilians like Pappalardo. The Paraguayans have been spying on them. The Americans have been asking questions, they hear. They are worried.

Consul Finnegan and his assistant receive Williams and Romeral with exceeding courtesy. They point out the blank spaces in the visa applications. Everyone regrets the clumsy oversight. Williams and Romeral fill them in. Their applications are now an odd mixture of handwriting and typescript. The Americans look over the forms and pronounce them quite satisfactory. They regret that they cannot issue the visas instantly, but there are too many painstaking procedures required. Bureaucracy, they sigh.

Not long after Williams and Romeral have departed, Finnegan sends an unwelcome message upstairs to the ambassador. It is worse than fishy, he says. First of all, he and his assistant know practically every official in Paraguay, and these two men are complete strangers. They do not look Paraguayan. They do not speak Spanish like Paraguayans. Finally, both men have just claimed the same hometown—a tiny village of perhaps two hundred people in a remote area of the country. The consul's Paraguayan assistant, who knows the village, declares that it is inhabited by impoverished, pure Guaraní Indians. The chances that such a village would produce two government officials licensed for international travel, especially a six-foot two-inch blond like Juan Williams, are zero, says the assistant.

Consul Finnegan agrees. He does not want his consulate to be pushed around anymore by the office of the Paraguayan President, no matter how loose the local customs are. To the consul, Pappalardo is notorious. The chief of protocol is an immensely wealthy man, having commandeered many secret concessions in the national economy. He receives a commission, for example, on each and every Ford automobile entering Paraguay. Worse, from the embassy's standpoint, Pappalardo is believed to have siphoned money out of the U.S. Treasury. The recent audit of an AID-funded reforestation project has shown that thousands of palmettos—hearts of palm saplings—somehow wound up planted on land owned by Pappalardo. The chief of protocol has also profiteered in AID wheat credits. All this, plus the visa fraud. Consul Finnegan declares that he will not issue the visas unless Landau explicitly orders him to do so.

The consul's attitude makes the situation all the more distressing for the ambassador. He knows Finnegan is correct. He knows that the responsibility for the false visas will be his alone, that there will be no chance of passing them off as a routine oversight, and that Finnegan's position will make it more difficult to report the matter to their mutual superiors in the State Department. At the same time, the atmosphere of this transaction is both tense and blatantly phony, in a way that tells Landau it is not a matter of money or ordinary corruption, as the consul fears. It feels more like an affair of state, a CIA operation. The ambassador resolves to cut a path between spy risk and protection. He sends down his orders: Issue the visas. Stamp them in the passports. Send the completed passports up to the ambassador's office on the second floor. Consul Finnegan complies with the orders, but he writes on the applications that the visas are issued directly on Landau's authority.

The ambassador takes precautions, too. He orders an embassy technician to photograph each page of the passports and to send the photos by pouch to General Walters that very day.

Shortly thereafter, Williams and Romeral arrive at the Foreign Ministry, next to the presidential palace. They find a long, red carpet rolled through the grand entrance and down the steps. The royal welcome has been prepared for a foreign ambassador, not for them, but the two agents feel no less honored when a functionary hands them the passports. Everything is in order, at long last. They deliver crisp, military acknowledgments and begin the long walk through Asunción—past the Chaco War Memorial and the downtown Plaza of Heroes, and on to the Plaza of Uruguay. The entire nation of Paraguay contains only a few dozen public telephones, and some of them are in the railroad station off this plaza. Romeral places a call to Chile. He uses code words and code names to report that the mission in Paraguay is accomplished. Then he hangs up and tells Williams that they have been ordered back to Chile for a while. They are not to proceed to the United States. Apparently their superiors now share their suspicions about the delays in Paraguay.

The two agents fly home after following instructions to tell the Paraguayans that they will probably go to the United States in two weeks or so. Word of this passes from Pappalardo to Landau, who is relieved. Now, if the report is true, he will have time to investigate their story and block their travel, if necessary. If the report is false, the two Chileans might be heading for the States already.

Landau drafts a cable to General Walters, laying out Pappalardo's version of events—Pinochet's request of Stroessner, Stroessner's gift of false passports, the commercial security investigation, and so on. Pointedly, he asks the general whether this is all part of a *quid pro quo* arrangement on the ugly spy scandal in Paraguay. Whatever it is, says the ambassador, he does not like it because of the implausible stories and the obvious conflicts with the State Department's duty to protect the integrity of international travel. Nevertheless, Landau reports, he has been careful. The photostats he has pouched up will enable the CIA to control the movements of the two Chileans, if that is desirable. Finally, the ambassador admits that he has not informed the State Department of these developments. He assumes they concern an Agency matter, and therefore he is treating it in strictest confidence, through CIA channels. But he would much prefer to tell the State Department, as is required of ambassadors, and he will do so unless Walters objects.

This last part of the message is the most painful to Landau. He is making himself somewhat vulnerable to Walters, who will realize instantly that the ambassador has excluded his own superiors from potentially explosive information. He has chosen to confide in the Agency, knowing that the step may be a fateful one. It may, for instance, make it more difficult to report the truth to the State Department later on. But the ambassador feels he has no choice. A report like this might cause a big stir at the department at a time when Landau does not have credible answers to the basic questions. His consulate might be asked to report on why it issued the visas. Self-righteous officials in Washington, with nothing to lose and little appreciation of entanglements in Paraguay, might chastise Landau for bending to Pappalardo. Above all, the department would be buzzing with the details of Pappalardo's juicy message, inevitably compromising what might be a real CIA operation. If it is real, it is unquestionably sensitive. Like most career diplomats, Landau is loath to allow that there are matters of foreign policy that the State Department should not even know about, but in this case he has been forced into one.

To send the cable to Walters, Landau spurns even his own classified, secure ROGER channel, as messages routed this way pass through the State Department on their way to the Agency. Instead, he summons the Agency technician again and orders him to send the cable directly to the CIA on the Agency's private channel. This is most unusual for an ambassador. In effect, Landau has become his own ad hoc station chief. Now, all he can do is wait for the Walters reply as he returns to the bustle of an ambassador's duties—the receptions and dinners, the paperwork and the administration of the embassy itself. For the most part, Landau has reconciled his stern determination to succeed with his distaste for the drivel of ordinary diplomacy. It has not been easy. Back in Uruguay, as a junior Foreign Service officer, he found the drone of cocktail conversation with his colleagues so oppressive that he was obliged to bum cigarettes, though a non-smoker, and burn the hairs on the back of his hand—just to keep awake, to have something to do. The remedy was effective, if not diplomatic, and Landau has made his way up to the level of ambassador, where the work is not so tedious. As the days go by without reply from Walters, the discomfort of the situation is itself an antidote to boredom.

A cable from General Walters arrives in Asunción on August 4. This seems an odd way to do business, says the general. He goes on to point out some peculiarities of Pappalardo's scheme. He shows no familiarity with it at all. The Agency sees no reason to meet with these particular Chileans in the United States, he concludes, adding that Landau should inform his superiors in the State Department.

This makes a sour turn for Landau. Pappalardo has deceived him. Landau is now left alone with responsibility for the false visas and with no answers regarding the absurd cover story, having seduced himself with worries about top-level clandestine affairs. His anger rises, but it must give way to calculation so that he can stop those phony passports before harm is done.

It will not be easy. Landau is in a tighter box than ever. He must now report to the State Department, but what can he say? He must tell the department to order a watch for Juan Williams and Alejandro Romeral at the United States borders, and he must get the photostats sent over from CIA to State. But all these documents have July 27 stamped on them as the date on which the visas were issued. It is now eight days later. How can Landau explain the delay? He can't possibly say that he has been waiting for Walters, especially now that the general has given no comfort to his beliefs about the operation. To report all that would make the ambassador look foolish, as well as out of line.

Ambassador Landau recalls that Pappalardo has been in Brazil much of the last week and that the chief of protocol has promised him further reports on this matter from the President. Painfully, on August 5, Landau drafts a cable to his boss, Assistant Secretary of State Harry Shlaudeman, in which he twists these last two facts into a plausible explanation of the entire affair. He tells Shlaudeman that Pappalardo had called on the twenty-seventh only to say that

Stroessner had a message for Landau regarding two visas pending that day in the consulate. This was all Pappalardo had said, Landau told Shlaudeman, but it had made Landau suspicious enough to have photostats made by the CIA as a precaution. Now, he continues, Pappalardo has returned from Brazil to tell a very fishy story about President Pinochet and Stroessner and undercover Chilean agents. Landau does not believe it, and he recommends to Shlaudeman that the two fake Paraguayans be stopped at the border if they try to enter the United States.

Landau's cable to Shlaudeman allows the ambassador to appear both vigilant and rigidly strict about visa matters. By this account, the visas had been issued "routinely" before Landau was informed that the Paraguayans were actually Chileans. The picture of the upright, rule-book Landau has not been an accurate one in this episode, extenuating circumstances notwithstanding, but it will be so from now on. Landau calls Pappalardo with a vengeance. He combines the stiff intimidation of his Viennese manner with the full authority of the American ambassador to inform the chief of protocol that the two visas are hereby void. The Chileans will use them at their peril.

A day later, with Shlaudeman's concurrence, he calls Pappalardo again and advises him to pass the word along to the Chileans: the United States will not be party to three-country visa fraud under false pretenses. He tells Pappalardo that he wants the passports back, to make sure they have not been used. That night, August 6, Landau attends a party at the embassy of Taiwan, where he runs into Colonel Benito Guanes, chief of the Paraguayan J-2. He finds out that Guanes has also been a party to the scheme. Hearing this, Landau tells Guanes of the American revocation of the visas and of his own personal displeasure over the incident, urging Guanes to demand that the Chileans return the false Paraguayan passports so that the U.S. visa permits in them can be officially canceled.

For nearly three months, Landau will badger Pappalardo and Guanes about the passports. On this specific request alone, he makes at least ten phone calls to Pappalardo. There is no satisfaction until October 29, when Pappalardo sends a courier behind his flourishes and fulsome apologies. Upon delivery, Landau finds that someone has ripped the photographs out of the passports, but otherwise they are intact. More importantly, the pages are all blank. They have not been used. He puts them in a drawer. No one has any idea that Landau, during the conflict with Coronel and Pappalardo, has preserved a vital clue in an international murder case.

2 ▣ CONCUSSION

From the pattern of leg wounds, Chief Medical Examiner James L. Luke and his colleagues would conclude that the young woman passenger in the front seat was riding with her right leg crossed over the left one, her body turned slightly toward the driver as though in conversation. Luke would find a number of things he had never seen before, such as the powdered hair. All the exposed body hair—the woman's eyebrows, the driver's mustache, the soft hairs on their arms and necks—appeared to be structurally intact even where the skin was burned, but at the slightest touch each hair would crumble to dust. Part of the blast had drawn the substance out of the molecules.

The fireball appeared and disappeared so quickly that the few witnesses would remember only a bright flash, if anything. Within a few microseconds, orange fire came up from the floor of the car to burn the left shoulder of the driver, to fill the car and singe hair and spill out the windows, and just as quickly to vanish. The fireball was sucked back into a concussion that jarred the back-seat passenger loose from his last clear memory—of a loud hissing sound, like steam coming off a hot wire. The concussion became the frozen moment which would seize and occupy the minds of distant strangers for years to come.

In the car immediately behind, two ministers from the Israeli embassy glided by the exploding automobile as it veered off to the right. Political counselor Eyton Bentsur stopped the car and looked

15

numbly at his companion as a long shower of glass and metal debris fell on the roof. When it stopped, the two of them tumbled instinctively to the pavement and checked themselves for wounds. Then they ran in a low crouch to the front of their car and peered back at the wreck through dark-brown smoke. In shock, the two Israeli diplomats thought *they* might be the targets of Arab terrorists. They stayed low, fearing secondary attacks.

A lawyer on his way to work, one car behind the Israelis, was stunned by a violent wave of air. It seemed to grab him by the lungs and slam him back against his seat. Then the sound hit him. When his mind returned a second or two later, the lawyer remembered seeing a blue car in flight, completely off the ground, and he remembered seeing it rock unsteadily back down on the ground and go into a skid.

The concussion left Officer Thomas A. Gibson semiconscious on the sidewalk in front of the Turkish embassy. He had no strength in his legs and would remember nothing of the next ten minutes. All he could reconstruct was that at nine-thirty-eight, by his watch, he had received a radio message relieving him of his post in front of the Romanian embassy. He had walked across 23rd Street, which enters Sheridan Circle from the southwest, and suddenly he found himself wobbling stupidly on the ground like a glassy-eyed boxer, holding himself up with his hands.

The economic attaché from the Greek embassy had just passed Gibson, walking in the opposite direction. He had no way of knowing that a NO PARKING sign, now pockmarked with shrapnel, might have saved him from serious injury. Instead, Vassilios Vassiacostas was dazed, squatting low, ears ringing, when he heard a loud crash. The crumpled blue car plowed into a parked orange Volkswagen and finally came to rest about twenty feet from Vassiacostas, having knocked the Volkswagen up on the curb. Still in a crouch, the unnerved Vassiacostas jumped away from the cars. He wanted desperately to flee before there were any more explosions or crashes. He started toward a building on his right but checked himself when he realized it was the Irish embassy. Even in a blind panic, Vassiacostas was enough of a diplomat to think of terrorism in Northern Ireland. He was afraid that the Irish inside might mistake him for the attacker. He turned quickly to his left, but something automatically told him that no Greek should seek refuge in the Turkish embassy at a time of violence, not with all the tensions in Cyprus. Vassiacostas hesitated in aimless fear before darting around the circle, running from tree to bush. He ran across Massachusetts Avenue into his own embassy, and only then did he realize that his left cheek was bleeding from a small puncture wound.

The concussion spread from Sheridan Circle with uneven force. To firefighter Skip Bingham, in the bathroom of a fire station six long blocks away through a park and many office buildings, it arrived like a sharp crack of thunder, loud enough that people were talking about it in the station. To anesthesiologist Dana Peterson, only two hundred feet from the blast, it sounded like no more than the backfire of an automobile. Peterson, late for a dentist appointment, was about to enter Sheridan Circle when she heard the noise off to her left. She saw the smoke cloud rising from the demolished blue car, and then she saw Vassiacostas crouching, moving furtively, shielding himself with something that looked like a small umbrella. From his behavior, Peterson thought maybe the sound had been gunfire. She pulled her car to the side of the road and parked.

Officer Charles Kucmovich was about to drive his Executive Protective Service cruiser into Sheridan Circle from R Street, about seventy yards to Peterson's right. The concussion reached him in its true proportion, full of noise and danger. "That sounded like a bomb," said Kucmovich's partner. The two of them surveyed the far side of the circle, where smoke was rising from the blue car. They felt a jolt of adrenaline when they connected the concussion to the sight of the mangled car and the smoke. The partner put the adrenaline on the EPS airwaves by telling headquarters that an automobile appeared to have exploded on Sheridan Circle. Kucmovich hit the cruiser's emergency lights and peeled out into the circle the wrong way, against the rush hour traffic. There was no other way to get there. Kucmovich frantically waved the oncoming cars out of his path. He steered the cruiser all the way around past the smoke cloud and screeched to a halt behind the wreck, parked diagonally to block two lanes of inbound commuter traffic.

None of Kucmovich's EPS experience—long, tedious hours patrolling Washington's embassy district for the uniformed division of the Secret Service—had prepared him for this, but somehow it seemed familiar. A horrid stench of gunpowder and burned flesh assaulted him even before he jumped out of the cruiser. He ran through the smoke toward the blue car and tripped over something in the littered street. He looked back to see a shoe lying near a rain puddle among a thousand bits of broken glass. Kucmovich saw the stub of a leg bone and a splayed mess of pulp protruding from the shoe, and he kept running. For an instant he was back in Vietnam, near the carnage he had hoped was forever behind him. Kucmovich smelled death less than a minute into the aftermath.

He could not open the left front door of the blue car. It was mashed shut. The foul air nearly hummed with aftershock. Kucmovich reached blindly through the smoke and tried to pull the injured driver from the floor of the car, but he was wedged tightly between the seat and the steering column. "This one is bad!" he shouted to his partner. "I can't get him out!" At that instant, Kucmovich heard a popping noise under the car. There were flames around the gas tank. He jumped back and motioned for his partner to do likewise. Kucmovich ran back to the cruiser and yanked out his fire extinguisher. He hesitated briefly, calculating the odds of a gasoline explosion, and then he dashed to the car to spray the flames. Half a dozen EPS officers were already in sight, arriving on foot and by cruiser from nearby embassy patrols. Others were on the way. Those closest to the car maintained a respectful distance until the fire was out.

A burly, redheaded civilian was paying no attention to the danger. He appeared from the sidewalk behind the car and charged around to the driver's window. His face was blackened, his shirt torn, and his hair was singed from the telltale blast of the fireball. He also tried to pull the driver from the car, straining his muscles as far as shock and hysteria would take them. But it was impossible. The young man looked to the sky in anguish. "Assassins!" he screamed. "Fascists!" He seemed to alternate between dazed fatigue and incandescent energy, erupting now and then with moans and cries.

EPS officers moved in to clear the area. One of them noticed the two Israeli diplomats, still kneeling behind the headlights of their car. The officer summarily ordered the Israelis to leave. Counselor Bentsur complied, but he doubted that it was wise for him to be driving off with all the metal fragments and other bits of evidence that were scattered on the hood, roof, and trunk of his car. They fell on the street in his trail.

"Somebody help me get Orlando out of here!" screamed the man with the singed hair. EPS officers went to him and said they would take care of it. They moved him aside, and he ran back around the car.

The woman passenger was lying in the grass in front of the Romanian embassy, having staggered and crawled from the car. Behind her, on the pavement near the orange Volkswagen, lay her right moccasin, a paperback novel, and thirty-seven cents in change that

had fallen out of her jumpsuit pocket. Beside them lay a man's pre-
scription eyeglasses in a brown case. At the top of the passenger
door, a foot forward of the handle, was a solid stream of fresh blood,
four inches wide, that divided into half a dozen trickles as it ran
down the door panel. The young woman's head had come to rest here
after the concussion, before she managed to heave herself through
the window.

Now she was lying on her side. Dana Peterson, on the ground beside her, pushed her head back, opened her mouth, and scooped out
clots of blood.

"Take some deep breaths," Peterson urged. The woman responded. Her breaths gurgled, however, because of the continuing flow of
blood. Peterson was still trying to clear out the air passages when
strong hands grabbed her shoulders from behind and began to shake
her violently. Peterson turned in anger and surprise.

"Save her!" cried the man with the singed hair.

"I'm a doctor," said Peterson. A quick read of the man's face told
her he was probably a victim, suffering from shock and extreme
emotional distress.

"Save my sweetheart!" cried the man, still holding the doctor.

"I'll do my best. Try to calm yourself," Peterson said firmly.

An EPS officer intervened, pulling the man a few feet off to the
side. "I'm a doctor," Peterson told the officer. She turned back to the
woman, whose breathing was weaker. Peterson examined her quickly in an effort to locate the cause of the bleeding. She found a great
many contusions and lacerations about the face, including a long cut
through the lower lip. The face was blackened by a sooty material
that would wipe away in some places but in others seemed literally
embedded in the skin. Peterson found similar wounds on the legs,
but there was nothing in her judgment that could account for the
bleeding. Then she saw two small cuts on either side of the windpipe.
She thought they might be small-caliber gunshot wounds.

Peterson checked for a pulse and found none. "I need to turn her
on her back," she told the EPS officer. But the distraught man
sprang ahead of the officer and helped roll the victim over. "Help
her! Will she be all right?" he pleaded. "I'll help you! Can I help?"

"Thank you. Try to be calm," Peterson replied. She nodded to the
officer, who pulled the man aside again.

Officer Kucmovich arrived with a resuscitator unit from his
cruiser. Peterson approved and urged him to hurry. Kucmovich assembled the machine and started the oxygen. Peterson began exter-

nal cardiac massage, leaning rhythmically on the woman's chest. Between pushes, she reached under the resuscitator mask to scoop out more blood, and she checked again for a pulse. There was still none. "This is hopeless," she told Kucmovich. "Is the ambulance coming?"

"It's on the way," Kucmovich said grimly. "That's probably it now." Three minutes or so after the explosion, there was a general din of approaching sirens.

Walter Johnson raced ahead of the other detectives. Jones, his temporary partner, was joking nervously that maybe they should take it a little easier, but Johnson continued to swerve past oncoming cars and sound his horn and squeal around corners all the way to Sheridan Circle from the spot near the White House where the call had found them. Johnson was in a rush. Part of it was the tone of the broadcast from police headquarters, where the news had been sent by direct telephone line from EPS. Part of it was Johnson's premonition. He was only twenty-seven, less than five years a policeman, but he already had a reputation for being on the scene of extraordinary events. Once, Johnson arrested a notorious fugitive who happened to rob a bank while Johnson was standing outside. Another time, a man viciously clubbed someone in the head just as Johnson was driving by. Things like that came along so frequently that Johnson worried for his safety. It was uncanny, and now he anticipated it again.

He roared into the circle and stopped near the place the Israelis had just vacated. Johnson was already shaken. When he jumped out of the unmarked cruiser, he dropped a folder full of papers on all his current cases. Scores of pages scattered in the street. He ignored them. The dark hanging cloud of smoke and the faces of the gathering bystanders told him the "automobile explosion" was real. He saw it was threatening to drizzle. "Grab the canvas!" he shouted to Jones. Johnson took his hand-held radio toward the perimeter of the circle, where an EPS officer was holding back the crowd. The officer waved Johnson by when he saw the badge on his belt.

Images struck him in a rapid blur as he ran. Glass, plastic, and metal bits crunching under every step. An orange Volkswagen. The unforgettable wrenching smell of the smoke. EPS officers grimly waving for him to hurry. A twisted blue car with its roof buckled high in the middle, like a pup tent. Johnson could not help wondering what he would find.

He saw hands just above the window line, and then he looked down at a middle-aged man with blank eyes who was opening and closing his mouth like a fish, gasping for air. The driver held both hands high in the air above him and was pawing about, as though trying to hold something. The man seemed to be crammed halfway under the car, his head just above the level of the seat, facing backward at an oblique angle, toward the left rear wheel. His look of simple puzzlement stamped itself on Johnson's mind. He had to clamp down on himself to function. EPS officers were telling Johnson they couldn't get the victim out of the car. "Hold on, mister," Johnson said weakly.

The door was jammed. Johnson looked for room to lift the driver backward, but the steering column interfered, even though it was pointing almost straight up. The car no longer had a dashboard. There was only a space framed by curled sheets of charred metal. Through the window, Johnson could see exposed shock absorbers and what had once been a transmission. He could also see down into the street, because the car had no floor.

Dropping to his knees, Johnson peered under the car and confirmed his worst fears. The driver's legs were not broken and bent: they were out of sight because they were absent, blown off at the knees. Johnson scanned the pavement around the ragged wounds. He found no sign of the lower extremities, but he did see a streak of reddish-black grease leading backward from the dirty pool of blood under the driver. Johnson's emotions took refuge in his first professional deduction: the driver must have fallen through the hole in the floor while in motion, and the car must have dragged the stumps of his thighs along the street, twisting his upper body around to its present position.

Johnson heard a desperate cry just behind him. "I was in the car!" shouted the man with the singed hair. "I was there!"

"Okay, okay," said Johnson. He turned in a hurry to Jones. "Take the witnesses," he said. "I've got the scene." EPS officers were calling out that there was another victim. Johnson ran around the car to confront the sight of a woman on the grass being treated by a black woman and an EPS officer. They were Peterson and Kucmovich. The latter was calling out for more oxygen. The cylinder from his small portable unit was running low. Johnson looked down at a scene of trauma and splashes of color—the victim's blue jumpsuit, the green grass, and a great deal of bright-red blood.

He had seen enough. Johnson called Second District Police Headquarters with his hand radio. He needed at least two ambulances, he barked. Siren noise made it difficult for him to hear any acknowledgment. A full box assignment of fire equipment was pulling up to the circle—four engines, two ladder trucks, a chief's car, and an ambulance—and they were adding their bass horns to the sirens. Johnson shouted into the radio for the mobile crime unit and the bomb squad. This didn't look like any accident. And Homicide, he added. "And anybody else you can think of!" he said. "This is a disaster area!"

Johnson drew a deep breath, having committed himself to the judgment that this was a monstrous crime. As he looked quickly around Sheridan Circle, he felt a cold chill of apprehension. The bomber probably had a view of the area when he struck, he figured, and might still be watching. Johnson saw the stately Victorian embassy buildings and the huge traffic jam and the wobbly-looking EPS officer being helped to his feet nearby. He was suddenly suspicious of everyone, especially the man who said he was in the car and who was now shouting incoherently on his way from one place to the next. "Hey!" Johnson shouted to several EPS officers. "Don't let that guy get away from here!"

Skip Bingham followed Engine Number 1 to the circle and parked his ambulance in front of the Turkish embassy. The firemen were supposed to go in first to check for smoke and for injuries, but in this case standard procedure was superseded by the anxious EPS officer who ran right up to Bingham. "We need you here!" he said. "There's a guy with no legs."

Bingham grabbed a resuscitator and a small ambulance kit. So did his partner, Vincent Catalano. As always, people shouted at them as they ran toward the scene. Bingham tuned it all out. All he wanted to know was how many bodies there were. How many bodies? Two, he learned. This meant he had to make a decision by "triage," the fire department's emergency method of setting priorities. Basically, those with the more serious injuries go first unless two or more people have life-threatening ailments—in which case the one with the best chance to make it goes first. Bingham ran to one victim and then the other. He thought the driver's chances were slim, the woman's good. He told Catalano to take the driver. On the grass, Kucmovich told Bingham he had run out of oxygen. Peterson said she was a doctor and there was no pulse and the victim had to be taken to the hospital immediately. Bingham got the oxygen going, checked the pulse, and ran back for the stretcher.

Detective Johnson was off to the side, trying to calm the man with the singed hair. "What happened?" he asked.

"They put a bomb in the car!"

"Who is they? Who put a bomb in the car?"

"The Chilean fascists did it! The sons-of-bitches!"

"What Chilean fascists did it? How do you know?" Johnson pulled out his notebook and pen.

The man looked pained. He wanted to tell it all in a second.

"Tell me," said Johnson.

The man saw the ambulance stretcher in the grass. He pushed his way past Johnson.

A second screaming ambulance pulled into Sheridan Circle, this one from the southeast, on Massachusetts Avenue. Officer C. A. Hebron of the Metropolitan Police Department (MPD) bomb squad pulled up just behind it. Hebron was known in the department for his laugh and his honest face and his friendship with Bruno, a German shepherd trained for explosives. Hebron and Bruno had worked together five years. Their job was to make sure there were no other bombs—no "secondary devices," as the training manual calls them. Hebron readied Bruno, and the two of them walked around the wrecked car and the Volkswagen. Bruno smelled no undetonated explosives. Then, with rope from the cruiser, Hebron began to seal off the area from gathering spectators.

Firemen from the trucks helped Bingham with the stretcher. They had it ready next to the female victim when Peterson halted them. She looked disapprovingly at the stretcher. "You can't put her on that," she said. "It has no back support."

"What?" cried Bingham. "That's what we always use!"

"I don't care," said Peterson. "I'm a doctor, and I don't authorize moving this woman until you get something under her back. Hurry!"

Bingham ran off in exasperation. He did this work every day, and he felt the field medic's traditional resentment toward higher medical authorities. He ran back with a spine support board from the ambulance. Within a few seconds, the stretcher was being hoisted in the back and the siren started. Peterson climbed in. The man with the singed hair tried to join her, but he ran into Bingham.

"That's my wife!" shouted the man. "I'm going with her!"

"No, you're not," said Bingham. "You'll just be in the way."

"I want to be with my wife!" the man persisted. "I was in the car!" He pointed toward the wreck.

"Yeah, sure," said Bingham. He was certain that no one could be walking around after that explosion. It occurred to him that this man might be the murderer.

"I *was!*" shouted the man. "Let me go with her!"

"No!" snapped Bingham, pullling the door shut. "You can't help. One of these guys will take you to the hospital."

As Ambulance Number 6 roared off, firemen pried open the driver's door of the blue car with a huge crowbar. They also popped the steering wheel off its column. An EPS officer was holding Private Catalano's oxygen mask over the driver's face. Even before the firemen pulled the victim out of the car, Catalano was under the car, groping in the ooze of the leg wounds with small tourniquet clamps, trying to stanch the rush of blood. Catalano soon sped off in the back of the second ambulance, working without hope. The driver no longer gasped for air. He showed a death pallor and no pulse. There was nothing left for the heart to pump. He had bled dry in less than ten minutes.

Kucmovich thought the man with the singed hair was out of his head. He might have a concussion or internal injuries. Kucmovich ushered him to the cruiser. On the way to the hospital, the man suffered fits of eerie calm interrupted by tears and expletives.

Detective Johnson was having doubts about police work. Grisly murder and rape scenes swept by him again. In particular, he could not shake an early memory of himself as a young scooter patrolman running eagerly into a neat back yard on an accident call, only to find an old man who had sat in a lawn chair and bitten the barrel of a rifle and blown parts of his head all over a white clapboard wall. That day haunted Johnson. As consolation, it provided sturdy evidence that he was not inclined to vomit on the job, and for this he was grateful. He had just seen a few officers on Sheridan Circle getting sick from the smell.

Johnson pushed his way through the police officers and hospital personnel who were already screening entrants to the emergency room at George Washington University Hospital. His partner, Jones, stalked the halls, taking down the names of anyone who might know anything about the victims or the crime scene. Johnson found the man he was looking for on a table in a small treatment room, wearing a green hospital gown. Doctors and nurses were treating him for facial cuts and abrasions, having removed a small piece of metal from his breastbone. While they were finishing the medical work, Johnson peered over the shoulder of an administrator and copied information from the inevitable admission form. It said: *Michael P. Moffitt. Date of birth: July 29, 1951.* There was another form for the female victim: *Ronni Karpen Moffitt. Date of Birth: January 10, 1951.* They were both only twenty-five.

Johnson resumed his interview. He fended off intruders and shouted to hold Moffitt's attention. Where did Moffitt work? What exactly did he remember of the explosion? What were the names of the
Chilean fascists? Moffitt started and stopped frequently. He related
mundane details of his schedule that morning, and he also blurted
out references to great events like military coups and assassinations
and battles between the hawks and the doves. Johnson scribbled as
fast as he could. Moffitt kept breaking down. He wanted to talk to
his friends. He swore at the murderers. And mostly he wanted to
know how his wife was. Johnson pressed him firmly, then rudely,
then cruelly. He was determined to learn the details now, while they
were fresh in Moffitt's mind—especially of the minutes before and
after the explosion. "Hey, look!" shouted Johnson. "There's no way
you're ever gonna get even unless you tell me everything!" Johnson
kept pushing, and as he did so, he felt desperately lost. He sensed
that he was in the middle of a fleeting opportunity to piece together
an incredibly complicated event. But there wasn't enough coordination. Chaos was winning. Every second the opportunity was unravel-
ing. He wondered why the Homicide guys hadn't come to take over.
Or the FBI. Johnson was only a junior detective. Fate had placed him
in the eye of another big moment, and all he could do was grill the
suffering man in front of him. Johnson kept at it. He had a premonition that the wife was dead and that Moffitt would not be able to
function when he learned it.

Sweat was pouring off Skip Bingham's face as he methodically
pounded Ronni Moffitt's chest. The driver's body lay in an adjoining
room. Dana Peterson sat outside, exhausted. At seven o'clock that
morning she had completed a twenty-four-hour shift in the operating
room, and now she was back at her own hospital.

Bingham was serving more or less as a manual laborer in the
midst of expensive technicians. Doctors worked over Ronni Moffitt
with feverish deliberation, while Bingham reached among them to
keep up the pace of the CPR. Five regular thrusts and then a pause
for a breath by the victim. Except there was no breath. Bingham
paused anyway. The doctors and nurses talked very little. They drew
blood and rushed to type it for transfusions. They started three IVs
to halt dehydration. They gave several injections of heart stimulants,
with increasing dosages. They made an incision just below the two
neck wounds and inserted a tracheostomy tube in order to pump oxygen directly into the lungs. None of these measures helped. Then

they sent repeated jolts of electric current into the chest between Bingham's poundings, placing the two electrodes over her heart. There was no visible response and nothing on the charts. The doctors knew what this meant. Time had worked against them. Finally, one of them drew a scalpel twelve inches across her chest—to clear hemorrhage and to get directly at the heart and lungs.

Bingham walked out of the room. His arms ached from nearly forty-five minutes of continuous pounding. He lit a cigarette in the hall. When he opened the hospital door to get some fresh air, bright lights hit him in the face. Microphones and television cameras dotted a sizable crowd. Bingham found himself staring at his own battalion chief, a lofty official known to show up only for promotions, parades, and four-alarm fires. "Don't say anything!" ordered the chief. A man in a conservative suit identified himself as an FBI agent and repeated the instruction. Bingham was astonished. The gore of the morning had made little impression on him. Young as he was, life in the fire department's ambulance had made him callous to the results of head-on collisions, shotgun blasts, knife fights, and babies bashed against hard walls. Bingham protected himself with raw jokes and cynical pleasures. In a way, it was all meat to him. But this reception was shocking beyond his experience. He could feel the pulse of the event. This was big, he knew. National news. Maybe international.

Bingham pushed his way toward a man he knew, a reporter for local Channel 5. "What's going on?" he asked the reporter. "Who's in there?"

"Some guy named Letelier," said the reporter. "An ambassador from Chile or somewhere. That's what we hear."

Inside, a doctor left the room a few minutes after Bingham. He made his way down the hall, steeling himself for the direct approach. "Your wife is dead," he told Michael Moffitt, and Detective Johnson's interview soon ended.

3 ▣ REACTION

One by one, the brass assembled in front of the Greek embassy. Their unhurried walks and deliberate expressions distinguished them from the hyperactive lesser officers. Captain Joe O'Brien, chief of the homicide squad, was there with his arms folded, revealing a large blue tattoo on each forearm. O'Brien was a freckled Boston Irishman who had spent twenty-four years in Washington's MPD, twelve of them in Homicide. He tended to speak in "yeps" and "nopes," and his reputation as a shrewd, solid cop was such that he had no known enemies inside the various law-enforcement agencies, which are notorious for professional jealousy. O'Brien's boss, the assistant chief of the criminal investigative division, was also there, along with the assistant chief of the traffic division.

These police executives were joined by the entire top echelon of EPS—the chief, deputy chief, and an inspector—as well as some civilian officials of the Secret Service, who were taciturn, almost clandestine. It was their job to make sure President Ford was not a target. Explosives experts from the Treasury Department's Alcohol, Tobacco and Firearms (ATF) Bureau joined the group. So did a couple of fire chiefs. Towering above them all was Neil Sullivan, representing the FBI's Washington field office (WFO).

Each new arrival shook hands with the other executives. Most of them already knew each other from similar conclaves in the past. A few months earlier, a man had been shot down on the White House lawn after vaulting over the fence, and within minutes representatives convened from these same agencies, plus the park police. Such large gatherings were unique to Washington, where special federal laws and the presence of official foreign personnel created a maze of conflicting jurisdictions. As always, the brass exchanged small talk and waited for facts to develop. They seemed unperturbed by the nearby pandemonium.

More than a hundred officers from the assorted agencies responded to Sheridan Circle within the first hour. Homicide detectives and regular detectives and FBI agents were interviewing each other, trying to make sense of the crime. A few common facts floated about, gathering force by repetition: the driver was an ambassador from Chile, which raised the possibility of political assassination, and no witness had yet reported seeing anybody that looked like the killer. Another fact came by radio from the hospital: Letelier had been pronounced dead on arrival. This meant the homicide squad was in. Word was relayed to O'Brien.

The mobile crime unit (MCU) was there with its evidence van, a kind of traveling laboratory. MCU officers spent little time looking for fingerprints. The bomb had been too destructive. Instead, they began to take photographs and gather debris. Their mission was to preserve all physical evidence, which put them immediately at odds with the fire department and the traffic division. Firemen yanked the gas tank out of the blue car. Then they hosed down both the tank and the car itself. The mobile crime officers could only grimace as bits of evidence were washed not only out of position but out of reach, down the sewer. They fared better with the traffic cops, who were anxious to relieve a massive traffic jam that had angry motorists backed up Massachusetts Avenue more than a mile, past Washington Cathedral. Every time the traffic officers tried to open a lane on the far side of Sheridan Circle, away from the bombed car, someone would shut it down again.

FBI agents took the side of the mobile crime unit and the detectives, against the traffic division. Arguments broke out. A police inspector who had no particular reason to be on the scene accosted a sergeant of homicide detectives, who did, and ordered him to leave the area. After loud protests, the homicide sergeant was forced to yield. He circled back again when the inspector moved on.

Carter Cornick and Al Seddon drove the official vehicle of the FBI's bomb squad up on the sidewalk near the circle. Traffic police promptly ordered them to move. They had trouble maneuvering in the tangle of official cars. Finally, they ducked under the crowd-control rope, flashing credentials. The smoke cloud still hung over the area, twenty minutes after detonation. Seddon got a quick briefing from the FBI agents already there and then ran to his counterpart in the police bomb squad, whom he knew. Cornick followed. He was "just off the boat" from assignment in Puerto Rico and knew hardly anyone in Washington.

The two FBI agents were concerned that there might be another bomb. Three years earlier, they had responded together to a car bombing on Magdalena Avenue in San Juan. Then, as now, the crime scene was roped off and the destruction awesome. Even before the command post had been set up, the inquisitive Seddon was poking around in a nearby culvert when he kicked a stray paper bag that turned out not to be empty. Seddon, to his horror, found the bag full of dynamite that was hooked up to a ticking clock. That second bomb had gone off just after technicians threw it into a special concrete-and-steel container on the back of the bomb truck. Ever since then, Cornick figured he owed one to Seddon.

The chief of the police bomb squad assured Seddon that the area had been combed by men and by dogs. Seddon crossed the sidewalk to report this to Sullivan in the conclave. The two of them conferred on matters of jurisdiction. As yet, there was no reason for the FBI to take part in the case, but Seddon had a few ideas based on the statutes under which the FBI bomb squad worked. Seddon roared off again under siren to find a pay phone. He made his first call to the office. In a clipped, emergency voice, Seddon asked a secretary to read to him the exact language of Sections 1116 and 1117 of Title 18 of the U.S. Code. Twice. There could be no mistakes.

At the crime scene, police detectives were beginning to fan out to knock on doors in search of witnesses, having exhausted the small supply of eyewitnesses and volunteers. Mike Pickett, as the first homicide detective to arrive, dispersed the group with informal instructions. Then he stared at his notebook. Among many interviews, there was one with a young scooter officer who said he had gotten in a few words with Michael Moffitt while Moffitt was reeling around the area in shock. "Embassy was out to get him and they did!" said Pickett's note. Which embassy, he wondered. Letelier's own embassy? Pickett mulled this over as he looked at a huge stone row house on the other side of Sheridan Circle. The blue car had passed it a few seconds before the bomb went off. Pickett shrugged. There was no getting around it. Somebody was going to have to go to the Chilean embassy—soon. Pickett did not want to go alone. He hated the task of notifying victims' families, and he did not feel comfortable with the idea of marching into a foreign embassy. So he asked Detective Ed Talbert to go with him.

A prim woman came to the door. Pickett identified Talbert and himself as MPD detectives. The woman, speaking English with a slight Spanish accent, identified herself as the social secretary. Talbert said there had been a bombing that morning. The woman nodded. Had she heard it? Yes, she had heard something, and everybody was watching all the people outside. Well, apparently one of the victims was a man named Letelier and he was the Chilean ambassador. The woman looked surprised but controlled. Was this Letelier's office, and had he just left there earlier that morning? The woman replied that there was a misunderstanding—Letelier was no longer the Chilean ambassador to the United States and had not been so for more than three years. Letelier was the *former* ambassador, she told them, having served from 1970 to 1973 under the previous regime. She told the detectives they were in the Chilean ambassador's official residence, not the embassy. The embassy itself was a few blocks away. Pickett wrote all this down and thanked the woman. So Mr. Letelier did not live there anymore? No, said the woman. She thought he and his wife lived somewhere in the Maryland suburbs, near Washington. Well, by any chance had Mr. Letelier *visited* the residence that morning? No. Was she sure? Yes, said the woman. Mr. Letelier never visited the residence anymore.

Al Seddon rushed back to Sheridan Circle with his report. It was all good, he told Sullivan. The Protection of Foreign Officials Act covered even former ambassadors. The State Department had said that Letelier qualified. His murder was a federal crime. "Okay, we're in," said Sullivan. "It's your ticket."

Seddon had just been given his biggest case, but he hesitated. It was a moment that would come back to gnaw at him. "Okay, but there's something I think you should know," he told Sullivan. He said he was taking a correspondence course toward a master's degree, and his exams were coming up that Friday. It was Tuesday. The case agent on something this big would be buried in paperwork for at least a week, and Seddon needed a little time to study. That wouldn't do, Sullivan interrupted. Better get somebody else. Seddon recommended Carter Cornick.

Now Sullivan hesitated. He didn't know Cornick. Seddon gave a quick sales pitch. Cornick was a ten-year Bureau man who had handled a lot of bank robberies and a few bombing cases. He was known as a "bird dog," a tenacious agent. Seddon knew him well and would vouch for him. Still, Sullivan hesitated. Was it possible that Seddon was trying to unload all the paperwork on a raw agent whom he could dominate by means of his extensive contacts in Washington? "He'll do all right," Seddon urged. Sullivan finally agreed. He dispatched Robert Satkowski, supervisor of the WFO bomb squad, to give Cornick the news. "Carter," said Satkowski, "it's your ticket. Will you run the crime scene?"

Cornick said yes and felt the weight of it at once. This was an intimidating crime, far from his usual one-pistol bank robbery. It was about to rain. The police had a big head start. Nearly fifty FBI agents were standing around the periphery of Sheridan Circle awaiting direction, and as a newcomer Cornick did not know who was good at what. On instinct, he decided to treat this crime like a bank robbery, although he hoped the case would be different in at least one respect: in bank robberies, as a rule, either you catch the suspects within the first few hours or you don't catch them for a long time.

As was his habit, Cornick tried to fix upon the most important tasks and then stick to them through the chaos. He was a man of order. He made up rules and homilies for any occasion, and then he repeated them to himself and to others. "We've got to get control of the crime scene," he told Seddon. Seddon agreed. He was passing the word among the FBI agents that they were in the case and that Cornick was the case agent—the one in charge. Cornick asked someone to summon the FBI bomb technicians. "Where is the debris?" he kept asking. Several policemen mentioned that cars had driven off with some of it. Cornick chafed at the inefficiency. "We've got to get control of the crime scene," he repeated.

Cornick and Seddon walked out into the huge grassy area inside the traffic circle. In the middle stood a life-size iron replica of Union General Philip Sheridan, on horseback. Cornick made up more rules. "We've got to make sure there aren't any more targets," he said. "And we've got to know the exact movements of that car." Was there a backup bomb waiting for Letelier at his office? Or for the Moffitts at their home? These things had to be checked out. Seddon was making a small sketch of the area. Every inch of it had to be searched.

Homicide detective Pickett had drawn his own makeshift map of Sheridan Circle on the back of a page in his notebook. He was standing near the orange Volkswagen, taking some final notes on the positions of the cars, when he heard the sound of a ferocious argument. It was coming from behind a large tree. Pickett looked around to see Sullivan going at it with the head of the local ATF office. Captain O'Brien was giving them plenty of room. The ATF man was making a strong claim for federal jurisdiction in the case, arguing that the FBI terrorism statutes would not apply until somebody tried to take credit for the act. Sullivan scoffed at this. He cited the Protection of Foreign Officials statutes. The ATF man retorted that there was not yet even a ruling of homicide. Letelier might have been transporting a bomb that went off by accident, for all that was known, and it was ATF's job to investigate the unauthorized use of dangerous explosives. Sullivan said the FBI was calling it a murder.

Pickett smiled as he listened to this debate among the feds. He beckoned to a fellow police detective. "Let the bastards argue," he said. "We'll take care of business." Pickett was looking at the nearby officers of the mobile crime unit, a renowned outfit that had been called in for forensic opinions on the assassinations of John Kennedy and Martin Luther King, Jr. The mobile crime officers waited for no orders and paid attention to no arguments. They walked methodically around the blue car. They carried self-sealing plastic bags for anything that looked like part of a bomb or a car or a personal effect. Each item was numbered, marked for location, and returned to the mobile crime van.

For Cornick, the paperwork began even before he organized his men. Supervisor Satkowski ran up to him. "We've got to get out a teletype," he declared. "We've got to give the Bureau something." Cornick sighed, looked around, and ran to the door of the Irish embassy. Using a telephone in the foyer, he dictated a breathless teletype for dissemination to headquarters and all FBI offices. Former Chilean ambassador murdered. When and where. Major Bureau investigation under way by agents on the scene. "And that's about it for now, honey," Cornick drawled to the secretary. To preserve his sanity in times of stress, Cornick impersonated a Virginia Cavalier or a Confederate cavalry officer. This was not difficult for him, as his family had occupied the same piece of Virginia land for three hundred years.

Cornick ran back outside into the middle of a late summer rainstorm. He and Seddon found shelter in a big ATF bomb truck. "A wet agent," Cornick told the group, "is a dumb agent." In the truck, Seddon was drawing an impressively detailed map of the area, correct to scale and "vectored" into quadrants. When the rain slackened, they collared every available law-enforcement officer and divided the group into four "search teams," based on the map. Some police officers snickered at the effort, calling it a junk patrol, since the mobile crime unit had already collected the items of value near the car. But they went along, placated by Cornick's assurance that the evidence would be delivered to the mobile crime van.

It was a little more than an hour after the concussion. The FBI officials had been cautious, bureaucratic, and imperious. They were also thorough. In this respect, the Bureau way was Cornick's. "Pick up everything," he urged—coins, safety pins, bottle tops. "The crime scene is here only once." No one could tell what might have been part of a bomb. The lab would discard the irrelevant material, but anything overlooked now would be lost. The search teams went over their pie-shaped areas twice. They swept the streets and the sidewalks. All the sweepings went into evidence bags. Then, with the help of the firemen, they went so far as to pump the water from the sewers and from the puddles along the curbs. From the pump tanks, the water was expelled through metal screens. Anything trapped in a screen went into an evidence bag.

Seddon and Cornick measured the distance between the bomb crater and the driver's door of the blue car—82 feet. That was roughly how far the car had traveled after detonation. The two agents found Cecil Kirk, head of the mobile crime unit, and Stu Case, the bomb man from the FBI lab, kneeling over the small crater. It was about the size of a cereal bowl. Curled bits of asphalt were scattered around it like wood chips. The lab men talked it over. Their preliminary conclusion was that the bomb had been constructed so as to direct its force upward. This reinforced Cornick's determination to push the search for debris into high places. "A bombing crime scene has a vertical component," he kept saying. The teams shook small trees, in case debris had landed on the leaves. They went up fire ladders and shook the limbs of the big trees. Then they eyed the roofs and window ledges of the surrounding embassies.

Mindful of protocol, Cornick cautioned that embassies were legally "foreign soil." Agents had no authority to search anywhere in or on them, even with a warrant. Cornick would have to ask permission. He obtained it from most embassies, but officials at the Romanian embassy—the one closest to the explosion—balked at the request.

Like everyone else, they were jittery, and they were not about to allow security officials from a capitalist country to trek through the private rooms upstairs. Cornick negotiated. What if the agents went to the roof on the outside, using fire ladders? This did not appeal to the Romanians either, but they finally agreed to a compromise. Two agents, no more, could go up a ladder to the roof, provided that they stayed briefly and took no cameras. Romanian security officers would be on the roof to make sure the Americans did not photograph or closely inspect the secret communications equipment.

A hook-and-ladder truck pulled around the corner, and two agents were soon climbing gingerly to the roof. As they ascended, the blinds snapped shut on all the embassy windows so that no one could see inside. FBI agent Perry Speevack stepped off the ladder and looked down. He was a hundred feet horizontally removed from the bomb crater in the street, and more than forty feet above it, but the roof was nevertheless littered with bomb debris. Speevack was dumbfounded. Hurriedly, in front of the Romanians, he picked up the ruptured frame of a Motorola car radio, along with assorted wires, an intact resistor, and bits of metal. He saw, but did not take, small pieces of flesh from the lower part of Orlando Letelier's legs.

Shortly after noon, Officer C. A. Hebron and Bruno finished their examination of Ronni Moffitt's car. They found no backup bombs. The car was parked outside the Institute for Policy Studies, where Letelier and both Moffitts had worked. Hebron took Bruno inside the five-story building. Stunned friends of the victims were in mourning. Some were crying; others were already on the telephone, answering a barrage of inquiries, notifying supporters, planning a press conference. Hebron worked Bruno in and out of the rooms among them. He heard a shout from above and ran up to the second floor. "Hey, C.A.!" called another K-9 officer. "Try your dog in this room!"

Hebron gave Bruno the alert command and turned him loose in the small cubbyhole, which was stacked with political reports and congressional documents. Bruno became quite excited. Instantly he began to whine and turn around in small circles. But he did not point his body stiffly or bark at anything, as he was trained to do in the presence of explosives. Hebron was puzzled. Bruno's behavior was not in the book. The other dog had acted the same way—excited but not decisive. Hebron called his superiors to the Institute by radio. When they arrived, a search of the room produced nothing to clear up the mystery. The technicians and officers remained apprehensive as the dogs moved on to other rooms.

Occupants of the building reacted to the patrols, becoming more than apprehensive. They would not have been comfortable with these intruders even on the calmest of days. IPS staff people had arrayed themselves against armed men in uniform ever since the early 1960s, when the Institute had been created to promote interest in world disarmament. In succeeding years, the Institute became well known as a liberal "think tank," producing studies critical of the Vietnam War and later of American national-security policies. In the late 1960s, FBI informants had infiltrated Institute seminars and sifted through its garbage in a campaign to intercept the Institute's plan of attack. The campaign had been unsuccessful, largely because the disparate intellectuals at the Institute seldom agreed on any plan or analysis. Nevertheless, they returned the hostility of the government and tended toward common sensibilities that went in and out of focus with the great issues of the day. Their sensibilities ran sharply against uniform dress, German shepherd dogs, policemen, wealth, and hierarchy—in favor of Hush Puppies, freedom songs, demonstrators, the poor, and political abstractions scribbled on a blackboard. Generally, in the past, Institute researchers had maintained a certain academic distance from their causes. They were committed and political, but they were not politicians. They cared about the Third World, but they did not live in it. They proposed and exhorted regarding matters of power from a margin of safety, as moral observers.

Now that thin margin of aloofness was shattered. Three Institute people—a leader, a researcher, and a fund raiser—had been bombed, two of them hideously murdered. Then men with dogs and guns were marching up and down the halls of the Institute, shouting orders and talking of bombs. It was unreal. IPS staff people followed the officers, out of bravery caused by mistrust. They were scared of a second bomb, but they were also suspicious of the police. Was all this a ruse? The dogs smelled a bomb. Was this part of a plot to say that Letelier's own friends had constructed the murder weapon? Such fears built one upon another. If a professional assassination on Sheridan Circle was possible, what could be farfetched? Institute people conferred among themselves. What if these guys were there to plant something? They needed time. Finally they told Hebron and the others to leave. No more searches. The policemen were perplexed. It was not safe to leave, they said. What harm could be done by a search? The Institute people insisted. Hebron left to report that the search had been obstructed. He still wondered what Bruno had smelled. His superiors wondered why Letelier's colleagues were so

uncooperative, and they debated about who would be blamed if there
was a secondary explosion in the building.

Five blocks away, arguments outlived the search at the crime
scene. The ATF officers wanted to run some tests on the car. FBI
Supervisor Satkowski wanted to take custody of the evidence bags in
the mobile crime van. And Cecil Kirk wanted to keep the area sealed
off until mobile crime officers could get a police helicopter in the air
to take some aerial photographs. Kirk's desires provoked the traffic
division into an ultimatum. There would be no more delay. There
would be no traffic jam through the lunchtime rush hour, as there
had been all morning, because traffic officers were about to move
out in force and wave the cars through Sheridan Circle.

This determination put pressure on the FBI and ATF. The blue car
had to be moved. No one could take the chance that a passing car
would bump into it and damage the evidence. FBI officials lodged a
firm claim to the car, again overriding ATF, and their victory suggested a compromise with the mobile crime unit. The police, having
sole jurisdiction over Ronni Moffitt's death, would take all the loose
evidence, and the FBI would take Letelier's car. Under this agreement, the mobile crime van packed up and left for the police evidence
room.

Meanwhile, Stanley Alexander, administrative sergeant of the homicide squad, called Medical Examiner Luke with the news that two
bodies were waiting at George Washington University Hospital.
Luke sent ambulances for them early in the afternoon.

At 1:08, a tow truck left Sheridan Circle with the blue car, heading
for FBI headquarters. The flow of traffic resumed after a delay of
three and a half hours, and for most people, things returned to
normal.

4 ▣ REFEREE

U.S. Attorney Earl Silbert called Don Campbell in the morning, while the radio reports and telephone calls about the bombing on Sheridan Circle were coming to him in thick bunches. It was imperative, said Silbert, to avoid repetition of the "Watergate problem." Campbell understood. Four years earlier, as line prosecutors, the two of them had failed to interject themselves firmly enough into the initial investigation of a break-in at the Watergate. As a result, a quarrel had festered between the FBI and the police, and some of the physical evidence was actually lost during the recriminations. That was a lesson.

Afterward, Silbert and Campbell had been obsessed with Watergate for more than nine months, until, just as the case was breaking open to spectacular national publicity, they had been replaced by the Watergate special prosecutor. Silbert and Campbell remained rather anonymously in the U.S. Attorney's Office, defending their performance as a good one that had been rolled over by a great tide of politics. Now they still spoke almost a private sign language based on the minutiae of their Watergate experience. Campbell didn't have to ask which of the Watergate problems was worrying Silbert. He promised his friend, colleague, and boss that he would assign a prosecutor to the case immediately, with full warning about the hazards of political, front-page investigations.

Campbell hung up the phone and sat back to contemplate his choice. His selection pool consisted of the combative lawyers who had survived in the harsh world of Washington's criminal courts, handling not only federal prosecutions but also the long gauntlet of rapes, murders, and misdemeanors that would normally fall to a district attorney. Young lawyers competed intensely for positions in the huge Washington U.S. Attorney's Office. Those who liked the work and compiled good records might win promotion to one of the two elite units, Fraud and Major Crimes.

Ten lawyers worked under Campbell in Major Crimes. Of these, he considered four for the Letelier-Moffitt case. They were distinguished from the others not by intelligence or legal skill, which are relatively equal in the upper levels of the prosecutor's office, but by more personal qualities. In Campbell's judgment, they were a little more dogged and contentious than the others. They hated to lose cases. They loved being correct. They would argue the slightest point with a lofty judge or a lowly witness. They would cajole, babysit, intimidate—perform all the myriad duties necessary to obtain convictions over the resistance of defense lawyers, under the scrutiny of judges, with the fragile cooperation of reluctant informants. They were prima donnas, known for temperamental fits of bombast in the office. In short, Campbell picked the four with the biggest egos. They all exhibited the traits of a prosecutor—touchy, given to detail—but each of them did so with his own personal style. In Campbell's mind, one was a commander, a forceful and exuberant personality who would either get his way or pitch himself into a fistfight if necessary. Another was a studier, who would outprepare his opponents. It was nothing for him to be laboring over papers in the office at three o'clock on a Sunday morning. The third was a charmer; the fourth a schemer.

Campbell soon eliminated the first two prosecutors, who, as work addicts, had accumulated such heavy case loads that they could not possibly add another full-time investigation. The charmer, Larry Barcella, served as Campbell's deputy and did not have so many cases, but he was prosecuting a special rape case. His trial blood was up. He would be occupied for weeks, maybe months.

That left the schemer, Gene Propper. He was only twenty-nine, a year or two younger than the other three candidates, but he had already tried more than fifty felonies, and only one jury had returned a not guilty verdict. That loss, Propper insisted, was President Nixon's fault, not his. The President, for political reasons, had ordered each U.S. Attorney's Office to fulfill a quota of "smut cases," and Propper wound up prosecuting the distributor of *Teenage Orgies*. The case was weak. Propper had recommended against taking it to trial. Then the judge excused any potential juror who objected to the sight of pornography evidence, so Propper had faced a jury of young men who liked looking at the pictures. Thus, at least, he explained the loss. Propper tended to defend himself with a mixture of relish and indignation that others found amusing. His intrepid secretary kept a file marked *Propper's Mistakes*, in which she recorded instances of incorrect legal citations, lost bets, misspelled words—nothing was too trivial. She was obliged to hide the file, knowing that Propper would object to every item.

Propper was new to Major Crimes. His reputation as a trial attorney was such that Campbell had brought him up from a felony trial section earlier in 1976 specifically to try the first of the cases growing out of an undercover operation called STING I. Police officers and FBI agents, posing as Mafia racketeers, had opened a major fencing business in downtown Washington. They secretly photographed every customer who came in to sell stolen property, and then one night they arrested 120 suspects in a great law-enforcement and media blitz known as the STING. Propper himself was the supervising prosecutor of STING II, or "Got Ya Again," which culminated in another mass arrest on the night of July 6, 1976. The press loved the flair of it, and the STING results encouraged FBI officials to expand their undercover operations into the area of political corruption, toward future campaigns such as ABSCAM.

Now, ten weeks after the STING II arrests, Campbell had seen enough of Propper's work to think highly of him. Campbell thought of Propper as a schemer because of his customary reaction to obstacles. He was best at cooking up schemes to circumvent them. He would go around by another way, and to do so he would try unorthodox moves. Once, stymied in the investigation of a murder conspiracy, Propper summoned to his office a marginal witness. Propper thought he might have seen something. The man was a street dude, afraid to talk, and he made fun of the bearded prosecutor with a small basketball hoop mounted over his trash can. Propper took offense, boasting that he was very good at basketball. The street dude was incredulous: no white boy in a coat and tie could be good at basketball. Propper offered a challenge. They would shoot ten times each right there on the spot. If Propper won, the dude would tell what he knew. Otherwise, Propper would let him go without putting him before the grand jury. The man accepted the gambit. They stood behind Propper's desk and fired paper wads across the room, envel-

oped by the heat of competition. Propper won, 9–6, and the astonished man kept his word. His information proved helpful, and
eventually there was a murder case.

In Campbell's mind, the only drawback in Propper's performance
was his low boredom threshold. He worked at two speeds—fast or
very, very slow. Either he was lost in an efficient frenzy or he was
bored. When bored, Propper would fidget, or he would wander into
Campbell's office and let fly at the dartboard. He held the office
scoring record. On the few occasions when he did not defeat Campbell and Barcella, Propper always explained why the outcome was a
freak of circumstance.

Campbell considered all this. He thought Propper was the best
prosecutor in the office for the case, as long as the investigation did
not bore him, and Campbell concluded that the Sheridan Circle bombing was hardly likely to be boring. Overwhelming maybe, but not
boring. Campbell tried to call Propper several times without success.
He searched the office, but Propper was not there.

About the time the FBI tow truck left the crime scene, Propper
was eating lunch in the basement cafeteria of the U.S. District
Courthouse, near the Capitol. A close friend, another assistant United States attorney (AUSA), joined him. They talked mostly about
their long-standing tennis rivalry and about subjects related to Propper's bachelor life. Titillation was much in the news. That morning's
Washington Post contained a long excerpt from the forthcoming
Playboy interview in which candidate Jimmy Carter confessed to
feelings of sublimated lust.

Propper saw Campbell prowling through the cafeteria and knew
there was business in it. Campbell was an easygoing man, with a
bald crown and a small red mustache, whose genial manner imparted
a family touch to the unruly prosecutors under his supervision in Major Crimes. He was a good administrator, but so low key in his approach that only an urgent matter would send him searching
downstairs in person.

Campbell made his way to the table and nodded hello. He asked if
Propper had heard about the bombing that morning. Propper replied
that it had already ruined his day. An FBI agent had called to cancel
a scheduled presentencing meeting on a white-slave traffic case, and
Ed Talbert had canceled a conference on a burglary case. Propper
said Talbert had told him the crime scene was gruesome and that
Talbert had already gone to interview the Chilean ambassador. The

FBI agent had told him not to say anything about the bombing because it had not been released to the public. Propper laughed. "I said, 'What do you mean, it hasn't been released to the public?' " he recalled for Campbell. " 'It's a huge bombing in the middle of the city. How are you going to keep something like that secret?' He said, 'Well, don't mention it, anyway.' "

Campbell asked what Propper had on for the afternoon. Propper said not much. Nothing in the grand jury. Every cop in town seemed to be busy on the bombing. Campbell nodded. "You better work on this one, then," he said. "You got it, Gene."

"Thanks," sighed Propper, pretending to be burdened.

"Homicide's already working the scene," said Campbell. "It looks like the Bureau wants in, too. Earl wants you to call them both as soon as you can. Make sure they don't start fighting and screw something up."

"I'll call O'Brien," said Propper. "Who's working it in the Bureau?"

"I don't know who the agent is," said Campbell. "But it's the bomb squad. The supervisor is a guy named Satkowski."

"Don't know him," said Propper.

"I don't either," said Campbell.

Propper was soon in his fourth-floor office, on the phone. Captain O'Brien promised to come straight over with a briefing. Someone in Satkowski's office said he was busy but would call back promptly. Propper was compiling a list of people to consult when O'Brien arrived. The captain ran through a quick summary of the known facts. Two of the three people in the car had died. Autopsies were under way. Letelier was a Chilean national and a socialist who had been an ambassador and a defense minister under the government that had been overthrown by the Chilean military in 1973. Letelier was living in exile in Washington, criticizing General Augusto Pinochet's military regime in Chile. Apparently, both Moffitts had worked for Letelier at an affiliate of the Institute for Policy Studies. Their car would not start the previous afternoon, Monday, so the Moffitts rode home with Letelier for dinner and then took the Letelier car home with them. They had returned to Letelier's house Tuesday morning, about six hours ago, and Letelier was driving the three of them to work when the bomb went off. Many leads were coming in, but none looked promising as yet. Mobile crime recovered two watches at the scene, a wristwatch and a pocket watch. It was possible that one of them had been used in a timing device to detonate the bomb. The lab would have to study it. Interviews were going on all over the place, and O'Brien would send copies of written statements to Propper as soon as they were typed up that afternoon.

Propper thanked O'Brien and called Satkowski again as soon as the captain departed. Secretaries fended him off; Satkowski was still busy. By now, Propper was fuming. He finally located a fellow prosecutor who had worked a case with Satkowski. The "book" on him was discouraging: Satkowski's bomb squad was full of intelligence agents who hated to disclose anything to anybody. Propper simmered briefly over this report. He placed a call to Medical Examiner Luke and then went down to talk things over with Earl Silbert.

Late in the afternoon, a homicide detective delivered a stack of witness statements and police reports to Propper at his office, and he lodged a police complaint against the FBI. Bureau officials had been calling all day for copies of the police reports, he said, but they were not willing to reciprocate by giving their own reports to the police. It was the same old one-way street. He figured the FBI agents would try to get the police reports from Propper if they could, and it would not be fair for Propper to take sides.

The detective left, and two FBI agents showed up within fifteen minutes to ask Propper for copies of the police reports. Propper replied that he would not pass any agency's reports to another agency until he was satisfied that there would be cooperation by all the parties, adding that he was disappointed in Satkowski's teamwork so far. He wanted to see all the people working on the case at eleven-thirty the following morning, in his office. They should pass that along. He said he expected everything to work out fine, and as a sign of goodwill he gave the agents a copy of Michael Moffitt's statement to the police.

Later, a tired James Luke called Propper with a preliminary autopsy report. He said Ronni Moffitt's death was a tragic fluke. The medical examiners had probed the small cut just to the right of her windpipe and recovered a paper-thin missile—about the size of a dime, metal, shaped oddly like something between a circle and a rhomboid—that had embedded itself in the muscles around the third cervical vertebra. The missile had severed Ronni Moffitt's carotid artery, causing her death. Had its path been shifted an eighth of an inch to the left or right, she would have survived, Luke concluded. Doctors had delivered the sliver of metal, the murder weapon, to the mobile crime officer who observed the simultaneous autopsies.

Most of the evidence recovered in the autopsy came from the other victim, Letelier. Luke said the exposed wounds from the traumatic amputations of his legs were filled with so much foreign material that the autopsy was not yet complete. Luke was obliged to proceed by taking X-rays to search for metal and by dissecting the exposed areas at intervals of a half centimeter. He had already given hundreds of items to the mobile crime unit, including coiled springs and bits of rock and rubber. Luke said mobile crime had delivered a right foot in its shoe late in the day. It, too, would require X-ray and dissection. The left foot was still missing. He would resume the next morning, and the work would probably stretch into a third day. He had never faced such a task. Most autopsies take only two hours.

As always, Propper asked Luke if anything struck him as a likely clue. Probably not, Luke replied. He knew from the bodies that Letelier and Moffitt had been relaxed, in normal riding positions, expecting nothing. Other than that and the high level of physical damage to Letelier, there was nothing instructive, but Luke wanted to consult other coroners. He had never performed a bombing autopsy. He knew the coroner who had worked the famous 1969 Weatherman bombing in Greenwich Village, and he knew another one who had worked the case of an Oklahoma judge who had been bombed by the Mafia. Luke wanted to ask them about the powdered hair and the smell. That might be something. The powdered hair might be unusual, indicating the heat and intensity of the blast. And the smell was no longer that of burned flesh but remained powerful and unique. Luke asked Propper if he had owned an electric train as a kid.

"Sure," said Propper. "How come?"

"Well," said Luke, "do you remember the way your transformer would smell when it overheated? That electric-heat smell?"

"Kind of," Propper said vaguely.

"That's the only way I can describe it," said Luke. "The smell is overwhelming. It's still around here."

Carter Cornick remained at the FBI's Washington field office until after midnight, running between his small cubicle and the night steno pool. He sent secretaries to the files to retrieve anything the FBI had on the names he had heard that day, such as the Institute for Policy Studies. He filled out the paperwork to get the case designated a "Bureau Special," meaning that he would be able to command the time of agents in Washington and elsewhere on an expedited basis. He dictated long lists of questions to be answered and of people to be interviewed. He listened to Al Seddon's account of the briefing he'd just received on Letelier from his contacts at the CIA. He discussed the meaning of the few leads already coming in, and as he did he tried to memorize the names of all the agents who had been involved in the work that day. He dictated teletypes to other FBI offices.

A secretary reminded him that the teletypes and all other official communications require a special caption for the case—a name. Cornick pulled the files on other bomb squad cases. The captions, he found, tended to end in BOM. He thought of possible prefixes, drawn from words connected to the case—Washington, Letelier, Sheridan Circle, Chile. Of these, he preferred CHILBOM. The first batch of CHILBOM teletypes went out overnight, after Cornick went home. He felt swamped by the details, the potential reach of the case. His initial goal was to keep from going under.

Early Wednesday, mindful of the enormous headlines the murders had generated that morning, a large number of FBI agents marched in for the boss's first daily CHILBOM meeting. Special Agent in Charge (SAC) Nick Stames presided, listening to the reports, approving or disapproving the day's assignments. Agents left in pairs on a multitude of tasks. Many went to reinterview all the police witnesses, as it was deemed unsafe for the Bureau to rely on the police version of events. Two agents rushed through traffic to Michael Moffitt's house. They were to check his story by leaving there at precisely eight-forty and driving to the Letelier house. Then they were to wait twenty minutes and drive by the specified route to Sheridan Circle, timing each leg of the journey. For precision, they were to do this on three different mornings, including the following Tuesday.

"Carter," said Stames, "you'll be working with somebody in Major Crimes, just like in Watergate."

"What?" cried Cornick. "I'm not working with any damn U.S. attorney! We've got enough headaches already." Cornick spilled out the traditional FBI resistance against sharing control of a case. He said he had never worked with the U.S. Attorney's Office before and in fact had never even heard of the practice. In his opinion, it was dangerously unprofessional to mix the investigative function with the prosecutive function. CHILBOM was an FBI case, he declared, and the Bureau should take a "finished product" to the U.S. attorney, nothing less.

"I know all that," said Stames. "But this is Washington and this is a big case. I want you to go over there and meet the bastard and co-ordinate with him!"

With the FBI posture toward the U.S. Attorney's Office thus defined, Satkowski returned Propper's call. He apologized for the delay. Propper said the police representatives were already there, waiting. Satkowski said they would be right over. Stames decided to send Assistant SAC Sullivan along to add rank to the delegation.

Sullivan, Satkowski, and Cornick grabbed chairs from the hallway and squeezed themselves into one side of Propper's office. Captain O'Brien and a police lieutenant sat on the other side. Introductions and handshakes were exchanged, along with nervous jokes about how a case like this could get everyone fired. To the FBI contingent, Propper's obvious friendship with the police representatives was mildly disconcerting, as was his appearance—young, bearded, an orange motorcycle helmet at his side, the basketball hoop over the trash can. Propper would never do at the Bureau.

He opened the meeting by saying that Earl Silbert had asked him to stay on top of the case from the beginning, that he would do so, and that he expected the law-enforcement people to bring problems to him. For the benefit of the FBI agents, he emphasized that Major Crimes had been specially designed to investigate as well as to prosecute. He and the other AUSAs there could write out a subpoena in five minutes and then escort a witness personally before a grand jury. He possessed grand-jury and subpoena powers denied to law enforcement, and therefore he expected to coordinate their strategies and forestall disputes.

There was tension in the room. Everyone was talking cooperation, but Propper was making a bid to run things and the FBI people were saying the investigation would be too big for anyone but the Bureau. It was O'Brien's turn to speak. "Well, the way I see it, I've got two unsolved homicides in my jurisdiction," he began. "I can't walk away from this case. We're gonna run out our leads, but this thing smells political. It sure doesn't feel like a local homicide. So when we run out of things to do here in Washington, which won't take long, we're gonna stay out of the political area and the intelligence area. We're not gonna push that. I've got plenty of murders."

Relief spread through the room. The police captain had declined the fight. The meeting broke up with Propper thinking that perhaps O'Brien was the wisest one in the group.

Cornick went back to battle the telephone and the paperwork. With Stames's approval, he had already initiated a series of an-

nouncements on local radio and television stations, soliciting the help
of witnesses and of people who had noticed anything that might be a
clue. Now Cornick was in the midst of a three-day barrage during
which countless members of the public volunteered their suspicions
to the FBI. Cab drivers called to report delivering strange foreigners
to the vicinity of Sheridan Circle over the past few days. A sheriff
called from a nearby county to report that nine hundred sticks of dynamite had been stolen from a storage depot the previous weekend.
A couple called to report that they had been having a drink at Cou-
steau's Bar a couple of weeks earlier when a rather sinister man had
intruded upon their conversation to say that he was a demolitions expert who had spent a lot of time in Uganda, Northern Ireland, and
other centers of terrorism. An Englishman called to report that he
had been standing on the roof of the British embassy, doing mainte-
nance work that he could not specify, when he had heard the bomb
go off at Sheridan Circle, and that an unmarked, low-flying helicopter had passed by within a minute thereafter from the direction of
the explosion and he could describe this helicopter in great detail. A
woman called to report that she had been stopped at a red light a
block from Sheridan Circle just before the bomb went off and she
had noticed a group of four men walking toward the circle, one of
whom was a tall Oriental who had given her a haunting, enigmatic
smile. A man called long distance from New Jersey to report that
while walking the previous night he had encountered two fishermen
who were talking about a big bombing in Washington, that one of
the fishermen said, "Wait till Carter and Ford get it," that he had
spoken up for Carter, Ford, and the United States in response, that
the fishermen had proceeded to beat him unmercifully, and that one
of them had a mustache and a foreign accent. Cornick processed this
last report into the FBI file called "Threats to the President and
Presidential Candidates." He assigned some agents to field such
leads, taking descriptions, and he sent other agents out for the obligatory interviews with victims' family members and co-workers, and
with people who worked near the crime scene.

Late that afternoon, Detective Pickett called Propper from a Ford
dealership. He might just have something. A woman named O'Connor had called Homicide to report that at four-forty-five yesterday,
the afternoon of the murders, she had been walking behind three
white females and two white males on Massachusetts Avenue. Just
as they passed the Chilean embassy, the woman said, the taller of

the two men turned to his companions and said, "I wonder if they would believe me if I told them I did it." Then they all applauded and got into a car, O'Connor reported, the tall man driving. Pickett said O'Connor had been alarmed enough to write down a description of the tall man and the license number of the car. Pickett had traced it that morning. The car was brand-new, sold the previous week by a Ford dealer. Pickett was standing there with the salesman, who remembered the transaction well because he had just received in the mail a copy of *The CIA and the Cult of Intelligence*, personally autographed to the salesman by John Marks, co-author of the book and purchaser of the car. Pickett thought it was very strange. The salesman's description of Marks matched O'Connor's description of the man at the Chilean embassy. This guy was a CIA expert, maybe a spy, said Pickett. What did Propper think?

Propper was already deflated after a surge of adrenaline during Pickett's report. The book thing didn't sound right, he told Pickett. Killers don't write books, as a rule, much less send them through the mail.

Pickett agreed. But there was something else, he said. The car Marks had traded in was still there at the Ford dealer, uncleaned, just as Marks had left it. As a precaution, Pickett had asked the bomb squad to take a look at it. Officer C. A. Hebron and his dog, Bruno, were there now. Bruno was going crazy around the trade-in car. He was an explosives dog who had never been trained for marijuana or any narcotic drug. Pickett was asking the bomb squad to crane the trade-in car down to FBI headquarters to search it chemically for bits of explosives. He was also taking the book to look it over.

Propper called Cornick to convey this lead. It was a gesture of trust. Cornick agreed that it was interesting but unlikely, and he reciprocated by telling Propper that he was having explosives troubles of his own. The Bureau lab people wanted to run gas chromatography tests on the room at the Institute for Policy Studies, he said, but the IPS people were denying them entry. The tests were quite sophisticated, as Cornick understood it, and it was vitally important to collect air samples without delay.

This wasn't the only problem at IPS, Cornick added. Letelier's colleagues there were refusing all FBI interviews except those conducted in the presence of an IPS lawyer. This was unacceptable. It would have a chilling effect, Cornick declared. Michael Moffitt had already told the FBI of a left-wing spy who was suspected of having infiltrated IPS, and there was talk of money trouble at the Institute. How could people discuss such things freely in the presence of a lawyer who could prepare people for the questions and report the answers?

Propper plunged right in on this issue the next morning when he and Cornick went to IPS for an audience with a lawyer named Robert Borosage, who stood his ground. Borosage was not a practicing lawyer but a scholar and an activist who had devoted his life to analyzing and opposing practices of American imperialism. Letelier's murder had shattered plans for his thirty-first birthday party, and now he was the emergency defender for IPS during the crisis.

Borosage told Propper that he had consulted with no less a figure than former Attorney General Ramsey Clark and that Clark had said IPS people should have the same lawyer present during all interviews. Propper replied that Ramsey Clark was wrong. Borosage said he was planning to consult William Kuntsler, Leonard Boudin, and other well-known radical lawyers. Propper replied that he didn't care who Borosage consulted, that they wouldn't affect the standard practice of criminal law in the District of Columbia. He explained that a single lawyer was not allowed to accompany multiple witnesses during FBI interviews, and he told Borosage that if IPS insisted on that arrangement he would have no choice but to subpoena all witnesses before a grand jury—where no one is allowed to have a lawyer.

Borosage told Propper he should understand that IPS had good reason not to trust the United States government, that IPS had a multimillion-dollar damage suit pending against the FBI, that Propper should not be so harsh on people who were in shock and had not yet even buried two of their friends. Propper replied that he would make allowances for grief, but IPS people seemed to function well enough on other things, such as press interviews. Propper said that while he and Cornick were waiting downstairs, a magazine reporter had chatted with them about his interview with Letelier's secretary. This irritated Propper because the same secretary had told the FBI that she was making funeral arrangements and wouldn't be available for a day or two. Borosage said the reporter and the secretary were good friends. Propper said that didn't matter: it was unacceptable that IPS people were talking politics to the press while saying that they didn't have time to talk with the FBI agents who were trying to solve the murders.

Cornick injected himself into the prickly discussion with the observation that everyone there shared a "commonality of interest" in solving the case. What was past was past, he said. Now everyone should work together. This would become Cornick's anthem in political disputes, and he would deliver it in his finest Tidewater baritone.

Borosage said that some of the Chilean exiles at the Institute were very much afraid of being interrogated at the FBI building. They thought they might be put away and tortured. Propper said he could understand why people not familiar with the American legal system might be afraid. He could arrange to have them interviewed somewhere else. Borosage said he would have to consult his peers at the Institute about the other issues.

As they left, Propper invited Cornick back to his office for a strategy session. Cornick declined. There was a crisis back at WFO. "Gene, have you read this morning's New York Times?" he asked.

"No," said Propper, slightly puzzled.

Cornick hesitated over the prospect of confiding FBI business to an outsider. It went against the grain of his training. On the other hand, Propper had just supported the Bureau at IPS. "Well, Gene," he said gravely, "the Bureau was criticized in there this morning. Everybody's henshit over at the Bureau. You have no idea what this means."

Propper asked what had happened. Cornick grimly said that a clergyman named Wipfler had called Congressman Donald Fraser to say that four agents of the Chilean secret police (DINA) had been spotted on a plane leaving New York for Chile just after the murders. The congressman had called the FBI, and Cornick had sent a teletype to the New York office requesting an immediate interview with Wipfler. An agent had driven to Westchester County to see Wipfler late that night. Before the agent arrived, however, an aide to Congressman Fraser called Wipfler to inquire whether the FBI had followed up on his information. Wipfler said no, whereupon the aide had called the Times in Fraser's name to criticize the FBI for sluggishness in the Letelier investigation.

Propper thought Cornick was making too much of a peripheral issue. "So what?" he asked. "You guys will just have to move faster if you don't want any heat."

"That's not the point, Gene," Cornick declared. FBI headquarters, he explained, was stacked with a layered maze of "nitpickers" and "drones," known collectively as the Bureau, all of whom would demand to know the exact reasons why the FBI had been criticized in the public press. The burden of the replies would fall on Cornick.

Cornick had another, more serious objection. The *Times* had named Wipfler as a source, and this was making Chilean exiles fearful. They did not trust the FBI in the first place. Now they had additional reason to fear that their names would appear in the newspaper if they volunteered information to FBI agents. The dreaded Chilean DINA could then target them, as they believed DINA had targeted Letelier.

It was a mess, Cornick lamented. As to the substance of the Wipfler lead, it was not promising. Reverend Wipfler had not seen the four DINA agents himself but had heard about them from a Chilean friend at the United Nations whom he was reluctant to identify for the FBI agent. This man, in turn, heard it from someone else. It would take several weeks to trace the report back through sources who wished to communicate with the FBI only through protective codes. In the end, the original source would not be able to identify or describe the four men on the plane, whom he had taken for DINA agents because of their shifty mannerisms.

At his office, Propper talked by phone with Detective Pickett, who reported that the lab tests on John Marks's trade-in car were negative. The car was clean. Moreover, discreet inquiries about Marks had established that he was a CIA critic, a former State Department official, and a friend of many people at IPS. Pickett wanted to drop the lead. Propper agreed. They speculated on the causes of Bruno's reaction. Officer Hebron could not explain the two errors on successive days except to say that Bruno might have gotten some possum or rat in his nostrils. The dog had a reputation for a "good nose." Several years earlier, after a daring midday post-office robbery, only Officer Hebron had the faith to chase Bruno down several miles of isolated railroad track on a scent, but he had been rewarded when Bruno walked in on three thieves at a warehouse dividing the loot. This case helped win Hebron and Bruno's promotion to the bomb squad. Except for the Letelier case, Bruno's record would be perfect until he retired from police duty in 1980.

Pickett believed O'Connor's report about what Marks had said on the afternoon of the murders, but he concluded that it was either a poor spy joke or a statement out of context. He told Propper that the homicide squad was running short of things to do, and Pickett planned to return to his regular cases by Friday.

Propper had reason to regret Homicide's departure. He knew that only the FBI possessed the vast resources and geographical breadth for something like the Letelier investigation, but the Bureau had already struck him as less congenial, less freewheeling, more encumbered by organization. He would miss the familiar contacts in Homicide. So, as insurance, he made several calls asking that Homicide remain on the case, even if only on a limited basis.

Neither Pickett nor Propper had any way of knowing then what repercussions would follow from the Marks lead. From the day of the murder on, Marks and his friends, including journalist Taylor Branch, were assisting IPS in a private investigation of the murders, driving all over Washington asking hotel clerks to help solve the Sheridan Circle bombing. Everybody had heard of it. Almost all the clerks opened up their registration lists, telephone logs, anything that might be useful. Marks and his colleagues checked for Spanish guests, especially Chileans, hoping to find one of the few known "war names" of DINA agents. They referred to themselves jokingly as "junior FBI agents," but they were also angry, driven, and on edge. They were afraid of being followed, and they were afraid of telephone taps by the FBI, DINA, or unknown groups of terrorists. So they spoke in code words from pay phones.

When Marks and his colleagues learned that the police were making vague inquiries about *him*, that police dogs might have been snooping around his car, they felt a fresh stab of suspicion. Might DINA or the CIA be conspiring to pin the murders on Marks, the CIA critic? Propper, for his part, thought the IPS people behaved strangely. No one could explain all the circumstances. Paranoia and odd reactions swirled around one another. The initial Marks lead became a harmless but suitably twisted introduction to the spy world.

Propper knew very little about the CIA, but he knew that the Agency's name was shouted about from the first day. Some people claimed that the CIA was the author of the murders, others that it was knowledgeable. The CIA's involvement in international assassination plots was a hot topic of news then, scarcely a year after the headlines and congressional investigations revealing CIA attempts to kill Trujillo, Lumumba, Castro, and other foreign leaders. A Senate committee had produced a sensational study of the CIA's undercover work in Chile, focusing on a campaign under Richard Nixon and Henry Kissinger to prevent the socialist regime of Salvador Allende from coming to power. Propper remembered bits of this from the newspaper. He planned to read up on Chile and the CIA in the Library of Congress. His boss, Earl Silbert, was giving him advice on the CIA.

"They'll spin you," warned Silbert. "They'll lie to you, especially the people in operations. That's their business. That's what they did to us in Watergate."

"That's great, Earl," Propper said sarcastically. "So what do I do?"

Silbert considered the problem briefly. "Well, I'd talk to Tony Lapham," he said. "He's the new general counsel over there, I hear. Tony used to be an AUSA. He's a good man. I'm sure he doesn't know everything that's going on over there, and his own people may not tell him, but at least he won't knowingly deceive you. That's something. I'd call him." Propper placed a call to Tony Lapham at the CIA and went home at the end of the third day, but the case followed him. A police lieutenant called to say that Detective Stanley Wilson would be allowed to work on the Letelier case indefinitely. This was good news. Wilson spoke Spanish, which would be helpful, and he had already worked with Propper on the case of a man who had murdered his own nineteen-month-old son on July 8, 1974, by beating him with an extension cord and kicking him down the stairs. The man was now in prison.

Propper called Carter Cornick at home to inform him of the contact he planned with Tony Lapham at CIA. Cornick was apprehensive about the idea. Lapham was a high official in a parallel and competing intelligence agency. It would take a month of up-and-down memos in the Bureau to agree upon such a broad request for cooperation, and even then the request would have to come from an FBI official of appropriate rank. Propper had shortcut all this with a single phone call. "Hold on a second, Gene," said Cornick. "I think you'll find with the Agency, just like with the Bureau, that you won't be allowed to see most of the stuff that really interests you. It's too sensitive, and you don't have a security clearance."

Propper did not hesitate. "What kind of clearance?" he asked. "I'll get one tomorrow. Who do I call?"

"I don't know," sighed Cornick. "Somebody in the Justice Department, I guess."

"I'll find out," said Propper.

"Gene, you are getting into the national security area, and things just don't work that fast," said Cornick. "For one thing, the Agency has a charter that explicitly prohibits those guys from getting involved in criminal cases. They can't get in there even if they want to."

"That's hard to believe," said Propper. "You wouldn't think we're working for the same government if that's what it says. It sounds like obstruction of justice. Who wrote that charter? We've got to change it."

"Hold on, Gene," said Cornick, somewhat exasperated. "You're talking about the entire United States government here. You can't go charging around like that. You've got to construct a foundation and then choose your moves."

"Maybe so," said Propper. "But I'm still going to see Lapham."

Propper settled back to watch the Thursday night presidential debate between Gerald Ford and Jimmy Carter. He found it so boring that it was a relief when the telephone rang. Detective Wilson was checking in. He turned on his confidential voice, as though speaking through his armpit into the phone. He told Propper, first of all, that he had located the mysterious umbrella man who had been seen by Dr. Peterson at Sheridan Circle. The umbrella man was scared and would speak only with Wilson, who went on to describe the Greek attaché's wound and his narrow escape on Sheridan Circle. Wilson said the attaché had been carrying a real umbrella, not a gun, but the story was a little spooky, anyway.

And there was more. Wilson said he had learned that the Turkish embassy used some of the most powerful radio transmitters in Washington, mounted on its roof. Apparently they used some specialized equipment to jam transmissions by their adversaries in the Greek embassy, just across Sheridan Circle. Wilson cleared his throat. And the real stuff, he said, was that he had obtained reliable information that the Turks broadcast their secret messages back to Turkey every morning beginning at precisely nine-thirty, Washington time. It was just possible that the bomb under Letelier's car had been a remote-control device and that the specialized frequencies from the Turkish embassy had triggered the blast.

There was one more thing, Wilson told Propper. All the evidence had not yet been delivered from the mobile crime unit to the FBI. Wilson had searched Letelier's briefcase, which had been in the back of the car, and discovered three very interesting cassette recordings. On the tapes, said Wilson, Letelier spoke for several hours in a long Spanish monologue, addressing a woman who had once loved him. Letelier sounded morose, confused, consumed by personal matters. Wilson thought the tapes might be important as a clue to his makeup and his worries, which might lead to the killers.

Propper agreed. He told Wilson to give the tapes to the FBI, whose translators and transcribers might turn them into English.

Wilson demurred: the police were not going to give the FBI any more evidence until the Bureau quit stalling and gave its interviews to the police. But Wilson agreed to hand over the Letelier briefcase to Propper as an intermediary. He would stop by in the morning.

After this first daily dose of Stanley Wilson's adventures, Propper returned to the presidential debates. The candidates were still blaming each other for the lagging economy. Propper turned off the television and picked up a thick file of press clippings and congressional speeches about the murders. More than thirty congressmen and senators had passionately denounced Pinochet's Chilean junta and called on President Ford to throw the full weight of the United States government against the killers, to make sure the whole world knew that terrorist murders would not be tolerated in the heart of Washington. The *Congressional Record* was filled with excerpts from reports by the United Nations and the Organization of American States documenting torture and repression by the Chilean DINA. These reports were so widely accepted in the world, and DINA so notorious, that Congress had already cut off all future United States military aid to Chile.

Among the items in the press and *Congressional Record*, Propper found copies of long letters from the co-directors of IPS to the attorney general of the United States in which the IPS people demanded a special prosecutor for the case. They argued that the United States government in general, and the CIA in particular, were too close to the Chilean junta for the citizens to entrust the investigation to the regular employees of the Justice Department, who are subject to political control by the administration. The letters raised the Watergate specter of political interference by high officials implicated in wrongdoing. This nettled Propper, as the letters implied that he was subject to manipulation and that he would permit politics to interfere with the investigation.

Everywhere Propper looked, high winds of political rhetoric were blowing through the case. Clearly, the murders received extra attention in the press because of a presumed connection to Chilean politics, which were a subject of great controversy in the United States. Conservatives had welcomed the military coup against Letelier's Allende regime as a great victory in the battle to prevent "another Cuba" in Latin America. Liberals, on the other hand, had pointed to evidence of CIA involvement in the coup and had denounced the United States government for abetting the overthrow of a democratically elected government.

Senator Edward Kennedy and other liberals described Letelier as a sensitive, refined economist and world citizen, so dedicated to the universal task of fighting hunger and inequality that the forces of fascist repression had seen fit to kill him. They made Letelier a symbol of justice. On the other hand, arch-conservative congressman Larry McDonald of Georgia denounced Letelier as a socialist—meaning Marxist—and therefore as a supporter of terrorism against law and order and America. McDonald went so far as to imply that Letelier might have been responsible for his own murder. The CIA might have prevented the bombing, he told the House, had it not been so weakened by criticism from Letelier and his ilk at IPS. His colleague Representative John Ashbrook of Ohio blocked a House resolution expressing simple regret over the murders. In the Senate, Jesse Helms defended the Chilean government against suspicion in the case. He advocated the "far more plausible" theory that Letelier had been killed by his own political allies. "Terrorism," declared Helms, "is most often an organized tool of the Left, used coldbloodedly for political aims. Leftist terrorists do not hesitate to use terrorism against the Left. . . ."

Much hyperbole was in the air even before the Letelier and Moffitt funerals. One person's saint was the next one's devil. Propper was not particularly interested in politics and never had been. Isolated as he was in prosecutions of street crimes and ordinary murders, he had never encountered anyone using politics to justify or explain murder. Now he faced a new obstacle to the development of leads—political propaganda. He noticed in IPS pamphlets announcing a memorial procession for the victims a lilting reference to Letelier as a gentle guitar player whose finger had been broken by DINA torturers in a concentration camp. Propper made a note to himself. He would ask James Luke to X-ray the fingers of the corpse to find out if there was evidence of old breaks. This was unpleasant and cold, but Propper would do it anyway. He was working on a murder case. Personal sentiments were subordinate to the overriding goal of solving it. To do so, he needed facts. To develop facts, he needed to know to what degree various sources would bend the truth for political effect or personal satisfaction. Propper also checked a statement to the FBI by an official of the Chilean government who described the concentration camp where Letelier had been held as "a sort of country club, in a resort area," and he found that, during Letelier's year there, several prisoners had died from malnutrition and exposure to the antarctic cold in the extreme southern part of Chile, in the Strait of Magellan.

Earl Silbert predicted that the case would bring great annoyance and hardship to Propper. Because it was political, many peripheral parties would want to direct and control everything about it, including the interpretation; and they would not hesitate to criticize the prosecutor, as they had done in Watergate. And because it was a terrorist crime, Silbert did not foresee success. "Give it your best shot," he told Propper. For confidence, Propper was thrown back on his lifelong irrational optimism. Its origins were obscure.

Propper was born in the Bronx and lived on Sheridan Avenue, the same street on which Lee Harvey Oswald once lived. This macabre coincidence was the only noteworthy fact of Propper's early years. His family moved to Long Island when Propper was six. A few months later, his father keeled over in the subway on his way to work in the garment district of Manhattan, and his mother went to work in the family belt business.

Propper attended a private school called Yeshiva Central, four hours a day in Hebrew and four in English. His mother was the Cub Scout den mother, and when Propper was twelve she married the scoutmaster of the Boy Scout troop. Propper gained an instant roommate and stepbrother of exactly the same age, who watched television all the time and still made straight A's without effort. Propper worked hard to make good grades. Things did not come easily to him. His mother let him stay up an extra half hour at night if he read a book. Generally, he excused himself early from dinner-table conversation—he fidgeted if he had to sit still for too long. He was somewhat withdrawn, and yet he was always making deals and wagers, setting goals for himself, jumping into fights with larger people. He doubted that he was as good as he claimed to be, but if he kept at it, he just might prove himself wrong.

Unsure what to do with himself when he finished college in 1968, he decided to go to law school at the University of Minnesota. It was the Vietnam era, and he was in Gene McCarthy country. His army preinduction physical was a riotous affair in which a guy who thought he had diabetes volunteered to produce a urine sample for everyone. When Propper passed the physical, he launched a tireless campaign to overturn the results, citing a recent severe knee injury from a skiing trip. Thirteen days later he sent home a victory telegram, and he would show his parents a folder labeled *The Kid vs. U.S. Army*. It was his first big case. He said he assumed all along he would win.

Shortly afterward, Propper went to a doctor to complain of a bothersome flu. Unexpectedly, and ominously, the doctor sent him to a hospital for a complete exam. After several days of tests, a doctor said to him, "I have bad news for you, I'm afraid. You're going to die."

"What else is new?" asked Propper.

"No. I mean sooner rather than later. You've got a very rare blood disease. It's always fatal. You have four to six months to live."

"I'm twenty-one years old!" Propper exclaimed. "I can't die. That's ridiculous."

"I'm sorry. There's nothing we can do for you." Three different specialists corroborated the diagnosis.

Propper got the same sad story at another hospital. Then, without telling anyone, he went to see a New York blood specialist during spring vacation. This doctor concluded that Propper either had the rare blood disease or an incredibly similar, nonlethal virus.

"Well, that's what I have," said Propper. It was true. The first hospital regretted the error and offered to forgive Propper's substantial bill if he would not sue. It was a questionable bargain, but the episode as a whole was another test of Propper's optimism.

Optimism was all he had in the Letelier case. He assumed that the bombers, unlike gunmen, had been nowhere close to the killings because they knew it was dangerous. So no one saw them. The bomb itself destroyed most of the evidence. The numbers were discouraging even in nonprofessional bombing cases, with less than a ten percent chance of arrest. This one looked political, so that Earl Silbert expected a fruitless ordeal. Hostile forces—maybe foreign governments—figured to be on the other side. Spy agencies seemed everywhere, and none of them was likely to help. Propper knew little Spanish, next to nothing of Latin America, and he was a virtual stranger to the cumbersome ways of the FBI. So far, he had been little more than a referee among competing bureaucracies.

"I'm gonna solve this sucker," he told himself. At times, he would pop out with the same announcement at the office, and Don Campbell would shake his head.

5 ▣ FIRST BLOOD

It is six years before the Letelier bombing. President Richard Nixon has been angry since September 4, 1970, when, contrary to all predictions by the CIA, Chilean citizens gave a plurality of their votes to the Marxist candidate, Salvador Allende. He has been even angrier since September 14, when the highest security review committee within the United States government concluded that it would be impossible to prevent Allende's ratification as president by the Chilean Congress. Nixon declares privately that he will not tolerate the creation of "another Cuba" in South America during his administration. He denounces the pessimism and timidity of the security committee.

On September 15, in the presence of Attorney General John Mitchell and National Security Advisor Henry Kissinger, Nixon summons CIA Director Richard Helms to the Oval Office and delivers an extraordinary speech, full of fire and determination. Helms takes notes that will become famous years later:

> One in 10 chance perhaps, but save Chile!
> worth spending
> not concerned risks involved
> no involvement of embassy
> $10,000,000 available, more if necessary
> full-time job—best men we have
> game plan
> make the economy scream
> 48 hours for plan of action

Helms has never heard anything like this. Nixon does not want to hear about the niceties or the problems. He wants a military coup to prevent Allende's accession to power. He wants it arranged within a month. And he wants to keep the plans utterly secret from the State Department and even the Pentagon, which he considers untrustworthy.

Within hours, these unprecedented marching orders create panic among the CIA officers stationed in Santiago, Chile. The station chief exclaims that everyone in Washington must be crazy. How can a coup be arranged on demand in a traditionally democratic country like Chile, which is no banana republic? Even if it could be done, how can it be kept secret from the American ambassador? Don't the people in Washington understand how an embassy works? Most importantly, how can his CIA people make clandestine arrangements with Chilean military officers without relying on the assistance of the American military attachés in the embassy? The attachés are the ones who spend all their time with the Chilean military, whereas the Agency people spend more time with politicians and Chilean journalists.

The station chief tries his best to comply with what he considers insane emergency instructions. After ordering internal secrecy even among his own employees, he canvasses them to find out who knows whom in the Chilean military. He takes it a step further: who knows a ranking Chilean commander well enough to broach the subject of a coup against Allende without much risk of a leak? Most of the CIA case officers gulp uncomfortably. There are very few military contacts already established at that level of trust.

A round of discreet inquiries brings disappointing results. Nearly all the Chilean officers express scorn for Allende, but most of them profess shock at the notion of a coup, saying that Chile is a constitutional country and that the military should respect the will of the voters as long as Allende respects the constitution. Some say that a preemptive coup would be treason. The few who show sympathy for the idea express great reluctance to take responsibility for moving first.

The station chief grows desperate, as the White House and CIA headquarters demand that he increase the pressure on the Chilean military, while at the same time the American ambassador, Edward Korry, orders him to have no contact with Chilean generals at all. Korry, in ignorance of the Agency's secret orders from President Nixon, demands the full emergency support of his CIA station for a different crusade against Allende—the one mandated by the top-level security committee in Washington. Working night and day, Korry is trying to pull off what is known as the "Frei Gambit." It is a complicated plan. Korry must prevail on the lame-duck Chilean President, Eduardo Frei, to resign prematurely after proclaiming that Chile is facing political disaster. Then the Chilean military can preserve order during the national emergency, and the Chilean Congress, stimulated by outright cash bribes from the United States, can use the crisis as a pretext to set aside the results of the election and return Frei to power for another term. Lawyers will be able to make tortured arguments that the gambit is technically legal.

On September 21, Korry sends a report to Kissinger on all the pressures his embassy is bringing to bear on the Chileans. "Frei should know that not a nut or bolt will be allowed to reach Chile under Allende," Korry tells Kissinger. "Once Allende comes to power we shall do all within our power to condemn Chile and the Chileans to utmost deprivation and poverty. . . ." Korry is warning the Chileans of aid cutoffs and credit squeezes, offering them a simple choice: support the Frei Gambit against Allende or face economic ruin.

While orchestrating this ruthless campaign, Ambassador Korry is also fighting a somewhat paradoxical rearguard action to make sure that the United States does not encourage an outright military coup in Chile. This would not only constitute an unconscionable intervention into the Chilean political process, he argues, but it would also backfire—it would provoke a unified Chilean protest against the United States, playing into Allende's hands. Korry is a volatile man who feels quite strongly about these distinctions in strategy. This is why he keeps demanding reassurance from his CIA station chief that the Agency is *not* promoting a coup, as is rumored.

The beleaguered station chief tells CIA headquarters that his employees simply do not have sufficiently strong relations with the Chilean military to carry out President Nixon's plan. This emphatic declaration causes a crisis in the new Chile Task Force, whose members Director Helms has handpicked for this emergency assignment. It is quickly decided to approach one senior Pentagon official on the basis of strictest secrecy, in accordance with President Nixon's instructions, and to ask permission to "borrow" one of the military attachés in Santiago. This is soon arranged.

The attaché,* an Anglophile and avid horseman with numerous

---

*Colonel Paul Wimert.

friends among the top Chilean commanders, is informally "detached" for temporary service under the CIA station chief, with orders not to tell any of his own colleagues within the U.S. Military Mission. And no one is to tell Ambassador Korry.

There is even greater confusion within the Chilean military, especially after word travels among the army generals that the United States favors a coup and that General Roberto Viaux is prepared to lead it. Viaux is somewhat tainted by the fact that he led an unsuccessful military revolt the previous year, seeking higher pay and more respect for the armed forces. Retired now, without a troop command, Viaux is still regarded as a leader of the hard-line anti-Communists within the army. Craftily, more hesitant generals discuss Viaux's proposals to test support for a coup.

On October 15, the CIA's deputy director for plans* goes to the White House to review coup preparations with Kissinger and Kissinger's principal deputy, Alexander Haig, who have been pressing the CIA Task Force almost daily. The deputy director says that the prospects are mixed. Now that the CIA station and the attaché have advertised American support for a preemptive coup, several well-placed Chilean generals have indicated that they will follow General Viaux's lead. But they will not lead themselves. They are paralyzed, everyone agrees, by the firm hostility of Army Chief of Staff General René Schneider, the highest-ranking general. The Chilean army is almost mystically traditional—more Prussian and hierarchical than most—and Schneider's opposition effectively dooms either a coup or the Frei Gambit.

After reviewing tactical options, Kissinger and Haig reiterate that President Nixon wants something done to stop Allende. Time is running out. The Chilean Congress will meet in nine days to choose a president formally.

By now, Viaux and the growing number of military conspirators around him have devised a plan to deal with General Schneider: they will kidnap him. They will blame it on leftist Allende supporters and thereby create a highly charged atmosphere throughout Chile. This daring move might allow a coup to "ignite." Alternatively, it might facilitate the Frei Gambit by giving President Frei a pretext for resigning. Hundreds of rumors swirl among conspirators in Santiago and from there up to the CIA Task Force and over to the White House.

*Thomas Karamessines.

The kidnapping of General Schneider is the catalyst for all schemes, but the conspirators face a new problem: Chilean soldiers will not physically attack a fellow Chilean soldier, especially a superior. The taboo is too powerful, even for soldiers who believe the move is necessary for the survival of freedom.

To circumvent this taboo, the military conspirators have resolved to employ some of the civilian paramilitary groups that have sprung up to oppose Allende. This idea is passed back to Washington through the CIA case officers and the well-connected attaché. Everyone is reluctant to use civilians, who are considered far less reliable than soldiers, but under the circumstances there is no choice. General Viaux and his associates are working with a group led by Enrique Arrancibia, a paramilitary commander in the new right-wing political party, Patria y Libertad. For the past month, Arrancibia and his followers have been dynamiting electrical towers, supermarkets, and other targets in a campaign to provoke the military into a coup. Arrancibia always sends advance communiqués to the newspapers in the name of the Peasant Workers Brigade, in an effort to incite public anger against leftists. This same covert technique will be used in the Schneider kidnapping, which is being rehearsed daily on the streets of Santiago.

Viaux's principal co-conspirator is General Camilo Valenzuela, commander of the Santiago army garrison. Both generals ask their American contacts for concrete assurances of support from the United States. With authorization from the CIA Task Force, the attaché informs General Valenzuela on October 20 that the United States will pay $50,000 for the successful kidnapping of General Schneider. Shortly after midnight on October 22, the attaché delivers the final load of special equipment for the kidnapping: three submachine guns, six tear-gas canisters, and gas masks. The submachine guns are "sterile," meaning untraceable.

That morning, on the third try, Arrancibia's men converge on General Schneider's Mercedes-Benz, forcing the military chauffeur to stop. Some conspirators jump from their own blockading cars while others spring out of hiding places. One of them shatters the back window of Schneider's car with a blunt instrument. The others demand his surrender. The attackers will later claim that Schneider grabbed reflexively for his side arm. In any case, they fire shots into the car, mortally wounding the general. Then they flee in panic.

The CIA's deputy director rushes to the White House to inform Alexander Haig that General Schneider has been shot instead of kidnapped. Martial law has been declared in Santiago. All of Chile is electrified, listening to continuous news bulletins. Haig learns that the CIA Task Force is optimistic in spite of the blunder, reporting that "a coup climate exists in Chile." In the crisis, General Valenzuela has been elevated to the command of the entire Santiago province. The positions of the major conspirators have been enhanced.

Suddenly it all falls apart. The assault on Schneider causes a tide of patriotic sentiment in Chile, as marching citizens and media commentators and politicians alike declare their support for constitutional processes. Within forty-eight hours, the Chilean Congress overwhelmingly declares Salvador Allende the next president of Chile. General Schneider dies the next day, and Allende soon leads a full-dress military funeral procession that reminds many observers of the John F. Kennedy funeral march in 1963.

In the aftermath, the commanders of the navy, air force, and *carabineros* (military police) are cashiered on suspicion of complicity in the plot. Generals Viaux and Valenzuela, along with many civilians and lesser officers, are convicted of criminal roles in the conspiracy. Enrique Arrancibia and many indicted conspirators flee the country ahead of murder warrants.

General Carlos Prats replaces Schneider as army chief of staff, pledging loyalty to the constitutionally elected president.

On March 2, 1971, Orlando Letelier arrives at the White House to present his credentials as Chile's new ambassador to the United States. President Nixon receives Allende's socialist envoy politely. "I am sure you agree, Mr. Ambassador," he says, "that no nation can in good conscience ignore the rights of others, or the international norms of behavior essential to peace and mutually fruitful intercourse." Letelier replies in kind.

———

September 11, 1973

At six-thirty in the morning, President Allende wakes his new defense minister, Orlando Letelier, to announce that the navy has revolted in Valparaíso. Letelier bolts out of his bed. He knows this might be the beginning of the coup. The rumors, violence, and nationwide strikes have been building for months. Allende says that the situation may be very grave, as none of his military chiefs is to be found anywhere.

Letelier frantically tries to locate his military subordinates, but he fails. The new army commander, General Pinochet, is considered a

wavering constitutional loyalist, who has been trying to calm muti-
nous officers. Letelier cannot find him, however. When he calls his
own office at the Defense Ministry, he is answered by Vice Admiral
Patricio Carvajal. This is strange. He wonders what Carvajal is doing
there. To Letelier's urgent questions about the navy revolt on the
Chilean coast, Admiral Carvajal replies that it is nothing serious
—navy units are merely readying themselves to react against any
disloyalty to the government. Letelier hangs up wanting to believe
Carvajal, who has actually transformed Letelier's offices into a command post for the coup.

Arriving at the Defense Ministry shortly after eight o'clock, Letelier sees groups of soldiers moving through the streets. Junior officers and enlisted men accost him just inside the main entrance to
announce that he is no longer defense minister. They place him under arrest and search him roughly. A few minutes later, they push
him back at gunpoint, toward a military vehicle for transport to an
army stockade. All the soldiers are tense, at the flash point of violence. By now, gunfire can be heard in Santiago.

Near the American embassy, *carabinero* units throw barricades
across the streets to stop all traffic. Some trapped motorists simply
abandon their cars and run. Bob Steven, a young American diplomat,
leaves his fellow bureaucrats in the crowded commuter bus and
presses himself against a building. Street battles have broken out.
Steven decides that it is less dangerous to push on than to go back.
He and a few others from his bus are the last ones to make it inside
the embassy, which is around the corner from La Moneda, the presidential palace. President Allende and his personal bodyguards are
battling the coup assault troops.

Allende refuses repeated demands for surrender made by General
Ernesto Baeza, commander of the Santiago garrison. Having learned
that practically all the armed forces from General Pinochet down
have joined "the treason," Allende makes a defiant radio speech
from the transmission room inside La Moneda, vowing to resist to
the end. "They have the power," he declares. "They can smash us,
but the social processes cannot be held back either by crime or by
force. History is ours, and the people will make it." This will be
Allende's last broadcast.

At eleven-fifty-six, on signals from Baeza and Pinochet, two of the
air force's Hawker Hunters streak through the air just above Santiago's downtown buildings, dip into Constitution Square, fire their
rockets into La Moneda, and make the steep climb around for another strike. Thousands of cowering civilians will remember the

screaming jets and the thunderous explosions as the most awesome military display of the coup. Even military commanders are impressed by the precision of the Hawker pilots, who put eighteen direct rocket hits into windows of the eighteenth-century Moneda.

Bob Steven tries to watch the attack from the American embassy, but stray machine-gun rounds keep coming in through the windows —even as high as the eighth floor. Firing is sporadic but indiscriminate, in all directions. Steven and his colleagues spend much of their time on their hands and knees, crawling in and out of offices, trying to avoid the broken glass. He worries frantically about his wife and three children, whom he will not see for three days.

Much of the top floor of La Moneda is in flames from the Hawker rockets, but puffs of smoke from the windows signal the continuing resistance. From his command post at Peñalolen, General Pinochet consults by radiophone with General Baeza and Admiral Carvajal. Baeza orders a renewed assault by his elite infantry school regiment, supported by eight Sherman tanks and cannons mounted on jeeps.

Shortly after two o'clock in the afternoon, infantry companies force their way into La Moneda. Small groups of them run upstairs through the smoke, covering themselves with bursts of submachine-gun fire. A blond Chilean lieutenant, René Riveros, suddenly finds himself confronting an armed civilian dressed in a turtleneck sweater. Riveros empties half a clip of ammunition into the President of Chile, killing him instantly with a string of wounds from the groin to the throat.

Military spokesmen are soon announcing the coup's success on radios all over Chile. General Baeza instructs regular police detectives to enter La Moneda to conduct a standard investigation of Allende's death. This move provokes the first major controversy among the new ruling generals, most of whom violently oppose any forensic examination by professionals. They want to present Allende's demise as a suicide. General Baeza objects that this is unmanly and that no such story can be maintained convincingly. The next day he will resign over this question, and only Pinochet will be able to persuade him to remain as the military government's new chief of Investigations.

Baeza is overruled on the afternoon of the coup. Inside La Moneda there is great confusion over what to do with Allende's body. In the end, it is placed in a metal coffin, which is then welded shut and flown to Viña del Mar for burial. Army, navy, air force, and *carabinero* doctors have already certified that his death was a suicide.

Meanwhile, nearly 100,000 uniformed soldiers and paramilitary ci-

vilians are sweeping through Chilean towns to locate and "neutralize" some 20,000 specified Chilean leftists. The violent chaos will last
for weeks before subsiding into a police campaign. Many on the lists
will be missed, but many others will be caught by mistake. Colonel
Odlanier Mena commands the sweep in Trapaca Province. Colonel
Hector Orozco commands in Aconcagua. Colonel Manuel Contreras
is in charge of the city of San Antonio. These officers, plus the other
Chilean leaders of the coup and Bob Steven, are destined to work
with and against each other in the Letelier investigation years later.

September 29–October 1, 1974

As one of the killers of General Schneider, Enrique Arrancibia has
been a hero to certain elements of the security forces in Argentina,
where he has continued his terrorist work during the Allende regime, making contact with officers of the Argentine intelligence service, SIDE. At SIDE's Campo de Mayo headquarters, Arrancibia has
formed alliances with unruly civilian gangs that are only too happy
to track down the Chilean leftists who flee to Argentina after the
coup. By 1974, Arrancibia is so well placed for operations in Argentina that Chilean army officers ask him to remain there on the payroll
of the new DINA.

Far above the terrorists and the unfortunate Chilean dissidents
who have fled to Argentina looms the political significance of General Carlos Prats, who has lived in Buenos Aires since the coup
against Allende. Like General Schneider before him, Prats had stifled conspiracies against Allende and had forced his subordinate generals to move against him. The college of Chilean generals formally
withdrew its support, and Prats's resignation removed the last political obstacle in the way of the coup. Since then, in exile, Prats has
maintained the reputation of a military constitutionalist and figure
of honor—admired by army officers, Allende supporters, and Christian Democrats. As such, he is a threat to President Pinochet, whom
he views as a man of mediocre talents.

General Prats has been talking to friends and to foreign reporters
about the memoirs he plans to write. He has been working on the
outline for months. Deeply humiliated and much reduced by what he
regards as the treachery of his former colleagues, Prats has struggled to preserve his sense of fairness and military dignity. Nevertheless, he does plan to comment, tangentially at least, on political
subjects by stating his belief that all Chilean soldiers of good conscience should work for the earliest possible return to civilian rule.

Colonel Contreras has resolved that Prats should not strike this blow against the new Pinochet regime. Early in September, an anonymous caller warned Prats that he would be killed if he followed through with his contemplated political statements. Since then, Arrancibia has been in Buenos Aires trying to find out about the general's intentions. They remain unchanged: he wants to finish the manuscript.

Arrancibia receives a historic order through his DINA liaison officer in Buenos Aires. This time there is no ambiguity, as there was with General Schneider: Arrancibia is not to kidnap General Prats; he is to arrange for his elimination.

He prepares for the mission with Nieto Moreno, a retired Perónist colonel who commands one of the civilian groups attached to SIDE. At Arrancibia's direction, Moreno's men follow Prats all over Buenos Aires, gathering information on his habits and associations. The men are experienced in the work. They are also ruthless and prone to extortion, however, and Arrancibia has tried to extract performance guarantees on them from SIDE officers. (Three of Nieto Moreno's men will be executed by Argentine intelligence officers within two years.) Early in September, he arranges the delivery of a large sum of DINA cash to Nieto Moreno's men.

At DINA headquarters in Santiago, the commanding officers wait anxiously for news of the mission's success. Instead, there are delays, more delays, and finally word that Arrancibia is having trouble with the Argentines. They are balking. Reportedly, some of them fear that the Argentine government will not tolerate the murder of such a respected Chilean general. The Argentines are squabbling among themselves about the safest method to accomplish the job. Some of them are complaining that the target is a good anti-Communist whose only crime is to be a rival of Pinochet. They say that for such a dirty, risky operation they may need more guarantees—more money.

These messages grate on Colonel Contreras, who has committed himself to the deed and therefore feels unbearable pressure. In the emergency, one of his aides, Pedro Espinoza, suggests that Contreras enlist an energetic young DINA consultant named Kenneth Enyart. This is the man who intercepted President Allende's private radio communications and who has already impressed Espinoza with technical innovations in fields ranging from electronics to explosives. Enyart is completely trustworthy. Moreover, he is already in Buenos Aires under a cover name. He can be called in quickly to solve the problems and meet the demands of the recalcitrant Argentines.

Contreras agrees. Espinoza's personal order goes to Enyart through DINA channels. A message soon comes back that the inexperienced civilian operative is meeting with the Argentines. Espinoza orders him to have no contact with Moreno or with Arrancibia. A few days later, Enyart sends back word that the stalemate has been broken. The mission will be accomplished.*

A bomb is placed in a simple cake tin and attached to the top of the gear box in General Prats's Fiat 125, so that the gear box will direct the force of the blast upward. Then it becomes a matter of waiting for the right moment.

On September 29, General Prats and his wife, Carmen, leave their

---

*The precise nature of Enyart's intervention with the Argentines is not publicly known and remains a matter of dispute. Sources within SIDE acknowledge the participation of Arrancibia and Nieto Moreno in the conspiracy against the life of Prats, but they maintain that Enyart found it impossible to solve the disagreements among the conspirators and was obliged to carry out the assassination himself. These sources offer no details about how he might have accomplished the task.

A more credible version comes from Chilean sources—among them several officers connected to DINA and CNI who initiated clandestine meetings with Eugene Propper early in 1981. According to the Chilean sources, Enyart's principal contribution was a technical one: he told the skittish Argentines how they could give themselves a greater margin of safety by using a remote-control bomb, and he was present when the bomb was constructed. Chilean sources state that Enyart did his work and left Buenos Aires for Montevideo, Uruguay, two days *before* the assassination. Thus, he was not in Argentina when the bomb was detonated. (The Chilean officers who contacted Propper maintained that President Pinochet approved the Prats murder in advance, at the instigation of Contreras, and that this fratricidal act helped ensnarl the Chilean government in a web of blackmail and corruption that still plagues the armed forces.)

"Kenneth Enyart" himself has provided contradictory accounts of his involvement.

On October 20, 1981, in conversation with one of the coauthors at FBI headquarters in Washington, "Enyart" became quite emotional when confronted with the accounts of the Prats assassination provided by Chilean and Argentine sources. "All I ever did," he said, "was to be a conduit for some funds in Argentina."

On October 23, 1981, inside a U.S. federal prison, Enyart denied having made the previous statement, claiming to have said instead that DINA had paid money to the Argentines for the assassination, that the Argentines had not performed, and that Contreras had become quite angry. "I did not say that *I* carried funds to Argentina," he repeated.

On October 28, 1981, Enyart denied making either of the two previous statements.

A few days later, he admitted the substantive truth of his remarks of October 23, although he still denied having made the remarks themselves. He said that he wanted to tell the truth but could not afford to. He said that he had to keep secret the details of his facilitative role in Buenos Aires in order to protect the lives of himself and his family. He has stated repeatedly that the Fifth Amendment will be his only protection in the Prats case.

apartment building on Malabia Street and drive to a meeting with friends only about five blocks away. They stay late into the night, returning to the apartment at nearly one o'clock the following morning.

General Prats leaves the car running as he gets out to open the building's garage door, which requires a key. His wife waits in the passenger seat. The garage door creaks open automatically. Prats walks across the pavement, his path marked by his headlights. When he leans over to re-enter the Fiat, the conspirators push the button.

The force of the blast propels the entire hood of the Fiat upward and across the street to the roof of a building some sixty-three feet above the pavement. General Prats is blown backward and killed instantly when his head cracks into the curb thirteen feet away from the car. His wife is mutilated and carbonized so badly that she cannot be identified by any known medical process.

Arrancibia returns to Santiago the next day, October 1. Enyart returns by way of Montevideo, Uruguay, so that Santiago police records will not show him entering from Argentina so soon after the mission. He lands in Santiago just after Arrancibia.

Within DINA, those with knowledge of the Prats operation catapult into positions of greater influence. They advance roughly in proportion to the degree of their involvement. Espinoza instantly becomes the line officer closest to Contreras, whose own hold over President Pinochet grows much stronger—soon Contreras's star eclipses that of army officers much his senior in rank. His immediate subordinates recognize that Contreras now believes he can pursue his considerable ambitions with near impunity.

As for Enyart, he is granted recognition as a full-time DINA officer, even though he is a civilian. He soon receives perquisites in excess of those due his rank—a car, a house, a large staff of DINA assistants. Enyart is given complete freedom to move about the DINA compound, which he had never been allowed to visit before. And within a few months, he is granted the privilege of meeting Colonel Contreras. The DINA chief pronounces the operation in Buenos Aires a complete success and says that Enyart has earned the gratitude of all patriotic Chileans.

6 ▣ A TEAM OF STRANGERS

Nine days after the Letelier murders, Propper drove west on the tree-lined George Washington Parkway through Virginia, just across the Potomac River from Washington. It was raining steadily as he pulled up to the checkpoint outside CIA headquarters. He gave his name, feeling queasily paranoid about the fact that this huge, looming spy agency had come into possession of his name and the essential facts of his life. They said it was necessary for security, but Propper felt as if he had been fingerprinted by a ghost. The guard finally waved him through the gate, and he drove on, barely able to see past his windshield wipers.

Cursing himself for forgetting his umbrella, Propper ran through puddles and rain to the entrance, where guards promptly accosted him again. He told them of his appointment for the briefing that was required before he could get a security clearance. They said he was at the wrong door. All visitors must obtain a pass at the main entrance. This was a staff entrance. Propper absorbed this and then asked the guards to take him through the building to the main entrance. That was not possible, they said. After arguing briefly on this point, Propper tried to go over the guards' heads by insisting that they call upstairs to the general counsel's office. They did, but it proved fruitless.

By now Propper was fuming. The guards did not have an extra umbrella, and by the looks on their impassive faces, Propper guessed that they would not be inclined to lend him one if they had. There was no alternative. He was obliged to go back out into the rain and run halfway around a building the size of a city block. He had intended to make a good first impression as a representative of the Justice Department, but the minions of secrecy were whittling him down even before he got inside their enormous bastion of white marble. Once he was admitted, an escort guided him down the grand hallway, past the chiseled inscription of the CIA motto: "And ye shall know the truth, and the truth shall make you free" (John 8:32). Propper was having his doubts.

In a small, windowless room, a score of applicants for clearances sat around a long table to watch a slide show, which flashed through maps, graphs, charts, and pictures in a showy, authoritative glimpse of the vast apparatus of government classification. At a carefully measured interval in the briefing, the security expert excused a number of people in the room, by name. Propper watched them leave and wondered what would happen next. Then the security man ran through more slides and more facts at a slightly higher level of intimacy with the workings of government. He excused a second group, and after a third round of slides, he excused a group that included Propper. Walking out of the room, Propper could not help eyeing the half dozen or so people who stayed for even higher levels of secrecy. The CIA escorts ushered him back into the rain.

The next day, he received a call from Stanley Pottinger, assistant attorney general in charge of the Civil Rights Division of the Justice Department. Pottinger introduced himself over the phone and said he had been speaking with representatives of the Institute for Policy Studies, who thought the Civil Rights Division should take over the Letelier case because of its political overtones. The Civil Rights Division offered certain advantages, said Pottinger, through statutes that made murder a federal crime as a violation of civil rights. What did Propper think?

Instantly guarded, Propper replied that he already had ample federal jurisdiction through the Protection of Foreign Officials Act, whose murder and conspiracy provisions carry maximum life sentences. In addition, he had two counts of first-degree murder and numerous related charges. The Civil Rights Division could prosecute none of these offenses, nor could its statutes bring to bear such severe penalties.

At this, Pottinger retreated a bit, saying he had not realized that Letelier was covered by the foreign officials law. It would be better for the U.S. Attorney's Office to hit the killers with the full weight of murder charges. Pottinger added that he wanted Propper to know that he and the Civil Rights Division were eager to help in any way they could.

Propper thanked him. It was time to be gracious, and Pottinger's offer of assistance clicked with the problem on Propper's mind. He was thinking of the rain and the intimidating CIA building, so he told Pottinger he was afraid he would not get cooperation from the Agency. Did Pottinger have any ideas?

Instant, warm confidence shot through the telephone line. The assistant attorney general replied that he happened to be a personal friend of the CIA director himself, George Bush. Pottinger called him "George." For him, the CIA director was only a phone call away. Would Propper like an appointment?

By that afternoon, he, Cornick, and Pottinger were scheduled for lunch with Director Bush at CIA headquarters on Monday. A Justice Department limousine would pick them up at noon. Propper whistled to himself. This was known in Washington as access. He called Cornick with the news.

"Whoa, boy!" cried Cornick. "That sounds good, but let me check. I don't think they'll let me go."

"Not let you go?" said Propper. "Why not?"

"They just won't," said Cornick.

"Who won't?"

"The Bureau, Gene. I've been trying to tell you. Listen, I'm a field agent. In the Bureau, a field agent is not even supposed to meet with a U.S. attorney, much less the CIA director. A SAC meets with a U.S. attorney, and only the FBI director meets with the CIA director. That's the way it is. Besides, there's a guy over in headquarters whose job is nothing but liaison with the Agency. If I want to know something from CIA, I'm supposed to ask him to find out for me. I can't go over there myself."

"That's crap," said Propper. "It's ridiculous. That guy doesn't know anything about the case. How's he going to talk to the people over there? He should be helping you out by getting you appointments."

"Gene, it's just not done," sighed Cornick. "That's all. I'm telling you. For me to go over there and meet the CIA director, I'd have to have a thousand supervisors sign off on it and there'd be a hundred drones standing around worrying the whole time."

"I can't believe it," said Propper. "I don't see how you guys ever get anything done. I haven't even told Earl about the meeting. If I were going to see the President, I'd tell Earl, I guess. But not the CIA director."

"Well, Earl is not the Bureau, Gene," said Cornick. "Let me give it a try, anyway. I'll get back to you."

Cornick called back shortly. He was forbidden to go. He did not bother to tell Propper that phone lines were buzzing up and down the Bureau hierarchy about the brash young assistant U.S. attorney who was meeting with none other than the CIA director on a Bureau case. The Bureau sensed ruin ahead.

On Monday morning, Propper went to Cornick's office to talk over his upcoming meeting at the CIA. At the Washington field office he did not find the gleaming, spotless, computer-and-glass layout he expected of the FBI. On the contrary, WFO was housed in the Old Post Office Building, one of the capital's oldest structures. It was quite impressive from the outside, having the appearance of a tall Bavarian castle tower, complete with round turrets and lookouts carved in the stone. On the inside, it was just plain run-down. Dirty plank corridors on each floor led around the ten-story column of air that made up the center of the building. Large rats were sighted frequently in the daytime. The building was served by two antiquated, handle-cranked elevators, which, like most of the windows, were reluctant to move up and down. On Cornick's floor, the fifth, ancient file drawers stood side by side around the entire corridor, covered with dust. One barnlike room on the perimeter housed all twenty agents in Cornick's bomb squad. They sat across from one another behind several long rows of tall wooden desks shaped like mechanical drawing boards. Supervisor Satkowski presided over a battalion of clerks in the adjoining room.

Propper stood next to an end desk, where Cornick was fighting stacks of paper on three sides. The two of them commiserated over the FBI bureaucracy. Cornick advised Propper not to hope for much from the CIA, quoting the Bureau line that the Agency never surrendered any information other than filler and boiler plate. Propper hoped for more. Cornick was skeptical, but said he hoped Propper would share whatever he got with the Bureau. Of course, said Propper. That was the whole idea.

Cornick nodded. He glanced around the room, in which Propper was a conspicuous sight, and then he hunched over slightly and said in a low voice, "Gene, we're gonna solve this case. Let me show you something." Propper understood that it was on the sly. He scanned a page under Cornick's arm. It was full of information about known international assassins, their records and suspected whereabouts. Cornick turned a page or two and then stopped. It was just a sample. "The stuff is starting to come in," said Cornick. "I'd like to show it to you, but my hands are tied until you get your security clearance."

"No problem," said Propper. He expected it to come through that very day. Clearances normally took at least forty-five days, but his was being processed in only one, he said proudly. Cornick nodded again. Propper was on a fast track. He wished him good luck with Director Bush.

When the limousine delivered Pottinger and Propper to the main entrance at CIA headquarters, they were met by escorts, given visitor's badges, and whisked into the director's private elevator. It opened directly into a suite of offices on the seventh floor, overlooking the forest that surrounds headquarters. Their hosts were there to greet them. Pottinger introduced Propper to Director Bush, and Bush introduced the two lawyers to Tony Lapham, his general counsel. Then, graciously, the director said, "Would you gentlemen care for some sherry?"

An old butler in a white coat served sherry and cheese hors d'oeuvres. Then the group moved into the director's private dining room, where an elegant table was laid on white linen. Propper looked over the menu—tomato juice, heart of lettuce salad, filet mignon, baby peas, wine—and wondered who was paying for it all. The prosecutor in him thought he might have a misuse of government funds case in front of him, but it was only a passing amusement. He reflected that this was certainly better treatment than he had received four days earlier.

When finally called on to state his business, Propper said that the Letelier-Moffitt murders were more than likely political assassinations, and that the investigation would probably move outside the United States into the Agency's realm of foreign intelligence. Therefore, Propper wanted CIA cooperation in the form of reports from within Chile, reports on assassins, reports on foreign operatives entering the United States, and the like. He wanted anything he could get that might bear upon the murders.

"Look," said Bush, "I'm appalled by the bombing. Obviously we can't allow people to come right here into the capital and kill foreign diplomats and American citizens like this. It would be a hideous precedent. So, as director, I want to help you. As an American citizen, I want to help. But, as director, I also know that the Agency can't help in a lot of situations like this. We've got some problems. Tony, tell him what they are."

Like Bush, Lapham was an Ivy Leaguer who took pride in his refinement. He came from an old San Francisco banking family. His brother was the editor of *Harper's* magazine. But Lapham could also be blunt and practical. He was no dilettante.

"The first problem," he told Propper, "is that every time we've tried to help Justice in the past, they've screwed us. They always promise us that if we give them this assistance or that assistance, they'll just use it for background, but the next thing we know, they're trying to make a witness out of our source. They're trying to put him in court. We can't attract and hold sources if they're afraid they'll get slapped into court."

"Well, that sounds legitimate to me," said Propper, "but I'm sure we can figure out a way to work around it."

"That's not all," said Lapham. "We got torn to pieces last year for domestic intelligence, so now everybody over here is gun-shy about reporting on Americans or any activities in this country. We can't do it. That's strictly out. The liberals don't like some things we do and the conservatives don't like others, and the way the rule book is now, we stay clean by keeping out of criminal stuff and domestic stuff. You've got a murder here in the States. That's both. That makes it tough."

"I see," said Propper. "But I can't believe there's not some way for you to get in this case. There has to be a way. If somebody comes into the country from overseas and assassinates people here in Washington, that's got to be your kind of work. They might do it again. Who else will stop it?"

"Sure," said Lapham. "That's a security matter. That's ours. But we don't know this is a security matter yet, and we'd have to investigate a crime to find out."

Discussion ensued. There was a chicken-and-egg problem. There were fine lines of definition, which Propper regarded as problems of semantics. He would label the investigation in whatever way would get him the most help. In the end, Lapham and Propper agreed that they could best handle the matter by an exchange of letters between the CIA director and the attorney general. They made plans to meet again to draw up the documents for their bosses. Director Bush ended the lunch on an optimistic note. "If you two come up with something that Tony thinks will protect us, we'll be all right," he said. Propper left, assuming things would work out. It struck him that the CIA, no less than the IPS, considered itself victimized on many fronts.

Cornick marched into the courthouse office less than an hour after Propper returned. Propper could tell he was in a business mood, for Cornick did not yell "Hi, honey" or carry on effervescently with the secretaries, as was his custom. Instead, Cornick leaned intently over Propper's desk. "Your security clearance came through. I checked the computer," he said. "Grab your coat, boy. We're gonna take a walk."

Cornick's manner was such that Propper went along silently, without the slightest protest. The two of them soon started walking around the courthouse block. They were within sight of Capitol Hill and the National Gallery of Art, circling the courthouse where Judge Sirica had banged his gavel and where elite reporters had camped out for months during the Watergate trials.

Keeping a wary eye out for passersby, Cornick spoke in a low voice. "You might as well know what you're in for," he said. "Gene, there are people in the United States government who get regular information about international assassins. I'm not just talking about the CIA, either. I'm talking about the Defense Intelligence Agency, the National Security Agency, various military attachés all over the world, and the Bureau. They use this information mostly to keep track of things in case of foreign travel by high American officials. They don't want these killers near Kissinger when Kissinger goes to Paris or somewhere."

"That's great," said Propper. "What do they say about Letelier?"

"Hold on a second," said Cornick. "I'm not saying you can use these sources, and I'm sure not saying you can trust them." He went on to describe an international underworld populated by double and triple agents, all playing with trick mirrors of reality. It was Graham Greene, filtered through the thick interpretive processes of the FBI and spiced up with some zesty lore from a Virginia romanticist. Cornick was an ardent bullshitter. He admitted it, and in fact he would talk at great length about his loquacious habits. FBI stenographers dreaded the sight of him and the sound of his long-winded dictations. A few months earlier, at his farewell party in Puerto Rico, the FBI employees had presented him with a bright-yellow crash helmet topped by a flashing red light, painted on one side with a steaming pile of brown manure and on the other with a long list of Cornick nicknames, such as "Secret Squirrel" and "The Mouth of the South." He was something of a rake in the Bureau, but when it mattered, he was also devoted to its orderly professionalism.

There was method in his spy monologue. He was afraid that the energetic Propper would get his hands on CIA material and fly off impulsively in many directions at once, and he was trying to forestall this by impressing him with the dangers, with the reasons for caution. "Gene, the first thing you've got to do is assess the veracity of the source," said Cornick. "Is he a valid conduit? What's his track record? Then you've got to assess the information itself. Can it be verified? Does it contain facts that you can use for corroboration? And finally, you've got to look at where the information will take you. A lot of these leads sound sexy as hell, but they only take you about as far as the end of your thumb."

Propper had been listening a long time. "From what you're telling me, it sounds like we're going to need a lot of help with all this verification. How many agents do you have in Chile?"

"Only one," sighed Cornick. "We've got a legat down there."

"Only one?" Propper sagged. "What's a legat?"

"Legal attaché. That's the FBI representative in the embassy."

"Carter, how can we investigate Chile with only one guy?"

"That's not the half of it," said Cornick. "That's just the good part. That legat doesn't even live in Chile. He's based in Buenos Aires. He covers Chile on road trips, and he also has to cover Uruguay, Paraguay, Peru, Argentina, and maybe a few others. I don't know. But I do know that the legats have absolutely no investigative power overseas. They can't question witnesses. They can't run informants. They can't even carry their FBI credentials down there, because they don't mean anything. They have no more authority down there than any private citizen. All they can do is maintain the best liaison possible with the local law-enforcement people."

"That's just terrific," Propper said sarcastically. "I can't believe this. How are we supposed to do anything?"

"The guy down there is one of the best in the Bureau, Gene. And one good legat is worth about a dozen of those spooks you've been talking to. The Agency itself doesn't have that many people in Chile."

"Well, at least they *live* there," said Propper. "For God's sake. What's the legat's name?"

"Bob Scherrer."

"Do you know him?"

"No. But everybody says he's solid. He's been there six years."

"Well, he may be great, but he's still one guy. That's not enough for something like this. I'll keep trying to get more people to work on this with us."

"Fine," said Cornick. "What are you going to do?"

"Well, I've got those two appointments at the State Department tomorrow. I've got to find somebody over there to help us. Beyond that, I don't know what I'll do."

"Well, that sounds all right to me."

"And I still think you should come with me to the State Department. It's stupid for me to go alone and then repeat everything. You've got to work with those people, too."

"Not a chance," said Cornick. "I've already checked into that. All I know is that the State Department did something to piss off the Bureau liaison man a week or two ago, and there's a freeze on. The State Department is off limits to everybody now."

"Because of something we did?"

"No, Gene, it has nothing to do with Letelier. It's some other thing. I don't even know what it is."

"That's crap! You mean to tell me that we can't work on our own case because of some bureaucratic squabble over in headquarters?"

"I'm afraid so. It won't last forever."

"We don't *have* forever, either. This stinks, Carter. We'll never get anything done this way. You've got to change this quick. It's simple."

"How's that?"

"You just don't tell them, that's all. You and I go over there and talk to the people at State, and you don't say anything about it. It's none of their fucking business, as long as you're doing your job."

Cornick eyed Propper as they walked along. He felt a warm flicker of temptation, but then he shook his head. "They'd find out, Gene," he said. "They're good at that. I know they would."

"So what?"

"So then they'd crack down on me, that's what. Once you've crossed them, they can make life miserable for you. Believe me."

Propper muttered to himself in frustration. Cornick returned to his national-security monologue for a half block or so. He thought he was making an impact on Propper with the extent of the Bureau's knowledge, but he could also tell that the impact diminished each time they ran up against the strict Bureau rules. This bothered Cornick. He and Propper were still feeling each other out, and he could tell that Propper sensed a contradiction between the Bureau's vast claims of prowess and the petty, tight restrictions on all its field agents.

"Don't get discouraged," said Cornick. "I promise you, the FBI will solve this case, probably by Christmas."

"Oh, really?"

"Count on it, brother."

"That's interesting, because I can't tell you how many people have told me it's unsolvable."

"Well, I think what they mean is that it's unprosecutable," said Cornick.

"What do you mean? If you solve it, why can't you prosecute it?"

"Well, it's going to be solved by sources too important to blow," said Cornick. "I suspect that's what'll happen. Sources will be out there in place, and their continuing information will be so important that we'll be better off keeping them there, knowing who killed Letelier but not prosecuting them."

This was heresy to Propper as a prosecutor, more distressing than the news of only one legat who did not even live in Chile. "No fucking way!" he whispered. "You can't *have* a more important case than a double assassination in the heart of Washington, D.C., Carter. What the hell are you going to save your source for?"

"Take it easy," said Cornick. "I'm just telling you how the big boys play ball, Gene. They're going to want to keep those sources to encourage other sources."

"Carter, if I thought we'd work our asses off on a case like this, and then, even if we solved it, we couldn't prosecute it . . . I mean, what is there in it? Why do it?"

"Well, maybe the satisfaction that we know who did it," said Cornick. "And maybe we can go to the jerks and tell them they better not do it again."

"You think *that's* enough?" cried Propper.

"Well, they'll know we know," said Cornick, in a low voice pregnant with intrigue. He had learned this line from Al Seddon, along with the better part of his spy monologue.

"Carter, if we find out what happened in this case, it's going to trial," Propper declared. "I guarantee it."

"No way," said Cornick.

"I bet you a dinner," said Propper, "at the restaurant of the winner's choice."

"You're on," said Cornick.

The first of many walks around the block concluded soon after four complete circuits of the courthouse. Propper returned to his office with a head full of the national security underworld. Larry Barcella casually asked what was going on. "Larry, I can't tell you. I really can't," said Propper. "You're not cleared." He left Barcella with a blank face. There had been no secrets in Major Crimes, where the family of lawyers protected itself in a stark world of hard criminals and autopsy photographs. Barcella's determination to be in on the news was matched by Propper's desire to tell somebody. Propper went home that night and talked for a long time into a tape recorder. Even then, in the privacy of his own bedroom, he spoke vaguely, in coded language, to guard against the possibility of theft or espionage. Cornick's dose was so effective that Propper remained secretive at the office, annoying his friends there. Within weeks, Barcella, Earl Silbert, and Don Campbell went in pursuit of their own security clearances.

The next day, October 5, Cornick arrived at Propper's office for a meeting with Stanley Wilson and an Immigration and Naturalization Service (INS) investigator from New York, Joe Schuman. Cornick was prepared to be unimpressed, and he was not disappointed. Propper, on the other hand, was eager. Wilson had promised him specific leads on the killers, saying that Schuman was a rich lode of information.

Schuman was an expert on Communists. He suspected their presence in countless places, including the FBI offices and the U.S. courthouse, where he was always on the lookout for hidden microphones. When the Chilean junta overthrew Allende and thousands of Chileans sought exile in the United States, the INS had dispatched Schuman to Chile on a mission to screen out terrorists from among the applicants. Since that assignment, Schuman had devoted himself to the study of the Chilean MIR, or Movement of the Revolutionary Left, a terrorist organization composed mostly of alienated young middle-class Chileans. MIR groups had campaigned against Allende, branding him as too moderate a socialist, and after the coup, these groups had been largely exterminated by the Chilean military. A few remnants of MIR were still in exile or underground.

Schuman suspected that one of these remnants had killed Letelier. He described the existing MIR network, listing the "cells" in New York, Washington, Chicago, Los Angeles, and many South American cities, the suspected leaders, the suspected meeting places, the power struggles, and so forth; but these details rested on such a thick foundation of supposition that the overall impression was somewhat vague. He would say, for instance, that a certain suspected MIR leader in New York owned a butcher shop, and then he would report the precise measurements of the butcher's shipping crates to buttress a suspicion that the MIR was stockpiling arms.

Cornick waded into Schuman's report after about ten minutes. "Do you have somebody telling you that the MIR killed Letelier?" he asked.

The pressure was on Schuman. He looked from side to side, a nervous security habit. "Yeah," he said.

"All right," said Cornick. "What do they say? How was he killed? Who did it?"

"Well, they haven't come up with those specifics yet," said Schuman, "but everything points in that direction. There are rumblings in the MIR. It makes perfect sense for them to knock off a moderate socialist like Letelier, especially since they can blame it on the Chilean military. It's perfect for them. Let me go over the MIR and the Castro Cubans for you."

As Schuman rambled on, Cornick rolled his eyes at Propper in mild reproach. He noticed that the prosecutor was no longer intent and fire-eyed, ready to pounce on the killers. Propper was already doodling on a pad, having sensed that this was not the great moment. The telephone rang, and Propper picked it up. He was not too busy to take the call, whoever it was, and Cornick was left alone on Schuman's long trail of Spanish surnames.

When the investigators left the office, Cornick shook his head and grinned, the vindicated professional. "Gene," he said, "you've got a couple of real live ones there. They are Commie-behind-every-bush types if I've ever seen them. They're worse than Seddon by miles."

"Okay, they don't have it yet," Propper admitted. "But you don't know they're wrong, do you? Have you ruled out the MIR or the far left as suspects?"

"No," said Cornick.

"So let 'em alone," said Propper. "Who knows? They may be right." He decided not to tell Cornick that he still planned to intercede with the bosses of Wilson and Schuman to obtain travel money for them.

"Come on, Gene," scoffed Cornick. "Those two guys couldn't track a bleeding elephant in six feet of snow. I'm telling you. Next time you get somebody who says he's going to solve Letelier for you real quick, have them call me, okay? Don't waste your time."

Cornick may have pushed his teasing too far. When Propper renewed his State Department challenge, the solid professional was in poor position to say he couldn't go because the Bureau wouldn't let him. Shortly, with misgivings, Cornick dared to follow Propper into the office of Louis Fields, director of the State Department's Office for Combatting Terrorism. Neither of them knew Fields or much of anything about the State Department, but the title of the office sounded attractive to them. They hoped to find an eager expert on the practice of terrorism in Latin America—someone who could school them in the clandestine affairs of Chile.

Fields was warmly polite to them, but he was also rather withdrawn. He kept emphasizing the special delicacy of international investigations, to the point that Cornick could almost sense Fields wondering why he had an FBI agent and an aggressive prosecutor in his office in the middle of the day.

"You know, Lou," Cornick interrupted, "your age is telling on you. I didn't think you were that old."

Both Fields and Propper were nonplussed by this sudden change of subject. "What are you talking about?" asked Fields.

"Come on, Lou," drawled Cornick. "That tie of yours goes back at least to the early fifties, maybe late forties, at Eljo's."

Fields lit up with surprise. Cornick had recognized in his attire—Weejun loafer shoes, gray slacks, blue blazer, blue tie patterned with little orange Cavalier roosters—the uniform of the Virginia aristocracy, and he joined Fields in an effusive reminiscence on the leading families of the state, on their experiences at the University of Virginia, on Eljo's, the renowned campus clothing store, and on many topics dear to the two of them but entirely alien to Propper.

Cornick's grandmother, Fields was interested to learn, was a direct descendant of President James Madison. His proud, ancient great-aunt still remembered enough of the old ways to be openly ashamed that a family member "toted a pistol" for the Yankee FBI. By her standards, gentlemen never carried guns. They carried swords, if anything. But young Carter Cornick had needed a job. He postponed plans to become a teacher and to write a historical narrative about the Eastern Shore Chapel. Cornick was a traditionalist with a slight rebel streak.

Cornick and Fields had exchanged hardly ten enthusiastic words on their rich common heritage before Propper began to fidget. The prosecutor knew by instinct that Fields was not the kind of State Department ally they were seeking.

"Goddamn it, Carter!" he exclaimed, when they finally escaped to the hallway. "It took you long enough to figure out he's not the one! My God! Not only did you beat around the bush, you walked *trenches* around the bush!"

"I know it, Gene." Cornick smiled. "But sometimes you've got to spend a little time to build up a rapport with someone before you know what they can do."

"Maybe so," fumed Propper. "But you could have done all that in five minutes and then asked the son-of-a-bitch about Letelier."

"A gentleman never hurries like that," teased Cornick. "Besides, it's not very often that I run into a fellow Virginian. Letelier can wait thirty minutes."

Propper did not settle down until they reached their next appointment, with John E. Karkasian, a State Department veteran of some twenty-five years. Karkasian was a Latin American specialist who had served many years in Chile, and he provided Propper and Cornick with their first comprehensive picture of Chilean politics. His experience included personal acquaintances not only with Letelier and all four leaders of the Chilean junta but also with practically every Chilean politician of note. Karkasian described Letelier as a smooth, charming man from one of Chile's best-known families, a man educated in the country's finest schools of military science, law, and economics. At the same time, Karkasian considered Letelier a rather shallow opportunist who spent most of his life as a socialist banker, traveling the hemisphere for the Inter-American Bank. Letelier had already lived ten years in the United States as a member of Washington's international community when, in 1970, the new President, Allende, asked him to stay on as Chile's ambassador. He returned to Chile only in the final months of the Allende regime's disintegration in 1973, just in time to be involved in the last desperate cabinet shuffles and to be arrested on the day of the coup.

As to the murders, Karkasian had no evidence, but he thought it unlikely that the Chilean government was involved. In his opinion, the leaders of the junta would not regard Letelier as a credible leader of a movement to unseat them, because Letelier was basically a political subordinate, a man for appointed office, whose political base in Chile would be severely limited by the fact that he had lived voluntarily outside the country for most of his adult life. Karkasian thought the Chilean leaders might resent Letelier's polish and his access to world media outlets, but he said they would consider him only a nuisance, not a threat. Karkasian said that even the politically unsophisticated Chilean generals would see that it would be disastrous to their interests to kill Letelier in so foolish a manner—in the United States, with the United Nations about to take up the issue of Chile's human-rights record, with the Chilean finance minister arriving that very day to seek financial aid, having only recently drawn attention to their disapproval of Letelier by canceling his citizenship. The assassinations had already wounded the regime, as anyone could have foreseen. The act was too crude for the generals, who were ruthless and Prussian in their suppression of internal dissent—but not stupid. Karkasian suspected that someone on the left or the far left had killed Letelier to make a useful martyr out of him and to discredit Pinochet. This, he said, was the prevalent view of the State Department.

Propper and Cornick went away from this briefing highly impressed. Many others, including Stanley Wilson and Joe Schuman, were disinclined to blame the Chilean government for the murders, but none of them possessed Karkasian's command of Chilean affairs. He seemed to know everyone in the country. And as he described the strengths and weaknesses of numerous Chilean leaders, of the Chilean economy, its political factions and tensions, he projected an air of certainty. Many clean, hard facts stacked up on his side of the ledger.

Cornick, in his cluttered roost at the Old Post Office Building, tried to incorporate some of Karkasian's views into his first official report on the case. Bureau officials were clamoring for something condensed on paper, and Cornick had been laboring for several days to produce what amounted to a book containing the basic facts and biographies, the crime-scene reports, and summaries of the essential interviews. Cornick had determined to interview each of the people mentioned in Letelier's address book, found in his briefcase, and this list alone ran to about 150 names, with locations spread from Moscow to California to Santiago, Chile. In addition, interviews were coming in from members of Letelier's family, his colleagues at IPS, and surviving members of Allende's cabinet. There were also interviews with various officials of the Pinochet government, who tended to disparage Letelier's character in savage terms and to blame the Russians for the murders.

In his report, Cornick listed samples of the conflicting opinions on what former Ambassador Letelier was like. His IPS colleagues eulogized him as a dedicated, peaceful revolutionary of great influence, possibly the next president of a free Chile. Their descriptions were glowing but somewhat arid, as though Letelier had been distilled from a political conception. Older friends put more flesh on him, observing that his charm and his powerful intellect had enabled him to suppress the conflicts between his socialist ideals and his taste for the good life. Some friends had noticed a change in Letelier after his year in the junta's prison camps. He had seemed more serious after his suffering, after his brush with death and with Chilean history. Living in Washington again for the last year and a half of his life —this time in exile—Letelier had been more at home with the notion that the core of his life was Chilean politics. He was a passionate critic of the Pinochet junta. Coincident with this change, however, many friends noted that Letelier was in something of a mid-life crisis. He was murdered at forty-four. Part of him remained in profound reflection, doubting everything—a state not uncommon to survivors of arbitrary arrest, deprivation, and psychological torture. Letelier's personal affairs were in a period of torment. Many of his friends believed that he looked to his wife, Isabel, for a constant renewal of moral strength.

No one seemed to dislike Isabel Margarita Morel de Letelier, not even her husband's enemies. Cornick already knew her as a woman of striking physical appeal and even more striking dignity. In her grief, before her husband's funeral, she had looked directly at the two FBI agents interviewing her and volunteered the information that Orlando Letelier had been having a prolonged affair with a Venezuelan woman that was "serious to the point of divorce." The affair had driven Letelier out of his home into a separate residence for most of 1976, she added, and they had reconciled shortly before the murders. In her quiet and yet outspoken way, Isabel Letelier said she wanted the FBI to know this as a sign that she had nothing to hide. She said it was possible that Letelier was having still other affairs, as was quite common for married Latin males. She told the spellbound agents that none of this had reduced her unreserved love for Letelier, or ever would. Nor could she ever believe that personal matters had anything whatsoever to do with the murders. She had loved Letelier in life, and now it was her sacred cause to prove that the Pinochet government was responsible for his death. By so doing, she would lay bare the utter moral depravity of the Chilean junta. Isabel Letelier approached politics with the same ardent conviction that she had given to the Catholic Church. For her, as for the radical clergymen of Latin America, the social and economic tenets of Marxism mixed well with religious compassion.

Cornick was inclined to believe Isabel Letelier's assertion that personal motives had nothing to do with the murders. Most murders arise from intimate grudges, but then again, most murders are not committed with bombs. As a rule, bombs meant politics to Cornick, not lovers. Nevertheless, he reported on the affair with the Venezuelan woman. Though a remote possibility, it could not be excluded without further investigation, especially after reports came in that the woman was a rich and influential person in Venezuela, related by marriage to the powerful governor of Caracas, Diego Arria. As such, she commanded her own bodyguards and the attention of the Venezuelan secret police. Letelier had called her "Queen." They had carried on their liaison in glamorous international style, meeting in Paris, New York, and the Caribbean. Such an affair was almost a matter of state, and it was not difficult to imagine its leading to dangerous intrigue, even murder. Cornick did not know enough to rule it out. The cassette tapes Letelier had made for the Venezuelan woman had not yet been translated. An American woman complicated things further by declaring that she had supplanted the Venezuelan as Letelier's mistress in the last months of his life, thereby provoking the Venezuelan's ire. The American woman feared that she might have been the cause of the murders.

The reports on Ronni Karpen Moffitt revealed a woman who was by age and inclination a latecomer to the Vietnam generation. She came from an Orthodox Jewish family in Passaic, New Jersey, where her father owned a delicatessen. Upon graduation from the University of Maryland in 1972, she taught elementary school for a year and then went to work as a typist in a Washington insurance agency. The job bored her. Seeking diversion in her favorite pastime, music, she applied for and obtained extra work at a place called the Music Carry-Out, which was part of the Mini-School, which in turn was a spin-off of the Institute for Policy Studies. The idea behind the Music Carry-Out was that if someone would provide a large room and a few musical instruments and a little inspiration in a diverse ethnic neighborhood, local musicians would congregate there spontaneously to play. IPS leaders had raised the money for this Washington pilot project during a phase in which they emphasized programs of decentralized community control. At the Carry-Out, Ronni Karpen organized a Bluegrass Night and a Jazz Night. She wrote funding proposals and proved to be such an enthusiastic, proficient worker that IPS officers gave her extra work at the Institute itself. The spirit of its political work attracted her. It was a new world. Toward the end of 1974, she felt secure enough in her varied IPS functions to quit her insurance job. A year later, the Music Carry-Out lapsed into insolvency, leaving behind two old pianos toward the payment of the last month's rent. After that, Ronni Karpen spent all her time and energy at the Institute.

Michael Moffitt was already there, doing research in international economics. His background and temperament contrasted sharply with hers. Moffitt was an Irish Catholic from upstate New York who had academic ambitions, a consuming interest in politics since childhood, and a fiery spirit that tended toward combativeness. "Everybody loved Ronni," he told the police and the FBI. "With me, it might be different." The two of them fell in love, caught up in each other and in the Institute's mission to reform the international economic order in favor of poor nations and to put an end to the kind of American interventions made infamous by the CIA. They shared a distinguished, inspiring mentor, Orlando Letelier, who operated in lofty circles. The explosion at Sheridan Circle occurred less than four months after their wedding, less than ten months after the bankruptcy of the Music Carry-Out.

Some officials of the Chilean government had already hypothesized that one or both Moffitts had been the intended victims of the explosion, not Letelier, and the head of DINA would later go so far as to suggest that Michael Moffitt had killed his wife and Letelier out of jealousy. Given the people involved, such thoughts seemed groundless, at best, but Cornick was determined not to overlook any conceivable motive for the crime. He wanted to be sure that no unexplored motive would come back to haunt him after he had moved on to more likely ones. So he sent agents out to interview Ronni Moffitt's acquaintances. None of them could imagine why anyone would want to kill her or her husband. Suspicion flickered only once, when a bizarre old boyfriend of hers from the insurance company days told the FBI that he still loved her and that he had sworn to kill her murderers with his .9 mm pistol, especially if they were black. The man said he "hated niggers worse than anything in the world." He seemed a little crazed. Cornick thought he merited a second interview. Two agents returned to find him in his kitchen, fondling a four-foot timber rattlesnake named George. The man said George would strike without a warning rattle. He said Ronni Moffitt had called him weird. He described her as "well-read, well-adjusted, and liberal," a woman who was too good for him. He understood that, and on second thought, he had decided not to kill her murderers. He said he knew a lot of her friends but couldn't remember them because his mind had been partially destroyed by amphetamines. The agents excused themselves hastily. They found out that he had been institutionalized as a mental patient. Doctors said he was harmless to anyone except possibly himself. Cornick finally decided that he could be eliminated as a suspect.

Cornick wrote and assembled his report during the remainder of the week, working whenever he could steal time from meetings and the flow of teletypes. Events great and small diverted his attention. On Wednesday, October 6, Venezuela-based Cuban terrorists placed a bomb on a Cubana Airlines jet before takeoff from the Caribbean island of Barbados. The plane exploded in the air and crashed into the sea, killing all seventy-three people on board. The passengers included twenty-four members of Cuba's fencing team, on their way home from a competition in Venezuela. The bombing became instant global news. Fidel Castro blamed the CIA and canceled the anti-hijacking treaty with the United States. The act would mark an end to the tentative moves toward détente between the two governments. At the time, the bombing was the second spectacular terrorist assassination in two weeks. CORU, a consortium of anti-Castro groups, claimed credit for the airline bombing. Cornick had reports that Cuban exiles might have been involved in the Letelier murders as well. Suddenly the primitive chill of terrorism no longer seemed distant for Americans, or even isolated in rare events. It was near, and constant.

Grisly details of the Cubana Airlines bombing spilled in on Thursday, October 7. That afternoon, Stanley Wilson and Joe Schuman walked into the Chilean embassy to talk over the Letelier case with two representatives of the Pinochet government. The Chilean diplomats responded warmly to Schuman's theories on the MIR, and the four men developed a hearty rapport based on suspicions that matched all the way down to exciting bits of obscure intelligence. Walking to lunch at Blackie's, they all pointed out the same plain building as a known hideout for MIR leftists. The Chileans pledged to help the Americans solve the Letelier case. Schuman wrote a report on the meeting and the lunch, describing the Chileans in his florid detective language as "very cordial and replete with the spirit of cooperation." When he and Wilson delivered the report to Propper, they found that a controversy had raced ahead of them.

The Chilean diplomats, apparently afraid that the American investigators were too good to be true, had called the State Department to make sure they were bona fide lawmen and not leftist spies. State Department officials had called Cornick to find out, and Cornick had called Propper, more than a little put out. He wanted to know what those two conspiratorial gumshoes were doing in so sensitive a place as the Chilean embassy. He could not think of anything more certain to bring calamity.

Propper found himself in a bind. Having known of their visit in advance, he had to defend their prerogatives as investigators. But he also agreed with Cornick's firm resolve not to advise Wilson or Schuman of any information developed in the investigation for fear that they would disclose it to potential suspects inside the Chilean government. Propper could only advise Wilson and Schuman to be more discreet, but he knew it was futile to hope that they would not get ensnarled with the FBI. He was glad Schuman was returning to New York. There was no time for such headaches.

On Friday, October 8, Propper went to the Justice Department for the big CIA meeting. Earl Silbert agreed to go with him in order to bolster the presence of the U.S. Attorney's Office. Tony Lapham and an assistant represented the Agency. A Justice Department delegation was led by Robert Keuch, deputy assistant attorney general of the criminal division. Keuch was the department's recognized national-security expert. He defended the government all day, and at night pursued a second career as an amateur actor and director. His youthful fondness for Barry Nelson parts was giving way in middle age to those played by Walter Matthau. He retained his droll wit and his actor's twinkle, but at the office he was a hard-liner on every issue of government power from wiretaps to preventive detention. As such, he could be a prosecutor's vital friend and helper, as Propper would learn. He had never met Keuch.

Stanley Pottinger welcomed the assorted teams of lawyers, showed them into a spacious conference room, and left them to work. Their task was to draft a letter from the attorney general to the CIA director that would enable the Agency to work on the Letelier case despite the flat prohibition against CIA involvement in criminal and domestic investigations. After considerable wrangling on legal fine points, the participants adopted a circuitous, backhanded approach. The attorney general would say that his criminal investigation of the murders had run into indications that foreign agents might have been involved. On that basis, the attorney general would ask the director to report on any aspects of the murders that might relate to the security of the United States against foreign intervention. Finally, closing the loop, the attorney general would remind the director that if the CIA should discover anything pointing to criminal activity, the Agency would turn it over to the Justice Department, of course, as required by law.

It took a long time to choose the correct words for this legal circumnavigation. Keuch and Lapham did most of the talking. Occasionally, when progress appeared to flounder, Propper would toss out practical encouragement. He was asked only one key question: "Do you really have anything that says foreign agents or foreign intelligence agencies are involved?" asked Keuch.

"Yes," said Propper. "We've got information coming in about a number of foreign groups and assassins whose methods fit this type of crime." He went on, winging it, and was happy no one pressed him.

When the meeting broke up, Keuch went to get the attorney general's signature. He had some doubts about whether Edward Levi, a stickler, would sign.

Propper felt immense relief as he hopped into Silbert's car. "How hard are your facts?" asked Silbert.

"Which facts?" asked Propper.

"The ones we used to call this an intelligence case, with spies and the CIA and stuff."

"Oh," sighed Propper. "Well, I wouldn't call those hard facts, exactly."

"What would you call them?"

"Well," said Propper. "More like shaky speculations."

Silbert closed his eyes and shook his head. Then he laughed. "You needed it, didn't you?" he asked quietly.

"Yeah."

"I figured you did," said Silbert. "I didn't want to get into it too deeply in there, because I figured if I asked you too many questions there wouldn't be any answers."

"Thanks," said Propper.

At the FBI, Carter Cornick finished his 500-page report and took it home to read once more over the weekend. He was proud of its order, of the methodical accumulation of facts and the methodical elimination of marginal possibilities. He was not yet in control of the investigation, but this was a start. The report contained only one tentative conclusion: "Investigation to date indicates Letelier was target of bombing, and that probable motive was political, although others (alleged financial irregularities and love affair with other than wife) considered feasible have surfaced."

Keuch brightened Propper's weekend with the news that Attorney General Levi had signed the final draft of the letter without hesitation. Couriers delivered it to CIA headquarters on Saturday, less than a week after the lunch meeting with Director Bush. In a government of nitpickers and redrafters and delays measured in years, this was motion of lightning speed. Keuch would present the letter to General Brent Scowcroft the next week and ask for the endorsement of the National Security Council.

Stanley Wilson called Propper at home to report the far less grandiose news that a prostitute had been arrested for murder in the District of Columbia. The hot part, said Wilson, was that he had recognized in her "trick book" the names of numerous known left-wingers and drug dealers, including none other than Carlos Altamirano. This meant nothing to Propper until Wilson explained that Altamirano had been head of the Socialist Party in Chile and was now supposed to be living in East Germany. He was a heavy, near the top of Schuman's MIR network of terrorists. Wilson had traced the number in the trick book to a tenement house in New York, and Schuman had checked INS records for him and come up negative. Altamirano, said Wilson, might have sneaked into the States to supervise a hit on Letelier. Wilson did not know yet whether Altamirano was still in the tenement, but he was checking. If so, Schuman had photographs of the real Altamirano that they could show around the neighborhood for identification. Propper told Wilson not to go anywhere near the guy without checking back, and he hung up. He thought it was just like Wilson to come up with a queer lead like that.

Cornick drove in from Virginia Monday morning to catch up on his teletypes. It was Columbus Day. WFO and all the rest of the government buildings were nearly deserted, but the few people there treated Cornick with the extra politeness due one of the condemned. He knew why. The first great leaks had occurred. On Saturday, *The Washington Post* had reported nearly all the details of Propper's arrangements with the CIA and a great deal about the FBI's general strategy on the case. Also, *Newsweek* published a startling item in the "Periscope" column of its Columbus Day issue: "After studying FBI and other field investigations, the CIA had concluded that the Chilean secret police were not involved in the death of Orlando Letelier...." Cornick could scarcely believe his eyes. First of all, there were no FBI reports other than the one he had under his arm. Second, there was nothing that he knew of to justify such a conclusion. Third, he knew the Bureau would set up machine-gun nests to defend itself before it would allow anyone from the CIA to review FBI reports on a criminal investigation. If anything, it would be the other way around: the Bureau would get the CIA reports. The item was ridiculous on its face, but that was irrelevant. This was a leak. From the Bureau's point of view, the *Post* story was a hundred times worse. Cornick could almost feel a tremble in the Old Post Office Building, before tomorrow's explosion. Glad it was a holiday, he drove home to spend the afternoon in seclusion with his binoculars and the southern migration. He was an experienced birdwatcher. It relaxed him.

In New York, Larry Wack spent the holiday with his fiancée, Elizabeth Ryden. Wack lived less than a block from the Manhattan FBI office and even closer to his favorite East Side bar. He was known to drink after hours with informants. Only twenty-six, with blond hair and a baby face, he looked like an ice-cream salesman but had a voice and personality straight out of Damon Runyon. Wack's manner was as abrupt as his name. He was the agent who drove up to Westchester after the Letelier murder to interview Reverend William Wipfler about the rumored DINA agents, and he did not understand why the bleary-eyed, intellectual clergyman was reluctant to name names. "What's the matter, Father?" snapped Wack. "Is it a confessional-type situation or something?"

Wack grew up just outside Trenton, New Jersey, where his father worked as a quality-control inspector in a war-matériel plant, hoping to reach retirement before the company found out that he was functionally blind. The elder Wack did the job well with his hands, but he knew his condition violated company policy. He encouraged his son's ambition to become an FBI agent, which was fixed permanently in Larry at the age of twelve, when he came into contact with an FBI clerk who was dating his sister. Young Wack wrote J. Edgar Hoover for a fingerprint kit and received instead a poster of Baby Face Nelson. Nevertheless, he kept up a lively correspondence with Hoover himself, went to see Jimmy Stewart in *The FBI Story* at least a dozen times, and applied for an FBI job during his senior year in high school, petrified that the omniscient Bureau would turn him down because his grandmother had sent chocolates to relatives in Germany in wartime. The Wack family was split evenly—half German, half Irish—and people said both sides were dominant.

He was pure FBI—but just barely, owing to a penchant for trouble. On his last night in Jersey, he and several buddies were celebrating their high-school graduation in an all-night joyride with a week's supply of moonshine, and in the wee hours it seemed like a good idea to expose parts of their bodies to the occupants of passing cars, one of which was filled with a group of unappreciative nuns. The local constable would not release Wack until he produced his official FBI acceptance letter, ordering him to report for training the next day. Wack became a clerk in headquarters at seventeen, just after the Washington riots following the murder of Martin Luther King, Jr., and was assigned to a section that handled subversives and political crimes. He attended night school so that he could become an agent, but he received his principal education in the bowels of the FBI, shuffling files on the Weathermen, the Chicago 7, the Wilmington 10, the King murder, the Kennedy assassination—anything that might require a report to Congress. There he learned Bureau lingo and sealed his dislike for Commies and hoods. His fiancée preferred not to hear about his cases.

They had an early dinner in Wack's apartment. Ryden left about seven-thirty and caught a bus down Second Avenue to the East Side terminal. She was a stewardess, on her way to work a flight that night. As she waited for the shuttle bus to JFK Airport, a thin man in a T-shirt walked up to her and said hello. He did not appear to be the sort of man with whom she wanted to encourage conversation, so she ignored him. An hour later, in an airport corridor, she was searching her purse for the key to the American Airlines Flight Crew Information Office when a hand grabbed her right arm and yanked her around into a hostile face.

"You tell your little friend Larry Wack to keep his fucking nose out of Chile's business or you won't be so pretty anymore!" hissed the man. "Boom! Boom! You know what I mean?"

"Yes, I know what you mean," gasped Ryden. She sank to the floor as soon as he released his grip. She shrieked for help as he vanished, and somehow, on the floor, drawing a crowd, she pulled out an envelope and wrote down the words and a description. It was the same man who had said hello at the bus station. He reeked of nicotine and venom.

Ten minutes later, there was hysteria in the Flight Crew Office. Airport police, fellow stewardesses, and American Airlines management personnel crowded around Ryden, who was trembling and crying and answering questions all at once. Her flight was delayed several times, and then it took off without her. Ryden would never be allowed to fly again. Airline companies considered the terrorist potential too great. A doctor showed up, and Larry Wack roared into the confusion ahead of half a dozen FBI agents. They blitzed the airport as best they could, and they took Ryden down to the FBI office after coming up empty.

A couple of hours later, the night supervisor had a small army of agents working. Some worked on teletypes, some took statements from Wack and Ryden, and others tried to track down more help—more agents, and especially George Dyer, the FBI artist. Wack called Carter Cornick at home in Virginia.

"Are you sure?" said Cornick. "Are you sure the guy said Chile?"

"Absolutely," said Wack. "And he made a noise like a bomb, and he looked like a fucking foreigner. Liz has got the description down well enough so we can get a good composite, I hope."

"My God, Larry," said Cornick. "Do you realize what this means?"

"I know what it means to me," said Wack. "It means some asshole is gonna get his face rearranged, that's what it means."

"Wait a minute," said Cornick. "Tell me what happened, Larry. Tell me exactly what happened." He sat down to recover his wits as Wack told the story. Nothing like this had ever happened in the Bureau, he knew. The few times FBI agents had been threatened were all renowned. It was always somebody under pressure, about to be arrested, who popped off at an agent.

"He scared the shit out of her, Carter," said Wack. "She can't even sit in her chair."

"I know, Larry. I'm sorry. But I want to know what you're planning to do."

"I don't think you really want to know," said Wack.

"No! I mean, what are you going to do about her? You've got to protect her. And you've got to protect yourself. They may come back at you again, and you've got to guard against it. This thing ain't over."

"Well, we got one of the female agents out of bed, and she's gonna stay with Liz in her apartment tonight. And two guys are gonna stay with me. I hope the fuckers do come back."

"You might want to think about getting her out of town for a while," Cornick suggested.

"She doesn't want to go anywhere, Carter. And tomorrow, assuming this composite comes out all right, we're gonna plaster it all over that bus station and all over the airport. Somebody had to see the guy."

"That's good, but I don't think you should be in on all those interviews yourself," Cornick advised.

"Why not?"

"Because if you catch the guy, all those 302s* will go to defense lawyers, and they'll see your name and impeach the evidence because of you. They'll say you had a personal interest in the case and can't be trusted."

"They might be right. I don't give a shit whether the guy gets convicted or not. I just want to find him."

"I do, too, Larry. That's great. But tomorrow you're going to want the guy to go to jail. I know how you feel, but you've got to do this right."

"Okay, okay. Can I go in there with Liz when they're doing the composite?"

"Sure you can. But goddamn it! I don't want to see your name on those 302s when they come down here."

A lot of extra agents showed up for the Letelier meeting the next morning at WFO. The FBI's clan spirit was aroused. Scores of agents were calling Wack from all over the country; many of them had never heard of him or the Letelier case before.

After the meeting, Nick Stames summoned Cornick to his office for a more private conference. It was the leaks, he said. People had been calling him all morning from headquarters. They had been calling Satkowski, too. They all assumed it was Propper. Some of them were drawing a straight line from Propper's CIA meetings to the *Post* story on CIA and FBI strategy to the Ryden threat. The story might have caused the threat by publicizing Bureau activity in the case. Anyway, headquarters was pissed off all the way up to Jim Ingram, head of the criminal division. Bureau people on the case were going to have to sign affidavits attesting to their innocence on the leaks, and Propper would have to be stopped if he was guilty. Stames wanted a written assessment by noon on the most likely sources of the leaks.

Cornick went back to his desk. He ignored a dozen messages from reporters and called Propper. Because of the time pressure on the leaks, he had to downplay the Ryden threat. Cornick passed along what was being said at the Bureau, and Propper denied it. Cornick said everyone was saying that Propper was a friend of the *Post* reporter. That was true, Propper admitted, but there were two reporters on the story. One of them covered the Justice Department, and

*Standard FBI interview form.

Propper therefore suspected one of the notorious leakers over in Keuch's outfit. They had all been aware of the CIA meeting. Besides, he said, the substance of the story itself would not hurt the investigation, even though the leak per se was bad. The notion that the story had caused the Ryden threat was idiocy. Propper thought maybe there was an FBI source somewhere, and there was back and forth jousting on numerous related points.

"And what about the *Newsweek* article?" asked Cornick. "What the hell is that?"

"You're asking me? It doesn't say anything in there about the U.S. Attorney's Office. It's all about the FBI and the CIA. You tell *me* what it means. I want all those reports."

"Gene, there ain't no damn reports."

"Where's the bomb report? It's a week late already."

"I don't know. They're working on it. Besides, it's irrelevant. Just because you're not in the story doesn't mean you didn't leak it."

"Come off it, Carter. You don't really think I leaked that crap about what the CIA has decided, do you? Why would I do that?"

"No, I don't think you did," Cornick sighed. "It just doesn't make sense, that's all."

"Well, some honcho at the Agency probably shot off his mouth to a reporter, and the reporter printed it. The story doesn't matter, anyway, so let's forget about it. Refer some of the calls to me if you want. I'll get rid of them."

"All right," said Cornick. "I'll tell you one thing, though. That kind of stuff is enough to make you think twice about getting any help from the Agency. I think you're pissing up a rope."

"Maybe so. We'll see."

Cornick went back to fend off the leak inquiry at the Bureau with qualified memos that leaned toward the predilections of those above him. He returned to Propper's office late in the afternoon with a full report and an update on the threat. Wack had half the agents in New York out on the street, he said. They had already come up with one Ulysses Spieth, a porter in the men's room at the East Side Terminal who claimed to recognize the face in the composite drawing. Spieth said the man had passed through the bathroom the previous night and remarked that he was on his way back to California, for what that was worth. In addition, said Cornick, Wack was planning to take Ryden through a rerun of her journey, hoping to draw some attention from the culprits. As cover for her, he had already commandeered six of the Bureau-owned taxis, a dozen undercover "beards," three or four sharpshooter women agents, and a small fleet of un-marked Bureau escort cars. Cornick feared what would happen if the man showed up.

One thing was certain, he said: Wack was in the Letelier case for keeps. Things looked bad at State, and he wasn't sure about the traveling legat in South America, but he knew they had a man in New York. Cornick had never met Wack. He hoped the younger agent would season quickly.

"Gene, the implications of this threat are mind-boggling," said Cornick. "Whoever did it had to know who Wack is, for one thing. He's only done thirteen interviews up there, he tells me. Then they would have to know where he lives. On top of that, they would have to find out the woman is his fiancée, or at least his girlfriend. And on top of all that, they would have to have the capability to follow her through New York City for an hour and a half. Either that, or they would have to know where she was going in advance. The upshot of it is that these people must have what amounts to an intelligence organization, and a pretty damn good one. They know more about us than we know about them. That's for sure. Plus, they're crazy. Nobody in his right mind would take the risk of getting caught like that when he's not desperate. Hell, the guy might have sprained his ankle or something right there in the airport and handed us the key to the whole murder case when they didn't have to! That's what gets me. They just did it to fuck with us, that's all. They're sending us a signal that they can and will do anything. They could come after any one of us."

"Come on, Carter," said Propper. "Don't get carried away."

"Especially you."

"Why me?"

"I'm not kidding, Gene."

"I'm not, either. Why should I worry? I'm not married or anything."

"You've got a girlfriend," said Cornick, referring to Propper's latest, a reporter for *The Washington Star*.

"They're not going to follow my girlfriend," scoffed Propper.

"They followed Wack's girlfriend."

"That's different. She spent a lot of time at his place, and his place is on the same street as the FBI office. And it's in New York."

"Look, Gene," said Cornick, "they're not coming after me. I live way the hell out in the suburbs. You've got a much higher visibility in the case. You've been in all the newspapers, you son-of-a-bitch. If they're coming after anybody, they're coming after you. How would you feel about having some protection?"

"Protection? You mean bodyguards or something? I don't want any of that. It would be a pain in the ass."

"I'm serious, Gene. You should think about whether it would make you feel safer. It can be done, I assure you."

"I know you're serious," sighed Propper. "That's what worries me. But I still don't want any protection. I'm a little paranoid, but not that paranoid."

Cornick took a deep breath. "Okay," he said. "I just wanted you to know."

"Thanks."

"And there's another solution to all this."

"What's that?"

"Well," said Cornick. "If your girlfriend really loves you, ask her to start your car." Cornick returned to his somber mood after a belly laugh.

Propper returned to the office after dinner that night to work on the pending indictment of a depressed uniform merchant who had put out a murder contract on his wife. It would go to trial in a few months. Propper still had a few cases working other than Letelier. He stayed late but worked poorly. When he left the courthouse, his mind was jittery, gnawing at him. He couldn't stop it. The sight of his car, parked in the dark, made it worse. Propper stared at it awhile. Then he opened the passenger door and took a flashlight out of the glove compartment. He opened the hood and shined the beam over the engine. Then under the car. He realized that he had no idea what he was looking for. If it was there, he would not know it. Finally, he climbed behind the wheel and sat there. It seemed foolish not to turn the key, but then again it also seemed foolish to do something like that to yourself. This was ridiculous. He closed his eyes, lifted both legs off the floorboard, and turned the key.

When the car started, he laughed out loud at himself, especially for lifting his legs. He knew that such a gesture would not have helped Letelier. He knew what the bomb would have done. Propper kept laughing, but he was angry. He told himself to either get on with things or drop the Letelier case.

7 ▣ FIRST LEADS

In a crisis, the Venezuelan secret police, DISIP, had come to depend on Ricardo Morales, a man who was already a legend among Latin spies. Though serving Venezuela in a highly sensitive position, Morales was a Cuban exile. This was odd in itself, but it was among the least surprising things about a man whose career was a mystery even by the twisted standards of espionage.

Morales had come recently from Miami to DISIP, where he replaced one of the men now suspected in the Cubana Airlines bombing. Though only thirty-seven, Morales had already lived the equivalent of several lives of intrigue, stretching all the way back to teenage service in Castro's military intelligence. He had survived numerous attempts on his life, which gave him an aura of invincibility, but the key to his reputation lay in his mysterious, smooth charm. He possessed a spy's gift for making people trust him—even people he had previously betrayed.

Morales attended a top-level meeting of DISIP in Caracas on October 15. The senior DISIP officials all showed signs of great stress, knowing that jobs—even lives—were at stake. One disaster after another had caved in on these men since the Cubana Airlines bombing nine days earlier. The two suspects in Trinidad, in utter dread, had confessed everything. They had come from Venezuela. They had made traceable phone calls back to Caracas. Their fellow conspirators were all in Venezuela. Worst of all, for the interests of the DISIP officials in the meeting, the suspects were saying that some of the conspirators were tied to DISIP itself—as DISIP veterans, DISIP informants, and friends of the DISIP high command.

President Carlos Andrés Pérez had been informed that the entire case was about to land on Venezuela—the jurisdiction, the two suspects, the suspicion of responsibility for seventy-three terrorist homicides, and the worst publicity imaginable. It could not be avoided. President Pérez was furious with the men in the meeting, his DISIP men, who had assured him that the best way to control the anti-Castro Cuban terrorists was to make a deal with them. DISIP allowed them to operate from Venezuela; in return, the Cubans promised not to strike against Venezuelans or targets in Venezuela.

Among South American presidents, Pérez was a leader among those pushing for détente with Fidel Castro. He was a spokesman for Third World causes, and he allowed Venezuela to become a sanctuary for democratic exiles fleeing military governments all over the continent. Pérez had personally invited Isabel Letelier to bring her husband's body to Caracas for what amounted to a state funeral, just two weeks ago. This was the liberal side of Pérez, but there was a pragmatic, fiercely anti-Communist side as well. He sold Venezuelan oil at high OPEC prices to rich countries and poor ones alike. His country provided exile to more than 50,000 anti-Castro Cubans, and Pérez had gone so far as to fill the upper ranks of his intelligence and secret police service with foreigners, mostly CIA-trained Cuban exiles. Their job was to accommodate the anti-Castro terrorists in private while Pérez accommodated Castro in public, but the jetliner bombing had now shattered the secrecy that was required for such a delicate arrangement.

At the meeting, the DISIP high command agreed on a two-step plan of action. First, they would arrest more than a dozen of the most active terrorists in Venezuela. On this, they had no choice. President Pérez had ordered a sweeping, highly visible crackdown. To comply, the DISIP officials drew up an arrest list and went about the dragnet in a manner unique to a spy world in which the government itself was riding a thin edge between law and terror. The DISIP officials divided the list among themselves and telephoned their friends among the intended victims, warning them in a gentlemanly way that they had a few hours to get their affairs in order before going to jail. The terrorists were advised that they might be better off there—for a while, anyway—and that they had only themselves to blame for making things "too hot" in Venezuela.

The second and more ambitious part of the plan called for Ricardo

Morales to initiate a one-man propaganda campaign that would deflect the glare of worldwide terrorist publicity away from Venezuela toward other countries. For his assignment, Morales drew on his accumulated knowledge of the political underworld. He saw to it that stories would appear stating that the Chilean government had sent assassins to Costa Rica, and that some of the assassins had planned to kill Henry Kissinger. Morales was well equipped to plant the sensational stories. He knew the assassins personally. Morales also called a radio station in Miami, where he was well known, and said on the air that the Cubana Airlines bombing was the work of CIA and FBI informants. This would spread suspicion in the case outside of Venezuela, and it would warn the American agencies not to get too righteous about the bombing. Morales knew that at least one of the principal planners of the bombing—his predecessor* in DISIP—had been in regular contact with the CIA for more than a decade. Morales also knew something of the workings of the CIA and FBI, having spent more than five years in the service of each agency.

His most successful propaganda ploy involved the Letelier murder, which had caused such a stir in the American capital. Morales planted a story about how Orlando Bosch—a Cuban baby doctor who was nevertheless the world's preeminent advocate of anti-Castro terrorism—had confided to close associates that the "Novo brothers" had killed Letelier. Morales knew that Bosch was a credible source. Back in 1968, when Bosch's amateur terrorism was not yet respectable among anti-Castro operatives in Miami, Morales helped Bosch with bomb instruction and then suddenly surfaced in court as an FBI informant and as the chief witness against the baby doctor, who went to jail. Bosch fled the United States six years later, soon after being released on probation. Bosch-style terrorism grew rapidly. By then, he was no longer a joke. Morales, having moved to his DISIP job in Venezuela, used his legendary charm to help convince the man he had put in jail that he should relocate in Venezuela and come to terms with DISIP. Now, after the Cubana Airlines bombing, the wheel had turned again. Morales signed the DISIP arrest warrant for Bosch, and after the October 15 strategy meeting, he went out with the DISIP party that escorted Bosch to prison. Then Morales sent his scoop on the Letelier murder to Venezuelan reporters. The story ran in Venezuela on October 18 and was picked up the following day in newspapers all over the world.

*Luis Posada Carriles.

Propper saw it in his morning *Washington Post.* Immediately he called Cornick. "Who the hell are the Novo brothers?" he inquired. Cornick was well prepared, as the same question had headlined that morning's daily meeting on the case. He told Propper that the brothers were leaders of a New Jersey-based anti-Castro group called the Cuban Nationalist Movement (CNM). Publicly, they were best known as the men charged with firing a bazooka shell at the United Nations building in 1964, during a speech there by Ernesto "Che" Guevara.* The shell had been a semidud, aimed poorly, and had plopped harmlessly into the East River. This daring but ill-fated attempt had drawn much attention and a few titters in the American press. In subsequent years, through numerous scrapes with the FBI, the Novo brothers retained a slightly clownish reputation. Until recently. Like Orlando Bosch, the Novo brothers seemed to have pushed their followers toward more substantial acts of terror in the last few years.

Cornick told Propper that CNM members were suspected of setting off a bomb on a Russian ship that was moored in the port of Elizabeth, New Jersey, just five days before the Letelier bombing. And three CNM members had been arrested for attempting to bomb the New York Academy of Music on July 24, in protest against a performance there by artists from Cuba. New York policemen claimed to have recognized a fourth CNM member fleeing from the scene.

"Did they get his name?" asked Propper.

"Yep," said Cornick. "They say they know who it is, but they didn't arrest him. Didn't have a good case, I guess."

"Was he still on the streets when Letelier got killed?"

"As far as I know, he was," said Cornick. "He's been mentioned in some source reports on the Russian ship case, Gene. His name is Suárez. But it's shaky stuff. I'm just getting the teletypes in."

"Well, I want that guy in the grand jury. Quick. While he's nervous and might spill something. I can get the grand jury tomorrow. You think your guys up there can find him?"

"Of course they can find him," Cornick declared. "Hold on. I'll be right over."

At this stage of the investigation, Cornick was still canvassing the Bureau—asking all offices for tips, suggestions, and criticism of his

---

*The Novo brothers were arrested at the scene of the crime, but criminal charges against them were dismissed because they had not been permitted to consult with an attorney before confessing to police.

approach. As a result, he was still buried in paper and had not yet
absorbed the reports on the Cuban Nationalist Movement. He and
Propper began to sift through them as soon as the subpoena went
out to New Jersey. Cornick soon had a better idea. He called Frank
O'Brien, an agent in the FBI's Newark office who had followed the
CNM for years and who knew the Novos well. O'Brien told Cornick
and Propper that the new lead didn't figure. From long experience,
he knew CNM leader Guillermo (Bill) Novo as an accomplished fund
raiser and public speaker, a man of considerable philosophical knowledge, who would blow out a store window or dent the hull of a Russian ship, but who was not a killer. Nor had Novo ever been known to
strike anything other than a Cuban target. They didn't care about
Chile. Where was their motive? O'Brien didn't believe they had one,
but he assured Cornick and Propper that he was already trying to
locate Novo at all the usual spots in New Jersey. Soon they would
see the account of an interview.

O'Brien seemed to know his man. Cornick and Propper discussed
his report and then began to prepare for the next day's grand-jury
session. Propper would ask the CNM man about the structure of his
organization. He would try to confirm the Newark agent's report
that Novo was the undisputed leader, who ordered bombings but
never appeared at the scene. He would ask the man why Orlando
Bosch would say such terrible things about the Novo brothers. In essence, Propper would fish for information and try to catch the man in
a lie. This was always one of Propper's goals. He knew that a proven
lie before a grand jury could be translated into leverage for the prosecutor.

The next morning, the subpoenaed man and his lawyer presented
themselves at Propper's office. Dionisio Suárez was a muscular man
who wore a neatly trimmed black beard and who smiled easily.
Suárez shook his head and wondered out loud why he had been called
on such short notice about a crime that had nothing to do with the
Cubans. He said he was accustomed to harassment by the FBI, however, and expressed hope that this latest episode would cost nothing
more than a day's pay. To Propper, Suárez seemed relaxed and soft-
spoken—a man of unusually professional bearing for a car salesman.
He sighed over the Academy of Music charges. He said he had heard
before that someone had seen him there, but it wasn't true. He told
Propper and Cornick where he had been, and he was cooperative in
all respects until Propper said it was time for the two of them to go
downstairs to the grand jury.

At this point, Suárez requested a Spanish translator to help him with the questions. Propper objected. He said Suárez spoke perfect English. Yes, said the lawyer, but Spanish was his client's native language and a translator would make him more comfortable. He wanted to be sure he answered all the questions properly. The lawyer's insistence put Propper in a quandary. To comply would mean delay, but to deny the request might taint whatever testimony Suárez gave. Propper offered a compromise: he would postpone the grand-jury appearance if Suárez would submit to a brief interview right then, in the office. Suárez agreed, and the discussion was under way when Propper was called out of the room for an urgent phone call.

It was Satkowski, the Bureau supervisor, and Propper knew something was wrong as soon as he heard the name. Ordinarily Satkowski would call Cornick, not him. Now Satkowski said there was new information coming in from New Jersey. Frank O'Brien was asking to be patched through to Propper.

O'Brien came on the line. Propper was instantly tense. "Gene," said O'Brien. "I may have something. My teletype is already on its way to Carter, but I thought you should know this yourself."

"Go ahead," said Propper. "Carter's right here. What is it?"

"Well, I finally tracked Novo down last night, and I interviewed him. And it was all the usual stuff until I asked him where he was on the night before the Letelier bombing. Then he said something very strange. He said, 'That is my trump card. That is the ace up my sleeve.' "

Propper felt a chill. "He said *what?*"

"I don't know what to make of it," said O'Brien. "He wouldn't tell me where he was. All he said was that was his trump card and the ace up his sleeve, and stuff like that."

"Wait a minute!" said Propper. "Hold on, Frank. I want Carter to hear this."

Propper pulled Cornick out of the interview and excused Suárez. O'Brien repeated himself for Cornick's benefit, while Propper's secretary typed up a subpoena for Novo. Cornick told O'Brien to stand by in Newark to serve it on Novo.

"Okay, we'll be here," said O'Brien. "But I know Bill Novo, and I still don't think he'd be dumb enough to get involved with anything like a double murder in Washington. I can't believe it."

"Maybe not," said Propper, who was gliding on excitement. "But what he said was dumb, Frank. It's stupid if he's guilty, and it's even more stupid if he's not."

But Novo was nowhere to be found. O'Brien couldn't serve the subpoena. Novo's friends and relatives were slamming doors on the agents. A freeze was on. Cornick advised O'Brien to gather more agents and "rattle some cages" in Newark and Union City. Agents should blitz the restaurants and bars, and they should knock on the neighbors' doors, making no secret of their desire to find Novo. Perhaps the agents should allow a little bit of gun to be seen on their hips.

It was midnight when Novo called the FBI. He was ready to talk. He had been waiting for Suárez to get back from Washington, but now he would say where he had been the night before the bombing. He had been with his wife. Novo agreed to meet O'Brien the next day and accept the subpoena. His older brother, Ignacio, was in Miami and would be pleased to accept his subpoena there.

Within forty-eight hours of Novo's call, Cornick received a late-night bulletin from another quarter. Larry Wack called from New York. "Carter," said Wack, "I just wanted to let you know that we're going in."

"Going in where?"

"Going into the Arica Institute," said Wack. "We've made the decision that we're going in. Now. We're gonna resolve this thing tonight."

Cornick heard the sounds of a bar or restaurant in the background on Wack's end. His internal warning system became engaged. "Wait a minute, Larry," he said. "Who's there with you?"

"Don't worry," said Wack. "I've got plenty of guys with me."

"Bureau guys?"

"A few. And some friends, too."

"Uh huh," said Cornick, now fully worried. "Hold on, Larry," he warned. "Now listen. I'm with you a hundred percent. I understand the significance of this to you and to the case. But you've got to do it right. Now tell me just what you've got since this afternoon."

The key thing, Wack replied, was that the doorman said the guy who threatened Liz Ryden was upstairs in the apartment at that moment. The previous day, Wack had shown the composite drawing to his daily quota of about fifty people, without success, but the last one, a doorman, had taken one look and said, "I know that guy." This alone had prevented Wack from sleeping that night. That was first. Second, the doorman said the guy usually wore jeans, sneakers, a T-shirt, and a blue windbreaker, which was precisely what Ryden had said of the man at the airport. Third, the doorman said the guy hung out in an apartment that faced directly toward the entrance to

Wack's building—which Wack took to be an ideal surveillance position. Fourth, the apartment where the guy hung out was rented to an outfit called the Arica Institute, which the doorman described as "some sort of cult or something." Fifth, the doorman said most of the people up there were Hispanic. Sixth, the registration records showed that the leaders of the Arica Institute had Spanish surnames and permanent addresses in California, where the porter in the men's room of the East Side airlines terminal said that a man who looked like the suspect claimed to be heading. This was pretty much where Cornick had left off that afternoon. Since then, Wack had gotten some reports from California. Seventh, the Arica Institute was named after the town of Arica, a province capital in the northern desert of Chile. Eighth, many of its members were Chilean nationals. And ninth, the doorman had called Wack at home with the news that the guy was upstairs now. He was more positive than ever. Wack was having dinner with about twenty of his buddies, and they were getting fairly well fired up to see the suspect for themselves.

"All right, now I understand," said Cornick. "But let me ask you something. If you take the guy downtown, what are you planning to book him on?"

"Obstruction of justice, under that standing warrant."

"Larry, you can't go busting in there to make an arrest. You don't have enough. You don't even have probable cause."

"Well, I'll get you some probable cause in about half an hour or so."

From there, an argument broke out. Cornick pointed out that the people who made the threat might have been using the Arica Institute as a cover. He thought Wack should play it low key and ask for an interview without his strike force. If the man looked like the composite, he could make the arrest later. Wack finally relented. He promised to call Cornick if any action ensued that night, and then he went back to his friends. He grumbled about how Cornick had pulled his "father-figure routine."

Some hours later Wack presented himself at the door of the Arica Institute. When it opened, he identified himself as an FBI agent and was invited into a room full of marijuana smoke and dim colored lights. A number of people were meditating on the floor. They talked to Wack of self-realization, dignity, and the beauty of life. None of them looked remotely like the composite. Wack became exceedingly polite. He showed the composite around. No one recognized it.

The next morning, a rather sheepish Wack called Cornick with the news. "Not even close," said Wack. "Nobody in that bunch is gonna threaten anybody."

Cornick was greatly relieved, after a long night worrying about shoot-outs and civil-rights suits and letters to the Bureau. He was also pleased that the matter had been handled correctly. He took it as a hopeful sign that Wack was curbing his Hotspur tendencies.

Sunday evening, Stanley Wilson called Propper from New York and launched into a coded monologue on the progress of his investigations in that city with Joe Schuman. They had unearthed numerous sources on the operations of the leftist Chilean MIR, and their information pointed toward the conclusion that Isabel Letelier had arranged her husband's murder for reasons that were both personal and political. Wilson explained how his inferences from scattered, independent sources were converging in that direction, but his speech was muffled and his references were oblique. He kept referring to "certain parties well known to you."

Propper could make no sense of it. He turned down his television and asked Wilson to start over. The detective complied, but his delivery remained so guarded that Propper asked what was going on. Was he in trouble? Wilson replied that he was in a crowded room and therefore could not speak freely. In that case, said Propper, Wilson should call him collect at the office in the morning.

The subsequent report was clearer but no less complicated. "Elements" of the MIR were thought to desire the elimination of moderate socialists like Letelier, and these elements were somehow knitted together with other elements that resented Letelier's treatment of his wife. Propper told Wilson he thought it was nonsense to believe that Mrs. Letelier was involved, but he encouraged Wilson to pursue his investigation of various political leftists who might have had reason to kill Letelier.

Two days later, October 27, Guillermo Novo arrived at Propper's office in response to his grand-jury subpoena. In Novo, Propper and Cornick encountered a rather dapper man, given to three-piece pinstripe suits. He was highly articulate and carried himself with suave assurance, unlike most of the murderers Propper had faced. In two respects, Novo was an oddity among the anti-Castro "action" men in the United States. First, he was not a refugee from the Castro government, having left Cuba in 1952, seven years before Castro took power. Also, he had never worked for the CIA. To some Cuban exiles he was an outsider trying to make up for the fact that he did not fight at the Bay of Pigs. Like most exiles, however, he felt he had led a life of persecution. He kept asking why it was the Cubans—always the Cubans—who got blamed for this sort of murder.

"Wait a minute, Mr. Novo," said Propper. "Look, don't say I'm starting out with a prejudice against you, because I'm not. I have never had a Cuban defendant before—never even had a Cuban witness. Until Suárez last week, I'd never even *spoken* to a Cuban except for my high-school Spanish teacher. I've always been a little bit anti-Castro, mostly because of him, but I don't have anything against you or any other Cuban, okay? You're in here because *another* Cuban said you did it. Orlando Bosch."

"Bosch is a liar and a traitor to freedom," said Novo, who began a diatribe against Bosch as an unstable, publicity-seeking drunk.

Propper interrupted. "So don't worry, then," he said. "All you have to do is tell us what you know. What is this crap about 'the ace up my sleeve'?"

"Look, I've had trouble with the FBI for years," sighed Novo. "I wanted to wait to speak with Suárez. He said it was all right. And then I told the FBI where I was. That's all."

"Well, then you won't have any problem answering the questions," said Propper.

"What are you going to ask me in the grand jury?" asked Novo.

"I can't tell you that," said Propper.

He and Novo soon took the back elevator down to the third-floor grand-jury room. The two of them went alone. By law, no outsiders were permitted inside the grand jury; the prohibition applied to defense lawyers and to all law-enforcement officers. Cornick waited upstairs in Propper's office.

Like most prosecutors, Propper observed witnesses closely on the way to and from the grand-jury room, and he believed that years of experience had refined his intuitions about which witnesses were likely to lie. Today, he thought, Novo was increasingly nervous on the way downstairs, into the medium range of anxiety. Beyond that, he couldn't tell anything.

An hour later, with Novo departed, Propper reviewed the testimony for Cornick. He said Novo had made "stupid" mistakes again. Novo was nervous. He took the Fifth Amendment selectively. He said he had never been to Trinidad, for instance, but he took the Fifth on travel to Chile and to Venezuela. In his questioning, Propper said he had only been fishing for information about Novo's organization and asking questions off the top of his head about possible connections to places and organizations he had heard about. He hadn't known enough to be more specific. Still, it was enough to make Novo nervous.

The next morning, Wilson and Schuman called Propper with urgent news: they had interviewed a New York informant who was so secret that Schuman would not allow a tape recorder or even a note pad. The informant's words could not be written down, because his speech patterns might betray his identity. The informant said that elements of the MIR hated Letelier, that Isabel Letelier had reason to hate her husband, and that Carlos Altamirano was believed to have been in the country to supervise the hit. Wilson and Schuman told Propper that they were closing in on Altamirano.

On October 29, the State Department sent over information about two Chilean agents, Juan Williams and Alejandro Romeral, who had tried to enter the United States by way of Paraguay. Cornick showed Propper the photographs and the two covering memos from State, in which the Chile desk officer explained the odd circumstances behind the photographs—how the American ambassador, suspicious of the two men, had ordered a technician to make photographs of the passports as a precaution, and how the ambassador ordered the visas canceled after learning that the two men were Chileans. Cornick said it was difficult to know what to make of the photographs. If these two men were involved in the Letelier murders, why would they travel through Paraguay? Most puzzling of all, why would they come to the United States on Chilean passports *after* the foul-up in Paraguay? The second State Department memo said that Williams and Romeral were believed to have entered the country at Miami on August 22.

Cornick was puzzled. As always, he tried to guide these two men through the known facts as though they were the killers. They had gone to Paraguay, perhaps so that the records would show two Paraguayans entering the United States—not two Chileans. Perhaps they had reasoned that the American authorities would be checking the identities of Chilean travelers. That made sense. But then, having been foiled in Paraguay, why would they put those same names on Chilean passports and come to the United States a month later? That would make sense only if they were certain their identities would never be cracked, but they had not behaved that way. They had been worried enough to try Paraguay. After failing there, they should have changed people, changed names. As killers, they would have to be brazen or foolish in the extreme.

At Cornick's request, the Immigration and Naturalization Service

(INS) furnished the FBI with a list of every Chilean who had entered the United States over a three-month period prior to the murders. But Williams and Romeral were not on the list. The State Department was wrong. No such people had entered Miami on August 22 or at any other time before the Letelier bombing. Cornick checked other United States entry sites with the same result: the men who had been foiled in Paraguay had not come to the United States.

"That's about as far as we can take it, Gene," said Cornick.

The new lead attracted Propper's attention. In his experience, new leads tended to be startling but indeterminate, like the first sharp tug on a fishing line. If patterns held true, the next few moves either yanked him into action or they did not feel right and his interest abated. Propper asked Cornick for copies of the photographs, but he felt the familiar letdown when Cornick told him the two men had not come to America. For the moment, Propper sensed much more promise in the Novo lead, where a specific accusation had been followed by Novo's defensive remark about the card up his sleeve. A few more confirming events and they might have something.

The same day, October 29, Ignacio Novo appeared before the grand jury. Like his brother, Novo was articulate and well dressed. He appeared without a lawyer to deny flatly any knowledge of the Letelier murders. Unlike his brother, Ignacio struck Propper as a relaxed performer in the grand-jury room, too much at ease for the average killer. Propper thought he was either innocent or very well trained. Ignacio Novo did nothing to advance any positive instincts about the lead that had come up from Venezuela.

Larry Wack worked throughout the last weekend in October. He rode the subway up into Cuban areas near 138th Street and Broadway, and he drove across the Hudson River into Union City, New Jersey. He worked alone, at odd hours, in the toughest of the Cuban business districts—all against the advice of the older agents in the New York office. Wack preferred street work and random interviews, even though his methods did not generate a volume of paperwork that would impress supervisors. He did not even bother to write up most of his interviews. As an agent, his strengths did not lie in file searches or identity checks or telephone work or directed interviews. His talent was that he could make an informant feel like a buddy and he could make a stranger want to be an informant.

Since transferring into the bomb squad the previous March, Wack had spent some time talking to Cubans about a mysterious group known as Omega 7, which had claimed responsibility for a series of bombings. Now Wack found himself nearly obsessed with Cubans. He suspected that the Novo brothers or their group, the CNM, might have carried out the threat to his fiancée.

Wack did not seem to mind getting thrown off a doorstep or insulted in a bar, and he did not mind trading idle conversation in a shoe shop. Usually, he would approach a friend of a known CNM member or a random Cuban businessman and say that the FBI had received a report that he or she "had connections to Omega 7." The idea was to keep the conversation going, and Wack would try to work in the idea that it would be terrible for good anti-Communist organizations to sink to the cold-blooded murder of innocent people like Ronni Moffitt. He was trolling for people who would complain about the Cuban Nationalist Movement for any reason.

It happened in a rush on the last weekend in October. A regular, unenthusiastic contact of Wack's suddenly asked if it would be possible to meet in a less visible place. Wack tried to be casual. He suggested a time and place. Then the contact threw him out loudly, as usual, and told him to quit harassing the freedom-loving Cubans. At the appointed rendezvous, the contact showed up and told Wack that Guillermo Novo was supposed to have a "covert contact" with the Chilean government—a man who had been in Union City on numerous occasions. Wack pressed for details—a name, a description, anything. He extracted nothing more, but he had already learned a lot. Wack worked in a fever the rest of the weekend. Incredibly, the very phrases "covert contact" and "covert link" seemed to loosen tongues. He found several sources who had heard of this person, two of whom claimed to have seen him in Novo's company. One said he saw the man with Novo in a restaurant a few weeks *after* the Letelier murders. He described the "covert link" as a tall blond Chilean, about six feet two inches in height, perhaps thirty years of age.

It would take Wack many days to coax his skittish sources into meetings with the FBI artist in New York. The sources refused to go to the Bureau; the artist was reluctant to go to New Jersey. Finally, Wack obtained a likeness that would become known as the "covert link" composite.

Propper thought Wack's news was a sign of life for the Novo lead. But it was vague. They had no name, and Novo might be able to explain the contact as an innocent one. Propper and Cornick also wondered why a Chilean agent would remain in the United States after the murders if he was involved in them. They asked Wack to go back to his source on that and make sure. Wack sent back a report: the source was certain that the blond Chilean had been with Novo in New Jersey several weeks after the murders. This news made Propper and Cornick adjust their hopes slightly downward, though they still considered the lead a promising one.

On November 4, two days after Jimmy Carter's narrow election victory over President Gerald Ford, an emissary from Isabel Letelier arrived at Propper's office to pick up the briefcase that had been recovered from the back seat of the bombed car on Sheridan Circle. It contained no physical evidence, and the FBI had made copies of the papers inside it, so Propper decided to release the briefcase and its contents to the Letelier family. With one major exception. Propper held back the cassette recordings in which Orlando Letelier had addressed the Venezuelan woman.

He did so at the request of Saul Landau, Letelier's friend and successor at the Institute for Policy Studies. Landau wished to spare Isabel Letelier from the intimacies on the tapes, in which Letelier had revealed himself to be an intellectual caught on the thorns of a bad romance—glum, repetitive, occasionally brilliant in self-analysis, sometimes scolding the woman for not wanting to get to the bottom of things, sometimes saying it didn't matter anymore. Propper understood why Landau would want to protect the widow and was willing to accommodate him, though the tapes were technically her property.

From Propper's standpoint, there was an extra incentive for complying with the request: doing so would help his working relationship with Letelier's friends and colleagues at IPS. Things had improved markedly since the threat to Elizabeth Ryden in New York, which produced several unexpected benefits. For the first time, Propper and FBI agents shared some of the paranoia at IPS, fearing that the Letelier killers might strike again. IPS people saw that FBI agents like Wack might become victims, too, and that agents were taking a personal interest in the case. The Ryden incident gave emotional substance to Cornick's old saw about how the "commonality of interest" between IPS and the FBI on this case should override the history of political antagonism between them. From this base, each side had taken several steps toward cooperation. Saul Landau and other spokesmen at IPS modified their public criticism of the investigation. Cornick, for his part, gave Landau copies of the Ryden composite. In effect, he was asking IPS to help identify the man who threatened her, and Landau responded eagerly. The composite was quickly distributed to IPS contacts all over the United States.

The spirit of cooperation was still new and tentative, but Propper thought it was already producing information that might be valuable. People who were otherwise leery of the FBI were volunteering what they knew. Propper persuaded one of them to confide in Cornick. Taylor Branch, Washington columnist for *Esquire* magazine, came to Propper's office and told Cornick of his quest to interview Orlando Bosch in a Venezuelan jail. Branch was twenty-nine, like Propper, and had written frequently about the CIA and about the Cuban exiles in Miami. His sources there had told him that the answers to the Letelier murder were in Venezuela. On the strength of this knowledge and his contacts, Branch had met with Isabel Letelier and with several of his own friends at IPS, and he had volunteered to fly to Venezuela. His trip had been arranged in great secrecy. Nevertheless, DISIP officers had snatched him out of the customs line at the Caracas airport. They had questioned him, followed him to his hotel, and refused to allow him to make phone calls. Then, at five o'clock in the morning, Branch had been dragged out of bed and thrown out of the country by none other than Ricardo Morales. Branch was still stupefied by the experience. What puzzled him most was Morales. He had known Morales in Miami and had counted on him to be a friendly contact in Venezuela.

"You're not the first one he's turned on like that," said Cornick. "You know that, don't you?"

"I guess so," said Branch.

"He's a dangerous man," said Cornick.

Branch held forth with his theories on the complicated treacheries of the terrorist underworld. To him, they meant that Cornick and Propper would inevitably come up against people who were informants for the CIA and FBI. That would make it difficult to proceed against them. That was why Branch and the people at IPS remained a bit nervous about confiding in the FBI, no matter how much they trusted Cornick.

"Let me tell you something, Taylor," said Cornick. "I'd arrest my own Virginia grandmother if she were involved in this thing. This is the biggest case in the Bureau right now. I'd arrest an agent, and nothing in the world would make me happier than to arrest a Bureau informant. Believe me."

"Even Morales?" asked Branch.

"*Especially* Morales," said Cornick, thinking about the angry denunciations of Morales that were coming up from the FBI office in Miami, where Morales was known as "the Monkey." Miami agents were saying that Morales had betrayed them, that he was a Castro agent, that he was trying to implicate the FBI in the Cubana Airlines bombing.

"Well, he must know something," Branch said with a sigh. "That's all I can figure."

"If he does, we'll find out about it," said Cornick. "Let me tell you something, Taylor. I'd take information from the devil himself on this case. And so would Gene. If the Monkey knows something, we'll be after him. If he's alive, that is."

"If he's what?" asked Branch.

"Keep this to yourself," Cornick said in his conspiratorial voice. "I don't want this to get out, okay? But we have a couple of reports that the Monkey may be lost somewhere in the Caribbean. On the *bottom* of the Caribbean. You see what I mean, don't you?"

"I guess so," Branch said weakly.

"Let me give you a piece of advice," said Cornick. "Don't go back down there. You have no idea how lucky you were last time, Taylor. Just take my word for it. Those people would think nothing of leaving you in a ditch somewhere with a bullet in your head, and within half an hour they'd have thirteen witnesses who'd swear it was an accident."

Branch shivered. "Maybe I shouldn't go," he said. He soon left Propper's office in a state of depression. The case led into an international swamp, he figured, and Cornick had implied that the government had little leverage overseas. Branch thought Propper and Cornick were outmatched. In that light, Propper's determined optimism about solving the murders struck Branch as naïve. Just outside the door, he overheard Propper answering the telephone. "Just give me the number of another phone near there, Joe," Propper said with some excitement. "And I'll get back to you." These words drove Branch to despair. He thought Propper was caught up in the same amateurish, pay-phone paranoia as were Branch and his friends at IPS. He would write as much in *Esquire*. Propper would take offense, and the two of them would not speak again for nearly two years.

Cornick was equally derisive of Propper's phone call, for different reasons. It was Joe Schuman, geared up for action, claiming to be on the trail of Carlos Altamirano. Schuman was moving from phone to phone with a team of INS agents, and he wanted Propper's approval to go in and bust Altamirano and whatever MIR people might be with him. As always, Cornick scoffed at the entire operation. He said Altamirano was living in East Berlin. Schuman insisted he was holed up in a Brooklyn tenement house at that very moment. He said the superintendent of the building had positively identified the man inside from the photograph of the Chilean socialist exile. Propper told Schuman that his source information was not enough to hold Altamirano or anyone with him on suspicion of involvement in the Letelier murders. But, said Propper, if the man turned out to be the right Altamirano, he would jump on the next plane to New York. Propper wanted to talk to him. He'd bring a grand-jury subpoena. Schuman could hold Altamirano as an illegal alien.

A few hours later, Schuman called again. He was deflated. His news deflated Propper. The man in the tenement was Carlos Altamirano, all right, but he was not Chilean and he didn't look anything like the photograph. Schuman tried to color his interpretation of the event in a manner favorable to the MIR investigation, but it was still a dead end. For the second time in a month, an errant doorman and an overzealous agent had combined to create false excitement. Cornick kidded Propper about Altamirano. Propper kidded Cornick about the Arica Institute. And the unfortunate Carlos Altamirano in Brooklyn was arrested.

Five days later, Cornick walked into Propper's office without his usual smile. This meant news of one kind or another, either hot or sour, and the two men were soon taking another stroll around the U.S. Courthouse. Cornick was talking about Ricardo Morales, the mysterious DISIP agent who had disappeared from Venezuela. He was getting more important. Morales had let it be known that the man "behind it all" was the head of DISIP's Preventive Services Division.

"You know what that is, don't you?" asked Cornick.

"No," said Propper.

"Gene, that's the division that prevents you from living," said Cornick.

"Oh," said Propper.

Cornick nodded gravely. "But that's not all," he said. "Wait until you get a load of this. Miami spilled it this morning. Gene, it turns out that the big Bureau source down there in Venezuela who's been confirming Bosch's Novo lead *is* Morales. And they didn't want to tell me."

"You're kidding," said Propper. "Morales works for you guys? Now?"

"That's right," said Cornick. "That'll give your thinking cap a workout."

"Carter, that's incredible," said Propper. "He's worked for Castro and the CIA and the Venezuelans, and now he's back working for the Bureau at the same time?"

"And God knows who else, Gene," sighed Cornick. "He's a pistol, all right. He works for us, and at the same time he's trying to blame the Cubana Airlines bombing on us. Not only that, we can't find him. He's called in to his contact, but he won't show up."

Propper was incredulous. "Carter, Morales has screwed you guys twenty ways from Tuesday," he snapped.

"That's true, Gene," Cornick said, trying to be patient. "Look, the Monkey was supposed to be our star witness in the MIBOM case. That's the one where the Bureau office down in Miami got bombed. But the Monkey didn't show up, and the guy got off. All the criminal agents are pissed. But the Palm Tree Peekers still love the Monkey."

"Who?" asked Propper.

"The Palm Tree Peekers," said Cornick. "The guys who always stand behind the palm tree with a bug in their martini glass but don't ever do anything."

This was the first indication Propper had of the rift between the intelligence and criminal sides of the FBI. Agents trained for intelligence work tended to refer to criminal agents like Cornick as Door Kickers or Handcuff Rattlers, implying that they were suited only for roughhouse work that required no sophistication. The Door Kickers, for their part, thought of the Palm Tree Peekers as a pretentious elite, self-absorbed in conspiracy and seldom accomplishing anything worthwhile, whose members used secrecy to avoid having to account for the quality of their work. Already, Propper and Cornick could see that Morales knew how to play one side of the Bureau against the other.

By the end of the walk around the block, the two of them were more resolved than ever to go to Venezuela. It was impossible to interpret a man like Bosch, the master terrorist, through so many screening agents, and it was even more impossible to interpret Morales.

The enigma of Morales helped Propper decide he was cold. "That's it, Carter," he said. "No more walks around the block. I can't take this weather anymore."

"That's all right with me," Cornick said with a smile. "I don't think your office is bugged, anyway."

Propper studied Cornick's face. He thought the case agent might be slightly serious. "It really isn't," he said.

No one could find Wack in the office that afternoon, because he was prowling after the "covert link" on his own. He had been pushing the blond Chilean angle for nearly two weeks when a friend who worked for a Spanish-language newspaper showed him news photographs of Guillermo Novo at political rallies with the head of the Chilean Mission to the United Nations. Wack took the news clips gratefully. The man in the photographs did not appear to have blond hair. To Wack, however, he was a Chilean with Novo and he wasn't bald, and these facts alone earned the man an interview. So Wack was sitting in the offices of the Chilean UN Mission on the afternoon of the twelfth, with the "covert link" composite drawing and the "Ryden threat" composite drawing in his coat pocket, along with assorted mug shots of suspected Cuban bombers. Having studied the "covert link" drawing one last time in the elevator, he was reasonably certain that the man in front of him was not the right one.

Bluntly, Wack asked Chief of Mission Mario Arnello if he knew Guillermo Novo. Arnello replied with finesse. Certainly, he said. He knew Novo as the leader of a Cuban exile group that had expressed friendship for the Pinochet government in Chile. Arnello praised Novo's qualities as a political statesman and public speaker, volunteering the information that he had appeared frequently with Novo at anti-Communist solidarity rallies.

Arnello seemed completely at ease. This was not the response Wack had hoped for. He would have preferred something defensive, bordering on a denial, after which Wack would have confronted Arnello with the news clips and perhaps some imaginary source information. Now Wack was forced to retreat as he probed here and there for clues. He asked about the duties of the UN Mission. He asked how many people worked in the New York office. Finally, at the close of the interview, he asked Arnello for permission to look around. Arnello, ever gracious, was pleased to assign Wack a personal escort for a tour of the premises.

Following his guide, Wack tried to behave like a casual tourist, but he stopped now and then to peer into a crowded office or to glance at the person he heard walking up the corridor behind them. No one looked like the "covert link." Wack asked how many employees were absent that day. About ten, replied the escort. Wack tried to conceal his disappointment. He knew how difficult it would be to devise enough pretexts to get a look at all those people. Finally, he left the Chilean Mission, annoyed by the thought that the "covert link" might have been out somewhere having a cup of coffee. Arnello, he concluded, was either innocent or very well trained.

On his return to the office, Wack found a stack of messages from Washington, but a call came in before he could respond to them. "Hello. Are you the Mr. Wack who just visited the Chilean Mission to the UN?" inquired a voice with a slight Spanish accent.

"Sure am," said Wack, reaching for his notebook and his pen.

"I work there," said the man. "Don't ask my name. I would like to talk with you. There are some things you should know."

"You name it," said Wack. "I'll meet you anywhere you say."

"Sunday afternoon," said the man, who went on to designate a rendezvous. He said he would recognize Wack, having just seen him at the offices of the Chilean Mission.

At the meeting, the Chilean described himself to Wack as one of many employees of the Chilean government who had become disenchanted with the Pinochet regime. Many months earlier, he said, an anti-Castro Cuban had presented himself at the Chilean Mission in New York to "offer his services." Other Cuban exiles had done so, on account of the fiercely anti-Communist posture of the new Pinochet government. But this particular Cuban had been special, said the Chilean. He had advertised himself as a member of an anti-Castro group that did not "play around." As proof, the Cuban had proceeded to open an attaché case filled with 8″ x 10″ photographs of targets demolished by bombs. According to the Chilean, the Cuban had then said, "This is some of our work in New York and Puerto Rico." The exhibition had not gotten the Cuban exile a job, but it did make him the gossip of the Chilean Mission. The Cuban, on leaving, had said that he intended to fly to Chile and make connections with the Pinochet government there.

Wack had been nervous before this encounter. He had paced around his apartment and worried about being followed or set up. Now he was calm by comparison. He asked a flurry of questions. Did the Chilean recognize any of the buildings in the photographs? Did he remember the Cuban's name or the name of his group?

The Chilean said no to all of these. But he did remember the Cuban well enough to specify what he had worn that day. He described the Cuban as well educated, relatively tall, perhaps thirty years of age, with a muscular build and short, light-colored hair.

"On the hair color again," said Wack, "would you say it was blond?"

"Almost," said the Chilean. "A little bit darker than yours."

Wack worried that he might not see the man again. After hesitating, he decided to show him a photo spread; there was no time to propose the idea through channels.

"Would you mind if I showed you some pictures?" Wack asked the man as he reached inside his pocket. "Do you recognize any of these guys?"

The Chilean looked briefly over the display and selected the composite of the "covert link."

"Take your time," said Wack. "You're sure?"

"There is no doubt in my mind. That's him."

Wack called Cornick to share the excitement. The notion of a blond assassin was coming at them from two independent sources. Cornick pointed out one major discrepancy—that the Chilean UN source called the man a Cuban. Was he mistaken? And if the man was a Chilean, why would he try to volunteer at his own UN Mission? Wack said the important thing was that the identifications be nailed down as the same person, regardless of nationality. There might be errors on a Latin's nationality. Cornick said Wack should go back to his sources and double check their stories and their identifications. Did he think the Chilean would be reluctant to meet him again?

"I don't think so," said Wack. "In fact, I think the guy might just flip for me"—meaning that the Chilean might agree to become an informant and work the Letelier case from inside the Chilean UN Mission.

Propper and Cornick were preparing to leave for Venezuela that week. Their pace was fast. They had to arrange for travel permits and for official receptions by State Department people in Venezuela. Cornick was practicing his Spanish. Word came in from New Jersey that Guillermo Novo had lost his passport and therefore could not comply with Propper's subpoena for it. (Propper thought he might have "lost" it in a river somewhere to conceal travel to Chile.) IPS people were still sending in identifications of the man who had threatened Elizabeth Ryden. Medical Examiner James Luke sent over the autopsy photographs of the bodies of Orlando Letelier and Ronni Moffitt. These allowed the investigators to see for the first time what they had only heard about—the carnage the murderers had produced. Propper had been prepared for the sight of them, but the pictures were even more ghastly than he expected.

Propper was studying his notes for Venezuela—what to ask Bosch, what to ask the Venezuelan DISIP. He was also studying the four likenesses developed thus far in the investigation: the composite of the man who had threatened Wack's fiancée, the "covert link" composite generated by Wack's Cuban Nationalist Movement sources, and the photographs of Juan Williams and Alejandro Romeral from Paraguay, about whose itinerary and contacts the Miami office had been unable to learn anything. Propper had nearly memorized the two faces, owing to the odd construction of the combination-lock security file cabinet he had commandeered for the Letelier investigation. It was built so that the second drawer had to be opened first in order to spring the locking rod for the other drawers, and there was a compartment for loose items in the front of the second drawer. Williams and Romeral lay there in two thick stacks of photographs, each stapled at a corner. The technician had photographed each page of the Paraguayan passports. The faces, which were actually photographs of the passport pictures, had been pulled out of order and placed on top of the stacks. Propper saw them whenever he opened his file cabinet. Williams looked as if he had dirty blond hair, and he had therefore drawn the greater interest of the two. But he did not bear the slightest resemblance to either of the composites.

On the sixteenth, the naval attaché of the Chilean embassy in Washington called the FBI to volunteer some information—in accordance, he said, with the stated wishes of the Pinochet government to assist the Letelier investigation by all possible means. This puzzled Cornick. Thus far, the Chilean government had done nothing but issue blanket denials of its own involvement in the murders, always blaming the Communists. The information was in the form of a letter, written in Spanish by Guillermo Novo and addressed to the Chilean consul general in the United States. Headed "July 5, 1976/In Exile," the letter berated the Chilean government at some length for shabby treatment of its allies among the Cuban "fighting exiles." Novo had written that this treatment was all the more incomprehensible inasmuch as the Cuban Nationalist Movement was supporting the Pinochet government "in all forms (publicly and privately, worthy of mention and worthy of silence). . . ."

This last phrase intrigued Cornick and Propper. It sounded like a Mafia code of behavior for hiding criminal acts. The letter as a whole was valuable, but it raised more questions than it answered. Why would the naval attaché hand it over? Was the attaché, like Wack's source at the UN Mission, disgusted by the possibility that the Chilean government might have conspired with Novo to murder Letelier? If so, why had he called the FBI to the embassy and handed the letter over so openly? Shouldn't he fear retaliation from the Chilean junta?

For now, the naval attaché's action made no sense. The only immediate effect of the letter was to increase interest in the Novo lead rather than to decrease it. This was the first tangible evidence of a relationship between Novo and the Chilean government. The letter made the Novo lead, Bosch, and the Venezuela trip even more worthy of attention. Morales was still missing somewhere in the Caribbean.

On November 18, the American ambassador in Caracas advised that the Venezuelan government had decided not to receive Propper and Cornick in that country. To Propper, the cancellation of the trip was not as surprising as the accompanying message from the Venezuelans. The Foreign Ministry in Caracas stated that Venezuelan law would not permit a formal interview with Orlando Bosch, inasmuch as Bosch had been charged with seventy-three counts of homicide in the Cubana Airlines bombing and was now "in the legal process." The Foreign Ministry added, however, that the government of Venezuela still wished to assist in the Letelier investigation because of its respect and affection for the United States. Accordingly, the government of Venezuela would arrange for Propper to interview Bosch under the following conditions: Bosch would be taken to a private place outside of his prison, without his lawyer, where Propper would be given access to him. In addition, both the government of Venezuela and the government of the United States must pledge to keep the interview secret and to deny its having taken place if necessary.

These conditions dumbfounded Propper. A deputy assistant secretary of state for Latin America explained that the Venezuelans planned to build a shack in the woods for a midnight interview and to tear it down again before dawn—if Propper agreed to the conditions.

"This is extraordinary," said Propper. "You mean I'm supposed to interview Bosch in the woods without his lawyer and then say I didn't do it?"

The diplomat replied that the Venezuelans had no choice. If Bosch's lawyers were to ask about the interview, the government would be forced to deny its existence or to admit that it had violated Bosch's legal rights.

Propper asked why Bosch couldn't sign a waiver of his rights and be interviewed voluntarily, like other prisoners. He understood that Bosch wanted badly to have his say with the American authorities.

Apparently not, replied the diplomat. The Venezuelans were saying that Bosch refused to be interviewed. That was even worse, said Propper. Did this mean that Bosch would be forced against his will into the shack in the woods, without his lawyer? Apparently so, said the diplomat.

Propper realized what a novice he was to this brand of international law. One government was proposing to another government to kidnap and forcibly interrogate a prisoner under the shadiest of circumstances, and to pledge mutually to lie about the entire affair if asked—all to protect the legal position of the prosecution in the Cubana Airlines case. Propper joked that the Venezuelan government would certainly go the extra mile to stay kosher.

The deputy assistant secretary pressed Propper for an answer. He said that the Bosch matter was of the utmost sensitivity for the Venezuelan government, and therefore, the American ambassador in Caracas wanted to resolve the matter as quickly as possible. In that case, said Propper, he could reply at once that the proposal was out of the question. The diplomat said the ambassador would be pleased by the refusal.

As always, Propper tried to view these developments in an optimistic fashion. There was still hope that the Venezuelans would arrange to have DISIP turn over information that might bear on the Letelier case—perhaps proof that Guillermo Novo had traveled overseas in violation of his parole. That would give Propper the power to put Novo in jail, which meant leverage that could force Novo to talk. This much was promising. In addition, Propper drew hope from the fact that the State Department and the Venezuelan government were responding to his questions on an expedited basis, at the highest levels, and that the Venezuelans had been willing to go so far as to break the law to help him.

Five thousand miles south of Washington, in Buenos Aires, the FBI's legal attaché held a much more cynical view of the Venezuelan government. Robert Scherrer assumed that the Venezuelans would do whatever was necessary to keep Propper and everyone else away from the volatile Orlando Bosch, and he scoffed at the notion that the Venezuelans would do so to protect Bosch. To Scherrer, the Pérez regime was trying to protect itself. Toward that end, its representatives wanted to keep Bosch as unavailable as possible, because he knew too much. Scherrer, after six years in Buenos Aires, had adapted to the grim probabilities of politics during a span of unprecedented terror in Latin America. As an American official, he was a target. On a gold chain around his neck, he wore a bullet that had been dug out of his armored car one night after an attack.

Scherrer was responsible for six countries and dozens of cases. In the roughly two months since the blast on Sheridan Circle, he had worked sporadically on the case, and his impression of the investigation was necessarily conditioned by the immense physical and cultural distance between the crime scene and his own theater of operations. He had not even learned of the murders through FBI channels. He read of them in the newspapers, because his official coding and transmitting equipment had been broken for some time. As a result, Scherrer had to wait until September 28 to send out his first dispatch, in which he reported on a meeting with an Argentine official.

The Argentine had told Scherrer of Operation Condor, a nascent program of cooperation among the military intelligence services of some Latin countries for the brutal purpose of locating and eliminating one another's fugitive terrorists and exiled dissidents. Both Scherrer and the Argentine knew that such cooperation had been going on for years, but the Argentine said that the ambitious leader of the Chilean DINA was trying to formalize and institutionalize the practice. There were three phases of implementation. In phase 1, the services of the cooperating nations would exchange information on the location of extremists. In phase 2, these people would be investigated by a team of agents, possibly from a third country. And in phase 3, yet another team of agents from perhaps a fourth country would carry out sanctions. The Argentine officer told Scherrer that the sanctions would include assassination. He said he knew of no such Condor operations as yet, but it was possible that the Letelier assassination had been a phase 3 Condor sanction.

Scherrer had not known what to make of this. Operation Condor was straight out of a spy novel, whereas the sanctions that Scherrer had heard so much about for years were ragged, personal, and sadistic. Condor was a favorite code word among spy buffs in Latin America. It was exotic. The methodical, bureaucratic teamwork contemplated for Operation Condor, as described by the Argentine, would require a radical departure from the jealous, nationalistic habits of the various intelligence services, as Scherrer had observed them. He decided to report the Argentine's information without evaluation.

The cable had caused a bureaucratic clash even before leaving the embassy in Buenos Aires. The State Department's deputy chief of mission called it "dynamite" and congratulated the legat, saying that the CIA station in Buenos Aires had previously reported something similar about Condor as an intelligence operation. But the Agency had not mentioned assassinations. When Scherrer's more complete version was disseminated in Washington, the human-rights people in the State Department would be up in arms, he warned, wanting to know why embassy people were listening to killers. Scherrer had replied that the matter was a simple one: the report was clearly intelligence, and therefore it should be disseminated. The Bureau would face criticism for reporting it. And Scherrer would personally take the responsibility for listening to killers.

Such concern over credit and blame was commonplace in American intelligence work. Indirectly, Scherrer owed his job to it. In 1970, FBI Director J. Edgar Hoover had played on President Nixon's dissatisfaction with the performance of the CIA, finally persuading Nixon to approve a small FBI legat program. Scherrer had gone overseas with the first wave of legats. During his first few years in Buenos Aires, he and all the other legats had been graded strictly on the number of "disseminable" pieces of intelligence they sent to headquarters each month. Hoover was competing against the CIA, hoping to regain some of the overseas domain he had lost nearly twenty-five years earlier, and his bizarre standard of measurement naturally created a glut of trivial intelligence reports. It had been a paper war, and the legats soon learned that a low-quality report counted just as much in Hoover's grading system as a good one. The system had been discarded soon after Hoover's death in 1972. Things were better, but enough gnarled bureaucracy remained at headquarters for Scherrer to be thankful that he was out of the country, on his own for all practical purposes. He took pride in the fact that he was farther from headquarters than any Bureau official except the legat in Hong Kong.

This distance had its drawbacks, however, as Scherrer realized when he wrote another teletype rebuking the New York agent on the Letelier case. Scherrer was having trouble making the agent aware of the difference between a Chilean and a Cuban. The New York teletypes coming down to Scherrer, by way of headquarters, conveyed the impression that the two were virtually interchangeable—on the order of a Kansan as opposed to a Nebraskan. Scherrer corrected him again. No credible Latin could ever confuse the two nationalities, he repeated. If the UN source had met a blond Cuban and the CNM sources had seen a blond Chilean, they could not be the same "covert link," as the New York agent wanted to believe.

This problem made Scherrer doubly aware of his isolation. He could not sit down with these people to correct such elementary mistakes. Finally, in exasperation, Scherrer called a friend in New York and learned that the agent, Larry Wack, was "just a kid." He asked his friend to straighten Wack out on the issue of Latin nationalities. Then he went back to his CHILBOM files, planning to write up a digest of his opinions thus far. Scherrer did not know the CHILBOM case agent, Cornick, but he was heartened by Cornick's habit of asking in teletypes for suggestions and criticisms. He did not seem to be a petty man.

On November 19, the day after Venezuela offered Propper a shack in the woods, Scherrer met in Buenos Aires with Colonel Victor Hugo Barria-Barria, the chief representative of the Chilean DINA in Argentina. Colonel Barria-Barria wanted to speak frankly about the Letelier assassination. It was true, he said, that the controlling powers of the Pinochet government had looked upon Letelier with contempt. That could not be denied. But those powers had not viewed Letelier as a threat to them, because he had lived too long outside of Chile.

Barria-Barria told Scherrer that he suspected the Venezuelan government of complicity in Letelier's murder. The governor of Caracas, Diego Arria, had flown to Chile in 1974 and personally asked Pinochet to release Letelier from prison. The DINA colonel added with sarcasm that Letelier had repaid Arria for this great kindness by embarking on an affair with a woman related to Arria, as everyone knew. An intimate transgression against a female relative would be a serious matter indeed to a high-ranking Latin official such as Arria. He might mention it to President Pérez or to his friends in DISIP, where the anti-Castro Cubans in charge were known to dislike Letelier already because of his many friendships in Havana. The Chilean government would continue to throw suspicion on the Communists for obvious reasons, he said, but he wanted to tell Scherrer in confidence that the Venezuelans were the more likely killers.

Cornick walked into Propper's office on the morning of November 24 with his daily update and a new item. Saul Landau was complaining that a prominent Chilean exile who worked for IPS had been followed the day before in New York. According to Landau, someone had followed the exile through Grand Central Station so clumsily and aggressively that the exile had asked a policeman to speak to the man. This having had no effect, the exile had left Grand Central, whereupon the man following him had hopped into a car. The exile had taken down the license number, and he had a description of the man. Landau thought the exile's life was in danger and wanted FBI protection for him.

The next day Cornick was back with a grin. "You won't believe this," he said, after closing Propper's door. "Guess who was following the guy up in Grand Central?"

"Who?"

"It was our people, Gene," said Cornick. "That license plate comes off a Bureau car."

"What do you mean it was our people?"

"It was the Bureau, Gene," said Cornick. "They were following the guy the Chilean was *meeting* in Grand Central. The son-of-a-bitch was meeting with a Cuban who is an officer of Castro's intelligence service. The upshot of it is that our Palm Tree Peekers were following Castro's spooks and this Chilean got mixed up in it."

"Jesus Christ, Carter," sighed Propper. "They did a damn good job of being discreet about it! They were so bad they got chewed out for spying by a cop. Can you believe that?"

"They weren't supposed to be discreet, Gene," Cornick said, a bit defensively. "They wanted the Cuban to know they were on him. That's what they tell me, anyway."

"Yeah, right," said Propper. "What are you going to tell Landau?"

"Well, that's a problem," said Cornick. "I can't tell him the truth because I can't tell him we were following the Cuban agent. Besides that, he would go apeshit if I told him it was the Bureau. My God! Those people at IPS would have a paranoid fit over that. I'll just tell him I've checked it out and it's under control. I'll tell him the FBI is on top of it."

Cornick did so. The incident amused him, but over the next few days he reflected on the possibility that the Bureau's intelligence division might be tripping across his investigation at other points unknown to him. This was a bothersome prospect. Cornick consulted Al Seddon, and he soon gained access to some of the intelligence files. Getting them required some adroit folder shuffling around the "guard dogs" in charge of the files. Cornick found no major revelations in the recent intelligence reports out of Newark or New York, but one day a Miami item took his breath away.

Cornick was still trembling when he dropped the piece of paper on Satkowski's desk. Satkowski read it and sagged back in his chair. "Oh, my God!" he said.

"Are you going with me to see Stames or do you want me to go by myself?" Cornick asked.

"What are you going to do?"

"Watch me," said Cornick. "I'm gonna stomp and raise hell all the way to the director if I have to. This FBI doesn't work that way, Bob."

In Stames's office, Cornick did not sit down. He paced while the SAC read the paper. One of the Bureau's most trusted Cuban informants, whose value and accuracy had been tested repeatedly over the years, had learned from a participant in the conspiracy that four leaders of the Bay of Pigs Brigade had flown from Miami to Washington on a certain day in early September. They had stayed in a motel in Alexandria, which the source named. They had met an official of the Chilean embassy, from whom they received a "hit contract" on Orlando Letelier. From Washington, they had assigned the contract to two of their soldiers, Alberto Franco and Raúl Martínez. These two men had blown Letelier up under orders from their superiors in the Brigade. Stames was shaking his head in dismay.

"Looks like we've got to have a fight," said Stames.

"I know," Cornick said quietly. "Nick, they've had that thing for three weeks now without telling us. They've cut the whole damn criminal investigative division out of this. I think that approaches criminal neglect."

"Absolutely," said Stames. "This is bullshit. You better write up something for headquarters on it. I'll back you."

Cornick's intention was to write a memo so hot that none of the intermediate supervisors at headquarters would dare to touch it —one that would still be smoking when it reached the desk of Jimmy Adams, the deputy associate director of the FBI. The diminutive Adams was known as "Little Jesus," the miracle worker, and was effectively in charge of the FBI's investigative operations, more so than Director Clarence Kelley. Adams outranked the heads of the criminal and intelligence divisions and thus could settle disputes between them.

Less than twenty-four hours after receiving Cornick's memo, Adams had summoned Miami agents to headquarters and sent them back again, having resolved the issue. Henceforth, he declared, the first priority of the agents handling the source would be to develop information for Cornick. However, Adams agreed with the Miami agents that the main security objective was to keep tight control over information that might jeopardize the source by revealing clues to his identity. Assistant U.S. Attorney Propper was mentioned several times as a potential source of leaks. Adams said they would not be tolerated. Cornick would tell Propper only what he needed to know, when he needed to know it for a legitimate purpose, such as issuing a subpoena.

Cornick called Propper. "I've got something hot, Gene," he said gravely. "It ain't the Arica Institute, either. This could put a bow around the whole case in a few weeks."

Propper was already fidgeting. "What is it?" he asked.

"Gene, I just can't tell you now," said Cornick.

"Is it Novo?"

"No."

"What is it, then?"

"Gene, I can't tell you just yet," Cornick replied. "We're working on it. I'll let you know in a few days. But it looks good. I'm telling you, it looks good."

Within a few days in December, word came back from the Alexandria office that the four Brigade leaders had in fact stayed at the hotel there, just as the source had reported. The Miami agents went back to the source, who was known to Cornick only as Tomboy,* and reported back that the Chilean official who had issued the contract on Letelier was Admiral McIntyre, the naval attaché—the same man who had given Guillermo Novo's letter to the Bureau in November.

This coincidence stunned Cornick more than any other development thus far in the roller-coaster investigation. Was it possible that McIntyre was the man behind the murders? Was he trying to infiltrate the investigation? Cornick had a legitimate brain twister. He let small pieces of this hot lead slip to Propper over the next week or so. "Gene, there ain't no Santa Claus and there ain't no Sherlock Holmes," he declared. "You need miracles in this business, especially with all the goddamn Palm Tree Peekers around."

Finally, Cornick could wait no longer. He shut the door to Propper's office and broke out in a smile. "Boy, I told you the Bureau would solve this case by Christmas," he said.

In Buenos Aires, Scherrer finished his digest of the case a few weeks before hearing of Tomboy's Brigade lead. He wrote a lengthy report to headquarters. Bombings of the kind that killed Letelier and Moffitt were the trademark of the anti-Castro Cubans, he said. In his opinion, one of the anti-Castro groups had carried out the murders for one of three reasons: (1) on contract from the Chilean DINA; (2) on contract from the Venezuelan DISIP; (3) on its own, to impress

*Not the correct code name.

the Chilean government while at the same time throwing blame on it, in retaliation for Chile's shabby treatment of Rolando Otero, the bomber in the MIBOM case.

The logic of it pointed to known contacts between Cuban exiles and Latin intelligence agencies, and Scherrer concluded that it was time to go see Colonel Manuel Contreras—head of DINA, one of the most shadowy, ruthless men in the world. Scherrer had not seen Contreras since the climax of the MIBOM investigation in May. All his dealings with the legendary Chilean secret-police chief—and virtually all his instincts about contacts between Chile and Cuban bombers—grew out of that investigation and Scherrer's victory in the spy battle over Rolando Otero. Thus far, it had been the supreme moment of his professional life.

8 ▣ SPY BAIT

The first warning comes from Ricardo Morales. "The FBI is closing in on you," he tells Otero, and Otero needs little persuasion. There are rumors of betrayal everywhere. His friends have scattered, and one of them may have turned over to a customs agent the typewriter he used for making bomb announcements to the newspapers. No one in Miami is thinking about Chileans or assassinations in Washington now, eight months before the Letelier bombing, but every newspaper reader in southern Florida knows about the mad Cuban terrorist, who, in a two-night spree, struck nearly every prominent symbol of legal authority—the police department, the FBI office, and the state attorney's office—along with the social security office, a bank, the state unemployment office, and even two post offices. The suspect also set off a blast in a locker at Miami International Airport. His daring and his assortment of targets have baffled authorities and terrorized citizens, many of whom are thinking twice about mailing letters, taking airplane flights, and visiting the downtown office district.

Otero must flee. There is no time to arrange for false papers or for much of a disguise—just an oversized hat and dark glasses. Otero returns to the Miami airport, where the bombings all started, and safely boards a flight to Santo Domingo, in the Dominican Republic. He realizes that his heart has been racing almost continuously for two months. Each time he shows his passport he fears arrest.

At the last checkpoint, it happens. Otero is led off to jail. All he learns is that the Dominican police have been asked to detain him by the American FBI. Morales was right.

In jail, Otero is visited by Frank Castro, the head of the National Front for the Liberation of Cuba (FLNC). Otero has made two hundred jumps at Castro's Golden Falcon Skydiving Club in the Everglades, and for years he has gone to meetings and helped plan "actions" for various groups under Castro's political leadership. But Castro has never given him a coveted membership in the FLNC itself. Until now. In jail, Castro tells Otero that he has finally earned his membership. He also tells him that he will be out of jail soon. Castro is married to the daughter of an admiral who is close to President Balaguer of the Dominican Republic.

The next thing Otero knows, he is walking out of the jail. It is a miracle, he thinks. Frank Castro greets him with a sly smile and says the Americans do not run everything. The battle is not over, he warns, because the FBI will be angry and will no doubt seek an indictment of Otero. American authorities will pressure the Balaguer government to extradite him. But for the moment Otero is safe, and the moment is all he can think of. Castro slaps Otero on the back, and Otero slaps back. He is exhilarated. Suddenly presidents are doing him personal favors. He may be arrested again tomorrow, or shot by an agent of Fidel Castro, but who cares now? Otero is enjoying himself on the edge. It makes perfect sense to him when Frank Castro suggests that their next move should be to summon a newspaper reporter. "Why not?" He laughs. They decide to make some declarations to the world and show people they are not afraid.

Castro calls Don Bohning, Latin America editor for *The Miami Herald*. Bohning pledges secrecy and catches the next plane to Santo Domingo, where he meets Castro and Otero at an open-air restaurant. The two Cubans are casually dressed and relaxed, sipping cuba libres. Castro is wearing his CIA-issue Rolex wristwatch, an emblem from the old days. Otero, Bohning will write, "looks like anything but the accused terrorist he is." In fact, Otero looks like someone who is enjoying himself immensely as he tells Bohning of his background. Otero says that the United States government trained him to fight Fidel Castro—to shoot guns and make bombs—but now the Americans have changed their minds and are trying to put Otero and his fellow exiles in prison. Otero says he feels betrayed. Then he shrugs. But that is business, he says, and now he is on vacation.

Bohning leaves to write a sensational story about the fugitive bomber who ignores the international manhunt to entertain in public.

For Otero, the repercussions begin even before the story hits the streets of Miami. Rival reporters have heard of the *Herald*'s scoop. Soon, half the Miami press corps is flying to Santo Domingo. Three local television stations have joined together to hire a Lear jet for their crews.

Before the hordes descend, Otero has second thoughts. It is nice to be so important, but a prolonged press orgy would certainly goad someone into arresting him. Flattery's rush gives way to panic. Otero bursts in on Frank Castro's bustling telephone area. "You are going to have to hold the press conference yourself," he says, "because I'm leaving."

Otero, through the window of his departing plane, sees the Lear jet land in Santo Domingo. It is a narrow escape. He laughs to himself that he is fleeing the press instead of the FBI. On the flight to Caracas, he remains both excited and afraid. He has only fifty dollars in his pocket and has become a fugitive terrorist, another of the famous exiles who have gone underground and international—men like Orlando Bosch and Morales. At last Otero has lived up to the expectations that have weighed on him ever since he was the youngest Cuban to land at the Bay of Pigs.

Morales, as promised, meets Otero's flight in Caracas and uses his authority to whisk him past all the customs officers and into a DISIP car, which, escorted by other DISIP cars, goes flying through the streets. Morales has embraced Otero on the runway and given thanks for his safe arrival. Now he offers Otero the hospitality of the Venezuelan government—a suite, free meals, a car and driver. But, he says, Otero's visit must be a short one. There is pressure from the Americans, and it will grow. Otero must leave Venezuela soon. In the interim, Morales and DISIP will try to find a safe place for him to go. "And while you are here, you must tell me what you're up to, my friend," says Morales.

In his apartment at the Anauco Hilton Hotel, Morales presses Otero about his plans—and about the bombings in Miami. Otero answers, figuring he has no choice. As for his plans, he says he is thinking of Chile.

This idea pleases Morales, who says that his organization in Venezuela, DISIP, is very interested in the operations of DINA, the Chilean intelligence service. DINA has been doing crazy things, such as contracting with a group of Cubans to shoot a Chilean senator and his wife in Rome, of all places—if the rumors are true. Morales says that he would be happy to buy Otero a plane ticket to Chile, and to pay him a salary of $300 a month, if Otero will go to Santiago, volunteer his services to DINA, and find out what they're up to.

"You mean you want me to be a spy?" asks Otero.

Morales only smiles. Otero asks questions and decides it is true. As he talks, he thinks. His services seem to be in great demand now that he is famous, and the prospect of working for both Venezuela and Chile, running anti-Communist missions, is a romantic one. On the other hand, Otero realizes that in a sense his choices are limited by his position—he can hardly afford to say no to anyone. To Morales, he says that he would never agree to accept the hospitality and assistance of the Chilean government of Pinochet and then spy on the Chileans. That would not be honorable. The Chilean government has been a steady ally of the Cuban exiles.

This answer does not please Morales, who explains that the Chileans will have nothing to worry about as long as they behave properly. Otero's services would provide some insurance, some intelligence. This would be only fair to Venezuela and DISIP in return for all the risk they have already taken to help Otero. Otero says he is grateful, but his principles will not allow him to ask the Chileans for help and then betray them. Morales smiles. Ever gracious, ever the protector, he says that he understands, but that there are limits to what he can do for Otero. He presses his argument through most of the night and then tells Otero they will discuss it further in the morning.

Otero cannot sleep that night. He knows that Morales has given him royal treatment and that Morales is the man most likely to help him, but he also knows that Morales might at any moment have him killed. Morales is renowned as a chameleon of intrigue, whose charm can instantly turn to wrath. Otero senses the violence coming from him, and he is frightened. He locks all the doors to his hotel suite. Then he strips all the beds for enough sheets to make a rope that will reach five stories to the ground outside. He sits next to a window until dawn with the sheet rope beside him.

The next morning, Morales returns with Orlando García, his boss. García is also a Cuban exile who has worked for the CIA, but he has been in Venezuela for more than a decade and is now head of DISIP, perhaps the closest adviser to President Pérez himself. Otero says he is honored to meet him. García says he is there to listen, and he does so as Morales repeats his proposition. There is a tautness about Morales that convinces Otero he was right to be afraid. Otero repeats his objections to García, who nods, thinks, and says there will be no problem. He says that DISIP is interested only in the protection of Venezuelan sovereignty, and therefore only in those DINA activities that might take place on Venezuelan soil. That's all he would like to know about. Anything else Otero might do with DINA would be Otero's private business, but García would feel entitled to know about anything DINA planned in Venezuela.

Otero, hesitating, looks at Morales and finds him smiling broadly. "You would not be a full spy," says Morales.

Otero is trapped, having just received a reasonable offer from a man who is effectively the highest law-enforcement officer in Venezuela. It is soon agreed. Otero tells García that he is worried about his personal security in Venezuela. Obligingly, García places three DISIP cars and a detail of bodyguards at his disposal. Somehow this makes Otero feel better, even though he knows from the previous night that his protectors and his enemies have become blurred in his mind.

García praises Otero's bravery and toasts their new partnership before leaving the details to Morales. In parting, he tells Otero never to set foot in Venezuela again while the heat is on. It is imperative that they do nothing that might compromise the new secret relationship between Otero and DISIP.

Alone with Morales, Otero asks whether security might permit DISIP to give him some false papers for traveling. Morales shakes his head. False Venezuelan papers are out of the question, and anything else would take too much time. Otero will be leaving for Chile that same night. There is much to arrange, including a secret form of communication between Chile and Venezuela. Otero manages to enjoy only one brief outing with his entourage of bodyguards before Morales escorts him back to the airport.

Morales embraces Otero and puts him on an Iberia Airways flight to Santiago, courtesy of DISIP, and then Morales himself boards a flight to Miami. There he places a call to his FBI contact. On the phone, Morales puts fear into his voice and says that his life is in great danger. It will be impossible to meet personally with the FBI man this time because of the danger and the press of time, but Morales wants the FBI to know that Otero is in Caracas and has admitted placing all the bombs on the night of December 3, 1975, including the one at the FBI office. Otero has also admitted that he bought all the clocks used as detonators at the same store at the same time. Morales hurriedly passes along a few more details, but then he breaks off the conversation. He promises to try to elicit more information, but for now he can only say that Otero is in the Anauco Hilton Hotel in Caracas and that Otero plans to leave soon for Chile.

This information, sketchy as it is, amazes the FBI man once again. Morales seems to have the entire bombing world wired to his ear. It is now January 24, 1976—less than forty-eight hours since Otero disappeared in the Dominican Republic, less than twenty-four hours since Bohning's *Herald* story exploded in Miami. The man handling Morales for the FBI swears that Morales is the best informant the Bureau has ever had. Agents huddle in the Miami office and try to figure out how to nab Otero in Caracas in a way that will not endanger their prize informant. It will not be easy, they know.

By this time, Otero is already in Chile, of course. Otero knows that Morales has been an informant in the past and that he is a dangerous man, but it never occurs to him that Morales might be telling the FBI about his journey. That would be too brazen, too perfidious, even for Morales. Otero would not have time to think such dark thoughts even if he were so inclined. There is too much pressure on him. DISIP has advanced him very little money. He must make contact with the Chilean DINA before his funds run out.

Otero decides to try the direct approach. He goes straight to the Diego Portales Office Building in downtown Santiago, where President Pinochet has temporary quarters. (La Moneda, the Chilean White House, is still a bombed-out ruin from the 1973 coup.) There, according to Chilean custom, any person from any station in life can ask for and receive an appointment with the President himself. Otero signs his name in the big red book, but he learns to his dismay that appointments take years. Officials laugh at him when he speaks of a quick one. So Otero walks over to the Ministry of the Interior, reasoning that the security apparatus comes under Interior in most Latin countries. This is his best hope, as there is no DINA listing in the Santiago phone book.

Soon Otero is in the office of an army captain who says he is head of the internal security unit in the ministry. Otero introduces himself as a Cuban exile whose superiors have authorized him to make contact with the Chilean intelligence organization in the hope of establishing a liaison for anti-Communist missions. "Your people have probably heard of me," says Otero.

The wide-eyed officer disappears into an adjoining room. While he is gone, Otero copies down the number of his private telephone extension. When the officer returns, still agitated, he tells Otero to return to his hotel and wait.

A few days later, Otero opens the door of his hotel room to face a contingent of four men and a woman. Two of them stand guard at the door while the other three invite themselves inside. The leader introduces himself as Major Torres. He introduces his tall blond companion as Captain Wilson. He does not introduce the woman. Otero watches her, however, as the two Chileans begin to interrogate him, and he decides that the woman taking notes is studying him closely. Whenever there is a break, she stares at Otero with an impassive face and twinkling eyes.

Major Torres welcomes Otero to Chile. His purpose, he says, is to conduct a background security check on Otero to find out who he really is and what he represents. His government must be careful, says Torres, because there are so many Communist spies and informants trying to infiltrate the Pinochet regime. He asks Otero a few questions about his background and purpose, and then he steps aside for Captain Andrés Wilson.

"Let's start with the 2506 Brigade," says Wilson. "Who are the leaders? What do you think of the security of the organization?"

Otero, a Brigade member, answers as best he can. Wilson goes on to ask about many exile organizations, including Abdala, the FLNC, and the Cuban Nationalist Movement of Guillermo Novo. He goes on for more than an hour. Otero thinks his answers satisfy Wilson most of the time, as they should, since he can speak with authority as an experienced Cuban exile activist. But Wilson remains skeptical. He asks Otero how the Chileans can be sure Otero is not a spy. Anyone can plant a bomb and pretend to be on the run, he says. How can the Chileans be sure Otero is even a member of the Cuban organizations? Does he carry an ID card for the Brigade or for the FLNC?

Otero bristles. "Don't expect me to carry an identification card," he says. "Do you carry one when you are on a mission? Do you think the CIA and the FBI carry cards? That is not very professional. You are an intelligence officer. I have given you my name. You should be able to find out all these things you are asking."

After a time, Major Torres interrupts Wilson in a friendlier tone. He tells Otero that he will be contacted again, soon. In the meantime, Otero should enjoy Santiago.

Almost a week passes, during which Otero tries to amuse himself and appear normal. Then a burly, redheaded man of about forty-five comes to the hotel and introduces himself as Marcelo Estrobel. He says he has something important to say but will not do so there in the hotel room. For security, he leads Otero out into the street and to a small restaurant. "Well, we have your assignment," Estrobel says bluntly.

Otero blinks in surprise. "You do?"

"Yes," says Estrobel. "Do you know who Andrés Pascal Allende is?"

"Sure," says Otero. "He is Allende's nephew."

"He is also a Communist and a terrorist," Estrobel declares. "We know he has been robbing banks in this country, but now he is in Costa Rica. We have asked the Costa Rican government to give him back to us, but we know they won't do it. As a matter of fact, we know they are going to release Pascal Allende soon, and he will go straight to Cuba. They will release him in the next few weeks. Your mission is to kill him before they do."

Otero is speechless, having never dreamed that he would be ordered about so roughly or so promptly. He has always expected a long series of meetings and trips and exchanges of intelligence.

"You have two weeks," says Estrobel. "Until February 22. After that, we will give the mission to another group. We are taking no chances."

"That's not very much time," says Otero, still trying to collect himself.

Estrobel dismisses this observation with a jerk of the head. "Pascal Allende is living with his girlfriend and terrorist companion, Mary Anne Beausire. She is a dancer, and she is very pretty, my friend. We want you to kill her, too."

"Kill her, too?" says Otero, stalling for time.

"Yes," says Estrobel.

"Well, let me tell you something about our organization," says Otero. "That is a problem. We don't mind killing him. We don't mind killing Communists, so that is no problem. But she is. Even if she is a Communist, we don't kill women. That is our professional code."

"The orders are to kill both of them," says Estrobel.

"I heard you," says Otero. "But we have never targeted women in an operation like that. We have targeted women in *other* kinds of operations, but nothing like that." He tries to laugh at his own joke, but Estrobel does not respond to the humor or to the sexual overtones. He only repeats the orders.

"Just a minute," says Otero. "I don't take instructions from you or anybody else in this country. I am here to make some kind of coordination with you."

"You are here to seek the support of my government," Estrobel reminds him sternly. "You are here to buy explosives and to seek a country of refuge. In return, you are offering your services on anti-Communist missions. This is your first mission. You are to kill both of them. You are to do it on your own resources and your own time, as a sign of good faith. After you've completed this first assignment, my government will show its gratitude to you and your people. We will support you with weapons and money. You will have *carte blanche*. But you have to do this first."

Otero stares at Estrobel and decides that he is the toughest, most abrupt man he has met in fifteen years of clandestine intrigue. "Look," he says. "You have to slow down. I'm trying to tell you that I have a few problems. I have a lot of FBI people looking for me all over Latin America. I can't just fly out of here on a difficult mission like this. And besides, I think my superiors would reject any order to kill a woman. We don't do that."

Estrobel seems to soften a bit. The two men argue about the assassination mission for the better part of two hours, speaking mostly of the justification for killing women in political war. Otero works his way into a stalemate. He says he wants a few days to think it over. When Estrobel leaves, he realizes that he will have to make the decision himself. He is too paranoid about wiretaps and surveillances to risk calling Frank Castro—or Morales.

A few days later Estrobel and Otero return to the same restaurant. Otero says he has determined to attempt the mission, on three conditions: first, he will need more time; second, he will not try to kill the woman; third, he will need false papers for travel.

Estrobel shakes his head slowly. No more time, he says. And no false papers.

"You are crazy," says Otero. "I can't move on my own name. Even here in Chile I have gotten in trouble with the police. They came to me and started asking me questions. I refused to answer them and told them to see Major Torres. So they didn't bother me. But they could have. In another country, I would have been caught already."

"No," says Estrobel. "You would have thought of something else. Use your own papers, or get some from somebody else. You won't have any problem."

Otero withers under the pressure. As a practical matter, he knows he has no choice. "I will take the chance," he says gamely. "But I will not target the woman."

"No problem," says Estrobel. "We are primarily interested in Pascal Allende. You do whatever you want about her. But if a bomb blows up his car and she happens to be inside with him, you know, as an accident, we will give you a bonus." Estrobel is smiling for the first time.

"Okay," says Otero. Estrobel hands him a brown envelope, in which he finds black-and-white photographs of both Allende and Beausire. Otero whistles to himself as he studies the woman. "She is a fox," he says, and Estrobel agrees. In the envelope, he also finds a paper with sketchy biographical material on the targets and another paper with a series of cryptic names and addresses. These, he learns, are the code names and the post-office boxes by which he is to communicate with DINA.

"And remember what I told you before," said Estrobel. "If you betray us with your mouth, we will kill you. Like that." He snaps his fingers.

"I understand," says Otero.

"Especially to the FBI," says Estrobel. "If you squeal to the Americans the way many Cubans do, we will kill you as a traitor."

"Don't worry," says Otero. "The FBI is my enemy almost as much as Fidel."

On the flight to Lima, Otero takes stock of his recent performance. He has reason to be proud. He has already accomplished DISIP's objective of penetrating DINA, and he has done so with results that will shock even Morales. On the other hand, he knows that his position is weak and he is expected to do the impossible. Already, his friends in Venezuela and Chile have taken advantage of his fugitive status to give him nothing more than two plane tickets and two life-or-death assignments. So far, Otero has managed to accept only half of each assignment, but the effect is the same. He cannot refuse anything, and therefore he is irresistible to spy organizations. If he is not killed by his enemies, he will only accumulate obligations to his allies. If the CIA were to catch him in Costa Rica, he fears, they would probably try to use him against the Venezuelans.

Otero decides that it would be too dangerous to go straight to Costa Rica, as the Chileans expect. But where else can he make the arrangements for the Pascal Allende mission? Where else is safe? After a time, he decides to go back to Caracas from Lima. This in itself is a measure of his desperation, since García and Morales have warned him not to come back. On top of everything else, he must worry about the Chilean DINA. If they are following him, they will surely regard it as a betrayal that he is diverting to Venezuela.

In the Lima airport, Otero imagines Tupamaros and FBI agents everywhere ahead of him, and he feels the Chileans behind. He changes his plane ticket for Caracas, wondering if DINA can trace him. Suddenly someone taps his shoulder and Otero whirls around, ready to fight.

"You forgot your sunglasses," says an old man.

Otero tries to collect himself. Then he scolds himself for poor tradecraft for having taken off his sunglasses at the customs booth.

The next day Otero fears arrest all over again at the Caracas airport. Then, standing in line, he spots a familiar face coming through one of the gates. It is none other than Orlando García. Otero is shaken by the coincidence. García seems to be equally distressed at the sight of Otero. He whisks Otero through immigration and off into a corner. "What the hell are you doing here?" he demands.

"Well, I picked up some very valuable intelligence down in Chile," says Otero. "And I think it's too sensitive to give you except in person."

García looks quite put out. "Well, I can't protect you in this country," he says. "You are a fool. Don't you realize that Kissinger is coming here in three days and all of Caracas is full of American security people? If they don't get you, our police will."

"What about the intelligence?" asks Otero.

"You tell Morales," snaps García. "He is my right hand, you know. But he is in Miami now." García sends Otero to Morales's apartment with a DISIP escort and instructions not to set foot outside until Morales returns.

While Otero waits in Caracas, Morales is in secret conference with his FBI handler in Miami. The agent is upset that Morales was not able to hold Otero in Caracas until an arrest could be arranged. Morales defends himself by citing all the pressures on him. His government, he says, wanted to get rid of Otero as quickly as possible, fearing that Otero's fanatical fellow Cuban exiles would set bombs off all over Venezuela if anything happened to Otero there. Morales says that his superiors ordered him to take Otero to the airport and that he had complied—not being able to tell them, of course, that he was also working for the FBI.

This mollifies the FBI agent somewhat. Then Morales confides that he has been able to extract more information from Otero about the Miami bombings, at no little risk to himself. Otero, he says, confessed to him that the bombings were an outburst of protest against "the system," as Otero saw it—a system that had trained Otero to fight, that had hooked him on conspiracy over the years to the point that Otero had to resort to the numbers racket, or *bolita*, to support himself, which he felt was degrading, and a system that then rejected Otero repeatedly when he tried to re-enter normal life. As to the fingerprint left on the airport locker, Morales says that Otero told him he had worn gloves to place the bomb but had taken them off, fearing that gloves would look too conspicuous in 80-degree weather. That was his only mistake.

In conclusion, Morales passes along the names of the people Otero had identified to him as accomplices, with some further incriminating information. It amounts to a believable confession, and Morales assures the agent that he will testify to it in open court. He signs a statement to that effect.

Amazed once again, the agent takes the statement to the Miami FBI office. Morales goes back to Caracas two days later, on February 15, 1976, and finds Otero waiting in his apartment. Otero has already decided that his situation is so desperate that he should give up the pact he has made with himself and with DISIP to report only DINA activities that affect Venezuela. Now, to protect himself, he becomes a "full spy" for Morales and tells him of his adventures in Santiago. Morales is impressed, especially when Otero hands him the brown envelope with the photographs and the codes. He smiles at Otero. "Well, my friend," he says, "what do we do next?"

Otero says that he has taken the liberty of calling Frank Castro for emergency help. Castro is already on a flight to Caracas. Morales seems pleased. It would be wise, he says, to consult with the head of the FLNC in such a situation. Morales goes back to the airport, and, surrounded by squads of his DISIP men, picks Frank Castro out of the incoming crowd and ushers him past customs and immigration.

The three men are soon in Morales's apartment, discussing the merits of the Pascal Allende assignment. Success, they agree, would benefit them all. Otero would earn a place of refuge in Chile. Morales would have a high-level penetration of DINA for his DISIP superiors. And Frank Castro's FLNC would move ahead of the rival Cuban exile groups that are jockeying for Chile's favor. On this last point, Otero recalls several of Estrobel's comments that made him think Orlando Bosch, the baby doctor, was heading the backup group Estrobel had spoken of. Bosch would be hunting Pascal Allende, too.

Privately, Frank Castro tells Otero that he would have preferred to consider the venture without the involvement of the devious Morales. But it cannot be helped, and Morales can offer certain help.

He can, for instance, use the DISIP intelligence system to pinpoint Pascal Allende's location in Costa Rica. At one point Morales leaves his apartment and comes back within hours to tell Otero and Castro that the targets are living in the Presidential Hotel in San José, Costa Rica. He gives them the room number as well. Otero and Castro are impressed.

After endless discussions of feasibility, tactics, and security, Otero turns to his companions and says, "Well, if we agree, let's do it."

They agree. Frank Castro says he has already raised the $10,000 they estimate will be required for the operation. He has forbidden Otero's participation in the actual assassination on the ground that Otero's face and name are too hot, too much in the press. So Castro has contacted two other FLNC "action men" and arranged for them to meet him in Nicaragua. From there they will go overland to Costa Rica. Otero, meanwhile, will go back to Chile immediately.

This is the only part of the plan Otero doesn't like. Mindful of Estrobel's warnings, he doesn't want to be in Chile if things go wrong in Costa Rica. But Morales has orders. García is annoyed with Otero for returning to Venezuela, so Otero must go. He can tell Estrobel that he has arranged with his superiors in the FLNC to have Pascal Allende assassinated. That should satisfy the Chileans.

Frank Castro leaves Caracas for Nicaragua on February 19. Otero flies to Santiago the next day and goes back to his hotel. He sends a coded telegram to Estrobel, asking for a meeting. Then he waits. No one contacts him. Otero sends more messages. After a week, he goes back to the army captain in the Ministry of the Interior and asks him to contact Estrobel. Then he waits again. Two weeks go by. He fights the temptation to use the telephone system to call Frank Castro. Otero walks the streets. The hotel bills eat up his money and he is forced to take an inexpensive apartment. He leaves a forwarding address at the hotel.

Finally, a knock sounds at the door. It is a DINA agent—one of the messengers Otero has met before—and Otero knows instantly that the news is not good. "Estrobel wants to kill you," says the officer. "He may do it when he gets back in the country. The entire operation in Costa Rica has been blown."

Otero, in shock, learns that Orlando Bosch has been arrested in San José, that his own name has been mentioned in the newspapers as a would-be assassin of Pascal Allende. The DINA messenger advises Otero to hop on the next plane to Costa Rica and kill Pascal Allende if he wants to live himself. Otero, cornered, replies that Chilean airplanes will blow up in the skies if any harm comes to him. A shouting match ensues, and the DINA officer breaks it off by stalking out. He says Otero will hear from DINA again.

Now Otero is frightened enough to forget about security. He calls Frank Castro with his story. "My life is not worth very much right now," he says.

Castro analyzes a hundred possible betrayals. The Chileans could have bungled. Orlando Bosch could have bungled. But the basic story is true. There are headlines all over the place. Bosch was arrested for plotting against the life of Henry Kissinger, as well as that of Pascal Allende! Otero's head is spinning. It is also conceivable that Frank Castro betrayed the operation. His name has not appeared in the stories. He has not been arrested. Otero suppresses the thought. He has to trust someone.

"It was the Monkey," says Castro, vowing retribution. No such punishment will help Otero, however. He is trapped. He cannot hope to escape from Chile against DINA's wishes. All he can do is sit tight and wait and hope that he can convince the DINA people that he is on their side, having shared their cause all these years. Otero goes back to his apartment, no longer the carefree fugitive who drinks cuba libres with reporters.

In Miami, Ricardo Morales has met again with his FBI handler on March 8 and confided to him further details of Otero's explanation of the Miami bombings. He has also related a sketchy but astonishing tale about how the Chileans tried to recruit Otero for an assassination mission against Pascal Allende.

On March 17, in Buenos Aires, Legal Attaché Scherrer receives a cable from FBI headquarters advising him that the MIBOM suspect, Rolando Otero, has reportedly fled to Santiago, Chile, in Scherrer's territory. The cable goes on to say that Otero may have been recruited by the Chilean DINA to assassinate Andrés Pascal Allende, nephew of the former Chilean President. Headquarters instructs Scherrer to make no inquiries whatsoever regarding this intelligence, and to take no action, as any move on his part might compromise the identity of a sensitive FBI source. For the time being, the information is strictly for Scherrer's private edification.

Scherrer does not know that the source is Morales, and he knows very little about Otero except that he is the famous terrorist who is supposed to have bombed the Miami FBI office. Still, the cable annoys Scherrer. It deprives him of a rare opportunity to do something about terrorism instead of merely absorbing the grisly facts. And Scherrer needs desperately to do something—for the sake of his own mental health, if nothing else.

It is a reasonable bet that Scherrer has been closer to more acts of sickening terrorism than any living American. His six years in Buenos Aires have coincided with a stretch of unspeakable internecine violence among the Argentines, during which scarcely a day passed without news of more kidnapped industrialists, deadly police raids, discoveries of mutilated corpses, executions of or by policemen, and daring bombing raids by the Marxist/Perónist Montoneros or the Trotskyite Popular Revolutionary Army (ERP) or the right-wing Argentine Anti-Communist Alliance (AAA). The violence was appalling even before the return to power of the legendary General Juan Perón, after nearly twenty years in exile, and it has become much worse since his death in 1974. There were 814 officially reported terrorist deaths before the end of 1975, and the number of recorded political assassinations in 1976 will reach 354 by May 1.

In letters and on home leaves, Scherrer finds it difficult to describe for Americans the atmosphere in Argentina, where the fear is pervasive and yet random, where the guerrillas and the police alike have made alliances with civilian criminals, and where all sides support themselves by extortion. Politicians and reporters in Argentina try to impose some meaning on the chaos by labeling the good guys and the bad guys, the right-wingers and the left-wingers, according to their views. Scherrer knows better, being privy to the government's own accounts.

His job is to conduct liaison with the Argentine law-enforcement agencies, chiefly Interpol and the Federal Police. Three of the Federal Police chiefs he has known have been assassinated—one shot, one blown up by a bomb placed under the mattress of his bed, and the third annihilated by a bomb that blew his 36-foot boat ten meters into the air, killing him and his wife. Shortly after the death of the third one, one of Scherrer's contacts at the Federal Police told him it was an inside job, set up by a sergeant on the chief's own staff. They had ample proof of the sergeant's involvement, said the contact, but it never occurred to anyone to arrest, try, and execute him. Instead, the Federal Police staged a shoot-out. They placed the corpses of Montonero prisoners in the back of a milk truck, which was driven past the sergeant's duty post at a high rate of speed. The sergeant and his colleagues ran after the milk truck, whereupon one of the colleagues shot the sergeant in the head. They fired a few rounds into the milk truck, and then the Federal Police announced to the press and public that two Montonero terrorists had stolen a milk truck and then been gunned down by valiant Federal Police officers, including a sergeant who was killed in the gun battle. Case closed. Word went out within the force that the sergeant had been executed, but there was no embarrassing publicity about the Federal Police. The sergeant's widow got her pension. And the entire matter was presented to the public in an acceptable manner, as a success in the war against the Montoneros.

Scherrer has heard dozens of variations on the milk-truck episode from his contacts in Argentine law enforcement, who are the people who concoct them. He receives the information because of his personal relationship with the officers, which is built on discretion. His ambassadors invariably appreciate the gruesome stories for their intelligence value. And occasionally Scherrer gets to draw on his relationships in matters that involve Americans. A year before the Otero case, for instance, Montoneros kidnapped a retired American named John Patrick Egan, who was serving as an American consular agent in the province of Córdoba, stamping visas. The Montoneros demanded as a condition of his release that four imprisoned Montoneros be shown on television to prove that they were alive and well. Scherrer went to his police contacts, who told him that three of the four had been killed already and that the fourth one was so badly disfigured from torture that he couldn't go on television. Scherrer told his boss, the American ambassador, that Egan was doomed. The Argentine government announced that the four Montonero prisoners were well but would not be shown on television, because the government would not negotiate with terrorists. The next day, Egan was dumped on a highway, wrapped in a Montonero flag, shot through each eye and horribly mutilated.

Scherrer knows that he must leave Argentina soon. As much as he loves the city of Buenos Aires and his position there in his own fiefdom, virtually independent of the Bureau, he realizes that the years of terrorism have worn him down. On numerous occasions, shooting has broken out in the neighborhood late at night, and Scherrer has herded his wife and their three small children down into the cellar in their nightclothes. The son of his wife's best friend recently disappeared and then turned up in the woods, dead, like countless others. Publicly, the Federal Police declared that the terrorists killed the young man, but they revealed to Scherrer in private that it was renegades from the Buenos Aires provincial police. This is the general pattern. The police blame their own killings on the Montoneros, and vice versa, and there are many extra killings that no one even bothers to blame anyone for anymore. In a showdown, Scherrer would side with the police, even with the corrupt ones, against the guerrillas, because the police are his colleagues and the guerrillas have branded him an enemy of the people. But this would be a choice of stark survival.

A week after receiving the Bureau cable about Otero, Scherrer watches the Argentine military move in to topple the floundering government of the dictator's widow, Isabel Perón. The level of violence quickly grows. It is now the anti-Perónist military against everyone else, and Scherrer's law-enforcement contacts advise him that it will be a war of extermination against Communists, Perónists, troublemakers, intellectuals, and their supporters. Civil restraints have been erased and petty hatreds let loose more than ever. Scherrer is glad to be from the United States, where things are done differently, and in that connection he decides that he must do something about the fugitive terrorist in Chile.

In early April, he sends a cable to headquarters stating that he believes he can force the Chilean government to extradite Otero to the United States for trial. By way of analysis, he writes that the Pinochet government already has a severe human-rights problem in the eyes of the world that Pinochet would like to overcome, and that Pinochet would therefore feel vulnerable to the threat of being publicly and officially denounced by the United States for harboring a wanted terrorist bomber. Scherrer does not believe that the Chileans would be willing to protect "the likes of Otero" at all costs. He predicts that they would give him up if subjected to enough pressure. Scherrer advises headquarters that he will leave soon for Santiago to begin applying that pressure.

Headquarters replies immediately with a rare and specific veto, ordering Scherrer not to mention Otero to anyone in Chile. Moreover, he is not even to set foot in Chile, lest his very presence raise alarms that might endanger the Bureau's source.

This cable annoys Scherrer beyond endurance. The source information—that Otero is in Chile—is so general that it could have come from thousands of people. It is not specific enough to endanger a source, in Scherrer's view. The real reason for the veto is that headquarters is committed to its own plan for extracting Otero, which involves having a U.S. attorney ask the State Department to revoke

Otero's passport as the first act in a long and complicated chain of legal events which might culminate in Otero's expulsion from Chilean soil. Scherrer thinks the plan is ridiculous.

Scherrer knows the very Chileans who would have to locate Otero and arrest him. He knows their customs, their language, and their relationships with rivals inside the Chilean government. Yet headquarters expects him to do nothing about the one terrorist case over which he can exercise legal jurisdiction. In effect, headquarters is telling him to remain a passive receptacle for intelligence about the seamy world of terrorism. Scherrer has had more than his fill of that as a foreigner in Argentina.

He does not challenge the headquarters cable. Instead, he contacts a trusted friend in the Investigations Department, Chile's equivalent of the FBI, and asks him to initiate a general inquiry about Otero. The next day, Investigations in Santiago sends a routine request to the local office of Interpol, asking who Otero is and where he has last been sighted. Interpol-Chile sends a cable to Interpol in the United States, as Otero is an American citizen, and that office forwards the request to FBI headquarters. In short order, Scherrer receives an urgent cable from headquarters, where alarmed officials want to know why Interpol-Chile is asking about Otero. How did they find out Otero was in Chile? To this, Scherrer replies blandly that Chile's Investigations Department must have learned about Otero from one of its sources. Then, secrecy broken, he prepares to fly to Santiago.

On Monday, April 12, Scherrer has a private cup of coffee in Santiago with one of the Investigations detectives who have been assigned to the Otero case. The detective is smiling. He says that Otero had been staying in room 711 of the Hotel Emperador until recently. Now Otero has moved to a suburb of Santiago called Providencia, but he still checks back at the hotel regularly for messages. It would be easy to arrest him, says the detective, except for DINA. Otero has already referred police to DINA when they tried to question him about his visa status. DINA's involvement will be a serious obstacle, but the detective says with a grin that for him it is also an incentive. He hates DINA. As an old police regular, he resents the way DINA tries to subvert normal detective work to politics. Colonel Contreras has won for DINA the right to take employees from Investigations and all other agencies of the Chilean government, and Contreras demands from his people an unswerving, blind loyalty. He expects DINA officers to bring him reports, gossip, and blackmail material from their old organizations, for instance, so that Contreras can build his own power base at the expense of the older branches of government. He has been extraordinarily successful. DINA exercises an electric power in Chile, similar to that of the Gestapo at the height of the Third Reich. It is admired by the faithful, privately resented by the constitutionalists, and universally feared.

After a candid strategy discussion with the detective, Scherrer goes off to see General Ernesto Baeza,* head of the Investigations Department. He already knows of Baeza's role in the coup and of his reputation as a straightforward military traditionalist, quite formal in business affairs. In Scherrer's estimation, Baeza is the kind of courtly official who would be offended if Scherrer were to let on that he knew Investigations had already located Otero. So he pays his compliments to General Baeza, as he has on criminal cases in the past, and informs him of the terrorist who has reportedly fled to Chile. Baeza nods along as though he has never heard of Otero. When Scherrer mentions that Otero may have been in contact with DINA, Baeza continues to nod and makes only the slightest show of annoyance. Scherrer knows that Baeza deeply resents Contreras, believing him to be an officer of inferior rank who used unscrupulous, dishonorable methods to advance himself at the expense of Baeza and Investigations, but he also knows that Baeza will never say anything openly critical of a brother army officer and government official. Baeza promises that Investigations will do everything in its power to locate and apprehend Otero for Scherrer.

A few days later, Scherrer is summoned back to Baeza's office. "I have something unfortunate to tell you," says the general. "It's about the terrorist you brought to my attention the other day, Otero. I'm afraid the case has been taken over by DINA, for national security reasons."

"National security?" says Scherrer. He suppresses an urge to snicker over the implications of this simple admission that Chile's national security is entangled with the fate of a man who stands indicted for bombing nine targets in far-off Miami.

"Yes," said Baeza. "Naturally, I can't be more specific, since it does involve national security. I can only assure you and the FBI that a complete and thorough search will be made for this man. I'm sure Colonel Contreras and his men will find him. They are quite resourceful."

"I hope so," says Scherrer, noting that the general is erect, unsmil-

*See above, pages 64 and 65.

ing, and that he speaks with only a trace of sarcasm about DINA's skills. Scherrer knows that Baeza knows that Otero has long since been located. Furthermore, Scherrer believes that Baeza has instructed his detectives to tell Scherrer so privately. But here, officially, Baeza maintains the dignity of the Chilean government.

"I'm sorry that I cannot report more definitive progress to you," says Baeza. "But my people will continue to monitor the situation, and I will let you know what happens."

"Thank you," says Scherrer.

"By the way," says Baeza. "Do you know of a man named Frank Castro?"

"Yes, I do," says Scherrer. "I don't know much about him, but I've seen his name in FBI files as a Cuban terrorist based in Miami. He is head of an exile group called the FLNC."

"That is interesting," says Baeza. "This man Otero may have been in contact with him from here in Chile, I understand. It might be helpful if you could provide us with more information about Frank Castro. I could see that it is passed along to the right people."

"No problem," says Scherrer, heartened by this indication that Baeza has not dropped the Otero investigation altogether. "I will get the information as soon as possible. You know best what to do with it. Needless to say, I have complete confidence in your direction of this case, General. I know that neither you nor any of your superiors in the government condone this kind of terrorist activity."

Not long after leaving Baeza's office, Scherrer meets confidentially with his friends in the Investigations detective force. His goal, he tells them, is to squeeze Contreras. He hopes General Baeza will take the information about Otero to President Pinochet himself, so that Pinochet will demand explanations of Contreras from above. At the same time, information about Otero should be planted in the various branches of military intelligence. The broader the dissemination of knowledge about DINA's involvement with Otero, he reasons, the harder it will be for Contreras to hide him.

The legal attaché soon leaves Chile. He has five other countries to cover, and the paperwork is building up back in Buenos Aires. He tells the detectives that he hopes to return in a few weeks with information from FBI headquarters about what Otero has been telling people in the United States.

With the month of March gone, and April slowly passing, Otero grows poorer and more desperate. He calls Frank Castro and begs him to wire money to his bank account in Chile. Castro speaks in shorthand whispers. He is worried about security. Otero is too hot, he says, with the FBI and the Chileans and everybody else. A bank wire is too open a transaction. Castro is looking for a more secure way to transfer funds. In the meantime, he reassures Otero, measures have already been taken to protect him. The organization will blow up airplanes and other Chilean property if any harm comes to Otero. Chilean representatives have been advised of this.

No money comes. Otero behaves erratically. On some days he walks the streets constantly, staying out in the open. On other days he never leaves his apartment. He has to stay in the apartment every night because of the Pinochet government's blanket curfew, still in effect nearly three years after the coup. A curfew, he realizes, is a serious handicap for a fugitive.

One night a handful of armed men push their way inside and begin to frisk Otero for weapons. He has none. Behind the agents, giving orders, Otero sees Andrés Wilson, the blond intelligence officer who interrogated him two months ago about Cuban exile organizations.

"You know there are responsible people who want to kill you, don't you?" asks Wilson.

"I'm used to that," says Otero, fighting panic. He did not like Wilson before, and now he sees a calm about him that is unnerving. Otero wishes Wilson were more agitated, because that would be more normal, and Otero associates normality with staying alive.

"Let's take a ride," says Wilson. To Otero, he speaks too quietly, as though he has done this before.

The agents shove Otero into the passenger seat of a car. A stocky, powerfully built man gets in behind him. Captain Wilson drives like a Grand Prix champion, peeling around corners and flying through downtown intersections with no thought of slowing down.

"That's one of the nice things about the curfew," says Wilson. "No cars on the street at night."

The engine whines as the car speeds up Cerro San Luis, a hill outside the city. Otero grows increasingly numb as he sees more trees and fewer houses.

Wilson suddenly throws the car across the road and skids to a halt on a turnout that overlooks Santiago. Otero sees the lights of the city in the distance. Immediately ahead he sees the tops of trees. They are on the edge of a bluff. Otero feels strangely peaceful. If the time comes, he tells himself, you can't avoid it. He starts to get out of the car.

"Stay where you are," says Wilson. He reaches under his seat and pulls out a small black box, which he places on the console of the car, behind the gearshift lever.

"That is a tape recorder," says Otero, somewhat addled by the tension.

Wilson ignores him and turns on the machine. "Now, why don't you tell me exactly where you have gone and who you have talked to since you left Chile to fail on your mission?" he requests evenly. "And pretend your life depends on being accurate."

Otero stares at the machine. Then he starts to talk. He tells Wilson about Morales and García and Frank Castro and the meetings in Caracas. He figures he is in no position to hold back information regarding the Venezuelans, just as he had figured he couldn't hold back about the Chileans on his last trip to Caracas.

When Otero finishes, Wilson looks bored and disgusted, as though he knew everything in advance. He turns off the machine, thinks for a moment, and then turns to Otero. "So you are given a mission of the utmost sensitivity by the service, and the first thing you do is tell a man like Monkey Morales?" he says softly, in mock disappointment. "A known informant?"

"I didn't have any choice," says Otero, with a sigh. "In my position, I didn't have any choice."

Wilson says nothing. Instead, he twists the ignition key and roars back down the hill just as swiftly as he drove up. No one says anything, least of all Otero, who soon finds himself looking at the door to his apartment.

"Get out," says Wilson. "You will be contacted."

Otero, in disbelief, manages to run inside, half expecting to be shot in the back. He does not sleep the rest of the night.

The next morning, Otero packs up his few belongings and leaves the apartment for good, having decided that he does not want to be contacted by DINA again. He will do the next bit of contacting himself, after enough time passes for tempers to cool. That morning, he makes his way to a small office on Viollier Street that serves as a meeting place for the Scorpions, a local parachute club. Otero has been making friends there over the past few weeks, trading yarns about skydiving. To ingratiate himself with the curious Chileans, he has gone so far as to confide that he is a man of some intrigue, and when pressed for details, he has admitted to the president of the Scorpions that he is wanted for blowing up two Spanish ships. In point of fact, this is a lie. Otero knows, like almost every Cuban exile from Miami, that Cuban commandos on a CIA mission did once at-

tack two Spanish freighters in the Caribbean—either by accident or
as a protest against Spain's decision to open commerce with Havana
—and that the attacks caused such a diplomatic fuss the CIA was
obliged to apologize to the Spanish government. But that was ten
years ago, and Otero had nothing to do with the attacks in the first
place. He has merely dressed up the stories in order to impress the
club members without giving up any real intelligence material. And
it has worked. The members seem to consider him good company, an
exotic foreigner who is exciting to have around. Now, when Otero
asks to use the club office as his home for a while, no one objects.
Otero agrees to help out with the chores. There is no bed in the office, but he doesn't mind sleeping on the floor.

A few nights later, hurrying back to the office before curfew,
Otero senses that he is being followed by a slow-moving car. He
speeds up and turns a few corners. The car is still behind. Otero
thinks it is a clumsy surveillance, as the agents are not bothering to
conceal themselves. When the parachute club comes into sight, he
breaks into a slow trot.

Three armed men step away from the door just before Otero
reaches it. He whirls to see the car screeching up behind him, doors
flying open. Otero flattens himself against the wall of a building and
raises his hands very slowly. He is soon staring into an array of gun
barrels. For some reason, his mind locks into the task of figuring out
the makes and models. They are all snub-nosed revolvers, he sees,
and he decides that one of them looks like a .38 Crowley.

"You are under arrest," says the leader. "Let's go inside."

The agents shove him through the door and throw him face down
across a desk. They are shouting among themselves about handcuff-
ing him, and then they are arguing over who forgot the handcuffs.
One of them yanks the laces out of Otero's tennis shoes. Then, to his
astonishment, Otero feels the agent tying his hands behind him with
his own shoestrings. He also notices that the agents are wearing
only dirty T-shirts, despite the cold night weather, and that one of
them is wearing heavy street shoes without socks. All this convinces
him that he has fallen prey to a gang of unofficial ruffians. He decides they are Communists.

"We are going to help you," says the leader in a menacing tone.

"I don't need any help like yours," Otero replies.

"But we can't help you unless we know everything," says the
leader. "So who are you involved with in Chile?"

Otero grimaces as one of the agents jerks his tied hands upward behind him. "I won't tell you anything unless you identify yourself," he says. "I want to see your identification."

The leader pulls a card from his wallet and sticks it before Otero's face. It says *Military Intelligence Service*, known in Chile as SIM.

"I don't believe it," says Otero. "What are your orders, then? What are the charges against me?"

"Well," says the leader, "we are thinking of charging you with blowing up two Spanish ships for the CIA."

"What?" cries Otero, realizing that one of the Scorpions has been talking to his captors. "You are crazy! Where is the ship? Where is the ship that was blown up?"

"You shut up and answer the questions," orders the leader. "I'll ask them."

Otero is gasping in frustration, now that absurdity has blended into the terror. "You say you are from SIM? You say you are an intelligence officer?" he cries. "You are on the moon! You don't know what's going on! You don't know who you're talking to! Let me tell you something: You are a lieutenant, but if you put one finger on me to harm me, you are going before the firing squad!"

There is a pause. The agents seem to be whispering among themselves. Otero thinks his speech has made an impression on them. He musters all the authority he can in that position and tells the lieutenant to contact DINA and ask for Major Torres. Major Torres will know what to do. The agents talk over this proposal, and soon they put a blindfold on Otero and drag him to a car outside. Otero tries to make a mental map of their route. He thinks he winds up in a house near the airport.

Some time the next day, the lieutenant returns. "Major Torres says he doesn't know anything about you," he declares.

Otero, still blindfolded, groans and calls out for his little telephone book, which the agents have confiscated. He directs the lieutenant to the name and number of the captain in the Ministry of the Interior, his original contact in Chile. "You call this man and tell him that I am Rolando Otero and I want to talk to Mr. Estrobel in DINA," says Otero. He fears Estrobel more than anyone in DINA except for Captain Wilson—more than anyone in Chile except for the uneducated gang of thugs who have been gloating out loud over the privilege of breaking his bones. Yet Otero appeals to Estrobel, of all people, in the hope that he might be susceptible to reason.

The lieutenant returns a few hours later. "You have friends," he says. Otero is elated. He does not even mind when he is dragged to a car again that night. At least he is moving, possibly to friendlier hands. Mentally, Otero is polishing up his excuses for Estrobel when he is pulled from the car and someone cuts the shoelaces off his wrists. Still blindfolded, he is guided a few paces and then shoved into a thick, overpowering stench. A door shuts behind him. Otero pulls off the blindfold to discover that he is in a small, windowless, concrete cell, alone. There is no latrine. A rotten wool carpet covers the floor. That night, he hears screams of agony nearby. He also hears thuds. Otero decides someone is probably being beaten with a rifle butt. Every few days, the screams drown out the wall tapping of the prisoners and the footsteps of the guards.

Making small talk with General Baeza, Scherrer promises to attend the graduation banquet of the Investigations Academy again that year and to present an official FBI plaque to the cadet with the highest scores on the target range. Then, getting down to business, he briefs the general on the Otero situation. There is a lot of new information. Scherrer has learned that Otero has been making phone calls from a certain candy store in Santiago. He has a list of the people Otero has called. He also knows the name of Otero's bank and his bank account number. And he has the numbers and addresses of various places Otero has been sighted, including a parachute club called the Scorpions. Scherrer says he will furnish all this in writing for General Baeza so that he can pass it along to the appropriate authorities.

"Very good," replies Baeza. "I am sure that this information will be of great benefit to Colonel Contreras in his search for the fugitive."

"I hope so," says Scherrer. "But I should tell you that there are intelligence stories in Santiago that DINA has already located Otero and taken him into custody." He does not tell Baeza that the intelligence stories came from Baeza's own detectives. This is by prearrangement to protect the general, who is not authorized to reveal what DINA has done.

"That is possible," says Baeza. "You will have to take that up with Colonel Contreras himself, since he is handling the case for us. I think it's time for you to meet him, Bob. You should go over there and talk to him personally. Tell him about this man Otero and what he is wanted for. I'm sure he'll understand your problems with terrorists."

"That sounds like a good idea to me," says Scherrer. "I hope I can get an appointment."

"I'm sure you'll get one," says Baeza, with just a trace of a smile.

"Good," says Scherrer. "I think I would tell the colonel that I have heard Otero has been apprehended and that I intend to remain here in Santiago until he is turned over to me."

"Well, if that is your information, you should consult with Colonel Contreras about it," says Baeza.

Scherrer is much relieved that Baeza has not protested against this message as too harsh and reckless. Instead, the general has given tacit approval for Scherrer to say he knows Otero is already arrested. Contreras will know this information has probably come from Investigations. Baeza is stepping up the pressure. Scherrer feels even better when the general offers an Investigations limousine and the escort of his personal aide for the trip to DINA headquarters.

Late that afternoon, Baeza's military aide guides Scherrer through checkpoints and into the DINA compound—a sprawling series of one-story buildings, connected by lawns and driveways, in downtown Santiago. They find Contreras alone in his office. He is not the coarse-looking martinet that diplomat gossip has led Scherrer to expect. Contreras is rather short and slightly paunchy, but in dress and comportment he is the essence of refinement. His suit (all military officers in DINA wear civilian clothes) is an expensively tailored pinstripe cut in the European style. He speaks formal Spanish, never uttering a word of slang. Already, after five minutes and a handshake, Scherrer knows more about Contreras than most spies in Chile do. Contreras's name never appears in the newspapers, and Contreras himself never attends diplomatic functions. He is a figure of great mystery in Santiago. Very few military attachés have ever met him. Only one officer of the Santiago CIA station has ever seen Contreras, and he has told Scherrer very little.

The office is airy and light, ten yards square. Matching pairs of French doors lead on one end to a garden and on the other to a private dining room, flanked by secretaries' offices. Everything about the ambiance is French—French Provincial chairs, the small French obelisk on the enormous oak desk, a French artist's sculpture of a woman's head in the corner, French lace curtains—except for the music that spills softly from speakers in a bookshelf, which is standard American Muzak. Behind Contreras's desk, there is a mural of a Chilean mountain lake. There are also two photographs—a medium-size one of all four leaders of the Chilean military junta and a much larger one of General Pinochet alone. Scherrer sees a political message in the disparity, knowing that Contreras has used DINA to strengthen Pinochet at the expense of the other three leaders. The only evidence he sees of an intelligence function is a television set mounted on the wall, showing a picture of the entrance to the DINA compound. By means of a console, mounted on his desk near the bank of telephones, Contreras can switch to other strategic views. He can even put President Pinochet's desk on the screen.

For fifteen minutes, Scherrer delivers an exposition on the MIBOM case and all the federal statutes and state laws Otero allegedly violated. Contreras plays absentmindedly with a slide rule as he listens. He explains the habit as a holdover from his years as a military engineer.

"Any bomb is bad," Scherrer concludes. "But we think Otero's targets bespeak the complete irrationality of the man. I'm sure you can understand our position. If a Cuban had come to Chile and placed a bomb in a locker out at Pudahuel Airport and then fled to the United States, you would be in our position. And you would probably come to us."

"Absolutely," says Contreras. "And we would want him back."

"Of course," says Scherrer. "We want Otero back the same way. And the reason I'm here is that General Baeza informed me that you are in charge of the case, and I've heard some unconfirmed good news that you have already managed to apprehend Otero for us . . ."

". . . Well, that's not quite true," says Contreras. "We did pick up a Cuban, and we ourselves thought it was Otero. But it was not. It was another Cuban. I'm sorry."

This news stuns and perplexes Scherrer, who tries not to show it. "Well, what was the Cuban's name?" he asks.

"I can't remember," says Contreras. "Quite frankly, I lost interest when I learned it was not your man Otero. I can get the name for you, if you like."

"Please do," says Scherrer.

"But I agree with you about how dangerous the Cuban exiles are," says Contreras. "We believe it was another Cuban exile here in Chile who took a shot at your ambassador's residence the night before last. Are you aware of the incident?"

"Of course," says Scherrer, further perplexed. "That's all people talk about at the embassy. But we had no idea it was a Cuban."

"Well, that is our information," says Contreras. "We believe it was a second Cuban striking out in protest against our picking up the first Cuban."

"What is the second Cuban's name?" asks Scherrer.

"We don't know," says Contreras. "We are still looking for him."

"Oh," says Scherrer. "I guess the first Cuban will probably tell you who the second one is."

"He probably would have," says Contreras, "except that we released him when we found out he was not Otero. We are trying to relocate him now."

"I see," says Scherrer, whose mind is literally spinning toward the conclusion that Contreras's story makes no sense. But he is off balance. He is not completely sure. In any case, he knows he is not in a position to challenge Contreras, to call him a liar. He has no proof. He can't even back up his report that Otero has already been arrested, because to do so he would have to cite Baeza's detectives. Contreras would want to talk with them. They would back down. Scherrer would have broken the rules.

For the next half hour, Scherrer asks questions about two Cubans he does not believe exist, offering to have their names run through the Bureau's terrorist files. Contreras, for his part, asks Scherrer who he thinks the other Cubans might be. They speculate at length on these matters, and in the end Contreras is looking for three Cubans instead of one.

Scherrer goes back to his hotel. That night, a strange woman calls his room and makes a number of social propositions, all of which involve Scherrer's leaving the hotel after curfew. He declines and then stares at the telephone, thinking it all quite bizarre. He is certain, at least, that he has captured Contreras's attention. The next day he reports back to Baeza, and the general assures him that Contreras will pursue the search for Otero. Later, in private, his detectives laugh at Scherrer's account of the Contreras meeting. They are certain, beyond a doubt, that Otero has been arrested. In fact, they know where he is. As to the story of the two extra Cubans, they are divided on its meaning. Some think it is simply a dose of confusion from Contreras. Others think Contreras was fishing for the name of the FBI's informant.

Scherrer reports the unhappy news to his own embassy, where Ambassador David Popper and his deputy, Thomas Boyatt, have become preoccupied with the Otero case for unusual diplomatic reasons. Secretary of State Henry Kissinger will soon arrive in Chile for the OAS Foreign Ministers' Conference, and Kissinger is sensitive about Cuban exile terrorists in light of Orlando Bosch's recent arrest in Costa Rica. Bosch has now disappeared again. The ambassador and Boyatt would be nervous enough about Secretary Kissinger's visit even if they did not know that Cuban terrorists were in Chile and in contact with the same Chilean security organization that is supposed to protect Kissinger's life there. Finally, they authorize Scherrer to try a gambit so daring they do not dream of telling their superiors in the State Department. Scherrer does not tell FBI headquarters, either. He knows the proposal would send the entire Bureau into an inconclusive flutter for months.

On May 6, Scherrer joins three embassy officials for a ride to the DINA compound, where they meet with their counterparts in DINA security. There is serious business on the agenda. The DINA officers want American assistance in providing security, not only for Kissinger, but also for the other foreign ministers and related dignitaries who will soon descend on Santiago. They have prepared a list of requests. First of all, they want a dozen metal detectors, such as are used at airports, for deployment at the entrances of the various buildings that will house the OAS conference.

"Excuse me," Scherrer interrupts, less than a minute into the DINA presentation. "I want to raise one very important matter before we go any further. The FBI has information that a Cuban terrorist named Rolando Otero is in Chile. We believe he is in DINA custody. Colonel Contreras told me the information was incorrect, but that was several days ago, and we believe he may be in DINA custody now. We also have information that Orlando Bosch is in Chile. We consider either of these men a threat to Secretary Kissinger's life. So far, this matter reflects poorly on DINA's abilities as an intelligence and security organization. If DINA cannot account for these two men, who have records of terrorist violence and who as Cubans would certainly stand out in Santiago, then the FBI will have to recommend that the secretary not come to Chile. Ambassador Popper agrees fully, and he has authorized me to tell you that without that accounting he will not allow Kissinger to come into the country. Basically, that's it: no Otero, no Kissinger. I wanted to tell you now so that we don't waste our time here if the secretary is not coming."

The man in charge of the DINA delegation* stares at Scherrer with his mouth partially open. He stares at his colleagues and then back at Scherrer. Without a word, he stands up and makes a T sign with his hands for time out. He leaves the room, which is across the DINA compound from Contreras's office.

Fifteen minutes later, the colonel returns and sits down. His face

*Lieutenant Colonel Luis Mujica.

shows signs of an extraordinary burden. "Top secret," he says in English. "We have him. Otero. We can't release him to you right now because we're using him to try to lure Bosch back into the country. As for Bosch, he is not here. He has left Chile. We thought you would have known that."

"Well, I don't know where he is, but we have information that he has been in Chile," says Scherrer.

"Not now," says the colonel. "We want to lure him back so we can deal with him." The colonel draws his forefinger very deliberately across his throat.

"I see," says Scherrer. "Well, I presume I will get Otero in a reasonable period of time."

"We'll try to hurry," says the colonel.

"Very good," says Scherrer, and the officers return to technical security matters almost as though nothing has happened.

Scherrer waits in Santiago more than a week. He goes to see General Baeza every day. The game is much more aboveboard now that DINA has admitted having Otero. But not completely. On one occasion, Baeza's military aide* stops Scherrer just outside the general's door. "It's going to be very difficult to turn Otero over to you," he says softly. "Will it be acceptable to have him dead?"

Scherrer blinks. His first thought is that the anteroom is bugged. "No," he says. "We want him for a trial."

"Well," says the aide, "Otero is a terrorist and a desperate man. If he resists us, our people will answer with deadly force."

Alone with Baeza, Scherrer decides not to mention the exchange in the anteroom. Baeza would never engage in that sort of conversation himself, he decides, but he might have put his aide up to it.

In any case, the conversation and the delay indicate that the struggle is not over inside the Chilean government. Freshly worried, Ambassador Popper and Boyatt help Scherrer spread the word around Santiago that DINA has promised to give Otero up. Press censorship favors their task: they don't have to fret about newspaper leaks because they know reporters are too frightened of DINA to write anything about Contreras. The Americans do what they can to keep up the pressure. By the time pressing business calls Scherrer back to Buenos Aires, they have begun to stall on preparations for the OAS conference, less than three weeks away.

———

*Lieutenant Colonel Jorge Aro.

One morning, Otero is summoned from his cell and blindfolded. Something big is happening. He can hear other prisoners moving around, too, and there is a lot of noise. Wagons are outside, and water is being splashed everywhere. They seem to be cleaning out the cells, and for that Otero is more thankful than he would have thought possible.

Suddenly he is being pushed along. Then he has to climb up in the back of something that turns out to be a truck. Many other prisoners are there. All of them smell bad. The guards warn the prisoners not to take off their blindfolds and not to make any noise. Then the door closes and the truck moves off. Otero cannot tell whether a guard is in the back with the prisoners or not.

The truck drives along forever, it seems. Then, after more walking in the herd, Otero is amazed to discover that he is back in his old cell. He yells along with everybody else who wants to know what the hellish ride was all about. The guards laugh. They say there is a big OAS conference coming up, and Chile agreed to allow an OAS Human Rights Commission team into its prisons for an inspection, to verify that Chile would be a suitable host. The commission visited the prison that day; the guards served as the prisoners.

A few days later, DINA officers appear outside Otero's cell to notify him that he will soon be released—deported to Peru. After that, he will be on his own. He will be leaving the next day. But nothing happens for a week. Finally, Otero summons a guard and tells him to pass along a message: he will not eat until he reaches Peru, as promised. His hunger strike is three days old when the guards blindfold him again and lead him out of the cell. Strange voices tell him he is bound for Lima.

A phone call wakes Scherrer at 2 a.m. on May 19, just four days after he has left Santiago. A voice says, "My Aunt Dina has a package for you."

Scherrer sits up in bed. The voice is familiar, and the message is cryptic but not difficult. "When?" he asks.

"Today," says the Investigations detective. "You better get over here right away."

By ten that morning, Scherrer has exchanged several cables with FBI headquarters and made plane reservations for three. (A DEA agent in Santiago has agreed to go along.) He has also gathered some special equipment for his overnight bag: handcuffs, a blackjack, a can of mace, and a few plastic spoons for the prisoner to eat with. Just before he leaves for the airport, the detective calls back to say that the package has been delivered. "I don't like the way he looks," he says. "He's dirty. I think he's been abused. I don't think he's gonna be too stable."

Thus warned, Scherrer flies to Santiago and goes straight to Investigations. The detectives take him to General Baeza's office. In the anteroom outside, they explain that the general has a special ceremony for expulsions from the country. They coach Scherrer on his lines and then send him in to face General Baeza and his tape recorder, which is running. The general announces that he has apprehended a fugitive from American justice and asks Scherrer what the United States would have him do.

Scherrer is soon at Pudahuel Airport, standing with the DEA agent in the doorway of a Braniff jet. He is trying not to let the moment get the best of him. Like most people involved in intelligence work, he fears naïveté and takes a certain pleasure in knowing about sordid realities far beneath the surface of public events. In many respects, he is a hard-eyed fatalist who holds very little sacred. His hero is Justice Oliver Wendell Holmes, who tried to view society as a harsh compact among animals. Still, having defined his own ground, Scherrer knows that he has never in twenty years with the Bureau put his intelligence training to such good use. He has never really arrested anybody like this or struck such a blow against the kind of sickening violence he has endured in Argentina. He is very proud to be an FBI agent.

Otero begins to tremble when he sees that the car is veering away from the Aeroperú jet toward the Braniff one, and he trembles all the way up the stairway.

"He's all yours. Keep the handcuffs," says the detective, handing Scherrer the key. Otero sees a blond man in a suit and knows he must be from the FBI. Scherrer sees a small, disheveled, unshaven man and knows he is the right terrorist.

He pushes Otero down into a window seat in the fourth row and buckles his seat belt. Then he identifies himself to the prisoner by name and title, and begins to explain why Otero has been delivered to the FBI. "I know," Otero interrupts. "You don't have to tell me."*

---

*Otero recalls the greeting quite differently, claiming that Scherrer said the following: "You son-of-a-bitch. I'm FBI, and I'm gonna take your ass back to the United States, and as soon as we land in Miami I'm gonna arrest you and throw your ass in jail. You're nothing but a terrorist and a loser, and I've nailed you."

Scherrer takes a breath, stands up, and turns his attention to the DEA agent, who is remonstrating with a passenger just across the aisle. The agent wants the passenger to move one row back so that he can watch Otero better, but the passenger, a businessman from New York, says he has paid for the seat he already occupies.

Otero silences the argument. He has reached around to unbuckle his seat belt, despite his handcuffs, and he has jumped to his feet, his back against the window. Suddenly he lets it go—all the fear in the airport and the terror and the jails and the betrayals. And the hatred of the FBI. *"Maricón!"* he screams, calling Scherrer a faggot. He screams it again and again. It is the shriek of a madman.

Still screaming, he kicks Scherrer two or three times in the leg when Scherrer tries to knock him back down in the seat. Otero stays up, bracing himself against the plane's bulkhead so as not to lose his balance. He is wiry, in paratrooper condition, and the flow of adrenaline makes up for all the days without food. He keeps screaming even after Scherrer kicks his feet out from under him.

Scherrer jumps into the seat on top of Otero, who bucks upward with such strength that Scherrer is thrown into the air. Otero has gone berserk, moving in every direction at once and screaming all the while. When Scherrer tries to clamp his right hand over Otero's mouth to stop the noise, Otero jerks his head and bites down into the knucklebone. Scherrer moans. Desperately, he tries to wrench his hand out of Otero's mouth. Many passengers are screaming.

The DEA agent vaults over the back of the seat onto Otero's chest, weighing him down with his two hundred pounds. Scherrer reaches into his coat pocket for the blackjack, and he begins pounding Otero on the bony parts of his legs and arms. After five or six hard blows, the fight leaves Otero as suddenly as it came. Scherrer feels the body go limp and finally pulls his hand from Otero's mouth.

He stands up and notices that blood is coming out of his hand in spurts. Some passengers are still screaming. One or two have vomited, and several will soon leave the aircraft for another flight. The pilot and all the flight attendants have entered the cabin. Quickly the flight attendants try to calm the passengers. One of them begins wrapping wet towels around Scherrer's hand. Another one brings Cokes. The DEA agent puts one to Otero's lips. He and Scherrer keep telling Otero to take it easy.

They also keep telling the pilot that everything will be okay. Scherrer's great fear is that the pilot will order them off the plane, as is his prerogative. Instead, the pilot winds up ordering that the rearmost eight rows of the plane be cleared for the trio. That way, he says, Otero can do anything he wants to and the agents will have room to control him.

Otero rises calmly when beckoned toward the rear, but suddenly he cries, "The FBI knocked out my teeth! The FBI knocked out my teeth!"

The New York businessman yells, "You goddamn terrorist! I wish the FBI had knocked out *all* your teeth!"

Scherrer pushes Otero toward the back. On the way, Otero screams, "There's a bomb on this plane! A bomb's about to go off! You're all gonna die!" His cries subside when Scherrer jerks the handcuffs upward from behind.

A flight attendant later collects Otero's watch and one of his teeth. Scherrer believes the tooth came from a dental bridge. He knows he is the one bleeding, not Otero.

In the air, a woman passenger walks back to thank Scherrer. She has a parrot on board that she is smuggling back to the United States, and the commotion helped save her from detection. She is very grateful.

Eight hours and fifteen minutes later, the jet will land in Miami. An ambulance and a throng of anxious law-enforcement officers will be there to meet it, drawn by the pilot's radio message about the wounded FBI agent on board.

Three weeks later, on June 11, Ricardo Morales will be so angry with his FBI handler for ruining his undercover operation in Chile and his reputation in DISIP that he will draw a policeman aside at a party. It was an FBI agent, he will say, who tipped Otero off that he should leave the United States. This offhand remark will entangle the FBI and the police and the United States Attorney's Office for months in obligatory internal investigations.

Three days after Morales's comment, Orlando Bosch, Frank Castro, and the leaders of half a dozen other Cuban exile groups will meet in the Dominican Republic to form their alliance, known as CORU. Afterward, Bosch will make his way back to Caracas, where Morales and Orlando García will meet him at the airport.

In July, anti-Castro Cuban exiles will retaliate against Chile for the expulsion of Otero, as promised. They will try unsuccessfully to bomb a 1975 Mercedes belonging to the Chilean embassy in Bogotá, Colombia—license number CD0064—and on July 24, they will bomb the Chilean Pavilion at Bogotá's International Exposition, injuring six people.

In August, Morales will ignore subpoenas to testify at Otero's trial. A federal jury will acquit Otero on all charges relating to the nine bombings in Miami. Scherrer, a witness, will take time to see a doctor before flying back to Buenos Aires. His hand will still be swollen and festering after three months. He will be back in Argentina a month later when the bomb goes off in Sheridan Circle.

9 ▣ CORNICK'S DOWNFALL

Scherrer arrived in Santiago with bittersweet memories of the MIBOM case. He would most likely be called again to testify at Otero's second trial, in state court, and he did not relish the prospect of another long journey to Florida. It would mean more days of waiting at the pleasure of trial lawyers. He would be denounced again by Cuban spectators who would see him as the FBI ogre who not only framed an anti-Communist hero but also knocked out his teeth. Otero was a terrorist to Scherrer, but he was a public hero to thousands of Cubans. He had been lionized in the media by civic leaders and elected officials, including the mayor of Miami. Scherrer expected another acquittal. His bloody hand and all his work would go for nothing.

He had a backlog of leads from headquarters. There were requests to verify source reports on various aspects of Letelier's life in Chile. There were half a dozen Cuban exiles who might have traveled to Chile; Scherrer was supposed to find out. And there were numerous fragmentary descriptions of Chileans who might have threatened Elizabeth Ryden at Kennedy Airport. Most of these came from Chilean exiles in the United States who had been imprisoned by the junta and had later made contact with Saul Landau at IPS. One of them remembered being tortured by a man known only as Colonel Robles. The source could provide only a partial description of the colonel. He could remember no first name, and Robles might be a false name, of course. Scherrer's job was to find out if such a person existed in Chile, and, if so, to learn more about him.

165

He worked on instinct. If a lead seemed unpromising to him, he attacked it directly, vigorously, and officially through normal channels. If it appeared promising, however, he became more cautious, almost paralyzed, and he relied on personal trust and unorthodox, devious methods. In short, he behaved more like a spy. The very nature of the case required such a paradoxical approach. Like the Otero case, CHILBOM presented Scherrer with the strong possibility that elements of the Chilean government had knowledge of terrorist acts, the disclosure of which would be embarrassing to the government even if it was not involved directly. Scherrer would be in the uncomfortable position of the foreign law-enforcement officer who is authorized to seek help only from his adversaries. He would be back in the scorpion's bottle.

On this first trip to Santiago since the bombing at Sheridan Circle, Scherrer encountered a relaxed, well-groomed, well-attended Contreras, who still toyed absentmindedly with a slide rule as he talked. Speaking in Spanish, Scherrer opened the amenities with some gossip about the ruthless Argentine intelligence services, to which Contreras responded warmly. The two men talked rather easily on this subject, both being insiders. Scherrer's purpose was to build up as much conversational speed as possible and then observe Contreras closely after raising the subject of Letelier. He wanted to see whether Contreras would slow down, choose his words more carefully, or otherwise betray discomfort.

When Scherrer abruptly announced that he was in Santiago to pursue leads on the Letelier case, Contreras smiled and said that he had imagined so, since it was well known that DINA had been accused of the murder in newspapers around the world. The charge was ridiculous, of course, and he welcomed the opportunity to say so personally to Scherrer, a professional who would readily understand why such a terrible act would have been foolish for DINA. As a matter of fact, Contreras added, DINA posted no representatives in Washington or anywhere else in the United States. If DINA officers did journey to the United States, naturally they would declare themselves openly to the FBI and the CIA, in the time-honored manner of mutually respectful intelligence services.

Scherrer detected no emotion beyond the usual controlled gleam of a smart intelligence man talking shop. There was no fear, no tightness. The delivery was off-handed and smooth. Contreras himself raised the subject of Letelier's death again by noting that much of the press information seemed to be coming from Venezuela. He pointed out that DINA had established relations with the Venezuelan DISIP and that he had flown to Caracas in September 1975 for an official exchange of information. The two intelligence services had agreed to hold the visit in strict secrecy, said Contreras, but headlines in Caracas promptly announced that he had come to Venezuela for the purpose of spying on Chilean exiles. The Venezuelans had committed an outrageous breach of trust, he said. They were difficult to deal with, especially since DISIP employed scoundrels like Ricardo Morales.

"I've heard of him," said Scherrer.

"The Monkey. The Monkey Morales," Contreras said contemptuously. "He is a real son-of-a-bitch."

"I've heard that, too," said Scherrer, who was studying the colonel's jaw muscles. For the first time, they had tightened.

"I have assets in Caracas," said Contreras. "Lots of them. And I can tell you with no doubt in my mind that the son-of-a-bitch who leaked all the information about me and the lies about my mission to the newspapers was the Monkey."

"That makes sense," said Scherrer.

"Believe me," said Contreras. "Let me tell you something, okay? There is some information and there is other information, you understand. This is no rumor, I assure you. We have the proof. The Monkey is an agent provocateur of Fidel Castro. He is a Communist agent."

"Are you sure?" asked Scherrer. He was impressed by this revelation from an intelligence chief. People in the Bureau were speculating along the same line.

"No doubt about it," said Contreras. "The Monkey is a very dangerous man. He affects the entire national relationship between Chile and Venezuela. It is not as good as it should be. We have to take special precautions just because of that one man. He is a plague on us."

"We should probably take precautions in the United States, also," said Scherrer, by now convinced that Contreras's hostility toward Morales was both genuine and noteworthy. It was seeping out from behind his broad, placid face. Scherrer could not help agreeing with what Contreras was saying, but he also knew that the DINA chief might be trying to impeach the character of Morales for a specific reason—namely, that Morales was both the conduit for the Novo lead in the Letelier investigation and the source of reports that Otero had been recruited in Chile for assassination missions. Scherrer wondered whether Contreras could possibly know this.

After the second or third cup of coffee, Scherrer said that high officials in Washington were very upset about the Letelier assassination and that he would have to investigate each of the many charges that DINA had been involved. He would have to explain them one way or the other.

That would be easy, Contreras replied. First of all, he was certain that no "responsible" person had made such an assertion, and he was even more certain that there could be no supporting evidence. Contreras reminded Scherrer that the American CIA was constantly being blamed for hurricanes, earthquakes, coups, wars, and all sorts of crimes for which it was not responsible. Wryly, he remarked that even Scherrer's own FBI was being accused of various "dirty tricks" by the newspapers and that he, Contreras, was wise enough to know how false the charges were.

Scherrer thought Contreras seemed more relaxed about the Letelier assassination than he was about Ricardo Morales. In fact, the DINA chief began to toss off bits of gossip and intelligence he had picked up about Letelier, mentioning Letelier's affair with the Venezuelan woman. He passed along as unsubstantiated the notion that Letelier had also been the lover of Ronni Moffitt, which, if true, would have provided both Michael Moffitt and Isabel Letelier with murder motives. Contreras stressed the fact that Michael Moffitt allowed his wife to sit in the front seat of the car with Letelier. This was very important, he observed, and it was fishy. No self-respecting male would take the back seat, leaving the front seat to his wife and another man. This, said Contreras, was the act of a cuckold, and a man in such a state would most naturally plot his revenge. Contreras reported that DINA officers were interviewing members of Isabel Letelier's family in Chile to find out whether she had known of her husband's alleged affair with Ronni Moffitt. Thus far, he said, the results were negative.

"Excuse me, Colonel," Scherrer interrupted. "I forgot something. My superiors in Washington asked me to make sure you received our letter of commendation from Director Kelley. Has it arrived?"

Contreras stopped to think. "Yes, Bob," he replied, pronouncing the name to rhyme with the biblical Job.

"That's good," said Scherrer. "The director wanted you to know how much the FBI appreciates your cooperation in the Otero case."

"It was nothing," said Contreras. "I did very little." He waited for Scherrer's next question, offering no more on his own.

The legat sensed that Contreras would have preferred not to receive the letter and took no pleasure in discussing it now. To Scherrer, this was a significant reaction. The letter had been his idea, and it was a move from the wiles of statecraft—to thank Contreras and DINA effusively for assistance in the Otero case, breathing no word of DINA's stubborn resistance. Scherrer adhered to the observances and the polite requirements, keeping the public reality distinct from the private one. By double meanings, one could communicate a great deal even while polishing the face of diplomatic acts.

"Well, you were very helpful, Colonel," said Scherrer. "You are too modest about your powers. But, speaking of Otero, you must be aware that many Cuban exiles like him have been in Chile. I only ask about Cubans because the Letelier bombing has all the trademarks of a Cuban exile bombing, and it's my job to learn about these Cuban activists. With your help, I need to find out where they were in Chile. And what hotels they stayed in. And who they talked to when they were here. Some of them say they had interviews with the President. That was in the newspapers. We have to find out about all this."

"Well, Bob, I will help you if I can," said Contreras. "But it will not be easy." Slowly, deliberately, he explained how difficult it was for DINA to keep track of Cuban exiles. Foreigners could come and go without DINA's knowledge, because as yet DINA had no control over the International Police at the Santiago airport. This was a sore point with Contreras.

Scherrer asked more questions about Cuban exiles and Contreras continued to dodge them, preferring to speculate further on the Letelier case. As to the notion that leftist Chileans might have ordered the assassination, the DINA chief broke into his first broad grin and shook his head in the negative. That would be practically impossible, he said, because DINA had destroyed the MIR and similar organizations. This achievement was a point of professional pride with him. "They were all penetrated," he declared. "Or destroyed."

Shortly thereafter, Scherrer excused himself. Contreras pressed him to stay, saying that he enjoyed talking with him. Contreras spoke expansively about the close cooperation he envisioned between himself and Scherrer, and he offered to have a private radiophone installed between DINA headquarters and the Chilean embassy in Buenos Aires, which could relay the signals to Scherrer. Contreras suggested that the two of them ring up the communications people and talk it over, but Scherrer made polite excuses and put him off until next time. He was eager to get outside the office and start making notes. Contreras had given him more than two hours of his time, four cups of coffee, and thousands of words with hidden meanings.

As Scherrer had expected, the interview had taken the shape of a ceremony almost Oriental in its strict observance of face-saving formalities.

About the time Scherrer boarded his flight back to Buenos Aires, Letelier's former mistress made the long journey from her home in Caracas to New York City. She did so regularly. On this visit, she had also agreed to see two agents from the FBI.

Cornick insisted on conducting the interview himself. Normally he delegated such tasks, even in Washington, but he sent word to the New York office that Wack should not proceed with this particular session until Cornick arrived. He wanted to be there. It was too valuable an opportunity to obtain insights into Letelier's character from the perspective of such an unusual source—a woman who reportedly spoke quite candidly of Letelier, without a political purpose that might color her memory. As Cornick explained it to Wack, the woman would most likely have been in the position of confessor to Letelier. She would know his strengths and weaknesses, his fears and aspirations. This sort of character information was vital, Cornick kept saying, especially now that the investigation had dragged into its third month. Obviously, he said, the case was not going to be solved by a lab miracle or a lucky break. They were in for the long haul. Only Propper and a few fools at the FBI were optimistic, he told Wack. Cornick wanted to show Wack exactly what he meant by the methodical approach. Besides, he wanted to meet the agent who had been making so much noise up in New York.

By prearrangement, the interview took place at a private apartment, where the two agents encountered a dark-haired woman of great beauty and presence, wearing designer clothes, jewels, and fur. They reacted quite differently to her. Wack marked her as a "classy dame" and plunged right in with his standard questions, fishing for clues, unknown enemies, threats, and strange occurrences around Letelier in the last months of his life. He would have completed the interview in a few minutes. Cornick, however, continued for two hours and most of a third one—trading stories with the woman, questioning her about her life-style and her social attainments, about Letelier and his habits. He complimented her poise frequently and likened her to some of the Virginia women he had known. Wack endured the process. When it was over, he told colleagues in the New York office that Cornick had obviously fallen in love with the woman. The case agent, he said, had gone so far as to assume the burden of writing up the interview himself instead of assigning the job to Wack, the junior man. This was unheard of.

Cornick drew immense satisfaction from the session. Leaving Wack with a promise that he would grasp the significance of the interview when he saw it on paper, Cornick flew back to Washington and told Propper that the woman was a gold mine, that she combined penetrating intelligence with regal comportment. "Let's put it this way, Gene," he said, "at the President's dinner table, she would know which fork to pick up." More importantly, she had provided insights that would bear upon the investigation. First of all, Cornick had no doubt that she was telling the truth when she said that she, not Letelier, had broken off their informal engagement. She had been content with the affair, without marriage, and certainly felt no wound to her honor. These facts weighed strongly against Scherrer's theory that the Venezuelan DISIP might have killed Letelier as punishment for having dishonored and rejected such an important woman.

Cornick reported that the woman saw Letelier as anything but a single-minded man. Letelier had been pushed from within in a number of directions, and he had possessed the charm and intelligence to excel in them all. He had devoted a large portion of himself to politics and what he had called "my Chilean affairs," but he had been equally driven by the notion that the fundamental questions are personal ones. Part of him had been an eternal optimist regarding the prospects for social justice in Chile. Part of him had been a fatalist in all things. The woman described Letelier's components as she had seen them: his inquiring mind and his compulsion to fairness had made him a socialist and a theorist; his overweening ego had made him assume a place for himself in the forefront of Chilean history; his wife, Isabel, shored up his ideological commitment; his conflicting belief in the sterility of politics drove him to seek mystery elsewhere. In the last week of his life, said the mistress, Letelier had spoken to her about his inclination to retire from politics. He had also denounced the Pinochet regime. He had told her that he felt he had reached a new plateau—that his reconciliation with Isabel felt right to him and that he felt less restless. He had also said he expected Pinochet to be in power for a long time.

To Cornick, all this meant that Letelier had been something of a dabbler—or, at any rate, that he had lacked the kind of consuming political ambition that creates embittered rivals. The man had been too personable. His interests had been too broad. It was understandable that many kinds of people had resented him for the ease with which he could change from jet-setter to revolutionary, but it was difficult to imagine how anyone would develop a hard, deep-seated hatred for Letelier personally. More than ever, Cornick believed he had been murdered as a symbol, but by someone who did not know him well.

The case agent felt as though he had just met the victim for the first time, and he considered this an essential first step. Over many hours, he labored to summarize the interview on paper in a way that would convey the flavor of it. He worked on the language. It was not easy to rise above ten years of experience with the standard FBI "pig-iron prose," but Cornick finally produced a lengthy report that he thought would set a fine example for the agents in the scattered offices working CHILBOM.

By coincidence, Cornick brought his draft into the office on the same morning that Scherrer's teletype arrived from Buenos Aires. The report on the Contreras interview filled thirty pages. "Look at this," Cornick announced to agents sitting nearby. "This guy is as long-winded as I am." He knew Scherrer only by reputation and from the few brief reports that had previously come from Argentina. This was his first full dose of the legat's work.

He soon tuned out the telephone hum and the clatter of shoes on plank floors in the big barnyard office as he read page after page of detail on the conversation with Contreras, the mysterious figure who had appeared in so many atrocity stories and who was now popping up in Cornick's investigative leads. As he read, Cornick actually found himself becoming excited, which was an unprecedented state for him as a consumer of dreary FBI reports. He was appreciative enough of a well-drafted report to realize that this one far surpassed his own in precision, without a sacrifice of insight. Scherrer supplemented his factual account with a long section of interpretive comments:

It was obvious during the above interview that Colonel Contreras held back with regard to DINA's knowledge of Cuban exile activities in Chile. . . . If DINA, in fact, was responsible for Letelier's assassination, Colonel Contreras gave no indication of concern or preoccupation, nor did his reactions betray him. However, little importance can be attached to Colonel Contreras's controlled, measured performance during the interview, since, obviously, Colonel Contreras did not rise to his present position of power by reacting emotionally to any problem or issue.

Legat believes that the U.S. government's and the FBI's message was clearly conveyed to Colonel Contreras with respect to our determination to pursue all investigative avenues to bring Letelier's assassins to justice.

Cornick dropped the teletype on his desk. He felt like congratulating himself. "Hot damn!" he cried. "We've got another professional working this case." To Propper, and to agent friends who did not mind an occasional joke on the Bureau, Cornick would express it differently. "That son-of-a-bitch Scherrer is far too intelligent to be an FBI agent," he would quip.

The interviews with Contreras and with the Venezuelan woman brought no hard clues, but they did help Cornick adjust to the prospect of a long investigation. By now, in December, Stames no longer held extraordinary daily meetings on the progress of the case. Agents began drifting back to other investigations. Cornick was pretty much on his own, although Seddon still helped and agents could always be commandeered to run down specific leads. The investigation had slowed to the point that it was requiring fourteen-hour days from only two people, Cornick and Propper. They had theories and even suspects, but they had no evidence and no clear picture of how the elements of the assassination plot had come together. The interviews renewed Cornick's optimism. He could imagine a thousand dramatic endings in which something in Chile clicked with something in Washington or New York.

Propper was too impatient and too bent on results to derive much pleasure from the elegance of a report or even from the savvy displayed therein by the interviewing agent. He was far more interested in Scherrer's discovery a few days later, December 6, that the International Police in Chile had confirmed Guillermo Novo's entry into that country. Novo had arrived in Chile on December 4, 1974, from Venezuela and departed on December 19 for Colombia, the records showed. This trip was a parole violation. If Propper could prove it had taken place, he could have Novo thrown back in prison. That would be leverage he could use to pry out more information on the Letelier case.

Propper focused on the Novo lead, taking aim at three specific prime sources—Novo, Morales, and Bosch. He wanted to put Novo before the grand jury again, but he decided to wait until he could marshal more evidence on the parole violation. As for Morales, his whereabouts were the subject of many rumors. Early in December, the Miami FBI office reported that Morales had been sighted in Miami and was not dead after all, but by the time Cornick sent word to Miami that Propper wanted a grand-jury subpoena served on Morales, he had disappeared again.

That left Bosch, the terrorist baby doctor, in Venezuela. Whenever Propper appealed through State Department channels for access to him, he received polite negatives from progressively higher levels within the Venezuelan government. This was an old bureaucratic trick, resting on the assumption that a person feels better when he is turned down by an important official. Each negative response was drafted impressively and mollified Propper—but only briefly. Propper knew that Bosch, Morales, and the travel evidence against Novo were all in Venezuela. The obstructions of that government began to irritate him, and he searched for a way around them.

Within days of the "shack in the woods" proposal of November 18, Propper telephoned the international law section of the Justice Department and questioned officials about the various methods of putting questions to Bosch under oath. The lawyers there sent him a book about a legal procedure known as Letters Rogatory, by which a court in one country asks a fraternal court in a second country to put questions to a witness. Propper had never heard of it.

He soon learned that the Letters Rogatory procedure was cumbersome and laden with protocol requirements. Officials of the international law section at Justice would review Propper's application for Letters Rogatory. Then, if it was approved, these officials would search for an appropriate federal judge. They would research the relevant Venezuelan law. They would ask Propper for facts and for information on United States law and jurisdiction. Then they would prepare drafts of the Letters Rogatory for circulation within the Justice Department. They would also prepare a draft letter for the attorney general, who was required to attest that the judge's signature was valid. When all this was approved, the State Department would be called in. Officials there would review the Letters for policy implications. The secretary of state was required to write a letter attesting to the signature of the attorney general, and the American ambassador to Venezuela was in turn required to attest to the signature of the secretary of state. Each letter of attestation depended on another. It was all very neat and diplomatic—and very slow. When all the drafts were approved, the State Department had to prepare official translations into Spanish. The full gestation period ran about six months.

After reading a few samples and a few handbooks on procedure, Propper rode his motorcycle to the State Department in search of a shortcut. He went from door to door and lawyer to lawyer until he ran into a young department man named Frank Willis, who turned out to be the lawyer who had received one of Al Seddon's emergency calls on the day of the Letelier assassination. The crime outraged Willis. He had kept up with the trickle of State Department cables on the investigation. Luckily for Propper, he also knew something about the procedures for Letters Rogatory. He told Propper immediately that it would be a fatal mistake to send the draft papers through the routine Justice Department liaison. He advised Propper to keep the papers in his own hands—literally. If Propper would bring them over on his motorcycle, Willis would show him how to "walk them through" the department. They could do it in a day or two.

All this was music to Propper. At last he had come upon a kindred spirit in the State Department. Willis volunteered to call people on the phone for Propper, to advise him how best to steer courses through the department, and to help him find other allies. Willis took a personal interest in the case. Propper thought everyone should behave that way as a matter of pride and official duty, but he knew that to many people an official attitude meant taking little interest at all. He was looking for the oddballs.

Propper took some sample Letters Rogatory home with him during the first weekend in December and wrote his own questions for Bosch. He was fishing for any detail of the murder conspiracy that could be corroborated—the names of accomplices, places of meetings, sources of the bomb components, anything. Willis took a copy of the draft to get a head start on the Spanish translation. Propper, meanwhile, took his draft of the Letters Rogatory directly to President Ford's attorney general, Edward Levi, who had asked to be kept abreast of major developments in the investigation. Levi approved the questions and signed his letter of attestment. Then Propper took the package to the State Department, where Willis was ready with the translation. Together, they walked in and out of offices. Little red ribbons were attached in the correct places. The completed Letters Rogatory left the State Department on December 14, by courier. On December 21, the American ambassador to Venezuela presented his compliments to the Venezuelan foreign minister and delivered the elaborate series of letters from high American officials to parallel officials in Venezuela, the ultimate design of which was to have Orlando Bosch brought into court to answer Propper's questions.

Propper himself reached Miami before the Letters' southward flight, having parlayed a speech on STING-style undercover operations into a visit there. He had learned from Cornick that the Bureau had a "case-breaking" lead out of Miami involving the Bay of Pigs Brigade, but he wanted to visit the city even earlier. It was the undisputed center of Cuban exile activities in the United States. He had noticed that bomb experts tended to live in Miami, along with smugglers and former Latin dictators. Ignacio Novo lived there. Rolando Otero had done his bombing there. A deadlier bomb had killed a legendary Cuban ex-senator and gang leader* in 1975. Orlando Bosch still collected money in Miami, his old operating ground, where he had once been arrested for towing a homemade torpedo through the city streets on a boat trailer. Miami was an occasional home for Ricardo Morales and scores of other Latin spies. In style, splash, and intrigue, the city was the American equivalent of wartime Casablanca.

Propper called ahead for an appointment with his counterpart in the office of the Miami U.S. attorney. After lunch, he followed Jerry Sanford back to his office, where he watched the sandy-haired young prosecutor take off his coat and his shoulder holster. Sanford put the holster and gun into his desk drawer. Propper disliked guns. He knew of no other AUSA who carried one.

"You really need that?" he asked Sanford.

"I'm the only guy in this office who works Cuban terrorism," Sanford replied. "You'd wear one, too." He continued his doleful briefing on the local crime wave. A dozen prominent Cuban exiles had been assassinated in the past two and a half years, he said. Drug-related murders were being committed at the rate of two and three a day, often with machine guns. Some Cuban activists were taking over the cocaine trade. Others were rebelling against the CIA and against moderate political leaders who they felt had betrayed their anti-Communist cause. The political groups often raised funds through smuggling, said Sanford, making it difficult to distinguish between a political assassination and a cocaine feud. It was all confused and very deadly.

---

*Rolando "El Tigre" Masferrer.

Sanford complained that the widespread approval of terrorists made his job impossible. Miami defendants had extensive political connections or huge sums of drug money, or both. He was afraid that the millions upon millions of illicit cash had corrupted the police and even some judges. He had lost the Otero case. He saw little prospect of solving scores of gangland murders. Rival Cuban leaders issued threats through the newspapers and carried them out in the streets. It reminded Sanford of Capone's Chicago, which was why he wore a gun.

On December 14, Larry Wack interviewed his first head of state, former President Eduardo Frei of Chile. He reported that the former President did not think the Pinochet government had ordered Letelier's death, but, on the other hand, could not rule out the possibility. In Wack's judgment, the interview was a failure. "That old buzzard didn't tell me a thing," he grumbled to Cornick.

On the morning of December 20, Cornick had read enough weekend teletypes to get a medium headache when Satkowski handed him the morning *Washington Post*, opened to Jack Anderson's column. "We got a big problem," he said gravely. "The Bureau's already called."

Cornick scanned the article, which was headed "Letelier's Havana Connection." He had expected this disaster for a couple of days, ever since Saul Landau had complained hotly to him that Anderson had obtained copies of the documents in Letelier's briefcase. It was a big leak. Now it was real. Cornick saw that Anderson sensationalized his scoop for his readers, calling the documents "secret papers . . . so sensitive that Letelier probably carried them to prevent their theft by the Central Intelligence Agency. We have seen some of these hush-hush papers." Anderson quoted from a letter written by Beatrice Allende, daughter of the late Chilean President, advising Letelier that he would be receiving a monthly stipend from the Chilean Socialist Party. Beatrice Allende, wrote Anderson, lived in Havana, Cuba, in exile. Therefore, Anderson concluded, Letelier's money was being channeled through Cuba, presumably with the approval of the Cuban government. To Anderson, this letter and others like it meant that Letelier "had been leading a strange double life." In effect, the columnist was saying that Letelier had been a spy for Castro.

After absorbing the shock, Cornick stormed into the office of SAC Nick Stames, where he proceeded to denounce the leak and the Anderson story in the strongest terms. "Nick, we're investigating this

damn bombing in a goldfish bowl!" he declared. "It's got to stop!"
Stames heartily agreed. Headquarters was demanding immediate answers. How many copies had been made of the papers from Letelier's briefcase? Who had them? Were they classified? Why had the
Washington field office neglected to take the approach that Letelier
might have been a Communist agent? Did AUSA Propper have access to the briefcase papers? It was assumed high and low in the Bureau that Propper had done the leaking.

By afternoon, Cornick was in Propper's office. "You've got to realize what we're up against," he said. "The people in the Bureau are
inclined to believe Anderson's column. They say, 'Well, Letelier was
a self-avowed socialist. He worked for a Marxist government. He
was getting this money through Cuba. So the fucking guy probably
was a Communist.' That's what Seddon thinks, Gene. And a lot of
others, too."

"So what?" asked Propper.

"You have to know what that connotes to the Bureau," said Cornick with a sigh. "If Letelier was a Communist, that's the worst.
That's lower than whaleshit, Gene."

"So what?" Propper repeated. "Does that mean it was okay to
blow him up on his way to work? What about Ronni Moffitt? Do they
think she was a Communist, too?"

"Hold on a minute," said Cornick. "I didn't say that. I'm just saying this will make it tougher, that's all."

"I disagree, Carter," said Propper. "First of all, I don't see how
this hurts the investigation. It doesn't have anything to do with our
real leads. It won't blow any sources. On top of that, I don't think it's
true that Letelier was a spy. Do you?"

"No," said Cornick. They did not believe Letelier had possessed
the character of a spy, in the first place, as he had been too independent to subordinate his will to anyone. Also, they decided that the secrecy of the contents of the briefcase had been wildly exaggerated
by Anderson in order to make his column more exciting. After all,
they reasoned, Letelier had taken the briefcase with him to work every day, filled with letters and old manuscripts and notes to himself
—and also with diverse items such as a black sleeping mask and a
bottle of aspirin. This was hardly the treatment one would expect Letelier to have given life-and-death spy documents. Finally, neither
Cornick nor Propper considered the Beatrice Allende letter a spy
communication. Spies don't carry letters around, they figured, especially letters about their compensation. Anderson's interpretation of
the "strange double life" seemed fanciful. More likely, Letelier had

been what he had openly declared himself to be: a socialist, with many friends and contacts in Cuba.

To Propper, this was all a sideshow. He advised Cornick to avoid a pointless and distracting leak investigation. When Cornick complained about the dozens of press inquiries on his desk, Propper volunteered to handle them. Government officials in the State Department, the White House, and elsewhere were already referring inquiries to him, the lowest-ranking available spokesman—as was natural in a case that presented political risks, few facts to stand on, and little prospect of credit. He said he didn't mind fending off the calls, and Cornick was only too happy to oblige him.

Among the most frequent callers was Letelier's successor at IPS, Saul Landau. Ironically, Landau had just returned from Cuba, where he had spoken personally with Fidel Castro about the Letelier case. To Propper, he protested that Anderson's column was calculated to "red bait" the Institute, to smear it by association with Castro, and, ultimately, to excuse the Letelier murders. Any mention of Cuban connections on the part of Letelier or IPS outraged him.

Propper thought Landau was playing into the hands of his critics by being so sensitive about his normal sympathies and associations. To Landau, this was political realism. He was fighting in the media to keep public attention focused on the bombing and blame pointed toward the Pinochet government. He was a political activist. Propper was a prosecutor. This basic difference caused tension that repeatedly undercut the tactical alliance between them.

"Gene," said Landau, "there are people in the United States government who do not want this case solved."

"I know that, Saul," said Propper. "There are all kinds of people around."

"Well, the point is that this is not an accident. This leak is exactly what you would do if you wanted to create an atmosphere that would make it easy just to forget about the case."

"So you think there's a conspiracy inside the government?" Propper asked skeptically.

"You call it what you want," said Landau. "I know there are people high up in the Bureau and elsewhere who are acting in concert. They're having an effect. You can't deny that."

"What do you mean, they're having an effect?" asked Propper. "They're sure as hell not having an effect on *me*, and I'm running the investigation. Who else matters? I can't see who they're having this big effect on."

"Wait a minute," said Landau, who thought Propper was both

puffing himself up and ignoring the power of officials above him in government rank. "Look, we're not worried about you," he said. "Or Carter. We know you're working. We trust you. So it's not personal. What I'm saying is that signals are being sent throughout the government, and the signals aren't good. The signal is that Letelier doesn't matter. Lay low. Take a dive."

"Let me tell you something, Saul," said Propper. "There is nothing in the world you can tell me that would make me work harder on this case. Or any less, either. None of it matters to me. I've looked at the autopsy pictures of Letelier and Moffitt, and they're the most horrible I've ever seen. I'd like to tell you those pictures are enough reason to work by themselves, but I've seen too many of them. They wear off. The real reason I'm obsessed with this one is that I like to win cases. I can't think of anything I'd rather do than catch the guys who did this and lock them up."

"I know that, Gene," said Landau.

"Now, you've been talking about all the subtle rewards people will get if they let the case slide," Propper continued. "You talk about how bureaucrats always adjust to the political attitudes higher up. I don't buy that in this case. But let's suppose it's true. What would I get? What would I get for easing up on the case? A two-thousand-dollar raise maybe? An in-grade promotion? Saul, that's *nothing!* And everybody would know that I'm the one who didn't solve the Letelier case. That's crazy. Saul, if Carter and I solve this case, I'll be a famous lawyer! With good reason, too, 'cause this is a tough one. And I'll win. You can't possibly give me any more reason than I already have."

This little speech confirmed Landau's fears instead of easing them. After nearly twenty years' work in a succession of leftist movements, he tended to trust only those motives that were political, that were grounded in an analysis of large-scale political forces and dedicated to the advancement of a cause. He considered Propper's motives non-political and therefore frail. To the extent that Propper's espoused commitment had a political tinge, Landau thought it was an individualist one, which he associated with selfishness, the profit motive, capitalism, and a host of other attributes that were foul to him.

The friction between Propper and Landau crackled often, then and later. It was of a special variety, fit for people with similar backgrounds and habits and with a common objective, but with clashing outlooks on the world. Like Propper, Landau came from a working-class Jewish family in New York City, and he was an ambitious, compulsive worker, something of a schemer, who looked for ways to cut a corner or two. But Landau was an ideologue—co-author of *The New Radicals*, an influential primer on movement politics in the 1960s. He was also a filmmaker with a number of titles to his credit, including an admiring documentary about Fidel Castro. Landau saw himself in a hemispheric political struggle that involved a murder case. Propper saw himself in a murder case that involved politics. To Landau, politics was a contest of ideas and interests, and governments were machines to implement the ideologies of the prevailing powers. At least to some degree, he thought the bombing case would be solved when and if the leaders of the American government pushed the right buttons and made the answers come out. In this light, Propper was a pawn and events like newspaper leaks occurred because they were willed by people in high places. Propper, for his part, took a much more haphazard view of government. To him, luck and skill shaped performance, and except in rare cases, things got done if the people at the working level bothered to push them.

Propper believed that Detective Stanley Wilson had leaked the briefcase papers to Jack Anderson. He knew from friends in the mobile crime unit that Wilson had made a copy of all the briefcase papers for himself. He also knew that Wilson had a consuming interest in spy matters, and that Wilson and Schuman were fond of the theory that the Letelier assassination was the ugly result of a quarrel among leftist spies. Anderson's "Havana Connection" story could be stretched to give backing to that theory. Finally, Propper knew that Wilson had been chafing somewhat since the embarrassing arrest of the wrong Carlos Altamirano in New York. He figured that Wilson had leaked the briefcase papers in a frustrated attempt to redirect attention to the Communist angle.

Cornick did not need to be told. "That's it for Wilson," he told Propper. "I'm chopping him off at the knees."

According to the information percolating up through the Bureau, however, Propper had leaked again. Officials noted that Cornick was defending him, and that Cornick and Propper were pursuing a course of dubious wisdom which had exposed the Bureau to criticism. People mentioned that the Letelier bombing might not be Cornick's kind of case. After all, he had become the case agent by a fluke. Perhaps Seddon would have been better all along.

Before the year was over, Cornick picked up signals that there was some dissatisfaction with his direction of the investigation. He tried to ignore them, but it was difficult. Morale dipped slightly. As time passed, sage heads in government and in the press began to nod and say that the Letelier bombing would soon become a faded memory, like all the other unsolved terrorist bombings and gangland killings. The work and the doubts were wearing on Cornick. Paperwork went on into the nights. Leak investigations kept intruding, and extraneous matters kept stealing his leftover time.

All these things were burdens. Cornick needed something to relieve them and to give meaning to his growing obsession with the case. He was counting on Tomboy, the highly placed FBI informant who had provided the Brigade lead. It was developing well, and it was pure FBI. If it panned out, both the work and the criticism would abate.

The crisis began to build on Tuesday, January 18, when Propper attended his first high-level conclave at FBI headquarters. Cornick himself knew some of the officials around the table only by name. They were all strangers to Propper, who was as tense as everyone else. The meeting had the atmosphere of a final council of war.

Cornick and Satkowski reviewed the progress on the Brigade lead. The motel in which the three Brigade members had stayed had been located just outside Washington, in Virginia. Agents had traced numerous phone calls through the motel switchboard, including several to the rural Georgia fortress of Mitchell Werbel, who was famous in certain circles as an international arms merchant and guerrilla-war enthusiast, inventor of the machine-gun silencer and a host of exotic, James Bond–style weapons, such as his swagger stick that could fire .22-caliber bullets.

While the Brigade leaders were in Washington, according to Tomboy, they had visited Admiral McIntyre at the Chilean Military Mission to protest what they called Chile's betrayal of Rolando Otero, a Brigade member. More importantly, they communicated their desire to postpone or cancel a DINA contract to murder an exiled Chilean newsman in Mexico City: there had been "too much heat" on anti-Castro Cuban activities in Mexico since July, when some of their operatives had tried to kidnap Fidel Castro's consul in the Mexican city of Mérida, in the Yucatán, killing a bodyguard in the process. McIntyre and the Brigade leaders made a deal: the Mexico job was off; they would kill a diplomat named Letelier instead.

For nearly an hour, Bureau officials reviewed what was known about the Brigade and its leaders. They knew that Propper planned to subpoena nearly a dozen more Brigade members, including the two reported hit men. The Bureau had his list. They asked him about the lines of questioning he planned and about his order of witnesses. Propper was impressed. It seemed to him that the FBI people were taking him into their confidence at last. He figured they had no choice but to do so, given his exclusive control of the grand-jury process. Still, he appreciated the show of partnership. For him it was marred only by a sense that some of the Bureau officials were slightly reticent, almost acting. Propper thought Cornick seemed a bit close-mouthed and crisp in speech—unlike his usual garrulous self. He told himself that this was nothing more than the result of pressure and anticipation.

Shortly after the meeting one of Bob Keuch's assistants in the Justice Department notified Propper that there would be another high-level meeting at FBI headquarters that afternoon. The announcement baffled Propper, who said he had just returned from the FBI.

At three o'clock, a larger crowd filled the same FBI conference room. Bureau officials disclosed the reason for all the theatric commotion: one of the men on Propper's subpoena list was none other than Tomboy himself! A security tangle had grown up around this single fact. The Miami FBI office had been extremely reluctant to give Tomboy's identity even to Cornick, and had done so only after seeing Propper's list. Then, over the previous ten days, FBI officials in Washington had conducted a heated debate about whether or not to tell Propper.

There were dangers either way. Uninformed, Propper might zero in on Tomboy as a suspect, and he might ask questions of other Brigade members that would tip them off. The Brigade members—including the four who would appear on Thursday—had been trained to discover informants within their own ranks. Propper's questions might reveal to them a knowledge of events that they could match with Tomboy's knowledge. An unwitting Propper might stumble into damaging information pretty much the way he had subpoenaed Tomboy in the first place.

If Propper knew about Tomboy, there would be a different set of risks. Knowing his identity, Propper would be obliged to behave almost as if he did *not* know—lest he arouse suspicion by speaking too much or too little of the man. He would have a very tricky role to play. And in FBI headquarters there were those who feared he would let something slip, deliberately or otherwise.

When, in the morning strategy session, Propper had mentioned Tomboy's actual name frequently, in connection with actions and mysteries that would, for peculiar reasons, make it likely that Tomboy would be compromised, Bureau officials realized that they had no choice but to include Propper. The participants in the afternoon meeting discussed the safe and unsafe areas of grand-jury testimony. Then they turned to a second issue: should Propper take Tomboy off his subpoena list? Again there were pitfalls either way. Not to subpoena him might in itself arouse suspicion, and it would deprive the Bureau of a proven means of stimulating informant reports. Bureau agents had found that it often helps to subpoena an informant, because the subpoena itself attracts attention within the informant's circles. Often the informant gets coached for his appearance by the guilty parties and learns a lot in the process.

Of course, it is also possible that the informant will be killed. Bureau officials reminded Propper and the Justice Department lawyers that the Brigade had recently acquired a reputation for viciousness. Less than two weeks earlier, on January 7, a former Brigade president and Miami civic leader who had denounced terrorism had been executed in his front yard. Before his death, the man had dared to testify before Jerry Sanford's grand jury on terrorist killings in Miami, and the street word was that Brigade members had not appreciated it. At this news, Propper felt new sympathy for Sanford, who now had one less witness and one more victim. He hoped the same thing would not happen to him.

During the meeting, an FBI agent suggested that it might be best for Tomboy to lie to the grand jury—provided, of course, that the government somehow excused the perjury. To this, Propper objected that it would put the government in the untenable position of suborning perjury, which might cause problems at any future trial. He pointed out that the government could legally agree not to prosecute Tomboy for perjury, but it could not prevent defense attorneys from citing Tomboy's lies under oath to impeach his character and his testimony. Bureau officials replied that this situation could not arise, for the simple reason that Tomboy would never testify at a trial. The Bureau would not allow it. He was too valuable an informant. Propper said he hoped Tomboy would not be called upon in a trial, but that he could not guarantee it. Bureau officials said he'd better. In the end, they strongly recommended that Tomboy's name be removed from the grand-jury list, and Propper agreed to postpone the decision. On this note, the meeting ended and tensions subsided.

Propper thought he had just seen a practical demonstration of the forces that create Palm Tree Peeking. Clearly, any step toward a grand jury or a courtroom brings nothing but pain, risk, and worry to informants and the government agents handling them, who always prefer to soak up information rather than to act on it.

As they left headquarters together, Propper enumerated for Cornick all the reasons why the FBI should have told him about Tomboy from the beginning. Cornick should have trusted him, he said. No wonder the case hadn't been solved by Christmas.

Cornick was rolling his eyes. "You've got to be kidding me," he said. "I hope you realize what I've been dealing with the last few days, Gene. You can see it now. I'm telling you, if anybody had even *suspected* that you knew who Tomboy was this morning at the meeting, they'd have made me walk the plank so fast you wouldn't have seen the splash."

On Friday afternoon, the day after Jimmy Carter surprised millions of television viewers by walking down Pennsylvania Avenue in his inaugural parade, Propper welcomed the four Cubans to his office. They all wore dapper three-piece suits and Sunday smiles. Three of them, according to Tomboy, had attended the fateful meeting with Admiral McIntyre in September. The fourth, Armando López Estrada, was a colorful figure who served as the Brigade's military director. López Estrada was a loquacious man who would appear shortly on national television with a bag over his head, speaking in menacing tones on behalf of the secret army waging war against Castro. Shortly after that, he would stand trial on charges of mounting a naval raid against Cuba for the Brigade, and he would win acquittal after two CIA operations officers testified favorably on his patriotism and government service.

Of the other three, the most striking was Bernardo de Torres, a giant hulk of a man who was an informal foreign minister for the Brigade. He groomed his mustache into a thin spiral that reminded Propper of Snidely Whiplash, the cartoon villain. De Torres traveled extensively in foreign countries, followed by rumors of arms deals and plots. Manuel Camargo, a small man with a wiry build, lived in Mexico City and was rumored to be in regular contact with the Mexican national police, narcotics officers, and also the CIA. Less was known about Roberto Carballo, the Brigade president, a slightly plump conversationalist who was jolly in spirit except when discussing the treatment of his compatriots by the FBI.

Carballo pointedly ignored Cornick and Seddon when they arrived at Propper's office, but the other three witnesses slipped quickly into banter about how much they had suffered at the hands of the FBI and how sorry they were that the Bureau was now helping to protect Castro. Propper admired their performance. He had been prepared for professionals—for men whose government experience was in some respects broader and deeper than his—but still he had not expected them to be so completely at ease. They were behaving more like guests on the Johnny Carson show than like target witnesses in a political assassination.

Propper tried to sober them up a bit before taking them downstairs, one at a time, to the grand jury. "We have to go now," he said. "But I want you to know that it'll be different down there than it is here with Carter and Al. I know you play games with the FBI in Miami. You've been doing it for years. That's all right with me. As the judge said in the Watergate case, you can lie to the FBI and there ain't much they can do about that. But if you lie in that grand jury, I'll nail your ass. I'm investigating a murder case. This is my first case with Cubans, and I don't have any grudges. But that's the way it is."

The four witnesses smiled warmly and said they understood. They said they had heard this many times before in Miami, when testifying to their "hometown" grand jury. One of them added that they certainly didn't mind testifying, and that in fact this appearance was nice because it allowed them to visit Washington again at government expense.

To Propper's further amazement, each witness grew more and more relaxed before the grand jury—in contrast with the behavior of Guillermo Novo. When Propper posed questions about the meeting with Admiral McIntyre, the three participants responded expansively. Of course they remembered the meeting, they said. They had protested the treatment of Otero by the Chilean government. They had discussed a supportive anti-Communist alliance between the Chileans and the Cuban exiles. They remembered details about McIntyre's manner and appearance. They described it as a "useful" meeting. But they didn't remember any talk about "jobs" for the Chilean government, much less about murders. That was preposterous.

It was all over by midafternoon. Propper, according to plan, offered the four witnesses a ride back to their hotel. A deputy U.S. marshal was in the building and agreed to drive them. The Cubans cordially accepted the offer. They signed papers to collect their witness fees and travel expenses, and then they departed with polite farewells.

Propper called Cornick, who had returned to WFO. "It worked," he said. "They're on their way with Ricky now."

"Good," said Cornick. "Everything is set. How'd it go in the grand jury?"

"Nothing. They all had a great time."

"That figures," said Cornick. "Those guys are slicker than owlshit. But maybe we can fool 'em now. It's worth the shot."

"I hope so," said Propper. "How many guys do you have on surveillance?"

"Don't worry," said Cornick. "You just stay near the phone. I'll let you know."

Cornick was in constant radio contact with the agents in the four squad cars outside the courthouse ready to follow the Cubans. He hoped the witnesses would make a stupid mistake, such as proceeding to an emergency rendezvous with contacts from the Chilean embassy. Cornick figured he had enough agents to keep up with them even if they switched cars, which they probably would do. It was a long shot. More realistically, Cornick hoped the Brigade leaders would say something to one another in the car. Propper's friend Ricky, the marshal, was black and was drawling in the best American dialect he could manage, but his real name was Ricardo. He spoke fluent Spanish. If the Cubans slipped up, Ricky would catch it.

Propper was pacing his office when Cornick called a few minutes later.

"Hi, Carter. Where are they?" Propper asked.

"I don't know, Gene," Cornick painfully replied.

"What do you mean, you don't know?"

"Just that. We haven't given up yet, but the bottom line is, we lost 'em."

Propper sagged down into his chair. "Where?" he asked.

"At the downtown Brentano's."

"Carter, that's only five or six blocks from the courthouse!"

"I know where it is," Cornick said testily.

"You're telling me you guys can't follow a United States marshal's car for six blocks in downtown Washington in the daylight? That's incredible!"

"I know," sighed Cornick.

"I mean, Ricky's got a radio!" said Propper. "There's a thousand ways you can follow him."

"It's not the car, Gene," said Cornick. "We know where that is. They got out of the car and went into Brentano's and disappeared. Out a back door, probably. We lost 'em on foot."

"How could you lose them on foot?"

"Gene, Seddon and those guys are not up on surveillance. Big-city surveillance is a sophisticated technique in itself. It's not as easy as it sounds."

"My God," sighed Propper. "I can't believe it."

Cornick signed off and went back to the scramble. FBI sirens were blaring all over Washington. One car screeched up Massachusetts Avenue to stake out the Chilean embassy, just in case. Cornick sent another car to watch the Cubans' hotel. Two others patrolled the streets near Brentano's. Nothing happened. Finally, in sheer frustration, Cornick himself drove to the airport. Fifteen minutes later, he saw the four Cubans pull up in a taxi.

That night, Propper and Cornick commiserated over the humiliation on the first full day of the Carter administration. It was a bad sign. Propper needled Cornick about the world's shortest surveillance.

"How about Ricky?" asked Cornick. "Did he overhear anything?"

"Nothing," Propper replied in disgust. "All they said was, 'Let us off at Brentano's, please.' In English. Hell, Carter. They didn't have *time* to say anything."

Cornick's fateful month began in the midst of the usual chaos. Propper was still angry over press reports out of Venezuela stating that Orlando Bosch had refused to answer the questions put to him from the Letters Rogatory. This news was not only a setback but an embarrassment. Propper was supposed to have been present at the questioning, but he did not even know it had taken place. Neither did the State Department in Washington nor the American embassy in Caracas. And neither did those people in the Venezuelan government who responded to official inquiries. At every level, Propper's huffy requests for verification met red faces and pledges to look into the matter.

Cornick, for his part, was investigating a tip from Michael Moffitt, Ronni Moffitt's widower. Moffitt had been getting telephone calls from a weird Texan named Woody who wanted to know whether Moffitt was still interested in the deal for five hundred million Chilean escudos. Moffitt had played along, learning after a string of calls that Woody's "deal" had been scheduled for consummation on the day of the blast at Sheridan Circle. Moffitt thought this might have been some sort of bait for Letelier, especially after Woody kept hinting that the money came from the CIA. Cornick had FBI agents scouring the streets of Houston for Woody, investigating what would ultimately prove to be a financial swindle unrelated to the Letelier case. Simultaneously, Cornick was studying the CIA's new response to Propper's requests, which revealed in general that nearly all the Cubans mentioned in the Brigade lead had extensive backgrounds of service to the Agency.

With all these things going in addition to the regular cable traffic, Cornick still hadn't acquired the habit of reading the morning newspaper. So he had no idea what Satkowski was talking about on the morning of February 1 when the supervisor greeted him with the cry "That fucking Propper has done it again!" Inevitably, it was another newspaper leak. A story on the front page of that morning's *Washington Post* disclosed that the Letelier investigators had evidence implicating the Chilean government and members of the 2506 Brigade. Cornick sighed as he read it. This was the first accurate glimpse of the investigation that had appeared in public. It revealed the names of no sources or suspects, but it did describe the Bureau's operating theory on the case. "The new focus of the Letelier probe," said the *Post*, "was discussed at a recent FBI headquarters meeting attended by Justice officials and FBI agents involved in the case...." This referred to the highly secret Tomboy meeting two weeks earlier.

Cornick was soon jumping up and down in Propper's office, saying that the Bureau had a simple interpretation of the story: the FBI, having trusted Propper at the meeting despite professional misgivings, was now getting its reward from Propper, who had promptly leaked the information confided to him. "This is confirming all their worst instincts about you, Gene," said Cornick. "And I hope I don't have to tell you who's taking the heat for getting you into that meeting."

Propper hotly denied being the leaker. He acknowledged receiving a phone call from the *Post* reporter the previous evening, but he said the reporter had already known the story. More importantly, said Propper, the story had originated with a reporter who covered the Justice Department, not the U.S. Attorney's Office. To him, this meant the story came from one of Keuch's aides who had attended the meeting. He pointed out that the story contained many small errors of fact that could never have originated with him. In short, he said, the source appeared to be someone who had attended the headquarters meeting but who knew little about the investigation. That meant Keuch's men. "I'm with you on this one," said Propper. "This kind of leak could kill us. People will know what we're thinking. They'll anticipate our moves."

Cornick went back to WFO, where accusations were flying and affidavits of innocence were being prepared for signature. He incorporated some of Propper's observations into his report, which nevertheless gave some support to those at headquarters who had already condemned Propper for the leak. Blame was circling, looking for a place to light, and everyone was shooing it away.

Outside the government, reactions to the *Post* story divided along political lines. Letelier's colleagues at IPS welcomed this leak as a substantiation of their beliefs. The Chilean embassy did not. On February 4, the chargé d'affaires sent an official note to Secretary of State Cyrus Vance protesting the *Post* article as an affront to Chile's honor. The chargé reminded Vance that the Chilean government had called for a thorough investigation on the day of the bombing, promising all the aid and cooperation that the American government might request. The chargé asked Vance to provide the Chilean government with an "official, reliable report" on the investigation. Within a few days, this request bounced from State to the Justice Department, and from there to Propper's desk.

Propper welcomed the Chilean request as the fortuitous result of a bad leak. It gave him exactly what he had been looking for: a pretext on which to approach the Chileans directly about the Brigade lead. On February 11, he and Cornick took deep breaths and rang the bell at the Chilean embassy. Neither of them had ever been there.

The diminutive chargé, flanked by a secretary and an American lawyer retained by the republic of Chile, opened the meeting on a note of pained reason, saying that his government was troubled by all the unfounded accusations in the press. The attacks were especially unfair, he added, because the government of Chile had desired justice in this terrorist crime as long and as fervently as the government of the United States—perhaps even more so, since the honor of his government had been impeached by those who did not know the truth. The chargé wanted to clear this up as soon as possible. His attorney agreed, saying he was sure the fair-minded Americans could do something to correct the unfavorable impressions caused by inaccurate news stories.

To this, Cornick responded with his standard speech about the "commonality of interest." "We both need to solve this case," he said, "because your government is receiving a lot of criticism, and it won't get any better until it's over. And if it's just a couple of bad apples in Chile, then let's get it out in the open and over with. That's what you need, and that's what we need, because we're not going to tolerate having people assassinated in our capital."

Propper was watching the chargé, whom he knew to be one of Stanley Wilson's contacts. Wilson, he figured, had no doubt lulled the chargé into a state of false security by stressing his suspicion of political leftists. Propper's reading of the chargé told him that the interim ambassador was a career diplomat, an intensely polite man who seemed congenitally fearful of unpleasantness and controversy. There would be no easy way to give him the news even if Propper were inclined to waste time trying to think of one, which he was not.

"Mr. Chargé," said Propper, "you asked our government for an update on the investigation. That's why we're here. I should tell you that it's not complete yet. We're not ready to indict anybody. There are people working on the case all over the world, and we will finish it. But right now all I can say is that I have evidence that persons in Chile were involved. Either in the government or not, I'm not sure yet. But our evidence is that Chileans were involved."

The chargé looked stricken and pale. "No, no, no," he said. "It can't be. Our government doesn't do things like that. The Chilean government doesn't do that."

"Well, that's the information we have," said Propper. "Maybe we can resolve it. I know for one thing that we need some cooperation from your naval attaché, Admiral McIntyre."

"Admiral McIntyre?" said the chargé. "You want to talk to Admiral McIntyre?"

"Not exactly," said Propper. "The FBI has already talked to him informally. We want him to take a polygraph."

Propper watched the chargé's face and saw signs of misery that bordered on hemorrhage. "A polygraph?" said the chargé.

"Yes," said Propper. "A lie-detector test."

"Like a criminal?" gasped the chargé.

"Well, at this point, more like a witness," said Propper. "Mr. Chargé, your ambassador has already written two letters asking for an investigation and waiving diplomatic immunity in talking to us, and in that spirit we would like to have Admiral McIntyre take a polygraph."

The chargé thought for a moment before speaking. "This is extraordinary," he said. "Are you absolutely sure it's necessary?"

"Yes," said Propper. "That's what we need. I can't keep the press from saying you aren't cooperating, but I can comment on some of the more outrageous allegations if you'll give me something to work with. I need something to be able to refute them. Right now I need the polygraph."

"I see," said the chargé. "Well, I don't control the military, you understand. On something like this, I will have to speak with my government. Perhaps I can give you a reply in a week or so. Is that satisfactory?"

"That's fine," said Propper. He and Cornick soon made their exit, much relieved.

Cornick started shaking his head when they reached the FBI car. "Well, you sure as hell didn't put any sugar on that medicine," he said.

"What do you mean?" asked Propper.

"I mean you crammed it right down his throat in about fifteen seconds," said Cornick. "I'd have softened him up a little more."

"I was perfectly polite," said Propper, taking slight offense. "I didn't say anything personally offensive, did I?"

"No," Cornick conceded.

"Well, you can't be too delicate when you're asking for a polygraph, Carter," said Propper.

Cornick mulled this over and began to laugh. "No, I guess not," he said. "I still can't believe we did it. Asking a foreign diplomat to take a polygraph is not exactly in the FBI field manual, you know."

A week later, with the request still pending, Attorney General Griffin Bell summoned Propper, Bob Keuch, and the FBI's Jimmy Adams to his office for a briefing on the Letelier case. Bell was new at his job, but already he had discovered that people asked him about the investigation nearly every place he went. He wanted to know what he could say for public consumption. A new media storm had arisen when columnists Evans and Novak had outdone Jack Anderson with their own lurid interpretation of the documents in Letelier's briefcase, announcing that "the hand of the Kremlin" had directed Letelier's life. Liberal commentators and congressmen who had enjoyed the leak of the Brigade lead were outraged over this one. Conservatives went the other way. The attorney general saw that demands for a new leak investigation were pouring in before the recriminations had died down from the last one. He wanted to know what was going on.

Propper was heavily outranked in this company. In effect, he was a lieutenant in the midst of two colonels and a general. As such, he recited for them the details of the major leads to date. The attorney general asked several questions about the Brigade lead, and then, after a few moments' thought, he turned to Adams. "Well, Jimmy," he said, "why don't you just surface your informant down there in Miami so Mr. Propper can bring an indictment in this case?"

Adams tried to conceal the sudden alarm on his face. "Well, sir, that's a possibility," he said, by way of delay, knowing that to make Tomboy testify openly would cause rebellion in the Bureau. It might also mark Tomboy for execution. And there was no telling what deep FBI secrets he might reveal in order to retaliate against the Bureau. Bell's straightforward suggestion was about the worst idea Adams could think of.

The attorney general was still smiling, awaiting a reply. "It sure would be nice to get this one over with," he said. "It would get rid of one of the albatrosses I inherited here—Koreagate and Letelier and Hoffa and the Helms case. We get more flack on those cases than all the rest put together. If you fellows think you've got this one figured out, why don't we just bring an indictment and let people know we've solved it?"

After enduring a long silence, Propper saw that no one else was rushing to speak up. "Well, Judge, that's what I want to do as soon as possible," he said. "But I don't think we've got enough evidence for an indictment yet. So far, the informant is all we have, and the information is technically hearsay. He didn't actually hear the orders being given to the alleged Brigade hit men, Franco and Martínez. He was all around the transaction but he was not actually a part of it. So we'd get killed with him as a witness. We believe him, but we've got to corroborate his information before I can seek an indictment."

The attorney general nodded, with a slight show of disappointment. "All right," he said. "What's your next move? Is there anything I can do?"

"I hope so," Propper replied. "On that meeting my agent and I had over at the Chilean embassy last Friday—that's still pending. If we can get the admiral to take the polygraph and he flunks it, then I think we'll have some leverage to use with the Chileans, and also with the Cubans. We need it with both. The Brigade leaders are very sophisticated, and we need all the pressure we can get to make one of them crack. Anyway, I think it would help a lot if you wrote a letter requesting that the Chilean government require Admiral McIntyre to take the polygraph."

This time it was the attorney general who perceived the drawbacks to a plan. He worried out loud about the kind of precedent such a letter would set. What would the United States say in the future when foreign governments asked American diplomats to take lie-detector tests in foreign criminal investigations? Would we always waive diplomatic immunity in the interest of cooperation, as Propper was trying to make the Chileans do? This was a delicate matter. Keuch and Adams were inclined to agree with the qualms of the attorney general, who finally asked Propper to look again for an alternative. If he decided he had to have the polygraph, more than likely he would have to induce the admiral to take it voluntarily—without an official American request.

"All right," said Propper, submitting to the refusal.

"Is there anything else?" asked Bell.

"Yes, Judge, there's one more thing," said Propper. "As I mentioned, I've been trying to go to Venezuela for four months now on the Novo lead. The Venezuelans have been stalling because they're so sensitive about having Orlando Bosch in their country. Well, last week they finally sent word that I could come down there and go through their police records on Novo and some other material. I think they did it only because we raised such a protest through the State Department about the way they've handled our Letters Rogatory. They needed to give us something, and this is it. If it's all right with you, I'd like authorization for foreign travel so I can go down there as soon as possible."

"I see," said the attorney general. "Is this fellow Novo part of that other matter with the polygraph and the Bay of Pigs people?"

"Not exactly," Propper replied. "He's part of another lead right now, but the two could be connected. We know Novo's connected to some of the Brigade people, and I believe he knows something about the murders. The problem is, I don't have quite enough to go after him on a parole violation. I know he went to Chile and Venezuela when he wasn't supposed to. The CIA just confirmed it. I can prove somebody with his name made those trips, but I can't prove it was him. I need a photograph or a witness, and I think I can get them in Venezuela."

"That's all right," said Bell, waving aside the details. "If you think you need to go on this case, it's all right with me."

"Thank you, Judge," said Propper. "I need to take my FBI agent, too, if that's all right. Earl Silbert doesn't think I should go to a South American country alone, and my agent knows the case better than anyone else."

"Fine," said Bell. "You take whoever you want."

Within hours, Cornick came into Propper's office on the run. "What the hell did you say to Adams?" he cried. "Stames just blistered my ass up and down his office! He said Adams called him so pissed they had to peel him off the ceiling!"

"What are you talking about?" asked Propper. "He didn't seem pissed to me."

"He wasn't pissed," said Cornick. "He was *henshit*, that's what he was! Nick said he was yelling and screaming about how you said 'my agent' this and 'my agent' that. He said, 'Who the fuck is Carter Cornick, anyway?' He said you made it sound like I was in your pocket and all I was doing was running out leads for you."

"That's bullshit, Carter," said Propper. "That's ridiculous."

"I'm serious, Gene," Cornick said. "Nick finally pounded his desk and said, 'Goddamn it, the FBI does not work for the U.S. Attorney's Office!'"

"Who said it did?" said Propper. "I can't believe this. Look, Adams *thanked* me at the end of the meeting, for Christ's sake. I saved the Bureau's fucking informant in there! The attorney general snapped his fingers and told Adams to use his source and bring an indictment just like that. And Adams just sat there and sucked his thumb until I bailed him out."

"That's not the point, Gene," said Cornick. "The point is, you can't say 'my agent' in front of those guys. I told Nick you say that all the time to my face and that's just the way you are, but it only made him madder."

"Carter, that's the pettiest thing I ever heard of," said Propper. "I can't believe it. These guys are supposed to be high government officials. I tell you what. You go back and tell Adams and Stames they can call me their prosecutor. I won't mind. This is ridiculous. These are supposed to be intelligent men."

"Don't get excited, Gene," said Cornick, seeing that Propper was becoming worked up. "I'm just trying to tell you that these guys are old Hoover guys. Nick is, and Adams sure as hell is. To them, there is a right way and a wrong way, and the Bureau's way is right. Investigators investigate, Gene. And prosecutors prosecute. When we finish investigating, you can prosecute. That's the way they see it. And the 'my agent' stuff is driving them crazy. I'm in deep water, I'm telling you."

A few days later Cornick relayed the first bit of bad news: he would not be going to Venezuela. Stames had forbidden it. The edict drove Propper into a tirade against the Bureau. Having suffered through months of delay on the part of the Venezuelans, he declared that he would not allow the Bureau to sabotage the trip. He would fight. Cornick would go. He had to, because Silbert would not allow Propper to go alone.

"That's just it, Gene," said Cornick. "Nick doesn't think you should go, either. He says our legat in Caracas can handle it."

"That's crap," said Propper. "Nick doesn't know what he's talking about. You know as well as I do that everything we've gotten out of Venezuela has come through the State Department. The legat down there hasn't done a thing on the biggest case in the Bureau. Besides, who does Nick think he is, trying to tell me I can't go? I've already got the approval of the attorney general. So do you."

Cornick sighed. That was part of the problem, he said. Normally, a request goes from the field office to the unit at headquarters, he said, and from there up through the section and the division to the director's office. And from there a memo goes over to Keuch or the attorney general for approval. That normally takes weeks. And at every level the supervisors have an opportunity to talk it over and to help shape the language that goes to the Justice Department, adding or subtracting conditions. Cornick explained that Propper had made a habit of short-circuiting this entire procedure by going to Keuch first. And now to the attorney general himself.

"So what?" said Propper. "I saved weeks, Carter. I'm just trying to make things go faster."

"That's not what matters to them, Gene," said Cornick. "You skipped them. You skipped about a hundred important people at headquarters. That's all they care about."

Propper said he would not stand for this sort of insanity. He vowed to launch a counteroffensive, through Silbert and Keuch. Through the attorney general, if necessary.

The second blow fell on February 23, just as Propper was leaving for the Chilean embassy to hear the chargé's answer about the polygraph. Cornick called at the last minute to say that Stames had forbidden him to go to the embassy. The FBI was withdrawing its support of the polygraph project, ostensibly for fear that it would jeopardize FBI legats abroad and the image of the Bureau among diplomats in Washington.

Propper flew into another rage, but in the end he had to call the Chilean embassy and make an excuse. He said he was sick with the flu. Over the next few days he kept canceling appointments on account of his "flu," while jousting unsuccessfully with Stames. Finally, he decided to go without an FBI representative. "Carter, I just want to get it done," he told Cornick. "There are a lot of people in the world who give polygraphs. Not just the Bureau. You can tell Stames I said that, okay?"

On February 28, Propper appeared at the Chilean embassy in the company of Larry Barcella, his colleague in the U.S. Attorney's Office. The two of them were old friends, having worked together for a year prosecuting major felonies in superior court without a loss. The judge who handled their cases had openly called them "Jesus Christ and Greasy Head," referring, with a judge's impunity, to Propper's beard and to Barcella's glistening hair. The judge had said they were quite a pair of characters. Their similarities were few. Each of them was an obsessive worker, and oddly, each of them had been falsely diagnosed as having a terminal illness. In Barcella's case, the hospital had gone so far as to mark his file *Deceased* without knowing that Barcella had gone home alive. Otherwise, the two prosecutors were aggressive lawyers whose styles reflected their personalities. Propper relied on his candor and chutzpah, whereas Barcella relied on his charm and his florid eloquence. He was a noted storyteller and the office romantic. As a law student, Barcella was once so starstruck by the beauty of a passing woman that he went straight to the blood bank to sell enough of his blood to buy a bottle of Rebel Yell bourbon, hoping to impress her. She did not drink, as it turned out, but he managed to marry her anyway.

At the Chilean embassy, Barcella said almost nothing. This was out of character for him, but he knew so little about the case that all he could do was listen. He was there as a potential witness, in case something was said that would later require corroborative testimony in court.

The environment made it difficult for Barcella to concentrate. They were in a dark parlor with twenty-foot ceilings and magnificent mantels and window casings, carved of dark wood. It made a sinister impression on Barcella, like a chamber in a dank medieval castle. Appropriately, he thought, the chargé was attended by a hefty woman who was at least six inches taller than he. Her blond hair was pulled back into a severe bun. She spoke English with a heavy German accent, and she seemed to prompt the chargé with his answers, in Spanish.

At one interval, Barcella leaned over to Propper and poked him in the ribs. "Gene," he whispered, "have you noticed the guy behind the door?"

Propper waited a few seconds and then glanced at the enormous parlor door. A man's head appeared behind it, in the shadows. Then it withdrew.

When the meeting ended, about all Barcella could gather from the back-and-forth was that the Chileans had denied the request. Propper could ask Admiral McIntyre to volunteer for a polygraph, but it would be McIntyre's personal decision. Barcella exercised his amazement all the way back to the office, embellishing descriptions of the scene at the embassy that would make "Ilse of the SS" a fearsome legend in the Major Crimes section.

"That was the spookiest meeting I've ever been to," he told Propper. "I was afraid they would take us downstairs and feed us to the Dobermans. You told me this case was weird, but I didn't think it was *that* weird."

"That's nothing," said Propper. "Don't be paranoid."

Two days later, the American ambassador to Venezuela saw Propper during a visit to Washington. Viron P. "Pete" Vaky was a scholarly, urbane Foreign Service officer, cut from the mold of the professional. He had no known quirks. His distinguishing trait was a propensity to identify with the foreign government to which he was accredited. It was a common affliction in the State Department, known as "clientitis," but Vaky's case was extreme enough to account for his professional nickname, "Flaky Vaky."

The assignment in Caracas suited the ambassador's talents, as Venezuela was becoming the most pampered country on the South American continent. American foreign-policy makers regarded its goodwill as essential for a number of reasons, not the least of which was Venezuela's position as the largest oil exporter in the Western Hemisphere. Also, Venezuela had one of the few functioning democracies in South America, and because of this, the American government tended to idealize Venezuela as a model for the Spanish-speaking countries.

Vaky told Propper that the Cubana Airlines case was an extremely sensitive matter for President Pérez's government, for obvious reasons, and that Propper would be welcome in the country only so long as there was no publicity about Orlando Bosch or the Letelier case. President Pérez was nervous about it and would require constant reassurance that Propper would not stir up any trouble. Toward that end, the ambassador said he would prefer to keep Propper's visit as quiet as possible, even within the government. It would be best handled as a diplomatic exchange arranged by the State Department.

There was no reason for the FBI's legat to attend the meetings, as his presence would be a reminder of criminal responsibilities.

Propper agreed. He was after Novo, not Bosch. Besides, under the circumstances the ambassador's skittishness about the legat worked to Propper's advantage. He would try to use it to force the FBI to put Cornick back on the travel list.

The next morning, Propper asked Earl Silbert to call Stames, with whom Silbert had a good working relationship. When the call began, Propper paced back and forth in front of Silbert's desk, listening and coaching. The conversation was friendly, though a little strained, until Silbert passed along what Ambassador Vaky had said about not inviting the Caracas legat to the meetings. From what Propper could overhear, Stames was protesting that it was vital for the FBI to have someone there, not only because it was an FBI case, but also because prosecutors do not know how to ask questions in that kind of situation.

"What do you mean, we don't know how to ask questions?" cried Silbert. "What the hell are you talking about, Nick? What do you think we go to law school for? What do you think we did in Watergate but ask questions? That's all we do . . . What do you mean an investigative question? What the hell is that?"

Propper stepped up his pacing. Silbert attacked for a while and then calmed down to say that Propper wanted to include the FBI and that it was only fair for the case agent to go. That meant Cornick. The attorney general had already approved it.

"Oh, he is?" said Silbert. He put his hand over the phone and whispered to Propper, "He says he's sending Satkowski down there." He turned back to the phone and spoke to Stames, half for Propper's benefit. "Oh, you want a supervisor, eh?" he said. "You want someone who can make decisions for the Bureau on the spot . . ."

Propper was making wild gestures of disapproval. He said Satkowski didn't speak Spanish. He said Satkowski was not as familiar with the case as Cornick. He said Satkowski wouldn't make any decisions on the spot but would delay things constantly to check back with Stames.

Silbert threw some of these comments in on his side of the exchange, which was moving rapidly by now. As he spoke, he snatched up a piece of paper and scrawled, "He says Carter doesn't speak Spanish that well—so little difference if any."

Propper could not contain himself. "Satkowski doesn't speak *any* Spanish, Earl," he said, so loudly that Silbert winced and motioned for quiet.

"Wait a minute," he suddenly told Stames. "He is? Are you sure? Don't you think you may be overreacting?" Silbert put his hand over the transmitter again. "He says Carter can't go because he's not the case agent anymore," Silbert told Propper. "He's off the case, as of today."

Silbert shrugged when the call ended. "I'm sorry, Gene," he said. "But he says it's an internal FBI personnel matter, and he's right. I can't tell him to put Carter back on the case any more than he can tell me which assistant I should put on a case. There's nothing I can do."

Propper remonstrated and cursed, mostly at the walls. "Thanks for trying, Earl," he said, and left.

His call found Cornick subdued, trying to make the best of it. "I tried to tell the bastard he's making a mistake," said Cornick. "But he wouldn't listen. It's really something. I love this man's Bureau more than anybody I know, but sometimes it's hard to take."

Cornick planned to ask for transfer back to the bank robbery squad. Before leaving, he embarked on a farewell report on the case, which would become a labor of affection. He would write that the Brigade lead was the probable solution to the case. Within a few days, he would call Propper to discuss the case informally, sounding rather forlorn, but he would not go back to Propper's office.

Al Seddon did. He visited Propper on his second day as the new case agent, having rectified the mistake he made at Sheridan Circle. The thin, mild-mannered Texan had always believed that Cornick and Propper were too straightforward, with their formal reports, grand-jury subpoenas, and efforts to obtain leverage over witnesses. He thought they were taking the standard Door Kicker approach, whereas Seddon preferred deep cover and the velvet touch of the spymaster. No twist was too bizarre. Castro could have had Letelier assassinated. So could the Israelis or the South Africans. Seddon had been known to mention suspicions of the Chinese Communists.

To officials at headquarters, the Seddon approach made sense. It would be contained within the Bureau. It would include a hard look at the Communists. It would prevent their being caught flatfooted by articles like the Anderson column. Most importantly, it would pull investigative control away from Propper.

As always, Seddon was helpful and polite to Propper, but somewhat reserved. "Things are going to be different from now on," he said.

10 ▣ CLOSE CALLS

The embassy car swerved back and forth along the winding road that climbed the hills around Caracas, carrying two prosecutors who were bleary-eyed from a long flight and from repeated briefings on the Letelier investigation. Propper had told the whole story three times or more and given Barcella little more than a persistent headache. All Barcella knew was that he was suddenly in a foreign country, once again a stand-in for Carter Cornick. He knew that Propper was having a fight with the Bureau, that Cornick had been canned, that the Bureau had insisted that Satkowski make the Venezuela trip "to oversee activities and provide appropriate direction to the Assistant United States Attorney." He knew that Propper had balked at this, weary of the collective wounded ego at headquarters, sending back word that Satkowski would not oversee anything. FBI officials had finally backed down, fearing that Satkowski would make the long trip only to be escorted out of the meetings as a crasher.

A small welcoming party greeted the prosecutors on the veranda of Ambassador Vaky's official residence, which afforded a magnificent view of sprawling, dirty Caracas. Introductions were made over coffee, cocktails, and hors d'oeuvres, and Propper soon fell into conversation with the leader of a two-man delegation from the Venezuelan government. A deputy minister of justice repeatedly emphasized the difficulties of providing access to information about Orlando Bosch, saying that the Venezuelan government had to take meticulous care to protect Bosch's rights, especially in an internationally sensational case such as the bombing homicide of the seventy-three passengers on Fidel Castro's plane. Bosch's lawyers, said the deputy minister, had consistently refused to allow anyone to speak with their client, and Bosch himself had snubbed the Letters Rogatory, as was his privilege. Propper kept saying he understood all this—which he did, having heard it from Ambassador Vaky. Barcella, meanwhile, said almost nothing. The speeches and the questions and answers made much less impression on him than the sight of the deputy minister's custom-made switchblade, which he kept opening and closing as he spoke.

DISIP's deputy director, a Cuban exile named Dr. Rafael Rivas Vásquez, spoke cautiously in the presence of the deputy minister, who appeared to be his security monitor, but Dr. Rivas returned alone the following day and got down to business. For nearly an hour, he answered Propper's questions about the operations of Orlando Bosch. As Barcella heard it, Rivas had a paradoxical relationship to the baby-doctor terrorist. On one hand, he was always finding Bosch in Venezuela with a pile of bombs and a stack of money, at which times Rivas would virtuously pitch Bosch out of the country. On the other hand, Bosch always seemed to be returning to Venezuela after writing Rivas a letter of his intentions, and Rivas always seemed to be meeting Bosch at the airport.

In telling of one such airport greeting, Rivas recalled that in early December of 1974 Bosch had arrived from Curaçao in the company of two other Cubans, Guillermo Novo and Dionisio Suárez. Rivas said he'd heard a lot about Novo but knew little of Suárez.

Propper became fully alert. He knew Suárez, he said offhandedly. Suárez worked with Novo. He had been the first man Propper had called before the Letelier grand jury, back in October.

Rivas recalled that the interior minister had been annoyed at the news of the arrivals and had given Rivas seventy-two hours to get the three Cubans out of the country. This had not been easy, said Rivas, because the Cubans had wanted to go to Chile and their travel documents had not been in order. Consequently, Rivas had been forced to spend almost the entire three days scrambling back and forth among the immigration office, the Chilean embassy, and the airline ticket offices. Finally, he had managed to get Bosch and Novo on a flight to Chile. Suárez could not get a Chilean visa, for technical reasons, and had to return to the United States.

"Do you think it would be possible to give me some information proving that Novo came through Venezuela?" asked Propper.

Rivas hesitated. "Just on Novo?" he asked. "Not on Bosch, too?"

"Just Novo," said Propper.

"That's good," said Rivas, apparently relieved. He thought for a few moments. "I don't see why not," he said. "He signed a lot of papers down here at the immigration office. There would be copies of his airplane ticket."

"That's great," said Propper.

"You wouldn't need to say where you obtained them, would you?" asked Rivas.

"No," said Propper. "But the documents would have to be certified. And we may need affidavits from some of the people who saw him."

"That would be more difficult," said Rivas.

"I understand," said Propper. "Let's just start with the documents, okay?"

Rivas seemed to be debating within himself, under pressure. "I think I can do it," he said. "But it will be difficult. In our business, it's much easier to provide the informal information than the proof, you see. That always causes problems."

"Well, it's very important to the United States," said Propper. "I'm pretty sure Novo knows who killed Letelier, and if I can prove he came down here in violation of his parole, I can get some leverage on him to make him talk."

"I see," said Rivas. "You really need it."

"Yes," said Propper. "Tell me, do you remember if Novo used his own passport? That would be the easiest way to prove where he went, but Novo says he's lost it. I don't believe that, but it doesn't look like we're going to get the passport. We need something else."

Rivas laughed. "No, I don't think you'll get it," he said. "I remember something about that. Novo said he'd have to get rid of his passport because of some kind of restrictions. He wasn't supposed to travel. He said he'd throw it in the river somewhere. I remember that."

"That sounds right to me," said Propper, glowing inside over this verification of his hunch.

The DISIP deputy director agreed to locate and deliver the travel documents Propper wanted. In response to Propper's questions, he resumed his story about Bosch, saying he had received intelligence some nine months earlier—in June 1976—that Bosch had convened Cuban leaders from all over the hemisphere at a secret meeting in Bonao, a small mountain town in the Dominican Republic. This was known as the "CORU meeting," at which the various Cuban exile factions hammered out an agreement to stop quarreling among themselves and to coordinate terrorist "acts of war" against the Castro regime and its sympathizers everywhere.

Propper had heard of the famous meeting, of course, but he did not know precisely what had occurred there. His accounts conflicted. He told Rivas that he would very much appreciate any information DISIP might have on the matter, since it was possible that Letelier's murder had been planned at Bonao.

Rivas seemed delighted at the prospect of sharing his information about the CORU meeting. There had been not one meeting but two, he confided—a large session at which various political differences were resolved, followed by a smaller "operational" meeting of the leaders of the principal CORU groups. The second meeting had been the more secret of the two, as responsibilities had been divided then and targets selected. Rivas said that the participants had been limited to Guillermo Novo, Frank Castro, Orlando Bosch, an unidentified member of the 2506 Brigade, DISIP's own Luis Posada, and Armando López Estrada.

Propper was taking notes. He recognized all the names, including that of López Estrada, who had been before the grand jury to answer questions about the Brigade lead. He told Rivas that this list was similar to others he had received.

At the operational meeting, Rivas said, the Western Hemisphere was divided into geographical zones, with each leader being assigned a zone for the missions of his group. One group, for example, was allotted South America, and this group had carried out the following bombings between July and October of 1976: the Air Panama office in Bogotá, Colombia; the Cubana Airlines office in Panama City, Panama; the Guyanan consulate in Trinidad; the British West Indies Airways office in Barbados; and, finally, the Cubana Airlines jetliner on October 6. Rivas ticked these explosions off from memory, adding the names of the actual bombers in each case.

Listening, Propper felt a surge of emotion. It excited him to feel so near his prey as he did when Rivas ticked off the crimes and the perpetrators, one by one. Propper thought he had been admitted at long last to the hidden recesses of terrorism. "What about Letelier?" he asked. "Do you have anything on whether Letelier was discussed at Bonao?"

"No," said Rivas. "I'm sorry."

"How about Novo's group, the CNM, and the Brigade?" pressed

Propper. "Do you have anything on the missions they were assigned?"

"Not really," said Rivas. "All I can tell you about Novo and the Brigade is that they were supposed to work in the United States and in the Caribbean. As I understand it, the Caribbean was agreed upon as a target of opportunity for all the groups. It's kind of a free-fire zone, as you would say in America."

"Well, do you know which group had Washington?" asked Propper. "Whose zone was that in?"

"I don't really know," said Rivas. "But there was a map. Maybe that would tell you."

"What kind of map?" asked Propper. "You're not talking about the street map, are you?"

"No, no, no," said Rivas, with a laugh. "Nothing like that. That street map is a fairy tale." Propper was referring to news reports that a map of Washington had been found in the office of one of the men arrested for the Cubana Airlines bombing. The stories said Letelier's route to work had been traced on the map in red ink. Rivas branded them fantasies.

"This is a different kind of map," said Rivas. "It's North and South America. These big zones are marked out on it."

"But you don't remember which one Washington is in?" asked Propper. "Is there a boundary in the United States?"

"I think so," said Rivas. "But you should see for yourself. I have a copy of the map, and I can give it to you if you like."

"That would be great," said Propper. "That might help a lot." He hoped the map would show a boundary between Novo's CNM in the North and the Miami-based Brigade in the South.

The meeting ended an hour later on a note of courtesy. Rivas said it might take him a few days to locate the map and the Novo travel documents. During that time, he would be happy to offer Propper and Barcella the services of two DISIP bodyguards and a DISIP car, so the Americans could sightsee in Caracas. Propper accepted the offer. After Rivas left, he and Barcella retreated to their hotel to brainstorm.

Barcella felt like an outsider, disoriented at once by the foreign environment and the Spanish language and the confusing facts and by the loss of all the familiar prosecutorial tools he enjoyed back in Washington. He thought everyone was behaving strangely, out of role. Ambassador Vaky was not there, but he had made it clear that he was more worried about Venezuela's sensitivities regarding

Bosch than about Propper's need to obtain evidence on a terrorist crime. The FBI's legat had not attended the meeting with Rivas, sending his assistant instead, and the assistant had neither said a word nor taken a single note. This baffled Barcella, who had never seen FBI agents work that way before. At first he was inclined to interpret it as some sort of Bureau retribution against Propper, but then he decided that the legat was taking his cue from the ambassador, not from headquarters.

"You can't worry about all that stuff, Larry," said Propper. "We're beggars down here. We have to take what we can get, and Rivas is giving us the map and the Novo stuff. If he does, the trip will be a success already."

"He hasn't done it yet," said Barcella. "I'll believe it when I see it."

"He will," said Propper.

Propper returned to unexpected emergencies in Washington. Officials of the Chilean government were angry, and so were the Venezuelans. The Chileans were upset about an address given to the United Nations Human Rights Commission in Geneva by Isabel Letelier, in which the widow said she had been told by Propper that DINA had killed her husband. European newspapers were displaying the story prominently, quoting Mrs. Letelier to the effect that she had received the news from Propper in a semiofficial manner—in the presence of the U.S. attorney general.

Chile's American lawyers had called Propper numerous times to protest, only to be told by his secretary, Cindy Grant, that he was not available. She had been under strict orders not to say that Propper was in Venezuela, or even that he was out of the country, lest stories appear that the Letelier prosecutor was in Caracas. This secrecy was one of the conditions imposed by President Pérez, relayed through Ambassador Vaky. Unfortunately for Pérez, however, the requirements of secrecy were no match for Chile's Washington lawyers, who had called friends all over town until they located someone who would tell them where Propper had gone. The news had relieved their anxious clients back at the Chilean embassy because it tended to make Venezuela look bad instead of Chile. Quickly Chile's representatives had leaked to American and foreign newspapers stories about how Propper was visiting Venezuela. These stories, in turn, had infuriated the Venezuelans.

Within a few days, one of Chile's American lawyers told Propper that the Chilean government was distressed about Isabel Letelier's speech in Geneva. The Chileans wanted a retraction or some form of recompense for the publicity, which was especially damaging to Chile's image because it mentioned Propper by name and sounded official. The lawyer, Tony McMahon, ended his appeal by asking what Propper was prepared to do to correct the injustice.

"Nothing," said Propper.

"Nothing?" said McMahon. "I don't see why. Her speech was wrong, wasn't it?"

"I don't know about the speech," said Propper. "But the news stories were wrong. I didn't tell her DINA did it. I told her we were investigating a number of possibilities, including DINA. She probably just exaggerated so she could say what she wanted to say."

"Probably so," McMahon agreed. "Then I don't understand why you can't just say so."

"I just did," Propper replied.

"No. I mean officially. My clients are entitled to a public statement that will correct the false impressions going around after all these stories."

"Well, I don't make official statements," said Propper. "Only the Department of Justice is allowed to do that, and it's against department policy to issue statements about ongoing criminal investigations. They never do that, for obvious reasons. They don't want to play twenty questions with the press over what they think is a good lead or a bad lead."

"I can see the policy," said McMahon, "but there must be exceptions sometimes. I mean, this is a serious mistake that has affected the image and standing of an allied nation."

"They won't do it, Tony," said Propper. "And I don't blame them. If they start, it'll never end. Look, there are millions of incorrect stories. Last fall, *Newsweek* said the CIA had reviewed our files and decided DINA was innocent, which was crap. It pissed off all Letelier's friends, but we didn't issue a statement about that one either."

"Yeah, but this is a government asking," said McMahon. "A government ought to get some consideration for a reasonable request."

"No way," said Propper, growing annoyed. "And even if they would do it, I'm not going to ask them. DINA hasn't helped me any, and somebody in DINA might have committed the murders. I don't particularly like DINA, if you want to know the truth. So why should I go to bat to get a statement to help those guys? Give me a reason why I should."

McMahon seemed to drift off in thought. "Well," he said, "I know you've been interested in getting a polygraph from Admiral McIntyre. Right?"

"Right," said Propper, instantly more curious, "but you know McIntyre has rejected it."

"Well, we might be able to help you get the admiral's polygraph if you can help us with the statement. How's that?"

"That's a reason," Propper said in a tone of congratulation. "You just gave me a reason."

"I know I did," said McMahon.

"Are you just saying that or is it a proposal?" asked Propper.

"Something in between," said McMahon. "I'll have to talk to some people before I can guarantee anything, but I think we can work it out if you're interested."

"I'm interested," said Propper.

After hanging up, he sat back to ponder the offer, which had surprised him as much as it had excited him. He wondered why the Chilean government seemed to be so sensitive about one press item out of the thousands that had appeared blaming DINA for the assassination. If the Chileans were reacting to Isabel Letelier's public invocation of Propper's name, that would indicate that they were extraordinarily solicitous of the United States government's goodwill. This might give Propper a psychological weapon against them. Propper also wondered what McMahon's proposing such a deal meant. Did it mean that McIntyre was innocent? Would McMahon's immediate bosses necessarily know if McIntyre was guilty? Might there be a struggle inside the Chilean embassy over this offer? Was it possible that McIntyre knew how to beat the polygraph?

Propper bounced hundreds of questions around, but he always returned to the notion that the prospective deal would be a step forward regardless of what happened. Already, he was curious to know what conditions McMahon would impose. He wanted to know whether the admiral would show up for the polygraph and, if so, how he would behave. Even if the admiral passed the test, truthfully denying Tomboy's allegations about his contact with Brigade leaders, it would be beneficial. If Tomboy was something less than the miracle informant the FBI people touted him to be, Propper wanted to know it sooner rather than later.

He pursued the deal over the next few days, negotiating with McMahon and arranging with Keuch for the Justice Department to issue the contingent public statement. Concurrently, Propper was trying to coax the Venezuelan government into transmitting the documents promised by Rivas. This was a delicate task, as the Venezuelans were still piqued over the publicity about Propper's trip, but packages finally moved through the diplomatic pouch. The CORU map arrived first. It looked the way Rivas had described it—a small map of the hemisphere divided by crude lines, without other notations of value. The North American line passed roughly through Washington, D.C., putting the murder site on a CORU border. Propper sent a copy of the map to the CIA on March 17, asking Tony Lapham to have the Agency files search for information about the Bonao meetings. He also asked Lapham to find out what the Agency knew about Admiral McIntyre. Did he work for DINA? McIntyre was much on Propper's mind as the polygraph talks progressed.

The bargain was all but concluded when the attorney general agreed to receive a delegation from the Institute for Policy Studies. The meeting took place on March 21, the six-month anniversary of the bombing on Sheridan Circle. Propper and Keuch mentioned this fact to Attorney General Bell before the IPS people were admitted to the office, warning Bell that he would most likely be taken to task for the fact that no progress had been announced. The IPS people would say that their patience was running low, and they would probably make a lot of demands. Keuch said this hurriedly, by way of preparation, as Bell tried to shift his mind from one meeting to the next. As usual, the attorney general was distracted by phone calls and whispered messages. Propper described Saul Landau, Isabel Letelier, Michael Moffitt, and some of the other IPS participants. He predicted that most of the talking would be done by the group's lawyer, Michael Tigar, whom Propper sketched as extremely smart and aggressive.

Keuch tossed in a dissenting view of Tigar, whom he called a troublemaker. He remembered facing Tigar in some of the celebrated political cases of the early 1970s, when Tigar argued vociferously that the government, represented by Keuch, had trampled upon the rights of various radicals and minority groups. The memory still nettled Keuch, who told the attorney general that he should choose his words carefully, because Tigar was believed to fight his battles through the press by means of cleverly twisted statements of the government's position.

Mention of the press captured the attention of Attorney General Bell. "They'd better not talk to the press," he said gravely. "This is supposed to be a private meeting, isn't it?"

"Yes, Judge," said Propper. "But it won't be private for long. Maureen Bunyan is standing outside in the hall, waiting to talk to them when they leave here."

"Who's Maureen Bunyan?" asked Bell.

"She's a television reporter," said Propper. "She's got a camera crew with her. Everything's all set up. I saw them doing a preliminary interview when I came in."

The attorney general made a sour face and drifted off in thought. "What am I doing meeting with these people?" he asked of no one in particular.

After a long silence, Bell's assistant, Frederick Baron, felt pressure to speak. He had scheduled the session after receiving a number of phone calls from IPS supporters who wanted it—preferably, they said, without Propper. "Well, sir," he replied, "they met twice with Attorney General Levi during the Ford administration, so we thought it would look bad if you refused to see them, too. It's more or less a courtesy."

"That's not a very good reason," Bell said gently.

"Well, I was against the meeting from the start," Keuch reminded Bell. "They'll just take advantage of it to hold a press conference and denounce the government and say we're not trying."

"That's not the point," said Bell.

"I know," said Keuch. "It just bothers me personally, I confess. I'd give anything to solve this case just so we could stuff it down their throats at IPS."

The attorney general was eyeing the clock. It was already past time. Another appointment was crowding in. "All right, let's get on with it," he said with a sigh. "Show them in."

The delegation filed in and were soon seated at the big conference table, giving speeches one by one. Some were simple reminders of facts and appeals for justice. Others were more abstract analyses of the historical forces that had produced the murders. Michael Tigar argued that Propper should be replaced with a special prosecutor and that CIA files on DINA and Cuban exiles should be obtained by force of subpoena rather than by request. He said it was the only way to guard against a conflict of interest. After a time, the attorney general cut him off. Tigar's argument had run into one of his pet peeves. Bell opposed special prosecutors on principle, saying that it didn't make sense for the government to protect its integrity by creating an office whose very existence was founded on doubts about the integrity of government. "There won't be any special prosecutors while I'm attorney general," Bell announced to the gathering. "As long as I'm here, we'll handle any case that comes our way."

Soon after this abrupt declaration, Bell expressed his sympathies for Letelier and Moffitt, his official determination to bring the murderers to justice, and his thanks to the delegation for its concern.

Thus excused, the IPS people unhappily filed back out into the hall. To them, Bell had seemed uninformed on the specifics of the case, ignorant about Chile, and arbitrary in his dismissal of the call for a special prosecutor. Some were put off by his Southern drawl, others by his way of seeming gracious and curt at the same time. Some of these opinions had to be harmonized and others suppressed in a huddle outside the attorney general's door. Then IPS spokesmen used the only weapon at their disposal—the press—to keep up the pressure on the government. They reiterated their demands and their disappointments in interviews, balancing them with praise for the attorney general's personal interest in the case.

Back inside, the attorney general was conducting a brief review. "Don't do that to me again," he instructed Frederick Baron in conclusion. "Those people have a grievance, but people get murdered in the streets every day all over the country. What am I going to say to the families of all the other victims? They'll want to know why I met with these people and not with them. It's the same thing I have with the Hoffa people. It's not the attorney general's job to meet with them. That's why I have assistants. They should handle the specific cases."

"Yes, sir," said Baron.

Bell turned to Propper. "That means you," he said. "You keep at it."

"I plan to," said Propper.

"And let me know if you run into problems," Bell continued. "You've got a big case. I don't want to hear six months late that you've been stuck on something, okay? You just call Fred here. He'll keep in touch with you on this case. He likes it, anyway."

"Thank you, Judge," said Propper.

"Is there anything I can do to help you now?" asked the attorney general.

Propper cleared his throat. "As a matter of fact, yes, there is," he replied. "I've got an FBI agent who's the only person in this whole world who knows the case as well as I do. He's done a bang-up job. But somebody in the Bureau took him off the case, saying he's too close to it. And that's crap. Pardon me, but it is. He's worked himself to death on the case, but that doesn't mean he's too close to it. Whatever that means. We've been making joint decisions on almost everything, and now it's hard for me to get things done with the Bureau."

Attorney General Bell was nodding along. He turned to Baron. "Call up Adams and take care of it," he said.

"His name is Carter Cornick," said Propper.

"Is there anything else?" asked Bell.

"No, sir," said Propper. "Thank you very much, Judge." He nursed a grin all the way back to his office. It took him some time to track Cornick down by phone.

"We've done it!" he cried. "You're back on the case."

"Bullshit," scoffed Cornick.

"I'm not kidding," said Propper. "You should be getting a call any day now. I bitched to the attorney general, and he told his assistant to call Adams and take care of it. Just like that."

Cornick was stuck between disbelief and fright. "Adams?" he said. "They're calling Adams?"

"He already did," said Propper. "Baron just told me he called and he thinks everything will be all right."

"Gene, you damned fool!" said Cornick. "I'm already off the case, and now you're going to get my ass fired!"

"What do you mean I'm going to get you fired?"

"They'll think I went around them and put you up to it," said Cornick. "They'll go apeshit."

"So what?"

"Goddamn it, Gene! The attorney general doesn't even know how to write a memo yet. You think the Bureau's going to get pushed around by *him?* Fuckin' Adams has been around twenty-five years, and he's buried more agents than you'll ever know . . ."

". . . You'll see . . ."

". . . For Christ's sake. You've really cooked me now."

Two days later, Cornick rushed into Propper's office wearing a look of awe. "Oh, these ain't the Hoover days anymore," he proclaimed. "I can see it now. Until now, when they took you off a case, there wasn't *anybody* who could put you back on. Bobby Kennedy was attorney general, but he couldn't even get a copy of the Bureau phone book!"

"Carter, what happened?" Propper asked impatiently.

"I'll tell you what happened," said Cornick. "I was out in the middle of nowhere chasing a fat lady fugitive, and the next thing I heard was Stames telling me to get my ass back over to the U.S. Attorney's Office on the Letelier case."

Cornick returned to duty just in time for a great explosion of misunderstandings, both in public and within the government. Admiral McIntyre inspired a number of them. In late March, Cornick notified the Bureau that Propper had secured the admiral's agreement to take a polygraph examination regarding the Brigade lead. The news was not well received at headquarters, where officials had remained in firm opposition to the entire polygraph project. Now, Cornick learned, things were worse. Bureau officials, resentful of Propper for his role in forcing Cornick's reassignment to the case, pointed out that the FBI could not very well show up to administer a polygraph the Bureau had not requested. To do so would make it seem that the Bureau gave polygraphs for other people, such as Propper. That would never do. The only way for the Bureau to proceed with the plan at all would be for FBI agents to visit the Chilean embassy and ask for the polygraph all over again, as though Propper did not exist. Cornick relayed this news to Propper and endured the inevitable burst of invective from the prosecutor, who objected that such a move would be not only foolish and redundant but also dangerous. It would give the Chilean embassy the impression of a weak, divided United States government.

"They'll think we're idiots, Carter," said Propper. "That's crazy."

"So what's new?" Cornick replied.

"Welcome back to the Letelier case," said Propper.

After much persuasion toward both sides, Cornick arranged to have an FBI delegation visit the Chilean embassy. He told headquarters that their mission was to propose the lie-detector test. He told Propper that their mission was to work out the details. He told the agents something in between.

On the morning of March 29, Propper arrived at the office before any of the other employees and was alone at his desk when the phone rang.

"Is Mr. Propper there?" asked a voice.

"Speaking," said Propper.

"If you don't get your ass off our case, you're gonna be in deep shit like Letelier," said the voice.

Blood rushed to Propper's neck. "Who's this?" he demanded. Then he heard a click.

Propper stood up and looked aimlessly around his empty office. Then he walked out into an empty corridor. There was no one to talk to. What was on his mind, aside from the raspy voice, was the fact that the call had come in on a private, direct line reserved for outgoing calls. The number did not appear in the phone book or on anyone's stationery. To Propper, this meant that the caller had either been in his office or knew someone who had been there. An hour later, he was telling all this to a swarm of FBI agents and security officers, who were bombarding him with questions he could not answer.

"How the hell do I know whether he was Cuban or Chilean?" cried Propper. "All I know is, he sounded funny."

Later, in private, Propper and Cornick tried to analyze the threat. They figured something must have triggered it—something recent. More than likely, the threat had come from someone who felt pressure. That might be one of the New Jersey Cubans. Propper had just subpoenaed Guillermo Novo and Dionisio Suárez back to the grand jury for an appearance the following week, hoping to lay the groundwork for a perjury charge by getting them to deny having gone to Venezuela. Novo's group seemed to be a possibility. So did the Brigade Cubans in Miami. With McIntyre's polygraph coming up shortly it was possible that a Chilean or someone connected with the Brigade lead had cracked.

Finally, as a long shot, Propper thought the threat might have come out of Venezuela. A young American reporter named Blake Fleetwood was then in Venezuela, by coincidence, to get a scoop for himself by interviewing Orlando Bosch in jail. He had stopped in to see Propper a few days earlier, on his way to Caracas. Propper had warned him by recalling the unfortunate experience of other reporters who had sought Bosch in Venezuela, but Fleetwood had seemed undaunted, citing his family connections to Venezuela and his acquaintance with Guillermo Novo. The reporter had intrigued Propper, who, on the off chance the mission might succeed, asked him to query Bosch on the Novo brothers and their involvement in the Letelier bombing. This conversation had taken place just several days earlier. Propper and Cornick wondered whether Fleetwood might have poked around in the right places and touched off a threat, but they couldn't quite imagine a convincing chain of events.

"Well, maybe it's nothing to worry about," teased Cornick. "They haven't got Wack yet."

Propper ignored this. "This isn't the kind of threat that bothers me," he said, trying to make the best of it. "When they call you up in advance, that's probably bullshit. If they were going to do it, they'd just do it. I don't want to hear from an informant that they're talking about it among themselves. That's what I don't want to hear."

Al Seddon missed all the stir over the death threat. He was driving out to rural Virginia that day for a visit with one of his old CIA contacts. The interviewee was a bomb expert. Unlike Seddon's, his job had been to use bombs, not just to know about them, and his personal history had bubbled along for years through coups and sabotage operations around the world.

The old bomb man, just retired, said he might have something really juicy for Seddon. Something strange had happened the previous September, he said. Another ex-CIA official had come to recruit him for a job in Libya, offering huge sums of money for little work. The man's name was Edwin Wilson, and the work he had spoken of involved explosives and great danger. Seddon's contact added that Wilson had displayed some of the wares he was using in his new, private, international bomb business. One of the items was a small plastic cylinder, about two inches in diameter and one inch in depth, from which Wilson had extracted a small electric circuit board, known in the trade as a "chip." Unfortunately, he had not examined it that closely, because he refused Wilson's contract and therefore didn't want to know too much. Anyway, he said, it appeared to be some sort of electrical timing device for a bomb, and Wilson had said that he possessed them in great quantities.

Seddon was interested. He discussed Wilson and hardware with his old contact as long as he could, and then he sped back to Washington. This was hot. Edwin Wilson sounded like a rogue spook from the Agency—involved with Libya, a country run by a maniac leftist named Qaddafi. And Wilson had been recruiting bomb men for missions in September of 1976, just before the Letelier bombing, using some sort of electrical timing device. This was all promising to Seddon, who had never believed the theory that the Sheridan Circle bomb had been detonated by remote control.

A quick FBI name check on Edwin Wilson turned up information that flashed in red. Lawyers in a small section of the Justice Department had been investigating Wilson for six months, trying to determine whether he should be prosecuted as an unregistered agent of the Libyan government. So far, FBI agents had come upon three CIA-trained Cuban exiles from Miami who swore that Wilson tried to recruit them for an assassination mission on behalf of the Libyan government, which the exiles had turned down after meeting with Wilson in Geneva on September 15, 1976. One of the Cubans had returned to Miami through Washington on September 19, 1976. Nobody in the Justice Department had made a connection to the Letelier case, apparently. To Seddon, the connection was obvious: the Cuban had been in Washington only two days before the murders of Letelier and Moffitt.

This was startling enough. But to an analyst of clandestine affairs like Seddon, the clue was even more tantalizing because it sounded so much like the Brigade lead. With only a few crucial changes, the information in the Wilson file would become a corroboration of everything Tomboy had told the Bureau. All that was needed was the last subtle insight to make the mental tumblers click into place. Was all the Libya talk a cover concocted by Wilson to hide his real mission, Letelier? Alternatively, was all the noise about the Chilean embassy and Admiral McIntyre nothing but a clever distraction to conceal Qaddafi's plot? Or was there another combination of players and motives? The elements for the solution of the mystery were all there in two parallel strands, too similar to explain as coincidence.

The excitement came at a bad time. Seddon was no longer the Letelier case agent. His supervisor and friend, Satkowski, had been rebuffed in his attempt to go to Venezuela. Satkowski's mentor, Nick Stames, and their allies at headquarters had just been firmly overruled in their effort to remove Cornick. By FBI rules, the Wilson file and the information from the old CIA bomb expert should go straight to Cornick, the case agent. Stames, Satkowski, and Seddon should surrender this hot new lead to the very agent who had so recently been forced upon them by Propper and Attorney General Bell.

This was too bitter a prospect. While the agents in Stames's personal circle generally carried on with their professional duties without regard to personal feelings, they could not completely ignore an opportunity to vindicate their judgment in the Letelier investigation. Technically, they reasoned, no hard information had yet connected Edwin Wilson to the Letelier case. Also, the discovery was Seddon's, not Cornick's, and the new information put the investigation squarely into Seddon's field of expertise—spies and double agents. It was precisely the kind of puzzle that should not be entrusted to Cornick, a Door Kicker. Any FBI intelligence officer could see that the situation required a more subtle approach. And any supervisor at headquarters could predict that if Cornick knew about the Wilson lead, Propper would soon find out, which would mean grand-jury subpoenas and leaks and a host of things unpleasant to both bureaucrats and Palm Tree Peekers.

So no one informed Cornick about Edwin Wilson or Seddon's interview. At least for the time being, it was deemed preferable to make discreet inquiries of the Justice Department lawyers handling the Wilson investigation. Satkowski knew people at Justice. So did Stames.

On April 4, Propper told Larry Barcella that hot news from Venezuela had been pouring into both his ears all morning. On one side, reporter Blake Fleetwood was just back from Caracas, with tapes of a six-hour interview he had conducted with Orlando Bosch. Propper was incredulous. Fleetwood said he had simply walked into the jail during visiting hours. (There were rumors, however, that he had sneaked in disguised as a priest.) Contrary to all the high-minded statements from the Venezuelan Ministry of Justice, Bosch had been positively eager to talk, Fleetwood reported, about terrorism, the Novo brothers, and his own collaborations with official Venezuelans —up to and including President Pérez. Fleetwood had agreed to let Propper make a copy of his tapes, and Propper wanted to have them by the next day so that he could play them for Guillermo Novo as a shock treatment.

On the other side, Propper told Barcella, the Venezuela desk at the State Department had been calling to pass along a series of unhappy messages from the American embassy in Caracas. Ambassador Vaky had learned of Fleetwood's miraculous interview, and far from rejoicing over its potential for assisting in the Letelier case and the war against terrorism, the ambassador was unhappy. He was unhappy because President Pérez was unhappy, and nearly to the same degree. President Pérez had ordered DISIP to arrest Fleetwood, but DISIP had failed. Fleetwood had slipped back out of the country with his tapes. The Venezuelan government sent word to the American embassy that Fleetwood was a CIA agent in cahoots with Propper. Ambassador Vaky was demanding an explanation. The Venezuela desk officer had just advised Propper that the ambassador would prefer it in writing. Specifically, Propper should address himself to Fleetwood's conduct as his "agent" and to the issue of whether the use of Fleetwood constituted a breach of faith with the Venezuelan government, being a sneaky tactic that would result in embarrassing publicity about the Pérez regime.

"That sounds like Venezuela, all right," quipped Barcella. As he and Propper fell into a tactical discussion on the use of the tapes, a phone call interrupted them.

Propper raised his eyebrows and put his hand over the transmitter. "It's Bob Woodward," he told Barcella.

Barcella pretended to be impressed. He twirled a forefinger in the air and mouthed the word "Whoopee," in tribute to the famous *Washington Post* reporter.

Woodward advised Propper that he was working on a story about the Letelier assassination. He had information that a principal suspect in the investigation was a former CIA officer named Edwin Wilson, who had been shipping explosives to the Libyan government and who had conspired with three Cuban bomb experts, one of whom had come to Washington on September 19, two days before Letelier was murdered.

"That's news to me," Propper said skeptically.

"It is?" said Woodward. "You've never heard of it?"

"Never," said Propper.

"All right," said Woodward. "But I hear that people over in the Justice Department have been investigating Wilson for a long time, and they think he might have been behind the Letelier assassination. In fact, they think it's so sensitive that they are intentionally keeping the whole thing from you. It makes sense that you haven't heard about it."

"That's impossible," said Propper.

"No, it isn't," countered Woodward. "I've been told that by reliable sources. The story's pretty hard that they're making Wilson a prime target in the case."

Propper was puzzled and alarmed. "Wait a minute," he said. "I'm telling you that Wilson *can't* be a target in the Letelier investigation, because I'm running it and I've never heard of him! I guess it's possible that Justice has something else going on Wilson . . ."

"It's more than possible," said Woodward. "It's true. I think it's clear that there are things going on that you don't know about."

"Quite frankly, I don't think so," said Propper, his conviction slightly shaken. "I can't believe that anybody in the Justice Department would keep information about the Letelier investigation from me."

"The people saying so are pretty high up," said Woodward.

Propper sighed. Woodward's tone was even and authoritative. "I'll tell you what," said Propper. "I'll find out if they're investigating Wilson. I can do that real quick. And if it's true that somebody's hiding stuff about Letelier from me, I promise you that I'll call you and say so. For quotation. I'll probably get fired for it, because I'm not supposed to talk to the press. But if they're hiding anything from me, I shouldn't be on the case, anyway."

"All right," said Woodward. "But I can't promise to hold the story."

Propper asked for time. After sparring and trading home phone numbers, they reached a brief truce. Propper hung up and turned to Barcella, who appeared overcome by curiosity. "Larry, you won't believe this," he said.

The next day, Guillermo Novo showed up to comply with his subpoena and preempted the drama Propper had planned by announcing that he would answer no questions before the grand jury. Novo would plead the Fifth Amendment as a protest against the government's baseless harassment of himself and his movement. He had instructed his two companions from the CNM to do the same. Propper played the Bosch tape anyway, just to study Novo's reactions. Novo flinched at the sound of Bosch's voice, but he did not lose his composure. Nor did he say anything, except that Bosch was infamous for his big mouth. Propper excused Novo and escorted the other two Cubans into the grand-jury room. Each pleaded the Fifth Amendment. Propper had never met Alvin Ross before. Ross impressed him as a rather coarse man, with a gravel voice, who seemed unable to endure silence. Ross kept making speeches about how much the FBI had mistreated him and how he would never crack.

Dionisio Suárez, by contrast, was consistently soft-spoken, as he had been the previous October. In waiting rooms, and again before the grand jury, he only smiled when Propper asked him whether he had accompanied Guillermo Novo and Orlando Bosch to Venezuela. It was a soft, gentlemanly smile. Suárez always said he was sorry, that he did not wish to make trouble for Propper, but he could not help—he would follow Novo's injunction to remain silent. Propper liked Suárez in spite of himself. Suárez's lawyer described him as a community leader in New Jersey—as the person who had received the pen with which the governor of New Jersey signed the Cuban-America Day proclamation. Propper believed it, and he felt some compunction when he warned Suárez to choose between answering his questions and serving time in the D.C. jail.

Suárez had scarcely departed when Cornick called to remind Propper that it was time for Admiral McIntyre's polygraph. Propper regarded the lie-detector test as the most critical moment in the investigation to date. Its outcome would affect his estimation of the Brigade lead, of the Chilean government, of Tomboy and the FBI, and all these in turn would affect the status of the Novo lead and even the new Wilson story from Bob Woodward. Leads would go up or down in importance. Confidence and suspicion would become rearranged.

Propper walked to the FBI's Washington field office in time to see Admiral McIntyre and Tony McMahon emerge from a long, black limousine. The admiral was out of uniform. He wore a conservative business suit and was immaculately groomed. As Cornick led the group into the creaky old hand-cranked elevator, the tension silenced everyone except the admiral himself, who was chatting confidently about how he was pleased to do anything that might help solve the Letelier case. Shortly thereafter, McMahon departed and McIntyre disappeared into a room with the polygraph operator.

"This is it, Carter," said Propper, who began to pace the corridor, stopping occasionally to peer through the dirty windows at the enclosed courtyard far below.

Ten minutes passed, then twenty and thirty. By then, Propper was lashing out against the ineptitude of the polygraph man and speculating incessantly about the implications of one outcome or the other. He was walking so rapidly that Cornick had trouble keeping up.

Inside, after laborious explanations, the polygraph operator was halfway through his questions, speaking in a slow monotone, like a speech therapist. "Do you know who killed Letelier?" he asked.

"No," said Admiral McIntyre, strapped and wired about the head, chest, and arms.

"Did you have a meeting with certain Cubans wherein they admitted carrying out assassinations for DINA?" asked the operator.

"No," said McIntyre.

When it was over, McIntyre left to shake hands with Cornick and Propper, who contained themselves in dignified poses until the Chilean was safely deposited in the elevator. Then Propper ran for the polygraph room, only to find the door locked.

"He must be figuring out the results, Gene," said Cornick.

"I thought he could tell by looking at the chart as he went along," grumbled Propper. "What's taking him so long?"

There was more pacing. Finally, the operator stepped out into the corridor, instantly attracting a crowd of two.

"Well, how does it look?" asked Cornick, trying to be casual.

"I'm not finished," said the operator. "But I know it's gonna be nondeceptive."

"Nondeceptive?" said Cornick, as Propper drew in a deep, cushioning breath.

"Yeah, I'm sorry," said the operator. "He only lied once, and that was on a test question when I asked him if he's ever done anything illegal in the service of his country. He said no, and the needle went crazy. That was a whopper. But he passed on all your Letelier questions."

Cornick and Propper walked off by themselves. They folded their arms and sighed back and forth. "Well, that's that," said Cornick.

"I guess so," said Propper. "I thought you said the Bureau would solve this case by Christmas."

Cornick looked at the floor. Then he smiled. "I didn't say which Christmas," he replied.

"Carter, this isn't funny anymore," said Propper.

"I know it, Gene," said Cornick. "But this test is not that big a disaster either. That's what I've been trying to tell you. They wouldn't have let him come over here if they knew he would flunk it. And even if he had flunked, we couldn't do much with him. We couldn't subpoena him, because of his immunity. All we could have done was to lean harder on people we're leaning on anyway. From an investigative standpoint, it wouldn't have taken us very far."

"I would have beat the Chileans over the head with it all the way to Santiago," Propper said, almost wistfully.

"Yeah, but it still wouldn't have solved the case, Gene," said Cornick. "It wouldn't have given us any evidence."

"Yeah, but at least we'd know we were on the right track," said Propper. "I could taste it. Now we don't know a fucking thing. We still don't even know what the bomb was made of!"

"Take it easy."

"And for all we know, Tomboy might be lying," said Propper. "That's one thing, Carter. Miami has got to polygraph Tomboy now, after this. They can't screw around with us anymore. They've been doing it for months."

"You know I agree," said Cornick. "I'll get the teletype down there tomorrow. After this, I know Stames will back me up."

"That would be nice, for a change," remarked Propper.

Cornick sighed. "Don't jump to conclusions," he said. "This test doesn't mean Tomboy is lying. He told us what he was told, and what he heard could have been wrong in some ways and not in others. Don't forget, he gave us the names of two killers. He could be right about them. Look, I still tend to believe him. I think the Brigade did it. As far as I'm concerned, this test means we're in the right church but the wrong pew."

Propper wrinkled up his nose. "What?"

"I said I think we're in the right church but the wrong pew," drawled Cornick.

"That's what I thought you said."

While the admiral was being polygraphed, Scherrer was sitting in a small office at the American consulate in Santiago, Chile, going through citizenship registration files. He was looking for Novo's al-

leged DINA contact, the blond Chilean, armed with some new information from Larry Wack. One of Wack's informants had reported
that the blond Chilean had been sighted at a restaurant and bar in
Union City known as the Bottom of the Barrel, a gathering place for
Cuban exiles. There, said the source, the blond Chilean's companions
had referred to him as "El Flaco," the thin one. And one of the companions, clearly boastful of his connections to such an international
operative, had remarked that El Flaco liked to fly airplanes and drive
fast motorcycles. He also said that El Flaco was a Chilean of mixed
parentage. One parent was an American. Or a German.

This vague report had passed from the companion to the source to
Wack, then to FBI headquarters, and finally down to Scherrer, who
thought he might make something of it. He knew from experience
that South Americans of mixed American parentage usually tried to
maintain their American citizenship, even in reserve, so that they
could travel to the United States on an American passport, free of
visa restrictions. He also knew that anyone who lived in Chile and
claimed American citizenship was required to fill out a registration
card at the American consulate. Therefore, reasoned Scherrer, the
blond Chilean might be registered. His parents could have registered
him years before.

Painstakingly, Scherrer examined each of the nearly sixteen hundred registration cards. Most of them had photographs pasted on
them, as required by the consulate. Scherrer compared the photographs and the biographical information with the source information
on the blond Chilean. It took him two days to finish the job, and the
result was a list of ten suspects. Now Scherrer faced the task of
checking them out—looking for a motorcycle rider or a political activist, hoping for an intelligence officer or a bomb man. His chances
were slim and the work was tedious, but at least Scherrer could investigate them legally, as Americans, without fear of being arrested
himself for espionage. In the Letelier investigation, this was a rare
consolation for him.

Some weeks later, he would report that all ten suspects checked
out without promise. Another long shot had failed.

Propper arrived at work the day after the polygraph in a depressed state, which worsened as he read the file on the Edwin Wilson case. There was indeed an ongoing investigation of Wilson's
activities on behalf of Libya, but the details in the file didn't seem to
point to the Letelier murder. There was too much travel to Libya and
too much involvement in the Middle East. And while the pattern of

facts was superficially attractive as a shadow of the Brigade lead, there were elements that did not fit Propper's conception of murderers. For one thing, the three Cuban exiles from Miami had *volunteered* to American authorities the information that Wilson had contacted them about the Libyan murder contract. Propper found it difficult to believe that they would assassinate Letelier and then, under no compulsion, seek out the FBI and CIA to place themselves in the middle of another murder conspiracy. By now, Propper had accepted the likelihood that the people he was after would be devious and crafty, like spies, but he still expected them to behave like killers. In his mind, this was over the line.

He called for an appointment with Tony Lapham at the CIA, saying that he had some new questions and some new people he wanted the Agency to check out. Lapham invited Propper to CIA headquarters right away. By coincidence, he said, he had just finished drafting the Agency's reply to Propper's questions about the CORU meeting, Orlando Bosch's terrorist summit conference the previous year. Lapham would be happy to exchange the old answers for the new questions.

"By the way," said Lapham, "there's not much in here on those meetings, so don't expect a lot. Most of what we have came from the Bureau, so you've already got it."

"Are you sure?" asked Propper, knowing something was wrong. "Carter's been telling me the Bureau has next to nothing."

Cornick paid his daily visit to the courthouse that afternoon, after Propper had returned from the Agency. He knew there was trouble as soon as Propper jumped up from behind his desk to commence his prosecutorial stalk. Cornick had no time to sit down.

"Carter, did you check the Bureau files on CORU yourself?" asked Propper.

"No. I had it done. I always do."

"How many times did they check?"

"Enough," snapped Cornick. "What's the problem, Gene?"

Propper thrust Lapham's memorandum into Cornick's hands. "Are those real Bureau file numbers there?" he asked.

"Yes," said Cornick. As he read, his formidable FBI presence shriveled. "Son-of-a-bitch," he whispered, backing out the door. "Don't say another word, Gene. You stay here. I'll be right back."

While Cornick was gone, Propper called one of the lawyers in the Justice Department's foreign-agents-registration section to say that he wanted to talk with Edwin Wilson and the three Cubans unless it might interfere with prosecution of the Libyan matter. The lawyer replied that Propper should go ahead. Justice did not appear to have a prosecutable case.

Less than thirty minutes later, Propper received a call from Bob Woodward. "I understand you've gotten permission from the Justice Department to question Wilson in the Letelier investigation," said Woodward.

"Who told you that?" asked Propper.

"I can't tell you," said Woodward. "But it's true, isn't it?"

"I'm not saying," said Propper, who despaired of giving a convincing denial. Woodward knew too much. "This is rather incredible," he fumed. "And I don't mind telling you, it pisses me off. A leak like this could really screw up the case."

"Then it's true?" pressed Woodward.

"I just told you I'm not . . ."

". . . If it's a leak that bothers you, it must be true, right?"

"Not necessarily," said Propper. He paused to compose himself. "Look, all I'm saying is that if it is true, and if I'm about to talk to Wilson and the Cubans, you could really screw it up by printing it. You'd tip them off about what I'm after, and they'd just get their stories together."

They sparred inconclusively, with Woodward chipping his way toward a confirmation and Propper asking for time. The call ended in a stalemate, short of a truce. Propper directed ugly thoughts toward the incontinent leakers in the Justice Department. Someone must have been on the phone to Woodward within minutes of Propper's phone call to Justice, he guessed.

Propper was mulling over Woodward's advantage when Cornick returned, carrying a file. "You won't believe this," he said, with a look of resigned disgust.

"Yes, I will," said Propper. "Nothing could surprise me."

"Well, headquarters did it to us again," said Cornick. "Miami sent all the CORU stuff up under a special intelligence caption. So it didn't show up when we searched the files."

"They gave it to the Agency, but they wouldn't give it to you?" said Propper. "Is that right?"

"I don't know what the hell happened," said Cornick.

"Oh boy," sighed Propper. "That's just great."

A rough weekend followed a bad week. On Saturday, Propper became thirty years old. He felt fifty. On Sunday, he debated whether to resubpoena Suárez and Ross, to seek their testimony again under a grant of immunity, and to throw them in jail if they still refused. Propper had never before jailed a witness for refusing to testify. The idea was repugnant to him, because Ross and Suárez were innocent, for all he knew. And the prosecutor's immunity power was extremely arbitrary. On the other hand, Propper knew the investigation was floundering. He had to increase the pressure. On Monday, he would write out subpoenas for Ross and Suárez, and apply to Justice for grants of immunity.

On Sunday afternoon, Propper was at home in bed with his steady girlfriend of the last few months when the phone rang. It was Bob Woodward. Propper bolted upright and whispered as much to the woman beside him.

"Bob Woodward?" she said, eyes wide.

"Shhh," said Propper, who then spoke to Woodward. "Listen, I still can't talk to you about this. The whole thing is at a very sensitive stage, so I can't say anything one way or another."

Propper was listening to Woodward when he heard a voice in his ear. "If you don't talk to him, you're not getting any," she said.

"What?" said Propper. "Just a minute," he said to Woodward. "What do you mean?" he asked of the voice.

"Just what I said," she replied.

Propper felt sorry for himself. "Excuse me," he said to Woodward.

"I don't really need any confirmation from you," said Woodward. "The basic story's solid enough to go with already, and I'm under pressure here to get it out. There are only a few little things I'd like confirmation on. For one thing, I've heard you had a meeting at the CIA and asked the Agency for all its files on Wilson and the Cubans. Is that true?"

Propper dodged and pleaded for delay of the story until he could question Wilson. Woodward outlined his story as it was already written. Parts of it were grossly inaccurate.

"This is ridiculous," said Propper. "How about this? If I confirm some things and correct some of the errors, will you agree to wait a few days until I can interview the Cubans?"

"I can't make any promises," said Woodward.

Propper sighed. "It sounds as if I don't have anything to lose," he said. "All right. I did meet with the Agency about the files, but I haven't gotten them yet. That's why I'm trying to get you to hold off a few days. And you're wrong about Justice hiding anything from me. This whole thing grew out of an unrelated investigation. And

Wilson's not the new prime target in the case. In fact, so far it doesn't look right to me."

"But you are about to call him in? Right?"

"I'm about to call in a lot of people," said Propper. "On a lot of leads. Wilson's just one."

When the call was over, Propper asked sarcastically, "How was that?"

"Great," she said. "What does he sound like?"

"Like an air hammer," said Propper.

Woodward's story ran on the front page of *The Washington Post* Tuesday morning under the headline EX-CIA AIDE, 3 CUBAN EXILES FOCUS OF LETELIER INQUIRY. The enticing CIA angle helped the story create instant news bulletins on airwaves across the United States, Europe, and Latin America. The Woodward by-line also enhanced the story's news value, as editors doubtless suspected that Woodward was cracking the Letelier case as a sequel to his Watergate achievements.

In Washington, a multitude of interested parties reacted to the story according to their own diverse lights. And they reacted quite strongly. The Woodward story, as the first public announcement of a major break in the case, served as a kind of lightning rod to attract the deepest convictions of the various players and commentators. Propper spent the better part of the day in hiding, but he could not avoid Earl Silbert.

"Civiletti wants to see you," said Silbert. "Right now. Over in his office."

"He does?" said Propper. Benjamin Civiletti was Keuch's boss, the assistant attorney general in charge of the entire criminal division of the Justice Department.

"Yeah," said Silbert.

"What for?" asked Propper.

Silbert shrugged. "Probably about the Wilson leak," he said.

Propper walked from the courthouse to the Justice Department and into Civiletti's office. He had never been there before.

Civiletti, who was destined to succeed Griffin Bell as attorney general, began speaking before Propper could sit down. "Listen," he said sternly. "The attorney general has a strict policy against leaks, as you know. He is personally concerned about this Woodward story that's come out. Very concerned. I am told you did it."

"What?" cried Propper.

"I am told you did the leaking," Civiletti continued. "And the attorney general has asked me to talk with you about it, and if he decides you did do it, I am authorized to take you off the case."

Propper's mouth was open. "You have got to be kidding," he said slowly.

Civiletti shook his head in the negative. "This is not an unserious affair," he said gravely.

"You think I leaked the story to Woodward?" said Propper, trying to speak softly. "The attorney general thinks that? My God, Woodward leaked the story to *me!* Let me tell you something. He called me one day in my office. I didn't know him from Adam. And he laid this story on me that was so fantastic I asked him to repeat it." Propper went on with his story, temper rising. "Now you do anything you want to me," he concluded. "But you tell me how I would know about Libyans independent of Justice or Woodward. If I leaked it to Woodward when he didn't know about it, who told me? It's not a U.S. Attorney's Office case!"

Civiletti leaned back in his chair. "Well, what do you think happened?" he inquired in a conciliatory tone.

"I just told you what happened," said Propper. "It leaked to Woodward right out of General Crimes. It's not the first thing that's leaked out of there, and it won't be the last."

"All right," said Civiletti, with a trace of a smile. "Let me remind you that the attorney general has a policy not to talk to the press in major cases. Thank you, Gene."

Propper walked back to the courthouse and straight into Don Campbell's office.

"Did Earl know why I was going over there?" Propper asked Campbell.

"Yeah," said Campbell.

"Why didn't he tell me?"

"Because he didn't want you to have six or seven blocks to get steamed up about it," said Campbell. "He was afraid you'd tell Civiletti to stick it and walk out."

"Well, maybe he was right," Propper conceded. "I almost got fired anyway."

Over the next couple of days, the *Post*'s major competitors ran stories debunking Woodward's account. While reporters would not admit to feelings of jealousy toward Woodward, they did seem more eager to challenge him in print than to acknowledge that he had scooped them once again on the big one. Propper confirmed for some

of them that the Woodward story was misleading: Edwin Wilson was
not the focus of the Letelier investigation. Woodward and the *Post*
remained silent, which rivals took as a sign of retreat.

The public face of the Letelier investigation was now more confusing than ever. It appeared that Propper and his government colleagues, after months of confidential endeavor, had suddenly leaked
word that Edwin Wilson was the key to the bombing and then just as
suddenly undergone a change of mind. To conservative observers,
this erratic behavior was a sign that the investigation was on the
wrong track. Columnist William F. Buckley, Jr., wrote a story entitled "Letelier: The Mysteries Nobody's Probing," in which he wondered why Propper and *The Washington Post* were ignoring the real
story—Letelier's Communist tendencies. The *Post*, in apparent rebuttal, published an editorial on April 14 entitled "Who Killed Orlando Letelier?" wondering whether there was a "political brake" on
the investigation. The editorial raised suspicion that the CIA might
be impeding the work with leaks and subtle manipulations.

Saul Landau and Letelier's former colleagues at IPS agreed with
the *Post*. Landau had recently coauthored a magazine article under
the confident heading "This Is How It Was Done." Beginning with the
revelation that "a high-level DINA agent landed in Miami on September 13, 1976, and met with a group of Cuban exiles," the article
traced a group of four unnamed Cuban exiles up to Washington, into
the Chilean embassy, where they received logistical information on
how to kill Letelier, over to an alley near the IPS building, where
they attached the bomb to Letelier's car, and then down Massachusetts Avenue behind Letelier for the hit. In essence, the article had
presented a dramatic expansion of the Brigade lead. Propper and
Landau had argued about the article. It was annoying to Propper because Landau had presumed to know what the government investigators knew ("In crucial areas," said the article, "our conclusions
and those of the Justice Department match exactly. . . .") and because he had asserted as fact what Propper only suspected ("The
names of most of the killers, their motives, and their *modus ope-
randi* are now known to the Justice Department. . . ."). After Admiral
McIntyre passed his polygraph examination, Propper tried again to
emphasize that the Brigade lead was only a theory, but he did not tell
Landau about the polygraph itself. Landau thought he was vague,
possibly dissembling.

Relations between them fluctuated violently over the first three
days of the Woodward controversy. Initially, Landau hailed the story
and praised Propper for unearthing Edwin Wilson. He began to

amend his account of the bombing to make room for Wilson, and he did so with alacrity, having always wanted to believe that someone from the CIA had been in on the plot. Landau immediately fed Propper a series of reports about Wilson from his own stable of unnamed informants, about whom he was nearly as secretive as was the FBI about Bureau informants. Wilson was in hiding, said Landau. He would never show up to face Letelier charges and had arranged with his buddies at the CIA to shut off the flow of Agency information to Propper.

Things changed drastically with the publication of the stories indicating that Propper was disowning the Edwin Wilson lead. Landau found this incredible. To him, it was an indication that the CIA had put in a quick fix to protect Wilson.

Propper was trying to defend himself on this score when a collateral disaster struck. The Justice Department's press office issued its first statement on the Letelier case at 3:00 p.m. on April 14, the day of the *Washington Post* editorial. To Propper's mortification, the machinery of the department picked that day to release the statement he had promised the Chilean embassy in exchange for the McIntyre polygraph. The language was dry and the objective unstated, but reporters had no trouble interpreting the department's official statement as a rebuke to Isabel Letelier.

"Why the hell did you do that, Gene?" asked Landau.

"Saul, I can't tell you," Propper tersely replied. "All I can say is that I did it to help the investigation. I got something for it."

"Like what?"

"I can't tell you."

"Well, I can't accept that, and you know it."

"Saul, read the statement carefully. It doesn't say DINA didn't do it. It just says no one told Isabel that DINA did it."

"I know what it says," said Landau. "And I know the public impact, too. The public impact is that Isabel Letelier is wrong, DINA isn't so bad, and the Chilean embassy has been cooperative. That's what it is. Where did that 'cooperative' stuff come from?"

"I got something for that, too," said Propper, rather lamely. At the last minute the Chilean embassy had agreed to furnish official, sworn documents on Guillermo Novo's trip to Chile.

"Well, I don't see you getting anything, and I see Pinochet and his thugs getting a lot," said Landau. "That's what I see."

Propper tried to enlist Cornick's aid to blunt Landau's suspicions, with little success. All Landau and his supporters could see was that, within the span of three days, Propper was responsible for backing off a CIA lead, for gratuitously contradicting the widow of Orlando Letelier, for giving comfort to DINA, and for complimenting the embassy of Chile—all in public. Not surprisingly, Isabel Letelier and Michael Moffitt would travel more frequently and speak more harshly in the succeeding weeks and months, giving speeches and making television appearances all over the country, and overseas as well, always calling for the appointment of a special prosecutor.

They saw the controversy over the Woodward article as a betrayal. The attorney general saw it as a leak. Commentators saw it as a conspiracy of the right or left. And over in the FBI there was a select group that saw it as a tactical lesson.

For Stames, Satkowski, Seddon, and their supporters at headquarters, nothing was going according to plan. It was not the prospect of a substantive failure on the Wilson lead that bothered them. They knew that failures happen. What bothered them was the laxity of security. No sooner had their confidential inquiries begun than they were reading in the newspaper about Propper's plans to target Wilson. As a practical matter, it was impossible to conduct a discreet investigation in conjunction with the Justice Department, because word inevitably would leak back to Propper.

This was the tactical lesson. Security would have to be much tighter if the Stames group wished to run its own clandestine investigation. Justice would be cut out. Cornick would be cut out. To eliminate Cornick, the flow of Bureau paper would have to be severely restricted because of his access as Letelier case agent.

In that same month of April, a crime reporter brought a certain Chilean citizen to the attention of Nick Stames, confidentially. The Chilean knew the personnel of DINA backward and forward. Not only that, the Chilean had the ability to institute wiretaps in Chile. He hated DINA and might, under the right circumstances, work undercover on the Letelier case. And he just happened to be in the United States at the time and would meet with Stames under proper conditions of security.

Stames, Satkowski, and Seddon all met with the Chilean, who impressed them more and more with every conversation. His knowledge of Chilean law enforcement and Chilean intelligence was staggering—as was his knowledge of the Chilean phone system. Seddon guarded against the possibility of a double agent by insisting that the man pass a battery of tests, including a polygraph.

Final approval was up to Stames, and he decided to go all the way.

They would operate the informant, code name Gopher,* in Chile. It would be one of the most highly secret operations in the FBI, confidential to the director and to agents trusted by Seddon, Satkowski, and Stames. Cornick would be excluded specifically, in order to prevent leaks to Propper. And the CIA must never find out, since the Agency would object strongly to an overseas Bureau undercover agent. The entire investigation—as well as Gopher's life—depended on the strictest observance of secrecy.

In ignorance of the Gopher operation, Propper was making calculations on a grittier, less exotic plane: he decided to put only one of the two Cubans in jail. Such a move would confuse the CNM membership, he hoped, and might even plant suspicion that the free man was a source. Also, the move would create only one public martyr instead of two. Propper expected a public outcry against the contempt-of-court jailing of Cubans who were regarded in their own community as anti-Communist freedom fighters. Propper wanted to leave one of the two witnesses out on the street so that he would be free to talk about all the excitement in Washington with his CNM friends—some of whom, Propper hoped, would be FBI informants. Half the game, Propper knew, was to maneuver the guilty parties into situations where they were near informants and had a lot to boast of or complain about. The other half was to make use of the informant information, which was often the more difficult of the two steps.

On April 19, still undecided as to which witness he would move against, Propper called Jerry Sanford in Miami about a technical matter on the parole revocation application he was preparing against Guillermo Novo. As an aside, Propper said, "Listen, Jerry. I'm immunizing these two guys tomorrow, Alvin Ross Díaz and José Dionisio Suárez Esquivel. What do you know about them?"

"Not much," said Sanford. "They're New Jersey guys. But I think I did hear in the grand jury some time that Díaz is called *Cepillo*. That's his nickname."

"What does that mean?"

"It means 'the brush,' " said Sanford. "It means 'hit man.' "

"All right," said Propper. "I'll go against Suárez then. I'll put him in jail and leave Ross on the street." This had been his inclination al-

---

*Not the correct code name.

ready, as he believed that Alvin Ross was the more talkative of the two men.

The next morning, Chief Judge William B. Bryant signed an immunity order for Alvin Ross and Dionisio Suárez in a brief ceremony Propper always called "the blessing." Then Propper escorted them back down to the grand-jury room. For him, this was the unpleasant part of his move. He liked Suárez much better than Ross, and he could not imagine that Suárez had been involved in Letelier's murder. Suárez was too civilized and urbane. His wife was a respected child educator, founder of the Head-Start program in Puerto Rico and board member of a dozen organizations specializing in progressive education for disadvantaged children. On the way downstairs, Propper was nearly pleading with Suárez. "Listen, you've got to answer the questions," he said. "Otherwise you go to jail, and nobody wants that."

Suárez politely refused to answer the questions and went off to jail. Propper found Alvin Ross outside in the corridor, fortifying himself with a speech. "I'm ready," said Ross. "I'm not gonna say anything."

"I'm not putting you in," said Propper.

Ross blinked. His lawyer asked why not.

"I'm just not," said Propper. "Not today."

Ross, the lawyer, and a large group of supporters that included Guillermo Novo's brother, Ignacio, went off to a press conference,* at which they explained that Suárez knew nothing about the Letelier bombing but had refused to answer questions as a matter of conscience, believing that Propper was on a fishing expedition that would require each Cuban exile to inform on the activities of the others.

Edwin Wilson came to see Propper the next day accompanied by his lawyer, William Bittman (who had become a minor celebrity during Watergate by picking up bags full of cash left for his client Howard Hunt). Propper found Wilson's denial of involvement in the Letelier bombing convincing, and he decided not to put him before

---

*FBI supervisors sent an agent to the event with instructions to pose as a news reporter. Legitimate reporters discovered the ruse and protested to Propper that it violated the attorney general's explicit pledge not to use the press as a cover for clandestine FBI operations. Propper thought it was also silly and needless, inasmuch as the press conference had been open to the public.

the grand jury. He did not believe, however, that Wilson was as pure and innocent in all matters as he claimed to be—especially after Wilson declared he wouldn't know a bomb detonator from a coffee maker. Cornick didn't believe him either. "That son-of-a-bitch is lying," he said, after Wilson and Bittman had gone.

On Monday, April 25, Al Seddon brought Propper a report that Ricardo Morales was scheduled to arrive that day in Miami from Caracas. This was hot. Propper had been waiting to get at Morales for months. The Bureau could have no objection to his questioning Morales, he figured, now that Rolando Otero had been convicted in state court even without Morales's testimony. Propper wrote up a subpoena ordering Morales to appear before the grand jury in Washington that Wednesday.

Cornick came into Propper's office the next day at a trot. The good news was that Morales had been served with the subpoena; the bad news was that he would probably ignore it, as he had ignored witness subpoenas in the Otero trials. "You won't believe this, Gene," said Cornick. "Guess why the Monkey came up to Miami?"

"I have no idea," said Propper, incensed at the thought that Morales might scoff at his subpoena.

"One of the bomb guys in Miami just told me," said Cornick. "It seems that the Monkey came up to address the International Association of Bomb Technicians down there. It's more or less an official group. And get this. His speech is called 'Bombings I Have Done.' "

"You're right, Carter," Propper said. "I don't believe you."

"It's true," said Cornick. "By God, it's true. I could never make that up. He was supposed to give a big speech to their convention down there. Bureau people are speaking, too. I say was, because the guys down there read him the riot act. They won't let a former Bureau informant give a speech like that. No telling what the Monkey might say."

Propper was holding his forehead. "Carter, I don't trust the Miami FBI office on this. They've got to *follow* Morales to make sure he gets on the plane to come up here, okay? Nothing covert or anything. Just surveil him right out in the open."

"I don't know if they'll do it," said Cornick. "But I'll try." He began making calls on one of Propper's phones. Propper called Jerry Sanford on the other. They spoke of Orlando Bosch and the latest rumors on Morales.

"By the way," said Sanford. "Remember what I told you about *Ce-*

pillo? Well, I've talked to some people down here and it's Suárez, not Díaz, who's the brush."

"*Suárez?*" cried Propper, scaring Cornick. "It can't be! I've already immunized Suárez!" He relayed the news to Cornick.

"Don't worry, Gene," said Cornick. "I'm not sure about that *Cepillo* stuff anyway."

Propper told this to Sanford, then turned back to Cornick. "Jerry says he's pretty sure, Carter," he said. "He's been talking to some FBI agent down there who says Suárez has killed more than seventy men. He used to give the *coup de grâce* in executions for Castro."

Cornick closed his eyes. "Hang up the phone, Gene," he said softly.

Propper thanked Sanford and hung up. "What's the matter?" he asked.

"Gene, the Bureau should have told me what they know about Suárez," said Cornick. "Not Sanford. It's just like the CORU stuff. We don't get coordination from headquarters. I've got to go rattle some cages."

"Go ahead," said Propper. "I'm going to Keuch. I can't take this anymore. Those guys are gonna kill us if we don't put a stop to this. Suárez has immunity, Carter. He could have walked into that grand jury and said, 'Okay, I killed Orlando Letelier and Ronni Moffitt.' And then he would have just walked right out of there a free man. I'd have tried to indict him anyway on independent evidence, but as a practical matter that's almost impossible. He could have walked."

Ricardo Morales did not show up the next day, and the Miami FBI office sent up a message asking Propper not to seek an arrest warrant. Propper told Cornick that he was weary of fighting, but that it was nothing that wouldn't be cured by solving the case.

11 ◪ BABY JACKAL

The female DINA agent has dark auburn hair, a petite frame, and a face whose beauty has only just begun to lose to middle age. She complains that there is no time to visit the Cloisters, the medieval museum in New York to which she remembers fleeing on hundreds of occasions to escape her overbearing mother-in-law. But that was several lifetimes ago, in the 1950s, when she was a frightened Chilean trying to be a beatnik and a Jewish wife at the same time. Now she is a secret agent with a long list of people to kill in Mexico City.

The mission occupies only part of her mind, however. She understands the reason for the blind haste, but she questions why they have to accept third-class lodgings in a cheap motel near the Lincoln Tunnel. She and her lanky blond partner are carrying more than $25,000 in cash for operational expenses—bestowed upon them personally by Colonel Contreras—but her partner does not want to spend any of it on questionable luxuries, such as a nice hotel. As always, he is practical to a fault.

She believes he is also far too tolerant of the brainless hatreds of the Cuban exiles, and she warns him that she will not listen passively to more talk of killing Jews or of Hitler's admirable qualities. Having heard little else from the potential recruits they have just rejected in Miami, she has decided that she doesn't care how important the Cubans might be for the mission: she will tell them off. If Novo's people behave that way, she will tell them her name is Ana Goldman and she will put on the large brass Star of David she always carries with her. In Chile, she has done so many times, just to silence the crudities of the ignorant militiamen she finds all too prevalent in DINA.

Her partner accepts all these declarations as the price of her approval, her quick-witted assistance, and her judgment. He says nothing in rebuttal as he drives their rented car through the tunnel into New Jersey for the rendezvous. They are to meet Guillermo Novo at the Four Star Diner in Union City, which turns out to be a bustling place. Having taken their seats, the two agents write their DINA names on a napkin—Andrés Wilson and Ana Pizarro. They hope Novo sees it, for he has no other way of recognizing them.

Not long after the scheduled time, two men walk by their booth and return to sit down unobtrusively. The one in the three-piece suit introduces himself as Novo. His companion is Dionisio Suárez.

Novo looks suspiciously at Andrés Wilson, who looks and sounds more Germanic than Latin, and he reviews the series of cryptic underworld messages by which the two DINA agents have been recommended to him. "As of now, I believe nothing," he says. "We have to be careful, you understand. Now tell me what you want."

"My superiors in the service have ordered me to seek your assistance for a mission," Wilson begins. He hints vaguely at the nature of the work, and he compliments the anti-Communist commitment of Novo's organization.

Novo appears unimpressed. "What kind of mission is it?" he asks.

"It is a mission of some personal danger, targeted against enemies of Chile," Wilson replies uncomfortably. "You will learn more, of course, if you agree to help."

"Where is the operation to take place?" Novo asks.

"Outside the United States," says Wilson.

"Where?" presses Novo. "We do not operate everywhere, you know."

"Mexico," Wilson replies.

"When?" asks Novo.

"Soon," says Wilson. "I cannot be more specific. I have already trusted you more than security allows."

"That is true," Novo says solemnly. "What kind of help do you want, exactly?"

"Documents, mainly," says Wilson. "Since the Mexican police are hostile to Chile, we don't want Chile to appear on any of our documents. We want American ones. And we'd like to borrow some equipment."

"What kind of equipment?" asks Novo.

"I can't tell you that now," says Wilson.

"And yet you are in a hurry," Novo says unpleasantly.

"That's true," says Wilson. "But we are also careful."

"So are we," says Novo. "And so far you haven't given me any reason to trust you or to help you."

"You will have to make your own decision about whether to trust us," says Wilson. "I am under orders not to make a show of my connection to the government. Therefore, I can't try to impress you with official contacts here in the United States. For this mission, I am on my own. But if you choose to work with me, you will see the powers behind us. You can minimize your risk until you come to believe that we are who we say we are. And I know why you should help us. You should help us because your movement has just committed itself in public to a war against Communism 'on all roads of the world.' For that kind of war, you need help, and there is no more powerful ally in that cause than the government of Chile."

"Chile has given very little assistance to the Cuban exiles who want to eliminate Castro," says Novo.

"My government has not responded favorably to every request," says Wilson, "but there are reasons for that. Many of your Cuban groups have been penetrated by Castro or by the CIA. That raises serious problems of security, and our service, DINA, is a new one. We have not had time yet to learn which groups can be trusted. That's why you had so much trouble when you visited Santiago."

Wilson waits for Novo's reaction to this disclosure that he knows about Novo's secret trip to Chile. Novo, however, makes no sign of surprise, fear, or pleasure. "Go on," he says impassively.

"I know that you and Suárez and Orlando Bosch came to Santiago just two months ago, in early December," says Wilson. "I know because I was there in the DINA foreign operations office when the call came in saying that you would be arriving. At the time, I knew very little about you or Suárez, but I recognized the name Bosch. I knew that his group was once penetrated by Monkey Morales and that as a result Bosch was sent to jail. I knew that Bosch's group, Acción Cubana, is suspected of being penetrated by the CIA. So I advised my superiors to be very wary of Bosch. In that way, I'm afraid I was responsible for the harsh treatment you received when you arrived. I apologize for that."

"That is all very interesting," says Novo. "But how do we know that you don't work for the CIA? What kind of assurance can you give us?"

"That would be very difficult to prove," Wilson observes. "What kind of assurance would you like?"

"Nothing you could say or do would convince me," says Novo. "We will have to do some checking ourselves."

"There is very little time," says Wilson.

"We need very little time," says Novo. "I should tell you that I am not offended by what you say about Bosch. He is a useful tool for the Cuban exiles, as a symbol, but he talks too much and is too much of a politician. Right now, we need soldiers."

"We are looking for soldiers, too," says Wilson.

Novo almost smiles. "Well, Dionisio here is the best there is in the world," he says. "He is much too valuable for us to lend him to you, but there are others. If you are not CIA, there are others."

"If that is your only worry, we'll have no problems," says Wilson.

Novo soon promises to contact the DINA agents at noon the next day with his answer. He insists that they check into a Howard Johnson's motel just outside Union City, so that he will be able to contact them there. They cannot contact him or Suárez.

At the new motel, Novo and Suárez watch the DINA agents check in to their room. Ana Pizarro appears unhappy, believing that they have trusted the Cubans too much by giving away their purpose and their location in exchange for nothing. Novo seems to understand her worries by telepathy. As he and Suárez are leaving, he bows politely to Pizarro and says, "Well, madam, I'm afraid that is a risk you will have to take."

Inside the motel room, Wilson says, "I think these guys are serious." Pizarro agrees, noting that Guillermo Novo is the first gentleman she has met among the Cuban exile leaders. She thinks he has the bearing of a nobleman.

The next morning, a half hour before the scheduled return of the Cubans, Pizarro is reading a novel and Wilson is sitting on the motel room bed when the door opens with a thunderous crack and three men burst into the room. They are wearing suits and elegant black leather gloves, and they carry what appear to be .45-caliber automatic pistols.

Wilson reacts instinctively to the shock by jumping off the bed to close the window curtain. He feels all three guns pointed at him.

"Was that a signal to your people outside?" Guillermo Novo angrily demands.

"What people?" says Wilson.

"The ones who might be waiting out there to trap us," says Novo.

"We don't have any people," Wilson says lamely.

"Good," says Novo. "Do you mind if we look through your belongings?"

Wilson does not reply to the rhetorical question. One of Novo's companions, Armando Santana, has already dumped the contents of their suitcases on the bed. He is sifting through the items in great haste. The third man, Dionisio Suárez, has taken a seat on the couch beside Pizarro. He holds his pistol across his knee and gives her a look of amusement that she finds more frightening than the shock or the guns. Pizarro clings to her novel.

Novo, pointing his gun at Wilson's chest, demands that Wilson surrender the keys to the rented car. He tosses them to Santana, who soon returns with some papers he has found in the trunk.

Novo looks through them in grim triumph. "You seem to have many passports under many different names, my friend," he says. "That is not very professional of you, is it?"

"It's part of the business," says Wilson.

"I don't think so," says Novo, holding up one of the passports. "You say you are a Chilean DINA agent, but this passport says you are an American named Kenneth Enyart. How is that?"

"I can explain it," says Wilson. "I have used that identity for the service."

"No, I can explain it," Novo says angrily. "You are CIA! You are trying to make us believe you are DINA, but you are CIA!"

"We are not CIA!" says Wilson. "We are DINA!"

Novo sighs wearily. "You understand that we have no alternative, don't you?" he asks, glancing at Suárez. Pizarro notices that Suárez is still smiling and that he has been sitting for some time in exactly the same position. She wonders if she will be allowed to write a note to her children.

"Wait a minute!" cries Wilson. "I can convince you that we are DINA, because I know things that only someone in DINA would know. When you and Suárez and Bosch came to Chile, I know for a fact that you were arrested at the airport and taken to the DINA interrogation center with hoods over your heads. Isn't that true? And you were questioned for nearly forty-eight hours straight. Isn't that true?"

"It was very unpleasant," Novo acknowledges. "And not very hospitable."

"But very professional," says Wilson. "And I know that the service decided to have nothing to do with you, mostly because of

Bosch. But they released you and let you move around Santiago. And you had numerous other contacts in Chile. And you even presented a written petition to the President himself, asking him to recognize your group as the Cuban government-in-exile. Bosch is still there in Santiago, waiting for an answer. And unless I miss my guess, he'll be waiting for a hell of a long time, because nobody wants anything to do with him. Isn't all this true? Doesn't it prove something to you?"

"Yes. It proves to me that the CIA probably has a man inside DINA," Novo says tersely.

"That's all?" says Wilson. "What do you mean?"

"Just what I said," says Novo.

Wilson walks nervously in small circles, under the watchful eyes of Suárez and Santana. Suddenly he snaps his fingers. "There's something else," he says. "There's a guy at the Chilean Military Mission in Washington who's helped me get some of my equipment delivered up here. You can call him. He'll vouch for me."

Novo considers the proposal and shrugs. "It can't hurt, I guess," he says, moving toward the telephone. He reaches the Chilean Military Mission and asks for Wilson's contact. Novo questions him about Andrés Wilson. "What does he look like?" he asks, eyeing Wilson.

Wilson is breathing more easily when Novo hangs up. "There," he says. "Now do you believe me?"

"No," says Novo. "Now I believe that the CIA probably has a man inside the Chilean Military Mission. That's what I believe."

Wilson rubs his eyes in frustration. "Well, it's against orders, but I guess we'll have to call Santiago," he says miserably. "They'll probably deny knowing us."

Pizarro suddenly leaps to her feet, drawing the attention of the guns. "I can't take any more of this!" she shouts. "If you are going to do something, then do it! But stop clowning around! You people probably believe that *chair* works for the CIA!"

Novo recoils slightly from the outburst. "You have spirit," he tells Pizarro. "But you have no idea how much the Cubans have suffered because they trusted the CIA."

"That's right, and I don't care!" says Pizarro. "We are DINA, and we have a job to do. If you are going to kill us, like the Communists want to, then go ahead and do it. I have lived long enough."

"We are only following the requirements of security," says Novo.

"That's how you see it," retorts Pizarro. "But that is not how DINA will see it if something happens to us."

"That's all right, Ana," says Wilson. "They are just trying to protect themselves. That's good, from our point of view. And I have used poor tradecraft by bringing more than one set of identity papers with me."

"You drop out of nowhere," Novo says tersely. "You speak with a strange accent, you carry an American passport, and yet you expect us to trust you?"

Novo asks a few more questions, while consulting his companions with his eyes. Then he walks to the bed and sits down, pointing his gun toward the floor. Tension seems to drain out of him. *"A veces, hay que perder,"* he says ("Sometimes, one must lose"). He repeats himself several times, in a resigned voice.

Turning to Wilson, he asks in a friendly tone, "What kind of material do you want?"

"Some explosives," says Wilson. "Preferably plastic. And some detonating cord and blasting caps. Perhaps some guns. And we would like you to send one of your men to Mexico with us to help carry out the mission."

"Do you propose to pay for this assistance?" asks Novo.

"If you like," says Wilson. "But I would rather accept it as a loan. The service will repay you with replacement material. Or perhaps we could work out an exchange of favors in the future."

"I would prefer it that way," says Novo. "If you stay here, you will hear from us soon." He and his men sweep out the door as abruptly as they had arrived.

Pizarro and Wilson stare at each other wordlessly for some time. "Well, I still think he's a gentleman," she says finally. "But I think we should get the hell out of here."

"No," says Wilson. "They are the first group that has shown any skill at security. I think they're what we're looking for."

Later that same day, someone knocks at the door of the motel room. Wilson opens the door and finds a large paper sack in front of his face. He takes it. A man is already running away, but Wilson decides not to chase him. Inside the bag he finds two and a half blocks of C-4 plastic explosive, two pistols, several blasting caps, and a roll of detonating cord.

The next day, Wilson and Pizarro fly to Miami to pick up a Dodge camper they bought. Wilson has hit upon the idea of driving into Mexico with the explosives and weapons in the camper, on the theory that the Mexican border police are unlikely to think of a camping family as foreign assassins.

He buys a hunting rifle with a telescopic sight. On February 12, he goes to an electronics shop in Miami and purchases a Fanon-Courier paging system—the kind used to "beep" doctors and other professionals for messages. Wilson knows how to modify the system so that a coded signal will detonate a bomb by remote control. He is proud of the modifications, which he has invented himself. From the electronics shop, he drives to Fort Lauderdale, home of a security-equipment firm called Audio Intelligence Devices, Inc. There, on behalf of the government of Chile, he spends nearly $13,000 on sophisticated electronic tracking and debugging equipment. Wilson arranges to have this material shipped to a DINA "front" company—Consultec, located in Buenos Aires—where he will pick it up after the Mexico mission. Then he drives back to Miami and helps Pizarro buy ordinary camping equipment for cover. They buy coolers, cameras, and sleeping bags—even a fishing rod.

By arrangement with Guillermo Novo, they drive to Miami Airport to meet a midnight flight from New York. When the passengers come through the gate, the two agents look for a man carrying a detached CB radio antenna. This will be their new partner from the Cuban Nationalist Movement, assigned to them by Novo.

The man with the antenna turns out to be young—only twenty-three—and quite reticent. He introduces himself by his operational name, Javier. He delivers blank driver's licenses and birth certificates from the state of New Jersey, and then he disappears on his own errands.

Meanwhile, on February 18, the third session of the International Commission of Inquiry into the Crimes of the Military Junta in Chile convenes at Mexico City. The leading Chilean speakers are Hortensia Bussi de Allende, widow of the former president; former Vice President and Foreign Minister Clodomiro Almeyda; Communist Party leader Volodia Teitelboim; and Socialist Party leader Carlos Altamirano. Other speakers include Allende's former ambassador to the United States, Orlando Letelier, whom President Pinochet released into exile some six months earlier, in September 1974.

Most of these Chilean leaders are on the target list Wilson received from Colonel Contreras. Pizarro knows none of them personally, but she hates them all. To her, they are the "rich liberals" who caused all the trouble in Chile and then left the poor people to face the consequences. She believes they deserve to die, and she explains her reasons to Javier.

But the would-be assassins are far behind schedule. Wilson had not anticipated the long trip to New York or the delays in Miami. By the time his camper is fully equipped, the meeting in Mexico City has long since ended.

At a public telephone, Wilson braces himself to report the failure to Santiago. He tells his story in coded language to Major Eduardo Iturriaga in the DINA foreign operations center. Wilson knows Iturriaga well, as does Pizarro. (Pizarro and Iturriaga's wife are old friends, having grown up together in La Serena, Chile.) To Wilson's relief, Iturriaga seems understanding about the delays. But he is also a soldier. He tells Wilson to hold the phone while he confers with "Mamo"—Contreras—and he soon returns with revised orders. "You are to do away with anybody on the list," he says. "Anybody who's still there. Whoever you can find. You are to make a demonstration that will show the exiles and the Mexicans that we will not tolerate that sort of treason."

"Yes, my major," says Wilson. "But it may be too late to find any of them. Even the permanent residents may have left Mexico."

"Try," says Iturriaga. "Hit somebody if you can. Those are your orders."

It takes Wilson some time to locate an IBM typewriter that can duplicate the typeface used on New Jersey driver's licenses, but soon he and Pizarro have fresh documents in the names of Ana and Andrew Brooks. Pizarro insists that they wait until late one afternoon—when the clerks at the Mexican consulate are tired and anxious to go home—and then they can obtain Mexican tourist cards without much scrutiny of their papers. A few days later they begin the long drive to Mexico City, on a camping trip with "Cousin Javier."

By now, their Cuban companion has relaxed somewhat. He has confided that his real name is Virgilio Paz, and he tells Pizarro that the mission has a special personal meaning for him: his father is buried in Mexico City. After Castro took power in Cuba, he says, his father was expelled from the Cuban army. Two years later, the elder Paz managed to take his family to Madrid, and later he caught pneumonia and died in Mexico—on the way to the United States. Paz blames Castro, Mexican doctors, and the American bureaucracy for the tragedy that struck his family when he was only ten. He says he has given himself to the war against Communism. He has killed for it, and he boasts that he can make a bomb with only a stick of dynamite and a twenty-dollar watch.

As to watches, Paz declares that no self-respecting Cuban owns only one. Every man must have an everyday watch and also a "dress" watch for the weekends, when the young ones party and spend money. Paz says that it is nothing for him to spend $200 on a Saturday night. He is fastidious about many things, including his clothes—only monogrammed dress shirts by Pierre Cardin—and his expensive cigars, which he smokes in the crowded quarters of the camper.

Wilson is much less interested in Paz's attire than in his aptitude for the technology of remote-control bombs. In Mexico, he is pleased to see that Paz is eager to learn about sophisticated delivery systems. He shows him how to remove the speakers from the Fanon-Courier receivers, and how to make other modifications so that the remote signal will set off the blasting cap and the detonating cord in a chain reaction that will produce enough flash heat to detonate the C-4. They test the system in the Mexican desert. Alone, a mile away from the camper and from Wilson's Fanon-Courier transmitter, Paz is impressed as he watches a test bulb light up on radio signal from Wilson.

Nearing Mexico City, Wilson tries an advanced experiment of his own. He wants to see if it is possible to encase the entire bomb in a resin plastic—almost like Styrofoam—that will make the deadly apparatus compact, portable, and innocent in appearance. The theoretical obstacle, Wilson knows, is that the liquid plastic gives off heat when the resin combines with the hardener. He wants to make sure it does not give off enough heat to detonate the bomb.

He carries out preliminary experiments in the camper. First he pours some of his liquid resin over a tiny bit of the C-4. Nothing happens. Then he pours some of the hardener over another bit of C-4. Again, nothing happens. Taking the next step, he combines a small amount of resin with hardener and pours the full ketone mixture over some C-4. The compound gives off a moderate amount of heat as it hardens into plastic, but there is no sign of chemical reaction with the explosive.

Wilson pronounces himself ready for the final test. First he builds the bomb, with Paz watching: he tapes the detonating cord and the modified Fanon-Courier trigger device around the blocks of C-4. Next he covers the safety switch and the electrical workings of the receiver with globs of plasticine, which he will remove when the plastic has hardened. Then he sets the entire apparatus on a platform of toothpicks that he has built inside a cake tin.

Everything is ready. After appropriately dramatic warnings to his companions in the camper, Wilson mixes a large batch of ketone and pours it into the tin until it covers the entire bomb except for the top of the plasticine.

Horror strikes quickly. The mixture begins to hiss violently and then to smoke. Instinctively, Wilson tries to pour the ketone out of the tin, but it is already too late. The plastic is too viscous. Wilson begins shouting incoherently through the dense smoke. He knows from experience that there is enough C-4 under his chin to scatter bits of himself and of the camper over several acres. The heat from the unexpected exothermic reaction becomes intense, and Wilson attempts to smother it with blankets and water. He senses vaguely that Paz has fled the camper in a panic.

Paz returns some five minutes later, after the reaction has died out of its own accord. He seems deeply chagrined. His flight has not reflected well on his machismo—especially in contrast to the performance of Pizarro, who stayed in her camper bunk with her book through it all, without saying a word. She tells a shaken Wilson that it was easy, because nothing surprises her. She tells him that all Mexico could disappear and she could find herself on a cloud, and her reaction would be, "Gee whiz. How can this be?"

"What happened?" Paz asks.

"I don't know," says Wilson, who is bothered by his technical lapse. "All I can figure so far is that the ketone may have reacted with the tape. That's possible. I should have tested the tape. I didn't think of that."

"How about the toothpicks?" asks Paz.

"It wouldn't react with the toothpicks," says Wilson. He knows that he can solve the chemical problem when he gets back to his laboratory in Santiago. For now, he will chip off the plastic and settle for a cruder bomb.

With the explosives packed inside waffle containers and stowed in the freezer, the camper finally pulls into Mexico City on March 15. They learn without too much trouble that the targets most likely to have remained in Mexico are Hugo Vigorena, Allende's ambassador to Mexico, and Pedro Vuskovic, Allende's minister of the economy.

Pizarro has heard that Vigorena is the treasurer of the House of Chile, a large hostel and meeting place for Chilean exiles in Mexico. She thinks he might be there, but she does not want to reconnoiter personally, because she and Wilson have several former friends among the Chilean exiles in Mexico. She is afraid they might be recognized at the House of Chile, so Paz volunteers to pose as a leftist Cuban and to find out what he can on the inside.

Paz returns with a great deal of intelligence. He knows where the leftist Chileans tend to eat and drink. He knows what hotels they stay in, and what they read. He even knows where they go to have their teeth fixed. No one, however, has told him anything definite on the whereabouts of Vigorena or Vuskovic. He only knows that the House of Chile is the site of almost constant meetings, youth classes, and study groups—and that it would be easy to plant a bomb inside.

"What for?" asks Wilson.

"It is a symbol," says Paz. "A symbol of Marxism. Cubans believe in symbolism."

"Well, I believe in orders," says Wilson. "We will not put a bomb in there unless we are sure to hit one of the targets."

"Why not?" asks Paz. "Didn't he order you to make a demonstration? Are you afraid? Look, I didn't come down here for nothing."

A new argument breaks out, with Pizarro supporting Wilson. Paz's mannerisms annoy her more than his words. She has noticed that Paz, whenever nervous, tends to collect spittle and to move it from one side of his mouth to the other. This revolts Pizarro, reminding her again of the Cuban groups she and Wilson scouted in Miami before seeking out Guillermo Novo in New Jersey.

Wilson uses his authority to veto the idea of bombing the House of Chile. To placate Paz, he suggests that they investigate the possibility of bombing the most symbolic target in Mexico City—the Cuban embassy. They spend a day on the task, driving and walking around the embassy, and they agree unanimously that it is an impregnable fortress, bristling with security equipment. Wilson thinks they may have been photographed already. In any case, he abandons the notion of attacking the embassy, and Paz becomes more surly.

In a last effort to salvage the mission, Paz and Pizarro walk into the office of a dentist they have been told treats the Chilean exiles. While Paz pretends to be in great pain, Pizarro takes advantage of the confusion to slip the dentist's rotary file off the secretary's desk into her purse. She and Paz then manage an escape before the theft is noticed. They are quite proud of the maneuver.

The file provides them with the names and addresses of nearly every Chilean exile in Mexico, it seems—except for Vigorena and Vuskovic. The operatives stake out some of the houses and follow some of the people. Paz proves to be adroit in his attempts to mingle with the leftists. When he learns that a certain official of the Mexican government is suspected of harboring sympathies for Pinochet, he and Wilson decide to visit the official. The rumors turn out to be true. After much discussion, Wilson reveals his Chilean connection and makes a pitch to the Mexican official to become a source of information for DINA. The official agrees, and Wilson pays him a handsome beginner's bonus out of his operational funds. In exchange he receives, along with related stories, unverified information that the President of Mexico has purchased a home for Allende's widow. It is a paltry reward, but Wilson knows that Contreras values intelligence with a high gossip content.

The three agents find themselves without much to do in Mexico City. One night they sit twice through the movie *The Day of the Jackal*. It is Wilson's favorite film, although he considers the character of the assassin far too wooden and he finds some of the schemes in the movie far too complicated to be practical in the real world. Nevertheless, he is willing to make allowances for Hollywood because he is entranced by the film's emphasis on technique—on the procurement of false documents, the selection and purchase of equipment and weapons, the dreary problems of travel. These things have become his own technical obsessions. He knows that his experience in Mexico, while unfortunate, has amounted to a crash course in tradecraft, as intelligence professionals refer to the accumulated wisdom of spies, commandos, and criminals.

A few days later, Wilson decides that they will accomplish nothing spectacular in Mexico. He tells Pizarro that he wants to abort the mission, though he fears the wrath of Contreras.

Pizarro agrees. "I have always known somehow that nothing would happen on this mission," she tells him. "Everything has been too unreal, as if it is out of a book or something."

The next morning the "Brooks family" heads north, with Paz grumbling in the camper.

Wilson does not realize it during the long drive back to Miami but his mission has already affected the underground diplomacy among the anti-Castro exile groups by raising Novo's prestige at the expense of Orlando Bosch. Hidden away in Santiago, still waiting for the Chilean government to respond to his overtures, Bosch sits down to write another letter of concern to his protégé Dionisio Suárez. Bosch senses that something is wrong. His letter, which will reach Suárez before Paz returns to New Jersey from Mexico, shows him to be as demanding as always, but more desperate:

Last night when you and Guillermo called me, I had been feeling sick for the past two days which, together with my mental depression and the fear that everything we say on the phone is being tapped . . . made me conclude the conversation, leaving many important things untouched. I'll try to explain them in this letter. Please pay close attention.

In the end, I'll make a historical revision of events. I have seen rulers, dictators, thieves, etc., direct the destinies of many countries and commit mortal errors and dishonesties of all kinds. Yet, in a few years, these countries received these men as heroes, forgetting the injustices they committed. . . .

I insist that we remember the 26th of July. In this sense, we have a lot to learn from the Communists. We are in a bad position—15 years of exile, treason, and indifference. We have to keep our heart and work intelligently. . . . I think it's inevitable that they are asking for money in my name. It is important for us to keep our silence and to create mystery about where I am, and what I am doing. Remember CHE. His two years of absence were more important than his own death. . . .

Perhaps you think that I am spending too much, but it is not true. The problem is this: since you left, everything has gone up threefold. The rent went up to 294,000 escudos. I have to pay 29,000 escudos for the hot water and the girl that helps because I have no strength to cook, wash, or anything else. The bill for the light is never less than 35,000 escudos. The gas went up, etc. . . .

For all of that, I ask you to put aside one or two thousand dollars for an emergency. . . . I want you to try your best and send me as much as you can in the next 72 hours. Later, we will pool everything—you know for what. You know I don't ask money for myself. I am happy fighting alone in this continent against thousands of Communists and murderers. . . . Please go see [name deleted] and ask him for $200. Ask him to give you his friend's name and ask him for $1,200. . . .

. . . Keep me informed about how things are going in Puerto Rico. And in reference to the copy of the letter I sent you . . . I ask you to read it so you can see the reasoning in the political and revolutionary order. . . .

Let me be clear about something: the rent is due the 7th. . . .

After many years of loyalty to Bosch, Suárez decides to ignore this letter. His allegiance is shifting toward Novo. He and Novo are tired of Bosch's nagging requests for money. In addition, Suárez knows that Novo is the more forceful of the two, though as yet he is much less famous. And Novo has already made the Chilean connection that Bosch has sought vainly for months.

In April, Suárez ignores Bosch's summons to a "mini-congress" in Santiago, for which he receives a sharp rebuke by mail on May 5. A few months later, he will receive what amounts to a draft notice from the anti-Castro leader. It begins: "The Cuban revolution ends its prewar process and actions, arriving at the sublime moment of historic deed. Nothing has stopped the conquering chariot of liberty." After several pages of florid, bellicose rhetoric, the letter comes to its point: "Under the existing conditions, after careful study of personal assets and responsibilities, the Treasury of Cuba demands of you the sum of $25,000 for the war."

Suárez has seen many of these letters, and he knows what it means: he is no longer one of Bosch's collectors and enforcers. Now he is a target.

Andrés Wilson returns to Santiago on May 17, 1975, several weeks after Pizarro. He carries more security equipment, including more Fanon-Courier receivers. In the laboratory, he prepares a one-page report on the Mexico mission for Colonel Contreras, whom he invites to his house for tea. Contreras accepts the invitation, saying that he wants to see the expensive DINA house that he has bestowed on Wilson as a reward for his services in 1974. It is big enough for Wilson's family and all his DINA equipment, and it also provides office space for Wilson's secretary, his chauffeur, and the other DINA personnel under his command.

At tea, Contreras interrupts Wilson's apologies about the failure of the Mexico mission. He tells Wilson not to worry about it. An effort was made, he says. An agent has been recruited in Mexico. An alliance has been arranged with the Cuban Nationalist Movement. Much valuable equipment has been returned safely to Chile. All these steps are positive ones, he says, and Wilson should not fret about missing the targets. He will have other chances very soon.

12 ▣ ALARMS FROM THE UNDERGROUND

Larry Wack was sitting at his desk when the call came from Hank Patovsky of the New York Secret Service office. The two men had a passing acquaintance. "Larry," said Patovsky, "are you the one who's been messing around with the Novo brothers?"

"Yeah," said Wack. "What's up?"

"You better come over here," said Patovsky. "We got a Cuban we busted for counterfeiting, and he's telling us some tall stories about Ignacio Novo. I don't know what this guy's talking about, but if it's bullshit it's major-league bullshit."

Wack took the first taxi he could find. The tone of emergency in Patovsky's voice was unusual, he knew, because Secret Service agents are loath to show any excitement to an FBI man. Patovsky was still showing excitement when he huddled with Wack outside his office. The Cuban was inside, he said: a con man, with a record of passing bad paper up and down the East Coast. Patovsky had arrested him a few days earlier, and to save himself, the Cuban had agreed to set up some of his associates in the counterfeiting ring. The big bust had occurred earlier that afternoon. Now it was dusk, and the Cuban was in a panic about his sentencing and about retribution from the people he had just handed up. Ricardo Canete was trying to further ingratiate himself with the Secret Service agents, and to do so he had been babbling about interesting things. One item stood out far above the others: Canete said his friend Ignacio Novo had been talking recently about killing a number of people, including the attorney general of the United States. "That's what he says," Patovsky told Wack in the hallway. "He says Novo's been talking about a hit list against Bell and Fiske and some guy named Prodder or something."

"Holy shit!" whispered Wack. "He's gotta mean Propper. That's the prosecutor on the Letelier case down in Washington."

"I don't know him," said Patovsky.

"Yeah, well, your guy Canete probably wouldn't know him either," said Wack. "He'd have a hard time making that up if he was spinning you. Have you guys reported the threat yet?"

"It's about to go out now," said Patovsky. "With Bell's name on it, it's gonna make a big splash."

"Yeah," said Wack, who drifted off briefly in thought. "I hope we can handle it so it doesn't get out. The whole thing might come crashing back down on your man Canete."

Patovsky smiled. "You wouldn't be thinking of making a source out of him, would you?" he asked. "Canete's a con man."

"I don't know," said Wack. "Mind if I talk to him a little bit?"

"That's the idea," Patovsky grinned.

Wack found Canete leaning back in a chair, wearing a suit and an open-collared dress shirt. Canete was in his mid-thirties, five feet nine, with an athletic build and Latin features that were handy in his trade—he could pass for a Greek, an Italian, a Spaniard, even a Moroccan. He spoke flawless English, and he spoke Spanish with the accent of his native Cuba.

Wack introduced himself. "Nice to meet you, Ricky," he said. "I hear you've been in touch with Iggie Novo."

"That's true," said Canete. "I've seen a lot of him the past couple of weeks. He seems to have something on his mind."

"Uh huh," said Wack, whose interest was rising. He was thinking about all the bartenders and shoeshine men he had interviewed over the past six months in an effort to identify the blond Chilean who was supposed to be Guillermo Novo's contact. Wack always thought the next interview might be the big break. Now, facing a talkative confidant of Ignacio Novo's, he could not restrain himself. "Have you seen a Chilean with him?" he asked abruptly.

"No," said Canete.

"Has he talked to you about a Chilean?" asked Wack.

"No," said Canete. "Iggie's been talking business, so he's been alone most of the time."

"Uh huh," said Wack, trying to conceal his disappointment. He consoled himself with the thought that at least Canete had not made up a story about a Chilean, as he might easily have done. This raised

Canete a notch as a prospect. "What kind of business has he been talking about?" asked Wack.

"Documents business," said Canete. "Iggie's been looking for some extra driver's licenses and stuff."

"Phony ones, I suppose," said Wack.

Canete shrugged coyly.

"You give him any already?" asked Wack.

"He wants more," Canete replied evasively.

"So you sell fake ID's, too, eh, Ricky?" teased Wack. "Not just fake money?"

Canete's smile revealed a little sheepishness and a lot of pride. "I could fool you," he said.

"Maybe so," said Wack. "What's this about the attorney general, Ricky? You can't play around with shit like that, you know. That ain't a petty con."

"I know," said Canete. "Look, Iggie just told me they're making a list. Like he was bragging. He said, 'If Guillermo goes inside, it's gonna be war.' He said, 'There'll be bodies all over the place.' He said, 'We're gonna get Prodder and Fiske and even Bell, if we have to.' That's what he said."

"What do you think he meant about Guillermo going inside?" asked Wack.

"Don't ask me," said Canete. "I guess there's maybe a rap about to come down on Guillermo, but I don't know. I sure didn't ask. When Iggie said that stuff, I didn't touch it. I didn't even want to hear it."

Wack asked a few more questions and then stepped back out into the hallway with Patovsky. "What are you gonna do with this guy?" he asked.

"Not much," Patovsky replied. "We've already made our deal with him. All that's left now is his sentencing. He wants us to say nice things to the judge, I guess. That must be why he's so helpful today."

"What do you think the judge will give him?"

"Six months," Patovsky guessed. "Maybe probation. He's got a pretty long record, but we didn't have too much on him."

"That's not much to work with," said Wack. "What's the maximum he could get on the charge he's got with you guys?"

"Ten years," said Patovsky.

"You think he'd believe me if I told him he's looking at ten years?" asked Wack.

Patovsky didn't bother to answer.

"I guess not," said Wack. "How about five years? Or three years?"

"I doubt it," said Patovsky. "Look, Larry, this guy's been around. But you can try. What have you got in mind?"

"I'd like to play around with him for a while to see if he can come up with anything," said Wack.

"He's all yours," said Patovsky. "I wasn't planning to do anything with him for a while anyway. It probably won't work out, but if it does, I want you to give us credit for one informant over at the Bureau."

"It's a deal," Wack said with a smile. "You got a room where I can talk to him alone?"

Wack was soon sitting in a small office with Canete. "Look, Ricky," he said, "we have reason to believe that the Novos might have been involved in Letelier. That's big stuff. Two homicides. If you can help me either prove it or disprove it, I'll try to help you."

Canete took on a queasy expression. "I'd really like to help you," he said. "But not on this. Not on those guys. You don't know them the way I do. They're too dangerous. Way too dangerous. I don't want to get involved."

Wack pressed gently for a few moments, playing the soft guy, speaking of his desire to help. Then he rose to leave. "Well, in a way I don't blame you, Ricky," he said. "I'm going now. It was nice meeting you."

"Nice meeting you, too," said Canete. "What was it you wanted me to do, anyway?"

Wack sat down again. "Well, I wanted you to get a little closer to them and find out what the hell they're doing," he said. "You got an in with the documents. Maybe you could get closer to them that way. What are they doing with those phony papers, anyhow?"

"I don't know," said Canete. "That's none of my business. You can do a million things with a good set of papers."

"I'll bet you can." Wack grinned. "Like travel. Has he asked for any passports? You think he might be getting ready to split for good?"

"Could be," said Canete. "Iggie did mention a passport, come to think of it."

"Whaddaya mean, come to think of it?" Wack demanded. "A passport is a big deal. You'd remember that. It ain't a library card, Ricky. Even I know that."

"I told you, they're dangerous," said Canete.

Wack studied Canete's face and decided that part of him—the con-man part—was tempted by the challenge of an undercover role of this magnitude. "This ain't a game, Ricky," said Wack. "I mean it might be a game for you to try to get close to them, but if they killed Letelier and the Moffitt girl, that wasn't a game."

"I know," said Canete.

"They use bombs, Ricky," said Wack. "Look, I'll be honest with you. I've had a lot of Cubans tell me, 'Fuck that Letelier. He was a Commie and I'm glad he's dead.' But I don't look at it that way. Whoever did this murdered those people in cold blood, with a bomb. That's a chickenshit way to do things."

"Well, I agree with you on that," said Canete.

"You think Iggie and his brother are capable of something like that?" asked Wack.

"Sure they are," said Canete. "They've been working up to it over the years."

"Well, they're a bunch of cowards, as far as I'm concerned," said Wack. "Whoever killed Letelier also followed the woman I just married out to the airport last year and threatened the shit out of her. They're crazy. They threaten women. They use bombs to kill innocent people. But I don't think they have the guts to go at you face to face. I don't think they'd come straight at me, and I don't think they'd go straight at you."

"I could handle them," said Canete, with some show of bravado. "It's not that."

"You got a wife and kids?" asked Wack.

"Yeah," said Canete.

"How many kids?" asked Wack, who proceeded to trade personal stories with Canete for nearly three hours. They spoke of threats, childhood feats, and the treachery of Fidel Castro. Wack's proposition remained in the background, but it was mentioned from time to time.

"Ricky, you're a real son-of-a-bitch," said Wack in a tone of high compliment. "You think writing bad checks is okay, don't you? You think passing counterfeit is okay, too. Right?"

"Hey, wait a minute," Canete protested. "I told you I didn't want to get involved in that stuff. Those guys pushed me into it."

"C'mon," said Wack. "And you're a blamer, too, aren't you? But at least you aren't a killer, and that's all I'm asking. And even if you had to kill somebody—and I hope to hell you never do—you wouldn't be a chickenshit bomber. You gotta draw the line somewhere, you know."

"All right, all right." Canete smiled. "Let me think it over for the night, but I'll try to give you a hand."

"Now you're talking," said Wack.

"I'll let you know by tomorrow," said Canete. "Because that's when I'm supposed to give Ignacio another batch of papers. I been working on them."

"You're kidding," said Wack, feeling a chill. He would have preferred to celebrate Canete's agreement to cooperate for a few days, at least, and build up the rapport between them.

"Look, Ricky," he said, "you've gotta stall him. You can't give him that stuff until you hear from me, okay? I gotta go all the way to the attorney general to get you permission to do something like this, you understand? Once that comes through, you're okay. You'll have some kind of immunity. But if you jump the gun, we'll all be in deep shit because you'll put the Bureau in the position of knowing about a crime in advance. We're in this together from now on, okay?"

Canete smiled. "Yeah," he said. "I'll wait. You really think the attorney general is gonna say it's all right for me to peddle paper?"

"Not to everybody," said Wack. "Just to Novo. I'm betting he'll give the okay."

"I shoulda gone to him before," quipped Canete.

Wack returned to the FBI office at nine o'clock, having skipped dinner. He wrote up a teletype on the Novo threat and another one requesting authorization for Canete to supply the false documents. Then he called Cornick at home.

"Jesus Christ!" said Cornick, on hearing the story. "Gene'll love this one. He's still recovering from the threat back in March. You think it's real?"

"I believe the guy," said Wack. "I just spent three hours with him, and we hit it off real well. Like we were on a date or something."

"My God, Larry!" said Cornick, who was still absorbing the news. "Now listen. You've got to take it easy with this guy. Play it cool and don't jump into anything. He might be playing you for a sucker. Let's take it slow."

"We don't have time to take it slow," said Wack. "He's supposed to make a delivery to Novo tomorrow. My teletype will be down there in the morning on the authorization for him. You've got to grease it for me."

"I can't, Larry," said Cornick. "I'm going to Miami in the morning to interview Monkey Morales. But I'll make sure it gets done."

Cornick soon woke Propper with the good news about Wack's new source and the bad news about the Novo threat against the lives of Propper, Bell, and the New York U.S. attorney. He promised to get Propper some FBI protection. Propper said that would be fine. "This is the worst good news I've ever gotten," he said. "Thanks a lot."

"Don't mention it, Gene," said Cornick. "And do me a favor, will you?"

"What's that?"

"Pat her on the ass for me."

"Carter, I'm alone!" Propper said. "There's nobody here. I wish somebody *were* here after what you just told me."

"Sure, you're alone," scoffed Cornick, who was susceptible to the belief that all men of Propper's Vietnam War generation socialized on the Hugh Hefner rotation system.

The next morning, May 10, a dual emergency broke out in the Justice Department. Jimmy Adams personally contacted Attorney General Bell with news of the threat on his life. Bell, in response, assigned a member of his personal staff to monitor reports about the threat. Meanwhile, the CHILBOM headquarters supervisor walked to the Justice Department with Wack's teletype and the authorization forms for the delivery of false documents. It required a crisis of this magnitude to dislodge him from his office at headquarters. These documents were special. They carried Canete's true name, which even Propper did not know. A leak of the informant's identity would not only expose Canete and injure the investigation but also, conceivably, add to the danger facing Attorney General Bell.

Late that night, Wack met Canete in a bar near the New York FBI office. They were both nervous, watching from their dark corner for suspicious strangers or dangerous friends. Wack told Canete that the authorization had come through. Canete told Wack that the rendezvous with Ignacio Novo was rescheduled for the next evening at a Chinese restaurant on Broadway.

Wack wanted to know more about how Canete and Novo had started doing business with each other. Canete explained that it had begun suddenly about two weeks earlier. Before that, he had lost contact with the Novo brothers and had been "out of politics" for years. Then he ran into Ignacio Novo one night, and Novo had implored him to rejoin the Cuban Nationalist Movement, of which Canete had been a founding member. Novo had seemed very tense, telling Canete that the CNM was in need of his skill at obtaining forged documents. At one point, Canete told Wack, Novo had mentioned important new friends and international connections who would be able to help Canete if he ever got in trouble. Novo's references had been vague but boastful. He had said something about how the CNM could smuggle people out of the country and get them in touch with DINA. "He said something like, 'We have good friends in the South, next to Argentina, and we have people in training there right now,'" said Canete.

"Hold it right there, Ricky," said Wack. "I thought you told me you didn't know anything about Chile. That's the first thing I asked you last night. Chile's next to Argentina, right?"

"Yeah," said Canete. "Don't get sore. You asked me about a Chilean, not about Chile. Besides, that was last night. I hadn't decided to tell you anything then, and if I had told you that, you'd have been all over me."

This answer did not satisfy Wack completely. "Don't make stuff up on me," he warned. "Ever. I'll find out if you do, and I'll bust your ass, Ricky."

"I'm not making stuff up," said Canete. "I promise you. This stuff is just heavy, that's all. Listen, those guys make a conscious effort to scare you. They're good at it. Last Thursday, Ignacio picked me up at the shoe store and took me for a ride. That's when he told me what kind of papers he wanted. And when he was driving the car he let his coat fall open to make sure I'd see that he was carrying an Uzi on a shoulder strap."

"An Uzi?" said Wack. "What's an Uzi?"

"It's an automatic rifle made by the Israelis," said Canete. "Fires 9 mm ammunition."

"You know that stuff?" asked Wack. "You saw all that under his coat?"

"No," Canete replied. "That's what he told me when I asked him about the gun, man."

"That's better," said Wack.

"Better for you, maybe," said Canete. "It's not so good for me. I think the damn thing had a silencer on it, and it looked like the barrel had been cut down some. It was real short, anyway."

"Okay," said Wack. "So Iggie is scary. I got it. Did he tell you anything about the guy he wants the documents for? Did he tell you his real name or anything?"

"No," said Canete. "He gave me a description and stuff to fill out the papers with, but he didn't tell me his name."

"Did you ask him?"

"No," said Canete. "That's not professional."

"Did he say why the guy needs the phony papers?"

"Yeah. I asked him that."

"What did he say?" asked Wack.

"He said the guy left a body behind," said Canete.

"He said *what?*"

"I didn't ask him any more about it after that," said Canete.

Wack took a deep breath. "Are you sure he said that?" he asked.

"Of course I'm sure," said Canete. "That impressed me a lot."

"I guess it would," said Wack. He asked to see the documents, which Canete had promised to bring along that night. The handiwork proved to be a New York State temporary driver's license, a Louisiana birth certificate, a certificate of baptism, and an army discharge form DD-214—all in the name of Frederick Pagan, age thirty-five. Canete explained that temporary licenses and army discharges were his specialty, as the blank forms were easy to obtain.

"That's great, Ricky," said Wack. "But look at this. You spelled 'honorable' wrong. It says here that this fellow Pagan got an 'honable' discharge. You screwed it up already."

Canete examined his form DD-214. "I guess so," he said. "Well, they'll never notice."

"An 'honable' discharge," laughed Wack. "You gotta do classier stuff than this now, since you're working for the Bureau, Ricky. You're gonna get me in trouble."

Cornick stepped off the plane the next afternoon and went straight to his roost in the Washington field office, where he sawed through some paperwork and dictated some reports and caught up on the latest hot news about Wack's new informant. Then he went over to see Propper. "You won't believe who was on the plane with us," he said.

"Who?" asked Propper.

"Your friend Stanley Wilson, that's who," Cornick declared. "With his partner."

"Stanley?" said Propper.

"Yeah, Stanley. He refused to say why he was going down there and what he was doing, as usual. But he didn't have to. Why the hell would a D.C. cop be going all the way down to Miami unless it's Letelier?"

"Well, he's probably got sources in the Brigade down there," said Propper. "That's a positive sign, anyway. At least he's not talking about how Isabel Letelier did it anymore."

Cornick studied Propper with suspicion. "That figures," he said. "You knew he was going down there, didn't you?"

"I knew he was going down there some time, yeah," Propper admitted. "But I didn't know when."

"Jesus Christ, Gene," said Cornick. "I thought we got rid of Wilson six months ago."

"Ronni Moffitt's still just a D.C. homicide case, Carter. You can't keep Stanley out of it."

"It's a disaster, Gene," said Cornick. "You mark my words. Wilson plus Letelier spells disaster."

"Well, he can't do any worse than the Miami office has been doing so far," said Propper.

"Oh, yes, he can," said Cornick. "He can do a lot worse."

"I sincerely doubt it," said Propper, shooing away the subject. "So what happened in Miami?"

"I'm not through with Wilson, yet," said Cornick. He shook his head and began to smile. "God, I wish you had been there, Gene. Before I got through being pissed off about finding Wilson on the flight, I looked up and saw Wilson and Seddon coming on to each other with these suspicious looks. They'd never met, but I'll swear it was almost chemical the way those two Palm Tree Peekers picked up on each other. The spook aura just pulled them together, like *thwoooop!*" Cornick clasped his hands together in the air. "They just loved each other. The next thing I knew, I looked up and they were sitting on the plane with their heads together. I couldn't have shined a flashlight between them, I tell you. And about halfway through the flight, Seddon came back and sat down next to me with this real worried look. He said, 'That guy Wilson is not what he represents himself to be.' I said, 'What do you mean, Al?' And he leaned over to me and whispered, 'He's on to a story about how some Russian code clerk disappeared this morning! *This morning*, and he already knows about it. Can you believe that?' So I said, 'Do we have something like that in the Bureau?' Al said, 'I don't know. I don't know what came in this morning. But how the hell does *he* know about it?' And he's looking at Wilson up there in the plane like he's the spy who came in from the cold. Al said, 'I worked on him, and I think he knows something. But he won't say how he found out. He's got to be Agency.' Al thinks he's a CIA contract employee."

"That could be, Carter," said Propper, laughing. "It's always been a standing joke around here that Stanley is the CIA representative on the homicide squad. And whenever anybody kids him about it, he gets really huffy and says, 'That's not funny!' Which of course only keeps it alive."

"Well, it's alive now with Seddon," said Cornick. "He's already checked on it, and some code clerk *did* disappear yesterday. They don't know whether he's defected to the Russians or what, but Al's going out of his mind trying to figure out how Wilson knew. He's gone out to investigate it."

Cornick spun a few more Seddon tales and then reported the big news of the previous day, the interview with the mysterious Ricardo Morales. He said Morales had lived up to all expectations. He was a smooth talker who had befriended and betrayed everyone from Otero and Bosch to the FBI, repeatedly, unscrupulously, and without any consistent motive that anyone could discern. Cornick said it was a good thing he and Seddon had gone down to Miami, because the Miami FBI office remained so entangled with Morales—fearing him, loathing him, almost worshipping him, depending on which agent was speaking—that Propper would have had to wait another eight months, and maybe eight *years*, before the Miami office would produce an interview with Morales.

It had not been easy to get anything out of him, Cornick advised. In fact, it had taken the better part of three hours and had required a good deal of cultivation and a little hardball. Morales had ignored a subpoena, and Cornick had made sure he realized that Propper might have him jailed, like Suárez. "That really got to him, Gene," said Cornick. "I told him it wasn't like Miami, where he can just ignore things. I told him I didn't think I could *control* you unless he really helped us out on Letelier . . ."

"So what did he say, Carter?" asked Propper.

"I'm getting to that, Gene," said Cornick. First, Morales had strongly denied that he had ever told anyone in the press or the FBI that Orlando Bosch had pinned the Letelier assassination on the Novo brothers, flatly contradicting the original and most persistent lead in the investigation. Moreover, Morales had told Cornick he doubted Bosch would ever say such a thing, because he and the Novo brothers were allies.

Second, Morales had told Cornick that Venezuela's agent at the CORU meeting in the Dominican Republic had been none other than Morales's predecessor in DISIP, Luis Posada, and that Posada had brought back to Caracas a complete plan of all CORU's future bombings, including the Cubana Airlines bombing, for which he was now imprisoned in Caracas with Orlando Bosch.

"If that's true, it's rather incredible!" said Propper. "No wonder the Venezuelans haven't rushed Bosch and Posada to trial." Propper launched into a tirade against the Venezuelan government, which was very much on his mind. A week earlier—just before Canete had surfaced in New York—he had finally received the official reply to the Letters Rogatory he had sent to Venezuela the previous December. The reply, as expected, was that Bosch had refused to answer any questions, but the reply also said that Propper had "failed to appear" for the questioning. Propper had not been able to believe that a court and a foreign ministry would lie that way, on an official document, and he pressed his friends at the State Department to find out if there was any chance that the Venezuelan government had attempted to notify Propper of a formal hearing with Bosch. The answer had come back negative.

Finally, Morales had told Cornick about two items that might substantiate all the street talk about how Cuban exiles had acted as violent agents of the Chilean DINA. He cited the shooting in Rome of former Chilean vice president Bernardo Leighton in October 1975, saying that a Cuban group called Zero had claimed credit for the attack. Zero, said Morales, was an "action cell" of the Cuban Nationalist Movement. An even better example, said Morales, was Rolando Otero. He told Cornick of recruiting Otero as a DISIP agent to find out about the Chilean DINA, and of Otero's return to Caracas with a DINA "hit" contract on Pascal Allende. Morales could not remember the name of the Chilean DINA officer who had been Otero's handler, but he said it was all in Otero's file at DISIP headquarters. Moreover, he said, there was a copy of Otero's "assassination package" inside a vault in the Foreign Ministry building in Caracas. The package contained photographs of Pascal Allende and his girlfriend, along with data about their habits and appearance.

Propper could barely contain himself as he listened to this part of Cornick's report. A DINA assassination package! A Cuban hit man! This was exactly what he needed! He jumped up to pace. Why hadn't Dr. Rivas told him about this in March, when he was in Caracas? Who were Otero's friends? Might they have killed Letelier while Otero was in jail? Propper was scheming to obtain the package from the Venezuelan Foreign Ministry. But what if Morales was lying? Cornick said you could never tell with the Monkey. If he had lied, what was his purpose? Propper felt torn between caution and nervous zeal. The excitement in the investigation was thick and palpable, with Canete's news coming down from New York and Morales's report coming up from Miami. But it was impossible to know what information to trust in the Letelier case, with no helpful eyewitnesses or physical evidence, with only the word of informants who were con men and conspirators themselves.

Propper sat down in his office to write what he called a Tactics

Memo. He tried to condense all the swirling rumors and informant reports into five typewritten pages, under two major headings: *2506 Brigade* and *Cuban Nationalist Movement*. The Brigade lead had suffered when Admiral McIntyre passed his polygraph in April, but Cornick had talked with agents in Miami and returned with renewed faith in Tomboy. Morales was now mentioning Frank Castro, who was active in the Brigade as well as head of the FLNC. Under *Cuban Nationalist Movement* Propper included all the Bosch reports on the Novo brothers and Wack's source information about Guillermo Novo's "blond Chilean" DINA contact. He added the information from the new Wack informant who was dealing with Ignacio Novo.

"These leads involve two separate anti-Castro Cuban groups," Propper concluded. "However, we are finding more connections between the two groups than was originally thought, so the leads do not necessarily conflict." Propper then posed a series of tactical questions: Should we proceed with the probation revocation hearing on Novo at the present time? Should we leave Suárez in jail? Should we subpoena Frank Castro, or give Morales a chance to work on him? Should we subpoena Morales? His tentative answer was yes to everything.

It was time to turn the screws, to send even more subpoenas to New Jersey and Miami, to put Guillermo Novo in jail and to leave Suárez there. He wanted to resolve the two leads while he had "the attorney general's complete personal attention," as Cornick joked, referring to the uproar over the threat.

That same afternoon, as Propper worked on his Tactics Memo, Larry Wack was engaged in an operation he had designed to test the reliability of Ricardo Canete. Wack was sitting alone in the back of a blue FBI van parked across the street from the Szechuan Taste West restaurant on the Upper West Side of New York. He had locked all the doors and rolled up the windows an hour ago, and he was still staring out a one-way porthole in the back of the van, which was filled with smoke. Wack chain-smoked Marlboros, as always, and he talked on the radio with Special Agent Cameron Craig, who was walking the street. Craig had a radio in his pocket and a small wireless receiver in his ear.

Wack was hoping the daylight would hold out long enough for good photographs, and he was hoping Canete wasn't taking the Bureau for a ride. He figured both things could go either way, until he saw something that made him pick up his camera and his radio at the same time. It was Canete, less than ten feet away. He was immediately behind the van and just far enough out into Broadway for Wack to see him. Canete waited for a break in the traffic and then crossed Broadway. He had been close enough for Wack to see in his hand a magazine with a photograph of a big, shiny motorcycle on the cover. Wack thought Canete seemed relaxed and composed—perhaps too much so.

Wack told Cameron Craig that the party was starting. Craig should not go too far away. One guy was there in the restaurant, and now they were waiting for the suspect.

Fifteen minutes later, Wack saw a new, very long Ford jerk to a stop in front of the restaurant. A man jumped out and ran into the restaurant, oblivious to the honks of the angry New Yorkers behind his double-parked car. Wack didn't get a good look at him, but he did notice the license plate on the car—DFE-1. From New Jersey. He knew this plate came from the series used by the New Jersey Ford dealership where Ignacio Novo worked. Wack could not quite believe it, having grown accustomed to useless, boring stakeouts. This was Ignacio Novo at work in his own element. Wack saw that a woman remained in the car. He alerted Craig and was just grabbing for his FBI snapshot of Ignacio Novo when he saw the man come running back out of the restaurant. Wack snapped a few photographs before the man jumped into the Ford and squealed off around the corner. If he had been carrying any forged documents from Canete, Wack didn't see them. He fought panic. Everything was happening too fast.

Canete did not emerge from the restaurant. Wack advised Cameron Craig to look out for the Ford, which he described, but he reminded Craig not to speak in reply. It was risky enough using a clean-cut, blond, FBI type like Craig in that neighborhood to begin with, Wack knew, and it would be disastrous if Novo were to spot someone like Craig on the street talking into a two-way radio. So Wack waited with his own thoughts. He felt relatively safe in the van, but he was not immune to paranoid speculations that his operation had been detected and that one of Novo's friends was standing just outside.

Then Wack saw the man and a blond woman turn the corner onto Broadway, on foot. Wack stared at his snapshot. It had to be Ignacio Novo, he figured. "They're back," he told Craig. "Everything's okay. Must have parked the car." He snapped a few photographs before the couple entered Szechuan Taste West. Then he waited. After fif-

teen minutes, he called Craig on the radio again and told him to go
into the restaurant on some pretext—to look at a menu, or to go to
the men's room—and to observe Novo and Canete together, if possible.

Wack saw Craig enter the restaurant. Shortly thereafter, Craig
came out again and signaled that all was well. Canete and Novo were
sitting together. Craig could testify to that, if necessary. Wack, feeling much better, spent the next half hour trying to keep the sun
from going down. He was restless, but he was also ready when Novo
and Canete and the blond woman came out of the restaurant together and began strolling up Broadway. Wack gave his camera a workout. He noticed that Canete was carrying nothing and that Novo was
carrying what looked like a magazine, rolled tightly in his hand.
Wack figured the phony documents for Frederick Pagan were inside.
Canete had delivered. Wack was soon motoring back toward the Bureau photo lab.

At a rendezvous the next morning, Wack nodded along as Canete
told how Novo had showed up with a blond woman whom Canete did
not know, and how he had slipped the documents to Novo in a motorcycle magazine. Not wishing to talk business in front of the woman,
Canete reported, he had given Novo the magazine when Novo was on
his way to the men's room, and Canete had then walked to the cigarette machine so that he could stop Novo on his return. Novo had approved the documents, Canete reported, and had ordered four more
sets of phony identity papers, specifying that one set should be completely "built up" with supporting bank accounts and credit references. Canete said he was still bargaining with Novo over the price.

"That girl must have thought you guys are a little weird," said
Wack. "You gave Iggie a motorcycle magazine, and he took off to
the bathroom with it, is that right?"

"Yeah," said Canete. "She didn't ask any questions. Look, she was
just along for the ride. Ignacio probably wanted to show her off.
She's probably seen a lot of stuff like that and knows better than to
ask."

"Uh huh," said Wack. Inwardly, he was quite pleased that Canete's report so closely matched what he and Craig had observed the
previous evening. Canete did not dramatize or exaggerate. There
was no talk of Uzis. Hopefully, Wack sprang his final test. "Did you
see a blue van out on the street last night?" he asked.

Canete looked puzzled. "Yeah," he said. "There was one parked
near my shoe store."

"I was in it," said Wack. "Watching you."

"Yeah?" said Canete. "I didn't see you there."

"That was the idea," said Wack. "Did you see anybody unusual come into the Chinese restaurant?"

Canete nodded. "Come to think of it, I did," he said. "There was a blond gringo who didn't eat anything and looked out of place for the area."

"That was my guy," said Wack. "We had you covered pretty good."

"No shit," said Canete. He stared briefly at Wack and then he broke into a wide grin. He slapped Wack fraternally on the back. "I *told* you I was gonna help you out, Larry," he laughed. "Didn't I? Didn't I do a good job?"

"Yeah, Ricky," said Wack, who was celebrating Canete's spontaneous pleasure over the news that he had been watched. If Canete had been plotting treachery with Novo, Wack figured, he would have betrayed some shock, some paranoia. Wack decided he had a good informant. He returned Canete's slap on the back, and soon he would deliver an initial informant's payment of $300 in cash. "You're doing okay so far," he said.

That same day, May 12, Al Seddon made one of his rare trips to Propper's office, where he closed the door. Without a word, he pulled a single sheet of paper from his coat and slid it across Propper's desk.

Propper read a nine-year-old French press agency news item out of Bogotá, Colombia, which announced that an American named Stanley R. Wilson had accused a fugitive American airplane hijacker of stealing secret documents concerning Castro spy activity in South America. The story said that Wilson "appears to be a member of the North American secret police—the CIA" and that Wilson had been living in Colombia with the hijacker until the latter allegedly absconded with the secret documents. In a parallel development, said the story, a third American had accused the same hijacker of stealing some underwater fishing equipment before he disappeared. The hijacker was reported to be seeking asylum in Havana.

Propper read the story twice and tried not to appear confused. "This is our Stanley?" he asked.

"Yep," said Seddon. "I don't have to tell you where that came from, do I?"

"I presume from the Agency," said Propper.

"No comment," Seddon replied.

"Well, how about telling me what it means," said Propper. "This story doesn't make any sense. If Stanley was working for the Agency, what the hell was he doing living down in South America with a fugitive hijacker? And why did he have secret documents on him to get stolen?"

Seddon smiled wryly. "Well, there are a number of ways to analyze it," he said. "The most likely one is that Stanley was trying to operate against this hijacker, who had already taken one plane to Cuba and was trying to go back. Wilson was probably trying to find out who the guy's contacts in Havana were. And the guy must have gotten wise and taken off with some of Stanley's stuff. That's the way I read it."

"Could be, I guess," said Propper. "But what kind of CIA agent denounces somebody in the press for stealing documents? He doesn't sound like an agent to me."

"You're right," Seddon declared. "That's the whole point. My guess is that Stanley was freelancing on an Agency contract, trying to get himself hired permanently. And let me tell you something. There's nothing more dangerous than somebody who tries to do spy work with a cop's training and a cop's mentality. Wilson's already causing trouble. He's still down in Miami. And I have information that he's going around spreading the word that the Bureau was involved in the Letelier assassination. The Bureau. That's what kind of guy he is."

"I don't believe that, Al," said Propper. "Stanley has his own ideas about how to do things, but he's not malicious."

"Maybe not. Look, I know he's your buddy. But I'm going to try to find out what he's up to, and I think you should be careful with him. You can keep that as a souvenir," said Seddon, referring to the mysterious news item.

A few hours later Cornick arrived with a report that Seddon had become obsessed with Stanley Wilson and talked of little else. Cornick was highly amused by the contest between the two Palm Tree Peekers, who, he said, talked and thought alike. The differences between the two grew out of the FBI's traditional condescension toward the police and the policeman's resentment toward the FBI. Otherwise, they were rival spooks—jealous and competitive, sustained by a common zeal for intrigue. "Gene, you know those Palm Tree Peekers all love one another," Cornick declared. "Maybe those two will keep each other occupied."

That night Propper received a call from Stanley Wilson in Miami. The detective said he had ascertained something of such importance that he must tell Propper immediately, regardless of the security risks both to the investigation and to Wilson's source, whom he would protect at all costs. Wilson wanted to swear Propper to secrecy.

"C'mon, Stanley," said Propper. "What is it?"

In whispers and hints, Wilson conveyed to Propper the information that a Brigade source had told him the Novo brothers were planning to kill Propper, Attorney General Bell, and New York U.S. Attorney Robert Fiske if Guillermo Novo went to jail.

Propper was aghast. Hearing the threat was just as chilling the second time—three days after the first time. It was a confirmation from another source, in another city. Also, Propper felt the jolt of a threat to security. Did Wilson know that the FBI had already learned of the same threat through Wack's new informant in New York? Did Wilson know somebody in the Secret Service who had leaked it to him? Propper decided not to let on to Wilson that he had already heard the threat, and he thought he sounded rattled enough to raise no suspicions in Wilson.

Propper asked how a Brigade source would know such a thing, as the Novo brothers were not members of the Brigade. To this, Wilson replied that Propper was wrong. The Novo brothers had not landed with the Brigade at the Bay of Pigs, but the Brigade had nevertheless admitted Ignacio Novo to membership the previous year—the year of CORU. It was a great honor to Ignacio, who lived part of each year in Miami. Wilson told Propper that the street word in Miami had it that Ignacio had gained admission on the strength of his own anti-Communist "operations," which were deemed a fitting substitute for combat service at the Bay of Pigs. The Novo brothers had many connections to the inner circle of the Brigade, said Wilson, who did not want to speak further about the source until he returned to Washington. In the meantime, he warned, Propper should be careful.

Ricardo Canete called Wack the next morning with his daily report, saying that he had made only brief contact with Ignacio Novo the previous evening. Novo, he reported, could not yet furnish passport photographs for the four sets of identity papers he had ordered from Canete, who told Wack he had not pressed the matter. Canete had to remain in character as a hustler and money-chaser. So he had told Novo that there was no real money in document forging anyway, and that he was content to wait, but he had expressed a renewed interest in a counterfeiting scheme he had heard Novo mention before. It involved counterfeit American money that Novo had said he expected to receive from Chile. For security reasons, Novo referred to it as a shipment of Chilean wine. Canete had repeatedly volunteered his skills for the job of passing the counterfeit as real money. Novo once again had offered Canete a chance at the distribution profits on the deal, which was still awaiting the shipment from Chile.

"Not much happened," Canete told Wack. "Everything's kind of on hold."

"You think he's suspicious of you?" asked Wack. "Did he say anything unusual?"

"He's suspicious of everybody," said Canete. "But I think he's just fucking around."

"Yeah, well, maybe you better wait for him to contact you next time," Wack suggested. "Let's take it easy for a few days."

"Okay," said Canete. "Oh. And by the way, I remembered something else. Not from last night. From a couple of weeks ago."

"What's that?"

"Those pictures you took of me reminded me," said Canete. "Ignacio showed me a picture once. Real quick. And he said, 'This is the cocksucker who wants Guillermo.' I didn't know the guy in the picture, so I didn't pay much attention. But I'm pretty sure it was you."

"Me?" said Wack.

"Yeah. I'm pretty sure."

"That's about as funny as a bloody nose," said Wack. "You're trying to bullshit me with a story like that. You expect me to believe that shit, that you all of a sudden remembered something like that?"

"I swear," said Canete. "I just didn't connect it to you until today, that's all. It looked like some kind of surveillance photograph or something. Those guys know how to do that stuff."

"Yeah, sure," said Wack. "What did the photograph look like, specifically?"

"It looked like you, that's all," said Canete. "Hey, don't get sore at me. I'm just offering you the information. All I remember is that it was some guy who looked like you. And he was walking in the street somewhere. And it looked like a rainy day. I think there were umbrellas in the picture. And the guy in the picture was wearing a real loud plaid sports jacket."

"What kind of sports jacket?" asked Wack.

"A real loud one," Canete replied. "With big checks on it. It was yellow with some red in it, if I remember right. I'm sure it was kind of ugly. Kind of tacky, really."

"Fuck you," said Wack.

"You got one like that?" asked Canete.

"Yeah. But I'm still not sure I believe you."

Wack cross-examined Canete on the photograph and then he wrote a teletype for Cornick, saying that he tended to believe the story but was not sure. Cornick concurred with Wack's opinion that they had no choice other than to act as though the story were true. Some of Novo's people might follow Wack to a rendezvous with Canete or with one of Wack's other informants. To guard against that possibility, headquarters and the New York office would soon agree that Bureau countersurveillance teams should cover Wack's clandestine meetings. Cornick urged Wack to keep his distance from Canete and to look for more ways to verify the informant's reports. "Hold his feet to the fire, Larry," he advised.

Cornick conveyed Wack's news to Propper, only to be outdone when Propper entrusted to him the information from Stanley Wilson. The news brought Cornick a fresh conundrum, wrapped in shock. He found it difficult to believe that Wilson could have discovered such precise intelligence so fast. But he managed to analyze the situation enough to isolate the two most likely explanations—both of which were extremely unpleasant. One possibility was that Wilson had learned of the threat through a leak in the Miami FBI office. If this was true, it would mean that security in the Miami office was a joke and that word might filter back to the Cuban exiles, who in turn might figure out that Canete was the informant. There were dire implications all over the place. And Cornick also knew that no one in the Miami office would ever admit to such a heinous offense as a leak.

The other possibility was that Wilson was telling the truth and had learned the information from a source in the Brigade, in which case Wilson's source would be just as well placed as Canete, and just as important. And Wilson would be right back in the thick of the investigation. This prospect depressed and alarmed Cornick, who figured that Wilson would guard the informant's identity with his life and force the Bureau to crawl to him for verification and further reports. Even worse, Wilson would no doubt come up with valid reasons why he needed to know everything Cornick was doing, the better to manage his prize source.

It was a rat's nest, Cornick and Propper agreed. And the situation demanded unorthodox maneuvers. For one thing, Cornick acknowledged that he could not very well report Wilson's information to the Bureau, because the Miami office would call Wilson a liar and would jump down the detective's throat in pursuit of his source's name. Wilson would not tell them. Friction and name-calling would ensue. Worst of all, Wilson would realize instantly that Propper had broken his promise to keep the information from the Bureau. Then Wilson would no longer trust Propper, who probably had the best chance to find out who the source was. Reluctantly, Cornick concluded that it was better not to inform the Bureau. Propper could then massage Wilson, telling him truthfully that the topmost levels of the United States government were in full alert over the threat to the attorney general, and that the FBI was activated, but that Propper had not given Wilson's name to the FBI. Then, treating Wilson with the utmost importance, Propper could coax him to reveal the name of his source in the Brigade.

Propper did this, employing all the blandishments and artifices he could think of—without success. Wilson protected his source steadfastly, adding that he would soon return to Miami for more information—provided, of course, that Propper would help him squeeze some more travel money out of the D.C. police department.

The overall informant situation, Propper realized, was gnarled in a maze of related "ifs." If Canete is lying to Wack. If Canete is telling the truth to Wack. If Novo is lying to Canete. If Wilson is lying about the Miami source. If Wilson is telling the truth. If Morales is telling the truth about Bosch. If Wilson is working for the CIA. Everything depended on the degree of confidence one felt in the conduits of information from an underworld, and every answer affected the others. The combinations could be manipulated so that one could believe that the case was on the brink of solution or that the investigators were floundering in a hoax that was partially of their own making. All Propper knew was that threats seemed to be bubbling up against him, which might mean that he was near a break, but he would never be able to separate the heroes from the charlatans until he possessed the elements of a murder case—the names of the killers and the probable facts of the conspiracy, such as where the killers stayed in Washington and where they obtained the components of the bomb that killed Letelier and Moffitt. Of all these he was ignorant, and in that state he could only grope around in a dark room of informants.

Propper had never been the sort to fret over shadowy complexities. His instinct was to concentrate on his next move and leave the troublesome possibilities to themselves. Accordingly, he devoted himself to the task of jailing Guillermo Novo. By all indications, Novo was the leader of the Cuban Nationalist Movement and the pressure point. Even a hint that he might go to jail had caused rumblings and threats from New York to Miami. This was a good sign. Propper focused on it.

On May 17, he sent four official copies of a motion for revocation of Guillermo Novo's parole to Federal District Court in Trenton, New Jersey. A court hearing was scheduled for early June.

Al Seddon dropped in at Propper's office on May 20, and again he closed the door for privacy. He was there to announce a breakthrough in the investigation. He said he had been checking with some of his contacts on the Stanley Wilson matter—on which, by the way, there had been no further progress—and in the course of things he had talked with a clandestine expert in bombs and electronics. This expert knew the transmission frequencies for all the commercially available remote-control devices that might be used to detonate bombs. In comparing them with a list of the most commonly used CB radio frequencies, Seddon and the expert had made the startling discovery that they matched almost perfectly. Seddon read off a long list of pairings as Propper scribbled notes. Seddon said the expert believed that the frequencies were too close for safety or control. The bottom line, Seddon declared, was that the bomb on Sheridan Circle had not been detonated by remote control.

This news discouraged Propper. Left alone, he pulled out a memorandum about the kinds of bombs Cuban exile terrorists had been known to use. It was a long list. There was the aluminum-foil detonator, with two pieces of foil touching a contact point connected to the bomb and each piece dragging under the car. When the car moved and the pieces touched, the bomb exploded. There were heat-sensor detonators, which could be rigged to make the bomb explode when the car engine reached a certain temperature. There were mercury-vapor switches, which would cause explosions when the mercury rolled to the contact points. There were even battery-deterioration bombs—used by Orlando Bosch, among others—that could be rigged to explode when the strength of a battery fell below a certain level. And, of course, there was an entire catalogue of time-device detonators, such as the "time pencil" that had been used in the old CIA

commando raids against Cuba and also, a decade later, in the bomb
that blew up the Cubana Airlines jetliner out of Barbados. All these
were on the list. Some of the devices were quite dangerous, some
crude, some sophisticated. But none of them offered the precision of
the remote-control device, which could be detonated with the touch
of a button and was therefore highly suited to the purposes of an assassin. All the other devices would have required an element of luck
to catch Letelier in the car at a certain moment. Propper and Cornick
had favored the remote-control theory because they did not believe
Letelier's assassins would tolerate that element of chance. Now,
after Seddon's piece of underground detective work, they were without a theory on the type of bomb used. Neither Propper's instincts
nor his reason favored any particular type, and the FBI lab report
was incomplete and inconclusive. Propper tried to forget bombs and
enjoy the weekend.

On Monday, May 23, Detective Wilson arrived at Propper's office,
complaining that FBI agents were still harassing him about his contacts in Miami. They wanted to know everything he knew, including
his sources, but they refused to tell him anything in return. It was
the same old one-way street, he said. Half jokingly, Wilson accused
Propper of throwing in with the Bureau. It was a mistake, he said.
The case would never get solved and Propper would wind up feeling
trodden upon, like a policeman. With a smile, he gave Propper a copy
of the police department's "semiofficial" FBI poem:

> We know who did it, but we can't tell you.
> We have his picture, but we can't show you.
> We know his address, but we can't take you there.
> We can't do any of these things, because we're too high in the air.
> We have a source who could, of course, close your case, that's true.
> But if we turned you on to him, then we couldn't be better than you.
> After reading this, you probably can tell just who we are.
> We won't bother to tell a lie.
> We're the high-stepping cats called the FBI.

"I don't need the Bureau to tell me what they're doing," Wilson
said slyly. "I have my own ways of finding out certain things. Certain pieces of intelligence information."
"Like what?" said Propper.
"Like Admiral McIntyre's polygraph," said Wilson. "I know you

guys gave the Chilean naval attaché a big super-secret polygraph about the Letelier case."

"What?" cried Propper.

"And I know it connects to the Brigade down in Miami," added Wilson. "That's what I'm working on."

Propper jumped up from his chair. "Stanley, this isn't funny," he said sternly. "That whole thing is classified. If it ever leaks out, we'll never get another damn bit of cooperation from the Chilean embassy."

"Everything is classified," grumbled Wilson.

"Yeah, well, this is one thing that *ought* to be classified," said Propper. "Stanley, I want to know who told you that. You can't fuck around on something like this."

An argument ensued. This time it was deadly serious. Wilson said he had to protect his sources, and Propper countered by saying that this looked like an *official* source rather than a Cuban exile who would fear for his life. Propper was intent, nearly possessed. He finally prevailed upon Wilson to reveal that he had heard about the polygraph from a secretary at the Chilean embassy. The detective refused to elaborate.

Wilson left in a bad mood, and Propper called Cornick. It took Cornick more than half an hour to calm down enough to discuss the matter. Then he argued that they had to move immediately. They had to go to the Chilean embassy and advise officials there of the security problem within their own ranks. It was an ugly move. The secretary might well be fired, and if so, she would blame Stanley Wilson for not protecting her, and Wilson would be enraged at Propper and the Bureau for betraying his confidence and for interfering with his investigation. All this would be bad, said Cornick, but the risk of doing nothing was even less attractive. If the polygraph story leaked to the newspapers, the Chileans would blame the Bureau and the Bureau would blame Propper. More importantly, the Chileans would have a pretext for refusing to cooperate further. In the end, Propper agreed. Cornick went to the Chilean embassy and returned with word that the Chileans were grateful for the warning. Later, they would tell Cornick that Wilson had been dating one of the secretaries, who admitted being the leaker. All this came down hard on Stanley Wilson.

On May 27, one of Scherrer's long cables arrived from Buenos Aires. "At present, we unfortunately have virtually no information from known Cuban exile travelers to Chile as to their activities and contacts in Chile," wrote Scherrer. "Legat believes Cuban exile travelers to Chile could be pressured through interviews with Bureau agents, grand-jury appearances, and the possibility of contempt citations, to make important disclosures as to what went on in Chile. Needless to say, the Chilean government will not make such disclosures if any Chilean government entity was involved."

Propper became annoyed even before he finished reading it. "What's all this pressure crap?" he asked Cornick. "What the hell does he think we're doing up here?"

"I guess he thinks we aren't doing enough," said Cornick.

"Carter, I'm putting those guys in the grand jury two a week," said Propper. "Suárez is in jail. Novo's going to jail next week. What the hell does he want me to do, torture them?"

"Maybe so," Cornick laughed. "Maybe he does. I think what he's really telling us is that it's up to us, because he's run into a stone wall down there with the Chileans. Listen to this: 'In recent contact with Chilean government officials, Legat has gained the impression that DINA has complete information on the Letelier assassination, but this information is being withheld for fear of embarrassing the Chilean government.' That's what he says."

"DINA has complete information?" Propper asked intently. "He said that?"

"Yep," said Cornick. "Complete information. Everybody's underlining it and going batshit at the Bureau. That's what kind of reputation he has. Everybody knows he wouldn't say something like that lightly."

"That's just great, Carter," Propper fumed. "He's saying DINA has complete information down in Chile, but we have to find out about it up here. Isn't that what he's saying?"

"Kind of," said Cornick. "But he's also giving us some hints. He's telling us what he needs if he's going to break any new ground down there. Listen to this: 'Until we are in a position to confront DINA or the Chilean government at a higher level with specific details as to the identities of Chilean government entities or individuals contacted by Cuban exiles visiting Chile, it is certain that no information or assistance in this regard from the Chilean government will be forthcoming.' The higher level is Pinochet, Gene. The President. Scherrer is telling us that Pinochet is the only one who can force Contreras to do anything. He's saying that if we can get him something to hit Contreras over the head with, he'll make sure it gets to Pinochet, so they won't have any choice. That's what he did in the Otero case, I hear."

Propper was paying no attention. "He said he's gained the impression that DINA has complete knowledge?" he said. "Is that right? He's *gained the impression*? Well, I've gained the impression, too, but it doesn't do me any good. What does that mean?"

"I don't know, Gene," said Cornick. "But I'll find out."

"You know, Carter, that cable doesn't really tell me anything new, but it makes me feel worse," said Propper.

"You've got to study these things, Gene," said Cornick. "Investigation is all a matter of perspective."

"Yeah, well, you study it," said Propper. "I'm going to put pressure on Novo."

On the morning of June 6, a small crowd gathered outside the courtroom of U.S. District Judge George Barlow, in Trenton, New Jersey. Cornick was there, along with Frank O'Brien and another agent from the Newark FBI office. Several parole officers and reporters were there, and so was Guillermo Novo's lawyer. But Guillermo Novo himself was late for the hearing at which the government planned to show why he should be jailed for violating the conditions of the parole he had received in 1974. (Novo had been convicted on charges of conspiring to bomb Cuban government property in Montreal, Canada.) His parole did not permit unapproved travel to foreign countries. As the minutes passed, everyone was trying not to worry. The lawyer said he had spoken with Novo the previous day, and Novo had promised to attend. Frank O'Brien said the same thing.

Propper was standing off to the side with Ignacio Novo, who was escorting a woman on each arm. "Where's your brother?" asked Propper.

"He'll show," Novo replied. "He's always a little late, but he'll show. I just talked to him."

"When?"

"This morning. A few hours ago. He'll show."

Propper nodded. Then he raised the subject of the negotiations he had begun a few days earlier, when Ignacio Novo had unexpectedly appeared in Washington on the day three Cuban Nationalist Movement members went before the grand jury. Propper had then made a proposition: he would see to it that the parole case against Guillermo Novo was dropped if the two Novo brothers and Dionisio Suárez agreed to take polygraphs on the Letelier case. Novo had said he was interested.

"What do you think?" asked Propper. "I'm not in a position to negotiate with you on the Letelier case itself yet, but I am in a position to negotiate on the parole thing. If you guys pass the polygraphs, I'll toss it."

"Those things can be rigged," Novo said with a smile. "By either side."

"Maybe so," said Propper. "But a rigged one wouldn't do me any good in the long run. And you guys don't have anything to lose. Look, Guillermo's going to jail. I've got him nailed cold. But all you guys have to do to get him out of it is to take polygraphs. And if the polygraphs say you don't know anything about the Letelier assassination, like you tell me you don't, then I toss the parole case and Guillermo walks. That's fair, isn't it? I want to prove to you guys that I'm not harassing you just for the hell of it."

"Yeah, right," said Novo. "Okay, I talked to Guillermo. And I can't guarantee that Suárez will do it, but me and my brother will do it. I have to talk to Suárez."

"You didn't do it in Washington the other day?" asked Propper.

"No," said Novo. "I was busy. There wasn't enough time."

"Well, we're running out of time," said Propper, who excused himself and walked over to the FBI cluster.

Cornick was growing edgy. "We've been on the phone, Gene," he reported. "We called Roy's Chevrolet, and they say he's not there and isn't supposed to be at work until tomorrow. His home phone doesn't answer."

"That's great," said Propper. "Is there anybody else you can call? I want to tell the judge we've made every effort to locate him."

O'Brien knew a few places. He and the other agent ran back to the phones. Propper turned to Cornick. "Carter, if he's taking a dive, we've got to move fast to catch him before he gets where he's going. Can you put out a bulletin now, just in case?"

Cornick shook his head. "They won't do anything without a warrant," he said. "The warrant will have a time stamped on it, so I can't jump the gun. If I call now, they'll just say I'm jumpy. They'll say Novo will show up late like Cubans always do."

Propper looked nervously at Cornick, the crowd, and the walls, as though consulting them on the next move. "Okay, that's it," he said. "That's it. I'll go get the judge. We have to get you guys started. The judge can always quash the warrant if Novo shows. They do it all the time."

Propper walked briskly into Judge Barlow's chambers and told a clerk he was ready to get started. Novo was more than half an hour late. Then he went back outside. The courtroom doors soon opened, and the crowd filed in. Propper waited outside as long as he could. O'Brien reported that the superintendent of Novo's apartment building had seen him leave early that morning. Propper and the agents watched Ignacio Novo and the two women and the lawyer enter the courtroom. O'Brien said that if they already knew Guillermo Novo was going underground, they had acted brilliantly all morning, pretending not to. Cornick and Propper agreed.

"Okay, let's do it," said Propper when he saw the judge make his entrance. On the way inside he whispered to Cornick, "Keep an eye on Iggie, will you?"

"Don't worry about it," said Cornick. He needed no further reminder that Propper was about to ask for an arrest warrant against Guillermo Novo with his back turned to the man who had promised to kill three men, including Propper, if Guillermo ever went back to jail.

Judge Barlow granted a federal bench warrant over the objections of Novo's lawyer. When Propper finished the paperwork with the clerk, he found that Ignacio Novo had gone. So had Cornick, who was on the telephone to headquarters, sounding the alarm, asking the Bureau to implement the standard fugitive procedures on Guillermo Novo, alias Frederick Pagan. In addition, Cornick asked the Bureau to give a special notification to the State Department, the CIA, and the FBI legal attachés in eleven foreign countries.

There was great excitement as the wires clicked and cables went all over the world, but for Cornick and Propper it quickly drained away. Their long-sought leverage over Guillermo Novo was being wasted.

"Don't worry, Gene," said Cornick. "We'll find the bastard."

Within twenty-four hours of Novo's disappearance, FBI agents reported that their informants were making numerous damaging allegations against Novo. This was natural, Cornick told Propper, because Novo was now a hot property, and also because informants have a tendency to dump on anyone who is on the run.

Two pieces of information were especially interesting. The Miami office sent a report that Novo had been involved in a bombing of the OAS building in Washington, which was significant in that it put him in the capital on a bomb mission. And Newark reported hearing that Novo and the CNM had been receiving arms shipments from Chile that were arranged through the Chilean consul in Miami.

While Cornick processed the rumors and false alarms of the Guillermo Novo manhunt, Propper spent some time at the State Department and soon devised a new international strategy. He would try to take advantage of an upcoming state visit by President Pérez of Venezuela, who was scheduled to have meetings with President Carter and a luncheon with Secretary of State Vance. Propper saw this as an opening. He would seek help from the very top of the government. Three days after the Novo hearing, he was drafting memos for both President Carter and Secretary Vance, appealing to each of them for help in obtaining the DISIP files on CORU and on the Otero assassination mission. "All the evidence gathered to date," Propper wrote, "has led to the conclusion that certain militant anti-Castro Cuban exiles are directly responsible for the murder. It is further believed that the assassination was ordered by the Chilean secret police (DINA), with whom these exiles have close connections, although less evidence of this fact exists." He added that the Venezuelan government had possession of vital information about the plans of the Cuban exiles before the Letelier assassination and about the nature of their contacts with DINA, and he asked Carter and Vance to seek help from Pérez himself, as other Venezuelan officials "have not been completely candid with United States authorities."

Propper sent them to the State Department, where Frank Willis, his ally there, had promised to help him squeeze the documents up through the bureaucracy toward the desks of the President and the secretary of state. Willis's task was not easy. Some officials at State were unhappy about the uncomplimentary reference to the Venezuelan government, and as for the White House, Propper received quick word that the President's staff would not even consider showing the President any paper longer than half a page. This made Propper fume, but in the end he managed to compress his argument and a summary of the investigation into the required length. Most of the original thoughts were still there, stripped of background, but they were packed so densely on the page that Propper could scarcely understand them himself. He worried about how it would read to someone unfamiliar with the investigation.

On June 22, Cornick brought Propper a pair of Scherrer's latest cables. Both were written in a rather prickly tone. Propper breezed through them and looked at Cornick. "You mean Scherrer really believes DINA didn't kill Letelier?" he asked, with some disappointment.

"That's what it sounds like," said Cornick.

"That's just great." Propper sighed. "And he doesn't think Otero was dealing with DINA either, does he? That's the implication in there."

"I'm afraid he doesn't, Gene," said Cornick. "That's what the second cable is about. Our friend Scherrer does a number on my interview with the Monkey. He tears it apart. He says Monkey's already told us three different stories on Letelier and a whole bunch of lies. He also says here that Monkey is lying to us about Otero's contact with DINA. He says it's possible that Otero *thought* he was dealing with DINA, but he wasn't. If he was, DINA would never have let him leave Chile alive."

"Jesus Christ, Carter!" said Propper. "He's got to be wrong about that! He'd better be. I'm right in the middle of busting my ass to get the President and the secretary of state to lean on Pérez to lean on DISIP to give me the Otero-DINA assassination file, and now Scherrer tells us it's all bullshit."

"I understand all that, Gene," said Cornick. "I'm just telling you what the man says. You've got to put it in perspective. The point is that Scherrer has a hell of a lot of expertise and experience down there. He's forgotten more than you and I will ever know. On the other hand, you've got to take into consideration the fact that he doesn't like Otero. Otero bit half his hand off, from what I hear, and a human bite wound is the worst there is. Scherrer also hates the Monkey. He thinks he's a Castro agent. All right? And to top it all off, he doesn't like the Venezuelans, either. He thinks they've been lying to us from the beginning to protect themselves in the Bosch case. So naturally Scherrer's going to think the Monkey is trying to put us on to some bullshit about Otero to keep us away from Bosch and Venezuela."

"So we don't really know, right?" said Propper. "The bottom line is, we don't know. Well, that does it. We won't know about anything until we see for ourselves. I'll send down a writ to have Otero brought up here so we can talk to him."

"He'll spit in your face, Gene," said Cornick.

"Maybe so," said Propper, "but he can't hurt me when he's handcuffed."

"He bit Scherrer when he was handcuffed," said Cornick.

"Well, Scherrer is an agent, and my writ won't say FBI on it," said Propper. "It'll just say me, and I've got a plan to deal with him."

"Oh, yeah? Tell me about it, Gene."

"I'll be nice to him," said Propper.

"What?"

"I'll be nice to him," said Propper. "I'll treat him like a gentleman. I won't drag him onto an airplane or anything. I'll just say, 'Look, it's all over now. I understand the Chileans mistreated you, and I'd just like to know what happened down there.' That's all."

Cornick was giving Propper a quizzical look.

"What's the matter?" Propper demanded.

"Nothing, nothing," said Cornick. "I agree with you. It can't hurt. So let's do it. I just think you've gone over the deep end, that's all."

Propper grinned. He was in a combative mood. If Scherrer was stymied by Contreras, he said, perhaps they could shake things up in Washington and introduce some new factors. Propper could ask for an appointment with the new Chilean ambassador, Jorge Cauas, who had a reputation at the State Department as an upright man of business who was supposed to revive Chile's economic reputation on Wall Street.

". . . Don't say any more, Gene," Cornick interrupted. "I hear the train coming. You want to give the ambassador a list of those Cubans, like Novo and Suárez, and ask him to have his government investigate what they did in Chile, right?"

"Why not?" asked Propper. "They keep saying how much they want to cooperate, don't they?"

"I don't care about them," said Cornick. "It's Scherrer. He ain't gonna like it if you go pushing your way into a police matter. That's his job down there."

"Well, I don't see how he can bitch after writing those cables," said Propper. "He keeps saying Contreras is stonewalling. He's damn near begging for help."

Cornick thought for a moment and then broke into a mischievous smile. "Well, what the hell," he said. "We'll all get fired over this case anyway. I think it's a good idea."

"Good."

"But the Bureau is going to go henshit on us, Gene," said Cornick. "You know how they feel about us hitting the Chilean embassy. My God, they've still got our legal advisors over there jumping up and down on my head because you want to subpoena the Chilean consul in Miami. They think it's illegal."

"Carter, I don't care what the Bureau legal advisors say. What can they do?"

"They can make a lot of noise," said Cornick. "They can write memos. And they can make me write memos. And they can pretty well make my life miserable. That's what they can do."

"So what?" kidded Propper. "You're used to that, aren't you? You don't even have to come to the embassy if they won't let you."

Cornick drew himself up with a show of dignity. "I'll be there," he declared. "Don't worry. I don't put up with that stuff anymore. I'll just handle it with my new method."

"What's that?" asked Propper.

"I'm going to tell the Bureau that you're a raving maniac. And I can't stop you. And you're going to subpoena the consul and lay it on this new ambassador no matter what the Bureau does. And I'll tell them there's no way to predict what abominations you might bring forth over at the embassy if I'm not there to watch you and tone you down. And I'll say I have to be there to protect the Bureau's interest. That always gets 'em."

"Okay, Carter," said Propper. "You tell 'em whatever you have to tell 'em."

"I'm glad you don't mind," said Cornick. " 'Cause I have to say some godawful things about you sometimes."

Not long after Cornick left, Propper received an unwelcome call from the State Department's Venezuela desk officer, who informed him that his superiors had rejected Propper's memo to Secretary of State Vance on grounds of excessive length. They refused to show it to the secretary until Propper reduced the length by half. It was a crisis, said the desk officer, as President Pérez was due in Washington within the week.

Late that afternoon a reporter from *The Washington Star* barged into Propper's office to make an important announcement: the *Star* would break a major news story about the Letelier investigation the next day. The reporter was there to offer Propper a chance to give a "reaction quote." He said he was sorry to have to give Propper the solemn bad news—a claim Propper doubted because of the glint in his eye. The story, said the reporter, was that the investigation was zeroing in on John Marks, co-author of *The CIA and the Cult of Intelligence.*

"For what?" asked Propper.

"For what?" echoed the reporter. This was not the response he had expected, apparently. "For the Letelier assassination. According to our sources, bombing material was found in the back of Marks's car on the day of the murders, and he was overheard bragging about having done it."

Propper started laughing, much to the discomfort of the reporter.

"Who's writing that story?" he asked. "You? That's a good one."

"Not me," said the reporter. "O'Leary. He's finishing it up back at the office. He said you could call him if you want to."

"O'Leary?" said Propper. "He should know better." Jeremiah O'Leary was a veteran Washington reporter.

"Doesn't sound like you think much of the story," said the reporter. "You want to call Jerry?"

"No, I don't," said Propper. "It's not worth the time. I think you should go back and tell Jerry I said to go ahead with the story if he wants to get laughed out of town. Tell him that lead was one of hundreds we discarded nine months ago, in the first week after the murder. Tell him the dog who supposedly smelled the explosives in the back of Marks's car is the same dog who smelled a bomb at IPS that day. The dog screwed up twice. The lab didn't find anything. Your story is a zero."

The reporter studied Propper's face for signs of deception. Propper, for his part, was struggling to address the matter seriously. "I don't know who your sources are," he added. "But it's either somebody who doesn't know anything about the investigation or it's somebody who wants to stick it to Marks. I don't know Marks, but if he ever asks me, I'll tell him I told you in advance that the story is bullshit. You guys better be careful."

O'Leary's story never ran.

On Friday morning, June 24, Canete met Ignacio Novo to deliver yet another set of false identity papers, this time in the name of Victor Triquero. Canete laughed about the name, which he translated roughly for Wack as "Tricky Vicky," but he did not laugh about the Chilean. Novo, he said, was leaving New York for Miami and then for South America, probably in the company of his fugitive brother, Guillermo. In his absence, Novo had told Canete, a Chilean would be coming to see Canete on business, the nature of which Novo did not specify. Canete would know the Chilean, said Novo, when the Chilean showed him a dollar bill torn in half. Novo gave Canete the other half, telling him to match it against the Chilean's bill. He also instructed Canete to call a CNM member named Alvin Ross if he had any "trouble" with the Chilean, saying that Ross knew the Chilean and could deal with him.

This news put Cornick into orbit. He wanted to have Ignacio Novo followed, on the assumption that Novo would lead agents to his brother. To accomplish that, he needed to put continuous surveillance on Novo in New York—all the way to the airplane door—and to make sure agents picked him up at the Miami airport and followed him. Cornick's most persistent rumors still had Guillermo in Miami, perhaps waiting for money and travel papers to flee into exile.

Cornick wanted to know about the Chilean. Was this Novo's "Chilean contact"? Was this the "blond Chilean"? If so, Cornick wanted him followed, photographed, and identified as soon as he came to visit Canete. This meant Wack had complicated arrangements to make. Having no idea when—or if—the Chilean would drop in on Canete, Wack might have to throw a stakeout on Canete himself, which would not make Canete happy. And he would have to be careful. Presuming that the Chilean had been trained in countersurveillance techniques, they were running a risk that the Chilean would detect the presence of the agents and conclude that Canete was an informant.

Finally, Cornick had to make sure Canete was telling the truth. It was no small matter to mobilize the Bureau for a stakeout and for coordinated clandestine surveillances in two cities. Supervisors and SACs would have other uses for the manpower. Wack and Cornick would have to override them—all on the word of a convicted con man. Naturally, Cornick worried that Canete knew how to let drop the one bit of information that would embroil half the FBI for weeks. Why would the Chilean stay behind in New York if the Novo brothers were fleeing the country? he wondered. Why would the Chilean need to contact Canete? Did it make sense that Novo would put so sensitive a person as a key Chilean agent in touch with the likes of Canete? Cornick asked such questions of himself and of Wack. He told Wack to put the fear of God into Canete, if possible.

In the midst of this, Cindy Grant buzzed Propper to announce that there was a Ricardo Morales on the telephone.

"Morales, calling *me?*" said Propper, of the man who had been ducking his subpoena since April and bedeviling his investigation from its very beginning. Propper had never seen or spoken to Morales.

"He says you know him," said Grant.

Propper recovered himself and punched onto the line, to be greeted by a voice that was at once smooth, low, and reedy in tone. Morales told Propper that he would like to visit him soon in Washington, making no mention of the subpoena or of the pressure from Cornick. He said it like an old classmate who wanted to drop by for a chat. He said that his life was in danger, as usual, that his position was a precarious one, but that he had been working to elicit information that would help Propper. He said he hoped to be in the capital within two weeks.

On Saturday, June 25, agents followed Ignacio Novo everywhere he went, until finally, that evening, they could report the number of the Miami-bound flight he had boarded. Cornick rousted the Miami agents to meet the plane and to resume clandestine surveillance.

Earlier that day, Wack kept a rendezvous with Canete and learned that Novo had dropped in on Canete Friday evening to say goodbye. Novo had mentioned the Chilean again, and he had warned Canete that a special team of CNM members would "blow the head off anyone who talks." Wack and Cornick decided not to put surveillance on Canete. They would spare the manpower, and Canete's nerves, until the Chilean made a contact. If he made one, he would probably make more.

The surveillance in Miami was still in operation on Monday, when Propper went rushing over to the State Department, cursing to himself. The Venezuela desk had lost the memo he had sent over two weeks earlier for Secretary of State Vance. Propper delivered another copy by hand and found the Venezuela desk in a state of crisis. President Pérez was meeting with Secretary Vance the next day. Propper learned to his dismay that his memo could not be presented to Vance without a covering memo from another State Department official—the higher the better. After a good deal of spinning around and bureaucratic maneuver, Propper got word that Terence A. Todman, Assistant Secretary of State for Latin America, had signed the memo, which was on its way to Vance.

Cornick arrived at Propper's office late the next morning, June 28, with news of a triumph. A couple of hours earlier, he said, Bureau agents had walked up to Héctor Durán, the Chilean consul, and handed him Propper's grand-jury subpoena on a Miami street corner. The agents said Durán had turned white. Cornick liked to think of the subpoena as a kind of artillery round, designed to soften resistance at the Chilean embassy before he and Propper arrived that afternoon to meet Ambassador Cauas.

It was a big day. The Cauas meeting would reach into Chile. The Vance-Pérez lunch would reach into Venezuela. Durán had already been subpoenaed. Subpoenas were out for several Cuban exiles. Agents were following Ignacio Novo in Miami, and Wack was on the Chilean watch in New York.

On the way to the Chilean embassy, Cornick tried to lighten the mood with exaggerated tales of the abuse he had heaped on Propper's head in his reports to Bureau superiors. Propper was in no mood for levity. He was psyching himself up to address the ambassador, which he did promptly upon the completion of introductions. Long before coffee or tea could be poured, and even before the sitting-room sofas warmed up, he announced that he had requested the meeting in order to seek the assistance of the Chilean government in the Letelier investigation.

Specifically, he said, he would like the Chilean government to search its files and conduct an inquiry as to the activities of Cuban exile terrorists who had sought sanctuary in Chile. The most notorious of these was Orlando Bosch, who was known to have lived in Chile more than a year. Propper also listed Rolando Otero, Guillermo Novo, and several others. He said he would like to know the names of the Chileans who had been in contact with the Cuban exiles, so that he could prove or disprove allegations that the Cubans had acted in concert with elements of the Chilean government in the Letelier assassination. Propper said he thought it was in the best interest of the Chilean government to cooperate fully and swiftly in order to resolve an ugly criminal matter before it did extensive political damage to relations between the two countries.

Propper and Cornick waited for a reply from Cauas, who leaned back in his chair to think for a moment. Then he said that the matter was indeed an ugly one and that he heartily agreed on the need to resolve it. He said he could not imagine what Cuban exile terrorists had been doing in Chile, but he would do his best to find out.

The two Americans were soon out the door, and Cornick was kidding Propper. "I thought you'd never get around to business," he quipped. The entire meeting had lasted less than thirty minutes.

Propper rose to his own defense. "Carter, I was perfectly polite in there," he said. "I didn't threaten him or anything. I called him Mr. Ambassador."

"Never mind," said Cornick. "Whatever you did, I think it got through to the ambassador. Unless he's a damned good actor, he doesn't like this stuff at all. I'd love to see the cable he's going to send down to Santiago."

"Well, the State Department tells me he's not real tight with the junta," said Propper. "He's respectable, and he's supposed to make Chile respectable up here. So maybe he'll make a stink to his own people if we show him enough of their dirty laundry."

"Well, we'll know something if they ship a new ambassador up here," said Cornick.

Propper went back to his office and spent the rest of the afternoon trying to find out what had happened in the *tête-à-tête* between Secretary Vance and President Pérez. This proved to be no easy task. The results were inside the secretary's head, and Vance was a busy man. Propper spent a lot of time on the telephone with the Venezuela desk officer and with Willis, trying to find someone of high position who could and would speak directly to Vance. He still had no answer late the next afternoon when Cornick dropped by with a bombshell.

The case agent had just heard it from Wack, who had just heard it from Canete: the Chilean had showed up. Canete was at his latest job, at a moped shop in lower Manhattan, when a man walked in and asked Canete if he had lost a dollar bill. Canete said he had lost part of one, and in due course the two men produced matching pieces of the same dollar bill. Then the man discussed mopeds knowledgeably for a few moments, advised Canete to keep his piece of the dollar on his person at all times, and left. The only comment he made having anything to do with nefarious activities was to tell Canete that he would be contacted by Alvin Ross. Canete described the man as tall, thin, and fair, almost Scandinavian, with light-brown hair worn over the ears. Canete said the man spoke good English and "non-Cuban" Spanish, and that he carried himself with a marked military bearing. While chatting casually, the man stood with his feet apart and his hands clasped behind him, in the "at ease" position.

"All right now, Gene," Cornick said intently. "If this is true, we've got a whole new ball game. This could be the link we've been looking for between the Novos and Chile. This could be the blond Chilean."

"He said the hair was light brown?" asked Propper.

"Yeah, but that could be close enough," said Cornick. "Wack's checking with his sources up there. And he's got to show Canete the composite. Novo could have *two* Chilean contacts, for all we know, but the point is that we ought to be able to nail this one. And if he's got any connection at all to the Chilean government, there's our leverage with the Chileans."

"You think the source is telling the truth?" asked Propper.

"What do you think?"

"He says this guy walked in with the dollar bill and talked about mopeds and then left? That's all?"

"Yep," said Cornick. "He could be testing the source, I guess."

"Yeah," Propper said, without much enthusiasm. "But I can't figure out why a Chilean would need to deal with a Cuban forger and con man in the first place."

"I know what you're thinking, Gene," said Cornick. "Something doesn't feel right about this. It's too good to be true. Wack's been busting his ass all this time to identify the blond Chilean up there, and all of a sudden his new source has a blond Chilean walk through the door. But the Chilean doesn't say or do anything we can verify, and all he does is give the source some spy mumbo-jumbo and the silent treatment, like something out of the movies."

"Well, if the source is lying, why would he do it?" asked Propper. "He couldn't be doubling back on us for the Novos, could he?"

"Damned if I know, Gene," said Cornick. "Some con men are compulsive liars, you know. They're incapable of telling the truth. They've always got to have something going."

"But some things he's told Wack do check out, right?"

"That's true."

"Well, we can't go on like this," Propper said irritably. "We've got to find out whether he's lying. This is too important."

"It won't be easy," said Cornick. "Wack's built up the relationship with the guy, and the problem could be that he's too close. There's a balance you've got to maintain with sources, and it ain't easy."

"I know it ain't easy," said Propper. "What are you going to do?"

"Well, I'll take a little trip up to New York and meet this guy with Wack," said Cornick. "And for starters, I'll threaten the piss out of him. The little bastard's got to know what he's looking at if he's lying to us on something this important."

"What's that?" asked Propper.

"I don't know yet." Cornick grinned. "But it's going to sound awful. I guarantee you that."

On July 6, Propper was interviewing a Cuban exile who had been trained as a CIA demolitions expert. He was also one of the three men allegedly approached by Edwin Wilson in the Libyan assassination scheme. He told Propper and Cornick that he knew nothing about the Letelier assassination but would be happy to cooperate any way he could. The investigators asked him about the kinds of bombs that might have been used on Sheridan Circle, and the man's conversation suddenly brightened. He talked expansively about detonators, charge composition, bomb-attachment techniques, and various ways to control the direction and spread of the blast. When he told how he and his friends still played with directional control by putting bombs in the ground, pitched to expel the force at an angle, and by competing to see who could stand closest to the blast, Propper and Cornick realized that they were speaking with something more than a bomb expert: this respectable-looking corporate executive was a bomb freak. The expert said you could stand amazingly close to a plastic charge if you knew how to control the direction of the concussion.

Propper asked the man if it was indeed impossible to operate a remote-control detonating device in an area of heavy CB radio traffic.

"Are you kidding?" said the man. "That's child's play. All you have to do is wire the detonator so that it won't go off until it gets *two* frequencies, or a combination of frequencies, in a certain order at a certain interval. Like a telephone number. You build in a little code so you can dial the bomb. That way you don't run the risk that some radio transmission will set it off. You should do that no matter where you are, as a precaution."

Cornick asked the man for his opinion as to the best method of attaching a bomb to the bottom of a car.

"Magnet," said the expert.

"How about tape?" asked Cornick.

"It can be done, but it's amateurish. Tape requires too much time on the target scene. And it's messy. The only reason to use tape at all is to secure a magnet to the bomb. Then you just slap the magnet up under the car where you want it. That way it only takes a second or two."

Propper asked the bomb expert to excuse him while he stepped outside with Cornick. "So much for Seddon's great discovery about how it couldn't be remote control," he whispered to Cornick.

"I know, I know," said Cornick. "Don't say anything to Al about it, okay?"

"Jesus Christ, Carter," said Propper. "Al was giving me all this stuff about how he'd gotten it from the supersecret experts over at the Agency. You think it's all bullshit?"

"I don't doubt that he got it from the Agency," said Cornick. "Al's honest as he can be. He's a Palm Tree Peeker, but he won't make stuff up on you."

"Well, how can he be so wrong, then?" asked Propper.

"Damned if I know, Gene."

"Al should have talked to this guy," said Propper. "He's a walking bomb manual. But as far as I'm concerned, anybody who plays with bombs like that is crazy."

"Yeah, but smart-crazy," said Cornick. "There's no way you see him having anything to do with Letelier, is there?"

"No way," said Propper.

"Me neither," said Cornick.

"Why'd you ask?"

"Well, I'd be happy to go up against anybody in this damn case," said Cornick, "but I'm just as glad it's not him."

"Yeah," said Propper. "Look, I'm thinking of showing this guy the crime-scene photographs of the car and the autopsy pictures."

"What for?" asked Cornick.

"I don't know," said Propper. "He might see something. I wouldn't put anything past him."

"It's worth a try, if he'll do it," said Cornick.

Back inside, the bomb expert said he would be happy to study the photographs and to suggest what conclusions he could. Propper unlocked his safe and pulled them out. The bomb expert spread them out on the table before him and then picked the grisly photographs up one by one, looking at them the way an orthopedic surgeon would examine a series of X-rays. It didn't take very long.

"Well, I'd say it was a mixture," said the expert. "Probably some plastic. But there's definitely some dynamite in there. Definitely some low-order explosive."

"How can you tell?" asked Cornick.

"From all these angles where things are bent and mangled," said the expert. "That's what we call a 'pushing effect,' which comes from a low-order charge. The C-4 plastic and any other high-order military explosive gives what we call a 'cutting effect.' All these angles would be much sharper."

"Why would anybody use a mixture?" asked Propper.

"That depends on who it is," said the expert. "Dynamite gives more bulk and stability to the bomb. And it's a hell of a lot easier to get."

"I see," said Propper. "Tell me, how many Cuban exiles would you say there are in Miami who know as much about bombs as you do?"

"None," said the expert, smiling. "But there are about a hundred who think they do." He soon left, promising to answer any bomb questions Propper or Cornick might think of later.

Two nights later, at two o'clock in the morning of July 8, the telephone roused Wack from a sound sleep. He mumbled something into the line.

"Larry, I gotta talk to you!" said a voice. "I'm sorry, but I gotta talk to somebody, and you're the only one who can help."

"What's the matter?" Wack asked Canete. "You sound like you've just seen a ghost or something."

"I wish I'd seen a fucking ghost," said Canete. "I wish to God that's what it was. Shit." He was panting.

"Go ahead," said Wack. "Tell me. Nobody's gonna be on the line at this hour of the night."

"I never thought it would get this heavy, I swear to God," said Canete. "But I was with Alvin tonight, and he told me he built the bomb that blew Letelier away."

Wack woke up instantly. "What? Don't fuck with me about something like that!"

"Just like that, out of the blue, I swear to God," sputtered Canete. "The asshole said, 'My latest bomb did a job on the Commie Letelier.' I told him to shut the fuck up, I didn't want to hear that kind of shit. But he just kept right on telling me stuff I didn't want to hear. I swear to God, I couldn't shut him up. I know you want to hear it, but I didn't want to hear that shit, Larry."

"Wait a minute, wait a minute!" said Wack. "I gotta get this while it's fresh. Right now. Are you all right? You're not going anywhere, are you? You're not outside or anything?"

"I'm going to Canada, that's where I'm going," said Canete. "No. No. I'm not going anywhere. You gotta tell me what to do, Larry. I'm in way too deep. This shit wasn't on the menu."

"Wait a minute! Wait a minute!" said Wack. "All right, let's go. Tell me what happened. Everything."

"Okay, so I go over to Ascione Motors last night about nine o'clock to meet Alvin," said Canete. "We have an appointment . . ."

". . . Wait a minute," said Wack. "That's last night, just a few hours ago? Thursday night? Tonight, really?"

"Yeah, just a few fucking hours ago," said Canete. "We have an appointment because Alvin wants more false I.D. . . .

"I had the stuff, but he just couldn't wait for me to get it typed up. So I go over there and the place is closed. And Alvin goes to the back of the store and comes back with a typewriter for me to use. And he's talking to me all the time about nothing special. And he sets the typewriter up for me at one of the desks and I pull out the blank papers and go to work.

"Okay? And I'm just typing away there, minding my own business. And while I'm doing it, Alvin is looking over my shoulder. He's too nervous to just sit there. And so he says to me, 'Hey, you're pretty good at that stuff, aren't you?'

"So I say, 'Yeah, pretty good,' and go right on typing along.

"And he says a few things to try to get me talking, but I'm still typing, you know, concentrating on my business. And finally Alvin says, 'Well, I can't do what you're doing, but I'm pretty good at making bombs.'

"So I say, 'Oh, yeah?' And I keep right on typing.

"And he says, 'Yeah. I'm pretty good with that stuff. I even made one out of a coffeepot one time.'

"So I say, 'Yeah, sure, Alvin,' kind of sarcastic, and I keep on working, like I'm not paying him any attention. You see?

"And he says, 'I'm not kidding.' He says, 'The latest bomb I built did a job on a Commie named Letelier. You heard of that?'

"So you can imagine what that does to me inside. I'm about to blow up, but I keep right on typing. And I say to him, 'Cut it out, Alvin, will you? Can't you see I'm working?' You know, like I think he's full of shit.

"And he says, 'I did.' He says, 'I'm telling you.'

"And I say, 'Sure, Alvin. How'd you do it?' I'm teasing him, you know?

"And he acts real secret and important and he says, 'I always use the C-4 plastic, 'cause it's easier to mold.' And he says, 'On the Letelier bomb, I used two timing devices, a clock and an acid backup. Just to make sure.' "

Wack interrupted Canete's breakneck monologue. "Wait a minute," he said. "What kind of clock? Did he say how he did these things and the technical part of how they're made?"

"No," Canete replied. "I'm telling you what he said. He just said a clock. A *reloj*. And an acid backup. That's all he said. And I didn't ask 'cause I'm not interested in that kind of stuff and he knows it."

"Okay," said Wack.

"Okay, so I'm still typing there, and I say, 'All right, Alvin. I'm fucking impressed. But anybody can build a bomb, I hear. That was a car bomb, right? Did you have the balls to put the bomb under the car?' And when I asked that, I was sweating that he's gonna get suspicious.

"But Alvin's too stupid, I guess. He just says, 'Well, I could have done it, but I didn't handle that part. The Brigade did it.' "

"Wait a minute," interrupted Wack. "He said the Brigade? The Bay of Pigs Brigade out of Miami?"

"Yeah," said Canete. "That's what I'm telling you. He says, 'Two guys out of the Brigade came up to handle that.' He says, 'The Shrimp Man took care of that. He and his partner.' He says, 'They do a lot of traveling, if you know what I mean.' I think he means they're heavies.

"So finally I stop typing and look at him, like he's finally knocked me over. Like he's finally done it and convinced me he's not full of shit. And I say, 'Knock it off, Alvin. I don't wanna hear that kind of shit.'

"And he kind of smiles, and he says, 'Okay.' And he says, 'We had three other jobs planned besides Letelier, but things kind of got screwed up. We were supposed to get a newspaper guy down South, but then the temperature in the South went too high and the Brigade had to shuffle things around at the last minute.'

"And I say, 'Come on, Alvin.' Kind of pissed off. Like I've already said I don't want to hear it. And he finally shuts up. And I finish the documents and give them to him. And after that I walked around on the streets in a fucking daze trying to figure out what to do. And then I called you. That's it."

"Holy shit," said Wack. "Holy shit, I can't believe it. Did he say anything else? Think now. Let's go back." Wack started questioning Canete. When he finished, the only additional detail that had emerged was that Ross had said something about the man who visited Canete at the moped shop. Ross called him "the colonel" and said he was a Chilean.

"All right, that's good," said Wack. "Don't worry about anything, all right? You did great."

"I gotta go get a drink," said Canete.

"Okay, but don't belt too many," said Wack. "We gotta go over this first thing in the morning. Like eight o'clock. I want to get this on tape. All right? Don't let me down on this one, okay?"

"Okay," said Canete. "Right now, I gotta get a drink."

Wack's phone call didn't find Cornick at his usual roost the next morning. Cornick was facing his own emergency at Propper's office, where U.S. marshals were due to deliver prisoner Rolando Otero at eleven o'clock. Incredibly, Ricardo Morales had called the previous afternoon to say that he would arrive in Propper's office at the same time.

Cornick and Propper hurriedly analyzed their predicament. They knew Otero had learned, through discovery proceedings before his trials, that Morales had informed the FBI thoroughly and regularly about his bombing activities in Miami. He might well regard Morales as the author of his misfortune. And Otero, according to Scherrer, was a violent, unstable man with a forty-year sentence and nothing to lose. Morales, for his part, was widely feared in the spy world and the underworld for his cunning and his violent outbursts, and it was believed that he was angry with both the FBI and Otero over the Otero case, which had caused him nothing but trouble with his employers in the Venezuelan DISIP. The investigators also knew, from Morales, that the two Cubans had not seen each other since the night in February 1976 when Morales put Otero on the plane for his second and last trip into Chile.

"One of them's the torch, and the other one's the powder," said Cornick. "We've got to play this one close, or we'll have an explosion in here." Cornick could not quite believe that Morales's arrival that day was a mere coincidence. He wondered out loud whether Morales had found out about the writ for Otero. Upon analysis, however, this seemed impossible. Even Cornick and Propper had been unable to predict when Otero would arrive.

Morales arrived first and was promptly whisked off to an empty office, where Propper got his first look at the famous double or triple spy. With his dapper appearance and round, smiling face, Morales hardly seemed like a hunted man. "I don't know why I keep working so hard for you after all the trouble it has brought to me," he said pleasantly, after introductions. "But I have some information." Morales disclosed that he had been pumping Frank Castro for Letelier intelligence, and that Castro had laid the murder on Dionisio Suárez, Ignacio Novo, and two Miami Cuban exiles. He said the assassination had apparently been a joint operation of Miami and New Jersey Cubans, and he was more certain than ever that the murder had been discussed at the CORU meeting in the Dominican Republic.

The phone interrupted Morales as he was trying to remember a few other tidbits of intelligence. Propper answered and told Cornick the caller was Wack. Something urgent. Cornick took the call in another office, leaving Propper and another agent, Tim Mahoney, to get acquainted with Morales.

Cornick was gasping as he listened to Wack's stunning report. "Larry, are you sure?" he asked. "Are you sure you got it right?"

"Yes," said Wack. "I got the whole thing down last night, and I got it again this morning."

"Are you sure *he* got it right?" asked Cornick.

"There's no doubt in my mind," said Wack. "You gotta hear him tell it."

"What was his reaction? What did he sound like when he told you?"

"He was petrified," said Wack.

"That's good," said Cornick.

"Yeah," said Wack. "It means he's probably telling the truth."

"There's not much in what he said that we can corroborate, though," said Cornick. "You think he'd be willing to take a polygraph?"

"Yeah, I think so," said Wack.

"My God, Larry, I've got to catch my breath," said Cornick. "That's the first real evidence we've had in the whole damn case."

"That's half the reason he's so scared, Carter. I'm worried about him. I'm gonna have to babysit the bastard every night now."

"That's all right," said Cornick. "It's worth it. You could have the whole case in your hand up there. When's the full teletype coming down on this?"

"It's already on the way."

"Good. My God. I'll read it over and get back to you this afternoon. Right now I've got to rescue Propper. We've got Monkey Morales in here now, and Otero's due any minute. I'm up to my ass in alligators, and they're draining the swamp. Any other day and I'd be right up there."

"Don't worry, Carter," said Wack. "I ain't going anywhere."

"God loves you, doctor," said Cornick. "You'll make a hell of an agent when you get a little older."

"Thanks," snickered Wack.

Cornick went back and summoned Propper outside for a hallway conference. Propper was clamping down on his excitement even as Cornick spoke. They both suppressed a desire to go shouting on the courthouse roof.

"You realize the implications of the Brigade stuff, don't you?" said Cornick. "We've had two leads all this time, and now they're the same lead all of a sudden. Right down to the Shrimp Man! That's got to be Alberto Franco. Tomboy keeps fingering Franco as one of the hit men on Letelier, and Franco is in the shrimp business. He's the Shrimp Man. There's the link."

"Alvin Ross isn't the leader, Carter," said Propper. "I know that. He didn't give any orders."

"I know that, Gene," said Cornick. "Wack says the source thinks Ross is only a wheel man or something like that. Errands and driving and stuff. But that doesn't matter. Ross is halfway to a confession."

"I know one implication," Propper declared. "We have to polygraph that source down in Miami. They've been stalling us almost a year."

"Don't worry," said Cornick. "I'll take care of it. We haven't had much leverage since the admiral passed the polygraph. I haven't been pushing it."

"I've got to get Franco back before the grand jury."

"I've got to go see Wack. He's sitting on a powder keg up there." Cornick took a few breaths. "But we've got enough to keep us busy right here. How's the Monkey?"

"He hasn't really said much more," said Propper. "He's been talking about why he's told us so many stories. He's still saying he never heard Bosch say the Novos did it. And I'll swear, Carter, I've seen a lot of witnesses lie, and I'm pretty good at spotting it. But I have absolutely no idea whether he's telling the truth or not. No idea. Everything comes out the same, and I wind up wanting to believe him."

"He's a smooth son-of-a-bitch, isn't he?" said Cornick.

"I told him Otero's coming in today."

"You did?"

"Yeah," said Propper. "He says he thinks he can help us. He might be willing to talk to Otero."

Cornick stared at Propper, almost reverently. "That's incredible," he announced. "He sticks his friend in the back with a forty-year sentence, and now he's going to have a little chat with him for us? The sheer nerve of the man amazes me. I told you, he's the slickest character I've ever met, Gene."

"He doesn't seem to look at it like that," said Propper. "He says Otero will understand what he did. It doesn't make any sense to me, but if Morales feels guilty or afraid to talk to Otero, I sure can't see it. Honest, Carter, he seems cool about it to me."

"That can't be right," said Cornick. "Well, let's go back in there and lean on him a little bit, so he'll think twice about trying to spin us. The game is complicated with the Monkey, because he's got so many cards to play. He's got his old Bureau service, and his knowledge, and the fact that he's a Venezuelan official. And he plays 'em all for himself. He'll go right back down to Caracas and tell the boys in DISIP that he's dealing with the case agent on the Letelier case —personally—and he'll tell 'em what leads we're looking into. And he'll be partly right, because he knows I can't afford to ignore anything he tells me. So I'm starting from a disadvantage. Your subpoena helps, but I've got to tell the Monkey that if he wants to stop having trouble from the FBI, he'd better be straight with us and help us. None of his stuff checks so far. It could all be bullshit. And I've got to tell him I'm only interested in the Letelier case, but I'd hate to see him get picked up on something else. He'll get the picture."

They went back in to see Morales, but very little time passed before they were buzzed again. Otero had arrived. Morales smiled brightly on hearing the news. He advised the investigators to hurry if they wanted him to speak with Otero, as his plane was leaving in less than two hours.

Cornick and Propper, whispering intently to each other, walked briskly into the reception area, where they found a large U.S. marshal standing on either side of a small, very skinny man.

As always, Otero held a book in his hands, which were handcuffed behind him. He was reading *Cops and Rebels* by Paul Chevigny, and soon he would include passages from the book in a newsletter called "Commentaries from My Prison Cell," which his friends regularly mimeographed and distributed to his followers in southern Florida. From this particular book, Otero would choose an excerpt that he thought came close to describing the motives of countless Cuban exiles who had begun as anti-Castro fighters and then adopted, over the years, the life of an informant or secret agent:

> I was very afraid of being arrested. I am terrified of the police, but I wanted to do "heavy" things, and have the security of not being arrested. I thought I could get away with a lot more, agitate more, without getting in trouble. I could make a speech that would radicalize other people, and if an undercover agent heard it, I would not be arrested. I could openly say that I was a violent radical. This way, I thought I could get the government to finance movement activities. I could give information about the government to the movement and not hurt myself.

Otero wrote like an eighteenth-century pamphleteer, cutting wide swaths through history and politics on a single page. In prison, his personal philosophy had gone into perpetual flux, as he struggled to reconcile his vituperative anti-Communism with his disgust for the Western world.

Propper and Cornick knew nothing of this confused personal odyssey. They saw a terrorist who had set off nine bombs in wanton disregard for the lives of those who might be near the blast, who then went on international assassination missions, and wound up biting through the hand of an FBI agent. They also saw someone who might help them learn about Chileans who dealt with Cuban exiles in matters of assassination. This possibility eclipsed everything else, and for that reason, Propper asked the marshals to remove the handcuffs. He also invited Otero to make use of the telephone, knowing how starved prisoners always get after months and years of stand-

ing in line for a single phone. Otero called his mother and his girlfriend.

"You don't know why you're here, do you?" Propper asked Otero
after the calls.

"It don't make no difference to me," said Otero.

Propper had no doubt of it. Otero seemed supremely indifferent to
everything. "It's about the Letelier case," said Propper.

Otero made no response.

"We are interested in what happened to you when you went to
Chile," said Propper. "Some of the people you met there may be involved in our case. We understand they mistreated you down there."

"Yes," said Otero. "But they didn't put me in jail for forty years."

"I know," said Propper. "But they gave you a pretty hard time,
didn't they? When you expected them to help you?"

"I expected the United States to help me fight Castro, too," said
Otero.

"I don't know anything about all that," Propper said. "And I don't
know anything about your case down in Florida except what I've
read. All I care about is Letelier. I can't hurt you on anything. I can't
help you much, but I can't hurt you either. And you might help me
nail some of the Chileans who hurt you. Okay? All I want to know
about is Chileans. I know you don't want to talk about any of your
Cuban friends, and that's all right with me. I won't even ask you
about them. I just want to know about Chileans."

"I will never talk about another Cuban," Otero said softly. "Never.
I got forty years now, and you can put another forty years on my
head if you want to. It don't make no difference to me."

"Okay, that's what I thought," said Propper. "No Cubans. That's
what I said. That's all right with me."

Otero made no response.

After a few more minutes in this vein, Propper and Cornick
stepped outside for a conference. Both of them favored giving Morales a chance to work on Otero, who struck them more like a sleep-
walker or a zombie than a madman. Otero needed to be energized.
"Gene, we can't forget that the Monkey's his handler," said Cornick.
"That's a powerful relationship, and Monkey has a gift for making
them come back to him after he's screwed them. I'll be damned if I
know how he does it, but he does. He might even help. He's already
done things a damn sight weirder."

Propper went back in to tell Otero that Morales was in the courthouse and had asked to see him. Cornick was having security night-

mares about what Otero and Morales might do alone together in the same room. He insisted that the marshals put the handcuffs on Otero, and then the entourage made its way down the hall.

"All right, if you don't want to talk to him, you just let us know," said Propper.

Otero made no response.

"You got him all right?" asked one of the marshals. "Okay if we go down to the cafeteria?"

"Yeah, I got him," said Cornick. "But I want you fellows to stick around for a few minutes. Right there and right there." Cornick pointed to positions just outside the door. He was speaking in a battle voice.

Cornick opened the door. Otero did not react to the first sight of Morales, who came toward him with a smile until he noticed the handcuffs. "Those aren't necessary," said Morales. "I can't talk to Rolando like this. Can't you take them off?"

"Sorry," said Cornick. "Not a chance. Prisoners are supposed to be handcuffed at all times in the custody of the marshals. We're not even supposed to leave you two alone."

Morales protested. Cornick stood his ground. And finally Morales took Otero inside and shut the door. Cornick opened it a few inches.

"Carter, take it easy," whispered Propper. "They're on the fourth floor, for God's sake, and this is the only door. They're not going anywhere."

"That's fine for you to say, Gene," said Cornick. "But if one of those guys throws the other one out the window or something, *I'm* the one who'll be writing memos for the next twenty years trying to explain why I left them in there alone without clearing it with the Bureau."

Morales glanced at the crack in the door and rolled his eyes in disgust. Then he smiled and gave Otero the Latin *abrazo*. "Rolando," he said. "How are you?"

"I am surviving, Ricardo," said Otero. "I am trying to explain my position to the people so that I can help the cause, you know."

"Like always," said Morales. He showed Otero to a seat. "I never thought they'd convict you," he said. "I'm sorry. I did everything in my power to stop it, and I think they'll overturn it on appeal, anyway."

"It's better to think they won't right now," said Otero. "Thank you for not showing up at the trials."

"I know you must be pissed off at me anyhow, my friend," said

Morales. "But you are wise not to make any threats or any show of it when you are in no position to do anything. But believe me. I warned you about the FBI. I was trying to protect you even with them. But that doesn't matter now."

"No," said Otero. "I know how you play, Ricardo. The FBI seems to think you are some kind of a superman. Maybe they're afraid we're going to escape and fly away."

Morales smiled. "Maybe so," he said. "The sons-of-bitches didn't want me to see you. I had to make some strong remarks to get them to back down. I wanted to see you and ask what's going on. Is there anything I can do for you?"

"You can get me some more books," said Otero. "I have a hard time getting them in jail."

"I'll speak to the people about it," said Morales. "Listen, I wanted you to know that I have decided to cooperate with Propper's investigation. I'm cooperating with him about the Letelier thing. It has nothing to do with Cuba, and the Chileans have turned into dogs."

"I know nothing about this Letelier," said Otero.

"They want to know about the Chileans."

"And you want to make sure I don't tell them about the involvement of the DISIP with me down there? Is that right, Ricardo?"

"I don't care," said Morales. "I'm not going to be on that job much longer. You have made one more job too hot for me, my friend." He laughed.

"I don't believe you will be fired because of me," said Otero.

"No," said Morales. "It's a long story. I can't tell you everything now, but I've got a lot of problems. Many people are after me, as usual. But you can tell them about the DISIP if you want to."

"What about the involvement of Frank Castro and the mission in Costa Rica?" asked Otero.

"I'm not talking about that," said Morales. "Don't worry."

"Well, I cannot cooperate as fully as you, Ricardo," said Otero. "But I respect your feelings."

Ten minutes later, Morales stepped outside the door, smiled broadly, and said, "He'll talk to you now."

Propper and Cornick looked at each other with relief, doubt, amazement, and hope. Cornick walked Morales out of the courthouse, trading indirect boasts of influence, and when he returned, Propper was making the pitch to Otero, asking Otero if there was anything specific he would like in return for his cooperation. Otero asked to be moved to a prison closer to Miami, to be nearer his law-yer and his friends.

"I'll try," said Propper. "I can't make any promises, but I'll try."

"I'll talk to you," said Otero. "I don't have no respect for the Chil-eans."

There was a rush for note pads, and arrangements were made to have phone calls held. But the marshals intervened before Otero could talk. They said the prisoner had to be back at the jail by three-thirty. Regulations. This was a fight Propper and Cornick knew they could not win, so they told Otero to try to remember things about his Chile trip over the weekend. They also asked him what kinds of books they might get for him. And when he was gone, Propper called the District of Columbia jail to make sure that prisoner Otero would never come anywhere near prisoner Dionisio Suárez.

On Monday, the prisoner returned with the marshals, and Otero talked in a low, bored monologue for nearly two hours, as Propper, Cornick, and Agent Tim Mahoney took notes. It was a dry summary of why he had gone to Chile and what had occurred there. Some things he could not remember, despite much prompting and many memory-stimulation techniques from Cornick. He could not, for ex-ample, remember the name of the Chilean captain who had ques-tioned him about the Cuban exile organizations. "He was a son-of-a-bitch," Otero kept saying.

When it was over, the three investigators sat alone. "There's no doubt in my mind that he told us the truth," said Cornick.

"Or that he was dealing with DINA," said Propper. "I think Scher-rer was wrong."

"Well, they *told* him they were DINA," said Cornick, hedging. "But they could have been lying."

"I don't think so," said Propper.

"I don't either," said Cornick. "I want to see what Scherrer's reac-tion is. But this thing is too detailed. It's worth its weight in gold from an investigative standpoint. It gives us a picture of how the for-eign side of DINA works, for one thing. And I'm telling you. This guy Estrobel makes me think that it's not always a cool rational deci-sion when they want to rub somebody out. He sounds like he's gone berserk, for God's sake. A guy like that could have decided to take Letelier out no matter how crazy it was."

"What about the blond captain?" asked Propper.

"I thought you'd never ask," said Cornick.

"Well, what do you think?" asked Propper. "Is it possible? Could it be the same blond Chilean Wack's chasing up in New York?"

"That ain't a long shot, Gene," said Cornick. "That's a shot in the dark. How many blond Chileans do you think there are?"

"We should try a spread," said Propper. "We have the composite from Wack. We have the composite of the guy who threatened Liz Ryden. We have the Williams and Romeral photos from Paraguay. We have a few other Chileans. You think you could put together a good spread by tomorrow, Tim?"

"Easy," said Mahoney.

In the interim, Propper went over to the State Department to pick up a memo from Terence Todman. "I don't know why the secretary did not raise the issue," Todman wrote, of the Pérez-Vance luncheon. "He was not opposed. Maybe he didn't find a convenient moment."

"A convenient moment!" Propper shouted to no one in particular among the State Department's Venezuela experts. "What the hell is that?"

He was not quite calmed down even by the next morning, when Otero arrived again. "We're going to show you some pictures," said Cornick, who ran through the standard instructions for photo ID sessions as Mahoney spread fourteen photographs on Propper's desk.

Otero looked at them no more than five seconds. Then he picked up the photograph of Juan Williams and handed it to Cornick. "This is the captain I told you about," he said. "But his hair was a little more blond than this."

Cornick closed his eyes briefly, but he did not faint. "You think that's the one, though?" he said. "The one who questioned you with Major Torres?"

"I know it's him," said Otero, without emotion.

Cornick, Mahoney, and Propper contained themselves until they could complete the formalities and walk outside. Then they exhaled and slapped each other and looked toward the sky. Lips quivered. "I've been doing photo IDs on bank robberies all my life," said Cornick. "And I know a positive ID when I see one. That was a hit, boy! That was a fucking hit!"

"I knew we would solve this sucker," said Propper.

Cornick's cable took two days to reach Scherrer in Buenos Aires. Scherrer cabled back immediately that the Juan Williams identification was a "momentous development." He said he might have been wrong about Otero.

Scherrer flew to Santiago that same day, July 14, and went to see General Baeza, informing him that Propper had gone to the Chilean embassy on June 28 and requested an investigation of Cuban exile activities in Chile. Baeza expressed surprise. He had not heard of the request. At this, Scherrer advised Baeza confidentially that the prosecutor was something of a wild man. Unless he got satisfactory answers about the Cubans—particularly about the contacts of Bosch and Otero—Propper might go to the American State Department and the politicians and possibly even the newspapers. The next day Scherrer gave the same message to Contreras.

On the same day that Scherrer met Contreras, Wack met with Canete in New York. He showed Canete the same photospread that Otero had viewed three days earlier. Canete picked out Juan Williams as "the colonel." But he could not be certain. Juan Williams was shown with a mustache and goatee. "The colonel" was cleanshaven. Wack called Cornick with a tentative confirmation: Juan Williams, the "blond Chilean" and the "covert link" to the Cuban Nationalist Movement, might still be in the United States.

Propper decided that it was time to communicate directly with the American embassy in Chile. He sent a memo to the deputy chief of mission on July 18 announcing that "the facts we currently possess indicate that the Chilean secret police (DINA) is responsible for the assassination."

Firemen and police officers struggle to remove Orlando Letelier (face and hand visible at the door line) from his car, minutes after the bomb exploded.

CLOCKWISE FROM LEFT: FBI Special Agent L. Carter Cornick. FBI Special Agent Larry Wack. FBI composite drawing of the man who threatened Elizabeth Ryden. Rolando Otero. Ricardo Morales. Cuban Nationalist Movement member Dionisio Suárez. FBI Legal Attaché Robert W. Scherrer.

Hoy, Vincente Vergara

CLOCKWISE FROM LEFT:
Eugene M. Propper on the streets
of Santiago in March 1978.
Ambassador George Landau.
Assistant United States Attorney
E. Lawrence Barcella, Jr.

CLOCKWISE FROM LEFT:
General Manuel Contreras.
Alvin Ross.
Virgilio Paz (left)
and Guillermo Novo at a
Cuban Nationalist Movement
reception in New Jersey.

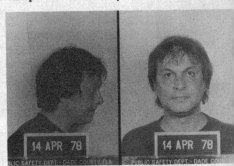

14 APR 78   14 APR 78

LIC SAFETY DEPT.- DADE COUNTY, FLA.   UBLIC SAFETY DEPT.- DADE COU

Hoy, Vincente Vergara

Hoy, Raul Montoya

UPI

CLOCKWISE FROM ABOVE: Don Campbell, Earl Silbert, and Seymour Glanzer, during the Watergate case, 1973. Inés (Mariana) Callejas de Townley, also known as Anat, Ana Goldman, Ana Brooks, Ana Luisa Pizarro, and Carmen Luisa Correa Letelier. Michael V. Townley after testifying in Santiago, Chile, 1978.

The faces of Michael Townley.
COUNTERCLOCKWISE FROM LEFT:
Juan Williams Rose, from
his special Paraguayan passport.
Andrés Wilson's Chilean identity card.
Hans Petersen's official Chilean
passport. Kenneth Enyart's
American passport.

Marcelo Montecino

Orlando and Isabel Letelier dance the traditional *cueca* on Chilean
Independence Day, September 18, 1976; at that time, Michael Townley
was assembling the bomb that would explode on Sheridan Circle three
days later.

13 ▣ TWO YEARS IN THE CATACOMBS

In DINA's second year, Colonel Contreras begins to concentrate on his war against external threats to the regime. Many officers from the first DINA group in Europe are returning home, their tours over, and Contreras is annoyed with their performance. As one replacement, he names Andrés Wilson. Contreras wants Wilson to go to Europe to recruit both brains and soldiers, to make alliances with those right-wing forces that will be most effective in neutralizing Chilean exiles and their European friends. The pace will be hectic and Wilson must do twenty things at once. The DINA chief has a number of specific projects in mind, and he reminds Wilson that he expects strict obedience to all standing DINA orders.

One of them is to kill Chilean socialist leader Carlos Altamirano on sight anywhere in the world. Like every other officer-grade DINA employee, Wilson knows that one of his predecessors in Europe incurred the wrath of Contreras for wasting an opportunity to do so. The miscreant admitted that he had been in possession of a gun, sitting in his car on a stakeout, when he saw Altamirano enter a hotel alone. He later reported to Contreras a number of circumstances that argued against striking at that time, but none of them saved his career.

Major Eduardo Iturriaga, head of DINA's foreign operations, briefs Wilson on the particulars of his new assignment. He responds favorably when Wilson asks permission to take along Virgilio Paz, of the Cuban Nationalist Movement in the United States.

Wilson flies to the United States on June 14—using the name Kenneth Enyart. He and Paz leave almost immediately for Frankfurt, where they begin meeting and evaluating the underground contacts Iturriaga has provided. Less than two weeks later, Wilson receives a terse emergency order to return to Santiago. Shrugging, he leaves Paz in Frankfurt and flies home on a mystery assignment.*

New emergency orders interrupt Wilson's preparations to return to Europe. This time it is a request originating with His Excellency himself, President Pinochet. A directive comes to Wilson from Contreras: he is to obtain photographs of British military installations in Northern Ireland, preferably of prison camps and interrogation facilities used for Irish political prisoners. Pinochet has decided to prohibit a scheduled inspection of Chile's own prisoner facilities by an international human-rights organization. He knows that he will be castigated in the world press for doing so, and he wants to fight back with evidence that his critics in foreign countries like Great Britain have human-rights problems of their own. He wants to accuse them of hypocrisy.

Wilson is given only eight days to produce the photographs. He contacts Paz by telephone and asks him to fly from Frankfurt to London to Belfast. He gives him the names of some DINA contacts in Britain.

A LAN Chile pilot brings the exposed film from London to Santiago one day too late for Pinochet's announcement canceling the human-rights inspection. Wilson develops the photographs himself—they reveal that he has somehow gained entry to restricted military installations as well as to the Maze prison, but the shots lack contrast and resolution. They reveal that Paz is a better spy than he is a photographer, and he resolves to teach him how to use a camera properly.

He flies back to Europe through Brazil on July 19, leaving DINA in controversy. Some officers believe Wilson and Paz should be congratulated for moving so swiftly on the assignment in Northern Ireland. Others think they should be censured for being late. Wilson knows that Contreras is in the latter group. The DINA chief is in a vengeful mood, obsessed by what he sees as a global weakness in the face of the Marxist enemy. He sees leftist generals in Peru, Communist leaders in Portugal, and leftists moving to take over Spain when Franco dies.

On the way to Frankfurt, Wilson stops in Rome to confer with

---

*The nature of this assignment is not known outside DINA.

DINA's most enthusiastic Italian contact, who is known as "Alfa."*
He learns that Alfa's Avanguardia Nazionale has assets and allies in
influential positions throughout Europe. It will be easy, they say, to
supply Wilson with all the explosives and firearms he may require in
Europe. Also, Alfa's people will funnel to Wilson a stream of intelligence reports about the activities of Chilean leftists in Europe. Wilson is grateful. He is under pressure to send as many such reports as
possible to Santiago. Contreras sees to it that a compendium of "hostile acts against Chile" is published regularly in Chilean newspapers,
as an unmistakable warning to the exiles that DINA is tracking their
activities all over the world.

In Frankfurt, Wilson returns to the job of eliminating Altamirano.
He meets Wolf von Arnswaldt, his contact there at the LAN Chile
office, and retrieves a Fanon-Courier paging system he has sent
ahead. This is the only piece of equipment Wilson has allowed himself to bring from Santiago. He and Paz collect the other components
of a bomb in Europe, but they do not assemble them. They keep the
parts scattered for security—stashed with DINA contacts, stored in
separate cars when Paz and Wilson travel together.

With Paz, Wilson tries to learn more about the character and habits of the socialist leader at the top of Contreras's list. Altamirano
has a reputation for eccentricity and irksome behavior even among
his own political allies. He is known as "Mayo," in reference to his
habit of eating mayonnaise with a bizarre variety of foods. The nickname also refers to Altamirano's alleged compulsion to spread himself thinly over a multitude of political positions. Within the Chilean
military, however, he is best known for the speeches he gave to navy
gatherings before the coup, in which he exhorted navy officers to organize against military disloyalty to President Allende. Since the
coup, the victorious officers have regarded these speeches as treasonous attempts to subvert the sacrosanct military chain of command.

---

*Code name for Alfredo di Stefano, who was first publicly identified as an associate
of Kenneth Enyart by John Dinges. The name di Stefano is in turn a pseudonym for
Stefano Delle Chiaie, also known as "The Black Bomber." Delle Chiaie founded the
neo-fascist Revolutionary Action Group in 1959, and in 1962 he founded the Avanguardia Nazionale. The latter group is the paramilitary arm of the Movimento Sociale
Italiano, the party in Italy headed by Member of Parliament Giorgio Almirante.

Police reports implicated Delle Chiaie in the December 17, 1969, bombing of a bank
on the Piazza Fontana in Milan, in which sixteen people died, but no charges were
brought.

Altamirano lives in Leipzig, but he frequently visits Frankfurt, Rome, Paris, and many other European cities to attend various political conferences. Wilson and Paz try to intercept him on several of the trips. They need to know his exact travel plans in advance so that they can plant a bomb in his car or his room. Altamirano repeatedly frustrates them. He travels erratically, almost whimsically, and he is always accompanied by two or three bodyguards. DINA informants among the Chilean exiles in Germany and France consistently fail to predict his movements. Wilson and Paz once spend two days at a hotel in Stuttgart, waiting for a victim who never arrives.

Fresh emergency orders arrive in August: Wilson is to drop everything and follow a European political leader* who has been making overtures of support for the Pinochet regime in Chile. Contreras does not trust the man. He orders Wilson to shadow him and to find out what he says to whom—find out if he is preparing to betray Chile. This assignment turns out to be so difficult that Wilson appeals for help.

Through Espinoza, he sends to Santiago for Ana Pizarro. She has a gift for infiltration, and he wants her to help penetrate the target's circle of acquaintances. Pizarro leaves Chile on less than forty-eight hours' notice. Her mission is of such importance that DINA chauffeurs, orderlies, and guardians materialize instantly to take care of her children in her absence.

Pizarro flies first to New York to meet Guillermo Novo. The Cuban exile leader, who has already dispatched Paz to Europe as an apprentice to Andrés Wilson, has agreed to provide false documentation so that Pizarro can travel on an American passport, posing as a Puerto Rican Marxist. As it turns out, however, the best Novo can deliver is the driver's license of a thirty-year-old Puerto Rican woman, crudely altered. Foul-ups and delays bedevil the effort to secure a passport, until Pizarro, under ferocious pressure from Santiago, departs on her official Chilean passport. Leaving Paz in Frankfurt, Wilson meets her in Luxembourg. She gets off the jet and treats Wilson to a rhapsody about a white-haired old man and his apple-cheeked granddaughter who enjoyed Pizarro's stories so much on the jet that they have invited her to vacation with them in Switzerland. Pizarro says she was tempted, and that the contrast between their wholesome family plans and her own grim DINA work has stimulated her imagination. She has already sketched out a short sto-

---

*Whose name is unknown to the authors.

ry based on the kindly, coal-eyed grandfather. She is also angry about the mix-up on the Puerto Rican documents. How can she infiltrate leftist Chilean exile groups in Europe when she is carrying an official passport from the Pinochet government?

Suddenly Iturriaga sends orders that Wilson is to abandon the surveillance operation and resume the effort to penetrate, frustrate, and divide the Chilean exile groups. Wilson is resigned to yet another abrupt shift, but he advises Iturriaga by coded message that the exiles seem to be doing a good job of keeping themselves divided. Wilson has obtained the minutes of some of their meetings, which show that the various exile groups have fallen prey to endless quarrels over money, personality, and minor points of political doctrine. Altamirano in particular seems to be a divisive rather than a unifying force, he says.

To this, Iturriaga responds tersely that the Service is not interested in Wilson's political opinions. His orders are to further divide the exiles through careful "disinformation" campaigns and to intimidate them by eliminating their leaders—specifically Altamirano. Wilson knows better than to protest, but he has no idea how to comply. Altamirano is too careful. He cannot be attacked securely. Only a suicide mission seems likely to succeed.

In Italy, Wilson explains his problem to Alfa, who has been in the business of illegal political operations for twenty years. To a man of his stature, a single slaying is a small matter indeed, but he rejects as foolhardy all Wilson's desperate schemes to shoot Altamirano on the street at the next opportunity. Escape is at least as important as the attack itself, he says, arguing that if the police managed to capture Wilson or Paz or one of Alfa's men at the scene of the crime, the damaging publicity would more than offset the gains from the elimination of Altamirano. The capture of a right-wing activist would unify Chilean exiles and other leftists all through Europe, he says.

Alfa shrewdly observes that the purpose of Wilson's mission is twofold: to demonstrate that DINA will not hesitate to strike silently and viciously at leaders anywhere in the world who advocate the overthrow of Pinochet, and to discourage the rise of unified Chilean opposition groups in exile. On both counts, says Alfa, Altamirano is the wrong target. He has heard Wilson speak of a far better one: Bernardo Leighton, a former vice president of Chile and founder of the Chilean Christian Democratic Party. Exiled in Rome, Leighton has become one of the most popular of Pinochet's critics-in-exile. Removed from ambition by advanced age and by an unassuming, avuncular personality, Leighton has excited little jealousy from the leaders of rival exile parties. Socialists and Christian Democrats across Europe and in the United States have responded well to Leighton's call for a return to civilian, constitutional rule in Chile, and in recent months Leighton's calls for a united opposition to Pinochet have also received support from Communist parties in Italy and other European countries. This threatens to bring about a unity against right-wing governments that has not been seen in Europe since World War II.

Leighton is one of Wilson's targets, on the list below Altamirano and Communist Party leader Volodia Teitelboim. The DINA operative has often heard his superiors refer to Leighton and other moderate reformers as "the Kerenskys of Chile"—meaning the constitutional democrats whose weakness paves the way for a Marxist rise to power, as in the Soviet Union. It is an axiom of Contreras's that if the Christian Democrats are allowed to bring civilian rule back to Chile, the Marxists will follow them within seven years. Contreras has vowed to erase that possibility.

Wilson finds Alfa's idea so persuasive that he explores it discreetly with other DINA contacts in Italy. Then he sends another message to Iturriaga to clear the Leighton attack in advance, explaining that Leighton threatens to become the "catalyst" for an anti-Pinochet exile coalition that will stretch across Europe. DINA readily agrees to the mission. Iturriaga demands immediate results. Something must be done to put fear into the exiles and to quell their conspiracies against the Chilean government, he says.

As Alfa has predicted, Leighton turns out to be a trusting man who makes no concessions to security. He and his wife, Anita, generally walk to the shops near their apartment, not far from the Vatican. They often ride buses to political meetings. When they go out in the afternoon, they sometimes walk home after dark. When they go to political meetings at night, friends sometimes bring them home after midnight.

Alfa says the Leighton mission will be easy, like a rabbit shoot. He agrees to undertake the dirty work for two reasons. First, he and his well-established network of professional anti-Communists feel some political threat from Leighton, who is urging Italy's Christian Democrats to make common cause with the parties to the left. Second, Alfa has seen that Wilson has one thing the well-established Italian groups lack: the backing of a country. Alfa has the tacit or open support of many mayors and businessmen. He has money and organization and skilled operatives of all descriptions. But he does not have access to the sanctuary or power that Contreras can offer—the assistance of a sovereign military regime with a kindred philosophy.

At a final meeting, Alfa agrees to the tactical details of a very simple plan, and he also agrees to act quickly. Wilson and his companions drive north toward Austria. They plan to be out of the country before the attack, in order to further insulate DINA from responsibility. They run into trouble at the Austrian border, however, when guards object to Paz's travel documents. His false papers do not include a passport. After much argument, the guards turn the trio back toward Italy. The Italian border guards, on second look, decide that they don't like Paz's papers either, and for a time the group bounces back and forth helplessly between the two checkpoints—unable to enter either country. In the end, they talk their way back into Italy.

Thus, by mistake, they are in the country on October 6, when Alfa's men watch Bernardo and Anita Leighton walk down a deserted street near their apartment. At eight-twenty, on signal, a man with a gun walks toward them on the street, passes them, then turns to fire from the rear. The first slug enters the back of Bernardo Leighton's neck and passes upward through his head, exiting on the left side just behind the forehead. Anita Leighton whirls in shock and catches the second bullet in the side. It passes all the way through her chest, clipping part of her spinal cord. The assailant disappears, leaving the Leightons in a heap on the cobblestones. All Alfa's men are out of Rome by nine o'clock. It was as easy as he promised it would be.

The next day, as headlines flash through Europe and South America detailing the vicious attack on the Leightons—both of whom lie critically wounded in a hospital—Wilson makes his way out of Italy. Pizarro goes straight to Santiago to make a preliminary report to DINA. Paz goes back to the United States.

Wilson flies to London. Now, alone, he is free to work on the most sensitive of the assignments heaped upon him by Contreras, Project ANDREA. Contreras anticipates war against the leftist generals in Peru, and he yearns to have his own secret weapon. By giving it to him, Wilson hopes to add to his reputation as a technical wizard who can accomplish practically anything in his basement laboratory. Wilson has promised to supply Contreras and DINA with a private arsenal for chemical warfare.

In Germany, he has managed a few hours' study of the early development of the organophosphate nerve gases, reading the reports on the pioneering research of a German scientist named Schrader. To Wilson, the import of these studies is that the Hitler regime never succeeded in mass-producing the deadly organophosphates Schrader discovered. They never found a safe way to handle the fluorine that was required for the process.

A team of British scientists headed by B. C. Saunders began competing with the Germans in 1941. In London, Wilson studies the work. He knows that the British, the Americans, and the Russians have stockpiled enormous quantities of the compound most suited to warfare. It is obsolete by the standards of the most modern weapons, but it will serve Contreras's purpose. Wilson makes inquiries at various chemical engineering firms, including one called Gallenkamp. He arranges to have equipment shipped from Gallenkamp to Chile. Within a very few days he is ready to leave. He is certain that none of the scientists and engineers with whom he has been discussing his interests will guess that his qualifications are nothing more than high-school chemistry and a knack for invention. By now, he can dash off the chemical formulas of every nerve gas produced in this century.

Reassuming his Enyart identity, he flies to New York to thank Guillermo Novo for the services of Paz, and he agrees to allow Zero, the ultra-secret execution arm of the Cuban Nationalist Movement, to take public credit for the attack on the Leightons. A Zero communiqué to that effect is drafted and approved by the CNM council on October 10—and distributed anonymously to newspapers. It is published in Spanish-language papers along with a cryptic sign that shows Leighton's initials, B.L., over a large zero.

The communiqué is intended to deflect suspicion from Chile and Italy toward the Cuban exiles, who in fact bear only the slightest responsibility for the attack. At the same time, it is designed to enhance the Cuban Nationalist Movement's reputation for ruthless daring. A hit on a foreign national in faraway Rome is dramatic evidence that the CNM means its public pledge to take the new war against Communism "on all the roads of the world."

In Miami, Kenneth Enyart finds that the "great war" among rival Cuban exile groups is continuing. Alleged CIA stooges and apologists for Castro are being executed, gangland-style, in what police call territorial wars of politics mixed with drug trafficking. Rolando Masferrer, an enforcer/philosopher of fearsome reputation from pre-Castro days in Cuba, has endorsed the terrorist war against "treason" in his newspaper, *Liberty*, declaring that Communists always understand dynamite. He has also written that Orlando Bosch is a "Communist" and that Guillermo Novo is nothing more than Bosch's enforcer. This is only one instance of heated disputes among anti-Castro rivals. Miami police have informant reports that Masferrer caught and disarmed Ignacio Novo one night outside the offices of *Liberty* and then directed his bodyguards to humiliate Novo by dumping him on the street without his trousers.

Enyart meets with CNM members in Miami. On October 15, only nine days after the attack on the Leightons, he drives to Fort Lauderdale to purchase more electronic security equipment from Audio Intelligence Devices, and he flies to Santiago the next day.

Returning to Chile, Enyart becomes Andrés Wilson again and prepares a lengthy report on his activities abroad. He tells Contreras that Paz has performed admirably, but he saves most of his praise for the Europeans. He describes the organizations of Alfa in Italy, of the Frenchman "Daniel"* in southern France, and of the Corsican Brotherhood in Corsica, Nice, and Marseilles, among others. These organizations have impressed even Wilson with their technical proficiency. In all modesty, he does not believe that they have any "solo" specialists as talented as himself, but they can quickly produce entire teams of specialists to work on big jobs. They have a history of doing so.

In addition, says Wilson, the European groups tend to operate on a military command structure. Many of the French members are veterans of the famous OAS group that rebelled against Charles de Gaulle's policies in Algeria and survived as a powerful right-wing secret network whose efforts to assassinate de Gaulle inspired the thriller *The Day of the Jackal*. Wilson declares that the European groups tend to have the military efficiency of the OAS and the trustworthiness of the Italian Mafia. All of them—especially the Corsicans—have histories of enforcing *omertà*, the law of silence.

These qualities make the European groups attractive as future allies for DINA. And there are others. The Europeans have ample local political protection, especially in Nice, Marseilles, and Milan. They

---

*Wilson's code name for Albert Spaggiari, a French political criminal who has belonged to numerous right-wing groups in Europe, including the OAS, the "Occident," Commando Delta, and the SS Weapons Brotherhood. He is believed to have tried to assassinate Charles de Gaulle.

think big: Alfa once led fifty of his men in an armed takeover of the Italian Interior Ministry in Rome, hoping to activate a coup. When it didn't work, Alfa simply led his men out again. The groups are powerful enough so that the European governments almost never manage to punish them even in the case of outright failure. This explains the existence of the industrial heroin labs operated by the Corsicans, and it enables the French and Italian action groups to mount enormous criminal/political operations. They kidnap wealthy leftists for ransom. They rob banks to obtain both the money and the embarrassing financial records of political leaders they oppose. As a result, the lower-ranking operatives are well paid and the more idealistic leaders concentrate on the political dividends.

Contreras finds all this quite attractive. He has heard some of it from his European specialists, but he is fascinated by the details of Wilson's new working relationships. He is especially interested in the bank operations. Contreras likes banks, as storehouses of both money and explosive political information. He admires the Europeans for thinking of them as political targets. Most of all, Contreras responds warmly to the European groups' desire for affiliation with a powerful national government that shares their belief that politics is an ongoing holy war against Marxism. They want the kind of sponsor that the CIA was supposed to be before the Americans developed scruples, and it is one of Contreras's driving ambitions to see DINA and Chile assume such international leadership.

On the morning of October 31, 1975, Rolando Masferrer gets into his car in Miami and is promptly blown to bits by a bomb. Parts of his body are scattered hundreds of feet in all directions, into the yards of neighbors. Miami newspapers splash the story across the front pages, partly because Masferrer occupies a romantic niche in Cuban history.*

That same day, in Santiago, a DINA militia squad breaks into the

---

*As a youth, in the 1930s, Masferrer went to Spain to fight against Franco. In the 1940s, he remained a socialist, but he became a gang leader for the Movement for Revolutionary Socialism (MSR) in Havana. In the 1950s, he flipped and became famous as "El Tigre," a senator and right-wing gang leader under President Batista. When Masferrer fled to Miami a few weeks after Castro came to power, U.S. authorities confiscated $17 million from his boat. In the 1960s, he achieved fame as the con man who persuaded many organizations, including CBS television, to invest in his fraudulent "invasion" of Haiti. In the 1970s, he remained all these things at once—con man, enforcer, anti-Communist, and expert on the early socialist thinkers in Russia.

home of Sheila Cassidy, a British doctor and Catholic novitiate nun who has lived some years in Chile. The militiamen shoot and kill Cassidy's maid because she is in the way, and they haul the doctor off to a DINA interrogation center, where she is stripped naked and tortured electrically on the *"parrilla,"* or "barbecue." The interrogators demand to know why Cassidy gave medical treatment to a leader of the leftist MIR, who was wounded in the leg during a shoot-out with a DINA squadron on the night of October 15. That man, along with MIR chief Andrés Pascal Allende and two female compatriots, miraculously escaped from the gun battle, and DINA has mounted a frenzied search for them. Cassidy says that as a Christian and a doctor she could not refuse treatment to any wounded person. She adds that she feels a missionary's devotion to the poor and the oppressed, and for that reason she does not want to tell DINA who arranged for her to treat the wounded fugitive. She knows DINA will kill them. Under protracted torture, however, she tells nearly everything she knows, and she maintains her sanity only by sharing her religious faith and political altruism with her fellow prisoners.

Wilson helps briefly in the search for Pascal Allende, but he spends most of his time assembling material for ANDREA. From Alfa he learns that all the Italians who took part in the assault on the Leightons are safe, and that the police are baffled, as usual. With Alfa's consent, Wilson passes some details of the attack to Virgilio Paz, for transmission to Guillermo Novo. These details appear in public a few days later as an appendage to Zero's third war communiqué,[*] in which Zero announces that it assassinated Rolando Masferrer because he was a Castro agent and a "divisive force" among the Cuban exile groups in Miami. The declaration goes on to say that Bernardo Leighton was shot in the back of the head with a .9 mm Beretta pistol. When published, the November 4 communiqué attracts the instant attention of Interpol and the Italian police, who know that the details are accurate and previously unknown to the public. (The Italian press had reported erroneously that Leighton was shot in the forehead, from the front.) Zero's credibility as a political execution

---

[*]Zero first appeared in 1974, to take public credit for the slaying of José Elias de la Torriente, a businessman and organizer of the "Torriente Plan" to overthrow Castro. When this plan failed ignominiously in 1972, after years of fanfare in Miami, many Cuban exile leaders endorsed terrorism and denounced Torriente as a "CIA stooge." A gunman shot Torriente on Good Friday, April 12, 1974, as he was watching *The Robe* on television.

group rises instantly, but no one can positively identify any of the group's members.

On November 7, Bernardo Leighton undergoes another round of surgery in Parma, Italy. He will survive, with an egg-size indentation in his skull. Anita Leighton remains partially paralyzed and will never walk again.

Later that month, Contreras accompanies President Pinochet to Madrid for the funeral of Generalissimo Francisco Franco. Now dead after thirty-six years as ruler of Spain, Franco has been Pinochet's political and military hero. Contreras decides to take advantage of the funeral trip to meet personally with Alfa.

The Italian eagerly accepts the invitation. He talks with Contreras at length about the resources and methods of right-wing political sabotage in Europe. In scope and detail, he goes beyond what Wilson has been reporting to DINA. Contreras is pleased. Pointedly, he does not refer to the Leighton operation, but he does express admiration for the dedication of Alfa and his men. Later, Contreras offers Alfa certain protections and privileges in Chile in exchange for Alfa's agreement to undertake sensitive espionage assignments against Peru and Argentina. He is satisfied that Alfa has enough military men among his operatives to carry out the missions both in Europe and in South America. Alfa accepts the proposal. He says he understands that to betray Contreras would mean war with the entire security apparatus of Chile.

When all is agreed, Contreras assigns Iturriaga and "Christian,"* one of Espinoza's espionage experts, to work with Alfa on the new missions against Peru and Argentina, and Alfa says he will be glad to keep working with Wilson from time to time.

Contreras manages to maneuver Alfa past all the overt functionaries of state into Pinochet's hotel suite for a private meeting with the Chilean President. The meeting consists mostly of pleasantries and mutual compliments between fellow soldiers in the war against Marxism. Alfa salutes Pinochet with the deference due a head of state.

Senior DINA officers whisper disapprovingly about the personal meetings with Alfa in Madrid, but no one is surprised to see that Pinochet and Contreras are more aggressive now that Franco has died. Pinochet sees himself as a historical re-creation of Franco. Not long after returning from the funeral, he denounces the nations of the

---

*DINA officer whose true name is unknown.

Western world for weakness and moral duplicity. The President singles out Great Britain for criticism, fighting back against pressure from the British government in the Sheila Cassidy case. In his laboratory, Wilson hears that Contreras has called for the photographs Paz took in Northern Ireland several months earlier. He soon sees one of them in the *Chilean* press, illustrating a story about Pinochet's denunciation of Britain. Wilson is disappointed in the photo selected, but he knows that its use will bring credit to Paz and himself.

In late December, millions of Englishmen watch Chile break into the news on the BBC. The Chilean government has finally released Dr. Cassidy, after nearly two months of quiet maneuvers by British diplomats, and her story of torture and horror in the DINA prison shocks the English public. Many Europeans have heard that the Chilean government has been charged with the use of torture against its own citizens, but those stories have never struck home like the Cassidy case—in which the most savage kinds of torture were applied to someone who was at once a British subject, a woman, a doctor, a pacifist, and an affiliate of the Catholic Church.

On December 30, 1975, the British Foreign Office gives official support to Cassidy's story by announcing the withdrawal of Reginold Seconde, Great Britain's ambassador in Santiago. In furtherance of the British protest, the Foreign Office announces that it will submit evidence in support of Cassidy to the United Nations Human Rights Commission. The Chilean embassy in London publicly denies all allegations of mistreatment.

In Santiago, Colonel Contreras sends an urgent order to Wilson: by whatever means necessary, he is to figure out a way to assassinate Andrés Pascal Allende, who has taken refuge inside the Costa Rican ambassador's residence. Contreras does not really care how it is done. To him, Pascal Allende is not only a traitor and a symbol of lingering opposition to the government but also the cause of international vexation to Chile through the Sheila Cassidy case. Pascal Allende and his young band of intrepid middle-class socialists pose no real threat to the regime, but their much-publicized travels and escapes reflect poorly on DINA's command of the country. To Contreras, as a military man, the absence of command is intolerable.

Through informants, Wilson finds that Pascal Allende spends a great deal of time inside the walled garden within the Costa Rican compound. But the walls are too high—and the surrounding buildings too low—for a sniper to get a clear shot into the garden. Most of the cruder methods, such as bombs and poisons, have already been rejected as too indiscriminate. Wilson labors to find something more inventive. Within a few days, one of the surveillance teams under his direction reports that the Costa Rican ambassador buys two kinds of cigarettes on the way home from work each afternoon. This is strange. Wilson asks the informants to find out about the cigarettes and soon learns that Pascal Allende smokes one of the brands the ambassador is buying.

Wilson then asks the informants to find out if anybody else in the residential compound smokes that brand. Meanwhile, on the theory that the new packs are going to Pascal Allende, he retires to his laboratory to see if he can build a bomb that will be light enough not to attract suspicion inside a cigarette pack and yet powerful enough to be lethal. He uses a special explosive called PETN, which is lighter but more stable than nitroglycerin. (It is the active ingredient in blasting caps.) After many unsuccessful experiments, he manages to devise a circuit-breaker detonator that will trigger the explosion when the cigarette pack is opened.

Wilson knows that there is some risk of accidental explosion, but he decides that the device is acceptable. The intelligence, on the other hand, is not. Informants have been revising their reports, and there is much confusion over who smokes what cigarettes inside the compound. Awaiting better information, he begins to search for alternative methods under great pressure. Contreras has ordered him to report to DINA superiors daily.

If possible, Contreras is even more intent upon capturing and eliminating Nelson Gutiérrez, the MIR leader whose leg wound had been treated by Sheila Cassidy in October. Gutiérrez has taken temporary asylum in the papal nuncio's official residence in Santiago,* one wall of which sits just across the street from the Costa Rican embassy. Wilson and several other DINA officers on the frenzied manhunt assume that Pascal Allende will try to move from the ambassador's residence to the embassy so that it will be easier to join Gutiérrez for an escape.

Taking a lesson from Alfa and from Daniel's French group, Wilson concocts an ambitious plan. He will try to tunnel into the papal nuncio's residence so that an assassin can enter surreptitiously on a weekend, when Gutiérrez is inside virtually alone. Informants say he

---

*The papal nuncio is the official representative of the pope at seats of government outside Rome.

sleeps on a sofa inside an office. He would be an easy target, and guards at the walls would be oblivious to the attack within.

The Europeans, Wilson knows, have been able to pull off large underground engineering projects to get at the money and intelligence locked inside banks, insurance companies, credit unions, and companies that do business with important leftists. The key to their success has been their ability to call on a number of specialists—electricians, masons, plumbers, engineers, architects, explosives experts—with the assurance that none of them will talk. They have accomplished amazingly complicated feats without a security compromise. Colonel Contreras, a career military engineer, sees no reason why DINA cannot do the same.

"Hermes,"* a DINA engineer assigned to Wilson for Project ANDREA, locates a set of building plans for the papal nuncio's residence. He and Wilson study them intently to find the safest route into the basement. They would prefer to tunnel in at a point near the Costa Rican embassy so that they can change plans easily if Gutiérrez and Pascal Allende go there. Planning a secret tunnel is tedious work. Many unforeseen obstacles arise. Wilson divides his time between the Gutiérrez project and the Pascal Allende project, and before either one succeeds he learns that both fugitives have slipped out of the country. The news infuriates Contreras.

Wilson resumes work on ANDREA. Storage cylinders and a large microwave oven have arrived from Miami. Most of the ingredients have come from England. Some of the chemicals have been procured in Chile. Special tanks of pure hydrofluoric acid are kept refrigerated, as are some organic salts of phosphorus. The first trials begin late in 1975, and the first stable product is obtained in tiny quantities the following year. Wilson has created Isopropylmethylphosophonofluoridate, a clear liquid organophosphate commonly known as sarin. It vaporizes upon exposure to the atmosphere, producing droplets that enter the body through the skin or lungs to interdict the neurochemistry that allows the respiratory muscles to work. Therefore, it is called a nerve gas. Microscopic doses are quickly lethal to human beings. Wilson knows that the United States and the Soviet Union have built missile forces armed with sarin-filled warheads.

He spends most of his time experimenting with delivery systems and with the durability of the compound. His mission is to develop a weapon that will be extremely lethal to large masses of people but

*A DINA code name for Eugenio Berrios.

whose effects can be localized within a relatively small area. The original idea was that it would be deployed along the short border with Peru in the north of Chile. Now, however, there is more concern about Argentina. A territorial dispute seems to be moving Chile toward a war in which its army would be overmatched. In that event, ANDREA would be used to guard the few passes in the Andes mountain range through which Argentine soldiers might pour into Chile.

By early 1976, Wilson's wife, Ana Pizarro, is criticizing him more stridently than ever. She thinks DINA is exploiting his skills. She says he is too eager to please and too enamored of spy work. For her, the clandestine wars have lost most of their romance, since she has seen for herself that DINA work requires a lot of personal contact with "ruffians." Wilson apologizes to her for his obsessive devotion to DINA. As he has done many times in Europe, he brings her a rose and says it will not always be this way.

Pizarro is more forgiving than usual. Her own disenchantment with DINA has been offset lately by successes in other pursuits. In late December, when the Sheila Cassidy case became public, she received (under another name) first prize in *El Mercurio*'s short-story competition for 1975. Her winning submission, "Did You Know Bobby Ackerman?" is the story of an aging Jewish tailor in Brooklyn, New York, who tells a young visitor about how his neighborhood has been taken over by Puerto Ricans and how, years ago, the tailor watched passively from the window as a gang of Puerto Ricans stabbed to death Bobby Ackerman, his son's best friend. The tailor wonders throughout the story if the Jews are a race of cowards. "Are we cowards?" he asks. "Only we, or the entire human race?"

El Mercurio's prize is the most coveted literary honor in Chile, and the award helps Pizarro see her DINA work in a new light. To be a spy—even a disenchanted one—*and* a prize-winning author is a delightful combination to her, because she can blend fiction and so many hidden truths of espionage. At times, she finds herself looking on the DINA people as mere characters in one of her stories.

Pizarro is not well disposed toward Colonel Contreras. For more than a year now Contreras has been promising to make Wilson a regular officer in the Chilean army, by special order of the President. Already, Wilson is the only civilian member of DINA who exercises command authority over officers and enlisted men of the regular Chilean armed forces. He has his own brigade within the service, named *Quetropillán*, or "Good Volcano," and he is regularly granted authority to command outsiders on special projects.

The actual commission never materializes, however. Wilson yearns for it. He has shaped himself to become a Chilean army officer. Once, when his prospects appeared particularly good, he went to tell Pizarro's mother that he had finally made it. Having determined to hold his optimism in check, he was bitterly disappointed when the ceremony was again postponed. Contreras, realizing that Pizarro is the more impatient and demanding of the two agents, pacifies her temporarily by giving her a diamond ring. Realism tells Wilson that there would be a revolt among the tradition-bound officer corps if he were to be interposed among them. The officers are notoriously jealous and conscious of rank. Wilson knows it is unlikely that he will ever receive his commission, but the promises keep coming.

"You've got to face it," Pizarro says sarcastically. "When they want something, you are an army officer. When *you* want something, you are only a civilian."

Wilson has many roles within DINA. One of them is to be chief informal expert on Cuban exiles, and therefore he is not surprised to receive a call in February from Major Victor Torres Pinto.* Torres runs DINA's Metropolitan Intelligence Brigade (BIM) in Santiago, a notorious outfit of roughnecks and housebreakers who excite Pizarro's strongest contempt for her colleagues. He wants Wilson to talk with a crazy Cuban named Rolando Otero, who has dropped into Chile on a self-proclaimed mission to establish a secret alliance between the Chilean government and Otero's Cuban exile friends.

Wilson and Pizarro agree to question Otero with Major Torres. The Cuban impresses them unfavorably, and after consulting by telephone with Guillermo Novo, Wilson recommends that DINA have nothing to do with Otero. He is more than a little annoyed to learn subsequently that DINA has sent Otero on a mission to assassinate Pascal Allende in Costa Rica. But he is hardly surprised. By now he knows that President Pinochet himself is furious at Pascal Allende and that Contreras, in a prideful rage, is so intent upon killing him that he thinks nothing of breaking into an embassy residence, or of violating the property of the Catholic Church. Wilson thinks Contreras has abandoned all considerations of security.

Frenzy over Pascal Allende is so widespread within the Chilean government that navy officers dare to compete with DINA for the privilege of killing him. They send another Cuban, Orlando Bosch, to Costa Rica on the same mission.

*This is the Major Torres whom Otero met above, page 136.

A month later, after both Otero and Bosch have failed miserably and brought embarrassment to Chile, Wilson cannot help feeling rather smug. He knows that the calamity would not have occurred if his superiors had heeded his judgment. Some weeks later, Contreras asks for his advice again. The FBI has learned somehow that Otero is back in Chile, and the Americans are exerting great pressure on Chile to give Otero up so that he can face criminal charges in the United States. Wilson argues stoutly that Chile should resist. He proposes sending Otero secretly to Argentina, where the Argentines will be happy to dispose of him if necessary. Contreras and Colonel Espinoza refuse to do so, pointing out that the Argentines would no doubt extract a full confession from Otero, and that the Argentines would not hesitate to blackmail Chile with the evidence of the Pascal Allende mission.

When Chile expels Otero to the United States in May, Guillermo Novo instantly takes out his wrath on Wilson, saying that influential Cubans are denouncing Chile at political rallies. Worst of all, Cubans are demanding an accounting from Guillermo Novo, who has been loudly trumpeting his "connection" to Chile. Now Novo feels politically obliged to denounce Chile's conduct in the Otero case.

This is especially embarrassing to Wilson, because Virgilio Paz is a guest in his home at the time. As a reward for Paz's services in Northern Ireland and on the continent of Europe, Contreras has invited Paz to Chile to receive a special DINA intelligence course and free medical treatment for his bad shoulder. Bureaucratic entanglements have delayed both these services for weeks, however, putting Paz into a quarrelsome mood even before the Otero controversy. The military government's state-of-siege laws have wiped out most of Chile's night life with a curfew, and Paz sorely misses the entertainment. He smokes cigars in the house and talks endlessly of Cuba, much to the annoyance of Pizarro. She finally banishes Paz from the family dinner table to the DINA kitchen downstairs. Paz takes this as another example of Pizarro's control over Wilson and resents it deeply.

It is all Wilson can do to smooth things over. He has long since discovered that there are many petty headaches in spy work. In June, he invites Guillermo Novo to Chile for a reconciliation. When Novo arrives, Wilson whisks him past the customs people and the International Police so that there will be no record of the visit. In this and many other ways, he and DINA show Novo the finest hospitality of an intelligence service. The DINA officers tell Novo that they are sorry about Otero and that they will understand perfectly if Novo attacks Chile in public. They expect it. Novo tries to be understanding. His worry is the publicity, he says, not Otero. "Why the hell didn't you just shoot the guy in the head and bury him?" he asks.

Wilson steers the conversation to the proposal that has enticed Novo to Chile in violation of his parole. It is a financial proposition in keeping with Contreras's conviction that there are better ways to finance his new network of anti-Communist operatives than by draining the Chilean treasury. Contreras wants to promote both international cooperation and economic self-sufficiency among the various groups—with DINA serving as a facilitator, contact point, and provider of refuge.

All officers in DINA's international section are under orders to promote this concept. In that spirit, Wilson tells Novo about a Dutch bank in Buenos Aires called Banco Holandés Unido. The Argentine intelligence group that helped DINA assassinate General Prats and his wife has agents inside the bank who can predict the movements of the bank president. Wilson and several DINA colleagues suggest to Novo that the CNM join the Argentines in an operation to kidnap the Dutch bank president for ransom. Such things are done every week in Argentina. The Argentines know how to blame it on leftist terrorists.

Wilson explains carefully that the fruits of the kidnapping can finance Novo's operations in the United States as well as anti-Communist activities in Argentina. He stresses that it will not be a DINA operation. DINA will only help, and take a small percentage of the profits. Wilson and his DINA colleagues plan to give those proceeds directly to Contreras as a surprise present. They know it will please him.

After considerable planning and a quick trip to Buenos Aires to meet his prospective partners, Novo agrees to advance $6,000 in seed money for the operation. He returns to the United States and sends the cash back to Wilson by way of a LAN Chile pilot. Paz takes the money to Argentina and obtains a receipt for it, which he returns to Novo from Santiago. Wilson arranges to have a *Grupo Rojo* ("Red Group") letterhead printed so that the Argentines can issue manifestos and ransom demands in the name of the fictitious leftist organization. He sends the stationery to Buenos Aires, and then it becomes a matter of waiting for the Argentines to move.

Paz grows restless in July as the Argentines keep delaying. He thinks he has been in Chile far too long. He has come to Santiago hoping to make a reputation for shrewdness and bravado among the DINA officers in training. He has needlessly brought to Chile a Colt

.45 Special Edition that he says was used recently on "a job." Conspicuously, he breaks the gun to pieces with a sledgehammer. As time wears on him, he gets to know some of Wilson's friends in the Metropolitan Brigade (BIM) of DINA. He becomes quite secretive about it—to the point that he does not tell Wilson or Pizarro when he gets involved on the fringes of an operation to pick up a suspected leftist named Carmelo Soria Espinoza. Soria is tortured, killed, and dumped into an irrigation canal in Santiago. The operation causes a much greater scandal than usual, because Soria was an economist who worked for the United Nations, but Contreras maneuvers successfully to take control of the Soria investigation away from General Baeza's Investigations detectives and protect his own men in BIM.

By mid-July, Paz is beginning to suspect that the Argentines plan to swindle the Cuban Nationalist Movement out of $6,000. Wilson thinks so, too, but he reminds Paz that DINA had not "guaranteed" the Argentines to the Cubans—it had merely introduced them and facilitated their arrangement. He tells Paz to take his complaints directly to the Argentines. He says the same thing when Novo calls from New Jersey to complain.

Wilson regrets that his Latin associates do not have the experience of his European contacts in matters of money. The Europeans operate more smoothly. From some of Alfa's associates living in Buenos Aires, Wilson knows that "Daniel," Albert Spaggiari, has spent May and June supervising a team of political criminals who are tunneling into the vault of the Société Générale bank in Nice. As planned, the operation will be presented to the public as the most spectacular bank robbery in history. Privately, Daniel hopes the documents seized from the vault will generate enough scandal to influence the upcoming French elections toward the right. Alfa hopes to finance his paramilitary operations for a year from the proceeds of the robbery. DINA might even get its hands on the secrets of some prominent Chilean exiles who use the bank.

On Sunday, July 18, the men who will become famous as the "Sewer Gang" break into the vault from the tunnel and weld the twenty-ton door shut *from the inside*. Before the bank opens the next morning, they haul off more than $10 million worth of jewels, documents, and securities from the personal safety-deposit boxes. They spurn the cash. As a publicity gesture, they tape to the walls of the vault some of the pornographic photographs they have found in the private collections.

Wilson will not hear about the robbery in Nice for a few days, because Colonel Espinoza sends him to Paraguay that Monday on another mission. He is to obtain Paraguayan passports and American entry visas for himself and another DINA officer. Unaccountably, things do not go smoothly in Paraguay. Officials at the American embassy in Asunción seems suspicious; DINA's Paraguayan contacts are disorganized; and both DINA agents are ordered to return to Santiago.

Wilson has reason to blame Contreras for both the foul-up in Paraguay and the controversy between the CNM and the Argentines. Both stem from overly complicated operations involving too many disparate groups, and this flaw in tradecraft is traceable directly to Contreras's obsession with international cooperation—with his desire to be the kingpin of a new anti-Communist consortium.

In August 1976, Wilson flies to Buenos Aires to meet with some of Alfa's men there, who fill him in on the details of Daniel's historic bank robbery in Nice. The Italians say that Daniel is looking for a temporary country of refuge, and Wilson replies that he could easily make the arrangements in Chile. On another matter, he goes to see the Argentines, who are procrastinating on the Banco Holandés operation. He urges them to go through with it or to refund Novo's money. Alternatively, he says, Novo would be willing to take his repayment in the form of detailed information about any daring operation against Castro Cubans in Argentina. Novo could use the information to claim public credit for the operation and thereby to build his group's reputation as a power among the Cuban exiles.

In late October, after the Letelier assassination in Washington, Wilson learns that the French police have arrested Daniel for the Nice robbery, on a tip from the American CIA. Wilson hopes the CIA has not discovered and similarly betrayed his own missions. He feels better as the weeks go by without any adverse developments.

Wilson has been assured that he will not travel overseas again until the international furor over the Letelier assassination dies down. Nevertheless, Colonel Espinoza orders him to Paris in late November as part of a mission to assassinate two Chilean journalists. Wilson becomes even more apprehensive when he learns that it is another of Contreras's cooperative missions with foreigners: he and Pizarro are to serve as "back-up" to a four-man team composed of two Argentines and two DINA agents. He voices his objections to Espinoza, but he does not dare to refuse a direct order. Espinoza's determination is firm and warlike. He says that Chile's enemies are resurgent in Europe. The Portuguese Socialist Party is holding a widely publicized congress, as is the Socialist International. Venezuelan President Pérez is in attendance, having signed an oil agreement with the Russians. Worst of all, a coalition of leftists is about to launch a pan-European newspaper out of Paris. The two Chilean targets*— one of whom is believed by DINA to be connected to the famous terrorist Carlos—are associated with the newspaper venture.

Wilson and Pizarro fly to France, with Pizarro complaining loudly about the new false passport DINA has supplied in the name of Carmen Luisa Correa Letelier. She thinks it is foolhardy and arrogant for DINA to use such prominent Chilean names, especially Letelier. She speaks bitterly of hubris in the service.

The two agents reach their assigned station in France only to learn that the entire mission has been scrubbed. Someone has betrayed the operation. The French security service has warned officials at the Chilean embassy in Paris that they are aware of the contemplated operation and will not tolerate it. Apparently, one of the Argentines in the Condor plan has told the American CIA, and the CIA has passed the word along to the French. This news makes Wilson even more nervous about the possibility that the Americans know of his deeds.

Under these circumstances, it comes as a shock to Wilson when Colonel Espinoza does not allow him to return to Santiago and instead orders him to Madrid. Espinoza sends a message advising that King Juan Carlos has agreed to allow the first legal congress of the Socialist Party since the Spanish Civil War. One of the visiting dignitaries in attendance will be the target who has escaped Contreras's designs for so long, Carlos Altamirano. Wilson and Pizarro are to assassinate him in Madrid. Espinoza points out that the job should be facilitated by some of Wilson's security contacts who are holdovers from the Franco regime.

Nearly in a stupor, Wilson and Pizarro spend four December days stalking the congress hall and the hotel in which most of the socialist guests are staying. They become even more convinced that their orders are insane or suicidal. All their target sites are teeming with security agents—not only the various Spanish services, but also the agents brought to Madrid by the glittering roster of foreign leaders: Willy Brandt of West Germany, François Mitterrand of France, Mário Soares of Portugal, Olof Palme of Sweden, Bruno Kreisky of

---

*The targets have not yet been identified.

Austria, Michael Foot of Great Britain, and many others. Altamirano never goes anywhere without a bodyguard on each side.

Wilson finally manages to learn Altamirano's room number in the hotel. Then, through contacts in the Spanish police, he finds out that it is a "blind"—that Altamirano is really staying in a different room. Wilson maneuvers to get closer. One evening he and Pizarro sit in a restaurant booth next to the one occupied by part of Altamirano's entourage. They speak loud Americanized English, hoping to overhear the Spanish conversation nearby without attracting suspicion. They want to hear something about the target's itinerary, preferably plans for some social outing in Madrid, but they hear nothing of the kind. The DINA agents continue to move on the fringes of the socialist crowds, watching the photographers and the reporters and the dignitaries. They grow ever more afraid of being picked up by any of a dozen security outfits. There is no time to communicate with Santiago by coded messages. Wilson's nerves are playing tricks on him.

He calls Espinoza to report on the latest frustrations in the hunt for Altamirano. Espinoza is becoming impatient. He listens to only a few of Wilson's explanations before interrupting. *"No me importa!"* he shouts. *"Mátalo! Mátalo!"* ("It doesn't matter! Kill him! Kill him!") Espinoza roars so loudly that Wilson winces and holds the telephone receiver away from his ear. Pizarro hears the shouting, too, from several feet away.

"Yes, my Colonel," says Wilson, but he begins to lose his military crispness as soon as he hangs up the telephone. Wilson knows Espinoza well. He has seen that officer stand toe-to-toe with his good friend and superior officer, Contreras, in arguments that have threatened to split the walls of the DINA compound in Santiago. Espinoza has an independent mind and a personality of great force, and for that reason Wilson is certain that he would not shout with such urgency unless he agreed with the order to kill Altamirano at any risk. Wilson already knows the strength of Contreras's hatred for the target. He realizes, therefore, that his failures are courting the united wrath of the DINA high command.

Pizarro expresses amazement that a gentleman like Espinoza could shout with such vulgarity and hatred. She believes the service should behave more rationally. Having made a decision of state to eliminate Altamirano for reasons of security, the commanders should constantly balance the benefits of that objective against the risk of failure or compromise. She repeats for Wilson her own motto for clandestine success: "First the head, second the head, third the head, fourth the heart."

Wilson defends Espinoza by arguing that the colonel's anger does not stem from a personal hatred toward Altamirano so much as from a desire to make sure that orders are always carried out efficiently. To Espinoza, the business of the military is to eliminate the enemy, and the business of the service is to do so secretly. Every time Altamirano attacks Chile in the European newspapers, Espinoza sees it not only as treason against the Pinochet government but also as evidence of DINA's continuing failure to do its duty. All this pressure is coming down on Wilson, but he believes that Espinoza is a man of honor who demands no more devotion of his subordinates than he will return to them in support. Like Contreras, Espinoza has the personal capacity to inspire a feeling of belonging to an elite military brotherhood.

At the conclusion of the congress in Madrid, Wilson and Pizarro resolve to follow Altamirano to his next stop, hoping to strike when they get away from the heavy security in Spain. They have alerted some of DINA's European contacts. When Altamirano enters the Madrid airport, Wilson and Pizarro are there to see what flight he takes. They follow him into the boarding area of a flight to Paris. Wilson stands behind a support pillar, waiting for the security men to leave, and when he finally moves toward a public telephone he bumps into someone. Recovering his balance, Wilson finds himself apologizing to Carlos Altamirano himself.

Wilson watches Altamirano say goodbye to someone and jump on the plane. To Pizarro, he explains his failure to strike as a consequence of unfavorable circumstances. Later, he will conclude that he lacks the nerve of a raw killer like Dionisio Suárez. Wilson has a taste for danger and risk in its more mannerly forms—without personal exposure to violence. He is an inventor and persuader. He can arrange an execution and will go so far as to take pleasure in the technical construction of the weapons, but he has never been present when his victims died. He thinks he is too deeply polite and middle-class for the task. Although Pizarro is not sure she respects this aspect of his character, she finds it interesting.

The DINA agents call Alfa's men in Paris and instruct them to follow Altamirano when he arrives there. If the Italians can track him until Wilson and Pizarro arrive on the next flight from Madrid, they will have another chance. As it turns out, however, they lose Altamirano somewhere in the Paris traffic.

Wilson and Pizarro return to Santiago and make an attempt to atone for their failure with a lengthy, detailed report on how persistently they tried to succeed. There are no more missions early in 1977, but the quarrels continue. Guillermo Novo keeps calling from New Jersey about his $6,000. When Daniel escapes from French custody in March by jumping out the window of a judge's office during interrogation, Alfa and Enrique Arrancibia fear some retribution because they have pocketed a large sum that Daniel entrusted to them for a bank robbery in Buenos Aires. Wilson tries to smooth things over. When the fugitive Daniel arrives in Santiago, Wilson makes arrangements for him to stay there without being molested. Daniel says he is glad to meet Wilson and looks forward to receiving advice on technical matters, such as the modification of walkie-talkies.

In April, a distressed Major Iturriaga summons Wilson with the news that *The Washington Post* has published a story claiming that a CIA operative named Wilson was responsible for the assassination of Orlando Letelier. Alarms have sounded throughout DINA. Iturriaga demands to know instantly whether DINA's role in the operation has been discovered.

Panic-stricken, Wilson calls Guillermo Novo, who gives him the details about Bob Woodward's story on Edwin Wilson, the renegade CIA officer who has been peddling arms to Libya.

Wilson soon walks back into Iturriaga's office with a big smile on his face. It has been years since he has felt such relief. "False alarm," he reports with a laugh. "They're after the wrong Wilson."

14 ▣ DOWNHILL AUTUMN

Two weeks after identifying the photograph of Juan Williams as "the colonel," Canete disappeared. Wack could not find him. Canete, having vacated the apartment he kept under an assumed name for general business purposes, proved difficult to trace. Wack's search was handicapped by the fact that he had to pretend to be hostile to Canete, planning perhaps to arrest him, lest people suspect that Canete was an informant. Canete's friends, acting in perfectly good faith to protect Canete, tended to develop amnesia whenever Wack asked about him. Within a few days, Wack was reporting to Cornick that Canete had gone underground, probably out of fear that he had gotten in over his head in the Letelier investigation.

Propper was awakened Saturday morning, July 23, by a call from the State Department's country officer for Venezuela. The official was making an effort to remain calm. He informed Propper that the President of Venezuela himself, Carlos Andrés Pérez, had just approved Propper's request for information on the Letelier case, and the secretary of state wanted Propper's immediate answer on how he planned to proceed. Propper hung up and reflected painfully on the fact that the Venezuelans had delayed and befogged the investigation for nine months, but now, suddenly, they were in a hurry.

In discussing their options, Cornick advised Propper not to count too heavily on assistance from the FBI legat in Caracas, warning him about the "legat shuffle."

"What's that?" asked Propper.

"Gene, don't tell anybody in the Bureau I said this, but legats have the reputation of never doing any work and giving everybody the runaround. As soon as they get overseas, they think they work for the State Department, and all they do is go to cocktail parties and play golf."

"That's just great," said Propper.

"The upshot of it is that we better not let the legat down there handle it, like the ambassador wants," said Cornick. "We might be sucking our thumbs waiting for him this time next year."

Propper flew alone to Caracas on August 4. There were no rooms available at the Hilton, and he wound up checking into a hotel so sleazy that his paranoia led him to wedge a chair under the door handle on the inside of his room. The next morning he accompanied the FBI legat to an equally run-down building, which turned out to be DISIP headquarters. Rafael Rivas Vásquez was waiting, and DISIP chief Orlando García soon arrived to parlay.

García's disclosures proved disappointing. He said he had been unable to locate the Pascal Allende assassination file that DINA had allegedly given Rolando Otero. He doubted that such a file existed any longer, if it ever had. As to DISIP's alleged informant at the CORU meeting, García acknowledged that it had been Luis Posada—a participant at CORU, DISIP veteran, and now the cellmate of Orlando Bosch—but García told Propper that DISIP had failed to debrief Posada between the CORU meeting and the Cubana Airlines bombing in October, so that, unfortunately, DISIP did not possess Posada's knowledge as to what had happened at the terrorist summit meeting. DISIP had nothing, therefore, on the two enticing leads that had required so much labor and endurance since Cornick's interview with Ricardo Morales in May.

It was not long before the DISIP leader was reminding Propper that his visit had been presented to the Venezuelan government as an *exchange* of information about terrorism—which meant that García wanted to ask some favors, too. Among other things, he wanted photographs of some of the major Cuban terrorists in the United States. Rivas Vásquez, for his part, solicited Propper's aid in getting his daughter admitted to the graduate program at Georgetown University in Washington. Propper said he would see what he could do.

The next day, trying to leave Caracas on an open first-class ticket, Propper discovered that all flights from Venezuela to the United States were booked until the following December. He argued as best he could with the few ticket agents who spoke English, but in the end he faced the prospect of being stuck in Caracas for four months. Fuming, Propper returned to the sleazy hotel and spent another night, not knowing where to turn for help. The FBI legat was out of town for the weekend, playing golf. Propper knew no other Americans, and the embassy personnel were mostly scattered for the weekend anyway. Finally, Propper called DISIP's Dr. Rivas Vásquez and asked for help. It was a call he would have avoided under any other circumstances. Rivas sent two DISIP escorts to take Propper back to the airport, where, after listening to a series of group conversations in Spanish, he learned that the influence of DISIP—plus an extra forty dollars in cash—would get him a seat on the plane. Propper endured this last humiliation and paid the bribe. Having come down to Caracas as a U.S. government official to receive crucial information from DISIP, he was now reduced to the plight of a confused tourist.

A few weeks later, even Propper came to acknowledge that his part of the investigation seemed to be slowing down. Wack was looking for Canete. Cornick was looking for ties between the Cuban Nationalist Movement (Ross) and the Brigade (Shrimp Man). The entire FBI was still looking for the fugitive Guillermo Novo. And Scherrer, down in Chile, was at work on the delicate task of identifying Juan Williams, the blond Chilean, without letting the Chilean government know what he was doing. Although these angles offered great promise toward the solution of the case, they had to be pursued blindly, as there was nothing in hand with which to work. "The scent is strong," said Cornick. "But the trail is cold."

Propper did not believe in bad omens, but he acknowledged that he and Cornick were suddenly on the defensive. In early August, they had tried to answer a barrage of protest from the Chilean embassy in Washington, where officials were incensed over *Washington Star* reporter Jeremiah O'Leary's story that a "high-ranking official" of the Chilean embassy in Washington had "recently" passed a lie-detector test in connection with the Letelier investigation. Propper speculated that O'Leary, whose brother worked for the D.C. police department, had made contact with Wilson, who was feeling disgruntled enough over his exclusion from the investigation to leak what he knew. Cornick did more than speculate. He denounced and declaimed, and he reasoned that the Wilson-O'Leary connection explained O'Leary's aborted story on the John Marks lead. Only a Palm Tree Peeker on the fringes of the investigation would have tried to leak a story that old and discredited, he declared.

On August 23, one of the Chilean embassy's American lawyers delivered to Propper the long-awaited investigative report on Cuban exile activities and contacts inside Chile—the one Propper had requested of Ambassador Cauas on June 28. Propper opened it eagerly, hoping that the document would renew his opportunities on the foreign side of the investigation. He found an English translation of an official communication from the Chilean government, marked HIGHLY CONFIDENTIAL. The document stated that Orlando Bosch had entered Chile on December 3, 1974, on Passport No. 85668 of the Dominican Republic, under the false name of Pedro Antonio Peña. It went on to report where Bosch had lived in Chile for nine months and when he had departed. As to his activities, the government of Chile declared: "The apparent activities of Mr. Peña were of an artistic nature, presumably a writer. He lived quietly and did not have much contact with his neighbors. There is no information that he might have taken part in actions against the Chilean government."

That was all. Propper felt as if he had been slapped. "You mean to tell me the Chilean government is asking me to believe that Orlando Bosch is an artist?" he gasped.

"I don't know," said the lawyer. "I didn't even know what was in there."

"My God," said Propper. "This is an insult. This is mind-boggling. I can't believe it. After all this investigation, they're saying Bosch is an artistic writer? What kind of writer, for God's sake?"

"How should I know, Gene?" asked the lawyer. "It's not fair to ask me. An artistic writer is something like a poet, I guess. I don't know the guy."

"A poet!" shouted Propper. "Bosch is a fucking terrorist! He's been bombing things for fifteen years! And they're calling him a fucking poet! Your client, the fucking Pinochet government, has the nerve to say it investigated the most famous terrorist in the Western Hemisphere and found out he's a poet?! That's outrageous! I'm telling you, they won't get away with it!"

"Take it easy," said the lawyer. "My client is the Chilean embassy, not the government itself. Look, the ambassador didn't write this report, and neither did I. We transmitted your request to Santiago, and now we're transmitting the reply. That's it. The ambassador can send another message down to Santiago for you, probably, if you want. That's it. You want me to tell him something for you? You want an appointment?"

Propper took some deep breaths. "I don't know," he said. "Just a second." He flipped through the remainder of the report and found equally terse, disingenuous passages on Guillermo Novo and Rolando Otero. Then he found another surprise. In closing, the document announced that "any further information that may be required from Chile must be requested through judiciary channels, in compliance with the established international legal procedure." The Chilean Foreign Ministry, on behalf of the Pinochet government, was declaring that it would do no more investigative favors for Propper.

The severity of Chile's rebuke sank in. Propper realized the futility of attempts to obtain cooperation by reason or appeal. Clearly, the Chileans would cooperate only under compulsion, and Propper did not have the facts with which to compel them. "No, there's no message," Propper told the lawyer. "Just tell the ambassador that I thank him for sending over the report."

Propper was still stunned when Cornick arrived that afternoon to read the Chilean report. "They just told us to go fuck ourselves," Propper said lamely.

Cornick was shaking his head. "They sure did," he said. "But they also told us something else. They told us they have a hell of a lot to hide. No government would put out ridiculous stuff like that unless they had to."

"Carter, I already *knew* they have something to hide," grumbled Propper. "That doesn't do us any good. What this says is that we can't prove it, and they don't give a damn what they have to say to keep on denying it."

"I know, Gene," said Cornick. "But that tells us something, too. We don't know shit, and we've already got 'em up on a high horse. That's something. They're already strung tight as hell, and that's when you make mistakes."

"Yeah, sure," said Propper.

As if to reinforce its rebuke to Propper, the Chilean Foreign Ministry soon sent the United States an unsolicited declaration on the Letelier case:

1. The Government of Chile has stated clearly and categorically that it did not have any connection whatsoever with the death of Mr. Letelier, and demanded at that time an exhaustive investigation be made of the matter.

2. The Government of Chile immutably reiterates what has already been expressed.

3. The Government of Chile does not possess any information or cir-

cumstantial evidence which might point to any Chilean citizen or foreign national, civilian or military, who might have had any connection with said death.

4. In view of the above, the Government of Chile believes that an investigation such as has been suggested by the Office of the U.S. Attorney General would be unfounded and unfeasible.

The Foreign Ministry went on to declare that Chile would henceforth respond only to formal Letters Rogatory.

Propper interpreted the stiff declaration as an attempt to cleanse the record on the Letelier investigation permanently, in preparation for President Pinochet's upcoming visit to Washington for ceremonies attendant to the signing of the Panama Canal treaties. The event would be a great hemispheric spectacle, a gathering in pomp of nearly all the heads of state in the Americas. Even General Stroessner would be there, making one of his rare trips out of Paraguay. For Pinochet, the trip would have the utmost political significance. In the full glare of worldwide publicity, he would appear as the equal of the other presidents, offering toasts and making the appropriate diplomatic statements. This would impart to Pinochet and his government a certain legitimacy they had lacked since the 1973 coup and the votes of censure in the United Nations. Clearly, thought Propper, Pinochet wanted to rise above the ugly worldwide suspicions in the Letelier investigation. The new declaration would enable him to say that the matter had been investigated and laid to rest.

Public impressions did not matter much to Propper, but he wanted to make sure that the United States government did not allow the Chilean government to disregard the Letelier investigation completely during the Panama Canal festivities. So he went to work on a memorandum for National Security Advisor Zbigniew Brzezinski, in which he summarized the evidence in a way that pointed directly at Cuban exiles and DINA. Then, for the first time, he put into writing his suspicions of Colonel Contreras and of President Pinochet himself. "It is very likely that an operation of this type would not have been carried out by DINA without the knowledge of its head, Colonel Contreras," he wrote. "Since Colonel Contreras's power is derived directly from his close personal relationship with President Pinochet, it is difficult to conceive of DINA carrying out an operation of this magnitude, with its obvious political ramifications, without Pinochet's knowledge and approval."

From there, Propper bluntly informed Brzezinski that although the Chilean government had repeatedly promised cooperation, its performance "evidenced a lack of good faith and a definite unwillingness to supply us with anything of value." He closed by asking Brzezinski and President Carter "to reiterate to President Pinochet the continuing importance to the United States government of obtaining the fullest cooperation at the highest levels of the Chilean government in eliciting information necessary to resolve this case." In short, he wanted President Carter to tell President Pinochet that Chile was not out of the Letelier investigation at all.

On August 28, a call from Chile reached Scherrer at his home office, at the American embassy in Buenos Aires. The legat was stunned to find himself speaking directly with Manuel Contreras, head of DINA, who said that a matter of great urgency had arisen. Contreras had already made a plane reservation in Scherrer's name. He wanted him to fly to Santiago immediately.

"I would be happy to come, Colonel," Scherrer replied. "But I can't. I don't have a visa, and it takes your embassy here at least three days to get me one."

"Forget about the visa," said Contreras. "I can easily get you into the country without one. Don't worry. Just come."

As soon as he hung up, Scherrer cabled headquarters in Washington for permission to travel under circumstances that were potentially embarrassing. Theoretically, Scherrer could be arrested for trying to enter Chile without his diplomatic visa. He thought it was a small risk, however, and he wanted to find out why Contreras was so excited.

Scherrer wondered whether Contreras wanted to talk to him about CHILBOM, the Letelier case. It was always possible, he knew, that Contreras's spies within the various branches of the Chilean government had told him that Scherrer had spent the past week in Santiago investigating the identity of Juan Williams, the blond Chilean identified by Rolando Otero. Working as discreetly as possible, Scherrer had established that no such person existed in the Chilean Registry of Citizens or in the records of any branch of the Chilean armed forces. He had found the same for Romeral, Williams's traveling companion on the mission through Paraguay. From this, Scherrer had concluded that the names Williams and Romeral were almost certainly aliases.

That previous week, Scherrer had also spent a great deal of time at the American consulate in Santiago, retrieving the documents submitted when two Chilean army officers under the names Williams and Romeral applied for visas to enter the United States. He had found them—two handwritten visa applications and two letters from the Chilean Foreign Ministry attesting that Williams and Romeral were officials of the Chilean government and would be traveling to the United States on official business. Scherrer had noticed another small puzzle in the larger mystery: the "Juan Williams" in Paraguay was six years older than the "Juan Williams" in Chile, according to the visa applications, and also six inches taller. Which description was accurate? Had two different people used the same alias?

On the plane to Santiago, Scherrer figured that he was now in a strong position to ask the Chilean government how and why its Foreign Ministry had vouched for two nonexistent persons, Williams and Romeral, in official communications to the American consulate in Santiago. The Chileans would be forced to explain. They would have to give up information about Williams and Romeral or lose face. So the option of making the demand had its attractions. On the other hand, it also had its drawbacks. Scherrer knew that the demand itself would telegraph to the Chileans the American interest in Williams and Romeral. If these two men were involved in the Letelier assassination, they might quickly disappear; they might be hidden anywhere in the world, or they might be killed.

This possibility alone was more than enough to make Scherrer hesitate before informing the Chileans of his interest in Williams and Romeral, and he perceived an even more basic drawback: he did not have enough information to open the contest. As soon as he asked about Williams and Romeral, the Chileans would maneuver to find out what the Americans knew. The game would begin in earnest. And inevitably the Chileans would learn that the Americans did not have even the most rudimentary facts necessary to place Williams and Romeral in a murder conspiracy. Scherrer did not know their true identities. He could not place them in the continental United States, let alone in Washington.

Scherrer toyed with various moves and combinations, and in most scenarios he envisioned the Americans losing for lack of follow-up evidence. By all calculations, he was not ready to raise the matter. He wondered whether Contreras knew this. It was difficult to believe that Contreras, the man who had brushed off Scherrer's persistent inquiries about Cuban exiles for nearly a year, would panic upon first learning that Scherrer was working on Williams and Romeral. It would make no sense unless there were a colossal misperception.

Scherrer racked his brain. Perhaps there was something obvious about Williams and Romeral that Contreras would assume Scherrer had already found out. Or perhaps Contreras's call had nothing to do with the two men. If not, what could be so important? Contreras had never called Scherrer before. Why hadn't he let an underling make the call?

At Pudahuel Airport, Scherrer was standing somewhat nervously in the immigration line when a blond man in civilian clothes approached him, looking official. He paid his compliments and said he was there to provide assistance. At his direction, subordinates fell into escort behind Scherrer, and they all marched around the immigration and customs lines directly into a DINA car under the command of the blond Chilean. Scherrer studied the man all the way to his hotel. Could this be Williams? Could this be *the* blond Chilean? Scherrer thought not. Contreras would never be so stupid as to send him to meet Scherrer. Besides, this man was only five foot six or so, with a very slight build. He did not fit the description of Williams. Still, it was crazy to be guessing. He resolved to cable headquarters immediately upon returning to Buenos Aires and to demand that the Bureau send him copies of the Williams and Romeral photographs. He should have had them long ago.

Late that same afternoon, Scherrer walked into Contreras's office in the company of Al Golocinski,* the State Department security officer. Contreras confessed at once that he had a problem. President Pinochet would be flying to Washington in a week for the signing of the Panama Canal treaties. Contreras's men were to serve as bodyguards and intelligence aides. And for peculiar, almost sentimental reasons, Contreras wanted to send a very large contingent of DINA people with Pinochet. Fifty-four men, he said. Most of them needed to travel under false identities, and all of them needed to carry weapons. Contreras was worried about the paperwork that would be required to get such a large body of armed men into Washington under aliases. He said he was determined that nothing would go wrong. He wanted no problems with the American authorities. He did not want any of his men to be denied visas at the American consulate in Santiago, nor did he want any of them arrested in Washington by U.S. Secret Service agents.

Scherrer nodded along impassively, but his mind was racing. Contreras's urgent problem was not CHILBOM after all, but, ironically,

---

*Golocinski would later become one of the American hostages in Iran.

it did involve false passports and visa snarls—the very CHILBOM issues that had been puzzling Scherrer for weeks. Scherrer's pulse quickened. He was being invited to help Contreras get agents into the United States, just as Contreras might have done for the Letelier assassination. This time, to be sure, the objective was not a criminal one. But the techniques might be the same, and so might some of the agents.

Mentally, Scherrer was scrambling to figure out if there was a way for him to get a look at the agents or to penetrate DINA's false identity operation. He and Golocinski explained to Contreras some of the bureaucratic mechanism he faced. Contreras would have to go to the Chilean Foreign Ministry and obtain a letter attesting to the official status of each of the fifty-four men. The Chilean Foreign Ministry would then forward the letters and accompanying passports to the American consulate, along with visa applications. As to the false identities, Scherrer advised Contreras that he should declare them openly to the FBI, the CIA, and the Secret Service as a matter of ordinary international procedure—and also to protect Contreras himself in case the consulate should question some of the visa applications. Finally, there were the guns. Scherrer and Golocinski explained that the Secret Service would demand to know the serial number of each gun and the name—true and cover—of its carrier. This was a must, they said, because the Secret Service would be jumpy having to deal with nineteen heads of state in Washington at once.

"There isn't time for all that," Contreras complained. "My advance team leaves this Friday."

"It is a real problem with so little time left, Colonel," said Scherrer, sensing an advantage. "Perhaps it would be easier if you sent fewer people. Surely the President doesn't need that many men for his security."

"I have to send them all," Contreras said firmly. "I want to reward them for their services to Chile. These men are the best, Bob. They are what you Americans call the 'cream of the crop.' Many of them will be leaving soon, because there is no DINA any longer, as you know. They deserve something. As a matter of fact, I will probably be leaving soon myself. The President's trip is for me the final big play. Our mission is completed. So perhaps you can see why I am determined not to fail either the President or my men."

"I see," said Scherrer, who knew that Pinochet had recently changed DINA's name to CNI (Center for National Information), in what much of the outside world was interpreting as a cosmetic move to spare Chile from the international disgrace attached to the name DINA. Contreras seemed to treat the change seriously, but Scherrer doubted that he would ever relinquish his power.

"Well, Colonel," said Scherrer, "we'll see what we can do to speed things up at the embassy for you. How long will it take to get the letters from the Foreign Ministry?"

"Days, probably," Contreras replied, making no attempt to conceal his disgust. "I was hoping you could arrange it so that we could send one letter for them all or something."

"Oh," said Scherrer. "Well, that will be more difficult. I don't think that's ever been done."

"I know," said Contreras. "But this trip is very important."

"We will explore the matter and let you know in the morning, Colonel," said Scherrer.

He and Golocinski were soon speeding back to the American embassy, laughing over how Contreras had finally slipped up. To Scherrer, it was an irony that the mighty Contreras had finally been humbled by bureaucracy and sentiment. He and Golocinski plotted how to take advantage of the first vulnerability either of them had ever seen in the intelligence chief.

They twisted many arms at the embassy the next morning, especially that of Consul Josiah Brownell. Before noon, Scherrer called Contreras with an attractive offer: if Contreras would collect all fifty-four passports and send them to the embassy, Scherrer would obtain the visas and the weapons permits. No Foreign Ministry letters would be necessary. The news delighted Contreras.

A courier delivered the passports directly to Scherrer in a valise. To the legat, it was a bag of treasure—all the top DINA operatives, complete with photographs and physical descriptions. First he flipped through the entire stack on the wild chance of finding a Juan Williams or Alejandro Romeral. Negative. Then he looked for officers with blond or light hair who were tall—at least five foot ten —and relatively young. There were seven who fit this description. Scherrer made a separate list of them. Then he turned all the passports over to an embassy technician, who copied all the photographs. As the camera clicked, Scherrer savored his coup. He was happy to see the relatively large number of ranking officers—captains, majors, and colonels.

When the work was complete, Scherrer took the valise to the American consulate. While waiting for the visas, he asked consular officials if there were any other official Chilean passports in the office being processed for visas. There were a few. Scherrer asked to see them and flipped through the small stack, looking for familiar faces or people who seemed military. He found nothing until he came upon a rather plump civilian named Morales Alarcón. Scherrer whistled to himself. "Fat Manny," he said. "You sneaky son-of-a-bitch."

It was Contreras himself. The phony passport had come over to the consulate that very morning. Clearly, Contreras was trying to obtain his own visa clandestinely, not wishing to be lumped in the valise with the other passports. Scherrer borrowed the Morales Alarcón passport long enough to have it copied. Thus, he obtained the only known photograph of the DINA chief.

The next day, Scherrer sent the valise and the fifty-four passports, all with United States visas stamped inside, back to DINA headquarters. Later, talking with a grateful Contreras, he took the opportunity to press his standard line about DINA's failure to account for the contacts of Cuban exile activists in Chile. "I have to say, Colonel," he told Contreras, "that you've put me in a difficult position with my superiors in the FBI. The Letelier case is a police matter, and I've tried to handle it that way with you. But the lawyer Propper has gotten more information on the Cubans through the embassy up in Washington than I've gotten down here working on a police-to-police basis. These questions won't go away until we resolve them."

Contreras seemed put upon—the more so now that he was freshly indebted to Scherrer. "I understand, Bob," he said. "But I assure you, it is a matter of no consequence. If there were something to it, I would know by now."

"That could be," said Scherrer. "But my superiors are asking me why I can't do as well as Propper. The Bureau has informants, as I've told you, who say that these Cubans came to Chile and were well treated by the Chilean government. The informants say DINA gave them training camps . . ."

". . . Well, that's ridiculous," said Contreras. "I can tell you that right now."

"Probably so," said Scherrer. "Don't misunderstand me, Colonel. Our informants aren't always right. They exaggerate, and they get things screwed up. But the problem is that we won't know what they're exaggerating about until we find out exactly what these Cubans did down here. We need the documents and the records to show precisely where they stayed and who they talked to."

Contreras sighed. "Well, that's not so easy to do, Bob," he said.

"Maybe it's easy for the FBI, but for us it's very difficult. Let's suppose that Guillermo Novo came down here and *did* see the defense minister. How could I find out about it? I could never presume to tell the minister to give me information about his affairs. How could I do that?"

"It's difficult," Scherrer agreed. "But as a start, we could at least verify that Novo stayed in a certain hotel and reportedly talked with a certain minister. Right now I have nothing but reports from informants who are not always reliable."

"Okay, okay," said Contreras. "I will get you the best report I can very soon. I will have it delivered to you in Buenos Aires."

"Thank you, Colonel," said Scherrer. "And have a good trip to Washington."

Before leaving for Buenos Aires, Scherrer decided to put in more work on a small matter that had been nagging at him: the identity of the blond Chilean who had met him at the airport. He checked his notebook. The man had introduced himself as Captain René Riveros of the Chilean army, currently attached to DINA. The man was a captain, like Juan Williams, and was blond. But his photograph was not among those in the fifty-four passports. Scherrer wondered who Riveros was. As a first step, he asked one of his Chilean contacts to check the National Registry of Chilean citizens. Word came back that there was indeed a René Riveros of the correct age and description who had attended the military academy and gone into the Chilean army. So, it seemed, the name was a real one.

Scherrer also knew—from the way Riveros had treated the flunkies around him at the airport—that the captain was a man of some influence. Perhaps he was the sort of trusted officer whom Contreras would call personally with the assignment of whisking Scherrer around the airport authorities. After spending nearly two days over coffee or drinks with various Chilean confidants, Scherrer found out what he wanted to know. Captain René Riveros was a private hero to certain members of the Chilean army; it was he who had killed President Salvador Allende during the 1973 coup.* This fact was still a radioactive state secret.

In Washington, conservative groups greeted the arrival of the Latin American dignitaries with large demonstrations in opposition to the Panama Canal treaties, calling them a giveaway of American

*See above, page 65.

property. Simultaneously, liberal groups demonstrated against several of the South American dictators themselves. At the largest of these demonstrations, crowds denounced Pinochet for oppression in Chile, and they also denounced President Carter for deigning to receive, and thereby to legitimize, Pinochet.

The Chilean President, moving in a security cortege from one elegant state function to another, remained insulated from the accusations, for the most part. Only once did ugly questions about the Letelier assassination intrude upon his diplomatic triumph. At a breakfast with selected members of the press, Pinochet sat next to Jeremiah O'Leary of *The Washington Star*. Most of the questions concerned the Panama Canal or the strategic balance of the hemisphere, but when O'Leary's turn came he said, "Mr. President, I have to ask this; did anyone in the Chilean government or the Chilean military have anything to do with planning or carrying out the Letelier assassination?"

Pinochet looked stiffly at O'Leary. "I swear on my honor as an officer that we did not," he replied.

When Pinochet returned to Chile, Propper tried to find out what had transpired between the two Presidents in the Oval Office. The most he could learn was that President Carter had indeed mentioned human rights and the determination of the United States to pursue the Letelier investigation, and that Pinochet had nodded and pledged cooperation. But the remainder of the hour had been filled with pleasantries and economic matters, and Pinochet had left the interview much relieved that it had not been worse. In fact, he had achieved a positive result, as became evident a few days later when the Carter administration announced that it was naming its first full-fledged American ambassador to Chile. The new ambassador would be George Landau, who would transfer from Asunción, Paraguay, to Santiago.

According to Propper's contacts in the State Department, Landau had been chosen only because he was due for reassignment and because he had a reputation for gaining the cooperation and respect of military governments in Spanish-speaking countries. Still, it struck Propper, Cornick, and Scherrer that the new ambassador to Chile would be the same man who had obtained—fourteen months earlier—the Williams and Romeral photographs in Paraguay. It was at the very least a coincidence—perhaps lucky, perhaps eerie.

"Don't worry too much about what it means, Gene," Cornick advised. "That and a quarter will buy you about half a cup of coffee."

Late on the afternoon of September 12, Wack was leaving the New York FBI office for home when he passed Ricky Canete going the other way. Wack did a double take and spun around in the entrance to the building. Canete, his prize informant, had been missing for fifty-two days, and now he had walked right past Wack into the FBI building!

Wack caught up with him. "Where the hell have you been?" he demanded.

Canete said nothing, but he gave Wack a look of extreme discomfort.

"You know this guy?" interrupted an FBI agent who was standing next to Canete.

"Yeah, Ron," said Wack. "I know him. Is he with you?"

"Yeah, he's with us," said Special Agent Ron Casedna, nodding toward another agent from the New York truck-hijacking squad who was standing on the other side of Canete. "You know him?"

"Yeah," said Wack. "He's Ricky Canete."

"Okay, that's it," Agent Casedna said grimly. "Canete, you're under arrest." He pulled out his handcuffs.

"Wait a minute!" cried Wack. "What the fuck is going on?"

Casedna was snapping on the cuffs. "We thought he was Canete," he said. "But he wouldn't say who he is, and he doesn't have any ID on him. Based on your identification, he's under arrest for ITSP [interstate transportation of stolen property]."

Wack gave Canete a scorching look. "What did you do, Ricky?" he asked.

"I didn't do anything." Canete shrugged. "I was just playing around with some mopeds."

Wack closed his eyes to help control his temper. "I thought you were coming to see me, you jerk," he said. Then he turned to Casedna. "Ron, can I talk to you for a second?"

Casedna and Wack stepped off to the side, where Casedna confided that Canete had ordered a truckload of mopeds from South Carolina, paid for them with a forged check, and then sold them in Brooklyn territory controlled by the Mafia. The hot-moped industry was jealously guarded by organized crime elements, some of whom were rumored to be making plans to eliminate Canete.

"We got a big problem," said Wack. "This asshole's been working for me on the Letelier case. He can't go to jail now."

Wack told Casedna the whole story upstairs. Then, while Canete was being booked and fingerprinted on the moped charge, he went to his desk and pulled out the photograph he had been waiting to show Canete all these weeks. It was Juan Williams, retouched by an FBI artist to show him without a goatee or mustache.

"That's the colonel, all right," said Canete.

"Yeah, I'll bet it is," snickered Wack. "I'll bet you'd say your grandmother looks like the colonel now that you're looking at five years."

"It's him," Canete insisted. "I'm ninety-nine percent sure."

"You better be," said Wack. "You think you're in trouble now, but if you screw me on this one, I'm gonna make sure you go away for the rest of your life."

Canete smiled. "Larry," he said, "have I ever lied to you?"

Four days after Canete's latest arrest, Wack met another of his elusive sources in a booth in the back of a bar in Newark. He showed the source the retouched Juan Williams photograph, mixed in with a number of others.

The informant held the photographs in his lap and flipped through them as inconspicuously as possible. "I think this is him," he said, handing Juan Williams to Wack. "But his hair was a little lighter than this."

Wack returned the photograph. "Take your time," he said. "You sure that's the guy you saw with Guillermo?"

The informant studied the picture again. "Yeah, that's him," he said. "I'm sure."

"How sure?" pressed Wack.

"Look, it was a year ago," said the informant. "But I'm telling you, that's the guy."

"Okay," said Wack, taking a deep breath.

"You don't seem too happy," said the informant. "I'm amazed you came up with this picture. I thought you'd be ecstatic about it."

"I don't know whether to hug you or kick you in the ass," said Wack. He pulled the informant's composite rendition out of his pocket and laid it on the table next to the Juan Williams photograph. "Look at your fucking drawing," sneered Wack. "Your guy in the drawing has jaws like a bulldozer or something. He doesn't look any more like the picture than I do."

The informant compared the two faces and then shrugged. "I'm sorry," he said. "What can I say? I'm better at recognizing faces than describing them."

"I hope so," said Wack.

In Washington, Propper and Cornick badly wanted to believe the two identifications. If true, they would make a vital piece of a very incomplete puzzle centering on one specific blond Chilean, of whom they possessed a photograph. Juan Williams—already tied to DINA by Otero and to the Chilean government by official letters vouching for his visa application—would be placed in the United States about the time of the Letelier assassination, in touch with one of the prime Cuban suspects, Guillermo Novo.

The investigators needed some good news, as their work had both slowed and soured in the two months since the Otero identification. And the trend was continuing. In the next week, IPS colleagues of the assassination victims would hold a public ceremony to commemorate the first anniversary of the bombing on Sheridan Circle. One year had passed. American authorities had arrested no one. The Justice Department had issued only one statement on the case, and that was for the purpose of rebuking Isabel Letelier. No leads or suspects had been announced, but the prime suspect in the eyes of the survivors at IPS, General Pinochet, had just been welcomed to Washington.

Propper could only grit his teeth over all this. He spent most of the anniversary week dragging medical records and computer cards into a spare office in the courthouse. He was using the office to store evidence in a complicated narcotics case that involved traffickers who sent a herd of stout "dieters" up and down the East Coast collecting amphetamine prescriptions from willing doctors who would receive a percentage of the enormous profits. Propper hated narcotics cases, but he had taken this one because of the doctors.

Don Campbell stopped in that week and asked Propper when he could take "another big one." He did so very gently and with a smile, as always, but Propper knew Campbell wanted him to carry more of a load. Privately, Campbell had been complaining to Earl Silbert that Propper was only going through the motions on his other cases, working at his slow speed, without zeal. Campbell assumed it was because Propper was daydreaming about the Letelier case.

He was not the only United States official who was beginning to look beyond the investigation, and others were fretting about how to manage the political ramifications of failure. Time, logic, and the string of recent investigative reversals led many people to anticipate a permanently unsolved crime—if they had not anticipated one all along—and in this sour atmosphere thoughts naturally turned to scapegoats and the apportionment of blame.

Propper was not immune to this. In the late summer, he had renewed his campaign to gain access to FBI informant files. To Cornick and finally to Bob Keuch, he argued that he should have access
to the raw information received from Bureau informants. Bureau officials, as always, rejected the idea as a violation of the sacred trust
between the FBI and its informants. Besides, they said, Propper had
been given everything of value from the files. To this Propper re-
joined that the Bureau had withheld informant information on many
occasions—citing the Alvin Ross material on the Letelier bomb and
the long delay in transmitting the original Brigade lead—and he added that FBI headquarters had been unaware, in many instances, of
the information in its own files. Propper's arguments did not increase his popularity at FBI headquarters, where it was none too
high to begin with.

In fact, officials inside the FBI wanted to see Propper fired. To
them, this prospect offered a number of advantages other than the
obvious one of removing the high-handed free spirit who had annoyed them from the beginning. They knew that a fired Propper
would be a blamed Propper, for one thing. But, more positively, they
believed that without the prosecutor they would have a much better
chance to close the case successfully by means of either Tomboy or
Gopher, their two special informants.

Satkowski took the lead in lobbying for Propper's removal with
Jimmy Adams, the number-two man in the Bureau. He played on
Propper's deficiencies as a suspected leaker, arguing that a leak of
Tomboy or Gopher material would bring disaster to the Bureau.
Adams, on several occasions, made the arguments to Keuch in the
Justice Department, asking for Propper's head. Adams was going to
Keuch about Propper at the same time Propper was going to Keuch
about access to Bureau informant files. Neither side trusted the
other. Keuch placated both of them, without telling Propper of the
Bureau's request.

Propper found out about Gopher largely by accident. Early in October Cindy Grant, keeper of the *Propper's Mistakes* file, burst into
Larry Barcella's office with an urgent message. "Larry, Gene's got
an emergency call from Bob Steven, and he's not here," she said.
"What do I do?"

"Who's Bob Steven?" asked Barcella.

"He's the guy Gene's been dealing with over at the State Department," Grant replied.

Barcella took the call. Steven asked his pardon for the intrusion and then asked Barcella if he had any idea why the FBI had just come to Steven's office to ask for a blank American passport.

"A blank passport?" said Barcella. "I don't have a clue. Who was it?"

"I don't know," said Steven. "He wouldn't tell me his name. That's what made me think he was some kind of nut."

"Wait a minute," said Barcella. "FBI agents always flash their credentials. Some agents I've known for five years *still* flash them whenever they come into my office."

"Well, this guy refused to tell me who he was," said Steven. "All he would say was that he was working on the Letelier case and he needed a blank American passport. He said it was an emergency."

"That's very weird," said Barcella. "What did the guy look like?"

"Well, he's thin, balding, late thirties maybe," said Steven. "Looks like some sort of intelligence guy to me."

"That sounds like Al Seddon," said Barcella. "He's one of the intelligence types over at the Bureau."

"So you know about this scheme?" asked Steven, with some distaste.

"No," said Barcella. "Frankly, I can't even imagine what's going on. But I know Seddon. I'll try to find out for you."

Barcella conferred briefly with Don Campbell before deciding on the direct approach. He called Seddon, who reacted with subdued terror. Barcella thought he could hear the air being squeezed out of Seddon's lungs.

"Uh, Larry, this matter is of the highest sensitivity there is," he said. "I really shouldn't be talking to you about it at all, but we desperately need a passport. We have to get somebody into a foreign country. That's all I can tell you."

"Sounds like you've got a problem," said Barcella. "Why don't you ask the boys across the river [the CIA]?"

"I can't tell you why," said Seddon, "but that's out of the question. Look, Larry, you've got to help me, and then you've got to forget we ever talked about this, okay? We never had this conversation."

"If you say so, Al," said Barcella. "It doesn't make any sense to me, anyway."

"And I'm sure I can trust you not to tell Gene," Seddon added. "He's not cleared for this."

"Sure," said Barcella, but he soon tracked Propper down by phone and told him the bizarre story. Propper said he had a vague hunch what it was all about. He called Steven to make sure no false pass-ports would be issued for the Letelier investigation without his knowledge, and then he went to Cornick and demanded to know what was going on. Cornick replied that the Gopher operation was too big for either of them to buck, being wired through the attorney general. Cornick, who had been excluded from the operation, admitted know-ing very little himself. This was a scalding humiliation to him as the CHILBOM case agent, but he tried to reassure Propper with prom-ises that they would find out the minute the operation produced a break in the investigation. The speech calmed Propper's indignation for a time, but he resolved privately to push even harder for access to Bureau files. He hoped he might find something in them that would provide an opening. This thought would make him boast that he would solve the case.

These comments made eyes roll at the U.S. Attorney's Office, where common gossip had it that Propper's investigation was sink-ing, but they were welcomed by Bob Steven, the new Chile desk offi-cer at the State Department. Steven was an unusual Foreign Service officer. After living through the coup in Chile,* he took a personal interest in the families of the Chilean citizens who disappeared into the hands of DINA. Throughout 1974, he made regular calls on Isa-bel Letelier, whose husband, Orlando, was then confined with other notables of the Allende government in the DINA prison camp on Dawson Island. When the Pinochet government allowed an Ameri-can crew from CBS to film interviews with some of the prisoners there—to prove the government claim that they had not all been murdered, as had been rumored in newspapers around the world —Steven went to the trouble of sending to the United States for a copy of the film. He invited Isabel Letelier and her four sons to the Steven home in Santiago (followed, as usual, by government security agents), where on a home movie screen they saw their husband and father for the first time since he had been arrested on the day of the coup. It was an emotional moment for everyone there, including Ste-ven. He also showed the film to relatives of other prisoners. His chil-dren became friends of the Letelier children. Two years later, in Washington, his son and one of Letelier's sons rode together in Lete-lier's Chevelle just a few days before it exploded on Sheridan Circle.

On leaving Chile, Steven had been posted at the American embas-sy in Buenos Aires, where he had kept up with the progress of the

* See above, page 64.

Letelier investigation by talking with Legat Scherrer, and he had ached for assignment to the Chile desk in Washington. When the assignment came through in August 1977, he quickly made contact with Propper and assured him that he would help the investigation any way he could. He told Isabel Letelier the same thing. From the very beginning, Steven made a habit of keeping Propper informed about political struggles within the Pinochet government. He called Propper regularly and sent him "night reading" from the State Department traffic out of Chile. And, astonished that no "Letelier case" file existed in his office, Steven set out to organize one. He told Propper that it would be a laborious task, because the general files were a mess—jumbled and incomplete and out of order. Nevertheless, Steven wanted to make sure that no bit of relevant information escaped the investigation.

Propper wished he could plant someone like Steven at FBI headquarters. The new desk officer changed his entire relationship with the State Department, where, in his experience, most officials spent their time being formal and vague and staying out of trouble. For Propper, the arrival of Steven was the best news since the discovery of Frank Willis.

On October 12, Scherrer answered his phone and heard a mysterious voice. "You don't know me," it said, by way of greeting, "but I'm a friend of Victor Hugo Barria-Barria. I need a visa. Can I come talk to you?"

Scherrer gave the voice directions to his office. Then he walked over to the window and looked down at the visa line, which stretched nearly five blocks outside the embassy in Buenos Aires. He figured the voice for a distant relative of Contreras's close aide Barria-Barria, someone trying to pull strings to get in the front of the visa line.

An athletic-looking Latin man soon arrived and handed Scherrer a business card showing him to be Enrique Arrancibia, an executive of the Chilean National Bank. "That's my cover job," Arrancibia told Scherrer. "I work for CNI. It's still DINA to me. I worked for Barria-Barria when he was here in Buenos Aires. Anyway, I need to go to California on business. Can you help me? I can't get in that line, because I have to leave tomorrow."

"May I see your passport?" asked Scherrer.

"Sure," said Arrancibia, handing it over.

"You are very candid about your work," said Scherrer, trying to be casual. He knew this face. "Tell me, are you going to the United States on a mission?"

"No," replied Arrancibia, smiling broadly. "This is real banking business. I promise."

"Okay," said Scherrer. "I think I can help you." He sent for a visa application, which Arrancibia filled out. Scherrer told him to come back in a few hours to pick up his passport. The visa would be stamped in it by then. Arrancibia thanked the legat effusively and left.

As soon as he was out the door, Scherrer went to his safe and pulled out the photographs of Juan Williams and Alejandro Romeral, which had arrived two weeks earlier from Washington. Scherrer put Romeral next to the photograph in Arrancibia's passport and whistled to himself. He could not match the faces exactly, but the resemblance was very strong.

He called Interpol-Chile and asked for a routine name check. Word came back quickly that there was an outstanding arrest warrant against Arrancibia for the murder of Chilean Army Chief of Staff René Schneider on October 22, 1970.[*] He was a fugitive from Chilean justice, and yet he was working for the Chilean National Bank and undercover for CNI. If he had killed an army chief of staff for Patria y Libertad, reasoned Scherrer, might he not have done the same thing to a mere former ambassador like Letelier?

When Arrancibia left for California, Scherrer sent an urgent cable to headquarters, transmitting the story and the number of Arrancibia's flight to Los Angeles the next day. FBI agents should grill him as soon as he stepped off the plane, said Scherrer, while Arrancibia was subject to the power of American law. He asked Cornick to monitor the interrogation personally.

Before any results came back from the United States, Scherrer flew to Santiago and obtained a copy of the police report on the Schneider assassination, which had itself become the subject of American news reports in 1975, when a select committee of the U.S. Senate reported on CIA assistance to the plotters against Schneider. What interested Scherrer at the moment were the police photographs of the numerous Chilean suspects. One of them,[†] who looked very much like Juan Williams, had been allowed to flee into Paraguay rather than stand trial for the Schneider murder. The idea

---

[*]See above, page 62.
[†]Juan Luis Bulnes Cerda.

jumped at Scherrer. Paraguay. Perhaps Williams and Romeral had
tried to enter the United States from Paraguay because Williams
was already there. In any case, he had something to work on: two
Patria men who had killed an important Chilean before. One of them
had gone on to work in DINA, the other to live in Paraguay. And
they looked like Williams and Romeral.

While in Santiago, Scherrer complied with instructions from headquarters to conduct discreet preliminary inquiries regarding extraordinary new leads in the case. The leads had been coming down for
months under special headings marked SINGULAR SOURCE. This
meant that the FBI informant was irreplaceable. Some of the cables
mentioned two or three different singular sources as the providers of
related bits of information. This made Scherrer suspicious.

He became even more suspicious after he discovered that many of
the Chileans mentioned by the new singular sources as suspects in
the Letelier case showed up on police indices as narcotics traffickers.
Scherrer noted skeptically that narcotics traffickers were not likely
to be involved in something like the Letelier assassination, and he reported to headquarters that the information so far made him doubt
the reliability of the "singular source." He used the phrase pointedly
to underscore his belief that there was only one source, not two or
three. To him, it was transparent that someone in the Bureau had
written the cables in a clumsy attempt to disguise one source as several.

Seddon and Satkowski, in Washington, hardly noticed Scherrer's
barb. They were too busy celebrating this first confirmation of leads
from Gopher, who had told them from the beginning that the Letelier assassination had been contracted out to Chilean narcotics traffickers by leading members of Patria y Libertad, some of whom had
official connections to the government. Seddon and Satkowski sent
down another batch of leads—slightly more substantive ones, now
that Gopher had passed the first test.

Scherrer received the cable and decided that it, too, was deceptive-
ly sourced. This was especially annoying because there was no way
he could tell who had written the cable—who was ignoring his protests. Scherrer finally telephoned the head of the legat section at
headquarters and, in language veiled for security, complained bitterly that deception had entered the Bureau itself. A fellow FBI agent
was trying to trick him, he said, which was not only unfriendly but
dangerously unprofessional. He said he could protect the source
more efficiently if he knew the identity. As it was, he might compro-

mise him by accident. In ignorance, he did not know which people and places to avoid.

To this, Scherrer received only the discouraging news that Enrique Arrancibia had sailed through his surprise FBI interviews in Los Angeles with alibis tight and composure intact. He could account for all his time and travel. Moreover, Bureau experts had determined that his face was not that of Alejandro Romeral.

Seddon and Satkowski did not run the risk of trying to explain the extraordinary security precautions they had taken for Gopher. The issue would soon be moot, they reasoned, and Scherrer would find out just how deadly a gamble they were taking. Gopher was on his way to Chile. Scherrer would find out quickly enough that the Bureau had tried to plant an informant in the innards of the Chilean government's security apparatus.

Shortly before October 20, Bob Steven decided to conduct an experiment. Although he instinctively trusted Propper's dedication to solve the Letelier case, Steven had compiled enough of the file documents on the case to know something was wrong. They contained explosive information, and Propper did not seem to be paying attention to it. Steven wondered why. Propper might be incompetent. His blustery indifference to rank and authority might be a façade, covering a blind deference to the fundamental order that could be rooted in political belief or timidity of character. Alternatively, Steven knew, the fault could lie in his own department—in which case Steven would find himself in a delicate position. To resolve the issue, he responded warmly when Propper asked to see the new Letelier file. Steven figured he would get a deeper reading on Propper's character very quickly.

Within an hour, Propper burst from an office at the State Department and asked Steven to step back inside with him. Steven followed him and took a chair. Propper was pacing. He did not seem to notice his chair or any of his surroundings. Steven saw that his head was bobbing nervously and he was fidgeting with his hands.

"Bob, somebody ought to have his ass kicked over here," said Propper, still pacing. "Maybe somebody ought to go to jail. I can't believe some of the stuff in there on Williams and Romeral and Paraguay. It says those guys *did* come into Miami! It says they worked at the fucking Chilean embassy up here! I never saw any of that stuff!"

Steven sighed. "I was afraid of that," he said. "Are you sure you got everything we sent over to the Bureau?"

"I know damn well I got everything Carter got," said Propper. "I don't know for sure if Carter got everything from headquarters, but I'd bet a lot on it. Those guys do stupid things sometimes, but there's nothing in here that might hurt the Bureau, and I can't imagine they would screw around with something like this."

"I can't, either," said Steven. "Then again, it doesn't make any sense that anybody over here would want to keep something from you on a case this hot. That's hard for me to fathom without the darkest of suspicions." Steven cleared this throat significantly. "The kind of stuff we don't like to talk about much around this place."

Propper studied Steven briefly before his indignation swept him back into pacing. "Dark suspicion ain't the words," he said. "Some of this stuff is straight out of Watergate." He jumped to the desk and flipped quickly through the file. "Look at this one. I never saw anything like that."

Steven looked at the memo, which was almost exactly a year old:

October 15, 1976

TO: ARA [American Republic Affairs]/John Keane
FROM: ARA/And/Ch/Robert S. Driscoll
THE PARAGUAYAN CAPER

1. I strongly recommend that we give these cables to the FBI intact rather than editing them. (A) The FBI knows we communicate by cable. They will probably ask for the originals. If they were to subpoena them, I do not know how we could resist. (B) The General Walters connection may or may not be important. Besides Stroessner, Colonel Manuel Contreras considers himself a bosom buddy of the General, I think the FBI should know. The General is an old hand. He can take care of himself. (C) If the fact that we had intentionally withheld information on the Letelier investigation became public, we would be subject to a storm of criticism. I recognize that we run the risk of leaks. In my judgment, we run greater risks if we appear to withhold information.

2. Please let me know if you want me to pass this information informally.

Ext. 22575

Propper was making a supreme effort to control himself, feeling whipsawed and betrayed. In one chilling paragraph, this memo showed him for the first time that there were deeper levels to the Williams and Romeral story in Paraguay; that there was a CIA angle to it; that Contreras himself somehow seemed to be involved, along with the CIA's retired deputy director, General Vernon Walters, and

—worst of all—that officials in the State Department may have discussed withholding evidence from him.*

Steven glanced at the memo and nodded. "I thought you'd pick that one out," he said. "Driscoll never showed it to you?"

"Are you kidding?" asked Propper. "He never *told* me, either! He could have mentioned this to me a hundred times, but he never did. He always acted like a conduit, like somebody else knew everything and his job was just to send me what they had."

"Well, he never served in Chile," Steven said of Driscoll, his predecessor. "So he probably didn't know everything. One of the crazy things around here is that we'd have a guy on the Chile desk who never served down there and doesn't really know the country. Besides that, he's kind of a strange guy."

"This is a lot worse than strange," said Propper. "It sounds like a cover-up. All that stuff in there about how the Bureau might find out anyway. My God, Bob, that's guilty fucking talk, and those guys are supposed to be *helping* me! This is a heinous thing here. It's an outrage." Propper noticed Steven's face and paused. "Well, you know what it is," he said, slightly subdued. "You know as well as I do."

"Well, it's a mystery, for one thing," said Steven. "It's not clear to me what's so scandalous about these cables he's talking about. And if they really are scandalous, I don't see why Driscoll would leave this memo in the files. All I can figure is that maybe he thought it would show him on the good side, because he's recommending that all the cables go to the Bureau."

"You've seen the cables?" asked Propper.

"I found most of them, anyway," said Steven. "I've tried to piece them together in a summary for you. How much do you know already?"

"I'd have to double check the files," said Propper. "But all I remember is that the State Department sent us the Williams and Romeral photographs along with a memo that said these two guys wanted to enter the United States on phony Paraguayan passports, and when Ambassador Landau found out about it, he canceled their visas so they couldn't travel. And he sent up the pictures. And the State Department also said these same two guys came into Miami on

*When questioned about these papers, Keane advised the authors that he could not recall the memo, and Driscoll said he could not remember how he had learned that Chilean agents entered Miami. In 1981, Walters told Congress that he had met with DINA's Contreras in 1976, about the time of the Paraguay incident. Asked why he had never mentioned this in his talks with U.S. Letelier investigators, Walters did not respond.

Chilean passports. But we could never confirm that. The FBI checked the INS records twice that I know of—once when we first got it and once when an informant identified the Williams photograph. And that was it. We couldn't put them in the country."

"Well, there's more to it than that," said Steven.

Propper pointed to the files. "You bet your ass there is," he said. "Driscoll's got another memo in there where he says Williams and Romeral were still in the United States *after* the assassination. It sounds like Driscoll knew them firsthand!"

"I know," said Steven. "Well, on the Paraguay story, the best I can make out is that Ambassador Landau first got suspicious of these two guys when somebody in the Paraguayan government *told* him they weren't Paraguayans. One of Stroessner's aides told Landau that Pinochet himself had asked Stroessner for help in getting Williams and Romeral up here as Paraguayans. The aide told Landau everything was okay because it had all been cleared with the deputy director of the CIA, General Walters. But Landau didn't buy it, and he canceled the visas."

"I never heard any of those big names," said Propper. "I'd remember them."

"Maybe everybody over here was worried that it would cause a stink in two countries down there if the Pinochet and Stroessner stuff went over to you guys and leaked. That's possible, but I don't think it's that simple. These memos sound scared. There's got to be more to it. I've tried to figure it out with what's here, but it's still a mystery to me."

"I don't need any more mysteries, Bob," said Propper. "I've still got mysterious threats and mysterious leads all over the place. Plus the assassination. The last thing I need is a new mystery over here. Look, if I have to go overseas on this case, I'll need the State Department to *help* me. I know a little bit about what it's like to get anything done down in South America. The last thing I need is a pissing match over here."

"I know," said Steven. "Well, I'll try to figure it out if I can. I know one thing that would help."

"What's that?"

"Well, these photographs didn't come up through the State Department," said Steven. "Not through our channels. Landau sent them to the guys across the river. I'd like to see their cables."

"The Agency?" said Propper. "I can work on that. What about Driscoll? Where's he?"

"On his new post," Steven replied. "Down in Venezuela."

Propper sighed at the news. "I might have known he'd be in Venezuela," he said.

Propper thumbed through the Paraguay memos with Steven until the very complexity of the concealment overwhelmed him. He asked Steven for copies of the Paraguay documents, which the latter provided without hesitation.

Later, Cornick said the whole thing sent chills up and down his spine. "It'll be a miracle if we ever solve this case, Gene," he declared. When he retrieved his records on the Williams and Romeral lead, he and Propper saw that there had been two communications from the State Department the previous October. In the first, on October 18, the Bureau liaison office received the photographs and a brief memo stating that Williams and Romeral had obtained U.S. visas in Paraguay, which had been canceled on discovery that their passports were fraudulent. In the second communication, ten days later, the State Department advised simply that "the two individuals subsequently entered the U.S. at Miami, on August 22, 1976, bearing A-2 visas issued at Santiago, Chile, in Chilean passports." The second report had brought on Cornick's first negative search of INS records, which revealed that no such Chileans had entered the United States.

Propper and Cornick noticed that the newly discovered "Paraguayan Caper" memo had been written just a few days before the first of these messages, which indicated to them that there had been a debate within the department over how much to tell the FBI. And, from the two skeletal messages, it seemed clear that the more secretive faction had won.

It also seemed that the affair had continued to bother Driscoll. On November 5, 1976, he had written Assistant Secretary of State Harry Shlaudeman stating that Williams and Romeral might pose a problem because they had come to Washington and might still be there. "I heard that they were in Washington working in the Military Mission as of ten days ago," Driscoll had written. On this memo, Propper and Cornick found handwritten instructions for Driscoll in reply: "Bob—don't cancel the visas, but inform the FBI."

Cornick told Propper there was no record that the State Department had ever told the Bureau that the two fake Chileans were in Washington or at the Chilean Mission. "We'd have torn the place apart," he said.

From Steven's file, they learned that concern over the Williams

and Romeral visas had lasted yet another week. There had been a
phone call on November 10 from the State Department's Passport
and Visa Office to the Latin American division, asking whether it
was desirable to seek out Williams and Romeral at the Chilean Military Mission and to revoke their visas, making examples of them for
flouting United States travel laws. And there had been a written reply on November 12 saying no, leave them alone.

"I can't believe it," said Cornick. "They had a regular correspondence going on over there about these two bastards, but they never
bothered to tell us they were in Washington."

"We still don't know for sure," said Propper. "We can't even prove
they were in the country."

"Gene, the upshot of it is that I've got to go back over to INS and
dismantle the place," Cornick declared. "They could not have entered
the country without giving an I-94 form to the immigration people
down there."

"Maybe they sneaked through," said Propper. "Maybe they handed in a blank form. There have got to be ways to get through."

"Yeah, but it wouldn't make any sense," said Cornick. "They've already gotten visas and declared themselves to the United States government as Williams and Romeral. And if they're coming up here to
look legitimate in the Military Mission, they wouldn't run the risk of
getting caught on a stupid immigration violation."

"Well, if they were coming up to kill Letelier, it doesn't make
sense to me that they would hang out at the Military Mission at all,"
said Propper. "And I don't see why they'd use the names Williams
and Romeral after screwing up in Paraguay. Why couldn't they just
pick out some new phony names? That doesn't make sense."

"Well, I don't understand it, either," said Cornick. "But they've
got to fuck up some time, or we won't catch 'em."

"I can't figure these guys as the killers," said Propper. "They're
too official-looking. But maybe they're the contract men. Maybe
they're the supervisors. Okay? And they come up to Miami and meet
with the Brigade people and put out the contract on Letelier. And
then they come up to Washington to supervise. And while they're doing that, they send the Cubans over to have an innocent conversation
with Admiral McIntyre, as cover. How's that? It gives the Cubans a
reason for being in Washington. And it allows the admiral to pass
our polygraph."

"That's possible," said Cornick. "But it doesn't explain why
Wack's informants saw Williams in New Jersey with Guillermo
Novo."

"Well, you can't have everything," quipped Propper. "Besides, we don't know how hard that ID is. The composite's way off."

Cornick became thoughtfully amused. "Gene, it sounds to me like you've come around to the Brigade lead at last," he said. "You might redeem yourself over at the Bureau yet. All you've got to do is say Tomboy's the greatest thing since sliced bread and you're sorry for leaking everything."

"Yeah, right," said Propper. "I'll believe the Brigade lead if we can nail Franco."

On October 20, Alberto Franco, the Shrimp Man, appeared in Washington to answer a grand-jury subpoena and submitted with his usual good humor to a preliminary grilling from Cornick. According to Tomboy's consistent reports, Franco had been the leader of the 2506 Brigade's two-man hit team for the Letelier assassination. And Alvin Ross had told Canete that he had met the Shrimp Man in Washington to carry out that mission.

"A lot of people have been saying you're the button man in this case," Cornick told Franco. "And we already know you've got the right credentials for the job. You know the right people down in Miami. You've had the right training with bombs from the spooks. So why don't you just make it easier on yourself and tell us where you were on the twenty-first of September last year?"

"I already told you that," Franco said wearily. "I was in Miami. I live there."

"Uh huh," said Cornick. "But they do have airplanes that fly up here from Miami, don't they? And they have motels to stay in over in Virginia, don't they? Can you prove you were down in Miami that day?"

"Probably not to you," said Franco. "Look, I'm sure they do have motels. I don't know what you're talking about."

"We'll see," said Cornick. "Would you be willing to take a polygraph on that?"

"Of course I would," said Franco. "I just want to get this thing over with, that's all. Why am I the one who keeps getting handed up?"

"Well, I've got one good reason in mind," said Cornick, who could appear both good-natured and menacing. In reality, however, he was in grave doubt as to Franco's guilt. So was Propper, as he led the witness to the back elevator and down to the grand-jury room.

Propper asked loaded questions about possible phone calls to the Chilean Military Mission in Washington and about possible motel registrations in northern Virginia, all of which Franco answered with aplomb. Then, abruptly, Propper handed the witness a grand-jury order compelling Franco to give the FBI a comprehensive handwriting sample. This was the bluff. The idea was to make Franco think the Bureau had recovered a motel registration form on which he had signed a false name. If guilty, Franco would fear being identified by the FBI lab.

In due course, the witness stepped outside the grand-jury room and into an office with Cornick and an FBI handwriting expert. He gave the sample and departed, shaking his head.

"Okay, Carter, that's it," said Propper in post mortem. "That guy didn't do it. Nobody is that cool."

"I know, I know," said Cornick. "I agree."

"This guy is not involved," said Propper. "That's all there is to it. I won't work on this lead anymore."*

"Yeah, Gene," said Cornick. "Don't even say it. We've got to go back and polygraph Tomboy."

"It's only been a year," cracked Propper. "I think Miami ought to get around to it soon. Right now, I don't care. I don't believe anything he says."

As always, there was a letdown after the elaborate trap sprang shut on thin air, but by the next day Propper was focusing again on Guillermo Novo, now a fugitive for nearly five months. Perhaps Williams and Romeral had flown from Miami to New York to meet Novo, he thought. Then again, perhaps the two Chileans had never come into the country. Cornick was having no luck on the record search. "Those INS guys couldn't find an Indian in a tepee," he said.

Within a week of the handwriting ruse, Propper received a call from a man in Miami who identified himself only as a friend of a reporter Propper knew. The Miami man said that the leader of a Cuban group in Miami wanted to talk to Propper about the Letelier case. He said the Cuban and his followers had themselves committed many acts of violence but that the leader would guarantee Propper's safety on the condition that he come alone.

"That doesn't sound like a very good idea to me," said Propper.

"Look," said the Miami man. "They're just as worried about being set up by the FBI as you're worried about being set up by them. This

*U.S. investigators would never develop any evidence indicating that Alberto Franco or Raúl Martínez was involved in the Letelier assassination. The names used here are not their true names.

guy just wants to talk to you, I'm telling you. I've known him for many years. He's a heavy. He's capable of doing Letelier, but I know he wouldn't harm you."

"That's nice," said Propper. "How do you know that?"

"Because if he was involved in Letelier and decided to go after you, he wouldn't have called me," said the Miami man. "Believe me. He'd just do it, and I'd never know. He sure wouldn't ask me to set up a scheme where I know who he is and your reporter friend knows who I am. That's crazy."

"So was the Letelier assassination," said Propper.

"Okay, that's a reasonable point of view," said the man. "All I'm doing is passing along the offer to talk."

Propper asked for time to think about it. A few days later he called his reporter friend and asked him to pass the word that he would be willing to meet with the Cuban leader alone, if the meeting took place in a public part of downtown Miami, in the daytime. It was agreed. Final arrangements were made in Miami. Propper did not tell Cornick about them. Nor did he tell his current girlfriend, who was then living in Fort Lauderdale. She would worry, he figured, and it was his gamble. Logic told him nothing bad would happen.

At the appointed hour, he was standing as directed at a certain display window of Burdine's department store in Miami, looking out at the midday traffic. Fifteen minutes later he heard a voice behind him say, "Mr. Propper, someone wants to speak with you."

Propper turned to see a Cuban male in his late thirties. His first thought was that the man had never been before his grand jury in Washington. "Fine," he said.

The man led the way out into the bright Miami sunshine and to a parked car. He opened the back door for Propper.

"Wait a minute," said Propper. "I thought we were going to talk here. That was the deal."

"No," said the man. "We want to go somewhere else."

A stab of fear somehow induced Propper to be extra polite. "I can understand that," he said. "But, quite frankly, if I go with you, nobody will know where I am. Somebody knows where I am here."

"Yes," replied the man. "But if you're concerned about your safety, the place doesn't matter. We could do it right now. But we're not going to. The person you are going to see will tell you things he doesn't want attributed to him. He doesn't want the Feebies to know he talked to you. So you won't see his face and you won't know where he is. Okay? Does that make sense?"

"Not really," said Propper. "I mean, it makes sense, but it's not really okay. How about if you tell me where we're going so I can tell somebody? I'd feel a lot better."

"No," said the man. "I can't do that."

Propper took an uncomfortable breath. "I wish you could," he said.

"I could have said yes and then lied to you and you wouldn't know the difference," said the man. "So what difference does it make, except that we're trying to be honest with you."

"Yeah, well, I suppose the place doesn't matter," said Propper, thinking furiously. Did the Cubans know he could be traced if anything happened? He looked around at the pedestrians and then slid into the back seat of the car.

The man jumped into the front seat. "You've got to close your eyes for a while," he said.

"Look," said Propper. "I don't know my way around Miami, anyway. So I won't know where you're going."

"You can read street signs as well as anybody else," the man said. "It's not so bad. I'm not asking you to be blindfolded. I just want you to put your hands over your eyes."

Propper blew nervously on his fingertips. "This is going to look pretty funny," he said. "Some guy driving down the street in the middle of the day with his hands over his eyes."

"It happens all the time in Miami." The man laughed.

This comment did not reassure Propper. He put his hands over his eyes, but as soon as he was in darkness and heard the engine start, he said, "I'm not sure I want to do this."

"If you want to get out, feel free," said the man. "But you'll miss some good information."

Propper swallowed. "I think I want to get out," he said.

"Fine," said the man.

Propper got out of the car and took several deep breaths. But when the car began to ease away from the curb, a compulsion forced him to run after it and rap on the window. "Wait a minute," he said. The car stopped. Propper hopped in, covered his eyes, and tried to keep his wits during a winding half-hour ride.

Propper got out of the car, hands still over his eyes, and was led by a touch on the elbow. It was like a child's game to him, but when he pictured himself walking through Miami that way, he felt an odd combination of emotions. He felt foolish and scared. If anything happened to him, his epitaph would be an ugly joke.

After stumbling through a doorway, Propper heard the man say,

"You can take your hands off your eyes now." He found himself in a small, brightly lit room with sofas and chairs—like the living room of a bungalow. Then, when he was led into the next room, all the lights went off. In the darkness, Propper could make out only the shapes of several men and of numerous rifles mounted on the walls.

"Congratulations for showing up, Mr. Propper," said one of the men.

"Thank you," said Propper. From the sound, he could tell it was a voice he had not heard in the grand jury. The man was sitting on the floor across the room, behind a chair, so that Propper could not see his face.

"I had doubts that I would see you," said the man.

"Right about now, I'm sorry I didn't have a couple more doubts," said Propper.

"Why is that?"

"I don't like seeing all those guns," said Propper. "On the walls."

"Don't worry about it," said the man. "You are going to walk out of here all right."

"I hope so," said Propper. "But I want to make sure you know people will be coming after you if I don't. I'm supposed to make a phone call to Washington by two-thirty. That's an hour from now. If I don't, my reporter friend will call your friend down here. And if they don't locate me within a reasonable time after that, they'll call the FBI."

"That's straight out of James Bond, my friend," the man said with a teasing lilt.

"Who are you?" asked Propper. "What group are you with?"

"Oh, come on, Mr. Propper," said the man. "I thought we were going to be friends. You don't think we did all this for fun, do you? I won't tell you who I am, and as far as I know, you won't be able to get back to this place. You'll just have the information I want to give you. Now tell me, why do you think the Cubans were involved in the Letelier thing?"

"Because of information we have from other people," said Propper, "most of whom are also Cubans."

"Well, they're probably Castro Cubans," said the man. "And they're probably trying to set us up. They've been doing that for years."

Propper paused briefly to think of Tomboy. Was it possible that the Bureau's top-secret informant had planted the Brigade lead at the behest of Fidel Castro? He had thought of it before, but the idea had only led him in circles. He shrugged it off. "Look," he said, "I can't tell you about the political convictions of all our sources because I don't know them. I know what they say, but I don't know what they might be hiding. Now, you guys always say that anybody you don't like is a Castro agent. That's fine with me. I think anybody who gives me information on the Letelier case is wonderful, whether he's Castro or one of you people. So let's forget politics for a second, okay? You guys are complaining because you think we're hassling you with no reason, right?"

"And we don't like it," the man agreed.

"Well, I'm telling you that the FBI agents working with me are not the ones you people have to squabble with every day down here. We're trying to solve a case, and I'm telling you there's no reason for anybody in Washington to try to screw any of you people."

"Then why are you doing it?" asked the man.

"Because we're getting information from anti-Castro Cubans that points down here."

"Well, it's wrong," the man declared. "The Cubans didn't kill Letelier."

"How can you say that?" asked Propper. "You don't speak for all Cubans. You can't possibly know what small groups of people might do."

"I'm saying that there is no group of Cubans in Miami that would have killed Letelier," the man insisted. "I would have known about it. Believe me."

"Oh," said Propper. "So you're just limiting it to Miami, then?"

"But you're calling a lot of people from Miami before your grand jury," said the man.

"That's not what I want to know," said Propper. "Are you saying it's not somebody from Miami?"

"That's right."

"Well, okay," said Propper. "I'm not sure I can take that at face value, but okay."

"You've heard about some of the things we do?" asked the man.

Propper hesitated. "Yeah, I think I know what you're driving at," he said.

"Well, there's a reason for them as old as war," said the man. "We're going to take that island, and if we don't, we're going to make the son-of-a-bitch's life as miserable as possible."

"Castro?" said Propper.

"The One," affirmed the man. "The Horse. *El Caballo*. If we can get him, we'll get him. If not, we'll fuck him as bad as we can. Bombing buildings? No problem. Bombing airplanes? No problem as long as there are no people in them. Killing Castro's people? No problem. But if it doesn't have any effect on the One, don't do it. That's why nobody from Miami would kill Letelier. I know."

"Yeah, but Letelier was a Chilean *socialist,* and I know for a fact that there have been connections between the Cubans here and the Pinochet government," said Propper.

"Sure," said the man. "We both hate the One. We're both anti-Communist. We want stuff from the Chileans, sure. They're not really giving us much, but they may. That's why we go down there. But we recognize that we can't go knocking off every fucking Communist leader in the whole world. We're only after one. And you're on the wrong lead if you think we did it."

"Who did do it?"

"Nobody down here," said the man. "You ought to quit harassing Carballo and Frank Castro and the others. You're not gaining any friends down here with FBI harassment."

"Yeah, well, you're not gaining any friends in Washington the way you hassle us about a subpoena," Propper retorted. "I bet you could find out who killed Letelier if you wanted to."

"Who cares?" said the man. "What has that got to do with Fidel Castro?"

"You guys know things besides Castro," said Propper. "Things aren't as neat and organized down here as you're making out. Like, what do you do with all these guns up here? What are you going to do with them? Shoot at a vacant building?"

The man made no immediate reply, and during the pause Propper reflected to himself that this had not been a brilliant line of questioning, under the circumstances.

"No, we don't shoot at vacant buildings," said the man. "But sometimes we need to scare people. There're all sorts of Castro Cubans down here, and there are people who will extort money from you, and people involved with drugs. And you have to protect yourself. You're not comfortable with all these big guns, are you?"

"No," said Propper. "I've been totally non-nervous through most of this, but I'm not overly comfortable at the moment."

"Well, I don't have much more to tell you," said the man. "If you want to contact me again, you can use the same method."

"Thank you," said Propper. "How am I getting back?"

"The same way."

"Hands over the eyes?"

"Unless you prefer some other way," said the man.

"No, I think a hand will do."

"Okay, my friend. And remember: no peeking."

Propper groped his way back out of the room amid general laughter. In the car, his original escort kept up a friendly banter until they reached the downtown area. "You can take your hands off now," he said. "So tell me, Mr. Propper, you're gonna take a look at the car when we drive away, aren't you?"

"Yeah," said Propper, "I'm sure I'll wave goodbye to you."

"Well, the car is stolen," said the man. "Besides, you won't be able to identify it, anyway."

"Well, at least I know what you look like," said Propper.

"Yeah, but after I shave, you won't know," said the man. "I grew this just for this meeting."

"Seems like a lot of trouble to me," said Propper, studying the face. "That guy didn't tell me all that much."

"Yes, he did," said the man. "He told you nobody down here did it. That's a lot."

"I'll have to think about that," said Propper. "You think he knows where else I'm looking?"

"I don't know," said the man. "How about if we let you out here?"

Propper looked around. "Fine," he said. "I'll just get a taxi."

The car stopped. "See you guys," said Propper, jumping out. When the car pulled away, he looked quickly for the number on the license plate. But there was no plate at all.

On November 7, Scherrer went to a small cocktail party in Buenos Aires honoring an Argentine army officer who had recently been promoted to general. During the evening, Scherrer found himself in private conversation with the Chilean army attaché. As casually as possible, the legat continued his delicate campaign to find out more about Juan Williams without letting the Chilean government know what he was after.

"You're the third or fourth Chilean I've met by the name of Mac-Kenney," Scherrer said pleasantly. "It's amazing to me that you see so many Irish names in Chile. Like O'Higgins."

"Yes," said the colonel. "Every time the British have cracked down in Ireland, some of the Irish have migrated to Chile. My mother's family emigrated from Ireland in the late 1800s."

"I see," said Scherrer. "Well, I've met a lot of people of Irish descent in Chile, but it's still hard for me to get used to the names. It's hard for me to think of you Irish as Chileans sometimes. For example, I've just made this new friend in Chile named Williams. His family is as Chilean as you are, but their name is Williams."

"Well, actually, the name Williams is of English origin," the colonel replied. "I agree that it sounds unusual in Spanish, but it is a very distinguished name in Chilean history. Especially in the navy."

"Oh, really?" said Scherrer.

"Yes." The colonel smiled. "There was a very famous captain in the navy named Juan Williams who claimed the Strait of Magellan for Chile in 1843."

"That's very interesting," said Scherrer.

"He is a great hero even now," said the colonel. "In 1843, President Bulnes sent the captain on a mission to claim the strait, fearing that one of the European powers would do so and take away an important part of the southern territory. So Captain Williams sailed in the warship *Ancud*, and he raised the Chilean flag on September 21, 1843. The flagship of a French expedition sailed into the strait the very next day, but Captain Williams was already there."

"It was a very close race, then," Scherrer said brightly. He was making some effort not to drop his drink or jump into the colonel's arms. "You know a lot of history, Colonel," he said. "Are you sure it was September 21?"

"Well, I taught history at the military academy," the colonel replied. "Yes, it was the twenty-first. It is a famous day in Chilean naval history. Even now, navy officers will toast Captain Juan Williams on that day."

"I see," said Scherrer. "Well, thank you, Colonel. You have given me quite an education. Tell me, do you think there is a party like this in Santiago to celebrate the promotion of General Contreras?"

The colonel stiffened and lost his knowledgeable glow. "I doubt it," he replied. "But I wish the general well."

Scherrer nodded. He needed no more to confirm that this colonel was one of the majority in the army who resented Contreras for establishing his own political brotherhood, separate from the army. Only three days earlier Pinochet had promoted Contreras to general ahead of many officers his senior. The new general was now an advisor to the President, nominally retired from intelligence work.

"Well, good luck, Colonel," said Scherrer, taking his leave. "I'm of German descent, myself. So I like seeing all the blond Germanic Chileans. But the FBI is full of Irishmen, and you guys are all right, too, I guess."

The colonel laughed, and Scherrer soon left the party. He could not sleep that night. Captain Juan Williams claimed the Strait of Magellan on September 21, he thought, the same day that "Captain Juan Williams," the blond Chilean, might have assassinated Orlando Letelier. Scherrer pictured a small group of navy officers hearing the news of the assassination and, as they always did on that day, raising glasses to "Captain Juan Williams" with thin smiles and a special feeling they would never forget. He wondered whether the killers felt driven to adorn their conspiracy with symbolic details from Chilean military lore.

Cornick and Propper shared a cold thrill over Scherrer's cable, but they agreed that the information would not mean anything until they could prove that Williams and Romeral had entered the United States. The INS computers had already registered a third negative response. Cornick, unsatisfied, had requested that INS order its clerical employees to search through the stacks of actual I-94 copies for the forms on Williams and Romeral. INS had responded that if the forms were there, they would have been entered into the computer. Cornick was still marshaling the bureaucratic leverage to force a physical search. Meanwhile, he was working through the FBI liaison office in an effort to find out how State Department officials—notably Bob Driscoll, the former Chile desk officer—had learned originally that Williams had entered the country.

There was little Propper could do in the search itself. He was working on his narcotics case when Detective Stanley Wilson dropped in late one afternoon. Propper had not seen Wilson since the flap over Wilson's female source inside the Chilean embassy. The detective had been thoroughly shut out of the investigation, but, as usual, he rebounded by means of his own unorthodox connections. After chatting with Propper about secret doings here and there, he advised that he had a thing or two up his sleeve and that he was on his way over to the Chilean embassy to ask his contacts there about a new suspect he had unearthed by the name of Williams.

Propper nearly vaulted over his desk. "What?" he cried. "Stanley, you can't do that!"

"Why not?" asked Wilson.

"My God!" said Propper. "We've been investigating that! It'll fuck it up if you tell the Chileans about that guy!"

"I got a picture of him," said Wilson.

"You're kidding!" said Propper.

"Nope," said Wilson, who could not resist an air of satisfaction over having struck so sensitive a nerve.

"Where'd you get it? What's he look like?" Propper demanded.

"From a source," said Wilson. "I don't have it with me."

"What source?" cried Propper. "Where's the source? This guy Williams has been blowing hot and cold for a year! What have you got?"

Wilson looked at Propper. "Just a source," he said, quietly but defiantly.

"Whaddaya mean, just a source?" cried Propper. "Stanley, this is too important to play games! We gotta know if it's a good source or a bad source! We gotta know if we can get some hard evidence that this guy Williams even came into the country!"

"I'm not playing games, Gene," said Wilson. "And I'll try to get the stuff for you if you tell me what you want. But I have obligations to my sources that I can't go back on. It's a source in Florida." Wilson paused, as if to weigh things in his mind. "It's in the Brigade," he added. "That's all I can tell you."

"You have a source in the Brigade who told you about a guy named Williams?" asked Propper, now nearly salivating with curiosity.

"Yep," said Wilson.

"All right, wait a minute, wait a minute," said Propper. "Let's forget about who the source is for a minute. You trust him, right?"

"Yes," said Wilson. "I haven't run that much stuff with him yet, but I trust him."

"Okay," said Propper. "Now, just tell me what the source said about Williams. I want to know what he said."

"Not much," said Wilson. "Not yet, anyway. He just said there's this guy named Williams who's the courier for the Chileans to the Cubans down there. And he said I ought to know about him for the case. And then he gave me his picture."

"Does the source know Williams?" asked Propper. "Does he know him personally? Has he seen him in Miami? Does he know where he stays down there?"

"Wait a minute," said Wilson. "I don't know all that yet. I don't know whether he knows Williams or not. I presume he does, but I don't know."

"You mean he might not even know the guy, but he gave you his picture?" Propper asked skeptically. "Where'd he get it if he didn't know him?"

"I didn't ask yet, Gene," said Wilson. "You don't understand how I'm trained to operate. Look, this guy drops a name and a picture on me and says I ought to know about it for the Letelier case, okay? Now, the way I look at things, if he wanted to tell me more he would have told me. Okay? That's the way these things work. I figure if he's fingering the guy, that's heavy enough for a Cuban in Miami to do. So he's probably scared shitless. And I figure the next step is up to me. So that's why I was on the way over to the Chilean embassy—I was gonna ask some of my contacts over there if they know this guy Williams. And I stopped in here on the off chance you might know something yourself."

"I'm glad you did, Stanley," said Propper. "If Williams is involved, that means the Chilean government is in this thing up to its ass. Believe me. And that means they'd probably kill Williams as soon as they found out we're on to him. Stanley, you might have really fucked up bad."

"Maybe so," said Wilson. "But it's the same old story. If you'd been telling me this stuff all along, this never would have happened."

"I *can't* tell you all this stuff, because a lot of it's classified and you don't have a clearance," said Propper. "Especially this stuff about foreigners. It's classified, Stanley."

"That's what I mean," said Wilson. "The same old story."

Propper sighed. "All right, look," he said. "You already know about this. The name, at least. We have to work this together. I can tell you that this guy Williams is important. We know he's DINA. I can't tell you how we know, but we know. And we have source information that he came up here through Miami and met with some of the Cubans in New Jersey. We can't prove it yet, though. That's why we need your confirmation so badly. I tell you what. If you can get me some confirmation that this is the same guy and some proof that he was in Miami, I'll see if I can clue you in on the rest of the lead. How's that?"

"I don't know," said Wilson. "It sounds like you want to tell me what to do and get me to tell you everything I know, but you don't want to level with me."

"Goddamn it, Stanley, I just told you a hell of a lot!" Propper exploded. "Carter would have my ass already. I'm taking a step to work together, and I'm telling you you're gonna be sorry if you fuck it up."

"How about if you take one more step?" asked Wilson.

"What's that?" asked Propper.

"How about if you call Captain O'Brien and get me another trip down to Miami?" asked Wilson. "I didn't know this lead was gonna be this important, and he might not take it from me."

"Done," said Propper. "But I want something back from you. I want to see that picture. I have to make sure it's the same guy."

Wilson looked rather pained. "I can't do that, Gene," he said. "Not without a release from the source."

"C'mon, Stanley," Propper implored. "Can't you call the source on the phone and get an okay? I've been looking at that guy's picture for months. I have to know if yours is the same one."

Wilson nodded and looked slyly at Propper's office safe. "You got it in there?" he asked.

Propper caught the suggestion. "Unh unh," he said, shaking his head. "I can't do that."

"Why not?" asked Wilson. "I don't want to *take* your picture. I just want to peep at it. I can *tell* you if it's the same guy. Come on. Let's quit playing games."

After some hesitation and further argument, Propper walked to his safe and opened it. He took the Williams photograph out of the stack in the front of the second drawer and walked around his desk to Wilson.

"That's the guy," said Wilson.

As Propper expected, Cornick flew into a tirade when he learned that such a critical clue had fallen into the hands of someone like Wilson. "This is it, Gene," he fumed. "This is the disaster I've been telling you about all along. That squirrel is gonna fuck up our last hope to solve this case. I should have done more than chop him off at the knees." He mentioned the gonads and the neck as more suitable spots. Cornick mistrusted the whole story. He wanted to see the "alleged photograph." Propper advised him not to underestimate Wilson. In the end, Cornick decided that the best way to answer all these questions was to identify Wilson's source. Working from a file he had built up on Wilson as a leak suspect, he began calling those people he knew had been in contact with the detective. He "cashed in all his chips," as he said, and asked them one by one if Wilson had said anything to them recently about a photograph.

Stanley Wilson was still in Miami a few days later when Cornick burst into Propper's office with triumph on his face. It was all a fraud, he declared. A friend of his in naval intelligence in New York had provided the first clue by recalling that Wilson had just asked him about a man named Williams and had said he got the photograph from a police detective in Miami. Cornick had figured this must be

Danny Benítez, the only police detective in Miami who had ever shown any interest in the Letelier case. Then Cornick had "rattled cages" in Miami to find out how Benítez might have gotten a photograph of Juan Williams, and to Cornick's surpassing disgust, an FBI agent had confessed under the weight of heavy evidence.

The story, as Cornick pieced it together, was that the Miami FBI office had received the Juan Williams photograph from Cornick weeks earlier when source information had come in that a Chilean DINA contact might be arriving in Miami from abroad. Cornick had asked the Miami office to cover the airport and look for someone resembling the Juan Williams photograph. But the Letelier case agent in Miami, ignoring strict orders from Cornick to show the Juan Williams photograph to no one, had given it to Detective Danny Benítez. The agent had been too busy to go to the airport.

"Gene, the upshot of it is that Wilson's got our own goddamn photograph," Cornick announced. "We thought we were getting a confirmation out of the Brigade, but he's got us chasing our own tail. The son-of-a-bitch. I could shoot him and Benítez."

"Wait a minute, Carter," said Propper. "If this is true, I'll be even more pissed at Stanley than you are, but I don't see what Danny's got to do with it. If the Bureau gives Danny a photograph of a possible suspect in the Letelier case, and Danny sees the police detective working the case, why shouldn't he give it to Stanley?"

Cornick looked disgusted. "Gene, that photograph had caveats on it from top to bottom," he said. "They weren't supposed to show it to *anybody*."

"Yeah, but those caveats went to the Bureau down there," said Propper. "Maybe the agent didn't tell Danny. We know the Bureau fucked up, but we don't know about Danny. I bet they didn't tell him anything."

"They all fucked up," growled Cornick, whose anti-police prejudice was at its height. For reasons of diplomacy, Cornick avoided the scene a few days later when an irate Propper confronted the detective.

Wilson had only begun to tell about his latest trip to Miami, throwing in all sorts of veiled clues, when Propper interrupted and demanded to see the Juan Williams photograph. Wilson declined, on the ground that the source was not quite ready to grant his permission, whereupon Propper lost what little patience he had stockpiled for the meeting.

"Damnit, Stanley!" he cried. "You better tell me who your source is! I think you've been spinning me! I don't think your source is from the Brigade at all!"

"What are you talking about?" asked Wilson.

"I think you've got our photograph," Propper accused. "I think you got it from law-enforcement people in Miami. Didn't you?"

"Gene, I can't play guessing games about who my sources are," said Wilson. "You know that. The Bureau won't do that. The Agency won't do that. Nobody will. Now, what is it you want to know, and I'll try to give you the information."

"Cut it out, Stanley," said Propper, waving his hand in disgust. "Don't give me that stuff about your supersecret sources. Just tell me if you got it from a policeman or any other law-enforcement officer down there, that's all."

"I already told you, Gene," Wilson said testily. "I don't talk about my sources. Look, I'm trying to help you out on this case, which is on the books as an open D.C. homicide, and every time I do . . ."

". . . No, *you* look, Stanley!" Propper interrupted. "We've known each other a long time, but this is more important than any of that. Now both of us have official duties, and I'm warning you that if you don't tell me whether you got your fucking information from officials down there, I'll slap you in the grand jury and ask you under oath! You got that? I'm not gonna ask you about Cubans or criminal sources who need protection or anything like that, but I *am* going to ask you about cops and FBI agents! And if you don't talk, I'm gonna slap your ass in jail right along with Suárez! You got that? You have no privilege whatever to hide official evidence from a grand-jury investigation, Stanley, and you know it."

"You just try it, Gene," Wilson said defiantly. "I'm not gonna give up a source to you or anybody else. And if you subpoena me, you'll never get a dime's worth of help from a cop in this city."

Wilson soon departed in a rage. The conflict quickly escalated into a war of innuendo, rumor, and pique that engulfed the Major Crimes unit and the homicide squad, pitting lawyer against cop. In an effort to resolve the dispute, a summit meeting convened a few days later in Don Campbell's office. Captain Joe O'Brien represented the police. Campbell, Propper, and Larry Barcella were on the other side.

Barcella told O'Brien that the FBI agent in Miami had admitted giving the photograph to Danny Benítez and that Benítez had admitted giving it to Wilson. "Stanley's got us chasing our own tail, Joe," said Barcella. "Gene thought he was getting a confirmation and all he was getting was his own information coming back to him.

And Stanley wouldn't level on it."

O'Brien sighed under the weight of facts. "Well, that's why I usually have Stanley on suicides and natural deaths," he said. "Look, he's good, but you gotta remember he has his own way of doing things. Larry, if Stanley was in this room right now and I picked you up and threw you out the window right in front of him, he would not close the case. However, in two hours I'll guarantee you he'd come up with a dozen sources—half of whom would speak Spanish, half of whom would have intelligence connections—who would give terrific information leading to the conclusion that I threw you out the window. And his story would be a hell of a lot more interesting than what really happened. But Stanley wouldn't be able to make an arrest based on the simple fact that he saw me do it. That's just the way he is."

O'Brien shrugged. The three lawyers exploded in laughter, and the crisis passed. In the end, O'Brien recommended that everyone leave Wilson alone. He would make sure that the detective pulled no more tricky moves.

Don Campbell waited a few weeks after the summit meeting. Then, after hesitating on several successive days and after further conversations with Earl Silbert on the same old subject, he finally called Propper and asked him to step into his office.

"Have a seat, Gene," said Campbell. He was very friendly but slightly nervous. "What have you got going on the Letelier case?"

"Not much," said Propper. "Is that what you wanted to talk to me about?"

"Yeah," said Campbell. "It seems to me that you've had a hell of a lot of ups and downs lately, and I just wondered if you have any idea what they'll add up to. You got any thoughts on where it's leading?"

"Not really," said Propper. "Lately, it's been mostly downs. A lot of it has been interesting stuff . . ."

". . . I know it's been interesting," said Campbell, nodding with a hint of boredom. This was a point he had often discussed with Silbert—that Propper understandably preferred the exotic, sexy, high-level stuff of the Letelier case to the more mundane cases on the docket.

"Uh huh," said Propper, sensing the squeeze. "Well, frankly I think the case is heading overseas," he said. "I have to admit that it doesn't look like the case will get solved here. Nothing's really happened in the grand jury for six months. I don't think the Cubans will talk. The Bureau's still looking for Novo. I'm not overly optimistic that they'll find him. And the Miami lead's pretty much dead, as far as I'm concerned. So that doesn't leave much for me to do. Lately, I've spent most of my time on other cases."

"What's left on Letelier?"

"Well, the Bureau's doing most of it now," said Propper. "I've had a few more grand-jury witnesses lately. I had Otero back up on a writ to take a lie-detector test."

"How did it come out?" asked Campbell.

"Well, it was very interesting," said Propper. "It came back 'Unable to Determine,' and the guy who gave the test said it was very rare. He said it was almost a flat line. He said Otero didn't care about anything one way or another. It made no difference to him whether he lied or not, so the machine got no response. I guess that's what happens when you're looking at forty years."

"What does it mean if the case goes overseas? Isn't that what you said?"

"Yeah," said Propper. "Well, it means the Bureau's got a big source who's supposed to be getting stuff out of Chile. And Scherrer's trying to identify one of the suspects down there who used a phony name. That's it. Basically, it's a last resort. Because if the case breaks in Chile, sooner or later we have to go to the Chileans for help. We don't have any power down there, and that means our suspects might disappear on us. Or the Chileans might just run circles around us. But right now it's the only alternative."

"Well, I know the Bureau wants to resolve it as soon as possible," said Campbell. "One way or another. Carter was in here the other day, and he told me he's under tremendous pressure to deactivate the investigation."

"He is?" asked Propper. "He said that?"

"Yeah," said Campbell. "He says it costs a small fortune to keep the investigation active as a special. And it's been way over a year now. So the Bureau wants to put things on a reduced basis. You know, they'll keep it open and investigate whatever comes up, but they won't beat the bushes every day. Carter says he doesn't think he can keep it going more than another month."

"I didn't know that," said Propper, amazed that Cornick had concealed this from him.

Campbell cleared his throat. "Well, Gene," he said uneasily, "quite frankly, I don't think he wanted to tell you. He knows as well as I do how much this case means to you ..."

"... It's not that, Don," said Propper. He started to say something and then stopped.

"They're talking about shutting it down around Christmas if nothing breaks," Campbell said.

"Well, I've got just a couple more things I want to try, and I can do them by then, I guess," said Propper.

"What's that?" asked Campbell.

"Well, Carter and I have been talking about sending Letters Rogatory down to Chile on the blond Chilean lead, for one thing," said Propper. "And I'd like to find out more about the Bureau's big new source before we let go. I've been pushing for that with Keuch. I want to look at the Bureau's informant files so I can say I believe everything possible has been done to solve the case."

"You think another month or two will be enough?" asked Campbell.

"I hope so," said Propper. "I may need a little more time than that. But not much."

"Okay, let's give it until Christmas, then, and see what happens," said Campbell. He invited Propper to work off his aggressions in a game of darts, but Propper, for once, refused.

Propper went back to his office in something of a daze and called Cornick. "I didn't know you were thinking about shutting down the investigation," he said. "I didn't know there was so much pressure from the Bureau."

"You must have talked to Don," Cornick said lamely. "Let me tell you ..."

"... No, it's all right, Carter," said Gene. "I think it's all right. We've got to bite the bullet some time."

"Exactly," said Cornick.

"I just think you should have talked to me first, Carter," said Propper. "I would have done that with you."

"I know, Gene," Cornick admitted. "He just called me in there and I told him the truth, that's all ..."

"... He said you came in to see him," said Propper.

"Well, Gene, to be perfectly honest, that's true in a way," said Cornick. "What happened is that we ran into each other and got to talking like we always do. And he asked me how things were going, and I told him not too good. And one thing led to another, and he asked me into his office to talk things over. That's what happened, in a nutshell."

"Uh huh," said Propper. "Well, we'll have to make things happen in a hurry."

"Don't worry, Gene," said Cornick. "We'll get it this Christmas. This is our year."

"That's what you said last year," said Propper.

15 ▣ GOPHER'S CHASE

The second Christmas of the Letelier investigation passed uneventfully. In Washington, Propper spent the last week of the year reviewing a file on Edwin Wilson, the retired CIA official who had popped up briefly as a suspect the previous April.* Shortly before the new year, he began a grand-jury investigation into Wilson's terrorist activities on behalf of Libyan President Qaddafi.

In Buenos Aires, Scherrer was analyzing Propper's State Department discoveries and the other scraps of information he had on the Williams and Romeral travel puzzle. He suggested that the State Department's Passport and Visa Office might have placed "stops" against travel by the two men, based on the orders from Ambassador Landau in Paraguay. In that case the I-94 travel forms on the two men might have been forwarded directly from the immigration department in Miami to the visa office in Washington.

Muttering to Propper about how the tent was being packed up and how it was time to take risks, Cornick had ignored the FBI's liaison office and gone straight to the visa office himself. There, as Scherrer

---

*Justice Department attorneys, having concluded that Wilson should not be prosecuted, had sent reports of their findings to the U.S. Attorney's Offices that could have had jurisdiction over cases against Wilson, asking each for a routine "letter of declination" to prosecute. By these letters, the prosecutors' offices would signify their agreement that Wilson should not be prosecuted. In the Washington U.S. Attorney's Office, Larry Barcella remembered that Propper had interviewed Wilson, and asked him to review the Justice Department report. Propper disagreed with the report's recommendation.

hoped, clerks finally unearthed records showing that Williams and Romeral had indeed entered the United States at Miami on August 22, 1976. This was the first indication that Juan Williams, the blond Chilean, had in fact entered the United States before the Letelier assassination. But the visa office no longer had the actual I-94 forms Cornick needed for evidence, having mailed them back to INS. In yet another twist, the clerks found that the I-94s had been mailed to INS headquarters in Washington rather than back to the Miami INS office, which explained why the physical search of the INS records in Miami had failed to locate anything on Williams and Romeral.

With all the pent-up fury of someone who has endured a long travail of bureaucratic frustration, Cornick demanded that a team of FBI clerks be allowed to go through the files at INS headquarters. This met with some resistance. Cornick threatened a subpoena from Propper, who advised caution on the ground that the INS was part of the Justice Department. Technically, he told Cornick, the attorney general might wind up in court defending a subpoena against himself. After further give and take, Cornick's team of clerks finally searched the records at INS headquarters and found the long-sought I-94s. No one knew why the information from them had never been entered into the INS computers. The best guess was that the clerks in Miami had mailed the actual forms before they had been entered and that the clerks in INS headquarters had not entered them either, assuming that they had already been put in by the clerks in Miami.

Propper and Cornick could celebrate only briefly, because INS records showed that Williams and Romeral had *departed* from Miami for Chile on September 2, 1976—some three weeks before Letelier was assassinated. Cornick called this news the last bump in the road. He and Propper tried to revise theories of the blond Chilean's involvement in the assassination. Had Juan Williams somehow reentered the country to meet Guillermo Novo later, when sources claimed to have sighted them? Alternatively, had Williams and Romeral merely ordered the murder? If so, would they have left so long before it was carried out? If so, were the sources who had seen Williams with Novo all wrong? Was it possible, as Scherrer had suggested, that there were *two* "Juan Williams" agents, that the one in Paraguay might not be the one who entered from Chile? If so, might one of them have entered under another name? Nothing added up.

On December 29, in Santiago, Scherrer took a momentous gamble. With headquarters' approval, he gave General Baeza the Williams and Romeral photographs and demanded both orally and in writing that Baeza locate the two men and produce them for an interview. By this act, Scherrer was telling the Chilean government just about everything that was known about one major lead in the Letelier investigation. The Chileans would know that the Americans had photographs of the two men. The Chileans would find out that the Americans suspected the two men because they had entered the United States on fraudulent official passports under circumstances that were doubly suspicious because of the bizarre incident in Paraguay.

Scherrer could only hope the Chileans would think the Americans knew more. He was opening the game on a bluff, hoping that the Chileans would fear the legendary, omniscient FBI enough to make a mistake. Beyond that, Scherrer hoped Baeza might use his influence subtly in the American's favor, as he had done in the Otero case nearly two years earlier. Scherrer knew that the straitlaced chief of Investigations hated terrorism and disliked DINA's Contreras—both for personal reasons and because he thought Contreras had dishonored the Chilean army. But, in a matter of this gravity, Baeza might feel compelled to take the photographs directly to Contreras and to conspire with his rival to resist and confound the American authorities. If he did, Scherrer knew he would lose.

The general was caught in a difficult position. If he did nothing, he would be blamed for allowing the investigation to grow into an ugly international scandal. If he tried to cooperate with Scherrer, he would no doubt find himself at loggerheads with powerful figures inside his own government. Baeza complained to Scherrer that Patria y Libertad had members scattered in high places throughout the government. They would find out about his investigation of Williams and Romeral, he said, and they would oppose him. Scherrer suggested that Baeza take the matter directly to President Pinochet for authority; the President himself should choose whether Chile would cooperate or suffer the consequences. Baeza promised an answer within two weeks, but the deadline came and went without results.

On January 4, Chilean citizens went to the polls for the first time since the 1973 coup and approved a referendum of legitimacy for President Pinochet.* Voting was mandatory. The referendum affirmed the leadership of Pinochet, but it did not mention the ruling junta at all. Navy and air force leaders denounced the vote as a grab

---

*Andrés Wilson and Ana Pizarro cast several ballots apiece in the referendum, using their various DINA names. They also cast ballots in the names of their minor children and in the name of their dog, Fifi, who voted as Fifi Wilson.

for power by Pinochet. Civilian leaders called it a sham. It was the first political dissent that had surfaced in the Chilean media since the coup, four years earlier. But Pinochet prevailed. A week later, he sent General Contreras to Buenos Aires as his personal representative in the delicate negotiations with Argentina over disputed islands in the Beagle Channel. International arbitration having broken down, there was imminent danger of war between Chile and Argentina. Troops were reported to be on maneuvers. To Scherrer, it was a bad sign that Pinochet would still entrust such a vital mission to Contreras.

In Washington, some FBI officials saw Scherrer's move on Baeza as a convenient preemptive action against Propper, who had wanted to hit the Chilean government with the Williams material himself by means of Letters Rogatory. These officials took great pains not to let Propper know that Scherrer would be taking the fateful step of giving the photographs to Baeza. They kept Cornick in the dark as well. Their motive went much deeper than a desire to keep the Williams lead under FBI control: they wanted to keep Propper out of Chile during the climax of the Gopher operation. They were largely successful, as Propper and Cornick did not learn of Scherrer's daring ploy for several weeks.

Gopher was hot all through December and January. The informant had gone back to Chile and was working his way into his old security apparatus, gaining access to files and to wiretap logs. By early December, Gopher was no longer reporting on the low-level Chileans involved in what he called "the network." He had worked his way up the organization to the active commander, whom he identified as a Colonel Robles. Seddon remembered and Cornick confirmed that Saul Landau had once mentioned a Colonel Robles as one of the many DINA officers identified by Chilean exiles as a leader in missions of liquidation. The agents pulled out the sketchy biographical details Landau had reported about Robles. Gopher's subsequent reports about the colonel fit in every respect.

"Robles" was a pseudonym, of course, but Gopher was moving closer and closer to his true identity. He reported that Robles was a high officer of Patria y Libertad who also served in DINA. He reported the telephone number in Santiago from which Robles conducted his clandestine business. He reported the true names of some of Robles's DINA associates. Startlingly, Gopher reported that one of them might "flip" and flee to the United States, with the proper guarantees of safety. He reported that Robles was a shadowy figure whose loyalties could never be pinpointed. He was part Patria and part DINA. He was either DINA's man in Patria or Patria's man in DINA. No one could be sure.

According to Gopher, Robles also ran a network of operatives who blended into the world of international drug smuggling. Some of the operatives were witting and some unwitting of the network's political purpose. Some were ordinary high rollers and drug financiers, who provided cover and occasional harmless favors, but among their associates were a few fanatically loyal political operatives waiting for orders from Robles. Sometimes the orders were to kill Chilean exiles.

In December, Gopher reported that one of his sources had overheard conversations in which associates of Robles said that the orders to assassinate Letelier had come from Robles through his network's "couriers." Most of the couriers lived outside Chile. Some of them traveled extensively, while others remained more or less in place. In late December, Gopher reported the names and addresses of two Robles couriers in the United States. One lived in New York, the other in Miami. Like Robles, they were people of many layers. They had respectable exterior occupations, behind which they occasionally fronted for drug operations, behind which they worked for Robles. They might go a year without receiving any instructions from Robles, but when the orders came, they asked no questions. Gopher reported that the orders to kill Letelier had come to the New York courier by means of a "dead drop" at Kennedy Airport. He gave the number of a post-office box there. Robles saw to it that instructions were left in the box for his couriers.

Wack, under peremptory orders not to say or do anything provocative, went to Kennedy Airport and prevailed upon postal authorities to disclose the name of the boxholder. It was registered in the name of a Martine Darragon, of Paris, France. Within days, the FBI legat in Paris reported that there was indeed a woman named Martine Darragon in Paris who was very rich and traveled extensively in the United States and Latin America. Inside the investigation, Darragon quickly became known as "the French Connection."

Wack spent most of January trying to locate the New York–based courier, whom Gopher had identified as a Chilean woman named Sánchez,* living on Wadsworth Avenue in the Washington Heights section of New York. Through Cornick, Seddon had sent Wack strict

*Not the correct name.

orders to find the woman without letting her know he was looking. Then Wack was to await further instructions. He was never to mention the name Darragon to anyone.

The Wadsworth Avenue address presented Wack with quite a challenge, as it served three huge apartment buildings that were nearly dilapidated. The occupants were transients, for the most part. No tenant had signed a lease in twenty years or so. The mailboxes in the downstairs foyers had been torn out, as a rule, and the superintendents usually took the rent in cash—when they could get it. Wack started poking around in the neighborhood. He dropped spending money in units of ten and twenty dollars on the local junkies and extracted a few false leads on people named Sánchez. He had coffee with the local postman and also with the relief postman, without success. Finally, he started knocking on doors in the buildings. He told people he was looking for an old relative and asked them if they might know anybody in the buildings who had been around a long time and would know everybody.

This ploy eventually landed him in the apartment of an old lady with white hair. Wack spent an entire afternoon getting to know her, drinking her laxative tea, and finally he decided he had no alternative but to trust her. In confidence, he asked the woman if she knew anybody in the building named Sánchez. The woman said there was a Mrs. Sánchez right across the hall. This news rocked Wack back on the sofa. He asked if Mrs. Sánchez was Chilean, and the old lady replied that she said she was from the Dominican Republic. Wack came back the next day and asked the old lady to recall everything she had ever heard Mrs. Sánchez say and everything she had seen her do. He wrote down the information, most of which was about babysitters. The woman said Mrs. Sánchez stayed home a lot, but occasionally she would go out. No one in the building knew much about Mrs. Sánchez, said the woman.

Wack went back to see her almost every day. He drank a lot of tea and heard a lot about the heating problems in the building, and occasionally he heard a new detail about Mrs. Sánchez. He sent the information to Cornick, who told him the significance of it might not be apparent but that he should stick with Sánchez. It was part of a bigger lead that was very hot.

"Okay, Carter, I'll do my best with this thing," Wack told Cornick on the phone. "But you don't want me to do anything on the Novos and the Chilean I've been working on? All that stuff's down the drain?"

"Well, it's on the back burner," Cornick replied. "This one looks pretty good. I can't tell you everything now over the phone, but stick with it. Something will break soon. We've got to force this thing to a resolution."

Cornick knew the Gopher operation was about to break. As the leads grew hotter and required more corroboration, he was drawn more and more into the agitation around Seddon. After months of obsessive secrecy, Seddon was opening up slightly because of the practical requirements. Even Propper knew by now that the new lead might well supersede all the others and bring him someone to prosecute.

For Nick Stames, the timing had been fortunate. Just as Gopher was implanting himself in Chile back in October, a position had opened up at headquarters for a supervisor in the terrorist unit handling the Letelier case. Stames had helped secure the promotion for Satkowski, and then he had moved Al Seddon up to Satkowski's job as Cornick's supervisor in the Washington field office, under Stames. By these moves, the three men who had originated and developed the Gopher operation were in place to control the flow of paper and information at both headquarters and the field office during the crucial stages, when any breach of security would be fatal.

By now, Al Seddon knew more about Gopher than anyone. He spent a great deal of his time sifting bits of information from the informant, comparing one angle with another. He also spent time "taking his pulse," as he said, trying to gauge the level of danger to the agent. Unquestionably, the risk had been growing rapidly. Gopher felt more restricted, more fearful of entrapment. There were signs of panic in his communications. Gopher kept saying he had to get out of Chile again quickly, before they killed him. Seddon tried to steady him until something broke with the identified couriers or until Gopher could come up with harder evidence against Colonel Robles. But Seddon was taking precautions. He began exploring with American air force connections the possibility of flying Gopher out of Chile on a "black flight," a plane with no markings or registration. He found that it would not be easy to arrange, especially since the CIA had been excluded from the Gopher operation all along. He and Satkowski worked harder as Gopher reported more progress in January on his campaign to persuade one of Robles's aides to defect. The aide would be a witness at the Letelier trial, as Gopher had promised all along. He would fly out of Chile with Gopher. If it was a trap, Gopher would not make it.

For Larry Wack, the chase began when a teletype and then a phone call came up from Washington: Legat Paris reported that Martine Darragon was leaving that very day for the United States. Her destination was Kennedy Airport in New York. The legat had obtained the flight number and nothing else. He had no photograph of Darragon, but he described her as very pretty, blond, in her early thirties. Wack's orders were to follow her, to report back at regular intervals, and to await further orders. He was not to lose her under any circumstances. This was top priority. Cornick and Seddon were leading an emergency task force in the Washington field office. Wack could call them for help, and he could commandeer all the agents in the New York office if he needed them.

By the time the message reached Wack, Darragon's plane was already in the air. Two hours later, Wack showed up at JFK Airport leading a team of thirty FBI agents riding in eight FBI vans and four cars. He carried extra copies of the composite drawing of the man who had threatened his fiancée, now his wife, at that same airport fifteen months earlier. He also carried copies of the Juan Williams photograph, the blond-Chilean composite drawing, and pictures of a dozen Cuban militant exiles, just in case. He had no idea who might meet Darragon, the courier, or where she might lead them, but he would soon find out. He had called his wife in great haste and told her not to wait for him, as he had done many times before. And he had told the perplexed Liz Ryden that he hoped the link turned out to be the blond Chilean, because it "would break my heart" if a year's hard work on the lead had been wasted.

After a quick, military-style briefing, Wack posted agents at all the exits from the Air France terminal and around the bank of post-office boxes in the main terminal. Then he and a small squad of agents went to the incoming immigration area, through which all the passengers on the Air France flight would pass. Wack located the immigration supervisor, flashed his credentials, and explained his problem bluntly. The supervisor agreed to help and called all the inspectors into a quick meeting. Each inspector was given a slip of paper with the name Darragon written on it, and the supervisor explained that when the passenger of that name came through, the inspector was to process her and then quickly and silently walk over to the supervisor and notify him. It was imperative, he stressed, that the inspectors do nothing that might let the woman know she was attracting attention.

When the flight came in, Wack was standing next to the supervisor, outside the immigration booths, as the passengers filed in on the other side. Agents stood around the outside trying to look like ordinary airport security people.

Suddenly Wack and the supervisor noticed something wrong in one of the immigration booths. The inspector, a middle-aged woman, had a stricken look on her face. She looked frantically around, as though seeking help, and then she pointed dramatically toward a blond woman who had just passed through her booth. Then, perhaps realizing her errors, the inspector covered her face with her hands.

"Holy shit," muttered Wack.

"Oh, no," moaned the supervisor. "I'm very sorry, Mr. Wack. Those were not my instructions. She will be disciplined. I'm very sorry."

Wack ignored the apologies. He was whispering into his radio in a near-panic, telling all the agents to fall in behind the blond woman in the fur coat, asking for reports from any agent who had seen signs that Darragon had noticed the overwrought clerk.

Darragon carried only a small piece of luggage. She walked out of the terminal, with agents strewn behind her, and jumped into a sedan that was parked immediately in front of one of the FBI vans. A man waiting for her in the driver's seat pulled quickly away.

The FBI caravan took up the chase and struggled through the New York afternoon traffic. As they drove, Wack relayed a description of Darragon and the license number of the car back to his supervisor in the New York FBI office, who relayed the information to headquarters and on to the task force at WFO. For the first few minutes, Wack thought the target car might be heading for the apartment buildings on Wadsworth Avenue, but then it turned north out of the city.

Two hours later, after dark, the car was still heading north on the New York State Thruway. Wack was in the lead car, about a half mile behind Darragon. The rest of the FBI fleet was about half a mile behind Wack, and many of the agents were grumbling over the radio. Their work shifts were ending. They had no idea where they were going. They were getting farther away from home. And a snowstorm was beginning. Wack asked for and received permission to let half the units turn back. He continued with a dozen agents in support.

An hour later, on a deserted highway in upstate New York, Wack was still peering through the snowflakes to see the taillights on Darragon's car. He lost them as Darragon crested a long hill, and when Wack's car followed over the top and down the other side, the highway abruptly ended. There were signs saying ROAD ENDS, and there was a highway patrol car sitting at the edge of the pavement. Wack grabbed the radio. "Slow down!" he shouted to the units behind him. They were converging rapidly from the rear. "Slow down! We just ran out of highway, and the target vehicle is doubling back on us!"

Agents' voices tumbled over the radio, asking what to do, as Wack watched the Darragon car make a U-turn at the bottom of the hill. It accelerated rapidly past the entire FBI caravan.

"Okay, take it easy, all units!" Wack called out over the radio. "We gotta make a U-turn just like they did. Everybody act like we just missed the last exit off the highway like they did! This could be a trick."

Wack's car was making its turn when the highway patrol car pulled into the way, flashers on. The patrolman ambled out of the cruiser and asked the driver for his license and registration. Wack uttered a string of obscenities and jumped out of the passenger door. "FBI!" he shouted. "We're on a surveillance! Let us through!"

The patrolman's jaw dropped. "Who are you surveilling?" he asked.

"That car up there!" shrieked Wack, pointing to the disappearing sedan. He jumped back into the car. "C'mon, let's go!" he commanded. "Go around the asshole!"

Wack's car roared off, fishtailing on the snow patches and burning rubber on the bare cement. On the radio, he heard agents behind shouting, "FBI! We're with them!" to the patrolman, one after the other.

"I can't believe that birdbrain wanted to know who we're surveilling," muttered Wack. "That's gotta be the only fucking car he's seen in the last three hours. Step on it!"

They went back over the hill and searched the darkness at high speeds for fifteen minutes, with different cars taking different roads. Finally, Wack called it off and directed all the cars and vans back to a rendezvous point. There was a lot of cursing and yelling and complaining about the lack of food, and there were theories on whether the targets had deceived them or made a mistake themselves. Wack reported the failure to his New York supervisor over the radio, and not long afterward the supervisor told him that headquarters was highly displeased. He offered Wack's team a chance to redeem itself. The target car, he said, was registered in the name of a man who lived in upstate New York. A name check was being run on him at headquarters. Perhaps Darragon was headed for the man's house.

"Not if they made our tail," said Wack.

"You got any better ideas?" asked the supervisor.

"No," said Wack. "It's worth a shot, I guess."

The caravan peeled off again, with Wack taking directions to an address that turned out to be a hilltop house in a remote area not far south of the Canadian border. The agents arrived there around midnight and stopped at the foot of the long, steep driveway. The house was barely visible in the distance, through the continuing snowstorm.

The agents got out of their vehicles to stretch their legs and reconnoiter. They searched the road at the foot of the driveway and found no target car. Most agents, including Wack, argued that the car could not possibly have gone up that driveway in the snow. There were no tracks. The general opinion was that the car had gone somewhere else, possibly to Canada, but Wack decided to climb the hill on foot—just to make sure.

One agent stayed in a car to man a radio. Ten others struggled up the steep grade behind Wack. The air was filled with muffled curses as agents, in their suits and street shoes, fell and scrambled, often pulling themselves through the darkness by grasping the branches of trees or bushes. Finally, they all reached the top and gathered in a small huddle to shiver and talk things over. Lights were on in the house, but there were no signs of activity. No car was parked outside. The group of agents sneaked in single file around the house to the garage and lifted Special Agent Danny Scott up to peer through a high window. It was too dark inside for him to see anything, but they all heard the angry barks of what sounded like a very large dog. The barks seemed to echo for miles through the still countryside.

Wack started half the agents back down the hill. The others stayed behind, sharing Wack's determination not to leave without knowing whether they had come all that way for nothing. One agent had brought a flashlight. Someone noticed that the garage door lacked about four inches of being closed all the way to the floor. Quickly the volunteers swept the snow off a patch of driveway next to the door, and the agent with the flashlight lay on his back and craned his neck so that he could see along the beam of the flashlight, under the bottom of the door.

"It's there," he whispered in amazement.

"Are you sure?" asked Wack. "Read me the numbers off the plate."

The prone agent did so; it was the car they had followed from Kennedy Airport. Wack led his group back down the hill and reported the triumph on the radio. Headquarters soon sent its congratulations for the recovery via the New York office, along with the welcome news that a relief team of Albany agents would take over the surveillance at eight o'clock sharp the next morning. By the time of this report, the dog had long since stopped barking, and Wack's group settled back to face the discomforts of the night. They had no food or coffee. No stores or gas stations were open for miles. They could not keep the engines on all night for warmth without running out of gas. So Wack fought the cold and carbon-monoxide poisoning by moving his entire group from one van to another at intervals. This also saved gasoline.

At seven-thirty the next morning, the lookout agent shouted the alarm, and all the others stumbled out of the running van into the cold. "They're leaving," said the lookout. Wack and all the other bleary-eyed agents squinted up toward the house and saw that the garage door was open. Soon the car backed out and started down the driveway. Wack's caravan took off after them. Agents who had made cracks all night about how much they would like to trade places with the man up there in a warm bed were now threatening over the radio to shoot the man for not waiting until eight o'clock. Others threatened to drop out of the chase and get some breakfast. Wack's posse was becoming unruly.

They survived only by dropping off one by one for frantic pit stops while the others kept up the tail on the target car. Each refueled car would catch up by driving at siren speed to make up for the lost time. In this manner, they succeeded in following the target car all the way back to Kennedy Airport in New York, by which time agents were yelling in disgust over the tortuous round-trip circuit. Wack, summoning his last reserves of discipline and control, led a ragged group of agents back into a terminal and watched Martine Darragon board a flight to Detroit.

It was the morning of January 26. In Washington, Cornick, Seddon, and Satkowski had been up half the night monitoring the progress of the New York surveillance. Now they threw themselves into the same task for Detroit. They obtained the necessary high-level clearances and burned the teletype wires to energize another surveillance team. Agents picked up Darragon's trail as she hopped into a car with another man and took off into the downtown Detroit area. By that time, agents from the Albany office were arranging to subpoena the telephone records of the man Darragon had stayed with in New York. Seddon, worrying about Gopher's personal security, worked overtime on emergency exit plans out of Chile. Satkowski tried to arrange for specially trained agents to take a surveillance photograph of Darragon in Detroit. All these schemes imposed on the time and energies of distant agents who knew nothing about the Letelier case, and so they required the maximum backup voltage from headquarters. Satkowski got it instantly from James Ingram, assistant director in charge of the criminal investigative division. Ingram would go to the director if necessary.

The surveillance men in Detroit missed a photo opportunity when Darragon went to a museum, Satkowski learned, and the next relayed report from Detroit put the Washington task force into a frenzy. Darragon had driven across the border into Canada! Agents of the Royal Canadian Mounted Police had agreed to pick up the surveillance there, but they would not assume the burden very long and they could not stop her if she left Canada by plane.

Cornick ran in to see his new supervisor, Al Seddon, who was equally alarmed. "Al, we have got to resolve this damn thing!" Cornick declared. "I don't think we can wait for her to take us to a Cuban or a courier or anybody else! If she's on to us and she's skipped the country, then she'll probably tip off the courier down in Miami. And if *she* skips, we'll be left with nothing." Cornick wanted to interview the courier in Miami. Otherwise, they might soon find themselves with access to none of Gopher's leads inside the country, where they were subject to United States laws and legal processes. Seddon felt squeezed. He saw the logic of Cornick's argument, but he felt a surpassing loyalty to Gopher down in Chile. Seddon feared that the Miami courier would alert the Robles network the minute an FBI agent called on her, and that the cunning Robles would identify Gopher's source in Chile, which would lead straight to Gopher. Seddon was in the grips of the agent handler's traditional paralysis. He disagreed with Cornick, but he did not object when it was decided to interview the Miami courier forthwith.

Cornick flew to Miami on half an hour's notice without so much as a toothbrush. After a long night of conferences and relayed surveillance messages, he summoned his courage the next afternoon and knocked on the door of the Miami courier.

Two hours later, he arrived grim-faced back at the Miami FBI office. It did not look good, he said, but he gave few details until he could report to headquarters that the courier was either innocent or incredibly sophisticated. She had betrayed no signs of nervousness or guilt at Cornick's appearance or his questions about various Cuban exiles implicated by Gopher. She had known some of them, Cornick reported, but she had been forthcoming about her associations. And, worst of all, when Cornick had asked the woman if she knew anyone in Chile, she had casually replied that she did. And one of the people she had named was Gopher himself—by his real name! She had said somewhat distastefully that the man was a habitual liar.

Cornick felt a powerful instinct that something was wrong. Seddon and Satkowski were undecided. The woman had said exactly what a cool, professional agent was supposed to say in that situation. She had defused Cornick's suspicions by sticking close to the facts while maintaining a calm innocence. As for her statement that she knew Gopher, there were a number of interpretations. One was that she was trying to sow doubt inside the FBI about its singular informant just at the moment when FBI agents needed to act decisively. Another was that her statement represented yet another sign of the network's twisted bravado, similar to the defiant act of blowing up Orlando Letelier within sight of the Chilean ambassador's residence.

On the phone, Cornick learned that there was urgent news from Detroit. Martine Darragon had returned from her foray into Windsor, Canada, and was now at the airport, waiting for a flight to Tampa, Florida. Her plane was being delayed by the same snowstorm that had hit upstate New York the day before. Detroit agents were trying to take advantage of the delay to get surveillance photographs.

At FBI headquarters in Washington, speculation was intense as to why Darragon would fly in from Paris, dash to upstate New York, fly to Detroit, dash into Canada, and now fly to Tampa, of all places. The most obvious and chilling explanation of the last destination was that Tampa was the home of Cuban Mafia boss Santos Trafficante, one of three gangster leaders once recruited by the CIA for assassination attempts on the life of Fidel Castro. Some of the Cuban exiles mentioned by Gopher as the action arms of the network's conspiracy against Letelier were associated with Trafficante's far-flung drug operations. It was possible, then, that Darragon was on her way to a rendezvous with one of Trafficante's lieutenants—or even with Trafficante himself. It was also possible that she might proceed from Tampa to Miami for an escape with the Miami courier.

Inside the FBI, those agents with the greatest knowledge of the

Gopher operation were under great stress by now from the uncertainty, the tension, and the lack of sleep. Cornick was among those who argued for making a move as soon as possible. They must arrest Martine Darragon, if necessary, before she fled the country again. He thought this was all the more necessary now that the Bureau had tipped its hand to the courier. Time was working against them.

That night Cornick got permission to fly from Miami to Tampa. The showdown would be there. Before leaving, he called a tired Larry Wack in New York. Wack had been watching the Wadsworth Avenue apartment building for unusual movements by the courier named Sánchez. Cornick told Wack that he could not say much over the phone but that he was about to join the chase after a certain Frenchwoman and he would appreciate anything Wack might remember about her looks or habits that might help Cornick in the event of a confrontation.

"Well, I'd go at her with all the cannons you've got," Wack advised. "She ain't just pretty—she looks like a goddamn blond movie star or something, and she acts like she owns the world. I'd say you'll have to get rough with her or she'll run over you."

"Thanks, Larry," said Cornick. "That might help."

"You gonna brace her?" asked Wack.

"Who the hell knows what's going to happen," said Cornick.

"Well, I hope you nail the bitch," said Wack. "My ass still hasn't thawed out from chasing her up that mountain in the snow."

Cornick arrived at Tampa airport an hour ahead of Darragon's flight and walked into a scene of near-chaos. Agents were milling about all over the concourse, trying to look inconspicuous. A number of them knew Cornick and asked him what the hell was going on that could have summoned their squad supervisor, Bobby Dwyer, from his family dinner table and brought all these agents there for a surveillance. Dwyer had commandeered a phone bank in one of the airport offices and was now a whirlwind of activity. He was calling in French-speaking agents and Spanish-speaking agents on an emergency basis. He was giving orders to the teams running the physical surveillance at the airport. He was on the phone to the Tampa police department, telling officials there not to be alarmed by the FBI siren squad that would squeal its way into the airport with the photograph of Martine Darragon that had been taken surreptitiously in the Detroit airport and then transmitted to the Tampa FBI office. The photograph was top priority. It had to get there before Darragon so that agents might use it for identification. And Dwyer was constantly on the telephone to headquarters. Agents in the airport said the Bureau had Dwyer cranked a mile up in the air.

Cornick tried to calm things as best he could by telling agents that the surveillance had been going on for two days and that it was part of the Letelier investigation. When the siren squad roared up, he got his first look at a woman who turned out to be even more gorgeous than he'd imagined. In the photograph, copies of which were being passed out hurriedly to the Tampa agents, the woman was shown walking through the Detroit airport in a lynx coat. About ten minutes after Cornick saw her picture, this same woman walked into the Tampa airport with the coat over her arm.

Two agents stationed at a car rental desk watched Darragon rent a Thunderbird, and as soon as she was out the door, they pounced on the clerk for the information on the rental form. Darragon had written that she would be staying in a St. Petersburg hotel. The agents took this news to Dwyer's telephone command post, by which time Dwyer and Cornick were alarmed over radio reports from the surveillance cars. Darragon was racing toward St. Petersburg at speeds of more than 80 miles per hour! The agents on her trail were afraid she would lose them. One agent said Darragon had her accelerator foot all the way into the carburetor.

Dwyer, acting on the car rental information, called a squad of St. Petersburg agents and ordered them at top speed to the hotel. "They ought to beat her there by at least fifteen minutes, if that's where she goes," he told Cornick. "I don't care how fast she drives."

It was now one o'clock on the morning of January 28. Cornick, mindful of Darragon's performance two nights earlier in New York, decided that it would be foolish for him to stay up the rest of the night listening to reports about how Darragon had gone to sleep. It would also be impossible, he knew, as he was about to collapse. This was his third night without sleep. Tampa agents half carried him to a room at the airport Holiday Inn, and Cornick fell on the bed in his clothes.

He was asleep when the squad of St. Petersburg agents burst into the hotel lobby and learned from the astonished night clerk that no one named Martine Darragon had a reservation for that night. And the hotel was full. If she planned to stay there, she would find herself in trouble, said the clerk.

The hotel squad was in radio contact with agents on the chase from the Tampa airport, from whom they learned that Darragon was heading straight for the hotel and was only minutes away. The agents on the hotel squad reasoned from the circumstances that Darragon was probably a drug dealer of some kind and would stay at the hotel with someone else—and that the someone else would most likely have an assumed name. It was imperative, the agents told the clerk, that they ascertain exactly where this Darragon woman went in the hotel and with whom she stayed. They ordered the clerk not to do anything to make her suspicious.

When Darragon walked briskly into the lobby a few minutes later, there was an FBI agent hidden in the small washroom behind the desk. He heard a cultivated, sultry voice ask, with a trace of a French accent, "May I have the key to Mr. Turner's room, please?"

"Ted Turner?" gulped the night clerk.

"Yes," said the woman. "I don't know his room number, but he's expecting me."

"I see," said the night clerk, trying to keep his wits. "Madame, it's after one o'clock, and I don't know that I should call up there at this hour. I don't have any notice here about you."

"Will you call him, please," the woman insisted. "It will be all right, I assure you."

Her manner was such that the clerk complied, and he soon gave the woman the room number.

An FBI agent fell in behind her as she walked to the elevator, where a uniformed bell captain took her bag and invited both of them inside. The bell captain started the elevator up to Turner's floor. He was wearing a gun under his uniform coat. The real bell captain was waiting out the event downstairs in the men's room, wearing his undershorts.

By prearrangement, the regular agent exited on the floor below Turner's, and the agent dressed as a bell captain offered to carry her bag to the room. He was nervous all the way down the hall, and his discomfort only increased when he stepped inside behind Darragon and saw a man in bed, holding up what appeared to be a bottle of champagne. "Hi, honey!" called the man. "What took you so long?"

Back at the Holiday Inn, the telephone dragged a groggy Cornick out of sleep. "Wake up, you bastard!" called Dwyer.

Cornick was wide awake before the story ended. "What the hell is she doing with Ted Turner?" he cried.

"Carter, I don't know," Dwyer said wearily. "It's *your* case. I was hoping you'd tell me."

"Oh, my soul," said Cornick. "I don't have the foggiest idea, Bobby."

"Well, I don't, either," said Dwyer. "All I know is that I've rolled the SAC out of bed at two in the morning, and now he's rolled fucking Ingram out of bed up in Washington. And Ingram's upset about Turner. The whole Bureau's lit up over him. And we're on the hot seat."

"Bobby, are you sure it's the same Ted Turner who owns all the TV stations and the baseball team in Atlanta?" asked Cornick.

"Positive," said Dwyer. "Down here he's better known as the guy who just won the America's Cup yacht race. He's down here to race down to Boca Grande and back tomorrow. That's the biggest thing in these parts all year."

"Oh, my aching ass," said Cornick. "What the hell are we gonna do?"

"Well, Ingram says keep the full court press on Darragon and don't lose her," Dwyer replied. "And hope she makes a move soon. I'll pick you up about six-thirty in the morning."

At seven-thirty, Cornick and Dwyer were standing beside Dwyer's car outside the St. Petersburg hotel. Turner and Darragon were inside having breakfast. Turner was wearing his skipper's outfit, and Dwyer was moaning over the possibility that Darragon would go aboard Turner's yacht, *Tenacious*, for the trip. Under the urgent orders from headquarters, that would mean that Dwyer would have to find a way to surveil the boat through 138 miles of open water on the Gulf of Mexico. The logistics were formidable. The coast guard was balking. And Dwyer was wrestling with the problem by radio to his SAC.

"Bobby, we can't let 'em go on that boat," Cornick interrupted. "We have to resolve this thing. It can't go on any longer. I want to interview her right now."

Dwyer tuned out the radio and the agents who were swarming around him with questions. "How would you get her away from Turner?" he asked.

"I wouldn't," Cornick replied.

"You're not going to brace Ted Turner, are you?" Dwyer asked warily. "Carter, he's got a lot of friends, and he's supposed to have a temper like a hand grenade. Suppose he calls the director?"

After agonizing consultations by radio with his SAC, Dwyer relented. When Turner and Darragon left the restaurant, arm in arm, Cornick took a deep breath and said, "Okay, Bobby, it's now or never. Let's go."

Supported by a few agents in the rear, they accosted the couple in the parking lot. "Excuse me, Mr. Turner," said Cornick in his most mellifluous tones. "I'm FBI Special Agent Carter Cornick of the Washington field office. This is Bobby Dwyer, of the Tampa office.

I'd like to talk to your friend here, Ms. Darragon, if you don't mind." Cornick was holding up his FBI badge.

Turner never flinched. He turned to Cornick with a broad grin and said, "Well, shit. Is she in some kind of trouble with the FBI?"

"No, sir," Cornick replied. "All I want to do is talk to her. We think she can help us in a major case."

"When you want to do it?" asked Turner.

"Right now, sir," said Cornick.

"Well, if you gotta talk to her, you gotta talk to her," Turner drawled amiably. "I gotta go race. You need to talk to me?"

"No, sir," said Cornick.

Turner turned to Darragon. "Well, honey, good luck," he said. As she was moving off with Dwyer, Turner winked at Cornick. "When you get through with her, send her back, will you?" He grinned. "She's a pretty good gal." Without another word, Turner strolled off to the day's race, in which he would finish second.

Cornick climbed into the back seat of Dwyer's car with Darragon and Dwyer. "Ms. Darragon," he said, "I'm the case agent for the investigation into the bombing death of Orlando Letelier in Washington September before last. Are you familiar with the incident?"

"I think so," said Darragon, frozen but poised. "I think I read something about it in Paris."

"I think you might be able to help me if you'll just answer some questions," said Cornick. "Is that all right?"

"I'll try," said Darragon.

"Okay, you're a French citizen, is that correct?"

"Yes."

"Now," said Cornick, "do you maintain any post-office boxes in this country in your name?"

"Why, yes," said Darragon. "Three of them, as a matter of fact."

"Three of them?" said Cornick.

"Yes," she replied. "I have one in New York, one in Miami, and one in Los Angeles."

"I see," said Cornick. "Would you happen to have the numbers with you?"

"I think so," she replied, looking more perplexed and more frightened. She found the numbers in her purse and showed them to Cornick. "I use them when I travel in the United States," she explained. "I guess I empty each one of them about twice a year."

"Well, can you tell me why you came to the United States this time?" asked Cornick.

"Yes," she said. "I came to be with Ted."

"I see," said Cornick. "But you didn't come straight to Tampa from Paris, did you?"

"No," she replied. "I went to New York a couple of days ago to see a friend I went to school with. He's a doctor."

"Would you mind telling me his name?" asked Cornick.

"Not at all," she said, and she told Cornick the name.

"And then where did you go?"

"I went to Detroit to see another friend," said Darragon, "and then I came down here last night."

"Okay, Ms. Darragon," said Cornick. "Can you tell me if you know any anti-Castro Cuban exiles in this country?"

"I beg your pardon?" said Darragon. She looked befuddled.

"Do you have any association with anybody in the Cuban exile community down here?"

"No, I don't," said Darragon. "I'm afraid I don't know what you're talking about."

"That's all right," Cornick said gently. "Just bear with me. How about Chileans? Do you know anybody from Chile?"

"Not really," said Darragon. "I've met a few people down there on skiing trips to Portillo, but I don't remember all of them. Most of them I just met in the ski lodge."

Cornick had been sinking inside for some time. "You travel a lot, don't you?" he asked. "Would you mind telling me where you're going from here?"

Darragon smiled for the first time. "I'm going to Festival down in Rio," she said. "I try to go every year. Last year, I missed it because I was out cruising in the South Pacific with Ted."

"I see," said Cornick. "So you've known him for some time?"

"Oh, yes," she replied. "I'm the one who caused all the problems at the America's Cup last year."

"I'm sorry," said Cornick. "I'm not familiar with that."

"Well, I'm the one the New York Yacht Club raised all the hell about."

Cornick cleared his throat. "Martine," he said, "you'll have to explain this. I'm not a sailor."

"Well, the board of governors of the club up there is very conservative," she said, "and they got all upset that Ted was defending the America's Cup while he was running around in public with a French-woman. But he told them all to go to hell. That's how he is."

"That's what I hear," said Cornick, who went on to ask her a few questions about her political beliefs. Dwyer asked a few questions, and Cornick came back with a few trick questions before telling her that it was all a big mistake. He apologized effusively.* By that time, he and Dwyer were suffering from the effects of her perfume and her beauty and her tales of life as an adventurer, world traveler, sailor, heiress, and owner of polo ponies. In the end, she relaxed enough to confess that she had been afraid the agents were going to arrest her for bringing her new lynx coat in from Canada without paying the taxes.

It took a while for the enormity of the boondoggle to begin to register on Cornick. He called Wack from Tampa. "Larry, it's a long story, and it's all bad," he said.

"What happened?" Wack asked eagerly.

"I don't know yet," said Cornick. "And for God's sake, don't tell the Bureau. But start forgetting everything you ever heard about Gopher. It's all turned to shit."

---

*U.S. investigators would conclude that all their suspicions of Martine Darragon regarding the Letelier investigation were completely unfounded.

16 ▣ THE FUSE

Scherrer's devastating report on Gopher was already at FBI head-quarters on the weekend that the chase wound up in Ted Turner's hotel room. From a bureaucratic point of view, the twenty-five-page teletype amounted to the equivalent of a nuclear warhead. Scherrer's unsparing account of his own recent misadventures over Gopher contained the following revelations:

—that "Colonel Robles's" supersecret DINA telephone number was in fact the telephone number of the Chilean Library of Congress in Santiago;

—that the Deputy Chief of Police in Santiago had complained to Scherrer about Gopher, stating that the informant had been going around Santiago claiming to be an FBI agent; also stating that Gopher was invoking Scherrer's name as his good friend and protector, and that Gopher had marched boldly into the Chilean phone company to order numerous wiretaps, sometimes in the name of various arms of the Chilean government and sometimes in the name of the FBI;

—that the deputy chief had confided fraternally to Scherrer that Gopher's behavior was so scandalous as to have attracted the attention of several intelligence organizations, including the CNI, which had Gopher under surveillance;

—that there was an additional reason why Gopher would not be able to flee easily to the United States; namely, that the U.S. consul in Santiago would never give Gopher a visa for U.S. travel because the U.S. Drug Enforcement Administration had placed a "hard stop" against Gopher's name;

—that DEA records in Santiago showed Gopher to be a former DEA informant in Chile, who had been terminated and blacklisted years earlier for double-dealing, flagrant misrepresentations, and "moral turpitude";

—that Scherrer had discovered, while reading through Gopher's three-inch-thick DEA informant file, a striking correlation between the names of Gopher's old narcotics associates in Chile and the names Gopher had been feeding the FBI in the Letelier investigation, which led Scherrer to believe that Gopher had simply strung the Bureau along with worthless clues from his own unsavory past.

This report was bad enough on its face. It demonstrated that Gopher's handlers had committed the cardinal sin of being duped by an informant in a monumental hoax. In Gopher's case, the security-conscious agents had assured the highest officials in the land that they had spent months checking the informant's credentials and his veracity. They had gone so far as to reassure Propper on this score, though they would have preferred to keep the operation entirely secret from him. Now, in excruciating detail from Scherrer, the informant was revealed to be not only a con artist in the extreme but also a discontinued DEA informant. This was especially galling. Drug informants are not known for their sterling character. Even the exemplary ones are generally drawn from the ranks of addicts and thieves, and for Gopher to have been singled out for moral turpitude in this element was a stunning negative achievement.

In Buenos Aires, Scherrer did not know about the Martine Darragon chase or the internecine battles over control of the investigation. Even so, it was doubtful that any Stateside news could have made him express his displeasure any more bluntly than he did in the cable. In his own world, several concurrent disasters had driven him to the brink of protest even before the Gopher fiasco. For Scherrer, January had been a terrible month, after two grueling years.

Since the 1976 coup in Argentina and since the Otero case in Chile, the level of violence in Buenos Aires had been so high that Scherrer's house was guarded continuously by uniformed soldiers. Terror was in the newspapers every day—and now it touched Scherrer and his family regularly. On July 2, 1976, he had arrived for lunch at the intelligence division headquarters of the Federal Police of Argentina only to find the eight-story building in ruins. A huge bomb had gone off minutes earlier, killing 145 people. In November, one of Scherrer's best friends in Argentina had been maimed for life when the nephew of a former police chief, working secretly for the Montoneros, had placed a bomb inside a police station in the La Plata area. Several others had been killed. In April of 1977, Scherrer and his wife, Rosemary, had attended the outdoor wedding of an army lieutenant, which was interrupted by a huge explosion. It turned out that the police bomb squad, which routinely covered such events in Buenos Aires, had become suspicious of a Donald Duck stuffed toy left on the sidewalk and had thrown it into the bomb chamber before it exploded so forcefully as to destroy the bomb truck.

Such events had continued throughout 1977, bringing home to Scherrer the fear of terrorism, as well as its eerie unreality. Even worse, he knew firsthand of the military government's response. Since the coup, the government's own terrorist campaign had become much better organized and much less discriminate. More or less official terrorists commonly executed entire families. Some of the same Argentine contacts who helped Scherrer prepare reports on terrorist attacks against Americans also told him proudly of the special disposal camp near the Paraguayan border. At times, Scherrer saw the bedraggled prisoners destined to be killed there. He talked to officers in charge of their torture and to others in charge of their transport to the camp, where the wasted prisoners were given shots of Brazilian curare. Soldiers took them up in army transport planes, gutted their bodies like fish, and dropped them into the Atlantic Ocean. It was something of an open secret among intelligence people and their friends, like Scherrer. Many distraught Argentines came to Scherrer for help in locating missing relatives, and many times Scherrer had learned from impassive contacts that the relatives had gone out of the plane into the seaward currents.

A number of the victims were Jewish. Anti-Semitism had always been strong in Argentina, but it had become grotesque since the coup against Isabel Perón. One of Scherrer's police contacts first told him of a place called the "hothouse,"* which was an old parking garage with a big skylight. The police used the hothouse as a hangout and as a place for the interrogation of prisoners, particularly Jewish ones. For effect, the police had adorned the walls with swastikas and pictures of Adolf Hitler—not because they were Nazis or even Nazi sympathizers, as they told it, but because the decorations had a powerful effect on Jewish prisoners.

One night not long after the 1976 coup, a police contact told Scherrer over drinks of the previous evening when a police posse had

---

*Not the correct name.

rounded up an old Jewish man suspected of Communist leanings. They had taken him and all his belongings to the hothouse. As the interrogation proceeded, some of the police officers put the old man's *Fiddler on the Roof* album on the record player and began dancing madly, mocking the old man's pain. Half in wonder and half in confession, the officer told Scherrer that the interrogators had brought in a bucket of excrement from the alley and started ducking the old man into it. Finally, a soldier had shot and killed the prisoner as he hung upside down by a rope.

As it happened, Scherrer knew the officer who was supposed to have fired the shot. He mentioned the murder to that officer, making it clear that he thought the story was false.

"That's all true," the officer said simply. "I shot him."

"What?" asked Scherrer. "What did you do that for?"

"Well," said the officer, "they would have killed him, anyway. It was like putting a horse out of his misery when he's got a broken leg."

"You really have a problem," said Scherrer.

"No, *they* have a problem," the officer insisted. "I don't have a problem. I did the Christian thing."

Scherrer reported the incident to Rabbi Morton Rosenthal of the Anti-Defamation League in New York City. Rosenthal specialized in the location of missing and abused Jewish citizens within South American countries, and Scherrer was invaluable to him in the task of locating Jewish citizens who had disappeared in Argentina. Late in 1977, a prominent Chilean banker and his wife had flown from Santiago into Buenos Aires and promptly disappeared. Rosenthal knew the couple and many of their friends, and so he had journeyed to Buenos Aires once again to seek Scherrer's assistance. After digging around, Scherrer brought back word that the Argentine Foreign Ministry had confirmed to him that the Chilean couple had been picked up by Argentine officers. But, the Foreign Ministry said, the couple had been released and had promptly gone to Uruguay and checked into a certain hotel, after which they had not been seen again. Scherrer reported this to Rosenthal as bad news, having heard this story many times before in the cases of Uruguayan terrorists. He did not think the Chilean couple had ever left Argentina. Rosenthal kept pressing for further word. The couple's family had already paid more than $30,000 in bribes to various mysterious Argentines, all of whom had failed on promises to deliver the couple alive.

Later in 1978, Scherrer would receive another terse, cryptic phone call from a contact from whom he would hear that the couple "*no existe más"* ("exists no more"), and he would pass this news on to Rosenthal so that the family would be relieved of the dreadful uncertainty and spared the expense of further bribes.

Shortly before Christmas, Scherrer had learned that the government of Venezuela was making plans to release its most famous prisoner, Orlando Bosch, after holding him without trial for more than a year. Scherrer confirmed FBI information that the Venezuelans had been making overtures to both Paraguay and Chile, hoping that one of these countries would accept Bosch as a refugee and thereby take Venezuela off the hook. For Scherrer, the choice of Paraguay was all too familiar. Twice before, he had worked with Ambassador George Landau to keep Paraguay from harboring famous international fugitives—Robert Vesco and Meyer Lansky—and both times he had been successful. When the internationally famous gangster/financier Lansky's flight had landed in Paraguay, Landau had watched with satisfaction as Paraguayan officials tore Lansky's Paraguayan visa to shreds and ordered him to reboard the plane.

Throughout January, Scherrer battled to thwart Venezuela's plans, sending warning telegrams to Landau in Chile and Ambassador Robert White in Paraguay. Both ambassadors brought the matter to the attention of their host governments. White reminded the Paraguayan foreign minister and the Paraguayan military intelligence chief that Paraguay's world image had suffered greatly for giving refuge to criminals, and more pointedly, he reminded them of their recent experience with a group of Croatian terrorists who had no sooner been granted safe haven in Paraguay than they assassinated the Uruguayan ambassador in a bungled attempt to kill the ambassador from Yugoslavia. This, White told the Paraguayans, was the reward of giving protection to terrorists. Landau delivered a similar message in Santiago with considerable effect.

Scherrer considered the mission a success until Ambassador Viron Vaky intervened from Caracas. Vaky, learning of Scherrer's moves, protested to the secretary of state and to the director of the FBI on the ground that the Bosch matter was an extremely sensitive one for the government of Venezuela and that, accordingly, all communications from the United States government pertaining to Bosch should be cleared with Vaky. In response to this, FBI headquarters relayed to Scherrer Vaky's prickly demand to know how and on what authority the two Latin governments had been warned not to accept Bosch.

Scherrer regarded this cable as the most egregious example of what he considered "clientitis" on Vaky's part. To Scherrer, the ambassador's behavior stopped just short of outright assistance to Venezuela in that country's effort to shirk its duty in regard to the most notorious bombing in the hemisphere, and he saw it as the same kind of protectiveness that had kept Bosch isolated from American authorities throughout the Letelier case.

Vaky's cable reached Buenos Aires in January, when Scherrer was preparing his report on Gopher and working on the case of the banking couple who had disappeared in Argentina. The events combined to drive Scherrer past the point of patience.

Scherrer stiffened the language of his Gopher teletype and sent a blistering cable to Washington on the Bosch matter. In the cable, he did not even ask headquarters for an opinion, let alone for approval. He simply asked headquarters to transmit to the secretary of state and to Vaky the message that Scherrer alone had been responsible for the warning messages to Chile and Paraguay; that Bosch was an international terrorist; that official United States policy was to oppose terrorism; that to implement this policy the United States government was supposed to keep indicted terrorists in the countries where they could be prosecuted for their crimes and out of countries of refuge, insofar as possible; and that, finally, Scherrer and the FBI would fulfill their duty in criminal terrorist matters such as the Orlando Bosch case without regard to the opinions of officials in the State Department. With this cable, Scherrer challenged Ambassador Vaky to a bureaucratic "pissing contest." He thought it was long overdue.

On January 30, two days after Cornick interviewed Martine Darragon in St. Petersburg, Scherrer received a teletype informing him that the State Department had notified Propper of its willingness to assist the prosecutor in transmitting Letters Rogatory to Chile. This news horrified Scherrer. He could think of only two possible explanations. First, Propper might be serious, trusting that the Chilean courts would be free to develop information about Juan Williams and Alejandro Romeral, in which case Propper would reveal himself to be hopelessly naïve about the freedom of Chilean courts under the military dictatorship. Alternatively, Propper might be sending Letters Rogatory as a mere gesture of suspicion toward Chile.

Either way, Scherrer thought Propper was about to ruin his campaign to obtain information on Juan Williams from General Baeza. He had never met the prosecutor. All he knew came from Bureau cables intimating that Propper was a prodigious leaker. From Scherrer's perspective down in the terrorist war zone, Propper looked like an incompetent who was ignorant of realities in South America, and as such, Scherrer thought he fitted in all too well with the FBI agents working the case. The legat was thinking of Gopher. Also, Larry Wack had recently asked Scherrer to obtain color photographs of Juan Williams showing front, left, and right views of his face. This request baffled Scherrer, who could not believe that Wack actually expected him to send readily available photographs of a man whose very identity had been the sole object of Scherrer's investigation for months. Furthermore, Wack had recently renewed his argument with Scherrer about whether Cubans were really all that different from Chileans. Scherrer felt as if he were dealing with extraterrestrial beings masquerading as officers of the government. He had doubts about Cornick. He knew from both experience and the teletypes that the entire Miami office had accomplished nothing. And, for good measure, he was still angry that incompetence or willful concealment in the State Department had delayed for a year the transmission of critical information in the Juan Williams puzzle.

The cable about the Letters Rogatory provoked Scherrer to take an unusual step. He placed a call on an open international telephone line to his boss, the supervisor of all FBI legal attachés, at FBI headquarters in Washington. "I'm sorry to call you like this, but I have to talk to somebody," he said. "You know that big bombing case we're working down here?"

"Yeah," the supervisor replied. "What is it?"

"Well, I keep getting jerked around down here because everybody up there is absolutely crazy," said Scherrer. "We have to do something about it. Where are we going with this friggin' case? People are doing things that make absolutely no sense."

"So what's new?" asked the supervisor. "Anything I can do?"

"I think we've all got to get together face to face, before this whole case goes down the tubes," said Scherrer. "We should have done it a long time ago. We've got to straighten things out before it's too late, and there are certain things I have to say that I can't put in writing."

"Oh oh," said the supervisor. "Like what?"

"Well, this isn't the place to discuss it," said Scherrer. "But basically, I want to tell Wack to straighten up and I have to tell Propper to quit screwing around down here in Chile when he doesn't know what he's doing. And I want to tell Miami that it's a disaster. And I want to tell our man in Caracas to put his pants on and start acting like a legat. Stuff like that. There are a whole lot of things that have to be said, and we can't do it like this. We don't know each other."

To Scherrer's surprise, FBI headquarters acted quickly and positively. The Bureau would underwrite a summit conference of all agents working the Letelier investigation, at which they could settle their differences. The conference was scheduled for March 6, in Miami.

Scherrer hoped that would not be too late. He flew from Buenos Aires to Santiago on a triple mission. He would renew his campaign to pry information out of General Baeza. He would ask Ambassador Landau to back him up in his controversy with Vaky. And he would "punch Gopher's ticket," meaning that he would openly disown the miscreant informant to police and intelligence officials throughout the Chilean government in order to minimize the chances that the operation would later blow up. He also decided to confess the bungled operation to Landau, lest the ambassador be caught unaware by Chilean officials.

In Santiago, the legat accomplished all his goals except for the first one. He called on one of General Baeza's deputies and learned that the general had extended his traditional January vacation through the entire month of February and would not return from the south of Chile until March. Scherrer could not believe it. He wondered whether Baeza was hiding from him. If so, he wondered what exactly Baeza knew about Williams and Romeral that so paralyzed him.

Scherrer knew Baeza's deputy fairly well. He asked the man to level with him, and then he posed a question: did the deputy think the implications of Scherrer's message and letter of December 29 had really gotten through to Baeza? The deputy replied that Baeza indeed understood the implications of what he was doing and had issued stern orders that his people should investigate in his absence. As a result, the deputy said he could report that Williams and Romeral were not real people. The addresses on their Chilean passports were nonexistent.

Scherrer listened to all this and bit his lip. "Julio, I don't think I'm making myself clear," he said evenly. "I already knew all that. In fact, I told General Baeza that everything on those passports is phony, and I told him that I thought those guys are army officers. What we're after is their real identities. We want to interview them."

The deputy shrugged. "They are not so easy to find," he said.

Scherrer told him to warn Baeza that time was running out.

The teletype reporting this discouraging interview reached FBI headquarters on February 7. Cornick showed it to Propper that same day, and the prosecutor jumped to his feet in a rage. "That's it, Carter!" he cried. "I'm not waiting for Scherrer another day! If that son-of-a-bitch down there is taking an extra month's vacation, screw it! We don't have an extra month! I'm filing this sucker as soon as I can."

"I know how you feel, Gene," said Cornick. "Believe me. But I've got my own problems over there . . ."

". . . Carter, we've been waiting over a month," Propper interrupted, pacing the office. "We can't wait another month. We just can't. Bob's not getting anywhere down there, that's all. It's not his fault, but he's not having any success."

"I know it, Gene, but he hasn't given up either," said Cornick. "Scherrer says the Chileans are going to tell you Williams and Romeral are poets, like they did with Bosch, and if we get their backs up, they'll tell us to stick it up our ass again. That's all. He wants to play it out his way."

"Carter, we've been over all this before," said Propper. "This time it'll be different. It won't be like Bosch or the Venezuela stuff. We'll go public for leverage."

"I agree with you," said Cornick. "But once we do that, we can't ever go back. We can only do it once. That's it. And you know as well as I do how little we have on these guys. So we'd be a hell of a lot better off if Scherrer can identify them and find out if we've got something that adds up or not."

Propper was shaking his head. "I know it would be better, Carter," he said, "but I don't think it will happen. So I'll take my shot."

Cornick let out a resigned sigh. "All right, let me ask you this," he said. "How long after you start cranking things up will the Chileans get these things? How much time do we have?"

"I don't know," Propper replied. "It took a month to get them down to Venezuela, as I recall, but I'll try to go faster this time."

"Fine, Gene," said Cornick. "I understand that. So how about if I tell Scherrer that we have tentatively decided to go ahead with the Letters Rogatory and he's only got until a certain deadline down there before it's too late to stop them. How about that?"

"Okay," said Propper. "That's all right with me. But make the deadline soon. I don't want to go too far down the road with the State Department people and then tell them we're not going ahead. Make it a week."

"Oh, boy," sighed Cornick. "The Bureau ain't gonna like this. Getting a deadline from a Commie-pinko prosecutor."

"Well, they can't hate it as much as I hate waiting, Carter," said Propper.

As soon as Cornick left, Propper called Frank Willis at the State Department to say that he wanted to go ahead with the Letters Rogatory to Chile, as planned. "But I want to come over there tomorrow and show you something," he added. "This time I want to do something a little different. I want to make them public."

"Make them public?" Willis said, with faint disapproval. "Well, I don't think you need a lawyer to do that, Gene. You need somebody else."

"I don't plan to leak it, Frank," said Propper. "Here's what I want to do. I want to divide the Letters Rogatory into two parts. Instead of one document, I want two documents. The second document has the actual questions for the court to pose to Williams and Romeral. I want to attach the photographs to that part and seal it in the regular procedure. Okay? And I want to take all the preamble and the greeting to the court and the reasons for the request and put them into a separate part that goes first. Like a cover letter. And I want to send both parts down to Chile, but I want to leave the cover-letter part unsealed when I file the whole document here in the courthouse. And then I'll advise the press that it's there."

"I never heard of anybody doing that before," said Willis. "It's kind of an official leak, isn't it?"

"It's not a leak if it's in the court record," Propper argued.

Willis laughed. "Well, I guess not," he said. "But I don't see what good it'll do you if you don't leak the questions."

"I don't *want* to release the questions, anyway," said Propper. "Because if enough people saw them, someone would realize how little we know and how much of a bluff this is. What I want to get out is the part of the cover letter that says why we want the questions answered. I've spent the better part of a month drafting it, and it pretty much says these two guys were in the middle of the Letelier assassination. I'll show you. I'm rather proud of it. And I guarantee you it will get a lot of publicity that will put pressure on the Chileans to answer the questions."

"I agree with that," said Willis. "Look, I never heard of a separate cover letter in any Letters Rogatory, so there's no legal precedent that I know of. But I don't see why you can't do it as long as you don't put any libelous statements of fact in that cover letter."

"I haven't," said Propper. "It's all by implication. You'll see."

Propper called Bob Keuch at the Justice Department and told him rather breezily of the unusual cover letter. Keuch asked if the idea was all right with the State Department, and Propper replied that he had checked it out with State. Keuch approved. The conversation lasted less than two minutes. Propper knew that Willis would be more surprised than anyone to learn that his casual comments constituted official approval by the State Department of Propper's latest scheme.

Late in the afternoon, Propper pulled finished drafts of the Chilean Letters out of his file cabinet, where they had been sitting for weeks. He and Cornick were proud of the questions, which they had formulated on a few facts and many speculative leaps. Propper had spent days on the language. Each question presumed an affirmative answer to the previous one. As a whole, the questions strongly implied that DINA, in general, and Juan Williams, in particular, were involved in the Letelier assassination.

Propper took them upstairs to the chambers of William B. Bryant, chief judge of the District Court for the District of Columbia. "I've got something for you to sign, Judge," he said, and he explained what the documents were.

Bryant nodded along. He was sitting behind his desk in chambers, still wearing his trial robe. After glancing over the document, he signed it in the appropriate place.

"Tell me, Gene, what do you think your chances are on this?"

"I don't know, Judge," said Propper. "Not really good, I'd say. This is a very tough case."

"I guess so," said Judge Bryant. "Well, I wish you luck. This case really needs to be solved. And always remember one thing: God makes the people who do this sort of thing make mistakes. All you've got to do is find them."

The next morning, Propper, Bob Steven, and Frank McNeil, Deputy Assistant Secretary of State for Latin America, devised a strategy for making the last shot as dramatic and productive as possible: at the same moment that Ambassador Landau handed the official Letters Rogatory to the Chilean foreign minister in Santiago, someone in the State Department would call in the Chilean ambassador in Washington and give him a "complimentary" copy of the Letters, along with a stern, dignified speech about how important it was for the United States government to receive a satisfactory response.

The only question was who would be the most effective State Department official for the role of speechmaker. In the status-conscious world of diplomacy, the rank of the official delivering a message mattered nearly as much as the content of the message itself. McNeil suggested that they shoot for the top and ask Deputy Secretary of State Warren Christopher. In some respects, Christopher would be better than Secretary of State Cyrus Vance, because the Chileans knew that Christopher effectively ran the day-to-day operations of the department, while Vance devoted his time to a few select issues, such as United States policy toward the Middle East. It was Christopher who had been most responsible for the Carter administration's decisions to vote against Chile in the United Nations and to cut off military aid to the Pinochet government. His name would transmit enormous voltage to Santiago.

Christopher sent them an uncommonly quick reply. He loved the proposal and went so far as to suggest little touches that might make his presentation more forceful. A court reporter should be present when the Chilean ambassador arrived, so that the State Department could furnish the Chileans with an exact record showing just how strongly the United States government felt about the Letters Rogatory.

In Santiago, the news of Christopher's planned cooperation dismayed Scherrer and Ambassador Landau almost as much as it excited Propper. Landau took it as a signal that the political forces in Washington were moving prematurely to accuse Chile of involvement in the Letelier assassination without sufficient evidence. This would cause Landau no end of diplomatic trouble. Scherrer thought he was about to lose control of the investigation in Chile—that it would move prematurely into the courts and the Foreign Ministry. In a last attempt to forestall this development, Landau ordered Scherrer to postpone his return to Buenos Aires and to visit Baeza's office daily. He was to bombard the deputy director under Baeza with increasingly dire warnings of what would happen if Investigations failed to identify Williams and Romeral. Meanwhile, both Landau and Scherrer would petition Washington by cable for delay on the Letters Rogatory.

Scherrer willingly complied. Through FBI headquarters, he wrung from Propper a promise to take no action on the Letters Rogatory until after February 15. In reality, this bought Scherrer only a few days and was not much of a concession from Propper, since the paperwork within the State Department would not be completed before then, anyway. But at least Scherrer had a firm deadline. He impressed it upon Baeza's deputy director every afternoon, with no good result. As time grew short, Ambassador Landau became so impatient that he ordered Scherrer to fly to Baeza's vacation spot in Puerto Montt and demand a satisfactory answer. Scherrer demurred on the ground that Baeza was making a clear and informed choice to duck the issue.

On the evening of February 15, Scherrer drafted a resigned cable to headquarters, admitting failure. His deadline having passed, he said, Propper and the State Department should proceed with their plans. Nevertheless, Scherrer could not resist noting for the record that he had "serious reservations with regard to the use of Letters Rogatory. . . ." He wrote that Propper's move would result inevitably in the dissemination of the investigative leads throughout the Chilean government, thus weakening the American hand without gaining any offsetting leverage through the Chilean courts. Under the military dictatorship, he added, the Chilean courts did not possess the power to act independently or with integrity on sensitive matters. "To think otherwise is to ignore the reality of Chile today," wrote Scherrer. "Letters Rogatory on Williams and Romeral have about the same chance of success as this projected tactic had in getting the Venezuelan government to have Orlando Bosch interviewed." Which was to say, no chance at all.

Propper ignored these barbs when they reached Washington the next day, for by that time he and his State Department contacts were in a frenzy. Christopher had informed them that he had an open time slot for the "ceremony" the very next day, February 17. Steven advised that they seize the opportunity even though it might mean a full night's work to prepare. There was much to do. Secretary of State Vance had not yet signed the Letters Rogatory, as required by international law. Steven undertook to handle that. When he succeeded, Frank Willis accepted the challenging assignment of making sure that the Letters reached Santiago by the following morning, so that Landau could deliver them to the foreign minister. Meanwhile, Steven was drafting cables for Landau on what he should say to the foreign minister and exactly when he should ask for the appointment, and Propper was drafting memos for Steven to use in briefing Christopher.

By evening, most of the memos had been written and the appointments made, but Willis was facing grim prospects. No diplomatic pouches would make it to Santiago overnight, and no special diplomatic couriers were available. Only one or two airline flights would be leaving the United States for Chile that night. Willis had already learned that no United States diplomats or military personnel would be on them. In desperation, he called a friend of his at the Air Transport Association and found out that his friend had a friend, a LAN Chile employee, who was about to leave for Santiago on one of the flights. Willis trusted his friend and the friend trusted the LAN Chile employee, so Willis left word of his intentions for Bob Steven and set out in a mad rush for Dulles Airport, carrying the Letters Rogatory.

When he arrived, he met the befuddled LAN Chile employee, who had been corralled by friends of the ATA executive. There was a great deal of excitement at the airport. People knew something important was going on, but no one except Willis knew what it was. He called Steven, who was having him paged at the airport. Steven didn't like the plan. He wanted to fly to Chile and back himself. By way of objection, he told Willis that he could never inform Landau that an international communication of this nature would be arriving in the hands of a foreigner who worked for the Chilean national airline. Steven wanted to know what he could tell Landau in his cable. Willis suggested that Steven write vaguely that the Letters Rogatory would arrive at the embassy and leave it at that. In the end, Steven relented and Willis handed the LAN Chile man a package ribboned and sealed in a manner befitting its diplomatic status.

Neither Willis nor Steven managed much sleep that night, but the next day's twin ceremonies went smoothly, as though they had been rehearsed for weeks. Landau, in his best formal manner and with full ambassadorial dignity, handed the Letters Rogatory to Foreign Minister Patricio Carvajal, and of course he gave no sign that he had fought within his own government to prevent the delivery. Almost simultaneously with this event, Ambassador Cauas walked into Warren Christopher's office in Washington to be greeted formally but cordially by Christopher and assorted aides. The court reporter in a corner set an unmistakable tone of austerity for the brief meeting, during which Christopher dryly recited the reasons for the Letters Rogatory, their purpose, and their importance to the United States. When it was all over, Steven reported to Propper that Christopher had performed magnificently. In his opinion, Christopher's normal monotone and expressionless face had been perfect for the occasion. Propper, who had not been allowed to attend, pressed eagerly for details. Steven recalled the hidden signs and slight mannerisms that led him to conclude that Cauas had been impressed with the weight of it.

Propper fidgeted all weekend. As gratifying to him as were the successful deliveries of the Letters Rogatory, the events thus far had been private ones held within the confidence of governments, and Propper therefore considered them mere preliminaries to the main event: the publicity. He was taking his investigation overseas reluctantly, but of necessity, and the press was the only weapon he could think of that might help him avoid the kind of impotence he had suffered as a foreigner in Venezuela. At the urging of Steven, Propper waited through Monday and most of Tuesday in order to give the Chilean Foreign Ministry time to transmit the Letters to the Chilean Supreme Court. When he could wait no longer, he took his copy of the Letters downstairs to the clerk's office and filed them. He made sure the clerk understood that only Judge Bryant's "cover letter" to the Chilean Supreme Court was public. Then he went back upstairs and called courthouse reporters to advise them that they might find something very interesting in the clerk's office.

The next day's headlines forever changed the character of the investigation. Both Washington newspapers, the *Post* and the *Star*, ran front-page articles on the "extraordinary public disclosure" with its "first public acknowledgment that the investigation had focused on members of the Chilean government." The story appeared on all three networks and spread into news outlets throughout Latin America and Europe, where press interest in the Letelier case had always been high. Michael Moffitt and Isabel Letelier were quoted widely in dispatches, welcoming at long last this official confirmation that the Chilean government was a prime suspect in the murders of their spouses. They urged the United States forward toward the seizure of positive proof. Reporters, naturally enough, played up the sense of impending confrontation between Chile and the United States that leaped out of the cover letter Propper had written in a manner brazenly calculated to generate news. Most stories quoted liberally from one particular portion of the letter:

3. It has become known to the Attorney General of the United States and the United States Attorney for the District of Columbia that two members of the Chilean military entered the United States one month before the Letelier and Moffitt murders. At least one of these men met with one of the persons believed to be responsible for these murders. Both of these men had previously obtained visas to enter the United States using fraudulent documentation from a country other than Chile. These visas were revoked by the United States on August 9, 1976,

after the fraudulent nature of the documents was discovered. They subsequently obtained official A-2 visas from the United States Embassy in Santiago, Chile, on August 17, 1976, by presenting Official Chilean passports. The A-2 visas obtained were TDY visas, which are multiple entry visas valid for a period of six months.

The information on the two men is as follows:

Juan Williams Rose
Address: Bustamonte 24, Santiago, Chile
Date of Birth: March 12, 1949 (the fraudulent passport lists the date of birth as October 18, 1942)
Official Chilean Passport Number: 528–76
United States Official Visa Number: 20530

Alejandro Romeral Jara
Address: Monjitas 613, Santiago, Chile
Date of Birth: May 25, 1950
Official Chilean Passport Number: 527–76
United States Official Visa Number: 20529

Photographs of these two men are attached to copies of the fraudulently obtained passports, which themselves are attached to the appended list of questions.

4. It is believed that these men have knowledge and information concerning these murders. It is therefore requested that you cause each of these men to appear in court and to answer under oath the written questions which are attached to this request. . . .

Cornick kidded Propper for managing to use derivatives of the word "fraudulent" four times within a single paragraph, and Propper, with a grin, replied that he had wanted to make sure no one would miss the challenge to the honor of the Chilean government.

Reporters from Rome, Paris, London, Mexico City, Madrid, and practically every major American city were calling all day and into the night, exposing Propper and Cornick for the first time to the press in a hunting mood. Even Chilean reporters were calling, which was something of a story in itself. Chilean newspapers had consistently parroted the government position that the Letelier investigation was a Marxist conspiracy insofar as it pointed any blame toward Chile. But now, for the first time, Chilean reporters became so caught up in the hard news and the mystery that they ignored restraints and joined the manhunt for Williams and Romeral.

Although he had been covering the Letelier investigation for nearly a year, Jeremiah O'Leary wrote none of *The Washington*

Star's early stories on the release of the Letters Rogatory. He was too busy trying to find out what lay behind them. With one look at the cover letter, O'Leary knew that there were major scoops to be gotten and that he was especially well qualified to be first. Having covered Latin America intermittently for thirty-five years, during which he had acquired a Mexican wife and a long string of official sources, he was determined to find out the name of the "country other than Chile" that had provided fraudulent passports to Williams and Romeral. The name would open up a whole new story angle on the third country involved in the conspiracy to assassinate Letelier. Also, for reasons growing out of his own best scoops in the past, O'Leary was determined to obtain the photographs of the two Chilean agents.

By the time the first stories appeared on February 22, O'Leary had already spent a day hammering away at his sources within the FBI and the State Department, without success. He called Detective Stanley Wilson and asked him to rendezvous for a very important drink at the Howard Johnson's motel across the street from the Watergate. O'Leary promised Wilson some news on the Letelier case.

Wilson kept the appointment. The excitement in O'Leary's voice and the secretive circumstances appealed to him. Also, for the first time in seven or eight months, Wilson knew that he would have something to contribute. O'Leary had mentioned on the phone that Propper was about to go after some Chilean named Juan Williams.

In the past, Wilson had provided O'Leary with a fountainlike stream of titillating secret connections and intelligence speculations, which seldom added up to a story. One of the stories Wilson was peddling—about the John Marks lead and how the police dogs had smelled explosives in the back of his car but were hushed up because of Marks's status as a famous CIA critic and a friend of Orlando Letelier—had enticed O'Leary to the brink of journalistic disaster the previous summer. Since then, the detective seemed to have run dry, and O'Leary's skepticism was renewed. He expected little of Wilson until the detective leaned across the table at Howard Johnson's and said that he had a copy of the Juan Williams photograph.

O'Leary showed no emotion. "I don't believe you, Stan," he said, in his gravelly voice. "Where did you get it?"

"I can't tell you that, Jerry," Wilson replied. "From a source. That's all I'm gonna say. But it's him, all right. I've got the photograph with me."

"You do?" said O'Leary. "Are you sure it's the same guy?"

"I know it's Juan Williams," Wilson said with calm assurance. "And I know it's the guy Propper's after. He confirmed it."

"All right," said O'Leary. "Let me see it."

Wilson at first balked at the idea, but after a long series of coy demands and an equally long litany of assurances from O'Leary that it would remain utterly confidential, the detective withdrew a photograph from his coat pocket and slid it across the table to O'Leary, keeping an eye out for suspicious bystanders.

"That's the same blond Chilean I mentioned earlier to you," Wilson whispered, as O'Leary studied the face.

"He doesn't look blond to me," said O'Leary.

"Me either," said Wilson. "But they say he's blonder than he looks here. Don't ask me how they know that. They've got sources, that's all."

"He looks like a Chilean to me," said O'Leary. "I've known a lot of guys who look like this down there. He won't be easy to identify."

"Well, he's one of the ones who went to Paraguay."

"Paraguay?" said O'Leary, trying to be nonchalant.

"Yeah," said Wilson. "They tried to come up through Paraguay for purposes of concealment, but things got screwed up and they had to come up another way. That's about all I know."

O'Leary gave Wilson a pregnant look. "Stanley, I know a lot of guys in the Paraguayan embassy and a lot of guys down in Asunción," he said. "I could go to them and identify this guy if you'll just let me have the picture for a few days."

"Not a chance," said Wilson. "You can't have the picture, Jerry. They'd have my ass so fast, believe me. They know I've got it. Propper does. I probably shouldn't even have shown it to you."

O'Leary winced painfully, and the decent side of him suppressed an urge to run out the door with the photograph. "Come on, Stanley," he said. "Look, this picture's getting around all over the place by now. Besides, how are they gonna go after these guys if they don't know who they are? You don't think these are real names, do you? They don't even know who they're looking for yet, and the pictures are the best way to identify them."

"Maybe so," said Wilson. "But I'm not giving you that picture. I've helped you enough. Now you know what it looks like."

O'Leary argued and pleaded for the better part of an hour, but Wilson refused to give in. O'Leary returned the photograph and departed. Within hours, he was huddling surreptitiously with sources inside the Paraguayan embassy.

Scherrer saw the headlines in Buenos Aires on February 23 and was stunned. He considered the publicity ruinous and ascribed it to stupidity or incompetence in faraway Washington. In fact, he thought it was probably another leak by Propper. It did not occur to him that Propper and Cornick had deliberately refrained from putting their publicity strategy in writing, for fear that officials in the FBI or State Department would veto the entire scheme, including Propper's invention of the separate cover letter. Propper, skating on the thinnest margin of authority, had told the fewest possible number of people and had minimized the effects of the plan even to them. As a result, the storm of publicity surprised Scherrer nearly as much as it surprised most Argentine readers.

He had little time to fume, however, because a call came that night from the American embassy in Santiago informing him that two officers of the Chilean air force intelligence service (DIFA) had made contact with the embassy and had urgently requested to see Scherrer about the Williams and Romeral matter. Scherrer flew to Santiago and reported to Ambassador Landau, who was as composed and articulate as ever, but clearly in the grip of sudden events in the Letelier investigation. Already, within twenty-four hours of the news leaks on the Letters Rogatory, the Chilean press was responding to the scandal and the air force was maneuvering against the government. Landau could feel the regime teetering slightly.

That afternoon, the two DIFA officers met Scherrer at the embassy and informed him that their service was attempting to identify Williams and Romeral so that accurate information could be turned over to the court conducting the Letters Rogatory procedures. Scherrer was uncertain as to their motives, but after some discussion he decided to show them the two photographs and also a copy of the letter in which the Chilean Foreign Ministry had vouched for Williams and Romeral to the U.S. consulate in August 1976. One of the DIFA officers instantly recognized Romeral as an army officer he had seen from time to time in various military offices. He did not know his name, having never been introduced to him. Scherrer studied the DIFA officer as he related this and decided he was probably telling the truth. Neither DIFA officer recognized Williams. They promised to try to identify both mystery agents, and they took the name of the Foreign Ministry official who had signed the letter requesting their United States visas. This man, Guillermo Osorio, might know who within the Chilean government had sponsored the agents.

Scherrer met almost daily with the two DIFA officers, in various places, but they made no more progress on the identification of Williams and Romeral than did the hordes of Chilean and foreign reporters who were scouring Santiago on the same assignment. The

officers did report one significant finding, however: Osorio had died
a few months earlier in a reported suicide, shot through the head.
The circumstances of his death were most suspicious. Osorio, a mild-
mannered career Foreign Service officer of sufficient rank to have
accompanied Pinochet on his 1977 trip to Washington, had been in
the company of Manuel Contreras and several Chilean generals only
hours before his demise. His body had been buried quickly, without
an autopsy. This raised the chilling possibility that someone had eliminated the one man whose name was connected in writing to those of
Williams and Romeral. Scherrer wondered whether Williams and Romeral would also wind up conveniently dead.

O'Leary kept pounding away at his sources, who were highly
placed in the government and close to the story he was after. His old
friend Harry Shlaudeman, for example, had been Assistant Secretary of State for Latin America during the fraudulent passport episode involving Williams and Romeral. From Shlaudeman and many
others, O'Leary pried enough information for a good story identifying Paraguay as the "country other than Chile," but he knew this
would be just a one-day scoop. The photographs, on the other hand,
would go around the world.

Two, three, four times a day, O'Leary called Stanley Wilson with
new arguments and new blandishments. He said he could understand
why Wilson would object to publication of the Williams photograph
alone, since the detective was known to possess it and not that of Romeral, and O'Leary promised over and over that he would not publish Williams unless he could use it to obtain Romeral and thereby
provide Wilson a measure of protection. To Wilson, this assurance
was good, but not good enough. He added further conditions.
O'Leary, happy to reach the stage of negotiation, promised much.
Finally, Wilson met him on a street corner and handed him the envelope. As promised, O'Leary swore that he would not print the photograph without Wilson's permission.

On the evening of February 27, O'Leary attended a diplomatic reception given by the State Department, at which the most visible and
newsworthy official was Ambassador George Landau—just up from
Santiago to attend a Chiefs of Mission session. Landau was surrounded by reporters and curious colleagues most of the evening,
but O'Leary waited long enough to steal a moment alone with him.
He knew Landau vaguely. O'Leary shook hands with the ambassador and promptly pulled out the photograph of Juan Williams. "Mr.
Ambassador, I'd like to know if you can confirm this photograph as

one of the ones you intercepted in Paraguay that's now coming up in the Letelier case," he said.

Landau stared at the photograph. Its likeness of a man called Juan Williams had gone on quite an odyssey since being snapped in the tiny Palau Brothers photo shop in downtown Asunción nineteen months earlier—from there to the Paraguayan Foreign Ministry, where it was affixed to a fraudulent passport; then on to the U.S. embassy in Asunción, where it passed beneath the technician's camera and went on to CIA headquarters in Virginia and from there to the State Department and eventually to the FBI; down to Miami and into the hands of Detective Danny Benítez, who gave it to Stanley Wilson; then back and forth across a dining-room table at the Howard Johnson's; and finally to O'Leary, who was now showing it to Landau, who for his own special reasons had caused the surviving copy to be made in the first place.

The ambassador looked back at O'Leary and gave no sign of recognition or alarm. In fact, he did not react to the photograph or to O'Leary's question at all, as though neither existed. Landau was quite good at this. In like manner, he could switch abruptly from cordial conversation to a determined, official monotone and declare that he could neither confirm nor deny whether there were any CIA officers employed in his embassy.

Landau's manner stifled all O'Leary's instincts to pose follow-up questions, and after a brief uncomfortable silence, Landau opened conversation cordially on another subject.

Earl Silbert had been talking to Don Campbell about Propper off and on for weeks, since Campbell's Christmas deadline had passed and Propper remained mesmerized by the Letelier case. During their few recent contacts, Propper had assured him that everything would be all right with the Letters Rogatory because he, Propper, was being allowed to draft many of the State Department cables going down to Chile and to talk directly with Ambassador Landau from the State Department. Moreover, since the explosion of publicity over the Letters Rogatory, Propper had informed Silbert that officials from all over the government, including the National Security Council, were suddenly demanding to be clued in on cables regarding the investigation, but that the State Department, citing Propper's authority, had actually decreased the distribution list for traffic rather than increasing it. The National Security Council's Latin America expert was being excluded on the word of a lowly assistant United States attorney, who thought the NSC man was a leaker.

"This guy's going around talking like he's running the entire State Department," Silbert complained. He told Campbell that Propper might be getting carried away by his zeal. This was heady stuff. If the investigation turned sour again, Silbert feared Propper's determination might drive him to make a mistake that would be magnified greatly by his new authority. If the investigation moved toward solving the case, on the other hand, Propper would need help. Either way, Silbert reasoned, it would be wise to assign a second prosecutor to the case—for ballast, assistance, and a second judgment.

He and Campbell called in Larry Barcella. Silbert started talking about the general down in Chile who had been "hiding" from the FBI and about the evasive answers the Chilean spokesmen were making on the Letelier case. He said he "smelled something" for the first time during the investigation, and he reminded Barcella of his policy since Watergate always to have at least two prosecutors on any major prosecution. Then he asked Barcella which of the Major Crimes prosecutors he thought could most smoothly join Propper. Somewhat taken aback by the gravity of the matter, Barcella began describing how Propper got along with the other prosecutors under Campbell's supervision—relations generally ranged from the contentious to the combustible.

Silbert interrupted him. "Yeah, you're right," he said. "None of those guys will do. So it's you and Gene."

"Wait a second, Earl," said Barcella. "I don't want to get in on this. It's Gene's case and he'll legitimately resent anybody who gets in on it now."

"No," said Silbert. "He'll resent anybody but you. You're his friend."

"I *know* I'm his friend, Earl," protested Barcella. "That's why I don't want him to resent me. It's his case. I've helped him a little, but it's his."

"I understand all that," said Silbert. "You're in, Larry. That's it."

Silbert and Campbell soon called Propper in and gave him the same speech. They asked him which prosecutor he would prefer to work with. Propper gulped and said that the only one he could think of was Barcella.

By afternoon, tensions were subsiding and the new arrangement was settling in. Barcella began reading Propper's CHILBOM files.

Scherrer walked with slight trepidation into the familiar office where he had met Colonel Contreras nearly two years earlier. Now

Contreras had been succeeded by General Odlanier Mena, a huge hulk of a man who had returned from an ambassadorial post in Panama to take charge of DINA, now called CNI. His deputy, Colonel Pantoja, had returned from a consular post in Argentina. They were the grim-faced new regime who greeted Scherrer on the morning of March 1, having summoned him urgently the previous night.

General Mena shook hands and introduced himself, but otherwise lost no time on amenities and went straight into a tirade. He told Scherrer that he was shocked and angered by the conduct of the United States government. Public disclosure of the Letters Rogatory had been a particularly irresponsible act, inasmuch as the United States lacked the basic investigative data necessary to frame intelligent questions. For that reason, said Mena, he believed that the Americans had issued the Letters for political purposes, and Chile would react accordingly.

Scherrer defended himself against this blast by stating that the Letters had been employed as a last resort, only after General Baeza had failed to provide any reasonable answers. He outlined his many contacts with Baeza. He also declared that the investigation was not political. The assassination itself might have been political, but the United States was determined only to solve the case and demonstrate that such murders would not be tolerated on the streets of Washington.

Calming slightly, General Mena admitted that Baeza must have failed to convey Scherrer's requests to the proper levels of the Chilean government. Scherrer responded that he had personally urged Baeza to convey his requests for information directly to President Pinochet, if necessary, because Scherrer felt the matter warranted the highest consideration of the Chilean government.

Mena nodded, seeing that Scherrer was giving no ground. "That may well be as you say, Mr. Scherrer," he said, "but I must ask you another question. You seem to be an intelligent man, and in your business you must know that certain elements in the air force have been trying to destabilize our government. Tell me, then: if you are not political in your objectives, why have you been meeting with officers of air force intelligence on this matter?"

"I can explain that, General," said Scherrer. "I was approached by officers who stated that they had information that might help answer some of the questions in the Letters Rogatory, and under my instructions I felt I could not refuse to listen."

"Well, we should get something straight, then," said Mena. "If you are going to handle this matter, you must handle it through CNI. We will answer your questions. President Pinochet has assigned to CNI exclusive jurisdiction in this case."

"Fine, General," said Scherrer. "I will initiate no contacts with DIFA or anyone else, but I must continue to listen to anyone who has specific information on the Letelier case."

Mena took a deep breath, seeming mollified, and changed the subject. He said that he had seen news stories implicating Cuban exiles in the Letelier killing, and he asked Scherrer what the basis was for believing that Cuban exile terrorists had been in touch with Chileans. This question stunned Scherrer more than any of the accusations. He replied that the subject of Cuban exile contacts in Chile had been almost the sole matter of conversation between himself and General Contreras since the beginning of the investigation. To this, Mena responded with a mixture of chagrin and annoyance that there was no mention of this in the DINA files he had inherited from Contreras. There seemed to be a great deal missing from the files, in fact. Contreras, Pantoja slyly observed, had built many bonfires before departing.

Later, left alone with Scherrer, Colonel Pantoja smiled fraternally. "You know, Bob," he said, "it makes me very uncomfortable to talk to you like this using *usted*. Why don't we use *tú*?" According to Spanish custom, Pantoja was inviting Scherrer to use the familiar as opposed to the polite form of the word "you."

"Very well, Colonel," said Scherrer. "Thank you."

"Good," said Pantoja. "Now, let me speak to you hypothetically. If—and I emphasize *if*—Williams or Romeral was involved in the Letelier assassination, I'm afraid it would be very difficult for us to deliver him to you. He would face at least twenty years in prison, wouldn't he? And the Chilean government would have certain obligations to defend him, don't you think?"

"Well, Colonel, I think that if one of those men was involved, it would be very difficult for Chile *not* to turn him over to the United States," Scherrer replied.

While Scherrer was dueling with Pantoja and Mena, O'Leary was achieving a final success in Washington. His personal relations with the "old South America hands" among FBI executives, such as Homer Boynton, went back more than three decades, and his access to leaks from the very top levels of the Bureau dated to a freak event in the 1960s. O'Leary had been interviewing J. Edgar Hoover when Hoover made the mistake of stepping out of the room, leaving

O'Leary within sight of a report on his desk showing that Director Hoover's weight was in excess of the strict standards required by the FBI. O'Leary had threatened to publish this fact. Clyde Tolson, Hoover's number-two man and alter ego, had pleaded with him not to, arguing that disciplinary morale would collapse downward through the entire FBI. O'Leary had agreed to hold back, and thereafter he had become a regular recipient of tips from inside the FBI. He joked that he had eaten off Hoover's fatness report for years.

Now O'Leary was after something deadly serious. He went to Adams, Boynton, Stames, and a dozen other men he knew. He told them all that newspaper publicity was the best and quickest way to identify Williams and Romeral. He said it was imperative to identify them immediately, before they disappeared. And when things got difficult, he said that he was going to publish the Williams photograph anyway.

O'Leary caused a great deal of soul-searching within the upper ranks of the FBI. There was some degree of validity to his arguments. On the other hand, there was also some risk to the lives of the suspects, and the Bureau hated newspaper leaks—most of the time. There was a lot of wondering how O'Leary had gotten hold of the Williams photo. Propper was strongly suspected as the leaker. If the leak proved instrumental in solving the case, Propper would no doubt take credit—which would be an unbearable insult, coming only one month after the humiliation of the Gopher operation. There were many reasons to give O'Leary the Romeral photograph. The truly damaging information had already been leaked. Besides, FBI officials knew that Cornick and Propper had debated and narrowly rejected the idea of releasing the photographs officially.

Finally, a phone call went out to O'Leary directing him to stand alone on the front steps of the National Archives Building at nine o'clock sharp the next morning. When the hour came, O'Leary saw an FBI car pull up to the curb. Bob Satkowski jumped out and walked briskly up the steps. He shook hands with O'Leary, handed him the photograph of Romeral, and walked wordlessly back to his car.

Spurning most food and sleep, O'Leary worked over his story in the tireless daze of a reporter who knows he owns the big one. When the story was nearly complete, he began the final rite—calling government officials to offer them the chance to give reaction quotes. O'Leary saved Propper for last. He knew the prosecutor would not laugh this time.

Propper jumped up out of his chair and began screaming through the telephone at O'Leary, threatening to hold the reporter responsible if the publication led to the deaths of Williams and Romeral. He said it would be unconscionable to run the story and demanded that O'Leary withhold publication. When O'Leary countered that the people likely to harm Williams and Romeral were inside the Chilean government and therefore already privy to the photographs through the Letters Rogatory, Propper hotly replied that O'Leary was in no position to say how widely the photos were distributed within the Chilean government or to judge the risks. Propper also shouted that he and the FBI were on the verge of identifying the men privately and would lose an immeasurable advantage if O'Leary and the *Star* threw the faces before the entire world.

"Well, I don't think it'll hurt, Gene," said O'Leary. "Besides, the decision to publish is out of my hands."

"Whaddaya mean it's out of your hands?" Propper demanded.

"My editor's got the story," said O'Leary. "You'll have to call her if you want to try to talk us out of the story."

"Who is she? What's her number?"

O'Leary gave Propper the information and then ran through the *Star* newsroom and up the stairs to the office of his editor, Barbara Cohen. He could tell from her stricken face that she was already on the phone with Propper. O'Leary began to gesticulate wildly in front of her face, making signs of support. He mouthed the words "No! Don't give in!" to her, as she fought Propper off with noncommittal answers.

The next afternoon, Friday, March 3, Propper walked into Barcella's office and dropped a copy of *The Washington Star* on his desk. Barcella gaped at the headline spread across the entire front page: U.S. THREATENING TO SEVER CHILEAN RELATIONS. Three pictures lay side by side beneath the headline: Letelier's mangled car appeared in the middle, rammed into the dented Volkswagen on Sheridan Circle; Juan Williams appeared on the left and Alejandro Romeral on the right. Then came a secondary headline: *Santiago Pressured to Cooperate in Probe of Letelier Murder Here*. Then came O'Leary's story, across six columns.

"Now they can blame you for leaks, too," said Propper. "You been talking to O'Leary?"

"Huh?" said Barcella. "Gene, I don't even know enough to leak this yet. That's ridiculous."

"Yeah, that's what they all say," teased Propper, who was wearing a sick, miserable grin.

While Propper commiserated with Barcella, the Juan Williams photograph was moving on the international wires, having been syndicated by the *Star*. Over the weekend, it would land on millions of doorsteps in the United States, Great Britain, France, Italy, West Germany, Argentina, Mexico, and Chile, among other countries, as part of the photograph's continuing journey. Sight of it would no doubt ruin breakfast for a tiny fraction of those readers.

On Sunday night the conferees trickled into Miami from points all over the hemisphere for the Letelier investigation summit meeting Scherrer had requested. They convened the next morning at the Miami FBI office on Biscayne Boulevard. As they milled around outside the main conference room, agents swapped war stories and introduced themselves to the Justice Department people, Propper and Keuch. The spectacular leak to *The Washington Star* brought a fine edge of anticipation to the group, as blame or glory seemed much nearer. Accusations about the leak were traded freely and not entirely in jest. In a corner, Scherrer was talking with the highest-ranking FBI official there, Deputy Assistant Director James O. Ingram. His obvious friendship with Ingram was noted by other agents as a surprise advantage for Scherrer in the upcoming battles.

Propper marveled at the Bureau's penchant for organization. Secretaries were coming in right on time with coffee and doughnuts. Each of the twenty participants found his name and title inscribed on the front of a folder that marked his assigned place around the enormous oval conference table. A water glass and several sharp pencils lay beside each folder, which contained blank legal pads, copies of the summary investigative reports prepared for the conference by the various FBI offices, and an official roster of the participants. Propper was studying it to make sure he knew all the agents when he happened to glance at Newark's Frank O'Brien, who was seated on his right. O'Brien was doing the same thing, but his printed roster seemed different. By closer scrutiny, Propper was astonished to discover that the two were identical except that Propper's name appeared second on his own roster and dead last on O'Brien's. He reprimanded himself for once again underestimating the Bureau's devotion to the minutiae of status. On realizing that the dual roster idea had probably required the time and mental effort of a $50,000-a-year FBI supervisor and numerous subordinates, Propper started laughing out loud and was obliged to stifle himself when the Miami SAC called the conference to order.

After the opening ceremonies, Satkowski took the floor and delivered a chronological recitation of the major events and leads pertaining to the case. Working from a stack of note cards, he wrote the most important dates on a large blackboard. Satkowski took about forty-five minutes to outline the major avenues of investigation, except for Gopher, a subject that was reserved for discussion at an FBI-only meeting the next day—without Propper and Keuch. Then he asked the spokesmen for the offices represented there to report on their own pieces of the investigation.

Frank O'Brien had just begun to speak for Newark when a secretary tapped Propper's shoulder and informed him that there was an emergency phone call. He tiptoed out of the conference to a room where phones sat on gray metal desks. Barcella came on the line when he pushed the blinking light.

"Have you heard about Juan Williams?" asked Barcella.

"What about him?" said Propper.

"Then you haven't. You're too calm," said Barcella. "Are you sitting down?"

"Yeah, I'm sitting on a desk," said Propper. "What is it?"

"They identified Juan Williams down in Chile, Gene," Barcella announced. "The blond Chilean turns out to be an American named Michael Vernon Townley!"

"What?" cried Propper. "How do they know?"

"He's an American," Barcella repeated. "It was in *El Mercurio* yesterday down in Santiago, and it's already in the *Post* up here this morning. They all say Juan Williams is this guy Townley. People are going crazy in Chile. I just got off the phone with Bob Steven for the third time this morning, and he says people are calling the embassy anonymously about Townley. A lot of people seem to know the guy. He's a fuckin' American! Can you believe that?"

"Not yet," said Propper. "What does Steven say? Does he believe it?"

"Yeah, he believes it," said Barcella. "The embassy's gotten too many calls agreeing with one another. Steven just got a teletype from down there. He's sending it over now. *El Mercurio*'s got a whole bunch of sources, apparently. And get this: there's a picture of a guy who looks just like Juan Williams in a Commie newspaper from three years ago. That was Townley. He was wanted for killing some guy when a right-wing group raided one of Allende's TV stations, or something. That paper said Townley worked for the Agency. It said Townley was an American spook, Gene."

"Oh, shit," said Propper. "Larry, call Tony Lapham."

"Who's Tony Lapham?" asked Barcella.

"He's the general counsel over at the Agency," said Propper. "Call Tony and tell him to start running a check on Townley."

"Yeah, right," snickered Barcella. "I'm supposed to call this guy I don't know from Adam and say, 'Hey, I'm Larry. Would you mind telling me if some guy named Townley who killed people down in Chile and probably killed Letelier was working for you folks over at the Agency?' Are you kidding me, Gene?"

"No, I'm not kidding," said Propper. "I think he'll tell you. They'll have to cough it up sooner or later, if it's true. Tell him I'll call him later today, but he can get going now. He's probably already started."

"I'll bet he has," Barcella said suspiciously. "Okay, I'll do it. But what the fuck do I tell all these reporters? This place is a madhouse. You picked a fine time to go down to sunny Miami and leave me alone. I can't even spell Letelier yet."

"Don't tell them anything," said Propper.

"Gene, they know more than *we* do about Townley," said Barcella. "The press has been on this for two days already! We're behind. They're down there combing the streets of Santiago now."

"Well, then ask them what they've heard," Propper suggested. When he returned to the meeting and whispered the story to Cornick, the two of them made such a commotion that they interrupted the drone of the conference. Propper and Cornick stumbled over each other's words to make a general announcement. Scherrer jumped out of his chair and ran over to them. With this, the conference broke down and a hum of excited conversation spread. Questions flew. Scherrer wanted to know whether the Chilean government had located Townley yet. Cornick wanted to know if Scherrer thought it was possible that an American was working for the Chilean intelligence service. Scherrer wanted to know whether State had confirmed the identification of Townley. "If he's an American who traveled to Chile, we've got to have passport records in Washington," said Scherrer. "Including a photograph. We've got to get on that."

Scherrer asked Propper if Ambassador Landau knew about the break. Landau, at Scherrer's invitation, had stopped by Miami on his way back to Santiago. The ambassador was hoping to attend the second day of the conference, but there was still some question about whether he would be admitted. Bureau officials who had been un-

easy about allowing outsiders like Propper and Keuch expressed
even greater reservation about an official of the State Department.

"Yeah, he knows," Propper told Scherrer. "Larry said Steven told
him he'd already called Landau. The ambassador found out before
we did. We're the last ones to know."

Cornick furiously scribbled notes to himself on what leads should
go out immediately. Agents were adding suggestions from all sides.
Propper and Scherrer were going back and forth about how much
stronger their position would be if Juan Williams were indeed an
American. It would be just like Otero, said Scherrer. With ample precedent, they could demand his expulsion—if he was still alive. Propper jumped on this dire possibility and asked Scherrer what the
chances were. "I don't know," Scherrer replied. "But I'll guarantee
you one thing: if this were Argentina instead of Chile, they'd already
have arranged an accident by now. Chile's different. There's hope."

Cornick rushed out to dictate his teletypes, and Satkowski finally
managed to bring the conference back to semiorder. A buzz lingered
in the room as the reports resumed. Cornick returned in time for the
presentation of the Miami office. An agent outlined his contacts with
Tomboy, the celebrated Cuban informant, whose Brigade lead was
still the favored one in the Miami office and at FBI headquarters
generally. (It was also the favored lead at the Institute for Policy
Studies, where Saul Landau and his associates continued to refine
their evidence and their theories.) Propper's mind was elsewhere,
having long ago decided that Tomboy was a fraud. Cornick was nodding along until the briefing agent described the January 1977
grand-jury appearance in Washington by the four Brigade members—the one after which the Bureau surveillance teams had lost the
Cubans in a downtown Brentano's. After that appearance, the Miami
agent recalled, Tomboy reported hearing that one of the four Cubans
flew from Washington to New York for a meeting with members of
the Cuban Nationalist Movement, including Alvin Ross.

Cornick's jaw dropped, and he interrupted the presentation shortly
thereafter. "Excuse me," he said. "Could you back up a little bit to
the part about the meeting with Alvin Ross? When did Tomboy report that?"

"I don't remember exactly," the agent replied. "But it was very
shortly after it happened. Some time in late January of last year."

Cornick was nodding as though dumbstruck. "Well, that's the first
I ever heard about it," he said. "It was never reported to Washington
field."

The briefing agent did not know what to say. Miami agents came verbally to his rescue, but they could not prevent the outbreak of a squabble. Most people in the room did not know what was going on. They kept asking why the disclosure was so significant, but they got little satisfaction because the briefing agents were swallowing their words and Cornick was too busy rolling his eyes at Wack and Propper. Only the lunch announcement interrupted the debate. On the way out of the room, Cornick was whispering about how the Palm Tree Peekers had done it again, suppressing for more than a year crucial information indicating a link between the Brigade and the CNM. A Miami agent, on the other hand, was growling to Scherrer about how stupid it had been for the briefing agent to disclose stuff like that.

During the afternoon session, Frank O'Brien stepped outside to take one of the emergency calls that seemed to be piling up at the switchboard. He learned from colleagues in Newark that they had just completed a search of Alvin Ross's abandoned place of business in Union City. The agents had hit paydirt, recovering what amounted to a bombmaker's lab kit. Ross had left behind a box of items that included blasting caps, detonating cord, and a bottle of potassium permanganate. The agents also found a long list of various arms and explosives, along with copies of letters written by Guillermo Novo to three different Chilean officials, including President Pinochet himself.* Newark agents told O'Brien that they were frantically trying to translate the letters.

O'Brien's news distracted the conference once again from its stated business. Larry Wack returned shortly thereafter from his own emergency phone call to announce that Ricardo Canete was claiming to have new information on the whereabouts and intentions of Alvin Ross. Clearly Ross was hot this day.

Propper soon came in again with a report that briefly eclipsed the others: there was a Stateside confirmation on Townley as the blond Chilean. Barcella had relayed word from Bob Steven that a marine sergeant had called the State Department to volunteer the information that he remembered the face of Juan Williams. He knew him as an American named Mike Townley, who used to hang around the American embassy in Santiago during the Allende regime, when the sergeant had been in Chile on embassy guard duty. The marine re-

---

*One of the letters was a copy of the letter delivered to the FBI by Admiral McIntyre in November 1976.

membered Townley as an auto mechanic who always had grease under his fingernails. Somewhat incongruously, the marine recalled,
Townley frequented a bar called the Red Lion, which was a kind of
poets' club. The marine also recalled that Townley was the son of a
wealthy American businessman, but he was not sure. The picture of
Townley remained blurry—a young American auto mechanic who
liked poets' clubs and was from a wealthy family. Propper and the
FBI men found it difficult to imagine such a man as an international
terrorist.

Then Cornick came back from the telephone and called for quiet.
"All right, I've got something," he declared. "That was Mahoney.
He's over in Barcella's office minding the store. He says it's like being buried in a foxhole under severe crossfire. Anyway, Mahoney
says a guy called the Bureau up there this morning and said he
might have information that would help the Letelier investigation.
And Mahoney talked to the guy, who had all the right connections
for security-type work. Believe me. The upshot of it is that this guy
told Mahoney he knows the guy in the newspaper identified as Juan
Williams or Mike Townley. But he didn't know him by either name.
He knew him as Kenneth Enyart. That's E-N-Y-A-R-T. This guy used
to work for an outfit in Fort Lauderdale called Audio Intelligence
Devices. He says it's kind of sleazy. Sells bugging equipment and so
forth. Anyway, he says he saw Kenneth Enyart at AID at least a
dozen times up through 1976. And here's the kicker. He says Enyart
was there to buy security equipment for the government of Chile.
Says Enyart is an electronics wizard."

A few of the Miami agents said that they knew about AID, which
was famous for selling sophisticated equipment to a strange clientele
made up of police forces, foreign governments, and various shady
elements masquerading under guises of legitimacy. AID was real.
Propper vowed to subpoena every piece of paper there, if necessary,
to find a purchase by Williams or Enyart or Townley. Now there
were three names being checked. Phone calls piled in on top of leads
going out, and the conference disintegrated. Grievances were forgotten.

That night, Propper sneaked Cornick up the back stairs of the Airport Lakes Holiday Inn and into the room of Ambassador Landau,
who had been on the phone quite a bit himself that day. Cornick
apologized for the stealth. There was no other way, he said, because
Bureau rules prohibited official meetings between agents of his rank

and a lofty ambassador. Propper dismissed it all as nonsense. He and Cornick swapped their version of the day's events for Landau's, and they agreed that some sort of fight was nearing over the right to question Townley. Propper said he would prefer to have Townley on United States soil, in front of an American grand jury. Landau replied that he would do everything in his power to make the Chileans produce Townley. He felt a personal stake in the effort to make the government of Chile account for the man it had sent to Paraguay.

The next day, at the FBI "housekeeping meeting," Scherrer argued that the tumultuous events of the previous day made it even more imperative that the FBI come clean with Ambassador Landau about the Gopher operation. Scherrer described Gopher as a land mine beneath the investigation. He asked his colleagues to imagine what would happen if the Chilean foreign minister told Landau that the American government had no credibility because it had been running illegal agents in Chile. Scherrer answered his own rhetorical question. Landau would deny it vehemently, falling into a trap that would ruin his own diplomatic effectiveness. Scherrer described this as an unacceptable risk, no matter how embarrassing Gopher was to the Bureau. "You don't screw around with George Landau," said Scherrer. "Not in his country. Chile's his country, and we can't do a thing there without him."

In the end, Scherrer prevailed. Ingram led a delegation to Landau's room at the Holiday Inn. Agents crowded inside, sitting on the bed and chairs. Propper waited in his own room. Landau, having been fully coached on the subtleties of diplomacy within the FBI, played his part perfectly. He pretended that he had never met Cornick before. And, as Satkowski delivered a terse and rather pained summary of the Gopher operation, blaming its failure on the informant, Landau reacted as though he had not heard it from Scherrer already. He said he welcomed the gesture of trust from the Bureau. When Ingram invited him to take part in the further deliberations back at the FBI office, Landau thanked him graciously but declined. "I must hurry back to my embassy tonight." Landau smiled. "You people have put it into an uproar."

That afternoon's conference turned out to be even less orderly than expected. Wack's partner called from New York with a report from Canete, who said that he had been in contact with friends of Alvin Ross and that Ross was going underground. So was another CNM member named Virgilio Paz, who until this report had been just one more of the CNM members Propper had called before the grand jury. Paz suddenly became hot. Meanwhile, news came down that Mahoney had obtained more details about Kenneth Enyart and AID. Enyart was reportedly on close terms with AID's owner.

That afternoon, an international phone call was patched from Santiago through the United States embassy up to the Miami FBI office. Scherrer picked up the phone and found himself speaking directly to Colonel Pantoja, who said he was flying that night from Santiago to Washington on an urgent mission and needed badly to speak to Scherrer about the Letelier case. Could Scherrer fly to Washington? He said the meeting he proposed was a matter of state and also a personal request from him and General Mena. Scherrer said he would be there. He told the conferees that things must be coming apart in Santiago.

The next morning, Wednesday, Bob Steven called Barcella with word that a Latin employee of the Organization of American States in Washington had called State with a tip that Romeral was actually a Chilean army captain named Armando Fernández Larios, who had a sister living in New York. He also reported a curious development. A woman in Santiago named Mariana Callejas was quoted that morning in a Santiago newspaper in an admission that she was Michael Townley's wife. This was strange, said Steven, because this same woman had appeared in Sunday's newspaper saying that she barely knew Townley and had not seen him since 1973. She had also described Townley as looking nothing like Juan Williams. Now she was changing her description and admitting the marriage. Her current statement said that she and Townley were "hapless pawns in a Marxist plot against the government of Chile." Steven ascribed the first statement to panic.

In Miami, the name Michael Townley appeared in the newspapers and provoked many volunteer calls to the FBI. People seemed to know Townley in Miami. The reports were sketchy, occasionally strange. Townley was a CIA agent. He was an AAMCO transmission mechanic—and a very good one. He was a friend of Cubans. He had not been around for many years. He was a nice guy. He was married to a Chilean. His father was a former international vice president of the Ford Motor Company, now working at Miami's largest bank. That struck a nerve. An agent confirmed that there was a man named Townley at the bank. Cornick said to hold off on an interview. Similarly, he said to hold off on interviewing the president of AID in Fort Lauderdale. He wanted to finish the name checks first.

By afternoon, the consulate in Santiago and the passport and visa office in Washington were reporting on their records. A passport had been issued to Michael Townley. He was thirty-six years old, from Waterloo, Iowa. His father, Vernon, was a businessman, now living in Boca Raton, Florida, near Fort Lauderdale. Michael Townley was registered at the Santiago consulate as an American living in Chile. Someone had apparently ripped the photograph off his registration card there.* The passport office was still searching for the photograph Townley had submitted with his application. Records also showed that Kenneth Enyart was an American from Dallas, Texas.

All the reports needed checking out, as the Townley and Enyart names might or might not refer to real people. Cornick sweated over the decisions on which leads to send out first. Now he could not afford to make a mistake. Wack was itching to get back to New York to check on Canete and to search for Alvin Ross and Fernández's sister. By this time, most of the Bureau executives from Miami and headquarters had long since departed. The strategy and fence-mending session had given way to the aftershocks of O'Leary's story the previous Friday.

Ambassador Landau was back in his office in Santiago. He called Steven late in the afternoon to report that President Pinochet was sending two high-level negotiators to Washington that night. The negotiators wanted to see Warren Christopher the next day. They also wanted to see Propper. Landau thought they probably wanted to work out a deal on the Letters Rogatory.

Steven sent an alarm through the State Department. This was very short notice. He wondered what to do with the Chileans. What should be said? When should the meeting be scheduled? How should they be treated? Before Steven could notify Propper or Barcella, another call came up from the embassy. It was another Juan Williams identification—this time from a Chilean businessman who said he was certain he had negotiated computer deals with Juan Williams. But this man did not know him as Williams, or as Townley, or as Enyart. He knew him as Andrés Wilson. State Department officials in the embassy reported that the source was quite reputable and sure of himself. They tended to credit his report, which, if true, would add a fourth name to the list.

---

*Townley himself had removed the photograph surreptitiously on one of his visits to the American embassy in Santiago. Thus, Scherrer had not seen the Townley photograph when he reviewed the registration files in April 1977. See above, pages 221–22.

Cornick groaned over this newest layer of identity and initiated yet another name check through the Bureau and the State Department and the CIA. He had very little time to do it. Propper was pacing, anxious to leave for the meeting in Washington. Having lost track of time for the better part of three days, Propper suddenly decided he was not where the work was. He pushed Cornick to gather up his piles of notes to himself, and very soon the two of them and Al Seddon were scrambling into the Miami Airport. The opening round against the Chileans would take place in Washington.

17 ▣ SHOWDOWN

Scherrer stepped off the plane from Miami into a Washington snow-storm. He was wearing his flyweight "legat suit," designed for the sweltering summers in South America, so he was still shivering when the WFO duty agent who had met the flight skidded across the ice and crashed into a parked car just outside the airport terminal. Several hours later, after enduring the accident report and a long drive to borrow an ill-fitting overcoat, he arrived at the Park Shera-ton Hotel on Connecticut Avenue and went up to Colonel Pantoja's room.

The CNI officer was quite upset about the O'Leary story and the sensational worldwide publicity it had created. He pointed to the newspapers that were spread out on his bed. "What about this, Bob?" he asked. "I thought we were professionals, working on a case, and the next thing I see is about the State Department prepar-ing to break relations with Chile. The State Department? Is this true? Is this whole investigation just a pretext for a political attack on Chile? Another one?"

"No, it's not, Colonel," Scherrer said grimly. "It's like I told you down in Santiago. The only reason the State Department got in on this thing is to transmit the Letters Rogatory, and the only reason for them is that we waited too long for General Baeza."

"Well, what about these stories and these threats?" asked Pan-toja. "We've seen them before. And I don't have to tell you that they're being used everywhere to hurt Chile."

433

"Well, I can assure you that the FBI didn't leak the story," said Scherrer. "And we sure didn't leak the photographs. That was stupid."

"Yes, it was," said Pantoja. "Who do you think did it, then?"

"Probably somebody in the State Department," Scherrer replied. "Look, I don't deny that the State Department has a foot in the investigation now. There's no way to change that. But we can minimize it. If you people will cooperate and help us resolve these questions about Williams and Romeral, we can keep them pretty well out of it."

"What about Propper?" asked Pantoja. "I've seen his picture in the newspapers, with that beard. He looks like a hippie to me. Do you mind if I ask you something personal, Bob?"

"No," said Scherrer.

"Is he Jewish?" asked Pantoja.

"I don't know," said Scherrer. "Probably so, but I don't know for sure. I just met him myself a few days ago. He's not a hippie, though. I can tell you that. I don't even think he's a liberal. He's a prosecutor. He doesn't give a damn about anything except solving this case."

Pantoja nodded doubtfully. "What about the beard, then?" he asked.

"I don't know about that," said Scherrer. "But a beard is not that big a deal in the United States. It's not like Chile. Even some businessmen wear them here."

"Perhaps so," said Pantoja, unconvinced. He informed Scherrer that President Pinochet was sending a team of Chilean envoys to Washington to meet Propper and to discuss the political implications of United States behavior in the Letelier investigation. Pantoja was on the team. He had come in advance to talk things over with Scherrer, whom he professed to trust. He had also come early in order to comb through the records at the Chilean embassy, where, to his surprise and chagrin, Pantoja had discovered many documents about requests from and replies to Propper concerning the Letelier case. None of these documents was in CNI files. It was just as Scherrer had said, he conceded, vowing that someone in the Foreign Ministry would be fired.

Scherrer invited Pantoja to join him for dinner, and the CNI colonel wound up flirting with a Spanish-speaking waitress. Ever the intelligence man, however, Pantoja told her he was from Ecuador.

The next morning, two Miami FBI agents drove up to Fort Lauderdale and called on AID president Jack N. Holcomb, a self-described soldier of fortune, security expert, and anti-Communist business-man. Holcomb did not like the FBI. A bristly, forceful man, he was not at all intimidated by the agents. He assured them that all his business was legal. He acknowledged that he had in the past sold equipment to the Chilean government, specifically to "the agency in charge of protecting the junta." Its representative, as he recalled, was about five foot eleven. He did not volunteer a name, but said he would look through his records.

That same morning, in Santiago, President Pinochet announced at a press conference that he was lifting Chile's state of siege, which had been in effect officially for four and a half years, since the coup against Allende. Pinochet did not link this liberalizing measure with the recent international publicity about the Letelier case, but he did speak on the latter subject. "This government has nothing to do with the Letelier crime," he declared. "I have the impression that this is a well-mounted campaign, like all campaigns mounted by the Communists, to discredit the government. When the truth is known, it will be seen that in Chile there is innocence."

In Washington, Propper followed Scherrer, Cornick, and the State Department representatives into a large conference room, where Pantoja was waiting with Pinochet's two special envoys, Undersecretary of the Interior Enrique Montero and Special Legal Counsel Miguel Schweitzer. Montero was an air force group commander and had been a fixture in the junta since its first day. Scherrer knew him fairly well, having helped arrange with Montero to get many drug smugglers expelled from Chile to the United States for trial. He also knew Schweitzer, who had represented many of those same drug smugglers. Schweitzer's father had been a Chilean minister of justice. He was tall, impeccably dressed and mannered, and spoke flawless English. Montero was shorter but equally distinguished in appearance, with jet-black hair and clear blue eyes. One of his daughters was a flight attendant, who, by coincidence, had bandaged Scherrer's hand during the Rolando Otero flight in 1976.

Montero, leader of the Chilean group, said he and his colleagues were there to urge that the Letelier investigation be free of political overtones, such as his government had detected in recent news stories. Schweitzer read the texts of resolutions by the Chilean minister of justice and the Chilean Supreme Court calling for speedy and faithful compliance with the Letters Rogatory. He also advised them of Pinochet's request for a separate investigation into apparent passport violations within Chile, and went on to explain Chilean legal procedures as they might apply to the investigations. Parenthetically, he observed that neither Propper nor any Chilean lawyer retained by the United States would be allowed to participate in the questioning of witnesses for the Letters Rogatory.

As soon as the State Department translator put this last statement into English, Propper interrupted. "Excuse me," he said. "Are you stating as a firm decision that I won't be allowed to be there?"

"That is correct," said Schweitzer.

"I see," said Propper. "Are you telling me that under Chilean law you are the one entitled to make that decision? And not the judge in the case?"

"I am telling you what Chilean law is," said Schweitzer, somewhat taken aback.

"Yes, but I want to know if your decision binds the judge in the case," said Propper. "I petitioned the court to be there at its discretion and not as a matter of legal right. So I want to know if the judge has the power to grant me that privilege. Frankly, I don't think it should be for you to determine."

"You're right, Mr. Propper," said Schweitzer. "The decision is up to the Chilean courts. I was being presumptuous."

"And even if the courts agree with Mr. Schweitzer, as I think they will," said Montero diplomatically, "I think my government may be able to work out a way for you to interview the same witnesses outside the formal court proceedings."

"Good," said Propper. "I would prefer to do both, but we must see these witnesses some time. We—the FBI agents and I—are the ones who know the Letelier investigation. We know the follow-up questions that should be asked, and because we know the particulars of what has gone on here in the United States, we will be able to detect errors and shadings of testimony that won't be apparent to people who aren't familiar with the case."

"I understand," said Montero. "And I'm certain that we will be able to accommodate you, because I'm certain that the government of Chile is completely innocent in this case. We will arrange something on the witnesses."

"Very good," said Propper.

Montero proposed a joint investigation of the Letelier assassination by the United States and Chilean governments, and invited Propper to come to Chile and see for himself the workings of the Chilean courts. Working together, he said, the two countries could more effectively control the deplorable leaks of information that had created a false image of Chilean guilt.

"Well, thank you for your invitation to Chile," said Propper. "I hope to take you up on it soon. First, let me say that I don't like the leaks any more than you do. Our grand juries are secret. There have been no leaks of information from any of the testimony I've obtained from dozens of witnesses I've put in the grand jury, as far as I'm aware. But we don't control the American press. I certainly can't control the opinions that appear in the newspapers. Most of it is speculation. A lot of it's wrong. And nearly all of it's political.

"I want to keep this investigation strictly within the United States Justice Department, where it belongs. It's a criminal matter. That's it. Somebody blew up two people with a bomb a few blocks away from here. They died horrible deaths right there in the streets in front of all those embassies. My job—the attorney general's job—is to find the people responsible for those deaths. I've handled a lot of murder cases, and what makes this one different is that a foreign government, represented by you people, is in a position to cooperate by producing witnesses. In a murder case like this one, I expect that cooperation from you just as much as I would from American citizens.

"Now, I've spoken to Mr. Christopher about this case, and I can assure you that he clearly understands his role and the State Department's role. That role is to oversee the foreign-policy aspects of the investigation. And as far as the Justice Department is concerned, there should be no foreign-policy aspects to the case as long as there is cooperation by those in a position to help. As long as Chile cooperates, State doesn't have anything to do except transmit messages and monitor the situation, which it has been doing well so far. I know you're upset about statements saying the United States is preparing to break relations, but I can assure you, and they will assure you, that is not true. That's just junk from the press.

"What is true is that the Justice Department will not back down on this or any other criminal case. If there are witnesses we believe can help solve this crime, we are determined to interview them. I welcome your offer to work jointly on this investigation. Since this crime did occur in the United States, giving me jurisdiction, I assume that you will give me anything you learn that might be of help. You can work through Agent Scherrer in Buenos Aires. He will be in Santiago whenever he's needed. You know him and so do I. We can all work through him to get this resolved quickly and legally."

Once the Chileans had departed, a jolly mood broke out among the Americans in the hallway. Frank Willis was patting Propper on the back, offering congratulations. So was Bob Steven. Even Cornick was tossing compliments. "I've been carrying Gene so long in this investigation that I'm stoop-shouldered," he declared with a laugh, "but I gotta admit that was the boy's finest hour in there. He had those guys convinced that he's on intimate terms with the attorney general and the President of the United States! It was beautiful."

Scherrer returned after bidding farewell to Pantoja and reported that Propper had made quite an impression. He said Pantoja had just told him Propper might not be so bad after all, despite the beard, and that in fact Propper reminded Pantoja of Abraham Lincoln. This comment drew a big laugh.

Propper was perplexed about all the fuss. He said he thought it had been a rather routine meeting between two sides on a criminal investigation. Nothing unusual had occurred.

"Nothing unusual?" said Willis, in disbelief. "Gene, you just treated those men like they were two ordinary guys from the Bar Association that you were trying to beat up on in a regular murder case."

"What's wrong with that?" asked Propper. "They *are* the opposing lawyers."

Willis shook his head. "They're also very high officials of a sovereign foreign government who have been sent here by their President on an urgent diplomatic mission," he said.

"So what?" said Propper, slightly on the defensive, as though he were being chided for failures in protocol.

"No, it's all right," said Willis, now convinced that Propper did not realize the impact of his manner on the Chileans. "But it is unusual in this business. Those guys don't get talked to like that very often."

"It was perfect," said Scherrer, trying to reassure Propper. "Every time you came down hard on how this thing is a Justice Department and FBI matter that you expect to be treated confidentially and professionally, Pantoja would be smiling at me across the table and giving me the thumbs-up sign. He loved it. The tougher you were, the more he liked it. To them it means you speak with authority and you'll keep the State Department out of it."

"It's not a State Department case," said Propper, as though stating the obvious.

"I know that, Gene," said Scherrer, "but *they* didn't believe it. Until now."

The next morning, March 10, Scherrer walked into the headquarters office of Jimmy Adams. Although the Bureau executive was eight or ten rungs above Scherrer in the hierarchy, the two of them had maintained something of a personal relationship since Adams had attended—and survived—an Interpol General Assembly in Buenos Aires during a time of rampant terrorism.

Scherrer told Adams he was leaving that afternoon for Miami and Buenos Aires and just wanted to say goodbye. "And there's one thing I think you ought to know about," he said. "I was planning to get it off my chest down at the Miami conference, but I didn't get a chance, because all hell broke loose. And that's this Gopher operation. Professionally it's the worst thing I've seen in my entire career. If you want to take the time when this case is over, you could study the file and figure out how bad it was. Number one, they obviously never checked that guy out with DEA, because DEA has a big headquarters file on him. Number two, they tried to deceive me about what was going on with phony double sourcing and stuff . . ."

Adams puffed on his pipe as Scherrer listed his charges against the operation. "Well, I agree with you," said Adams. "We weren't on top of it well enough here at headquarters, either. It shouldn't have gotten that far along before we caught it. I'll take some of the blame."

"Well, that's not the point," said Scherrer. "The point is that it could have really screwed up the investigation down there. But it didn't, thank God."

"How does it look?" asked Adams.

"I think we'll solve it," said Scherrer. "And I'll admit I never thought that before."

Adams smiled through the pipe smoke. "When?"

Scherrer hesitated slightly, knowing that any estimate would be a boastful guess. "Give us a month," he said.

Adams opened his eyes slightly wider but otherwise kept nodding and puffing. "How about the U.S. attorney?" he asked.

"Propper?" said Scherrer.

"Can you work with him?" asked Adams. "Some of our guys have had nothing but trouble with him."

"Sure, I can handle him," said Scherrer. "No problem."

"Okay," said Adams. "What do you need?"

"Nothing right now," said Scherrer. "Just let us work it a little bit. We may have to do some unorthodox things. I don't mean anything illegal, but we won't get anywhere if we have meetings about everything and get every move cleared in advance through channels. I think you've got to let us go some on our own."

Adams thought only briefly. "You've got it," he said. "Just call me if you have any trouble."

That same day, in Santiago, two Chilean lawyers appeared at the American embassy and asked to speak to a political officer, to whom they delivered an unsigned declaration. The lawyers vouched for the author of the declaration, who they said was very frightened but wished to offer information anonymously. In the declaration, the man said that he recognized the photographs of Michael Townley and his wife, Mariana Callejas, that had appeared recently in Santiago newspapers, and he also recognized their street address in the mountainside suburb of Lo Curro. He said he had been there to do business with Townley, who had described himself as a CNI employee and also as the representative of a company called Karbel, which was bringing money into Chile through London banks for investment. In the declaration, the man gave many details of Karbel's business profile, including its connections to the Chilean government. He also said that Townley had always gone by another name—Andrés Wilson. Mrs. Townley had always been Mrs. Wilson. He said Townley was widely known by that name in Santiago.

This was the second mention of Andrés Wilson. There was also the name Kenneth Enyart. In Fort Lauderdale that day, an FBI agent went to see AID's Jack Holcomb for the second time, to find out if Holcomb remembered anything further about his firm's dealings with the government of Chile. Holcomb told the agent that AID kept strict records of who entered and departed its premises, for security reasons. The company maintained a time clock to record the exact times of visits by authorized persons. The company also kept a log of all telephone calls made from AID. From these records, Holcomb had retrieved punch cards and time sheets showing that Kenneth Enyart, representing the government of Chile, had been inside the AID plant on numerous occasions during 1975 and 1976. Specifically, he showed the agent a card indicating that Enyart had punched into the plant at 8:25 a.m. on September 21, 1976, and had departed at two that afternoon. Therefore, it seemed obvious that Kenneth Enyart could not have been in Washington that day blowing anybody up.

Holcomb conceded the possibility that Enyart was a false name. If so, he said, the falsehood reflected on the government of Chile and not on the integrity of his company. Holcomb said he always required official letters of authorization before selling security equipment to foreigners, and he showed the FBI agent a letter authorizing "Mr. J. Andrés Wilson or Mr. Kenneth Enyart" to make purchases on behalf of the government of Chile. The letter bore the stamp of the Chilean Interior Ministry and the signature of Undersecretary

Enrique Montero. This was the third mention of Andrés Wilson.

The agent took this information back to the Miami FBI office, thinking that the customers at AID sounded legitimate and that Kenneth Enyart was another dead end for the Letelier investigation. He reported it to his supervisor, who incorporated it into a teletype for headquarters. Anything relating to Letelier was hot enough for a teletype.

Meanwhile, another Miami agent was interviewing Michael Townley's father, J. Vernon Townley. The elder Townley spoke with the worldly detachment one might expect from an international vice president of a large bank—more so, in fact. He told the interviewing agents of his business career as president of Ford-Chile, of Ford-Venezuela, and of Ford-Philippines, and of his subsequent shift into the banking world in 1972. Against this backdrop of corporate success, Vernon Townley bluntly told the agents that his older son, Michael, had run away from home at the age of eighteen and had had little to do with the family since. Michael, said the elder Townley, had run away because he wished to marry a Chilean woman and the family had not approved. Townley described his other two children as well. He said his daughter had married a Japanese man named Fukuchi and lived in Tarrytown, New York. His younger son lived in Pompano Beach and had a business called Mark for Carpet Cleaning, which was a one-man show and was not doing well.

Vernon Townley added dryly that his son Michael did not have a college education, that he did not know where to reach him in Chile, and that the last time he had heard from Michael had been several months earlier, when his son had called wanting to borrow money. He did recall that Michael had a private pilot's license. Other than this, Vernon Townley said he did not think he could be of help to the FBI. The agents left, not far ahead of the newspaper reporters who began to descend on the elder Townley. "My life and my son's life have very little connection," he would tell them.

In Washington, Cornick and Tim Mahoney spent that afternoon interviewing the man who had first volunteered the name Enyart to the FBI, connecting Townley to the company called Audio Intelligence Devices. The man said Holcomb sold all sorts of sophisticated equipment, including remote-control devices that could be used to detonate bombs. He also said that Holcomb was very gruff and ardent in his private war against leftists of all kinds, and that Holcomb would probably refuse to volunteer information that would incriminate anyone, especially his customers. The man recalled that Enyart/

Townley had dealt personally with Holcomb, often calling him directly from Chile, and that many of Townley's shipments from AID had been hand-carried to pilots of LAN Chile, for transport to Santiago.

Back at WFO after the interview, Cornick began to worry that the Miami agents might not realize what they were dealing with in Jack Holcomb, so he called the supervisor of the Miami anti-terrorist squad to warn him. It was then that Cornick learned of the interview that had already taken place that day—of Kenneth Enyart's airtight alibi and of the letter from the Chilean undersecretary of the Interior.

Of all the revelations, the one that stunned Cornick most was the name Enrique Montero. The official who signed the letter to AID vouching for Enyart/Townley was the same man Cornick had just seen leading the Chilean delegation at the State Department! If Montero had signed such a letter, the investigators would have a hook into the upper reaches of the Chilean government.

Cornick composed himself enough to shout over the telephone that the Holcomb material was definitely not routine and that somebody had better turn around and go back up there and grab all those documents. Why hadn't they been taken already? Had Holcomb resisted or asked for a subpoena? The answer was no, but by now it was Friday evening and too late to return until Monday.

In New York, Larry Wack was busy that night. Since returning from Miami, he had located Ricardo Canete and pumped him up for another run at his contacts in the CNM. Canete had offered many smooth apologies, and then he had said he couldn't find Alvin Ross. Wack said Ross had just showed up at a preliminary hearing on charges of having assaulted his girlfriend and therefore could not be in hiding. Still, Canete insisted that Ross was not responding to any of his messages. Wack suggested that Canete contact Virgilio Paz instead, now that Canete had heard that Paz was planning to go underground.

"But I don't know the guy," Canete protested. "What am I supposed to do? You want me to call him up and say, 'Hey, I hear you're thinking of going underground on the Letelier rap. Why don't we get together?'"

"Very funny," said Wack. "No. How about this? You call him up and say you're desperate. You can't find Alvin, and you've just been told you're gonna get subpoenaed before the Letelier grand jury on account of your CNM connections. And you wanna know what to do. How's that?"

"It might work," said Canete. "But he's gonna want to know who told me that. I can't just say I heard it on the streets."

"You tell him I told you," said Wack. " 'Cause I just did. Ricky, you're about to be subpoenaed. You're in my territory, so it ought to make sense."

At ten o'clock that night, Canete was waiting for Paz at Gino's restaurant in Union City. To identify himself, Canete took out his cigarette lighter with the thunderbolt emblem—sign of a founding member of the Cuban Nationalist Movement—and placed it on the table. He noticed two Cuban males, who entered the restaurant, looked around, specifically at him, and then departed. Figuring these two for Paz's reconnaissance people, Canete thought rightly that Paz would be along shortly.

Paz soon entered in his customary cloud of cologne, wearing a sports jacket and an expensive monogrammed shirt. He walked over to Canete's table and examined the lighter. Canete thought he looked young, trim, handsome, cool—and very tight underneath.

"Ricky, how are you doing?" asked Paz.

"Fine," said Canete. "Nice to meet you. Have a seat."

Paz sat down and looked around cautiously. "What's going on?" he asked.

"This asshole named Wack called me from the FBI and said he's gonna subpoena me for a grand jury down in Washington," said Canete. "What do I do?"

Paz looked sternly at Canete. "Button," he said. "That's what you do."

"Okay," said Canete.

"Look, we'll be meeting Alvin a little later," said Paz. "He wants to talk to you."

An hour later, Canete and Paz were sitting downstairs at the Bottom of the Barrel restaurant in Union City when Alvin Ross joined them. The three of them ordered drinks and Canete acted scared, which was easy for him to do. He said he had never faced a federal grand jury before. He was worried about what the feds knew, about what they would ask him. He complained about Ignacio Novo's poor security habits. Ignacio talked too much, he said. His audience nodded along through his worries. Paz seemed to become more calm as Canete became more jittery. Finally, in a period of silence, Paz leaned over to Canete and said quietly, "We did Letelier."

Dumbstruck, Canete said nothing. He turned slowly to Ross, who was nodding his head in the affirmative.

"Yeah, we did it," Paz said, with a slight smirk on his face. "We know it, and they know it. But let them try to prove it."

This was why Canete would have to "button" before the grand jury. Paz watched Canete stew over the new dimensions of his problem for a few seconds and then said, "Come on, Ricky. I want to show you something."

"Okay," said Canete.

Paz stood up and looked at Ross, who was wearing a black knit seaman's cap. "Lend Ricky your hat, Al," he said.

Canete put the hat on without question. On Paz's order, he also put on a pair of dark glasses and realized that he was about to go somewhere incognito. Outside, in Paz's car, Canete sat in the passenger's seat and did not move when Paz leaned over and tied one of his monogrammed handkerchiefs around Canete's neck. "I hope you don't mind this," Paz said as he pulled the seaman's hat down over Canete's face and sunglasses, and pulled the handkerchief up to tuck it under the hat. "It's for security," he added, almost playfully.

Half an hour later, Canete found himself being walked inside something warm enough to be a building, treading on wood and on concrete through twists and turns, down at least two sets of staircases, the last of which was a spiral one. When Paz finally yanked off the hat, Canete found himself in a very small room with windowless walls covered by pegboard. There were five or six machine guns lined up on a rack. A bazooka and an assortment of shotguns and handguns lay on the floor, surrounding heavy crates that Canete assumed were filled with more guns and grenades and all kinds of explosives.

After Canete's eyes adjusted to the light, Paz let him study the arsenal briefly and then said, "You see what we can do, Ricky. So now you know that when you get to the grand jury, you haven't heard anything. Seen anything. You don't know anything, see? Because it's not only you, Ricky, it's your family, too."

Canete nodded glumly to Paz, who suddenly broke into a grin and slapped him on the back. "But I know there's no need of that with you," he said fraternally.

Not long afterward, Paz removed the seaman's hat again and Canete found himself back at the Bottom of the Barrel. Not long after that, he was alone at a pay phone, calling Wack. It was late on Friday night, at the end of one full week since the appearance of the Juan Williams photograph in O'Leary's article.

Wack worked all day Saturday, on adrenaline. From Cornick's leads, based on newspaper stories out of Santiago, they located the sister of Captain Armando Fernández Larios. Fernández was the man identified as the Romeral who had gone to Paraguay. His sister was a naturalized American citizen, living in Manhattan. Wack and Special Agent Neil Herman spent the better part of two hours with her on Saturday and learned that she had last seen her brother in the United States during the summer of 1976, when he came up on a vacation. On that trip, she said, she had accompanied her brother constantly and therefore knew positively that he had attended to no business of any kind. Mostly he had played tennis.

Wack and Herman then drove to Tarrytown, New York, on a lead growing out of the interview with Townley's father the previous day. They found Linda Fukuchi at home and engaged her in a long and similarly innocent chat. Fukuchi said she knew very little about her brother, as he was older and had run away from home when she was quite small. She said she had last seen her brother about three years ago, when he had passed through during a visit to the States.

All day Sunday—when he wasn't "holding Canete's hand" while the informant waited to be recontacted by Paz or Ross—Wack studied his notes on the two interviews. He decided he wanted to talk with both women again. Late Monday afternoon, he made the long drive back to Linda Fukuchi's house. She said she was still bewildered by all the publicity about her brother. Friends and even strangers had been calling about articles in *The New York Times*.

Wack pulled out his copy of the Juan Williams photograph, which he had forgotten to bring to the Saturday interview. Fukuchi said it looked like her brother, all right. She kept shaking her head, and Wack kept inviting her to help solve the mystery. He asked many of the sly questions he had planned, but received few answers. All Fukuchi could add about Townley was that she remembered hearing that his wife was a Chilean woman who was at least ten years older than Mike. That was about it.

Wack probed for memories of the visit Townley had paid his sister about three years earlier. Fukuchi couldn't remember anything except that it was very brief and unexpected. Then Wack tried another ploy. He asked whether Townley had made any phone calls from Fukuchi's house during the visit. She couldn't remember that, either. Wack asked whether she kept her old phone bills, by chance, and Fukuchi replied that she did. She started rummaging through drawers. Wack said he'd like to take a look at her bill for September 1976, if she could find it.

Fukuchi finally unearthed a tattered record of her toll calls for that month. Wack looked it over and felt his knees grow weak. "You got any friends in Union City, New Jersey?" he asked Fukuchi.

"No," said Fukuchi. "Not that I know of."

"How about Cliffside, New Jersey?" asked Wack. "You know anybody there?"

"No," said Fukuchi.

"How about your husband? He know anybody?"

"Not that I know of. Why?"

Wack showed the bill to Fukuchi and pointed to listings of four calls. "You sure you don't know anybody who would call you collect from Union City?" he asked.

"Positive," said Fukuchi. "Hardly anybody ever calls us collect."

"Uh huh," said Wack. "Would you mind if I took this?"

Fukuchi looked at the phone bill. "Of course not," she said. "As long as I could get a copy."

Wack hesitated. His mind was tumbling. "Nah, it's not that important," he said. "I'll just write down these numbers and check them out. I don't want to take your property unless it means something."

"I don't understand any of this," said Fukuchi.

"I don't either," said Wack. "But you keep hold of this, okay? Put it somewhere where you can find it."

"I'll put it right here in the top drawer," Fukuchi said obligingly.

As soon as he got inside the Bureau car, Wack grabbed the arm of Jimmy Lyons, his stand-in partner for that day. "Son-of-a-bitch!" he cried, eyes bulging. "That's a fucking gotcha!"

Wack's manner frightened Lyons, who thought he might be having a seizure. "What's the matter?" he asked.

"Look at that son-of-a-bitch!" cried Wack, pointing to his note on the call to Cliffside, New Jersey. "I don't know about those collect calls from Union City, but I *recognize* that motherfucking number. That's Guillermo Novo's apartment! Some son-of-a-bitch called Guillermo Novo's apartment from that phone in there at 6:16 p.m. on September 19, 1976. That's a day and a half before the murder down in Washington, and I'll bet my ass it was Townley!"

On the long drive back to New York, Wack rolled down his window to shout now and then, just for the release of it.

Wack's emergency phone call shocked Cornick almost as badly as the news of Paz's confession, four nights earlier. Cornick went into a numb, fatherly mode—as he usually did when he was reeling. "Larry, are you *sure*?" he asked. "Let's not make a mistake now."

"Yeah, I'm sure," said Wack. "I checked the number already. It's Novo's."

"September 19?"

"Yeah. 1976."

"My God," whispered Cornick.

"Son-of-a-bitch," said Wack.

"Let me ask you this, Larry," said Cornick. "Did she give you the phone bill? Do you have it in your possession?"

"She said she'd give it to me. But I didn't take it. She was almost *too* willing. I was afraid she'd claim I stole it later and get it suppressed. So I didn't want to take any chances. We gotta get a subpoena."

The next day, the news sent Propper into a fit. "Carter, she's a *witness*, not a defendant!" he shrieked. "Nobody can move to suppress anything she gives Wack! He should've taken it! She might destroy that stuff!"

There was a lot of frantic phone calling. From New York Telephone Wack learned that the company's own toll records were routinely destroyed after a year. Wack notified Fukuchi that the September phone bill was now considered evidence and warned her of the penalties for tampering.

Just after agents collected the Fukuchi telephone bill, word came from the Newark FBI office that two of the collect calls to Fukuchi's house had come from a pay phone in Union City that was located in a restaurant called the Bottom of the Barrel. More red flags went up.

From Miami, that same day, word came that agents had visited Jack Holcomb for the third time and finally obtained photocopies of the AID records on Kenneth Enyart's visits to the company. The agents also obtained a copy of the letter authorizing Enyart to make purchases for Chile.

"Gene, it's coming at us from both directions at once," Cornick told Propper. "That's the way it ought to be. We're tying Chile to Townley and Townley to the Novos."

Propper, Cornick, and Barcella spent hours that night trying to construct a plausible theory of the assassination from the new evidence. They could place Townley in New York on September 19, in contact with Guillermo Novo. And they could place Townley in Fort Lauderdale on September 21, at the time the bomb went off on Sheridan Circle. But they couldn't place Townley or anyone else in Washington. Something was wrong. Cornick directed ugly suspicions toward Jack Holcomb. Some reports already made him out to be a rather hard and sinister character, in the business of intrigue. "I'll bet that son-of-a-bitch is in this up to his ass," said Cornick. "And he's falsified the records to give Townley an alibi."

Scherrer arrived in Santiago on March 15 and went into conference with Ambassador Landau, who said that Dr. Miguel Schweitzer, Chile's special counsel, had just advised the embassy of dramatic news: the men identified as Townley and Fernández did in fact travel to Paraguay as Williams and Romeral, but they did *not* go to the United States. Instead, Schweitzer revealed, two *other* Chileans had assumed the Williams and Romeral identities and had traveled to Miami on the date mentioned in the American Letters Rogatory. Schweitzer was trying to make the tangle of identities sound simple. Now, said Schweitzer, there were four men involved instead of two. One Williams and Romeral set had gone to Paraguay but not to the United States. In fact, said Schweitzer, Captain Fernández had never been to the United States in his life. The other, newly discovered Williams and Romeral set had indeed gone to the United States in August 1976, but their mission had been only to deliver new "service codes" to the Chilean Military Mission in Washington. Schweitzer said that the two who had gone to the United States could easily prove that they had nothing to do with the Letelier assassination. Therefore, Schweitzer expected to dispose of the Letters Rogatory by the end of the week. He expected a statement from the United States government recognizing Chile's full cooperation.

The story sounded shaky to Landau, but there was no question that the Chileans were about to take the offensive. Scherrer could expect to be "mousetrapped" with the two new Chileans at his meeting with General Mena.

The next morning, March 16, Scherrer went alone to Contreras's old office at CNI headquarters for a meeting with Mena, Pantoja, and Montero. Mena was in an expansive mood and said that the mystery had been solved. He told Scherrer the story of the two "extra" agents and announced that CNI had recovered their passports. They were secret, he told Scherrer, because the matter was still before the Chilean courts, but he would show them to the legat in confidence as a sign of cooperation.

Scherrer took the red official passports from Mena and examined them in the presence of the Chilean officials. The passports appeared to be authentic, bearing the same names, numbers, and dates of travel as were specified in the Letters Rogatory. Then Scherrer saw the photographs. Both the new Williams and the new Romeral were familiar to him somehow. Scherrer struggled not to show his surprise or the mental strain of the effort to remember who they were.

Handing the passports back to Mena, Scherrer said, "That is very interesting, General. But those men are not mere couriers."

"You know them?" asked Mena.

"I recognize their faces," Scherrer said matter-of-factly. "The blond one in the Juan Williams passport is Captain René Riveros. General Contreras once sent him to Pudahuel Airport to get me into the country without passing through the International Police. Captain Riveros is a very important man, and is very close to General Contreras.* The other one is also close to Contreras. In fact, the general told me he was part of DINA's 'cream of the crop.' I can't remember his name, but I have it back at the embassy. I have his photograph, too. General Contreras gave me his passport in the group of bodyguards who accompanied President Pinochet to Washington last year. The photograph you have there shows the same man."

The three Chileans stood silently for a moment, clearly surprised. "So you know these two imposters?" Mena said quietly.

"I know Riveros," said Scherrer. "I've never met the other one, but I have records and a photograph of him. Contreras gave them to me."

"Contreras gave them to you personally?" asked Mena, in disbelief. "He personally gave you photographs of DINA agents involved in secret missions?"

"I helped him get U.S. visas for the bodyguards," Scherrer explained. "General Contreras and I discussed the matter personally, and then he sent the passports directly to me by courier."

"That is very interesting," said Mena. He gave his colleagues a look of annoyance, as though tabulating Contreras's acts of stupidity. Then he turned back to Scherrer and confirmed the legat's identification of Riveros. He also identified the other man as a Captain Mosqueira. These were the two men who had entered Miami on August 22, 1976, as Williams and Romeral, he said. These were the two men who would be questioned pursuant to the Letters Rogatory.

"Thank you very much, General," said Scherrer. "But I should tell you that our primary interest is in the other two men—the ones who went to Paraguay. Particularly Townley."

Mena sighed. "We have been looking for him," he said. "I can assure you that we are mounting a nationwide search for Mr. Townley. We have received information that he might have fled to the south of Chile about March 1. His wife and children are still at home in Lo

*See above, page 65 and page 340.

Curro. We know that. And we will find Townley sooner or later. But he is not the Juan Williams who went to Miami."

"I understand that," said Scherrer. "But he has been to the United States. In fact, we have information that Townley was in the Miami area, representing DINA. He made numerous purchases from a company there that specializes in electronic equipment, including the kind that can be used to detonate a remote-controlled bomb. That's one of the reasons we would like to question him in particular."

General Mena mulled this over. "This is very confusing," he said. "You acknowledge that Townley is not the Juan Williams who went to Miami, but you want to question him anyway on the basis of information connecting him to DINA. May I ask what is the nature of the information?"

"Certainly," said Scherrer, who was ready to play his trump card. "Townley made his purchases in the name of Kenneth Enyart from a company called Audio Intelligence Devices. We have witnesses who have identified Enyart as Townley. And the FBI has a copy of a letter from the Chilean government to the company in Fort Lauderdale authorizing official purchases of security equipment. I do not yet have a copy of the letter. It will take a few days to get down here. But I do have the text of it, and I can read you what the letter says, if you like."

"Go ahead," said Mena.

"All right." He glanced briefly at Montero, who seemed curious and impassive, like the others. "It's dated January 29, 1975, and written on official stationery from the Ministry of the Interior," said Scherrer, who noticed a sharp movement of surprise from Montero. "It's addressed to the president of the company, a man named Jack Holcomb, and the text is as follows:

> By this letter we hereby authorize the firms Prosin, Inc.; Prosin Ltda. or Consultec Ltda., as represented by Mr. J. Andrés Wilson or Mr. Kenneth Enyart and/or any agent they may individually or jointly name, to make inquiries and request information pertaining to the products of your firm.

"The letter bears the official stamp of the undersecretary of the Ministry of the Interior," Scherrer continued. "And it's signed 'Enrique Montero S.' "

Montero was already on his feet. "That's not my name," he said sharply. "I have always signed my name Enrique Montero Marx, which is my true name. Always. I do not remember ever signing such a letter. This is impossible."

Scherrer winced slightly and continued in a monotone: "My cable describes the stamp as a circle with a star in the middle and words around the border."

"That sounds like my seal," said Montero, "but the name is incorrect. The last part of the name." He was walking back and forth. His colleagues were giving him looks of puzzlement tinged with suspicion.

"I doubt that you did sign it," said Scherrer. "But we have to find out who did."

"What are those names again?" snapped Montero.

Scherrer told him. "We have information that this Andrés Wilson may be another alias for Townley," he said. "That would make three—Williams, Enyart, and Andrés Wilson. There may be others, of course."

"I don't remember those names," said Montero. "I really don't. Or the company. But I sign many letters every day. I will try to remember." He sat down, attracting pained looks.

"It appears that someone from DINA may have obtained Mr. Montero's stationery and forged his signature, I'm afraid," said Scherrer.

"That would reflect very badly on the integrity of our government," Montero said, through barely concealed rage. "I will prove to you that I did not sign that letter and I did not even know about it. Furthermore, we will find out who did."

"Thank you," said Scherrer.

Mena cleared his throat and said, "Under the circumstances, Mr. Scherrer, I wish to reassure you that these two official passports are genuine." He called for a member of his staff to bring in an ultraviolet light, under which Mena placed the red passports. The stamps showing the U.S. visas reacted to the light, indicating that they were probably genuine ones.

When the meeting broke up, Montero insisted that Scherrer accompany him back to his office at the Ministry of the Interior. Almost desperately, Montero asked Scherrer to look through the letters in his files—even the classified ones—to attest that the signatures appeared in a different form from that of the letter to AID. Then he insisted on providing Scherrer with samples of his handwriting so that the FBI laboratory could compare it to the signature on the AID letter. The undersecretary of the Interior said that he would submit to anything—even to this humiliating act of giving samples like a criminal suspect—in order to prove his innocence.

Scherrer returned to the embassy to confer with Ambassador Landau. They agreed that the Chilean government was likely to come forward with the "new" Williams and Romeral quite soon, without producing Townley. The Chileans might try to answer the Letters Rogatory quickly and then drop the Letelier investigation as a *fait accompli*. To guard against this possibility, the Americans needed the authority of the Justice Department to deny instantly that the Chilean response was legally adequate.

Landau drafted a cable that night urging Propper and Cornick to fly to Santiago as soon as possible. No public announcement should be made. Secrecy and speed were of the essence, as critical legal situations were likely to arise within the next few days.

While Scherrer was springing the AID letter on the Chileans, Propper and Barcella were in the grand-jury room taking the testimony of "Carlos Casado." Canete had assumed this false identity for his own protection. Even so, Wack sat upstairs in the courthouse fretting about leaks that might get Canete killed. Canete himself was trembling and perspiring nervously in Propper's office, but in the grand jury itself he suddenly acquired a stage presence. He captivated the grand jurors with a dramatic account of Alvin Ross's July 7 "bomb speech" and of the evening when Paz showed him the arsenal.

"By God, he's a born witness," Barcella said when it was over. He could not resist a dramatic re-enactment of Canete's testimony for Wack's benefit, with himself in the role of Canete. Wack, who could see that the prosecutor in Barcella was lusting to put Canete on the stand, only muttered that his prize informant's life would be worthless if he appeared in open court.

In Manhattan, during Wack's absence, two agents carried out a bit of investigation that couldn't wait for his return. They went to a little radio shop near Grand Central Station, carrying a purchase receipt that had been among the items recovered from Alvin Ross's abandoned office ten days earlier. The receipt showed that an Alejandro Bontempi, from Buenos Aires, had bought nearly a thousand dollars' worth of radio equipment in 1975. The shop clerk said he remembered the transaction as an odd one. Deciphering the receipt, he told the agents that Bontempi had bought four units of a radio paging device commonly used to beep doctors and other professionals for messages. Bontempi had said he was planning to take the items back to Argentina.

The agents thought they might be on to something. By now, they knew from Wack that it was possible to modify such paging systems so that the receiver would activate a bomb instead of a harmless message beeper. So the agents asked the shop clerk if he would mind looking for Bontempi in a photo array. They spread six mug shots on the counter of Grand Central Radio, and the clerk picked out Virgilio Paz.*

On Sunday, March 19, Scherrer reserved a VIP airport bus and pulled out onto a runway at Pudahuel Airport to meet the flight from the United States. He snatched Propper, Cornick, and Seddon off the stairs of the airplane for a quick, private journey through the International Police to the waiting embassy cars, telling them these maneuvers were designed to avoid the Chilean press, which had picked up rumors that an American delegation had been dispatched to Santiago. The travelers, dazed by their thirteen-hour flight, followed Scherrer's orders without a word.

On the long drive into the city, Cornick, Seddon, and Propper took in the endless expanses of flat agricultural fields. Much of the foliage and grass was of a particularly brilliant and yet soft shade of green, unfamiliar to Americans. Men worked in the fields behind horses and spindly, primitive plows, and the embassy cars would occasionally pull around a horse and cart or an old man carrying an A-frame filled with hay. Then the Americans entered the city and the scenery changed abruptly to billboards, shop windows, traffic jams, and well-dressed pedestrians. Had it not been for the Spanish signs and the preponderance of miniature European automobiles, the visitors might have thought they were arriving somewhere in the United States. Propper felt as if he had traversed about three centuries since he had arrived at the airport. His car took him directly to Ambassador Landau's residence, while Seddon and Cornick were delivered to the San Cristóbal Hotel, a sleek new building with a façade of gently curving glass.

Once the newcomers had checked into their rooms, Scherrer called Cornick into his. "All right, what the hell is Seddon here for?" he asked.

Cornick told the sad story. Just as he and Propper were on the point of leaving for Chile, SAC Stames had announced that Seddon would be the FBI's emissary to Santiago. Cornick would not go. He

*The clerk said that Alejandro Romeral also looked familiar.

did not have enough rank to deal with foreigners. Seddon did. Besides, Cornick was a "cowboy" and Stames wanted to send someone more palatable to FBI headquarters. After a long quarrel with Propper and Barcella, Stames reluctantly consented to send both agents, on the understanding that Seddon would be the senior man.

Scherrer was visibly annoyed. "Nick's got a lot of nerve sending Seddon after what they did to me on Gopher," he said. With that, Scherrer stalked into Seddon's room. "Al, this is nothing personal about you, but I resent the hell out of your being here," he said bluntly. "You don't represent Bureau interests down here. I do. The Chileans are very sensitive about too many foreigners coming down here to intrude. So you've got two choices: you can either turn around and fly back home or you can stay here and get a suntan by the pool. Pretend you're not in Chile. Because you're not going to any of the meetings. The ambassador will back me up. So will Adams. I've known you a long time, and I'm sorry you wasted your time. But that's the way it is. This is too important to be screwing around with Stames's bullshit."

On the way to the embassy, Cornick opened his locked briefcase and began pulling out papers—interviews, documents, teletypes. Speaking in a low voice, he began with the dynamite—the calls from Fukuchi's phone to Novo and the Bottom of the Barrel, and the confession by Ross and Paz to Canete. Then he moved on to the mere bombshells. Townley's last passport photograph had been located and matched against that of Juan Williams. Perfect fit. Ignacio Novo had called Wack late one night at home and warned the New York agent to quit "harassing" the CNM. Canete had testified before the grand jury, persuasively. The AID material had been pried out of Jack Holcomb and checked out. There were now *three* identifications of Kenneth Enyart as Townley. After the bombshells, Cornick pulled out what he called "the fodder," such as the interviews with relatives of Townley and Fernández, the FAA's record of Michael Townley's pilot lessons, and a sheaf of news clippings. He had not even identified it all when the car reached the embassy.

"I'm telling you, the ground is trembling up there, Bob," said Cornick. "You can feel it."

"I can tell," said Scherrer, still absorbing the headlines. He reached for the copy of the Montero letter of authorization to Jack Holcomb of AID. As Cornick repacked his briefcase, Scherrer examined the markings, the stamp, and the signature. "Beautiful," he said, mostly to himself. "This thing will put Montero on our side."

At the embassy, Ambassador Landau greeted Propper and the two agents with the news that *El Mercurio* had published an editorial denouncing Propper's request to be present at court hearings in Chile as an affront to Chilean sovereignty. Also, Landau told the group, Chilean reporters were already calling the embassy on tips that Propper had entered the country. They might follow him and harass the Americans. The newspapers might try to whip up nationalistic sentiment against the "intrusion" by foreigners.

"It was probably some of the International Police at the airport who tipped them off," said Scherrer. "Are the reporters asking about the FBI, too?"

"I don't think so," said Landau.

"Sorry, guys," teased Propper.

"I'm sure someone recognized the beard," Landau said wryly. "You won't be able to go anywhere without being recognized."

Cornick briefed Landau on the new evidence putting Townley in the United States two days before the assassination, in contact with Guillermo Novo, working for DINA. For the first time, the ambassador realized that the Chilean government would not—or should not—be able to explain the bizarre Paraguayan episode innocently. It now seemed that Pappalardo might have involved Landau in a murder plot. The thought of it made Landau bristle.

The following morning—Monday, March 20—Propper enjoyed his first breakfast at the American ambassador's official residence, a sprawling modern structure laid into a hillside. He found its elegant appointments somewhat overwhelming. There were American flags in the entry, gardens, a swimming pool, and delicious food served instantly when the ambassador's wife, Mary Landau, rang her dinner bell. In his bedroom, Propper found on the telephone a listing of extensions for him to dial various valets, cleaners, and maids. He began to be attracted to an ambassador's life.

Propper did not have long to dwell on these pleasures. After breakfast, he went to visit Juana González, the judge designated to handle the Letters Rogatory proceedings. Propper told the judge, who looked more and more pained as she heard the translation, that he would do whatever was necessary to get to the bottom of the murders. He told her that he expected some irregular behavior from the Chilean government on the Letters Rogatory, and that the United States would not stand for it. Her actions would be watched by the entire world, he said, not just by people in Chile.

Shortly after leaving Judge González, Propper joined Cornick and Scherrer in a drive to CNI headquarters, where Montero, Mena, Pantoja, and Schweitzer were waiting. The teams traded compliments, and General Mena promptly began the business. He announced that President Pinochet himself had ordered his cabinet officers to get to the bottom of the questions raised by the Letters Rogatory and that the CNI had located a second set of agents who had posed as Williams and Romeral. Mena paused occasionally so that Scherrer could translate for Propper. Cornick was struggling to keep up with the Spanish on his own.

Mena also announced something of a breakthrough in regard to Captain Fernández, the man who had gone to Paraguay with Townley. "I have interviewed Captain Fernández personally," he declared. "As you know, in the past he has categorically denied that he has ever visited the United States. I can now tell you that he has changed his story. He has admitted to me that he did in fact go to the United States in the summer of 1976, after the Paraguay incident. This is a very serious matter. He had lied to me and perhaps caused officials of my government to mislead you. I apologize for that. I can only hope that you will take this as evidence of my own determination to find the truth."

"Yes, General," said Scherrer. "This is very significant. Did he say why he had gone to the United States?"

Propper, noticing that everyone in the room had suddenly become intent, could not restrain himself. "What'd he say, Bob?" he asked.

Scherrer tried to answer Propper and maintain eye contact with Mena at the same time. "He said Fernández admitted he did go to the States after Paraguay," Scherrer said quickly, in English.

Propper jumped. Ten questions were stifled in his throat when General Mena continued in Spanish.

"No, Mr. Scherrer, he did not say why he had gone to the United States," Mena said. "First he said it was personal. He said it was a reward to him for his previous services to the DINA. Then when I asked him if that meant DINA had paid for the trip, he refused to say."

"He refused you, personally?" asked Scherrer, clearly showing his amazement that an army captain could refuse a general.

Mena's jaw muscles were very tight. "His answer is unacceptable," he said. "Captain Fernández insists that the trip was personal, and yet he also insists that he can say nothing about it without the permission of his superior officer at the time, General Contreras."

"But Captain Fernández is attached to CNI now, isn't he?" pressed Scherrer.

"Yes," said Mena.

"Doesn't that mean that you are his commanding officer and not General Contreras?"

"Yes, it does," Mena acknowledged.

"Well, correct me if I'm wrong, General," said Scherrer, "but as I understand the rules of the Chilean military, an officer owes his allegiance to his current commanding officer, not to his previous ones. No army could operate on such a principle of organization. Am I correct?"

"That is correct," Mena said tersely. "That is why his answer is unacceptable. What I am telling you is that Captain Fernández maintains a fierce loyalty to General Contreras that is not in accord with military practice."

General Mena declared that he and his colleagues had much work to do with Fernández, for obvious reasons. With that, he invited the Americans to return the next morning.

"Very well, General," said Scherrer. "But before I go, I want to show you some evidence I promised last Thursday. Special Agent Cornick has brought it down from Washington with him. It's the material from the security firm in Fort Lauderdale relating to Townley, who, as you know, is the main focus of our attention."

On the coffee table in front of him Scherrer spread the records showing Kenneth Enyart's purchases from AID, his phone calls, and the times of his visits. He retrieved these after the Chileans had perused them. Then Cornick handed General Mena a copy of the controversial Montero letter. Scherrer commented soothingly that the signature bore no resemblance to Montero's own but that the forgery must be investigated. Finally, Cornick gave Mena an extra letter that had been recovered from Holcomb. This one was signed by a José Fernández on official stationery. It authorized Kenneth Enyart to make inquiries about triangularization equipment, which could be used to trace the origin of radio transmissions.

General Mena accepted the two letters and ushered his guests to the door. None of the Americans knew when they left that José Fernández was the operational alias of President Pinochet's own chief of telecommunications. Scherrer had his photograph in the batch from those DINA officers who accompanied Pinochet to Washington, but he did not recognize the name.

When the car pulled up to the embassy, a crowd was gathered outside. A number of people cried, *"Fiscal! Fiscal!"* It was the Spanish word for prosecutor. Reporters with notebooks surrounded the bearded *fiscal* who had come down from America. Santiago was buzzing with the news, and so many reporters had pestered the embassy and the Chilean government for confirmation of the rumors that Landau had seen fit to announce Propper's arrival officially.

Propper pushed his way inside, but he could not resist tossing a wave or two back toward the throng.

"Oh, my Lord!" cried Cornick. "Now we're in for it. With Gene's ego, he'll quit his job and move down here."

Upstairs at the embassy, Landau asked Scherrer to step into his office. The ambassador reached into his desk and pulled out two Paraguayan passports. "I think you better have these," he said. "After hearing the evidence Carter brought down last night, I decided to go through the boxes I still have packed up from Paraguay. And I found the original Williams and Romeral passports. I wasn't even sure I still had them. You can see that the photographs have been ripped out. That's how they were when I got them back to cancel the visa stamps."

Scherrer stared at the actual fraudulent passports that Propper had made so much of in the Letters Rogatory, and he discussed an idea that he had been developing with Propper and Cornick. Suppose that Contreras had sent "Williams and Romeral" through Paraguay as cover for a mission to the United States but the mission had been aborted because of troubles in Paraguay. And suppose Contreras got word from the Paraguayan government that the U.S. visas were no good and that Landau wanted the passports back. In that situation, asked Scherrer, was there any way for Contreras to have known that the passports had already been photographed inside the United States embassy in Paraguay? No, Landau replied. Contreras would have to believe that the only copies of the photographs were in the passports themselves.

In that case, Scherrer continued, it would make sense for Contreras to tear out the photographs before sending the Paraguayan passports back to the Paraguayans for delivery to Landau. By doing so, Contreras would protect the faces of his agents Townley and Fernández. He would think the Americans had no record of the faces, and all that would remain of the operational mix-up in Paraguay would be the names Williams and Romeral. To "cleanse" these names, Scherrer suggested, Contreras might then have sent two different men to the United States under the names Williams and

Romeral on an innocuous mission. That way, if the American investigators ever raised questions about the mysterious episode in Paraguay and the agents named Williams and Romeral, Contreras could produce the two innocent men.

"That's what they're trying to do now, I think," said Scherrer. "And it would have worked perfectly except that we have the photographs from Paraguay. They must be beating their brains out trying to figure out how we got them."

"A lot of people think the CIA knows everything," Landau said with a smile. "We should play on that." He told Scherrer he had never dreamed that the bizarre incident in Paraguay might have been part of a murder plot. He could scarcely believe it. Now the ambassador was beginning to accept the possibility that the Chileans and the Paraguayans had tried by deception to involve him personally in a heinous crime. He told Scherrer that he was determined to get at Townley and discover the truth.

That night, Scherrer showed the phantom passports to Cornick and Propper. The three investigators kept staring at the mystery documents—especially at the page from which the Juan Williams photograph had been torn. Scherrer told his colleagues of his impression that Ambassador Landau would throw the full weight of his authority behind the investigation, along with a strong personal commitment. "We're lucky as hell," said Scherrer. "He doesn't really have to do anything except report what we're doing to the State Department. Most ambassadors would try to stay out of something like this."

A crowd of reporters and curious citizens lined the approach to CNI headquarters on Belgrado Street the next morning when the embassy car arrived bearing Cornick, Scherrer, and the *fiscal*. Straining against the security guards, they shouted questions and greetings to Propper. The Americans realized that the Chilean government was no doubt unhappy about such glaring advertisements of the location of its secret service. But the regime was helpless —temporarily, anyway. The reporters were turning out in droves to cover the big international story, acting as though they were on a long-overdue holiday.

In Mena's office, Scherrer apologized for the commotion as he and his colleagues took their seats on the sofa. The Chileans, except for Mena, sat in chairs on the opposite side of the coffee table. Mena himself stood behind them. "I have something very important to tell you," he announced, in a manner that hushed the room. "It is very secret for now, but this afternoon the news will shake Chile. Last night, the President of the Republic summoned General Contreras for a private audience. Based on the information supplied by you concerning the activities of Townley in the United States and the purchase of equipment at the company in Florida, the President questioned General Contreras and found that General Contreras lied on several occasions. Therefore, the President demanded Contreras's immediate resignation from the army. The public announcement today will say he voluntarily resigned, but I can tell you he was fired."

There was silence. Then Scherrer turned to Mena. "Can you tell us specifically how he lied? It might be relevant to our investigation."

Mena shook his head in the negative, smiling slyly. "It is enough to say Contreras is fired," he said. "Excuse me, gentlemen. I have urgent business to attend to."

Mena walked out of the room, leaving shock waves. His Chilean colleagues then commented almost reverently on what a historic moment this was for Chile, given Contreras's enormous power. They said it was a sign of the beneficial impact the American investigation was having on Chile.

Propper waited for as many translations as he could stand and then said, "That's terrific, but where is Townley? He's the one we're interested in."

Miguel Schweitzer, the Chilean special counsel, looked at Propper in mild disappointment. "The search for Mr. Townley continues," he said. "I can assure you. But let me explain that, from a Chilean point of view, General Contreras is a thousand times more important than Townley, who is a minor functionary."

"Townley is more important to me," said Propper. "You invited me down here to see the progress of the investigation, and Townley is the reason I came. Not Contreras."

"I understand that, Mr. Propper," Montero said, "but surely you can appreciate that we have been overtaken by events here. We are now involved in a political crisis for the entire country."

"I can see that, Mr. Montero," said Propper. "But I am only interested in a criminal investigation, as I assured you in Washington. I can't concern myself with Chilean politics or American politics, and I certainly can't help it if Contreras lied to the President. I only want to see Townley."

General Mena returned to the room just as Scherrer mentioned that he had been investigating Consultec and the other Chilean companies mentioned in the Montero letter to AID. Montero and Mena looked at each other as though holding a visual debate. "You need not bother with that investigation," Mena said grimly. "We can confirm for you that those companies are cover firms for DINA, and now for CNI. They are still active, as far as we can tell. We've just checked the records."

"That is true," said Montero.

"I see," said Scherrer, trying not to show satisfaction. "Well, that tends to confirm that Townley was carrying out sensitive overseas missions for DINA. If not, how would he know the names of those firms?"

"Yes, Townley worked for DINA," said Mena. "And we will find him for you. But let me tell you something. Right now, we are after much higher game. I can tell you confidentially that General Contreras will be interviewed by another army general this afternoon and tonight and as long as it takes to get answers." Mena added that Contreras had burned or stolen many critical items from the CNI files, and that this only made the charges against the former general all the more serious.

"That is very interesting, General," said Scherrer. "But I must emphasize that *Fiscal* Propper's first objective in Santiago is to question Townley. Perhaps General Contreras can tell you where he is. I must tell you that my sources have said that officers within CNI *already* know where Townley is, General. They say CNI has known all along."

"That is a lie," General Mena said testily. "You said 'sources,' Mr. Scherrer. Are you saying that you are operating informants in Santiago against the CNI?"

Scherrer hesitated, knowing that this question raised the treacherous subject that had plagued him throughout the investigation. If he, a foreigner in Chile, acknowledged that he was directing informants to make inquiries within the Chilean security service, he would be admitting to classical espionage. Mena would be perfectly justified in placing him under arrest. "No, General," Scherrer replied. "I do not have informants here."

"Then how do you know anything about where Townley is?" Mena pressed.

"I have friends," said Scherrer. "I don't have informants, I have friends."

Mena studied Scherrer coldly before remarking that Scherrer's "friends" must be lying. He said abruptly that he had urgent business and invited the Americans back that afternoon.

At the embassy Ambassador Landau listened to the reports and said, "I think they're getting scared. They're going to try to sell Contreras's firing as a tremendous conciliatory gesture on their part. We've got to say, 'So what? What's that supposed to do for us?' "

The three investigators went back to CNI that afternoon and hammered away on the theme that Townley must be located to answer the Letters Rogatory. The Chileans kept saying that Chile was a big country and that the search was difficult. And they grew increasingly annoyed. They said they were moving on many fronts at once. For instance, they said, they were preparing to deliver Williams and Romeral to the Supreme Court judge soon to answer the Letters Rogatory.

"Which Williams?" asked Scherrer. "Which Romeral?"

"The ones who went to Miami," said Schweitzer. "Captain Riveros and Captain Mosqueira."

"That is unacceptable," Propper declared flatly.

"Those are the wrong ones," said Cornick. "They're not the ones in the pictures. We want Townley and Fernández."

"We are doing our best to comply with your numerous requests," Schweitzer replied tightly. "You have asked our government to produce men who went to Miami under those names, and now we are about to do it."

"That's great," said Propper. "Let's question them, too, but as far as I'm concerned, the Letters Rogatory won't be complied with until you produce the men in the pictures. We included those pictures for a reason."

"I'm sure you did," said Schweitzer, straining to be polite. "But the language of your document specifically asks the Chilean court to produce the two men who went to Miami on August 22, 1976. Is that not correct?"

"Yes, that's correct," sputtered Propper, "but you know good and well . . ."

". . . And that's what we're doing," Schweitzer declared. "No one can deny it."

"Technically, you're half correct," fumed Propper. "But we also asked the court to question the men in the photographs we sent down. We're still interested in Townley and Fernández. If you produce only those other two guys, it will be a fraud."

"That's not true," said Schweitzer. "Speaking for the government of Chile, I must officially protest your words. We will produce the men you asked for. We will fulfill both the spirit and the letter of your judicial request."

"It doesn't sound like it," Propper replied angrily. "Look, I want to warn you right now. Those two ringers don't have any connection to the Letters Rogatory as far as I'm concerned. We'd like to question them informally, but it won't have anything to do with cooperation on the Letters. You do what you want with them. But I'm telling you right now that if those guys show up in court as Williams and Romeral, I am going to instruct our Chilean attorney to stick the Paraguay photographs in their faces right there in the courtroom and say, 'Is this you?' And then he's gonna walk right out of there and denounce the whole thing as a fraud. That's what's going to happen. I hope you don't elect to do that."

While Propper, Scherrer, and Schweitzer were arguing over the identities of Williams and Romeral, Major Eduardo Iturriaga, one of Michael Townley's closest friends from DINA, stepped outside CNI headquarters and made a phone call that would have enlightened both the American and Chilean negotiators. He dialed the Townley home and, by code, got Townley to come to the phone. "Another search party is leaving," Iturriaga said. "It'll be there in about an hour."

"Shit," said Townley. "Does General Contreras know?"

"He knows," said Iturriaga.

"He's got to *do* something," said Townley. "I've got to move. This won't work anymore."

"Why not?"

"Because I think they've got the house staked out," said Townley. "And they've probably got the phone tapped."

"Those are reporters around there," said Iturriaga. "And I'd know about a tap. Don't get paranoid."

"I'm *not* paranoid," snapped Townley. "There are all kinds of people around here and some of them aren't reporters."

"How do you know?"

"I have ways," said Townley. "Anyway, I refuse to climb that hill again. You tell my general that I'll just surrender to Mena's men the next time they come. I'm tired of this."

"Wait a minute," said Iturriaga. "I'll call you back."

Townley waited. Long ago he had installed two water storage tanks on the hillside above his house to increase the water pressure, which was otherwise quite low. For two weeks, since the Americans had begun to close in, Townley had climbed into a water tank to avoid CNI search parties. Iturriaga and other Contreras loyalists inside CNI always warned him. Townley was frightened, but until recently he had almost enjoyed the game. He had his gadgets, his friends, and his wits. It was easy to outsmart the reporters and the CNI foot soldiers—so easy in fact that Townley had often thrown on a scarf and a motorcycle helmet and dropped in at the homes of friends, who were always astonished to see how casual Townley was despite the manhunt.

Now it was not so easy. Iturriaga called back. "Don't worry," he whispered. "I'm going with the search party. I'll lead it. You stay in the house and hide in the closet of your bedroom. Okay? I'll make sure they don't find you."

"All right, but that won't help next time," said Townley. "The general has got to do something."

Iturriaga hung up. Not long afterward, he rapped sharply at the door. Townley's wife, Mariana Callejas, began screaming at the CNI search party as the men filed in behind Iturriaga and began searching the house. She denounced them for frightening the children and for refusing to believe her when she said Townley was not there.

Iturriaga stomped into the master bedroom and flung open the closet door. He winked at Townley. Townley winked back. Iturriaga slammed the closet door and began poking around under the bed. Then he took up a station just outside the bedroom door and shouted, "He's not in here! Hurry up!" And when the men filed out, they endured another volley of abuse from the lady of the house.

Ambassador Landau interrupted the strategy session as soon as he heard that the Chileans planned to bring the "ringers" to court to answer the Letters Rogatory, in spite of Propper's warning. "Things are reaching the crisis point," he said. "I think I'd better pay a call on the foreign minister myself." He instructed his secretary to seek an immediate appointment.

That same afternoon, March 22, Landau walked alone into the Foreign Ministry and told Foreign Minister Carvajal* that Mena had admitted that Townley was a DINA agent, and that Townley had been in contact with the Cuban exiles believed to have committed the murders. He said it was "inconceivable" that the Chilean government with all its resources could not locate an American like Townley in Santiago. If Townley was not produced by the next day, Landau declared, *Fiscal* Propper would leave Chile and tell the President of the

*See above, page 64.

United States that his mission was a failure because of lack of cooperation from the Chilean government.

Landau also warned the foreign minister that it would be a "sham" and a "mockery of justice" if the Chileans tried to claim that they were meeting their legal obligations by sending Riveros and Mosqueira to answer the Letters Rogatory. He told Carvajal that the United States would have no alternative but to denounce the sham publicly. He said that such a course of action would not be in the best interests of either government.

Returning to the American embassy, Landau reflected that Carvajal's information had seemed "about three days behind the power curve." By bringing him up to date, Landau had made certain that the Chilean government's leadership was aware of the risks ahead.

Propper was surprised to hear about one part of Landau's threat. "Excuse me, Mr. Ambassador," he said. "I hope that doesn't mean you expect me to talk to President Carter. I've never met him, and I doubt that I could get in."

"You could if you had to," said Landau. "Besides, the point is simply that you and the Justice Department will be unhappy with Chile if they don't produce Townley. And you'll say so publicly. That's all that's necessary."

"I know," Propper said painfully. "But Justice would never say that. They almost never make public statements. Besides, even if they did, they'd never say I'm unhappy with Chile. How can I be unhappy with Chile? I'm just an Assistant United States Attorney."

"That may be what you are up there," said Landau. "But down here you're the *fiscal*. We have to play on that and build it. I have deliberately referred to your visit as the 'Propper mission' in all my dealings with the Chileans. We want to maximize the impact on them if you leave and say you're unhappy. That's a dignified, effective protest. It doesn't give away any evidence and it doesn't call them any names, but it will put the pressure on them."

"That's good," said Propper. "But the State Department has got to say it. You people have press briefings every day."

"Don't worry," said Landau. "We'll get it out in the appropriate way."

That evening, the Americans waited to hear what happened at the Chilean court, where the Chileans were to bring "Juan Williams" and "Alejandro Romeral" before Judge Juana González. There was suspense on two questions: would the Chileans follow through on their plan to produce the wrong people? And if so, would Judge González accept them as legitimate and thereby place the authority of her court behind the ruse?

As it turned out, the Chileans made their attempt in spite of all the warnings. Riveros and Mosqueira walked into court. But Judge González refused to accept them. On a motion from Alfredo Etcheberry, the Chilean counsel for the United States, she dismissed the two officers on the ground that they were not the ones desired by the United States for questioning. She called on the Chilean government to produce Townley and Fernández. The hearing ended in a standoff.

The following morning, Foreign Minister Carvajal welcomed Landau, Propper, Etcheberry, and Deputy Chief of Mission Tom Boyatt to his office. Mena, Montero, and Schweitzer were there on behalf of the Chilean government. After amenities, the foreign minister said he had invited the parties because of complaints he had received from the Americans that Chile was not cooperating in the Letelier investigation. He asked Mena to present the Chilean side.

Mena gave a prepared speech, stating that Chile had been very cooperative thus far. It had produced three of the four men who had used the names Williams and Romeral. The Chilean investigation had been rigorous enough to have repercussions at the highest levels of the Chilean security establishment. And Mena was confident that his men would locate Townley sooner or later. He said Santiago was a big city. He said he had just learned the previous day that Townley had hired a Chilean lawyer.

When Mena finished, Carvajal recognized Landau, and Landau turned to Propper. "Go ahead," he said. "Tell them why you're unhappy. I'll translate for you."

Propper began to address the foreign minister in what he thought were appropriate tones. Ambassador Landau translated a few sentences, but appeared to grow more agitated. Finally, he turned to Propper again and said, "That's not it. You're being too diplomatic. You've got to tell the foreign minister how bad it really is." Propper was stunned.

Landau addressed the foreign minister on his own, in Spanish, while Boyatt translated simultaneously for Propper, in a whisper. "Excuse me, Mr. Foreign Minister," said Landau. "We have a very serious situation on our hands, and I want to make sure you have the force of our views. Frankly, I'm very annoyed by what I've just heard. It's inconceivable to me that the Chilean government has not been able to find Mr. Townley or even learn about his lawyer during the week Mr. Propper has been here. Inconceivable. Half of Santiago knows. They seem to be giving press interviews all the time. And for goodness' sake, I can't imagine that a six-foot two-inch *gringo* would be that difficult to find.

"Yesterday your people told us that Townley's wife had not been interviewed because she has a privilege under Chilean law. Mr. Etcheberry tells me that's not true. Your people also said that the *carabineros* were out looking for Mr. Townley, but I've asked my people to stop *carabinero* officers on the street and ask them, and none of the *carabineros* seem to know anything about it. There are no rewards, no announcements or pictures in the newspapers. Frankly, I don't believe your people are trying very hard. And we have Chileans calling up the embassy to say that your security people already have Townley in custody. I'm afraid this is a pattern of conduct, Mr. Foreign Minister, that makes it impossible for you and me to do our jobs. Just last week, you relied on your security people and told me that Captain Fernández had never been to the United States, which was false. I regret that, and I know you do, too. But these things keep happening . . ."

Propper could tell from the faces in front of him that the ambassador's speech was having a powerful effect. Boyatt was moved to comment. "He's sticking the knife in," he whispered.

Landau was still going: ". . . Mr. Foreign Minister, you and I are charged with keeping the relations between our two countries on a cordial and dignified level. We must assert ourselves now, because the FBI and the CNI are fighting with each other. Their squabble has already turned a criminal case into a matter of unfortunate publicity, and it will get worse if we don't take action. I'm afraid Mr. Propper here is going to have to go back to the United States tonight and tell the President that Chile has not cooperated. That Chile has deceived us about efforts to locate Mr. Townley. And I'm afraid his report might wind up having serious repercussions on our diplomatic relations. Which is a tragedy. To me, it would be a tragedy if you and I allow our relations to be dragged down by policemen who are either incompetent or deliberately deceitful . . ."

"Now he's twisting the knife," Boyatt whispered in awe. "He's really twisting it."

As evidence of that fact, Propper saw that General Mena's face was turning bright red. He thought it might explode with anger.

When Landau finished, the foreign minister asked him to stay a minute and excused everyone else. Montero overtook Propper at the door and drew him aside in the corridor. "Don't worry," he said in English. "You will have him within three days. Please don't say or do anything rash when you get back to the United States."

Propper's eyes opened wide. "Then you have him?" he asked. "He's not missing?"

"You will have him within three days," Montero repeated. "I guarantee it."

On the way out, Etcheberry remarked that only the American ambassador could have gotten away with what Landau had said.

That evening, after a flurry of last-minute messages, the three investigators drove through Santiago to pick up their belongings—and Al Seddon. Along some city blocks, crowds turned to wave toward "the *fiscal*'s car," as it was known. Propper, who made a point of sitting next to the window, flashed a "V" sign through the dark tinted glass. Cornick teased Propper for behaving like Winston Churchill.

Propper looked indignant. "You heard the ambassador," he said. "My public image is vital to the case."

"Don't give me that," scoffed Cornick. "You love it."

"That may be"—Propper smiled—"but it helps the case."

Once Seddon, Cornick, and Propper had departed for Washington, Scherrer flew back to Buenos Aires to spend Easter Sunday with his family. On Tuesday, he received a call in his office at the embassy from a man who identified himself only as "Gerónimo." It was Pantoja, calling from Santiago.

"Bob," said Pantoja, "you know the man you're looking for? You better come back here quick. We are about to produce him."

"Are you sure?" asked Scherrer.

"Positive," said Pantoja.

"Sure enough that the *fiscal* should come down, too?"

"Absolutely," said Pantoja. "You should all come now."

"Okay," said Scherrer. "But I want to warn you: the *fiscal* is already pissed. If he comes all the way back down to Chile and the man is not produced, I don't want to be responsible for his reaction. It might affect our entire relationship with Chile."

"He will be there," said Pantoja. "I guarantee it."

"Do you have him in custody?"

"Don't worry. We are taking care of him," Pantoja cryptically replied.

Scherrer's phone call created instant pandemonium in Washington. Propper wanted to leave that very night. The arrest warrant wasn't ready. Press people were all over the office. Silbert wanted a briefing. Barcella wanted to go, too. Propper said he was sorry but that would be impossible because of the Seddon precedent. Airplane tickets and visas were secured within hours. Meanwhile, Barcella dictated a warrant for Townley's arrest as a material witness in the Letelier murder. Under pressure, he and Propper had decided that they did not have enough to support a warrant on any criminal charge related to the murder.

Even the material-witness warrant made Cornick nervous. He balked at signing the required affidavit. "Larry, you'll get me thrown in jail!" he protested.

"What's the matter?" asked Barcella. "Everything in there is true."

"Well, kind of." Cornick grimaced. "But it leaves a lot of implications."

"Carter, we don't have time for this," said Barcella. "Your plane is leaving. We've got to go sign the thing in front of the judge. I'll get you out of jail."

Propper and Cornick left for Chile that night, but news of the trip leaked even faster. As a result, the *fiscal* waded into a throng of fifty radio, television, and newspaper reporters when he stepped off the plane the next morning, March 29. It took him ten minutes to push through to the embassy car. On the way, Propper answered only one of the questions thrown at him. When a reporter asked how long he would remain in Chile, Propper said, "As long as it takes."

At the embassy, Ambassador Landau reported that the Chileans had come up with a new obstruction. Pinochet's special military prosecutor, General Héctor Orozco, had gotten into the act and was secretly questioning Townley even as Propper stepped off the plane. Townley would be "unavailable" for several more days, but in the meantime, the Chilean government had consented to produce Captain Fernández for an interview.

On the evening of March 30, Propper, Cornick, Scherrer, and an American translator sat alone in Colonel Pantoja's office with the man who owned the face that the Americans had known for so long as the Romeral who went to Paraguay. Scherrer began by advising Fernández of his rights. Fernández waived them. Seeming nervous but tightly competent, he admitted going to Paraguay on a DINA mission with another DINA agent, whom Fernández said he knew vaguely as Mike. He said he had received his orders for the Paraguay mission directly from Contreras, and that the purpose of the mission had been to contact CIA Deputy Director Vernon Walters in Washington to receive intelligence beneficial to Chile. Fernández said the arrangements for his mission to Paraguay had been made by DINA's director of operations, Colonel Pedro Espinoza. (This was a DINA name the Americans had never heard.)

Fernández admitted making a subsequent trip to Washington and to New York in the summer of 1976, accompanying a female DINA agent who had a mission to perform. He said he was never informed what the nature of her mission was, and because of intelligence protocol, he had never asked. Fernández said he had amused himself on sightseeing trips and had spent most of his time visiting relatives until leaving from Kennedy Airport on September 9. He said he remembered leaving quite well, because, as he was waiting to board his return flight, he saw Mike deplaning from Santiago, walking down the international concourse in the middle of a large group of *rabinos*.

At this point in the monologue, Cornick jumped to his feet. "Wait a minute! What's going on?" he cried in Spanish. Then he turned to Scherrer and said in English, "Bob, what the hell does he think he's trying to pull? Saying this guy Mike got off the plane in a bunch of rabbits, for God's sake."

Scherrer held his forehead with one hand. "Carter, *rabinos* means 'rabbis,' not 'rabbits.' He said Mike got off the plane with a group of Jewish rabbis."

Cornick turned red. "Excuse me," he said. "I knew there was something wrong."

A sober atmosphere was re-established, after which Fernández recalled that he had said hello to Mike in passing, and that Mike had known the personnel of LAN Chile Airlines well enough to have them upgrade Fernández's ticket to first-class status. Fernández said he remembered thanking him for that and engaging in idle conversation before his flight's departure. But he insisted that there was no talk then or ever of Letelier.

At the embassy, Scherrer and Cornick dictated a report on the Fernández interview. They studied the transcript and discovered numerous small contradictions in his story, but they knew they didn't have enough independent evidence against Fernández to force him to be more candid. Their target, as always, was Townley. The Chileans were stalling again, even after giving solemn pledges to produce Townley for an interview. Ambassador Landau was saying that the case was about to blow open into the ugliest of public scandals.

Under such pressure, the Chileans revealed that matters on their side were even more tangled than the Americans expected. After another shouting match the next day, March 31, General Mena drew Scherrer off to the side. "I want you to know something," he said softly. "We are at a critical stage right now, and I am a little bit worried about Townley's security."

Scherrer blinked at Mena. This was an extraordinary admission. "You are?" he said. "I thought you said you have him under guard now."

"We do," said Mena. "We have a triple guard assigned to his house and his person night and day. But I must be honest. There are people who want to see him dead. If something were to happen to him, it would bring extreme embarrassment to the Chilean government and to me personally."

"That's true," said Scherrer. "Then why don't you take him into custody? He can't be safe as long as he's loose in his house."

General Mena sighed. "I can't," he said. "There are no charges pending against him."

Scherrer studied Mena. He was inclined to believe him, although it was jarring to hear the head of the mighty CNI say that legal niceties stood in the way of an arrest. Scherrer thought the hidden power of General Contreras might be protecting Townley's civil liberties. "What about the passport charges?" he asked. "Couldn't you arrest him on those?"

"No," said Mena. "If he and Fernández acted under orders from Contreras, then under Chilean law Contreras is responsible. I'm afraid I can't do anything without your help."

"My help?" said Scherrer.

"Yes," said Mena. "Couldn't you get a warrant for his arrest in the United States? I might be able to hold him on that."

Scherrer responded positively, but he did not tell Mena he already had the warrant.

Propper was in favor of using the warrant immediately. The original plan had been to save it until all possible information could be gleaned in Chile and then to spring it after the Letters Rogatory hearings. Propper wanted to escalate his demands. He thought Townley's Letters Rogatory hearing would be unproductive since the witnesses had already practiced their responses. It appeared that the Americans would get little or no information out of Townley on Chilean soil.

The Americans returned to CNI headquarters that same afternoon and presented Mena with a copy of the warrant. Scherrer formally requested that Townley be expelled from Chilean territory so that the arrest warrant could be served on him in the United States. Propper, growing ever more fearful that the entire investigation might soon be snuffed out along with Townley's life, said that he would be pleased if the expulsion could take place that very night.

The Chileans seemed surprised by the instant production of the American warrant. Montero said it would be impossible to expel Townley so quickly, because the Chilean government needed him to fulfill its legal obligations under the Letters Rogatory. Propper said these could be accomplished in less than a day. Scherrer added that he need not remind Montero how rapidly and efficiently the Chilean government had acted to expel foreigners in the past. Montero replied that Townley was different. He was married to a Chilean. He was connected to the Chilean intelligence service. His case was connected to that of Fernández. Montero said this was all very sudden.

"Wait a minute," said Propper. "The fundamental fact is that this man is an American. He's wanted in the United States. He's in this country illegally on a false American passport. So he's ours. The other issues are irrelevant. You give us Townley, and then we'll discuss everything else without all this pressure."

The argument went on until nearly eight o'clock that evening, but in the end Mena and Montero agreed. Townley would go to the United States as soon as possible. Hasty phone calls were made. Mena sent out an order commanding Townley to appear the next morning, on Saturday, to answer the Letters Rogatory. The judge would come to CNI headquarters to take the testimony, because Chilean intelligence officers were by law exempt from appearing in court. By act as well as word, this would be an admission of Townley's official status in Chile.

Ambassador Landau called Montero several times that night. He thanked the undersecretary for Chile's cooperation. He also urged repeatedly that Townley be placed under arrest so that nothing tragic could happen at the last minute.

The Americans wondered what Townley knew. Through all the frustration of March, they had consoled themselves with the thought that Townley must be vital to the case because the Chilean government was so reluctant to produce him. Now that Townley was going to be handed over alive, the Americans began to have doubts. Why would the Chileans give him up? Might Townley actually be a mere mechanic and technician for DINA, in keeping with the reports coming out of Miami that he had worked there as an AAMCO transmission repairman?

Despite such second guessing, Propper could not suppress a rush of optimism. On Saturday and Sunday, both Townley and Fernández were whisked through the Letters Rogatory hearings. There were signs of great haste. Scherrer and Cornick drafted cables to FBI headquarters, warning that they might be bringing Townley into Miami any day and that Cuban exiles might try to kill him anywhere in the United States. They suggested that Townley be incarcerated in a military base instead of a jail. The base would provide greater security, they said, and it might also create an impression that Townley was cooperating with the government, which might raise the panic level among his Cuban contacts. A more intense psychological warfare was starting.

Propper celebrated these events by inviting the steadiest of his Chilean female admirers to a clandestine tryst at the ambassador's residence. In light of Propper's position and diplomatic protocol, the couple was obliged to avoid the guards stationed outside the residence. The woman sneaked alone on foot across a golf course and up a hillside to the wall that surrounded the grounds. From the inside, Propper helped her scale the wall and led her inside the residence through the front door.

The optimism vanished the next day, April 3. Scherrer, Cornick, and Propper went to CNI headquarters for what they thought would be a last meeting to arrange the details of Townley's departure that night. Instead, Miguel Schweitzer said problems had arisen that would delay Townley's expulsion for as long as two weeks.

"Two weeks!" cried Propper. "That is absolutely unacceptable. I'm not waiting two weeks. Your own people have said Townley might not survive from day to day, so how can you talk about delaying two weeks?"

Montero interrupted in a conciliatory tone. "You have to understand something, Mr. Propper," he said. "The President understands and our government understands that we will run worldwide propaganda risks if we hastily turn Townley over to you. The Marxists of the world will criticize Chile for bowing to the forces of United States imperialism."

"What's that got to do with anything?" asked Propper. "Why should you care what the Marxists say if you're doing the right thing?"

The meeting ended in a stalemate. The news alarmed Ambassador
Landau, who interpreted it to mean that Contreras was fighting
against the decision to expel Townley. The focus of the pressure was
Pinochet.

That night President Pinochet held a press conference at which he
repeated his assertion that no one within the government of Chile
bore any responsibility in the Letelier case. He also declared that the
resignation of General Contreras had nothing to do with the case. At
the same time, Pinochet announced that some four hundred political
prisoners would be freed soon. This news appeared the next morning
in Santiago, along with leaked stories about how Chile had complied
with the American Letters Rogatory and how the two Chilean agents
had had nothing to do with the assassination. Alongside these stories, there were others in which Townley's lawyer attacked Propper's visit as an insult to Chilean sovereignty and the rule of law. He
called on Chileans to grant Townley immediate Chilean citizenship in
order to better resist the intrusions by the American bullies.

Landau, sensing that the currents were shifting rapidly against
American interests, went to the Foreign Ministry twice that day and
said that the investigation could not be contained within legal channels for two more weeks. The press was building up the political confrontation. Townley's lawyer and other prominent Chileans were
attacking the motives of the United States. Before the end of two
weeks, he warned, the State Department would be obliged to fight
back with dramatic diplomatic actions that might include damaging
revelations about Chilean performance in the investigation.

Once in the morning and again in the afternoon, Landau listed all
the benefits that would accrue to Chile upon Townley's immediate
expulsion—and all the dangers that would follow delay. In the end,
the ambassador won from Mena and the Foreign Ministry a promise
that Townley would be expelled immediately upon American acceptance of certain conditions.

After Propper reached a tentative agreement that night on the
conditions for Townley's expulsion, he and Landau drafted a cable to
the State Department to spell them out: first, Deputy Secretary Warren Christopher must agree to meet with Montero and Schweitzer
the next day, in Washington; second, the State Department must announce publicly that Chile had cooperated with the investigation;
third, the U.S. Justice Department must agree that any information
derived from Townley or Chilean sources would be used only for
criminal prosecutions and not for political propaganda. Unless these

conditions were met, said the cable, the Chileans would refuse to expel Townley. Landau reported that he believed a statement of cooperation could be shaped to fit the truth, within the bounds of diplomatic license. Propper thought he could negotiate an acceptable agreement for the Justice Department. He rushed to the airport to join Montero and Schweitzer for the long flight back to Washington, hoping to settle the wording of the agreements on the airplane.

Landau's forceful intervention seemed to have restored the promise of a quick expulsion, but no one, including the Chileans, seemed to be sure what would happen next.

The next day, Propper and Barcella marched into Earl Silbert's office for a briefing. "You look terrible," Silbert told Propper.

"I ate the salad down there," said Propper. "Mrs. Landau said I shouldn't have done it, and I guess she was right."

"He's so corked up he doesn't even know he's sick, Earl," said Barcella. "The Chileans are going to give us Townley."

"It looks like tomorrow," said Propper. "A couple of the Chileans flew up with me to work out the details. Larry and I have to go over to State this afternoon to meet with Christopher. You want to come?"

"Do you need me?" asked Silbert.

"No," said Propper.

"Then tell me when it's over," said Silbert.

At the end of the next day's negotiations at the State Department, the two sides emerged from Christopher's conference room with draft copies of two statements. At the last minute, the Chileans had insisted that the State Department press release be modified to say that the Chileans had cooperated "efficiently" as well as "fully." In return, Propper and Barcella had insisted on an addendum: "We expect this cooperation to continue."

The second document was the draft of an agreement between Earl Silbert and Enrique Montero. Silbert, on behalf of the United States, agreed to provide Chilean representatives access to Townley in the United States. He also agreed not to use information obtained from Townley or other Chilean nationals for purposes other than criminal prosecutions. Montero, for Chile, agreed to send to the United States any information the government of Chile subsequently obtained relating to the Letelier assassination.

Propper slept fitfully that night. The next morning, he and Barcella took the draft of the "Silbert/Montero Agreement" to Silbert, who made a few modifications.

"I've got only one question for you guys," said Silbert. "Where do I get the authority to sign a treaty with a foreign government?"

"I was hoping you weren't going to ask that," said Propper.

"Yeah, well, I just asked it," said Silbert.

"It's really not a treaty, Earl," said Barcella. "It's more like an agreement, an understanding. It's not really a treaty."

"You call it anything you want," said Silbert. "But I'm signing an agreement with a foreign country as a representative of the United States. That sounds like a treaty to me, and I'm just the U.S. attorney for the District of Columbia."

"Yeah, but the Chileans don't know that, Earl," said Propper.

Silbert looked quite displeased. "Look, you two," he said. "I know you're under a lot of pressure, but I'm not signing this thing until you find out what authority I have."

Propper and Barcella rushed off to consult Frank Willis at the State Department. Willis told them that Silbert was correct—the agreement was technically a treaty—but that Silbert or any other U.S. official could sign it legally, provided that he submit the document to the U.S. Senate within sixty days. This news failed to reassure Silbert, who asked the prosecutors to seek further approval at the Justice Department.

Bob Keuch soon heard the story. Propper said the agreement was perfect—it would get Townley without giving up anything. Under the agreement, Silbert would not block access to Townley, but Townley or his lawyer could refuse to see the Chileans. Silbert was agreeing not to use Chilean information for anything other than prosecution, but prosecution was Silbert's only authorized function in the first place. "Earl's agreeing not to be a propagandist," said Propper. "That's it. We're not giving up a thing." Keuch agreed.

Propper and Barcella called Schweitzer and Montero at the Chilean embassy to say that Silbert was ready at any time that day for the signing ceremony. The two Chileans replied that there might be a delay. They said there were some problems in Santiago. Propper and Barcella waited fretfully by the phone.

FBI special clerk Sadie Dye was spending another afternoon in the bowels of the State Department, sifting through old visa applications. It had taken weeks to obtain permission for her to conduct a search within the department, and she had been going through stacks of poorly organized records for days. She was after the original papers—not the computer record—because she wanted the attached photograph. Finally, that afternoon, she located a visa application from 1973, in the name of Kenneth Enyart. Dye placed its photograph next to the Juan Williams photograph and the visa application photograph for Michael Townley. They all matched.

Propper and Barcella were still waiting when a call came in from Danny Benítez in Miami. Propper figured Benítez was after gossip about his adventures in Chile, like many others who were calling, but he took the call on the off chance that Benítez might have heard something on the whereabouts of Guillermo Novo, who had been a fugitive now for ten months.

"Hey, Gene," said Benítez. "Did you ever speak to Cornick about getting some pictures of Novo down here?"

"Yeah," said Propper. "Months ago. They didn't give 'em to you?"

"No!" said Benítez. "They keep telling me I can't have them. Some kind of secret."

"Danny, it's not secret!" said Propper. "Novo's a fugitive, for Christ's sake. I'd like to see his picture in the newspapers!"

"I know," said Benítez. "That's what I told them. But they still won't give me Novo's picture."

"Okay, Danny, tell you what, I'll mail you the picture. Forget the Bureau."

"That's great," said Benítez. "He might be down here. I wanna put him in jail. All the terrorists are dopers, anyway. I wanna put 'em in jail." This was Benítez's favorite phrase.

"I'll send you Ross and Paz, too," said Propper. "I've got some extras, and we've heard they just went underground."

Propper put the photographs in an envelope and addressed it to Benítez. Then he resumed the wait. Schweitzer and Montero kept stalling by telephone.

By the middle of the afternoon, Scherrer and Cornick knew something was wrong, too. They had been panicked all day by the Chilean government's last-minute request for a legal document formally requesting Townley's expulsion, and when they took the document to CNI headquarters, they received a further surprise from General Mena. There would be no expulsion that night, said the general, who seemed weary of the pressure. He told Scherrer and Cornick that Townley was being expelled formally, by a legal procedure that allowed him to appeal the order to the Chilean Supreme Court. Townley would have twenty-four hours to do so. This was Friday, so the expulsion could not take place until after the weekend.

This was bad news. Under Chilean law, Townley could have been informally tossed on an airplane without any legal recourse, like Otero and many drug smugglers in the past. Was this delay a trick? All the Americans knew was that the conflicting signals pointed to a continuing struggle over Townley's fate at the highest levels of the Chilean government. Colonel Pantoja told Cornick and Scherrer that the expulsion order had already been signed by the minister of the interior, but there was an ongoing debate. General Mena was still in President Pinochet's office at the Diego Portales Building late that night. As Pantoja spoke, he received a call from Mena. Grim-faced, he took it in another room. Afterward he told Scherrer and Cornick again that it was all right—Townley would be arrested that night.

Michael Townley was planning to go on television on that evening of Friday, April 7, to appeal to the Chilean people not to be taken in by the diabolical plots of the Americans. To make the arrangements, he and his wife drove to his lawyer's office—with an armed CNI guard in the back seat and a carload of guards following behind. Townley found the lawyer quite agitated. The television press conference was off, he said. He also said he had been at CNI headquarters that day and that things were very, very dangerous. Finally, he told Townley that he had received an official summons ordering Townley to appear immediately at Investigations. This might be good, said the lawyer. Investigations wanted to send Townley to a court hearing in the south of Chile. He might be able to hide out there until the Letelier case died down. This had been Contreras's plan all along.

"I don't want to go down there," Townley said quietly. "I don't think I'd get there, and if I did, I wouldn't live very long."

"Mike, you have got to tell Mena everything!" Mariana Townley cried. "He has the power of the law! He's the one dealing with the Americans, not Contreras. If you tell him everything, he'll never send you to America. Never."

"I can't do that," said Townley. "I can't betray my general." He was trapped. To confide in Mena was to betray Contreras. It was also to confess, to give up.

"Don't be stupid," said Mariana. "Contreras has already betrayed you. He has refused to take responsibility for his men, as an honorable general must do."

"I know," said Townley. "But he has not lost anything, either."

"You call this not losing?" said Mariana. "What we're in? Contreras is the one who wants you to go! You're loyal to him, but you're afraid he might repay you by killing you. You call that not losing?"

Townley waffled. The lawyer said they had no choice but to honor the summons to the Investigations Department, to drum up support in the Chilean press, and to help Contreras manipulate things with Pinochet and the courts. He joined the caravan for the drive to the Investigations building. Mariana waited in the car. When Townley did not return after an hour, she ran into the building and tried to find him, without success.

In a panic, she drove home and found twenty CNI men in her living room. One of them introduced himself as General Mena and said he had expected to see Townley himself.

"Why would you expect that, General?" she replied venomously. "Mike went to Investigations as he was supposed to. He *always* follows the instructions of the Chilean authorities. So he is not here. Your men are with him. They're supposed to take him down south."

"I'm afraid not," said Mena. "He is being expelled to the United States."

"I don't believe it," she said.

"We cannot help it," said Mena. "It has to be done."

Mariana Townley flew into a rage. She told Mena that he was a fool, that he was betraying Chile, that he didn't know who Townley really was, that Pinochet and Chilean law would never allow it. Then she ran into her bedroom and returned with a letter.

"I want you to give this to the President," she said sternly. "Mike doesn't know about it, but I have written this letter to make sure you and the President know exactly what Contreras has done and what Mike has done, always under orders, and what we know. I will not allow this to happen to Mike. He is the last person who should be blamed. And believe me, if anything happens to us, proof of the things in this letter will be told to the world!"

Mena took the letter. "Your husband has a right to appeal the expulsion order to the Supreme Court," he said stoically. "Maybe something favorable will happen."

"The judges will do what they're told to do," said Mariana. "You just make sure the President reads that letter tonight. Now give me my DINA car and my driver. You can at least do that. I want to see Mike." By now, Mariana Townley hated Contreras, but she retained the habit of Contreras's partisans, who still used the name DINA. It was an insult to Mena. He granted her demands.

At the Investigations building, she found Townley under guard in a holding room. The lawyer was there. So were Major Iturriaga and a number of Townley's old friends from DINA—who had been disarmed before entering the room. All of them, including Townley, had been shown the expulsion order and were in shock. Several were in tears. The lawyer said he felt betrayed and kept apologizing for having advised Townley to come.

Mariana Townley said, "They cannot send you to the United States. They will not! I won't let them." She spoke with leaden determination.

"I hope not," Townley said vacantly. "But I think they will."

The others sought to reassure him. Rumors were flying. Two parachute regiments loyal to Contreras were supposed to be making preparations to rescue Townley at the airport. Others might come that night to Investigations. Contreras was seeing the President. This was all a show to get rid of the Americans.

None of these seemed to please Townley. "I wonder when they're coming for me," he kept saying. "I will disappear, that's all."

The lawyer said he and Mariana would appear before the Supreme Court early the next morning, on an emergency basis. There would be an uproar in the press. The Chilean courts would protect Townley, once the President was squeezed by the true facts. Mariana told Townley about giving her letter to Mena. This upset him. She said it was for the best and left with an oath that she and the lawyer would succeed in the morning.

In Washington, at nine o'clock that night, Larry Barcella's phone rang. It was Propper. "Larry, Schweitzer just called me," he said. "They want to sign the agreement tonight! He says things are coming apart in Chile."

"That's great, Gene," sighed Barcella. "We waited for them all day, and now that I'm home with my feet up, drinking a Jack Daniel's, of course he wants to sign it!"

"We don't have any choice," said Propper.

"Where's Earl?" asked Barcella.

"I don't know," said Propper. "One of us can sign for him if we have to."

"Which one?" asked Barcella.

"You're closer to the embassy," said Propper. "And you've got the papers."

"Gene, tell me the truth," said Barcella, "are you getting laid at the moment?"

"No," said Propper. "I wish I were. I'm sick. And you're closer."

After a call to Silbert, Barcella was soon driving down Massachusetts Avenue, thinking eerie thoughts about how he was traveling the route Letelier had taken to work and was heading for the forbidding place where he had met "Ilse of the SS" more than a year earlier.

Someone escorted him into the ambassador's office, where the Chilean ambassador greeted him, as did Montero and Schweitzer.

"Things are very confused in Santiago," said Schweitzer. "I just talked to General Mena on his car telephone, and no one is sure what's going to happen."

"Very confused," added Montero. "We have talked to the President several times today, and even he is uncertain about the facts."

"Wait a second," said Barcella. "I thought the whole idea of this agreement is that we know what's going to happen. We're going to get Townley."

"I know that's what we assume," said Schweitzer, somewhat painfully. "We have an agreement with you. But if we can tell them it's already signed, you will have completed your part and we'll have no choice but to turn him over."

"If I sign, do we get Townley?" asked Barcella. "Is it firm? You guys have got a deal with us and with Christopher and the State Department. If there's no Townley, this thing will blow sky high."

"We are aware of that," said Schweitzer. "And we are willing to sign the agreement. We want to tell Santiago it's already signed."

Barcella decided he had nothing to lose. He took the final copies of the agreement out of his briefcase. Montero signed for Chile. Barcella signed Earl Silbert's name and put his own initials beside it in tiny script.

In Chile, the next morning, Scherrer went up to his room after breakfast. The phone rang. An excited DINA officer identified himself and said he was calling on behalf of General Mena. He said Townley was on the way to the airport. Scherrer and Cornick should leave at once. Delay could be fatal.

After a quick, deep breath, Scherrer called Ambassador Landau at home with the news.

"What do you think?" asked Landau.

"I don't trust him," said Scherrer. "They've changed everything. It's an Ecuadorian flight, not a United States carrier. It stops in Ecuador. Chile and Ecuador are very close. They could arrange something so that the Ecuadorian army could take him from us when we stop there."

"Yes, but we better take a gamble on it," said Landau. He barked orders to one of his aides to send a car immediately for Scherrer and

Cornick. Then he spoke again to Scherrer. "If it happens, it happens."

"I don't think we can make it," said Scherrer. "The plane's about to leave, and we haven't even packed or notified the Bureau."

"Forget all that!" cried Landau. "Just leave! I'll talk to you on the car telephone."

Scherrer grabbed his guns, spoons, handcuffs, and blackjacks. He also grabbed a ticket the embassy had bought for Townley in the name of Mark Johnson. Then he ran downstairs and shocked Cornick. The two of them ran to pay phones in the hotel lobby, followed by the ever-present reporters. Scherrer tried to confirm the news with contacts in Investigations, where all was pandemonium. The embassy car arrived before they could accomplish anything. Scherrer and Cornick looked helplessly at each other and jumped in. Reporters tried to follow.

Landau called on the car telephone as Scherrer and Cornick were speeding to the airport. He said he had checked with Etcheberry and satisfied himself that the United States could not be held responsible for violation of Townley's right to appeal the expulsion. Landau also said he was calling the U.S. ambassador in Ecuador to warn the Ecuadorians against foul play there.

An Investigations car met them at the airport and escorted the embassy car out onto the runway where the Ecuadorian plane was filled with waiting passengers. Scherrer and Cornick jumped out. The Investigations Department officers said they did not have Townley—he was coming in another car. The FBI agents talked to some embassy people Landau had sent to meet them. The flight was due to land in New York about midnight, and they wanted word sent to the FBI to have Wack and every agent in the area out at Kennedy Airport to meet them. The plane should not go near the terminal, for fear of Cubans. They should take Townley off at an isolated spot on the runway.

Scherrer and Cornick climbed the stairs and waited, talking security with the flight crew. American and Chilean officials gathered at the foot of the stairs. All of them saw a lone car pull out onto the runway and drive slowly toward them.

A tall blond man got out of the car, hands handcuffed in front. On signal, he walked through the crowd and up the stairs. His face was blank. Scherrer knew the detective behind him. The detective gave Townley to Cornick and the key to the handcuffs to Scherrer. "This is him," he said in Spanish. "You owe us a pair of handcuffs."

18 ▣ PIGS IN THE WINTERHOUSE

On October 17, 1960, Mariana Callejas and her bohemian friends reluctantly enter the American residential neighborhood in Santiago to retrieve a compatriot Chilean artist who is attending a party at the stately home of Vernon Townley, an American industrialist. On leaving the party, members of Callejas's rowdy crowd give thanks that they have escaped the garish opulence of the house, which, like almost all American houses in Santiago, looks to them like an embassy, and they tease their young friend for having gone there. Then, somewhat to everyone's embarrassment, they discover that the newcomer who has jumped into their red convertible is none other than the host of the party, Michael Townley. He is only seventeen, and knows nothing of Camus or the books of Panait Istrati, the Romanian novelist, but he is obviously so smitten with Callejas that he has abruptly left his own friends and is now wordlessly staring at her. He continues to do so all night, through discussions in bars and in the homes of the piano player and the photographer, and he follows Callejas to a group breakfast the next morning and then through a full day at the beach. To the amusement of her sophisticated friends, he gives Callejas a red rose, follows her to her mother's home, and, a few days later, asks her to marry him.

At first, Callejas thinks it is a joke. She tells Townley that she is already married, that he is still a kid, and that she has three children. Townley, undaunted, begins taking her young children on outings to the park. He tells Callejas that she must marry him. He is determined.

When Callejas finds her first job in Chile, having lived nearly ten years abroad, Townley continues his courtship by visiting her every day at her office. He is an unemployed high-school dropout, but Callejas sees that he is very bright and rebellious, like herself. Townley sends her a red rose every day and follows her to lunch from a discreet distance. Her friends tell her not to look at him—that he will finally get the idea and leave. "He's staying away," Callejas jokes to her friends, "about two meters away." Townley sits near her office. He is always courteous, but quite persistent.

Unable to be harsh with Townley, Callejas flees to her older brother's home in La Serena, where she grew up. Townley learns her destination by stealth and hitchhikes up the Chilean coast to the small city, where he makes inquiries on the street until he finds the correct address. Back in Santiago, Callejas's friends are tiring of the joke. The Polish piano player, who is becoming rather famous, drafts a declaration of independence that Callejas signs in front of the group, promising to have nothing more to do with the callow young American. But by now Callejas has begun to apologize whenever she is impolite to him.

Townley promises to take care of the children as his own and to support her somehow. He points out that he can attend to all the practical matters that befuddle Callejas and her friends. She has no doubt that this is true, for his skills in electronics and mechanics are already renowned among small circles in Santiago. In his own way, he is as precocious as she was. She is proud of having read her first classic, *Crime and Punishment*, when she was eight. At that age, Townley built a functional, homemade telephone transmitter and receiver.

She tells him to go home to the United States and enroll in a college. Failing that, he should go with his parents to Venezuela. Ford has just promoted his father for outstanding achievement in Chile and transferred him to Caracas. Townley, however, refuses to go along. He says that he was uprooted from all his friends once before, only three years earlier, when he came to Chile and found a strange language and hardly ever saw his father anymore. Now Townley is defying his parents. He will not go to school, nor will he accompany them to Venezuela. He will stay behind, alone if necessary, but he would prefer to be married.

Callejas doubts that Townley has the nerve to go through with his rebellion, but part of her responds to his predicament. Ten years earlier, when she was exactly his age, she had forced herself to flee her home and her country for no comprehensible reason, and to do so she had arranged her first marriage of convenience. Townley—if she accepted him—would be her third husband.

In 1950, Callejas was afraid to tell her father, a minor magistrate in the Chilean civil service, that she had dropped out of high school. For months, she arose every morning and put on her navy-blue suit and her white blouse and pretended to go to school. Actually, she was looking for an office job suitable to her family's station in life. In Chile, it was strictly forbidden for young middle-class girls to accept menial work, such as waiting on tables in a restaurant. Nor could they leave school without their parents' permission. It made no difference that Callejas had not really meant to quit school and had only done so because her favorite teachers, a couple named Feinsilbert, had been fired by a principal who resented the influx of Jewish refugees from Hitler's Europe. Young Callejas impetuously and clandestinely followed them to a school that proved too difficult for her. The Feinsilberts, whom she idolized, shared the secret that she was out of school. They also corrected some of her girlish apprehensions about the world that had just been shattered by the great war. They told her, for instance, that not all Germans were Nazis. This was a great relief to Callejas, who had feared that Richard Tauber, her favorite tenor, would never be permitted to sing again.

By then, Callejas had read many books on her own and had developed some ideas about how to construct a just global society. In that light, her deep fears that her parents would soon discover her truancy appeared trivial, and she resolved to break with social expectations on a larger scale: she would get married, and she might even emigrate to the new nation of Israel. One day she told her perpetually understanding mother about her truancy, her new husband, and her conversion to Zionist socialism. As she expected, her father banished her instantly from the family. Callejas managed the shock of transition bravely until Pablo, the husband she had recruited to help implement her plan, suddenly declared that he would rather be married to one of her high-school classmates. Pablo's family had the money and the inclination to push an annulment through the Catholic bureaucracy. The marriage had lasted only three months, and Callejas, at the age of seventeen, found herself already married, unmarried, out of school, and a pariah. So she decided to make use of the Feinsilberts' connections and squeeze herself onto the next boat for Israel, becoming part of the Exodus.

She joined her first kibbutz, Nan Kitzuphim, and began laboring to build the perfect socialism. Meanwhile, she learned Hebrew in special classes and picked up some conversational English by reading *The Saturday Evening Post*. And she tried to avoid the first ugly controversies that marred her vision of the primitive, harmonious life in the kibbutz, where the founders, it was said, had seized for themselves special eating privileges and the softer, more administrative jobs. The founders were also accused of looking down on non-Jews and on refugees from a few unpopular countries, especially Iran. In the end, most of the new arrivals were farmed out to build their own kibbutzim on the frontiers, where they were grouped by nationality. Callejas found herself in the Negev Desert with refugees from North and South America, building the kibbutz from nothing. Conditions were better in that there was no established hierarchy to fight, but they were worse because of the constant military danger. Egyptian soldiers and desert Arabs frequently raided the kibbutz. Callejas carried a Sten gun on regular night patrols before her eighteenth birthday.

By then she was known as Anat, having rejected as too Catholic her given name, Inés, and her nickname, Mariana. She also made a practical adjustment to the harsh life on the frontier, where the men outnumbered the women four to one, and where many of the refugees, with tattoos and vacant stares from the Holocaust, had little use for the sexual reservations of a proper Chilean girl: more or less for defensive reasons, she married Allan Earnest, an idealistic American agricultural student who had migrated to Israel from Cornell University. After the wedding, they danced the hora around campfires.

Less than a year later, around those same campfires, the kibbutz split apart when its council passed an edict that all members must declare themselves either Israelis or citizens of the world and forsake all formal ties to less enlightened countries. Twenty of the fifty members, including Anat and Allan Earnest, left over this issue. The new couple relocated in a *moshav*, a land collective that permitted home ownership and other expressions of individualism. Taking advantage of this freedom, Anat put up the only Christmas tree in the *moshav*, in 1951. She said she missed Chile, her paradise lost—for the food, if nothing else. In Israel, there was no sugar or coffee. What passed for coffee was actually a concoction of meal boiled in water. To Anat, working in the kitchen, everything smelled like fish —including the soap. On the night shift, she would thrust only her hand through the kitchen door and rattle a pot until she could hear no more little feet running around inside. Then she would go in and pick the mouse turds out of the oatmeal.

The new nation remained in a perpetual state of war, and in 1952 the Israeli army drafted Allan Earnest, who, as a pacifist, did not wish to serve. He was still recovering from wounds suffered when a land mine exploded beneath his tractor, and he said he had come to Israel to grow things, not to fight. On mutual agreement, he and his new wife said painful goodbyes to their friends and caught a boat to Chile, taking with them their infant son.

Arriving on her mother's doorstep, Anat became Mariana again. She was still only nineteen, but she had seen a great deal and had her first romantic ideal parched out of her. Her mother apologized to her father for the new husband she had brought home, and her mother also apologized to the couple for the conduct of the disapproving magistrate, who remained upstairs and refused to greet them. Although Callejas remembered him as the man who used to take her on walks in La Serena and greet all passersby with kindly, paternal words, she still feared him. To her, he was rigidly anti-Communist, anti-Nazi, anti-Zionist, and anti-Catholic. At the age of ten, when she dared to make her first and only confession to a Catholic priest, and when she returned home upset because the priest had asked her questions about sexual practices she did not understand, he had told her, to the dismay of her devout mother, that she should expect nothing better from Catholicism and its priests, who were not normal because they did not marry.

She thought her father was in favor of only one thing: the strict code of manners and morality that upheld the dignity of the Chilean middle class. To that, he demanded a fierce obedience. He required even the middle-aged daughters in his household to be home by eight-thirty each night. He called everyone, including his wife and daughters, by the formal Spanish word for "you." He made a science of the correct behavior toward servants. Magistrate Callejas was only a minor landholder of meager financial standing, but like many Chileans he spoke often of his heavily propertied relatives. He went so far as to trace his ancestry back to the original conquistador himself, Francisco Pizarro—founder of Peru, colonizer of Chile.

She was not really surprised when she and her new husband received a stiff welcome from such a man. The couple soon took another boat—to New York. They shared an apartment in Washington Heights with Allan Earnest's mother, who complained regularly that her son had brought home a *shiksa* and a foreigner who couldn't speak English. Mariana Earnest escaped during the day to watch acting classes at various schools, dreaming of the theater. As her English improved, she read short stories in *The Atlantic* and *The New Yorker*. She soon wrote stories herself and managed to show them to a number of literary people, including an American poet who lived in Greenwich Village surrounded by a talkative entourage and often did not eat breakfast until after dark. He encouraged her as an unusual young woman who had already carried guns in Israel and read a lot of books. She called him and his friends her salvation from boredom.

In 1957, she and Allan moved to the Long Island suburb of Uniondale, with their three babies. At first, she tried to drive into New York once a week to visit her friends on Bleecker Street, but the distance and her new responsibilities made this impractical. She hated being a housewife, almost as much as she hated her brief commercial experience as a waitress at Tony's Italian Restaurant. She fled to Chile once, and then, after a desperate effort to reconcile with Allan in New York, she left with the children and landed once again on her mother's doorstep. She told no one, not even her mother, that she never intended to go back to the United States or to her husband again.

This third return to Chile took place in 1960. She kept writing short stories and quickly introduced herself to a circle of artistic friends that centered around the photographer and the piano player. This energized her again, but she had no money and no career. She feared that weakness would compel her to return to Uniondale unless she could form some sort of attachment in Chile.

Callejas marries Michael Townley on July 22, 1961, with the photographer as the best man. The piano player and some of his associates refuse to come, on the grounds that she is being silly. None of the parents attends. The Townleys have already taken their other two children, Linda and Mark, to Venezuela, where the elder Townley is directing the extraordinary corporate feat of building a Ford assembly plant from bare ground to full production within the span of fifty weeks. Even the gentle Mrs. Callejas boycotts the ceremony. She opens her home to Michael, Mariana, and the three small children—along with her unmarried son and two full-time maids—but she avoids speaking to Michael for nearly six months, until after Christmas. Every time he enters the house, she scurries upstairs to her semi-invalid husband. From there, she communicates with the household through the maids.

Townley is not allowed upstairs until the stern old magistrate Callejas dies, and even then it is only because the family does not have the money to buy the licenses required to ship the body to the north of Chile for burial. He solves the problem by building a crude casket himself and transporting it clandestinely in a truck. In this crisis, his practical daring earns the first measure of respect from his mother-in-law.

Michael Townley persists through all the discomfort. The needs of the young children require him to grow up instantly, and he pitches himself into the task of becoming a provider, selling sets of *Collier's Encyclopedia* to wealthy families who read English. He repairs automobiles and electrical appliances as a sideline. In 1962, he finds himself in a nasty dispute with a future president of Chile, Eduardo Frei, who, as Townley sees it, grandly offers to buy a set of encyclopedias but then changes his mind and refuses to pay for it when Townley delivers the order. In later years, Townley will recall the incident as a fitting introduction to Frei and most other Christian Democrats, whom he will regard as vacillating, irresponsible politicians.

In 1964, his father uses his burgeoning influence within the Ford Motor Company to help secure for his son a managerial position in Ford's Peruvian subsidiary. Townley goes to Lima ahead of his family to find a house to live in and to test himself with his new responsibilities. Four months later, he returns to Santiago, having quit. He is not sure whether the fault lies with himself or with the Peruvians he was supposed to have supervised, whom he describes as slow and listless in comparison with Chileans.

The financial struggle resumes, and then in 1965 Townley finds the break he has been looking for. He becomes the sales representative in Chile for Investors Overseas Services (IOS), the mutual-fund conglomerate whose spectacular success has attracted worldwide attention and worldwide investment. Although it is technically illegal for Chileans to invest money outside the country, nearly all Chileans of the upper strata wink at the restriction.* Many of them become Townley's eager customers, amassing paper fortunes, and the sales representative himself attains prosperity so quickly that at first he

---

*Because of legal restrictions, Townley and the other IOS salesmen in Chile kept business records under fictitious names. This was his first use of a pseudonym.

has trouble spending the money. He moves his growing family (a new son, another on the way) into a spacious house in the suburb of La Reina, where Mariana superintends her own household, with a landscaped garden and two live-in maids. It is the only period of enjoyable domesticity thus far in her life. The Townleys spend more time skiing. Townley himself combines his mechanical gifts with his derring-do behind the wheel to modify and race an Austin Mini-Cooper at terrifying speeds. He finishes first-in-class and seventh overall in his first major race, a road rally through the mountains of Peru.

In 1966, his father wins another promotion and prepares to move from Caracas back to Santiago as president of Ford's subsidiary in Chile. Townley, having succeeded at long last on his own independent course, hopes to make peace with the family and to overcome their resentment of Mariana, whom they blame for his decision to ignore his education and stay behind in Chile.

Everything falls apart, however, when rumors begin to circulate that IOS is on the verge of bankruptcy and that one of its directors, Bernard Cornfeld, may have swindled investors out of millions of dollars. Panic quickly breaks out among Townley's customers, many of whom come beating on his door with informal redress on their minds. They have no legal claim against him over the disappearance of their illicit investments, but they demand that he prove his innocence. They want their money back. Townley goes into hiding when no one at IOS answers his increasingly desperate letters. Finally, the danger to him is such that he is obliged to leave everything and flee to the United States. The family joins him there after he promises Mariana that they will return to Chile in a few years, as soon as it is safe. His parents arrive just in time to be left in the sour aftermath of his hasty departure. Townley fears that his creditors will demand satisfaction from his father. If so, his father will never acknowledge it.

The family finds shelter with Townley's grandparents in Pompano Beach, Florida, where Townley tries his luck selling Ford trucks. When he is fired, he concludes that few people buy trucks in tourist-oriented Florida. Then, a twenty-four-year-old quasi-refugee with four small children, he accepts work under pressure at an AAMCO auto transmission shop in Miami's Little Havana. Somewhat to his surprise, he enjoys the steady work. He excels both in the actual repair work and soon in the management of the other employees. Slowly and laboriously, he prospers. Within two years, he acquires an ownership share in another AAMCO shop in nearby Hialeah.

For her part, Mariana Callejas enrolls in a creative-writing class at Miami University and quickly makes another group of literary friends. As in New York more than a decade earlier, the American intellectuals differ from their Chilean counterparts in that they see themselves as political leftists, whereas her Chilean friends have fled Communism in Eastern Europe, for the most part, and see themselves as bohemian, anti-Communist individualists. To Mariana Townley, these political labels make little difference. As yet, she does not even know the names of the presidents of Chile or the United States. She describes politics in her own way as something both moral and personal—as a romantic cause.

In Miami, many of her new friends have joined the New Party of Florida. They write and agitate against the Vietnam War, for abortion rights, for birth control, and for the presidential candidacy of Senator Eugene McCarthy. Callejas agrees with all these stands, partly because she is a renegade Catholic and partly because she believes that the anti-Communists of the world should fight their own battles without bullying or bossing from the Americans. She says, and writes, that the Americans have no business fighting in Vietnam as long as there are no Russian soldiers there. In the privacy of their home, Townley agrees with her, but otherwise he neither says nor cares anything about politics.

Generally, southern Florida is inhospitable to the views of Callejas and her literary friends. During the October 1969 nationwide protests against the Vietnam War, she joins a motley crew that marches through the streets of Miami, heavily outnumbered by hostile Cuban exiles who shout, spit, and throw tomatoes at Callejas and her fellow demonstrators. She returns their anger with at least equal measure. Like many Chileans, she has always looked upon Cubans with a certain condescension. She finds them gaudy, crude, unreserved, sweaty—altogether too "tropical."

Occasionally, such opinions cause trouble for Townley, who has many Cuban exile customers and employees at the AAMCO shop. On the day of the Vietnam Moratorium, when she asks him to close the shop in solidarity with the national protest, he replies that he might as well close his business permanently—it would infuriate his Cuban customers. Callejas hotly replies that she has no respect for the alleged anti-Communist commitment of the Cubans. If a Communist like Castro ever threatened to take power in Chile, she declares, she would struggle to get *into* the country, not out of it, so that she could fight. She thinks the Cubans live in Miami for the money. "If they hate Castro so much, why are they here?" she demands. "They are all like dogs barking behind a fence!" More than once, she says such things to a Cuban, and Townley tries to smooth things over.

She longs to return to Chile and is mildly concerned about President Frei's land-reform program there. For her class at Miami University, she writes "Pigs in the Winterhouse," which she and Townley and her teacher unanimously regard as her best story to date. It is an allegorical horror tale about a struggling man who works his entire life in the Chilean countryside to build his farm and his family, but when he is old, his land is overrun by marauding pigs. The old man looks on helplessly as the pigs ruin his crops, his house, and, finally, his winterhouse—the tiny, delicate sun house in which Chileans of refinement grow flowers in the winter. The pigs lay waste to the winterhouse in what the teacher describes as a beautifully written picture of utter defilement.

Townley understands that the story is about President Frei's incipient land-reform program in Chile, which has been designed to reduce the extremes in Chile's distribution of wealth. As in many South American countries, a small number of families and corporations control the vast bulk of Chile's wealth. Far beneath them in economic power is the relatively large and aspiring middle class, and then, living almost in another century, is the huge separate class of peasants and menial laborers. The United States government has been urging Chile to shift some land to the peasant classes as a means of heading off social upheaval. Frei's program is a moderate one, but it is assailed by the political left as too little and by the right as an unholy assault.

Only the most enormous landholdings have been expropriated thus far, with compensation paid to the owners. Neither Mariana Callejas nor anyone in her family has even a small parcel that might be seized, but she knows people who do and she reacts violently against the very idea. To her, it is a revolt of the servants in alliance with the opportunistic, wealthy politicians, such as Frei—all manipulated by the United States. It threatens to ruin the flowers, the finest aspects of civilization.

On September 4, 1970, the entire Townley family stays up late listening to Chilean election returns on Spanish-language radio. When the Marxist candidate, Salvador Allende, wins a plurality of the votes, a shocked Callejas weeps for the first time she can remember.

"I don't want to live there under Allende," Townley says sadly. "I guess we can't go back."

"We *must* go back," she retorts. "I must go back now more than ever." An argument breaks out. She accuses him of forgetting the promise he made to her in the wake of the IOS scandal—that they would return to Santiago permanently as soon as it was safe to do so. She says he has lost his homesickness for Chile. He says it would mean selling everything, uprooting the children again, and starting over in Chile, where he has never had an easy time making a living.

On October 21—the day before the Schneider assassination—she flies alone to Chile and lands once again on her mother's doorstep. "I guess I've always been afraid of being locked out," she says, happy to be back in Chile. As it turns out, she and Townley have country-club acquaintances among the civilians recruited by the military leaders to take part in the conspiracy against General Schneider. All of Chile, she finds, is excited or outraged by the conspiracy and the accession of Allende. Some of her wealthier friends are packing suit-cases and closing bank accounts—preparing to go into exile before the collapse of the fundamental order. She ignores them to look for a house. Her husband is unhappy, but she knows he will bring the children to Santiago as soon as he can dispose of their possessions in Mi-ami.

Townley calls the Miami office of the CIA and offers to go to work for the Agency in Chile. A CIA representative takes biographical information but fails to recontact him. Townley decides he is not want-ed. He flies to Santiago in January and quickly despairs of finding work. He thinks he has the tools and the skills to build custom-made boats, but no one is starting businesses in Chile. He repairs a few cars on the street in front of the new house, but he decides that there are not enough automatic transmissions in all of Chile to support a shop like AAMCO. Despondently, he tells Callejas that financial ruin is imminent. He also confesses that he has taken a lover in the Unit-ed States. Callejas absorbs the news quietly, stoically. She says she isn't surprised, that Townley has been following her for ten years, that perhaps he should seek the bachelor youth he never had.

In April, Townley flies alone to San Francisco. He moves in with his girlfriend and finds a job quickly in an AAMCO shop. Nearly every night, however, he and Callejas exchange anger and remorse by telephone. Within a month she flies to San Francisco herself, bringing the two younger children as emotional collateral for all contingencies. On discovering that the new couple plans to get married, she flies into a rage. "You son-of-a-bitch!" she shrieks at Townley, "why didn't you tell me? I wouldn't have come!"

Townley breaks off relations with the woman, but Callejas soon catches them during a secret tryst. She packs to return to Chile, but Townley thwarts the move by hiding her passport. Negotiations resume. One of Callejas's best friends, an avid supporter of Allende's new "Chilean way to socialism," flies up from Santiago to act as intermediary and offers the opinion that the marriage is irretrievably broken. Townley considers suicide, driving through San Francisco at high speeds. He abandons the idea after once banging into a guardrail.

After three months of battle, the exhausted couple reaches a tentative agreement to try again. Callejas and the children return to Santiago in July. Townley stays behind to close up his American business affairs once again.

In Santiago, Callejas re-establishes contact with the old bohemian crowd and concludes that they have aged in spirit. The piano player has married and divorced several times. All of them are absorbed in private pursuits that Callejas now finds selfishly artistic and unresponsive to the national political crisis. Impulsively, she investigates the political parties opposing Allende. She scorns most of them because of their conservative ties to the Catholic Church. She still retains the anti-papism of her late father, of her bohemian circles on both continents, and of the kibbutzim in Israel. Only one party, Patria y Libertad, is nonreligious enough for her tastes. It is new, authoritarian, national socialist in philosophy, and supportive of paramilitary action. Its youth are training for sabotage and street demonstrations against the Allende regime. This militancy attracts her more than anything else, for she is ready to fight.

When Townley arrives from San Francisco that October, he finds that she is conducting workshops and discussion groups almost nightly in their living room for young members of Patria y Libertad. She has taken on a younger generation of bohemians for instruction. Their oldest son takes part, as do many of his friends among the middle- and upper-class Chilean teenagers. Callejas criticizes some of them as juvenile delinquents masquerading as revolutionaries. She forces them to analyze the Allende regime and the disintegration of the country. She helps them plan street demonstrations. In her spare time, she writes an article or two for Patria y Libertad. She describes its propaganda magazine as "a brick" and labors to improve its quality, complaining frequently to Townley that the Patria leaders are amateurs in most respects, and too timid as well.

While sympathetic to Patria's objectives, Townley remains aloof from Callejas's "hobbies," as always, so that he can concentrate on the task of establishing himself financially. He renews his effort to start a boat-building business, finding semireliable partners with whom he buys vessels for renovation. Townley frequently drives to the port city of Valdivia, where he overhauls motors and electrical systems. The projects are highly speculative and bring in no income.

Ironically, Callejas and her family profit handsomely from the economic woes of the Allende government she is trying to destroy. The Chilean economy is falling apart. The rate of inflation, which actually declined during Allende's first ten months in office, is now skyrocketing from 20 percent a year toward a peak of 200 percent. Many consumer goods have disappeared from the shelves, and black markets are springing up. Any Chilean with American dollars can sell them "unofficially" for an enormous premium in Chilean escudos. The Townleys have American dollars arriving by mail each month—payments from the sale of the AAMCO shop in Hialeah and also checks from Allan Earnest, who, more than ten years after losing Callejas, is still volunteering support for her and for their two children. His checks are small, but currency values become so skewed under Allende that the Townleys—by selling their checks to Chileans with bank accounts in the United States—pay the equivalent of $4.50 per month rent for their house.

In December 1971, 50,000 Chileans—mostly women from the most fashionable neighborhood in Santiago—march through the streets shouting slogans and banging cookware together to raise a terrifying din, in what will become famous as the "March of the Empty Pots." Allende's supporters denounce the marchers for blaming economic shortages on the government, when in fact the privileged classes themselves are sabotaging the economy in order to force Allende from power. The marchers think otherwise. They blame Allende's alien, Marxist programs for crippling Chile's productive capacity, and in a remarkable near-riot they surround the presidential palace and run wild as long as they can. They call Allende a traitor, a coward, and worse. The respectable women of Chile are aroused.

Mariana Callejas and her followers in Patria youth agree with them. Moreover, Callejas feels a particular loathing for Allende as a hypocrite. It is bad enough, she says, that Allende loves only the poor and urges the peasants to steal property rightfully belonging to productive citizens, but it is even worse that he does so while living in luxury himself. Callejas says that she lives only ten blocks from the President's home and that she knows how, even in the midst of shortages, he manages to obtain the best cuts of meat for his own table. She says that Allende has always worn only the most expensive suits, that he owns more than a hundred pairs of shoes, that he drinks only Chivas Regal.

As she begins to spend more evenings with "my boys" from Patria, Townley admits to pangs of jealousy. She urges him to join them. Townley says he agrees with everything they are doing but demurs on the ground that he is not a politician or a Chilean. He says he must work. Besides, he says, the street actions of the Patria youth are childish. They throw rocks through windows. Their Molotov cocktails are primitive. He would do it correctly or not at all.

He is nettled, challenged, and tempted. Some weeks later, he agrees to make a "technically correct" Molotov cocktail as a model. He consults some of the chemistry journals to which he has always subscribed, and he finds ways to assemble the proper ingredients —sawdust, potassium nitrate, sulfur, oil, gasoline, and ether. Then he conducts experiments to determine the exact proportions that will maximize temperature and noise. His new formula dramatically raises the firepower of what Patria's paramilitary chief Manuel Fuentes calls the "White Terror" against the Allende government.

Townley is pleased with the precision of his work, and Callejas is proud of his contribution. By June 1972, Townley no longer goes to Valdivia to work on the boats, because he has thrown himself into Patria's campaign against Allende. Almost instantly, his home becomes a communications and explosives laboratory. He learns how to "sweat" nitroglycerin crystals out of dynamite and how to produce a dozen different effects with the same amount of TNT. He designs and builds "secure" radio equipment for the use of Patria leaders, and he astonishes even himself when he figures out how to intercept and record the radio messages between President Allende and his personal bodyguards. These and other feats quickly bring the top three leaders of Patria y Libertad into the Townley home. They want his services, saying that no one else has his technical gifts or his imagination. Townley agrees to work under Fuentes on the condition that he remain insulated from Patria's mass membership—which he considers unwieldy, paralyzed by numbers and hesitation. Townley wants to get more done in small groups. "When I do something," he tells Fuentes, "I really *do* it." Fuentes has no doubt that this is true.

He can almost feel Townley becoming larger, a commander and an inventor, as though all his gifts were designed for this role.

That summer, the Townleys become a whirlwind. He passes special dynamite to Fuentes, who in turn gives it clandestinely to the operative who throws it over the wall into the compound of the Russian embassy. Together with his daughter's boyfriend, Townley sets fire to the government-controlled Quimantu Printing Company. He cooperates with groups that blow up sections of railroad track to block freight shipments, and he plans to blow up a television tower on Cerro San Luis. Callejas often rides with him on missions ordered by Fuentes. She always speaks softly and seems strangely oblivious to the danger. Townley once turns around in the car to find that she has lit three Molotov cocktails simultaneously. During the general strike in October 1972, Townley creates a one-man Molotov-cocktail factory in his back yard, producing hundreds, and his oldest son helps use them to immobilize passenger buses in Santiago. By then, Townley is sending young Patria operatives on "blind" missions to pick up nitrates or to stake out potential targets. He carries a .45 pistol on missions. When some of the members of Callejas's Patria youth workshop admit that they are too squeamish to kill anyone, Townley tells them to shoot for the legs. The guns are only for emergency, he says—in case they encounter a guard or a night watchman. No one has been seriously hurt in his sabotage operations, but the pace is building and he knows it is only a matter of time.

In the late summer, when sabotage and government blackouts combine to silence nearly all the radio and television stations in Santiago, Callejas makes a devilish proposal: why can't Townley build a homemade radio station? The idea eventually takes hold of Townley, who doubles the challenge by resolving to build a portable radio station. It must be small enough to fit in the back seat of a car. Fuentes approves of the project and assigns two Patria technicians to help. Townley succeeds in a very short time and installs the radio transmitter in his Austin Mini-Cooper.

One night late in October, the Townleys drive to a preselected neighborhood in Santiago and park. Townley turns on the transmitter, and for the next seven minutes the inhabitants of the surrounding homes listen to anti-Allende speeches and to renditions of patriotic songs written by Callejas. It has all been prerecorded. The clandestine radio soon becomes a sensation in the Santiago newspapers, which gleefully report the Allende government's failures to locate and neutralize the treasonous, unlicensed transmitter.

The Patria leadership is nearly as disturbed as the Allende regime, for different reasons. Fuentes angrily accuses Callejas of putting the clandestine radio into operation prematurely, without authorization. He says he wanted to accumulate twenty transmitters so that they could cover all of Santiago. He says he wanted to use the transmitters as a private means of communicating with Patria members. Callejas has ruined all those plans by leafleting neighborhoods and transmitting on her own. Worst of all, says Fuentes, she has invited leaders of *all* political parties opposing Allende to submit recorded messages for her broadcasts. Even former President Frei of the spineless Christian Democrats is being heard! he sputters. He says that the radio belongs to Patria and to no one else, and that Callejas has committed an outrageous usurpation.

Callejas replies coolly that Fuentes wants to control the radio himself because he is jealous of its success. She refuses to surrender it. The transmitter is well hidden. She and Townley will keep the broadcasts. She will continue to write songs and to receive clandestine recordings from spokesmen for all opposition parties. Townley shrugs. He tells Fuentes that it is not his idea and that political messages are Callejas's field.

For weeks, they continue to broadcast. Police dragnets always miss them. Whenever Townley sees a police car in his rearview mirror, he turns to Callejas and begins to neck enthusiastically, as though they were only another amorous young couple. They find the experience romantic in many ways.

Roberto Thieme, Patria's number-two man, bursts into their home one night to sound the alarm. "You've been discovered!" he cries. "The police will be here any minute! We've got to hide the radio!"

Callejas only smiles. "I don't believe that," she says quietly. "And if they are coming, it's because you told them to."

No police arrive. Thieme is enraged that he has been unable to trick the Townleys into surrendering the radio. He and the other Patria leaders agree that they would purge the headstrong couple if Townley's expertise wasn't so valuable.

Patria stages a fake airplane crash and a funeral for Thieme in January 1973, so that he can move more freely about the country. Thieme and other Patria leaders are already conspiring with military commanders to overthrow the Allende regime by force. Townley can scarcely believe it. The whole thing has been too much fun. At times his operations seem like nothing more than illegal adventures, but he cannot deny that he has helped bring about a fear and economic chaos that may soon provoke the military to act.

On new orders from Fuentes, he and the two technicians who helped construct the clandestine radio drive to the Chilean city of Concepción, where the broadcasts of a conservative Catholic television station are being jammed by Allende supporters. Political arguments rage over who is doing what and over whether the jamming or the station itself is more illegal. Townley's mission is to trace the jamming signal to its origin, and then to find a way to enter the building in which the jamming equipment is located.

He accomplishes the task smoothly, as he has done before, but there are a few annoying developments. One of his companions attracts undue attention to himself by loudly offering pieces of chocolate to other guests in their Concepción hotel, and on the way back to Santiago the police stop Townley for speeding. He tells them his name is Juan Manuel Torres but that he has misplaced his driver's license. After some squirming and much fast talking, he returns safely and gives a purloined building key to the leader of another Patria team. The other team goes to Concepción that Sunday and destroys the jamming equipment. On its return, Townley meets with the leader and learns that it had been easy except for one minor problem: the raiders had run into an old drunk in the building. They had tied him up and given him a large injection of morphine to keep him quiet.

Panic breaks out within Patria the next day when the government announces that political saboteurs have killed an old man in Concepción. The police have tips that point toward Patria operatives as the culprits in the murder. The manhunt becomes big news in Chile, as Allende supporters point to the incident as proof of Patria's depravity. When police close in on Townley's two technicians, having traced them from the hotel, he seeks help from the head of Patria, Pablo Rodríguez, who says that he can beat the charges in court. Townley is not so sure. He is an American. He will be branded as a CIA agent. He had been part of the overall operation, even though he had not known about the old man. Rodríguez promises to help, but then he avoids Townley, who feels betrayed.

One night, while in hiding, Townley sees police stop and interrogate his oldest son in the street. He knows they are looking for him. He decides, over the strong objections of Callejas, that he must leave the country. He takes a bus to the south of Chile, in disguise. Then he walks for several days across the mountains into Argentina, bribing border guards with bottles of pisco. On April 2, 1973, he lands in Miami with empty pockets.

Callejas is left behind to face the police detectives. She resents Townley for ducking the fight, the more so because she knows that she and the family must also leave. She packs up the house, storing things at her mother's, and takes a flight to Miami in June. To her immense relief, the police do not try to stop her at the airport. She thinks it is because she has charmed one of the detectives in the Concepción case.

This time it is different in Miami—they are both committed soldiers in the war against Allende. Townley yearns to get back to Chile. In an ordinary Miami phone book, he finds the number of the local CIA office and calls again to offer his services as an operative. Specifically, he tries without success to interest the CIA officer in the radio system he has devised to intercept Allende's private communications.

At the AAMCO shop, he conspires busily with Cuban exiles whose clandestine lives he has previously ignored. In search of arms and explosives for shipment to his Patria allies inside Chile, he finds himself negotiating with representatives of a ubiquitous Cuban exile named Ricardo Morales, who wants to trade the material for Patria assistance in a plot to assassinate two of Fidel Castro's close associates when they visit Allende in Chile. Various complications doom the exchange.

In June, Townley buys champagne when he hears that Patria will attempt a coup against Allende. It fails, and Pablo Rodríguez flees Chile. On firmer notice in September, Townley stores up even more champagne, and he hosts a great celebration when the armed forces eliminate Allende on September 11. Throughout Miami, anti-Communist Cuban exiles are spontaneously toasting the overthrow of the Marxist regime. For the first time Callejas thinks Cubans may not be so bad after all—even if they do spit too much.

She has a seat aboard the first commercial airplane allowed to land in Chile after the coup. There is much merriment on the flight, as the returning exiles wave Chilean flags and sing patriotic songs. Only a few Chilean women, dressed in mourning, do not share the joy. Callejas lingers over the sight of them, which she finds surreal. It is difficult for her to imagine that the end of Allende has saddened anyone, but it must be true. She has heard that the Chilean military has executed 10,000 leftists in the first week.

Back in Miami, Townley is arranging his affairs so that he can take the children to Chile again. The CIA man has not contacted him.

Townley decides that the Agency might be worried about the out-standing murder warrant against him in Chile. Townley is worried, too, despite Callejas's assurances that such problems are forgotten in the new Chile. As a precaution, he resolves to re-enter the country illegally under a new identity. A friend of his named Kenneth En-yart, who has no thought of ever traveling abroad, agrees to lend Townley his birth certificate and social-security card. With these, Townley manages to obtain an American passport for himself as En-yart. His children practice calling him *"Tío Ken"* in Chile and "Uncle Ken" in Miami.

Townley and the children find that Callejas has already left her mother's for a house in the Providencia section of Santiago, and she has enrolled in a new creative-writing class under the tutelage of En-rique Lafourcade, Chile's most famous novelist. Townley drives down to Valdivia to check on the boats he abandoned eighteen months earlier. He is looking for work.

All this is normal for the re-entry. Otherwise, everything has changed. The Townleys and most other Chileans remain in the after-shock of the coup. Townley's outlook is exceptionally bright.

By coincidence, their new landlady is a mistress and confidential informant to Colonel Pedro Espinoza, an army intelligence officer. She is highly impressed to learn that Townley is Patria's famous "Juan Manolo," who, with Callejas, a year ago pestered Allende and entertained all Santiago with the elusive clandestine radio. She says she knows a lot about them, from Espinoza, and within a few days she announces that Espinoza would like to meet them.

Despite his civilian clothes and his warm smile, the colonel who ar-rives at their house is a man of rigid military bearing, with business on his mind. "So you operated the clandestine radio?" he asks. When the Townleys admit it, he says, "I'm proud to meet you. I was in charge of the army intelligence unit that was supposed to track you down. But we didn't try very hard."

A bond grows with winks, smiles, and an exchange of yarns. Espinoza shows great interest in Townley's electronic and explosive inventions, of which he has heard many reports. When Townley ex-plains why he and Callejas often worked as a male and female team on clandestine missions, he approves of both the reasoning and the results. He says that intelligence people tend to be far too tradi-tional. He admires their pluck, their patriotism, and Townley's tech-nical imagination.

At their second meeting, Espinoza gets down to business. Having served as the officer in charge of the personal security of the inner circle of generals who planned Allende's overthrow, he confides, he expects to play an important supporting role in the new Chile. Specifically, he will be one of the officers organizing the central intelligence outfit, DINA, that will defend the new regime against its enemies in Chile and abroad. President Pinochet has selected Espinoza's patron and longtime friend, Colonel Manuel Contreras, to assemble the personnel for DINA. It will be a strictly military organization. Nearly all its employees will be career soldiers. But Espinoza says there is room for a few exceptional civilians who are willing to mold themselves according to the discipline required in an organization built on both secrecy and military command. He offers positions in DINA to Townley and Callejas.

They accept eagerly. It is a new romance and a great honor. Instead of being amateurs, they will work under the aegis of the government itself. This excites them, but they have few illusions. Espinoza has said that it will be war. He says that only an elite command can carry out the ugly but necessary requirements of state. It has always been so, he says. The polite forms of government are merely window dressing for the public, but the actual survival of Chile in these historic times depends on force, loyalty, cunning, and the harsh laws of security.

Townley agrees. He has concluded that the constitutional norms of his native country are a historical aberration resulting from the peculiar circumstances in eighteenth-century America. He knows that many influential Americans agree with him but cannot say so in public. Both he and Callejas have accepted what they call "paternalistic feudalism" with a zeal that will serve them well.

Townley educates himself in DINA. He quickly discovers that it is a young and unsophisticated organization that invites ideas for improvement. As usual, he thinks big. He wants to design and acquire a special press so that DINA can print its own false identity papers. He wants to install special electronic equipment to protect President Pinochet against eavesdropping by potential enemies. He experiments with explosives at the DINA practice range.

Callejas is dismayed to find that there are very few gentlemen in DINA. Colonel Espinoza is one of them. To her, most of the others are uncouth militia types whom she would not invite into her home. Townley says she is too critical, as usual.

They hear many times that their ultimate boss, Colonel Contreras, established a tone of unbending obedience around him even before

DINA was created. After the coup, as military commander of the port city of San Antonio, Contreras became dissatisfied because longshoremen were unloading sorely needed food supplies only one bag at a time. He summoned a number of the foremen and directed them to have their men unload two bags at a time. The foremen refused and suggested that he take the matter up with union officials, whereupon Contreras shot several of them in the chest. The food bags began moving more rapidly off the ships.

Unfortunately, this is the kind of work needed to restore Chile, they say. Townley and Callejas expect to play only supporting roles, but they perceive the grim nature of the task. Many pigs remain in the winterhouse.

Townley receives a full set of identity papers under his new DINA name, Andrés Wilson. They are dated June 9, 1974. Callejas selects an operational alias in honor of the exalted pedigree her father claimed: Ana Luisa Pizarro.

19 ▣ A BLUFF
AND A PRAYER

Not a word was spoken until the plane left the ground. Cornick put Townley in a window seat and sat down beside him. In the air, Cornick showed Townley the warrant and said he would be arrested the moment the wheels of the plane touched American soil. Then he read the prisoner his rights even though he was not yet under arrest. He said that Townley was in more trouble than he could imagine. He advised the prisoner to come clean quickly and make things easier for himself. Repeatedly, Cornick warned Townley that he would not get off the plane in one piece if he caused any trouble.

Townley began to cry softly. He recovered quickly and announced with military formality that he had done his duty and would not have anything to say until he could speak with a lawyer. Cornick abandoned his effort to browbeat Townley into a confession after observing that it only strengthened the prisoner's resolve.

"I know how you feel, Mike," said Scherrer, leaning across Cornick. He would play soft cop, handling Townley gently. "Your own people have just betrayed you and kicked you out of the country to face this all alone. You don't owe them a thing."

Townley looked at Scherrer. "I don't understand it," he said miserably. "I can't believe this is happening." He said nothing for nearly half an hour, and then he began to cry again spontaneously. He apologized to Scherrer. After drifting off into his own world again, he turned to the FBI agents and asked, "What's going to happen to Fernández?"

504

Cornick looked significantly at Scherrer before making a reply. "He's in a lot of trouble too, Mike," he said. "You know that as well as I do."

"He's going to have to answer for his involvement in the Letelier assassination just as you are," Scherrer added.

Townley did not deny it. "This is a disaster for Chile," he said. "My God. I'm afraid it could lead to an institutional crisis within the Chilean army, and that could lead the generals to move against the President."

"They should have thought of that before they started running around killing civilians," said Cornick.

Townley ignored him. "You have no idea what this means," he said numbly. "There are still all kinds of Christian Democrats buried inside the government, and if Pinochet goes, they will take advantage of it to push for a return to a Frei-type constitutional government. And the Marxists will be right behind them. I guarantee it."

"Mike, we don't know anything about that one way or another," said Cornick. "Our job is to solve the Letelier case. That's why we came after you."

Townley's face hardened instantly. "You can't prove a thing," he said.

"Let's not talk about it now," Scherrer said soothingly. "This isn't the time or place."

Hours later, as the prisoner was conversing easily on neutral subjects, Scherrer leaned over to begin a ploy. "Mike, I want to speak personally for a minute, okay?" he said.

"Sure," said Townley.

"I can tell that you've been in the intelligence business for some time," said Scherrer. "So have I. All right?"

"If you say so," said Townley.

"We've already discovered that I know some of the same guys in Argentina that you do," said Scherrer. "And I was kicking Iggie Novo's ass in New York ten years ago. So we both know Cubans."

"Maybe so," said Townley.

"I'm not trying to get anything out of you now," said Scherrer. "What I want to do is to talk to you as one professional to another. We're going to have a long, miserable flight if we can't trust each other at all, and we have to go with you every time you take a piss. Right now, I'd like to know if I can have your word as a professional not to make any trouble while Carter and I go talk to the pilot about security."

"I won't make any trouble," said Townley.

"That's good enough for me," said Scherrer.

He and Cornick walked to the front of the plane to confer privately. "There's no doubt in my mind that we've got the right guy," whispered Scherrer, making an effort to conceal his excitement.

"Mine either," Cornick replied. "He's worrying about his friend Fernández. He's even worried about Pinochet. The guy's acting guilty. You got any ideas on how we can get him to admit it?"

"Not yet," said Scherrer. "I think we've got to treat him like an intelligence officer, not like a criminal, and play him slow."

The two agents agreed to stage a bit of theater. Accordingly, they went back to Townley, and Scherrer soon said that he trusted the prisoner enough as a fellow professional to allow him to make the trip without his handcuffs. Cornick protested at first, saying that both he and Scherrer could be fired for taking the cuffs off. He agreed to do so only after making Townley promise never to tell anyone in the FBI.

Engine trouble caused an unwelcome layover in Quito, Ecuador, during which airline officials herded all passengers, except for the prisoner and the two agents, off the plane. U.S. embassy personnel came on board to tell Cornick that his messages had been received —that the agents' belongings would be picked up at the Santiago hotel and forwarded to them, that Townley's wife had already been asked to bring clothes to the embassy for forwarding to him in the United States.

Townley noticed that an Ecuadorian air force unit had come onto the runway in jeeps. Soldiers stood at attention all around the plane for the full duration of the layover. Townley was impressed with all the security the Americans could command. He had already told the agents that he feared a sniper attack against him at any of their future stops.

In the air again, Townley began to talk more personally to the agents, especially to Scherrer. "Where did you grow up?" he asked.

"In a lousy section of Bedford-Stuyvesant in New York," Scherrer replied. "With a crime rate you wouldn't believe."

"Well, I didn't have anything like that," said Townley. "In Iowa and Michigan I used to go to an old-fashioned ice-cream parlor with my father and have chocolate sundaes. He and I used to mow the lawn together back in the early 1950s. We had one of the first big power mowers back then, and he rigged up a pulley system so he could support me while I pushed the thing on steep banks of grass. I had a very pleasant life until I was thirteen or fourteen."

"Until you got to Chile," Scherrer prompted.

"I guess so," said Townley. "Everything changed then."

Not long after midnight, a flight attendant tapped Cornick on the shoulder. He followed her to the pilot's cabin and learned to his astonishment that the plane had been ordered by radio to land at Baltimore, where FBI squadrons would be waiting for Townley and his escorts. The pilot said he was under strict orders not to let the regular passengers know of the diversion until after it was accomplished. Neither Cornick nor the pilot knew that the extraordinary diversion plan had been originated by Larry Barcella, in Washington.

While the flight attendants gathered excitedly in the front of the plane to receive instructions, Cornick whispered the news to Scherrer, who told Townley. A voice soon came on the intercom and announced to the dozing passengers that they were beginning their descent into New York. This caused much stirring and grabbing for hand luggage. When the plane swooped low enough for the lights of a city to become visible, Scherrer loudly pointed out New York's George Washington Bridge. Nearby passengers asked him to show them the Empire State Building.

Scherrer smiled to himself. Actually, they were flying over the Chesapeake Bay near Baltimore, two hundred miles south of New York. "Put the cuffs back on, Mike," Scherrer told Townley, allowing the prisoner to rehandcuff himself.

Cornick heaved a big sigh when the wheels finally touched the ground. He turned to Townley and advised him that he was under arrest. "I'll tell you the rest later," he said. Passengers were scrambling for the doors. The flight attendant was trying vainly to make them return to their seats. Finally, she and her colleagues pushed the crowd far enough back so that the agents and Townley could make their way to the door.

As the plane taxied on the runway, Townley knocked on the door to the pilot's cabin. When it opened, he leaned inside and said, "Captain, I want to thank you for the safe flight and for the courtesies you and your crew have extended to me."

The pilot nodded blankly toward Townley and then gave Scherrer a quizzical look, as though to ask how such a polite young man could be a dangerous criminal.

On instruction, the pilot parked on the runway, far from the gates. A string of FBI cars sped out to meet the plane, red lights flashing. The agents led Townley down the stairs toward the lead car. Behind them, the flight attendant was telling the bewildered passengers that they were not in New York after all.

Cornick called Propper at four o'clock in the morning. "We got him, boy!" he cried. "We tucked him in at Fort Meade with about five hundred guards. I'll tell you all about it in the morning. Go back to sleep and pat her on the ass for me, will you?"

Propper was up early the next morning—Sunday, April 9. It was his birthday. He knew Townley would be the most welcome birthday present of his life, and the very idea of meeting the "blond Chilean" thrilled him. One way or another, he would find out what Townley knew about the Letelier assassination. Even before hearing Cornick's report on the long flight with Townley, Propper felt by instinct that Townley was involved. But he did not know how. His best guess was that Townley had been a DINA courier to the Cubans. It was also possible that he was merely a technician who worked on the bomb, or that he had only indirect knowledge of the assassination plan.

None of it mattered to Propper—as long as Townley was involved. He could not bring himself to contemplate the possibility that Townley's clandestine visits to the United States had been unrelated to the murders. This was too horrible a prospect. It would wipe out all the clues and all the labors in Chile. Propper knew that Townley was probably his last hope for answering the galling mystery of how the bomb had reached Sheridan Circle.

He drove to the courthouse and rummaged through the files in his office. When he found the items he wanted, he put them into a file folder and drove on to Fort Meade. Army guards admitted him and showed him to a conference building near the stockade.

Propper waited outside until an FBI car drove up. Townley emerged between Scherrer and Cornick. All three of them looked sleepy, but Propper hardly noticed. He was transfixed by the first sight of the man whose face had stared at him so long from the second drawer of his file cabinet.

The tension of the moment dulled Cornick's mind. His manners took over. "Gene, this is Mike Townley," he said, as though Propper didn't know.

Townley extended his hand to the *fiscal* and smiled. "Nice to meet you," he said.

This was not what Propper had expected. He shook hands. "Nice to meet you," he replied. "Your lawyer and the magistrate are on their way for the hearing."

Scherrer led Townley inside. Propper lagged behind with Cornick. "I can't believe this," he said.

"I can't either," said Cornick. "Don't try to figure him out yet, Gene. Two days ago he was at home in Santiago in bed with his wife. He doesn't know what hit him."

"Good," said Propper. "By the way, Carter, where is it?"

"Where's what?" said Cornick.

"The confession."

"What confession?"

"You promised me you'd get a confession on the plane," said Propper.

Cornick snickered. "That was a joke, Gene," he said.

"I know, but what did you get?"

"I got Townley," said Cornick.

"Yeah, but I need a confession," said Propper. "I need it bad."

"Don't worry," said Cornick. "Bob and I are working on him."

Ironically, the man who showed up to represent Townley at Fort Meade was Seymour Glanzer, who, along with Earl Silbert and Don Campbell, had been on the original team of prosecutors for the Watergate burglary case. Glanzer had been retained on the recommendation of James Weck, the Townley family lawyer in Florida. At the hearing, Townley admitted his identity and agreed to be removed to Washington, within the jurisdiction of the judge who had signed the arrest warrant for him. Afterward, Glanzer said he'd like to have some time to get acquainted with his new client.

At the entrance to the military stockade, Propper drew Glanzer aside. "Seymour, I want to show you something before you go in there," he said, reaching into the file folder he had brought with him from the courthouse. "I don't think you or anyone else realizes what we're dealing with. You can look at these pictures and see for yourself."

Glanzer found himself staring at color autopsy photographs that seized his innards and shook loose all his worldly composure. He was naturally pale, but now he became ghostly white as he saw the mangled corpses of Ronni Moffitt and Orlando Letelier.

Propper was looking away. "I've tried dozens of murder cases, but I still can't handle these particular ones," he said gently. "This was a horrible crime."

Nodding wordlessly, Glanzer returned the photographs.

"You can show them to Townley if you want," said Propper. He escorted Glanzer into the conference room and withdrew, leaving the file folder on the table near Townley. Scherrer and Cornick were waiting outside, admiring Propper's tactics. Both of them had seen Glanzer's face turn sickly. Propper said he had done it for the psychological effect on Glanzer, whose practice had been largely confined to white-collar cases. "Seymour's not used to that kind of stuff," said Propper.

When Glanzer left the conference room an hour and a half later, he encountered Cornick and Scherrer near a soft drink machine. He gave each of them a look of profound sincerity and extended his hand. "Congratulations," he said hoarsely. "You've done one hell of a job."

Neither Cornick nor Scherrer knew what to say. They mumbled their thanks and watched Glanzer walk over to Propper and repeat himself.

"Congratulations?" said Propper. "Nice job? What does that mean, Seymour? What did he say?"

"He said it's a crazy world, Gene," said Glanzer. "In so many words, that's what he said. You know better than to ask exactly what he told me. You and I have got to talk. We've got to sit down and talk."

"I just want to know if you and he are inclined to cooperate or whether you'd prefer to go to trial against us and those pictures," said Propper.

"That's what we have to talk about," said Glanzer. "In a few days. He wants to talk to his family and his wife. She's coming up from Chile." Glanzer was shaking his head. "We've got to talk," he repeated. "The world is sure as hell full of crazy people." He walked out, promising to call the next day.

Cornick and Scherrer joined Propper. "That man was in a daze," said Cornick. "You think it was the pictures or what Mike told him?"

"I don't know," said Propper. "I think both, and I'd give anything to know what Townley told him. He probably told him how the murders went down."

"Well, there's no doubt in my mind that we've got the right man," said Cornick.

"I don't doubt it either," said Propper. "Now all we need is some evidence."

On Monday, officials at FBI headquarters called the Secret Service and arranged to borrow Vice President Mondale's bulletproof limousine for the day. They used it to transport Townley from Fort Meade to the courthouse in Washington for his bail hearing. All parties kept the hearing secret. FBI agents sneaked the limousine around to a rear basement entrance, but American reporters had the area well staked out and did not miss their first opportunity to glimpse Townley.

Privately, Seymour Glanzer told Propper and Barcella that he would not press for Townley's release. "In the next few days, we're either going to cooperate or I'll ask the judge to let him go," said Glanzer. "In the meantime, I want him protected as much as you do. He's not safe outside."

At the hearing, however, Glanzer objected strenuously when Propper asked for a $5 million bond. He said the figure was outlandishly high. He said it was a travesty and that Propper was trying to railroad his client. In the end, the magistrate ordered Townley held without bond at all. To Propper and Barcella, the episode meant that Glanzer would fight for his client in ways that were unpredictable and theatrical. He was trying to keep them off balance.

The next few days passed in a blur. Glanzer often called to say that the government had only five days to put Townley in the grand jury or the material-witness warrant would expire. The prosecutors challenged Glanzer on the law. And they bluffed by saying that they would indict Townley rather than question him before the grand jury. They kept telling Glanzer that they would prefer to make a deal, however, and that they were ready to talk. At this, Glanzer would stall. The two sides were feeling each other out behind poses of confidence.

On Tuesday, Earl Silbert asked for a briefing, now that the whole world knew Townley had been snatched from Chile. "What are we going in with against Townley?" he asked, referring to the upcoming negotiations with Glanzer.

Propper and Barcella cleared their throats often between mumbles, but they managed to give their superiors an accurate account of a bleak prospect. They said they could tie Townley to DINA. They could prove that Townley had violated U.S. passport laws and that he had been in the United States before the bombing. They probably could prove that he had been in contact with Guillermo Novo, and they could argue by inference that Townley had flown into New York to arrange a hit contract on Letelier with Novo and the CNM. But they did not possess a shred of evidence to support that inference. They had nothing that tied Townley to the murders, and in fact, they did not know how the murder had actually been carried out. On the present evidence, Barcella summarized, they might squeeze a murder indictment against Townley through a grand jury, but he was sure that any competent judge would quash the indictment for lack of evidence.

There was an uncomfortable silence before Silbert said, "That's what I was afraid of." Then there was more silence. The prosecutors did not need to say much to each other. They all knew that if Glanzer and Townley refused to bargain, challenging them to prove a case in court, Townley would go free. He would walk out of jail within a week. Needless to say, his release would be difficult to explain to the families of the victims and to the reporters who were bombarding them with questions on when the case would be solved.

Propper could not bear the thought. "It's not that bad, Earl," he said optimistically. "Seymour wants to make a deal. So does Townley, I think. We've just got to keep the heat on them."

As a bluff was unavoidable, the prosecutors fell into a discussion of tactics—what to say to Glanzer if and when the defense lawyer came to bargain. They stressed among themselves that they should always speak as though they knew Townley had been right in the middle of the murder plot against Letelier. But they should keep it vague, because they knew very few supporting facts. They should never guess about specifics, because Glanzer presumably knew the truth by now and would pounce on any error they made. They had to appear strong, but they could not reel off the prosecutor's string of supporting facts. They had to appear willing—but not desperate—to make a deal.

While the prosecutors plotted their approach to Glanzer, Scherrer and Cornick drove to Fort Meade every day to work on Townley. They had to be careful. Propper and Barcella had warned that they could not interrogate the prisoner without Glanzer present. They should not even attempt to elicit information from Townley. Glanzer would find a way to suppress it in court, and he might even argue successfully that the illegal confession had tainted other evidence.

Mindful of this injunction, Scherrer and Cornick went to Fort Meade to talk, not to listen. They wanted to nurture in Townley's mind the idea that he had been snatched out of Chile because the omniscient Americans knew exactly what he had done, and that Townley would never see the outside of a jail again unless he struck a bargain with Propper. Together, Scherrer and Cornick dropped ominous hints into their conversation. Some of them were wild exaggerations or outright lies. They told Townley, for instance, that the FBI had penetrated the Cuban Nationalist Movement with many informants, one of whom was traveling with the fugitive Guillermo Novo. They said the Bureau had the case wrapped up on the domestic side and that they had gone after Townley to find out what had happened in Chile.

Most of the time, however, the two agents tried to ingratiate themselves with Townley. They brought him books and a toothbrush, sent his messages, contacted his relatives. Scherrer kept up the small talk on events in South America. He and Townley talked Chilean politics. Townley said he was lonely, cut off from everything. He said he appreciated Scherrer's company. Scherrer treated Townley like a high-level espionage defector—not like a suspected murderer. Now and then he would remind Townley that he was in a lot of trouble and would do well to cooperate, to get it over with.

Mariana Townley left Chile on Tuesday, April 11. For three days Santiago newspapers had featured her shrill denunciations of the Pinochet government. "What is terrible is that they used my husband," she declared. ". . . I am sure that President Pinochet and high officials did not know who my husband really was, what he did, and what he knows. If they had known, they would not have expelled him." Alongside these stories were others quoting the president of Chile's Supreme Court, who said angrily that Chile's summary expulsion of Townley was a gross violation of his rights. President Pinochet also appeared on the front pages, promising to return civilian rule to Chile sooner than expected. In one paper, the Chilean President reiterated that the Chilean government was innocent of all complicity in the Letelier assassination. In another, he phrased it more carefully, with regal detachment. "The intelligence services serve the government," he declared. "An unpleasant situation affecting them is their problem. Not mine."

Before Mariana Townley landed in the United States, Cornick and Scherrer learned that she was not reserving all her wrath for the Chilean government. Townley confided that she was pouring some of it on him—for being stupid, for making the wrong moves in Chile, for trusting too much. And of course she hated the *fiscal*. Townley thought she was generally angry toward everyone. As much as he longed to see her, he waited with some trepidation.

At Baltimore-Washington Airport, Scherrer greeted her with a large bouquet of yellow roses. She took them suspiciously, not knowing what to say. Inside was a note from Townley, telling her that the flowers were the FBI's idea but that he loved her anyway. Mariana

Townley read it and said nothing to the agents. She was silent on the drive to Fort Meade, where Scherrer and Cornick left her alone with her husband.

Scherrer considered the flower gesture a success. If nothing else, it made Mariana Townley stop to wonder what was going on. Scherrer thought the psychological warfare would be won on the accumulation of small things. He knew that Michael and Mariana Townley would soon realize that they were trapped in a hopeless position—amid bitter hatreds, the force of the law, vicious struggles for power, and desperate desires to silence a potential witness. They were utterly dependent pawns. In such a state, Townley needed to throw in his lot with someone—with the Cuban exiles, with the Chileans, or with the Americans. Cornick and Scherrer wanted to make sure he and his wife understood that the Americans were the only ones who would not kill him.

Outside the conference room, Scherrer told Cornick more tales of his experience with potential defectors. While caught and undecided, they tended to make childish, petty demands, he said. A potential defector urgently wants to know how his new protectors will treat him. So he tests them. Townley was fitting the mold perfectly, said Scherrer. He had asked them to bring him a special kind of stretch socks. He had asked them to call Mariana in Chile to ask her to bring him two bottles of pisco, the Chilean national beverage. He had asked a hundred other favors, many of them silly, and the agents always made an effort to comply.

When Mariana Townley left for the night, the prisoner called for Scherrer and Cornick. He seemed agitated. He said he needed to talk with someone from "the service" or from the Chilean military. Specifically, he wanted to talk with General Orozco, the military prosecutor in Chile who had questioned him for sixteen hours. Scherrer told Townley this would be no problem and promptly placed an international call to Orozco in Santiago. The two agents sat beside Townley as he told the general that the FBI was closing the Letelier case and that he had major decisions to make. Townley said he urgently needed to discuss his obligations to the Chilean government—and the Chilean government's obligations to him. He said he didn't want to do or say anything without first obtaining orders, and he all but begged General Orozco to take the next flight to the United States. Orozco made no commitments. Townley was distressed when he hung up.

Cornick called Propper to tell him of the fresh signs that Townley wanted to cooperate. "He's dying to do it, Gene, but he's a procrasti-

nator," said Cornick, who passed along Scherrer's character reading
on the prisoner. According to Scherrer, Townley's desire to talk did
not come from remorse over the murders. It came from fear, from a
soldier's need to reattach himself after being rejected by his commanders, and from a defector's urge to make himself sound important by telling of his exploits.

Earl Silbert, his principal assistant Carl Rauh, Propper, Barcella,
and Don Campbell—the five prosecutors trying to obtain Townley's
cooperation—all knew Glanzer well, and they had conducted a thousand plea-bargaining sessions among them. Nevertheless, the
charged emotions and legal vulnerabilities of this case made one issue so delicate that the prosecutors discussed it delicately even
among themselves. This issue was the proffer—the off-the-record
statement of evidence commonly made by each side at the beginning
of plea-bargaining sessions. Glanzer was entitled to hear a proffer of
the government's evidence against his client. If he asked for one, it
would be embarrassing for Propper and Barcella, who had very little
evidence to reveal. They would have to be vague, but no amount of
verbiage would deceive a lawyer as sharp as Glanzer. They hoped to
avoid giving a proffer at all.

The prosecutors were entitled to a reciprocal proffer from
Glanzer. According to the ritual of plea-bargaining, they would say,
"All right, this is what we've got against your client. Before we even
discuss a deal, we've got to know what he can do for us. We're not
buying a pig in a poke. What will his testimony be?" And Glanzer
would be obliged to reveal what Townley knew about the Letelier assassination. Because this information would incriminate Townley,
the prosecutors would pledge in advance not to use it against Townley if the plea-bargaining negotiations were a failure.

To the prosecutors, a proffer of Townley's testimony was a chilling notion under any circumstances. It was already painful enough
for them to contemplate the possibility that Townley might go free
for lack of evidence. It was even worse to think that they might find
out exactly what had happened at Sheridan Circle in a proffer from
Glanzer and then, in the event negotiations with Glanzer failed, be
honor-bound to say nothing of what they knew—not even to the relatives of the victims who had been so brutally murdered. By the odd
contortions of the plea-bargaining system, the prosecutors would become secret parties to the very criminal knowledge they had labored
so long to bring to public light.

Late Wednesday afternoon, Glanzer arrived with his partner

Barry Levine. After amenities, Glanzer took the initiative. "Earl, I
just want you to know something," he said grandly. "You and Don
will understand what I mean when I say my guy is good. I'm telling
you, he's better than John Dean was in Watergate. A lot better. He
can give you the top and the bottom, just like Dean. He can testify
about the guys at the top who gave the orders, and he can also testify about the guys at the bottom who carried them out. The parallels
are amazing, but I'm giving you my word that our client is better
than John Dean."

"That's great, Seymour," said Barcella. "But John Dean never
killed anybody." By prearrangement among the prosecutors, Barcella had agreed to play the role of the hardliner.

"That's not the point, Larry," said Glanzer. "The point is that he
can give you the whole package. He's just about the only government witness you'd need. He's the best star witness I ever saw."

"Okay, Seymour," said Silbert. "I'll take your word that Townley's
like Dean. What else have you got?"

"*Better* than Dean," Glanzer emphasized. "You won't believe this
guy, Earl. I'm telling you, what he's got to say will knock you out of
your chair. You remember how stunned we were on that April day
when Dean first came in and told us all in secret about the Watergate cover-up? Well, I'm telling you that was nothing compared with
Townley."

"All right, Seymour." Silbert smiled. "Would you care to go into
the specifics?"

"No, I'm not going to make a proffer," Glanzer announced.
"That's the first thing we should get straight here. I don't even want
to discuss it."

"What?" said Propper, in disbelief, masking his delight. "How do
you expect us to offer you a deal blind, Seymour? That's not fair and
you know it."

"Well, you'll just have to take my word that he's better than John
Dean," said Glanzer.

"Well, it's conceivable that we'd take your word because Don and I
know you so well," said Silbert. "But I don't like it. I'll have to think
about it. In a case like this, that's asking a lot."

"And you're sure as hell not gonna get a proffer from us for nothing," said Barcella. "We'll just say we got a better case than you
guys had against John Dean."

"Bullshit," Glanzer retorted. "You guys won't give me a proffer
because you haven't got a goddamn thing. The best you got on my
client is a couple of passport charges."

"Wait a minute, Seymour," said Barcella. "First of all, that's not true. We got your guy on a double homicide. Second of all, we've got him cold on *ten years* of passport charges."

"Yeah, but you'll never get any time out of them," said Glanzer. "It's a first offense. I'll get him probation and a fine, and you know it."

"Not on this case," said Barcella. "This is no ordinary passport case."

"So what?" Glanzer asked heatedly.

"So we'll pile them on top of two first-degree murder charges and about a dozen conspiracy and bombing charges, that's what!" said Barcella, opening the bluff strongly. "Seymour, what I'm trying to tell you is that we've got your guy. We know what he did. We know he came up here from Chile. We know he met with Guillermo and the Cuban Nationalist Movement people in New Jersey and New York. We know he set the whole thing up with them. And we know about his expertise with bombs and electronics."

"Yeah, but you can't prove any of it," Glanzer said.

"Seymour, don't tell me what we can prove and what we can't prove!" shouted Barcella. "You don't have to do the time—Townley does. We got him. Maybe we've only got a fifty-fifty shot at him at a trial on the murders, but you put that on top of a hundred percent shot on the passport violations and that's a hell of a chance for your man to take."

"Oh, cut it out, Larry," said Glanzer.

Propper interrupted. "Wait a minute, you guys," he said. "Look, Seymour, we want Townley to cooperate. You know that."

"Then you'd better offer a hell of a deal," said Glanzer. "He's that good a witness."

"I don't know how good a witness he'd make," said Propper. "But I do know he's right in the middle of this. That's obvious. There are millions of people in Chile, but we went down there and came back with just one—Townley. We did that for a reason. And what Larry is saying is that if you lose in a trial, Townley will never see the light of day."

"That's not quite what I'm saying, Gene," said Barcella, less soothingly. "What I'm saying is that we don't have to make a deal with your fucking client, Seymour. If you walk into court against Gene and me, we're gonna put your man's ass in jail for a long time."

"Oh, cut out the tough talk, will you?" cried Glanzer. "I've been on the other side of that bullshit so many times it bores me."

Silbert's eyes had been closed during the fireworks, but now he intervened. "Now wait a minute, you guys," he said. "We're not getting anywhere with this." Silbert tried to mediate, and the pattern was set for the next hour. Glanzer would say white. Barcella would shout black. Propper would say gray. And Silbert would say let's not argue.

In the end, Glanzer said, "Look, there's no sense talking anymore now, because Townley wants to see this goddamn tin-star general from Chile. He won't do anything before that."

"Orozco," said Propper. "We know about that."

"Okay," said Glanzer. "And he wants to talk with his wife and his family. Even if Barry and I recommend that he cooperate with you guys, we're not sure he'll do it yet. But I think he will."

"That's good, Seymour," said Silbert.

"I'm not making any promises, though," said Glanzer. "I'll get back to you, maybe tomorrow. I just wanted you to know how good a witness this guy would make. He's the only one who can give you the big shots. You guys have done a good job so far. Don't screw it up now."

In the post mortem among the prosecutors, Silbert sounded an optimistic note. "I think Seymour's getting close to a deal," he said. "Otherwise he would have rejected the whole thing by now. We may get out of this without offering immunity after all."

"Immunity?" said Barcella weakly.

"Yeah, Larry," said Propper. "What else would we do if Seymour comes in here like gangbusters and stonewalls it? It's late in the game. We've got no case. And if we have to give Townley a free ride to solve the case or let him go and *not* solve the case, what's the choice?"

"He'll make a terrible witness if he gets a free ride," said Barcella. "Nobody will believe him."

"But a bad witness is better than no witness," said Silbert.

"We wouldn't have any choice," Propper said numbly. The vision of a free Townley and a disintegrated investigation suddenly paralyzed him. Silbert's words made the nightmare seem real.

"Look, that's the absolute worst case," said Silbert, rebounding from the gloom. "I don't want to hear any more about immunity. When we're talking with Seymour, it's out of the question. I think we're going to get some time out of Townley."

"Where we lucked out was the proffer," said Barcella. "When Seymour said he refused to give us one, I wanted to go out and blow a trumpet or something. Then Gene jumped on Seymour's head, and I was afraid he would bully Seymour into giving us one."

"I had to act pissed off, Larry," said Propper.

"I know," said Barcella. "Just don't be too good at it, okay? You scared me."

"It worked okay," said Propper. "But I don't figure it. How come Seymour wouldn't give us a proffer, Earl?"

"I don't know," said Silbert. "He must have a damn good reason, though, because it means he has to negotiate without knowing exactly what we have. Maybe Townley's worse than we think, and Seymour doesn't want to have to tell us."

In Miami, Danny Benítez's regular partner was eating alone in a restaurant that day when he thought he saw a familiar face. At first, Detective Humberto Rapado was not even sure of the name, but the face nagged at his mind enough so that Rapado left money on the table to cover his bill and followed the man outside. The mystery man was one of three Cuban males who had just finished a meal together. Suddenly Rapado remembered the name: Novo. Benítez had shown him a picture of the fugitive only two days earlier.

Luck was with Rapado. The three men stepped into a new Lincoln Continental and drove past the spot where Rapado had parked his unmarked police cruiser. Rapado followed the Lincoln through the Miami traffic toward the airport, wondering what he would do if the three men tried to board a flight.

To Rapado's relief, the Lincoln pulled into the parking lot of an apartment complex near the airport, and the three men went inside one of the apartments. Then the detective walked across the street from his makeshift observation post and looked into the Lincoln. On the passenger's seat he saw a clipboard holding several papers, including a new automobile registration form. The name on the form was Alvin Ross.

Detective Rapado remembered the name. Benítez had shown him Ross's photograph along with Novo's, from a package Benítez had just received in the mail from Propper and from friends in the New York City police department. These were suspects in the Letelier case.

Rapado could not reach Benítez until nearly two o'clock in the afternoon. Excitedly, he relayed the news. "I spotted Novo's face and Ross's car," he said.

Benítez pounced on the break. "How sure?" he asked.

"I'm pretty sure it was Novo's face, but he was wearing a wig," said Rapado. "I'm not a hundred percent sure. I didn't see Ross's face, but I saw his name in the car. They're checking the license now. It's a New Jersey temporary. Must be new."

"Fantastic!" said Benítez. "Did you tell the Feebies?" He was referring to the FBI.

"Yeah," said Rapado, without enthusiasm.

"What'd they say?" asked Benítez.

"They don't believe it," said Rapado. "They say Novo's supposed to be somewhere up in Jersey."

This disgusted Benítez. "The pansies," he growled. "They don't know where he is. So what are we supposed to do, forget about it?"

"They want us to put them under surveillance until we can get a positive ID," said Rapado.

"That figures," muttered Benítez.

By the next morning, April 13, New Jersey officials had confirmed that the Lincoln was newly registered to Alvin Ross. Rapado's lead heated up. FBI cars joined Dade County police units on the surveillance.

Word of the possible sighting reached Cornick and Scherrer at Fort Meade. Townley was in the conference room with his parents, who had arrived from Florida that morning and trained looks of cold contempt on the agents who had brought their son out of Chile. During the Townley family's private interview, Cornick was on the phone to WFO, to headquarters, and to Miami. In the crisis, everyone was agreed that there could be no mistakes. The Miami agents *must* make sure it was Novo. They must not lose him. They had to make sure they arrested him legally.

As to Ross, Propper and Barcella began calling prosecutors in New Jersey, knowing that Ross had been near indictment there on charges of storing explosives and making destructive devices. Could the New Jersey prosecutors quickly get before a judge with enough evidence to justify an arrest warrant on those charges?

At Fort Meade, Scherrer and Cornick were debating an escalation in their psychological warfare against Townley. They wanted to predict Novo's arrest to Townley—and to make the arrest sound like a routine event, a natural consequence of the FBI's omniscience in regard to Novo's movements and deeds. They told the two prosecutors of the possible benefits from such a move, and of the obvious risks: if the man sighted in Miami turned out not to be Novo—or if the man was in fact Novo but managed to get away—then Townley and Glanzer might begin to realize the weakness of the forces against them.

"What difference would it make?" asked Barcella. "If everything goes wrong down there, you can keep the news from Townley until everything's over up here, anyway. Go ahead. The *fiscal*'s ass is so far out on a limb that another mile or two can't matter."

Propper did not think this was funny. "Your ass, too, Larry," he said, but he agreed with Barcella's conclusion.

Cornick and Scherrer, who had risks of their own to worry about, had resolved to make several new pitches to Townley when they saw a transformed couple emerge from the Fort Meade conference room. The mother had been crying, and even the ramrod-straight Vernon Townley appeared visibly shaken. Once again, Cornick and Scherrer assumed he had made some sort of confession, and they ached to know the details.

Back with Townley, the two agents dispensed favors and resumed their practiced, idle conversation. Scherrer chose the moment to begin the drama. "You know, Mike, there's something I ought to tell you," he said in a hushed, conspiratorial tone. "Whatever you and Glanzer are planning to do—you'd better do it quick. Take my word for it."

Cornick was frowning almost violently.

"Why?" Townley asked Scherrer.

"Because we're going to roll up Novo soon," said Scherrer. "We've got an informant on him that we can't leave out there any longer. It's too dangerous. So we're about to pull them all in."

Townley studied Scherrer intently, waiting for more. Cornick intervened. "That's enough, Bob," he declared. "That's informant information. Don't tell him another word." Cornick turned to Townley. "Mike, forget you ever heard that," he said gravely. "It could get us in a lot of trouble."

Seymour Glanzer walked alone into Silbert's office that Thursday afternoon for the second negotiating session with the prosecutors. Both sides knew that time was running out on the material-witness warrant. Each side would be forced to make a move soon unless an agreement could be reached.

Before Glanzer could fully warm to the subject of Townley's superiority to John Dean as a witness, Barcella interrupted. "Wait a minute, Seymour," he said. "I can't take any more of this. John Dean went to jail, didn't he? Why don't we start with that and talk about Townley?"

"That's true," said Glanzer. "Dean did go to jail, but not for long. You'll note that I haven't asked for immunity."

"That's a good thing," said Propper, "because we wouldn't even consider it for Townley."

"Of course not," Silbert declared. "You guys know better than that. For a crime of violence, we wouldn't even talk if you asked for immunity, Seymour."

"Well, I want damn near it," said Glanzer.

"Look," said Silbert. "This is a double homicide. We say Townley's involved in it, and you say Townley's involved in it. For that kind of crime, he's got to serve at least a reasonable period of time."

"What kind of time are we talking about?" asked Glanzer. "I want some kind of cap on it from you guys. I want a cap on the sentence before we deal. We're not going to leave the sentencing to the judge."

"We can't guarantee that the judge will buy it," said Propper. "We can agree, but it might not mean anything."

"That's all right with me," said Glanzer, "as long as the cap on the sentence is part of the deal. I want to be able to say to my client, 'Look, you won't have to serve any more time than this.' If the judge wants to reject the sentence, he has to reject the whole deal. And we start over."

"Just a minute, Seymour," said Carl Rauh, a man whose soft-spoken manner seemed at odds with his harsh views. "I just want you to know that I think this man ought to go to jail for the rest of his life," he said politely. "He shouldn't ever be out on the street again. He killed people he didn't even know. He's as cold-blooded as they come."

"Well, he's not going to jail that long and you know it," Glanzer told Rauh, who did not reply. Rauh assumed a pose of aloof disapproval, as though representing the claims of the silent victims.

Don Campbell broke into the discomfort. "Look, we can't very well talk about time until we agree on what he's pleading to," he said. "Let's get that first."

"I think he should plead to one count of Title 1116," said Propper, "murder of a foreign official."

"No way," said Glanzer. "He's not gonna plead to the murder itself."

"Why not?" asked Barcella. "He's a murderer, so he should plead to the murder."

"He's also the first one here to make a deal," said Glanzer. "So that's out; 1116 is out."

"How about conspiracy to murder a foreign official?" asked Silbert. "The conspiracy count would cover everything he did."

"That's Title 1117," said Propper.

"That covers the whole ball of wax," said Silbert.

"That sounds better," said Glanzer. "What's the time on that?"

"Up to life," said Propper. "It carries a life maximum."

"That's just what I mean," said Glanzer. "That's no good. We need a cap way the hell below life. We won't go in and take a chance that the judge might sentence him to life. That's ridiculous. We've got to have a cap."

"What kind of cap are you talking about?" asked Silbert.

"I think twenty years," said Barcella. "I could live with that, maybe."

"Well, I couldn't," said Glanzer. "The man's not going to do twenty years."

"We're not talking about a minimum twenty years, Seymour," said Barcella. "We're talking about a *maximum* twenty years, so he could get parole after seven years."

"I know that," said Glanzer. "But forget it. He won't take twenty years. We'll take our chances in court before we'll do that."

For the next hour the lawyers argued numbers. Glanzer preferred a sentence similar to the one given John Dean for the Watergate cover-up—one-to-four years. Barcella argued for twenty. Propper generally advocated a numerical compromise, and Carl Rauh spoke up every ten minutes or so to say he thought Townley should go away forever.

The two sides found themselves arguing about a proposed nine-year sentence, which would make Townley eligible for parole after three years.

"Seymour, let me tell you something," said Barcella, "I deal with the Bureau of Prisons every day, and I should tell you that he'd be better off with a ten-year sentence than with nine."

"Why's that?" Glanzer asked skeptically.

Barcella went on for ten minutes about the complicated, contradictory parole rules, in what would later become known as the "New Math" speech. His objective was to reach a sentence in double figures, knowing that it would sound more palatable to a jury. The result was that Glanzer accepted the ten-year maximum. He said it didn't make him happy, but it was possible. The prosecutors said the same.

"I think Townley will take it," said Glanzer. "But it'll take time. He wants to talk to people."

"Let him think it over," said Silbert. "But just remember this, I'm thinking it over, too. You've got an offer, but we can withdraw it any time until he signs it."

Glanzer departed, and the prosecutors nearly collapsed at the release of tension. They made nervous speeches to one another about how the deal was a good one under the circumstances. All of them, especially Propper, found it impossible not to dwell on the central question: would Townley sign? Now, with the entire investigation hanging in the balance, Propper's normal impatience grew into a fever.

When Townley heard of the offer, from Glanzer, he bombarded Scherrer and Cornick with requests for phone calls: to Mariana Townley, to his parents, and to James Weck, the Townley family lawyer in Fort Lauderdale. After the calls, Townley paced and brooded in his cell. Then he summoned Scherrer and Cornick.

"I'm going to tell you something," he said. "But first I have to have your word that you won't tell Propper. I mean it."

"What for, Mike?" asked Cornick.

"I can't tell you that without telling you what it is," said Townley. "But it's important."

Cornick and Scherrer withdrew to consult privately before agreeing to Townley's condition. They decided that Townley needed to play spy, that he needed to conspire with someone, and that it was a good sign that he wanted to do so with them instead of with the Chileans or Cubans. They would agree to take Townley's oath; they could always violate it if he told them something heinous.

Townley made them swear on their professional honor. "Okay," he said. "I'm inclined to sign the agreement. Weck thinks I should. I think I should. But I don't want you to tell Propper, because I want to make some changes in the agreement. If he knows I'm going to sign anyway, he won't agree to make them."

Cornick and Scherrer decided that they could abide by their oaths in most respects. Cornick called Propper. "Gene, I've got some bad news and some good news," he said. "The good news is that Townley's family lawyer told him your offer is a damn good one. That impressed Townley. The bad news is that Townley got the lawyer to fly up here in the morning so he can talk it over some more."

"What the hell does he want to talk to him for?" snapped Propper. "He doesn't know criminal law."

"That may be, Gene, but he still wants to talk to him. And he's still after Orozco. He says he won't sign anything until he gets an order releasing him from his secrecy agreement."

"Shit!" said Propper. "What does he think he's doing? He's a criminal suspect, not a movie star!"

"Calm down, Gene," said Cornick. "You've got to be nice to this guy Weck. He'll call you tonight. You and Larry should take him up to Meade tomorrow. And don't worry. Townley's going to talk."

"How do you know?"

"It's all part of the big picture," laughed Cornick. Propper didn't laugh at all.

Danny Benítez had joined the surveillance at four o'clock that afternoon for the night shift. Rapado was asleep, so his partner was Detective Ignacio Vásquez, known on the police force as "the Hulk." Vásquez was half a foot taller and even huskier than Benítez. Neither detective had eaten all day—owing to steady work on other cases—and they became bored and very hungry as they watched the Lincoln from across the street. Occasionally they chatted with the two FBI agents who were sharing the watch.

The three suspects had been inside the apartment all day. Nothing was stirring. Shortly after dark, Benítez made a run to the Burger King nearby and returned with six cheeseburgers, two large Cokes, and a load of fried potatoes. He knew something was wrong before he opened his car door. Vásquez was arguing with the FBI agents. Panic had struck. Benítez jumped into his car with the bag of food.

"They're moving!" said Vásquez. "All three of them! In that brown Chevy." Benítez and Vásquez drove off in pursuit of the three suspects, who were heading toward Little Havana.

"What about the Feebies?" Benítez cried over the radio. "Aren't they coming with us?"

"No!" said Vásquez. "They say their orders are to stick with the Lincoln."

"What for?" cried Benítez. "If they're all in the Chevy, what are they watching the Lincoln for?"

"That's what I asked them," said Vásquez. "They say they're not moving."

"The bastards," said Benítez. "What if we lose them?"

"Forget it," said Vásquez.

The driver ahead shot through the traffic at high speeds, and the detectives, driving without their headlights, fell behind. Only by chance did they see what they thought was the brown Chevrolet pulling into the parking lot of La Hacienda restaurant.

Vásquez stopped across the street and waited while Benítez walked over to verify the license number and to take a peek inside the restaurant. He returned to say that the three suspects were sitting calmly at a table near the window, ordering dinner.

"Let's eat, too," said Vásquez. He and Benítez opened the Burger King bag and found that both Coca-Colas had spilled during the chase. The cheeseburgers and french fries were floating in a sticky mess.

Benítez radioed for reinforcements and then settled back miserably with Vásquez to watch the suspects have a meal. "I'll bet they're eating steak," said Benítez.

"Forget it," said Vásquez. "Look, while they're in there in good light, we should try to get a positive ID. You know the pictures. You go in there and take a look. I'll keep an eye on the car."

Benítez went inside and pretended to look at a menu near the cash register, hoping that none of his friends on the restaurant staff would come by. Glancing over at the suspects, he recognized Alvin Ross immediately. Although another of the suspects was wearing thick-rimmed glasses and a longish wig, with bangs, Benítez was relatively certain he was Guillermo Novo.

He thought the third man was Virgilio Paz, but he couldn't get a look at the man's face. Benítez retreated to a pay phone near the cash register and called his mother as he waited for the suspect to turn around. He called several other people to pass the time, but the man he thought was Paz never let him get a good look at his face.

Two hours later, Vásquez and Benítez led three other police cars on a surveillance run behind the brown Chevrolet, which led them to the Sensation Club—a discotheque known as a rendezvous point for drug smugglers. A few hours later the surveillance team followed the car to the home of a woman who had lost one husband and at least one boyfriend in narcotics-related homicides. Such murders occurred almost nightly in Miami as a by-product of the $5 billion smuggling trade.

"These guys are dopers," Benítez concluded. "We gotta bust 'em." He restrained himself, however, knowing that the FBI wanted a warrant on Ross and some positive proof on Novo before making a move. His team followed the suspects back to the apartment building just before three o'clock in the morning. A fresh unit of FBI agents was there watching the Lincoln, which had not moved.

Benítez was called back to duty at nine o'clock the next morning —Friday, April 14. He found eight FBI agents and half a dozen police officers clustered around a makeshift command post near the apartment building. They were all waiting for word to come through the Miami FBI office that the warrant for Ross had been signed. Then they would move in on the apartment and arrest Ross, and they would question the other two men to find out if they were Novo and Paz. Benítez kept saying it was about time. All the officers were nervous, in anticipation of the bust. They planned logistics and wondered whether the men inside were heavily armed.

There was still no news on the warrant at eleven o'clock, when one of the FBI lookouts called over the radio to say, "Better hurry! They're moving!" He said the three suspects were outside the apartment loading suitcases into the trunks of the Chevrolet and the Lincoln.

Ovidio Cervantes, the FBI's Miami case agent for CHILBOM, struggled to make command decisions. The warrant still had not come through. This news caused much cursing. Cervantes shouted orders over the general noise among the officers: they would follow Ross and move in for the arrest when advised by radio that the warrant had been signed. Several officers protested the plan. Cervantes tried to establish order. Just then word came that the three suspects were splitting up. This called for a new plan. Cervantes shouted that he and two other cars would follow Ross's Lincoln. The others would follow the brown Chevrolet and attempt to interview the occupants to determine whether one of them might be Guillermo Novo.

Cervantes jumped into his car and roared off as the other officers argued about how they would "interview" someone like Guillermo Novo. Benítez and several others wanted to arrest him.

The lookouts were shouting over the radio. The Lincoln had just taken off toward Little Havana at high speed; the Chevrolet had turned the other way and was heading toward the command post.

Cervantes and his backup car passed the Chevrolet, which came by the command post while Benítez and the other officers and agents were jumping into their cars, still arguing about what to do. The Chevrolet turned right, toward the airport road.

Benítez and his group were just about to pull out in pursuit when they heard shouts over the radio: the Lincoln had just executed a squealing, high-speed turn and was now heading back toward the command post! The Cervantes group did the same.

"They've spotted the tail!" shouted Benítez. "Or they're dopers!"

He knew that the U-turn was a standard security measure on large smuggling runs.

Benítez and his party were obliged to wait just off the road, fuming, while the Lincoln and the Cervantes group roared past them and turned toward the airport road, just as the brown Chevy had done. By now the Chevrolet had a big head start. The cars in the Benítez party scattered in many directions, and it took the FBI agents and police officers some time to report to one another by radio that the Chevrolet was gone.* They had lost it.

Fortunately for the chase team, an FBI agent named Connelly was just arriving late on the scene. He came on the radio to say he thought he had seen a brown Chevrolet entering the parking lot of the Airport Lakes Holiday Inn. All cars on the Novo surveillance converged there to find a car with the correct license number. Sighs of relief went up, along with vows that the suspects would be arrested before they had a chance to escape again.

The lead FBI agent, George Kiszynski, called by radio for an undercover FBI agent—someone who could enter the Holiday Inn surreptitiously to look for the suspects. Benítez and the police contingent called by radio for backup squad cars of uniformed officers. The mixed posse abandoned all efforts to be subtle, and soon the parking lot was teeming with uniforms and with plainclothesmen carrying rifles. The FBI undercover man went inside and reported by hand radio that the two suspects were having breakfast, apparently oblivious to all the commotion outside.

Meanwhile, the officers heard Cervantes shouting for help over the car radios. The Lincoln was heading north on the Palmetto Expressway at speeds above 80 miles per hour. Cervantes was falling behind in the traffic. In desperation, he asked the police to radio ahead to units in the northern suburbs of Miami. Finally, a marked car from the town of Medley caught up with the Lincoln and pulled it over. Cervantes came up from behind, supported by units of FBI agents. Alvin Ross jumped out of the Lincoln and surrendered. In the Lincoln, the officers found a Derringer pistol, a .45-caliber automatic, two .38-caliber Smith & Wessons, a book of poems by Federico

---

*Lacking a common radio frequency, the FBI agents and police officers were obliged to communicate with one another by relaying messages through dispatchers at their respective offices. Naturally, this caused delay and confusion. At that time, each of the fifty different law-enforcement organizations in the Miami area insisted on having its own frequency, with the result that officers could not speak directly with anyone from a different agency or jurisdiction.

García Lorca, a Gucci travel bag, a three-post weighing scale, and a large plastic bag full of white powder. Police officers said it was cocaine.

Back at the Holiday Inn, the undercover FBI agent had not returned and the men outside were getting jumpy. Suddenly one of the two suspects emerged from the lobby and walked to the brown Chevy. He was just opening the trunk when an FBI cruiser and two police squad cars converged loudly within a few feet of him. The startled suspect fell back against his car. Donald Dumford jumped out of the cruiser, identified himself as FBI, and told the man not to move.

While this suspect remained pinned against the Chevrolet, a dozen officers poured into the lobby of the Holiday Inn, guns drawn, shouting, "Police! FBI! Don't move!" The desk clerks and several hotel guests shrank back against the walls.

The third suspect was nowhere in the restaurant. All the invading officers, now worried about the FBI undercover man, began to search frantically. Benítez ran into the men's room and kicked open all the stalls. He was debating whether to do the same in the ladies' room when an elevator door opened and the third suspect stepped into the lobby, in the custody of the FBI undercover man.

Outside, the two suspects were quickly surrounded by some thirty lawmen from different organizations, and the lawmen in turn were surrounded by a growing crowd of spectators. George Kiszynski pushed his way through to the second suspect and asked for his name.

"Victor Triquero," said the suspect.

"I'm with the FBI, Mr. Triquero," said Kiszynski. "We want to find out who you are and what you're doing here. Do you have any identification?"

"Sure, no problem," said the suspect. He handed Kiszynski a driver's license in the name of Victor Triquero.

Benítez pushed his way through the crowd and put his nose a few inches from the suspect's. "This is Novo!" cried Benítez. He shouted into the suspect's face that a "Tricky Vic" alias might work against the *gringos* but not against a Cuban cop.

"Take it easy, Danny," said Kiszynski, seconded by several officers in the background.

"This is Novo!" shouted Benítez. He pulled out his photograph of Guillermo Novo and held it up beside the suspect's face. "See?" cried Benítez. "This is Novo!"

Officers peered at the photograph and several were inclined to agree. The suspect said, "I don't know anyone named Novo. My name is Victor Triquero."

Benítez stamped on the pavement. Veins were standing out on his neck. "You're Novo!" he shrieked, thrusting his hands into the suspect's pockets. He pulled out a receipt from the Sensation Club and a newspaper clipping about the arrest of Michael Townley. The clipping mentioned Guillermo Novo. "See?" cried Benítez. "Last night you were at the Sensation Club and you ate at La Hacienda! You were wearing the same tan suit you're wearing now, and you were wearing a wig! You're Novo!" Benítez turned to Kiszynski. "If you don't arrest this guy, I'll arrest him!"

Kiszynski was in a conference with several other agents. Benítez couldn't stand the wait. "Okay, Novo, you're under arrest for displaying a fraudulent driver's license!" He handcuffed the suspect while Kiszynski tried to calm him down.

"The FBI is not saying you're Novo," Kiszynski told the suspect as he was being led off to an FBI car. "We just want you to go with us to the office for questioning."

"Wait!" cried Benítez. "So he can walk away again? Bullshit! I arrested him! He's going to jail! I don't care what happens! He's going to jail!"

Beside himself with rage, Benítez stomped through the crowd to the other suspect. "I bet you're Paz," he said. "Gimme some ID."

"I don't have any ID," said the suspect. "I just gave it to the other guy."

Benítez looked around. There were at least twenty officers nearby. "*What* guy?" he demanded. "I don't care! Gimme some more ID!"

The suspect reached nervously into his wallet and handed Benítez a driver's license in the name of Manuel Menéndez.

"Okay!" said Benítez. "Is your name Manuel Menéndez?"

"Yes," said the suspect.

"Wait here!" Benítez commanded. He went to ask for a name check by radio. Before he could get to his car, a police sergeant stopped him and said, "Danny, take it easy. I've already checked that guy's ID and it's okay."

Benítez looked at the driver's license in the sergeant's hand. It was in the name of Héctor Rivero. Benítez took both driver's licenses, stomped the pavement some more, and put his nose into the suspect's face. "You gave us two different driver's licenses, you son-of-a-bitch!" he cried. "You're under arrest for using a fraudulent driver's license! Whoever you are, you're going to jail!" Benítez handcuffed his second prisoner. An FBI agent told him to take it easy.

"Have you arrested him for anything?" Benítez asked.

"Well, we're going to talk to him down at the office," said the agent.

"That's great," said Benítez. "But he'll be arrested when you do, 'cause I'm arresting him right here."

Two hours later, at the Miami FBI office, one suspect was still insisting that he was Victor Triquero. No one realized that his identity papers had been provided by FBI informant Ricardo Canete. The suspect would not break.

Inside the Fort Meade stockade, FBI Agent Tim Mahoney escorted Townley, in handcuffs, into the back of an army jeep. The driver took them to a helicopter pad where an FBI helicopter was already revving its engines. Mahoney helped Townley climb in. They were the only two passengers on the flight down through Maryland and Washington, across the Potomac River (where the pilot narrowly missed a high-tension power cable), and into Virginia.

At the Quantico helicopter pad, Stames, Satkowski, Cornick, and Scherrer watched Mahoney deliver Townley into the joint custody of the U.S. marshals and the U.S. marine authorities at the new Quantico brig, where security was much tighter than at Fort Meade. Two marshals would be with Townley at all times. Marine officers welcomed Townley stiffly and marched with him inside, where they ordered him to remove all his clothing for a body search.

At the Miami FBI office, agents were swarming over the Lincoln and the Chevrolet for fingerprints and contraband. Benítez was marking evidence. Agents had taken statements from Alvin Ross and Manuel Menéndez, but Victor Triquero would say nothing. He resembled Guillermo Novo, but he held to the Triquero identity and demanded to be released or informed of the charges.

When he heard of the impasse, Benítez went into the interview room and read the suspect his rights. "I don't give a damn what these guys have on you," he declared. "I've got you for a fraudulent driver's license. I'm gonna take you to jail and book you as a John Doe, and it may take you ten years to get out! You can't make bond until you prove who the hell you are."

Taking the suspect and his possessions, Benítez drove to the Dade County Jail, where he photographed the possessions and filled out a

John Doe booking slip. Benítez wrote "00000" in all the spaces for biographical data. Then he took the suspect to the cellblock. "I got a John Doe arrest," he told the jailer. "This asshole won't tell me who he is. I know he's Guillermo Novo, but I'm gonna book him as a John Doe because there's a conflict in his ID."

"That won't be necessary, jailer," said the suspect. "My name is Guillermo Novo."

"Are you sure you're not going to change your mind?" Benítez asked. "You don't want to be Triquero anymore? Do you know who the hell you are?"

"Yeah," said Novo, "I'm Guillermo Novo."

"Okay, that's better," said Benítez. "Now I've got to change the booking slip."

The FBI dispatch that reached Cornick at Quantico did not mention a contribution by Benítez or any other police officer. It said merely that the Miami FBI office had arrested Alvin Ross and a man who was now positively identified as the fugitive Guillermo Novo.

Cornick shouted hallelujahs. He called Miami for details about the third suspect, who was identified as a convicted drug smuggler. Then Cornick and Scherrer sat down to plan more theater for Townley.

In Townley's cell, Cornick interrupted the casual conversation. "Mike, we didn't come in here to entertain ourselves today," he said. "Bob and I wanted to give you a little advance warning. We picked up the Cubans today in Miami."

Townley's face became instantly tight. "Which ones?" he asked.

"Guillermo," said Cornick. "And Ross, too. It'll be in the papers tomorrow. You can ask Glanzer, but we wanted you to know early. Now it's every man for himself."

Townley, who took nothing from Cornick at face value, turned to Scherrer for confirmation. "It's true, Mike," said Scherrer.

"The rats are leaving the ship," said Cornick. "That's why Bob's been pushing you to make up your mind."

"They'll never talk," said Townley.

Scherrer was wincing, shaking his head. "They won't have any choice," he said. "Besides, they're drug people. They were caught red-handed with a lot of drugs they were trying to sell to get money to run with. They're drug people, Mike. They're not professionals."

Scherrer and Cornick left the cell. Townley sent for them almost immediately and said he wanted to talk to General Orozco again, right away. Obligingly, Scherrer called Santiago.

As the two agents stood beside him, Townley told Orozco that it was imperative for him to speak in person with Orozco or someone else at the highest levels of Chilean military authority. Townley said he wanted to cooperate with the FBI and that he wanted to explain himself to Orozco. He said he wanted someone to guarantee the safety of his family in Chile. He also told Orozco that he wanted someone to release him from his DINA secrecy oath so that he could speak freely to the FBI about the Letelier assassination.

Scherrer took the phone from Townley and spoke in Spanish. "General Orozco?" he said. "This is Scherrer, the legal attaché from the FBI. We met in Santiago. I'm here with Townley, and I want to make sure you understand how important this is."

When Orozco promised Scherrer that he would fly to the United States the next day, Saturday, Scherrer and Cornick sent Townley to his cell and called Propper at the courthouse. "Let me tell you something," said Cornick. "That helicopter move today had an amazing effect on Townley, and the timing was incredible. Believe me. That military stuff gets to him. Now he's down here where you can eat off the floor and the marines spit-shine the whole place every five minutes. Then Scherrer and I hit him with the Novo bust. That did it. He's ready to sign. He's been frantically calling Glanzer. And the upshot of it is that you and Larry better find Glanzer and we can be done with this thing."

"Don't worry, Carter, we'll handle it!" said Propper.

"That's all I wanted to hear, boy," said Cornick. "Good luck." He hung up and turned to Scherrer. "I still can't believe we got Novo today of all days—after all these months," he said. "God must be an FBI agent."

Townley prowled his cell at Quantico all day Saturday, smoking cigarettes continuously. He wanted Orozco to hurry. He wanted to sign. He wanted to change the agreement Glanzer was fashioning with the prosecutors.

Scherrer and Cornick showed Townley newspaper articles about Novo's arrest the previous day. They underlined passages that told how guns and drugs had been found in Ross's car. They also told Townley in tones of great significance that Manuel Menéndez had been released already, on minuscule bond. Smiling, they said they could not imagine how such a thing could have happened.

Neither Cornick nor Scherrer knew then that Menéndez had been released because of an oversight. In the chaos after the Novo arrest, no one had bothered to check the federal indices on Menéndez, and

Menéndez had bailed his way out of jail before anyone discovered that he was wanted on federal heroin charges. But Townley seemed to believe—falsely—that Menéndez had been the FBI's informant.

Townley said he wanted to sign, but he kept changing his mind in fits and starts. And he kept proposing new conditions for his agreement with the United States. He backed away from some of them, but he insisted that his wife, Mariana Callejas Townley, be immunized from all prosecution in the United States. Otherwise he would not sign.

Glanzer relayed this condition to Propper and Barcella during their telephone marathon over the weekend. It puzzled the prosecutors, who had never had any reason to suspect that Mariana Townley had been involved in crimes. They kept telling Glanzer that the arrest of the Cubans made it a new ball game. Time was short. They might withdraw their offer to Townley and make a deal with the Cubans. It was no time for Townley to dream up new conditions.

"You won't need to make a deal with the Cubans," said Glanzer. "Townley's the best thing you could ever want. He can give you the big shots in Chile. The Cubans can't do that."

"Yeah, but they can give us Townley," said Barcella. "They can turn a fifty-fifty shot at Townley on the murders into a ninety-ten shot. We could worry about the big shots later, just like you did in Watergate, Seymour."

"Look, you guys have got a good deal if you don't blow it," said Glanzer. "My client has asked for a reasonable assurance that he won't have to worry about his wife getting arrested every time she comes to visit him in the United States. What's wrong with that?"

"What do you mean, what's wrong with that?" asked Propper. "Seymour, it makes us a little paranoid that he wants to stick her in here at the last minute. That's what's wrong. We're not going to give her a free ride now and then turn around to find out she's killed somebody we didn't even know about."

"She didn't kill anybody," said Glanzer. "But she may have worked for DINA. She may have slipped in and out of the States on false passports. That kind of stuff."

"That may be," said Propper. "But we will not give her total immunity. We don't know anything about her. We've talked to Earl. The best we'll do is to immunize her for all crimes she may have committed in the United States except for crimes of violence. We're not going to take a chance of immunizing her for a murder."

"That sounds okay to me," said Glanzer. "I'll talk to Mike."

Draft sentences were exchanged and modified through the night and into the next day. Propper and Barcella confided to each other that they would go crazy if it didn't end soon.

Scherrer and Cornick were waiting at National Airport with officials from the Chilean embassy when General Orozco arrived, accompanied by Pantoja. After handshakes and greetings, the Americans and Chileans went to the Chilean ambassador's residence, just across Sheridan Circle from the spot where Orlando Letelier died.

There Scherrer told Orozco that the FBI was closing in on the Cubans who had carried out the assassination. Townley wanted desperately to cooperate in order to spare himself a life sentence in prison. All that stood in the way was Townley's desire to be officially relieved of his secrecy obligations to the Chilean government.

"That's all it is, General," Scherrer summarized, in Spanish. "He wants a few little things from you, such as your assurance that nothing will happen to his family in Chile. But basically all he wants is for you to order him to tell the truth. He wants to do it."

Orozco seemed pained. "I see," he said. "But I'm afraid I can't make such a deal with him. I don't have the authority."

"I don't understand, General," said Scherrer. "You are the military prosecutor in charge of the Letelier investigation in Chile, and you are a general of the Chilean army. Why can't you simply tell Townley to tell the truth?"

"It's not that simple, Mr. Scherrer," said Orozco.

"Maybe not," said Scherrer. "But I must warn you that that's the way *Fiscal* Propper and the State Department will look at it. If Townley is willing to talk, which he is, and the only thing that's stopping him is that you refuse to order him to tell the truth, the United States will view that as obstruction on the part of the Chilean government. You are the ranking member of the government with regard to the Letelier investigation. If you can't tell Townley to tell the truth, who can?"

Orozco sighed. "Well, I suppose I should talk to this man Townley again," he said.

Several hours later he was at Quantico, accompanied by Scherrer and Cornick and greeted by Propper and Barcella, along with Mariana Townley, the Townley parents, Barry Levine, and Seymour Glanzer. Townley himself came in from the cellblock. It was quite a reunion. A few of the pairings greeted each other frostily, at best, and Mariana Townley was on cordial terms with no one, including her in-laws. But overriding matters of business were at hand.

Townley asked to be alone with General Orozco, and the two of them were excused to an enclosed courtyard within the brig. All the others remained in the conference room, near the entrance to the cellblock, and wondered what was going on in the courtyard.

Orozco came in after an hour and a half. "I have just heard many very shocking things," he said. "But I have released him from his secrecy oath. He can tell you about what happened to Letelier."

Everyone stirred. Mariana Townley and the defense lawyers went out into the courtyard to consult with Townley. The lawyers called Propper and Barcella over for last-minute talks on the agreement, while Orozco carried on a conversation with Scherrer.

"I will need to take an official statement from him for the military investigation in Chile," said Orozco. "I would prefer to do it at the embassy."

"I'm afraid that would be impossible, General," said Scherrer. "We can't allow Townley to go to any embassy. He might try to claim asylum as soon as he walked through the door."

"Very well," said Orozco. "This is a military base. Perhaps I could convene a court of inquiry here. I'd like to do so at once. Tomorrow, if possible."

Scherrer consulted with Propper and Barcella, who insisted that Townley sign the agreement and tell his story to the Americans before testifying to Orozco. The general relented on that point. By then, Levine and Glanzer were in from the courtyard to remind everyone that Townley wanted his secrecy agreement put in writing before he signed. Orozco looked very pained but nodded. "I will consult with Santiago tonight," he said.

The meeting broke up. Orozco took Scherrer aside. "There is no way Santiago will authorize me to put such an order to Townley in writing," he said.

"Even an order simply stating that he should tell the truth?" asked Scherrer.

Orozco's face showed heavy pressure. "*Especially* such an order," he said grimly. "You know what is involved here. When I tell them, they will never do it."

"Well, General, I can't tell you what to say to your government," said Scherrer. "But I can tell you that you should authorize Townley to talk somehow. If you don't, the State Department is going to announce either that you refused or that your government refused. Either way, it's a disaster."

The next day—Monday, April 17—Barcella and Propper drove to Quantico with the final copies of Townley's plea agreement. Townley had been jittery all day about Orozco. He wanted to see the written secrecy release, but Orozco was nowhere to be found. Scherrer assumed the general was staying away from Quantico altogether, in the hope that Townley would sign Propper's deal without a written order to talk. Finally, Scherrer tracked General Orozco down at the Chilean embassy. Orozco said he was having difficulties with the authorization from Santiago.

"Well, then, this whole thing may blow up in our faces in about ten minutes, General," said Scherrer. "I'm going to get Townley, and I'm going to put him on the phone. The responsibility is yours. You tell him what you want to."

Scherrer could almost hear Orozco being squeezed. "I will tell him that Santiago has approved and that I will get an official letter to him as soon as possible," said Orozco.

"Very good," said Scherrer. He put Townley on the phone. Townley appeared to be moderately relieved.

The Townleys and the defense lawyers had asked to be left alone in the Quantico conference room. Obligingly, Cornick watched Townley from the far end of the room, out of earshot. Then he and Scherrer and the two prosecutors stepped out into the courtyard. It was late afternoon.

Glanzer came out within five minutes. "My client has decided to sign the agreement," he said.

The four investigators looked numbly at each other, trying not to show anything. "That's great, Seymour," said Barcella. "We just happen to have a few copies for him to sign."

Glanzer soon returned with signed copies. Only then did the investigators let go. They slapped each other on the back. All of them claimed to have known this would happen. Barcella said it wasn't quite real yet.

"Well, I know you guys want to hear what he has to say," said Glanzer. "I guess we can get started on that tomorrow."

"Not a chance, Seymour," said Propper. He was pleasant but nearly bubbling with determination. "I've been working nearly two years for this. Feels like ten. We're going to start this tonight. Right now."

Glanzer and Levine shrugged at each other. "Okay," said Glanzer. "Let him say goodbye to Mariana. He'll tell you the story. But let me warn you, he's very nervous. He likes to walk around and smoke while he talks. He can't do it any other way. So don't tell him to sit down, and don't tell him he can't smoke."

Propper grinned. "Seymour, let me tell you something," he said. "I don't care if he strips and stands on his ear—as long as he talks."

The defense lawyers went back inside to prepare Townley. Cornick went outside while they were gone and returned with a sickly look on his face. He was walking lightly, with pain, as though afraid he was crushing kittens with every step.

"What's the matter?" asked Propper.

Cornick swallowed. "You're not going to be happy, but I've got to tell you this," he said. "Stames is outside. He just said this is an investigative stage of the case, and the Bureau should take Townley's statement. And you and Larry shouldn't be there."

Propper started laughing, which only added to Cornick's discomfort. He turned to Barcella. "I know how you feel, believe me," he said. "But I want you to know how Nick feels, too."

"Gene, Carter's serious, I think," said Barcella. Propper could not stop laughing. "Look, Carter," said Barcella, "I should have known Nick would show up now. It's perfect. Look, I know how I feel, and I know how Gene feels. We both feel you should tell Nick to go fuck himself. If anybody's not gonna be there, it's gonna be him."

Propper stopped laughing as Barcella was trying not to start. "I thought he was kidding," said Propper. "I think you should tell Nick we worked it out with Seymour, and we're not sure the Bureau ought to be there."

Stames left in a huff. A few minutes later, the defense lawyers and the four investigators were in the conference room, sitting at schoolroom desks—the kind with small note-taking surfaces for right- or left-handed students. Townley was walking back and forth in front of them, wearing blue jeans, touching his face a lot, and smoking heavily. He paced silently for several minutes, unable to speak the first words.

"Go ahead, Mike," said Levine. "Just tell them what happened."

20 ▣ FULL CIRCLE

"You will be traveling today," says Espinoza. "Lieutenant Fernández, will be returning from Kennedy Airport tomorrow. You should make arrangements to meet him there to receive the preoperative intelligence."

"Yes, my colonel," says Townley. He is sitting alone with Espinoza in a car on the outskirts of Santiago. This means business. The two men, with their wives, have known each other socially for several years now, and they see each other regularly at DINA headquarters, but for matters such as this one Espinoza has always arranged a private meeting.

"Have you been talking to the Cubans?" asks Espinoza.

"Yes, sir," says Townley. "But I haven't mentioned any missions, of course."

"And you still think you are on good terms with them?"

"I think I can reason with them, yes, sir," says Townley.

"Good," says Espinoza. "I want you to explain this mission to them. You are to get them to undertake it for us, and then you are to leave the country. I don't want you there when it happens. If possible, I want it to look like a street mugging or an accident. Something quiet."

"If that's not possible, are you prohibiting the use of explosives?" asks Townley.

Espinoza almost smiles. "No," he says. "If you have to, you have to. I want it done. But if you use explosives, you'd better be ready to stand on the other side of my desk and convince me that it was absolutely necessary."

"Yes, my colonel," says Townley, feeling the weight of the mission. It keeps coming back to him. This is the third time Espinoza has spoken of it since the mission was aborted in Paraguay. Now it is an order. As always, Townley's face seems to grow longer and thinner, more impassive, when he is afraid.

Moments later he jumps out of Espinoza's car and into his own. He soon walks into his house and abruptly tells his wife to repack his suitcase. He will be going to New York after all. Mariana Callejas, who has only recently unpacked the suitcase on the assumption that the Letelier operation has been canceled, protests, but Townley is moving too fast to hear her. His urgent manner sends whispers through the whole house. The servants and the children know that he is leaving again.

Townley rushes downstairs to his laboratory and begins rummaging through the cardboard boxes on one of the shelves. He finds the experimental new electric matches and snips the connector wires off a handful of them. The matches fit snugly inside a half-empty pack of cigarettes, and they look much less suspicious than ordinary blasting caps. Townley also retrieves a box of cold capsules from the upstairs bathroom. He empties a dozen of them and replaces the medicine with lead azide, a powdery white chemical that serves as a "booster" to an explosive charge. The capsules go in Townley's shaving kit.

After some thought, Townley checks into the guarded DINA storage facility for Project ANDREA and with great care takes just enough sarin to fill the small Chanel No. 5 perfume bottle he has brought with him. He tints the clear liquid nerve compound so that it looks very much like the perfume. The Chanel label is still on the bottle. Townley seals and recaps it. He knows that under certain circumstances the sarin might be the ideal instrument for his mission. Someone might be able to throw the bottle into Letelier's car or office window, for instance. Or, if a female accomplice could seduce Letelier, she might be able to open the bottle and leave while he was in the shower. Townley wants to prepare himself for as many options as possible.

He sends his chauffeurs and orderlies scurrying around Santiago all afternoon. One of them returns with an envelope full of American cash—$900: $600 for general expenses and a $50 per diem for six days. Townley protests this as a niggardly sum, but does not expect to be gone long. Another aide returns from the DINA documentation center with the completed new "Hans Petersen" passport and identity card. Townley flies into a rage when he hears that the credit cards and the international driver's license are not ready. They should have blanks on hand, he says. How will he rent a car? Anger makes him drive even more rapidly than usual to the automobile club in downtown Santiago. He resents having to do this himself, but he knows people at the club and there is no alternative. It takes him a little more than an hour to obtain a new international driver's license in the name of Petersen.

Townley proceeds to the travel agency to pick up his airplane ticket. A couple of the clerks, who know him as Andrés Wilson and as Kenneth Enyart, suppress smiles when he comes in as Petersen. This is a new one to them. Townley makes a mental note to renew his protest against DINA's policy of using the same travel agency for all tickets. He feels put upon, having to compensate for all the bureaucratic insanity in the service.

From downtown, he makes an international call to Fernando Cruchaga at the LAN Chile office in New York. He alerts Cruchaga to his arrival the following morning and advises him that someone will come to the LAN Chile office at Kennedy Airport to ask for Andrés Wilson. Cruchaga should make him comfortable and let the man know that Wilson will be there. Townley also asks Cruchaga to call Virgilio Paz with the message that he will be arriving.

At home again, he makes sure that the three newspaper photographs of Orlando Letelier are in his suitcase. After attending to numerous other last-minute chores, he eats a hurried meal with Callejas and the children and says goodbye. He boards the plane with the electric matches in one pocket and the Chanel No. 5 bottle in another. This is risky, he knows, but he decides that it is better than sending them with a LAN Chile pilot, as he normally would do. The bottle might be broken in an accident, or an unwitting LAN Chile employee might want to sniff the perfume. He knows that the sarin would kill everyone on the plane if its fumes escaped into the cabin.

Twelve hours later, approaching an immigration desk at Kennedy International Airport, Townley consoles himself with the thought that he is only a little bit more nervous than he has always been at international borders. For some reason, these places have unnerved him since he was a child—even when he was using his own name and carrying no deadly contraband. It takes an extra effort to appear casual as he hands his official Chilean passport to the immigration inspector. He returns the inspector's polite nod and then watches as the man flips through a book and begins running his finger down a page. Townley knows this is the American government's watch list.

The finger stops abruptly beside a name, and Townley's heart has already frozen by the time the inspector looks up at him. Suddenly alert, the inspector moves the Petersen passport closer to the book for comparison. He looks at Townley again and then reaches for something that Townley fears is the telephone. Instead, it turns out to be an I-94 form. The inspector stamps an entry on it and staples the form to the Petersen passport. Like all other foreign travelers to the United States, Townley will be required to surrender the form when he leaves the country.

When the inspector smiles and returns the passport, Townley takes a few steps and a very deep breath. But he remains shaken. There is clearly a Petersen on the watch list, he reflects. It could be another person. Or, ominously, it could be that the inspector's instructions are to let Petersen through and then notify the CIA or the FBI. Glancing back, he sees that the inspector is on the phone. He loses strength as he imagines the inspector's call to the authorities.

Townley walks to the most remote customs table in the international receiving area. His confidence begins to return when he breezes through without a search, but he does not move ten paces before a LAN Chile employee runs up to him. "Andrés!" he calls cheerfully. "I'm glad you're here! I've been wanting to talk to you!"

Townley reacts with such a ferocious look that the man swallows uncomfortably and then slinks away like a fool, as Townley keeps walking. He hopes the customs attendant has not heard him called Andrés instead of Hans, and when he sees Cruchaga approaching with a big smile, he decides not to give him the chance to make the same mistake. Frowning violently, he shakes his head from side to side as Cruchaga draws near. "Don't talk to me here, Fernando," Townley orders. "Meet me outside."

Safely in the LAN Chile ticketing area, Townley drops his duffel bag and gives Cruchaga an enthusiastic *abrazo*. "Sorry about that," he says warmly. "I'll explain later." Cruchaga says no problem, taking it as part of the mysterious spy game. Townley goes out of his way to apologize to the other LAN Chile employee as well. He is now making a conscious effort to behave gregariously—just in case he is being watched. While trading jokes and handshakes with several other LAN Chile acquaintances, he notices an odd pair of men at the ticket counter. One of them is a stiff-looking blond man in a business suit. The other is in dungarees, looking disheveled. They worry Townley.

Cruchaga leads him upstairs to the executive lounge for an introduction to Enrique Gambra, the new manager of the LAN Chile office in New York. "I am very pleased to meet you, Don Andrés," says Gambra, giving Townley a significant look. Cruchaga looks equally pleased to have delivered such a legend to his new boss. Townley replies benevolently. It amuses him that Gambra, a business executive many years his senior, addresses him by the archaic royal title Don.

Gambra insists on giving Townley a tour of the executive suite, and then he announces that he has made reservations for lunch at an elegant French restaurant. "Thank you, Mr. Gambra, but I don't really want a French meal," Townley replies politely. "As ridiculous as it may seem to you, what I really want is a malted milk, a hamburger, and french fries. The first thing I always want when I come to the States is good old American junk food. I can get a fine French meal in Chile."

This response takes Gambra by surprise, but he keeps smiling. "Of course, Don Andrés," he says. "We will have a hamburger."

After lunch, Townley sits in Cruchaga's office and leafs through the new Radio Shack catalogue. A phone call makes Cruchaga beam. "Someone is asking for Andrés Wilson downstairs," he reports with satisfaction.

Townley walks downstairs to greet Lieutenant Fernández, who is standing between two women. Fernández is trying to look like a tourist. Tennis rackets protrude from his luggage. One of the women is his sister; the other is a DINA agent named Liliana Walker.* Fernández presents Townley to them as Andrés Wilson, and the two men excuse themselves at the first opportunity. They walk upstairs to a private office near the LAN Chile lounge.

Fernández gives Townley a homemade street map of Washington and several handwritten notes. Then he picks a few random items off a desk and begins handling them compulsively. Fernández always needs something in his hands, Townley knows.

---

*A DINA pseudonym. Her true name is still unknown to American investigators. "Walker" is reported to have been a member of the leftist MIR, who "flipped" to work for DINA when her life was spared. Her immediate superior in DINA is said to have been an officer named Bentjerot, but her loyalty ran strongly to his boss, Colonel Pedro Espinoza.

Fernández speaks quietly as he delivers a crisp report. "That's his address there," he says. "And the license number of his car. His wife has another car. That one is his. He drives it to work. They live north of the city in Maryland. Here on the map. And he drives to his office this way, down this route. He parks right here in an alley, next to the office building."

"An alley?" says Townley.

Fernández knows what Townley is thinking. "Yes," he says. "It's very poorly lit at night, and he sometimes leaves work after dark. That's the best place I've seen so far."

Townley nods. Fernández begins pacing. "I don't think his house is a good place, because it's on a dead-end street, with lots of dogs and neighbors nearby," he says. "You might get him at night when he comes home, but it would be difficult."

"Okay," says Townley.

"All the people I've talked to say he will screw anything in skirts," says Fernández, with a glint. "So you might be able to get him to a motel if your people have any bait. That would be the best. But they'll have to find a woman a lot better than that idiot they sent up here with me."

Townley notes the disgust on Fernández's face. "No good?" he prompts.

"No," says Fernández. "She won't follow orders. She's given me nothing but trouble."

"Did she make any contact with him?" asks Townley.

"Not even close," says Fernández.

"What's the matter, Armando?" asks Townley. "You seem more nervous than usual."

"Nothing," says Fernández.

"How is your father?" asks Townley.

"Very bad," says Fernández. "I'm afraid he may die before I get home. They say he is in a coma."

"I'm sorry," says Townley. "I hope he makes it."

"Thank you," says Fernández. "I guess I wasn't getting anything done up here, anyway."

"That's all right," says Townley. He is not sure of Fernández's original orders, because of DINA's compartmentalization policy, but he thinks Espinoza might have ordered Fernández to carry out the mission alone—once Liliana Walker lured the victim into a compromising situation. Townley prefers this interpretation, because it would mean that DINA has been forced once again to turn away from its prideful army officers to a civilian—him. But he likes Fernández personally. "Have you had any security problems?" he asks.

"No," says Fernández.

"I think I have," says Townley. He tells of the watch list and of his continuing worry that the CIA has been aware of their movements since the fiasco in Paraguay six weeks earlier. Townley asks a few more questions about the target. Then he puts the papers into his pocket and beckons Fernández to the door. "I want to show you something that worries me," he says.

In the corridor, Townley makes animated conversation with Fernández as he looks around. "See those two guys over there?" he asks, describing the blond executive and the hippie he had seen earlier. "I saw them downstairs when I first got here. And they're still around. They don't look right to me."

At Quantico, nineteen months later, Townley interrupted his narrative of these events* to look suspiciously at the four investigators sitting at school desks in front of him. "I *still* think those guys were watching me from the minute I came into the airport," he said sourly. "Which would mean the Agency had to have somebody high up in DINA. *Very* high up."

Propper and Barcella looked numbly at the two FBI agents. The idea of such a surveillance was preposterous to all of them, but no one wanted to say anything. They wanted Townley to keep talking. They had made a pact among themselves to conceal any shock or surprise the confession might cause, in order to encourage Townley to believe that they had known everything all along.

Not to be brushed off, Townley put his hands in his pockets and stared at the floor until he forced an answer.

"Could be, Mike," Cornick said evasively.

"Come on," Townley protested. "You can tell me now. I've signed the agreement. This has been bothering me a long time."

After an uncomfortable pause, Scherrer spoke up. "Why don't we go into that a little later, Mike?" he suggested. With a wink and a look, he communicated to Townley that this was a matter best dis-

---

*Townley only summarized the story at Quantico, and for years afterward he continued to withhold crucial details of the version presented here. He did not tell U.S. investigators that he brought a bottle of the nerve compound sarin with him on the Letelier assassination mission, for instance. Sarin was first identified and confirmed as a reserve means of killing Letelier in October 1981, by one of the coauthors.

cussed privately among the intelligence professionals and not in front of straitlaced lawyers.

"Okay," said Townley. He started walking again.

Fernando Cruchaga vouches for Hans Petersen's credit at the airport Avis office, and Townley is soon speeding toward New Jersey in a rented car. He is worried about being followed. He might well be compromised already as an agent, he realizes, and the security of the mission itself may be jeopardized. If the Americans know he is here, and are smart, they will follow him so that they can obtain photographs or other incriminating evidence of the conspiracy. Townley blames Fernández's nerves for making him more jittery than ever.

In Manhattan, Townley takes a detour into the garment district. For the next half hour he drives in special patterns designed to tell him whether he is being followed. He pushes through the traffic in clover leafs and figure eights, always looking to see whether he encounters a familiar car when he doubles back across his own trail. In the end, he is satisfied that the chances of a surveillance are slim, but he repeats the maneuvers in New Jersey—just in case someone is waiting to pick up his trail on the south side of the Lincoln Tunnel.

At Virgilio Paz's apartment, Townley receives an *abrazo* and an introduction to Paz's new wife, Idania, who is manifestly reserved toward her husband's political associates. Paz has already complained to Townley that she lacks the discipline and the capacity for sacrifice that he requires. But she is spirited enough to join them for dinner. When she leaves to change clothes, Paz turns briefly to business.

"What's up?" he asks.

"Orders," says Townley. "I need you to arrange a meeting for me with Guillermo as soon as possible. This is something heavy."

"No problem," says Paz. "But you are not the most popular man around here with the Cubans, you know. This may not be the right time."

"I know," says Townley.

"Is it in Europe?" asks Paz.

"No," says Townley. "Here. In Washington."

Paz stares into his drink and raises an eyebrow almost imperceptibly. This is the only concession he makes to the boldness of the idea. "Who?" he asks.

"One of Allende's cabinet ministers," says Townley. "A guy named Letelier."

"I've heard of him," says Paz. "Don't worry. I will speak to Guillermo." He says nothing for a moment and then takes a long breath, as though to dismiss the subject. "Well, my friend," he says, smiling. "I see there will be no more months of boring vacation, like in Chile. Here we will show you a good time."

Paz does not speak another word of the mission that night. The three of them go to the Bottom of the Barrel for dinner, which is plain food and strong drink, mixed with loud conversation and frequent visitors to Paz's table. Many people pay their respects to Andrés Wilson.

As the evening wears on, Townley keeps thinking about his cover plan. He wants to stay two or three days in New York, persuade the Cubans to undertake the mission, and then return to Santiago by way of Miami. He has decided that a quick visit to his sister in Tarrytown would make a suitable pretext for his trip. At eleven o'clock that night, he excuses himself from Paz's gathering and places a collect call to his sister from the pay phone in the basement at the Bottom of the Barrel. The ensuing conversation is awkward. Linda Fukuchi has not seen her older brother for many years, and she has lived in a different country than he for most of her life. Suddenly he is calling to announce that he is already in the United States and wants to visit her.

Virgilio Paz puts a hand on Townley's elbow and interrupts his phone call. Townley turns to find a lot of noise and an insistent audience. He apologizes to his sister, saying that he will have to call her back. When he hangs up, Paz slaps him on the back and introduces a husky man named Alvin Ross.

"We have talked on the phone, haven't we?" says Townley.

"Yes, we have!" Ross says grandly. "And I am very glad to meet you. We may have our little differences, but I have a lot of respect for Andrés."

After half an hour of glad-handing and bar jokes, Townley calls his sister again and explains himself as best he can.

The next afternoon Townley and Paz are sitting in the Four Star Diner when Guillermo Novo and Dionisio Suárez join them. Townley is reminded of his first meeting with the CNM leaders in the same restaurant some nineteen months earlier. Now, as then, Novo is quite skeptical of Townley's ideas. "We have gone through a lot together, my friend," says Novo. "I trust you, and I understand you, but I am questioning our alliance with Chile. We have done our part. We have helped you wherever we could, in many countries. And what have we gotten in return? Your country offered training and medical assistance for Virgilio, but it didn't work out. You called me all the way to Santiago at great risk to myself, and then the mission you asked us to join in Argentina fell through. Your friends in Argentina have cheated us out of the money, and we have wasted a lot of effort. Worst of all, your country betrayed Otero and Bosch. It is in the *newspapers* now that Chile has issued an arrest warrant for Bosch! How do we know you won't treat us like Otero and Bosch if we ever need you?"

"We've gone over this before, Guillermo," says Townley. "You would never behave the way those two did. Otero dug his own grave. He came to Chile on his own passport, so there was no way to deny it. Then he betrayed his mission to Monkey Morales. Frankly, I don't understand why this issue still troubles you so much, Guillermo. Chile made a mistake. I admitted it. It was certainly not done to hurt you or your movement."

"It's not me personally so much," says Novo. "I don't give a shit about Otero. You know that. But we are a political movement, and many of our supporters are upset. They don't know you. Andrés, we have married our approach to the government of Chile. We have built up the idea of an international anti-Communist alliance among the Latins, and we have told all these groups, 'Hey, if you get into trouble, we can take care of it. We'll send you to our friends in Chile.' Then you do these things to Bosch and Otero *in public!* You've put us in an impossible position."

"But you have to understand that Bosch and Otero put Chile in a difficult position, too," says Townley. "Bosch took a Chilean passport with him on that mission to Costa Rica. That was his idea—or the navy's idea—not DINA's, and it was stupid. Once he did that and got himself arrested, Chile had no choice but to issue a warrant for his arrest on the passport charge. It was as inevitable as day following night."

"No, it wasn't," says Suárez. "You are missing the point. Bosch failed. We all know that. He screws up a lot. But Bosch is our flesh. You should never have issued that warrant. Chile did that to protect Chile. You should have said you didn't know anything about that false passport."

Townley does not quarrel with Suárez, who rarely speaks. "I see your point," he says.

"We do not believe you can act selfishly in this movement," Suárez continues. "That's what Chile has been doing. If we agree to help you in your mission, we will not take money for it. You know that."

"I know," says Townley. "I have already told my superiors that."

"Our problem is the nature of the partnership," says Novo. He carries the burden of the debate for the next hour, pausing only when the waitress brings food or clears dishes. Townley always tries to move the subject toward the mission, and Novo returns to the complaints of the Cuban Nationalist Movement. In the end, he informs Townley that he cannot make such a momentous decision on his own. Townley must present his case that night to the full executive committee.

Soon after leaving the restaurant, Townley places a call to his wife in Santiago. He tells her to pass word to the service that he has made contact and that he thinks everything will work out. "But it's a bitch," he adds. "They've been putting me through it."

Townley drives into Manhattan that afternoon and discovers an eerie coincidence: Orlando Letelier will be making a public appearance that night in New York, just before the secret meeting with the Cubans that may determine his fate. The occasion is the third anniversary of the coup against Allende. Chilean exiles and their supporters will rally to call for a return to civilian rule. Letelier and others will speak. American folksinger Joan Baez is the feature attraction. All these facts are on the posters that Townley examines as he walks around Madison Square Garden.

He debates going to the rally himself. It would be nice to see the target in action, he thinks. He is curious. Also, he thinks he might gather impressions that would buttress his presentation to the Cubans that night. He could describe for them more vividly how dangerous Letelier has become as an exile leader in opposition to Pinochet. And he thinks it would impress the Cubans to hear that Andrés Wilson has walked right into the enemy's camp.

After toying with the idea, he rejects it as unprofessional. He does not want to run the small risk of bumping into someone who knows him from Santiago—one of Mariana's literary friends, possibly. Besides, he doesn't want to contribute the price of a ticket to Letelier's cause. He rips one of the posters off a railing and takes it back to his motel.

Orlando and Isabel Letelier check into New York's Algonquin Hotel at three o'clock that afternoon. Friends arrive to greet them. Letelier says he is pleased with the posters he has seen advertising that night's rally. He predicts a good crowd at the Garden's Felt Forum.

Shortly after arriving, Letelier returns the call of a wire-service reporter and receives the stinging news that the Chilean military gov-

ernment has issued a decree revoking his Chilean citizenship. The
generals have publicly stripped him of his national birthright. Letelier is speechless. He listens in silence as the reporter reads the text
of the edict, which states bluntly that Letelier's attacks upon his
country have brought on the forfeiture. The decree cites his lobbying
campaign against a Dutch loan to Chile and some of his public criticisms.

"I was attacking the government, not the country," says Letelier.
"This is impossible to believe. Pinochet thinks he is a king."

By that evening Letelier's shock has been refined into anger. "Today Pinochet has signed a decree in which it is said that I am deprived of my nationality," he declares to a crowd of five thousand
people at the Forum. "This is an important day for me—a dramatic
day in my life in which the action of the fascist generals against me
makes me feel more Chilean than ever . . . I was born a Chilean; I am
a Chilean; and I will die a Chilean. They were born traitors; they live
as traitors; and they will be known forever as fascist traitors!"

The crowd responds with applause and with emotional cries of support. Letelier, introducing Joan Baez, invokes the spirit of the martyrs who have been killed by the military government, and he
declares that their common cause is gaining strength. The Pinochet
regime is weakening within Chile, he says, and is completely isolated
internationally. "The solidarity of the American people in favor of
the restoration of democracy and human rights in Chile must continue to grow," he concludes. "That solidarity is paramount to us.
We will never rest until we achieve the overthrow of the fascist regime in Chile."

At Quantico, Townley had trouble remembering the names of all
the Cuban exiles who had filed into his room at the Château Renais-
sance motel that evening of September 10. "There were about seven
or eight of them," he said. "Guillermo introduced them to me, but I
remember the tension better than the names or the faces. The atmosphere was a little bit charged, I would say." Townley tried to smile
at his own understatement.

The investigators nodded casually as Townley paced in front of
them. Propper and Barcella, thinking of a future indictment, yearned
to know the names of all the participants in this crucial conspiracy
meeting, but they forced themselves not to show Townley their interest.

Townley closed his eyes to re-create the scene, and he moved his hands in the air as though to place the Cubans where they had been. Townley had sat on one corner of the bed, with Paz and Suárez along the foot of it to his left. Novo had been just to his right. The newcomers had pulled chairs into a semicircle in front of him. Most of them had straddled the chairs backward, facing Townley, with their arms resting atop the chair backs. The motel lamps had given poor light to the room.

"I remember the face of the guy who was sitting right in front of me," said Townley. "He did almost all the talking for them. He was an older man. And I can remember his face because he looked just like one of Chile's television commentators. I can see him. But it's funny, now I can't even remember the name of the commentator."

Cornick looked up from his notes, unable to bear the digression. "Don't worry about it, Mike," he said. "We've got photographs of all those guys. We'll take care of it later."

"Okay," said Townley, who seemed annoyed with his memory.

"Just go on with the story," Cornick urged gently.

Sitting on the bed, Townley takes a breath and plunges directly into business. "I am here to ask you to do it," he says. "I am asking you to eliminate this man as a threat to Chile and to the movement we share. My orders are to seek your assistance and to leave the country once you have accepted the mission. We trust you to carry it out. The service has already taken care of the preoperational intelligence. We know his habits. We know where he lives and how he drives to work. He parks his car in a dark alley. I believe it would be easy to get him there and leave him like the victim of a mugging. We also know that he chases skirts. Perhaps you could approach him that way, but I believe it is unnecessarily complicated. The point is that it must be done—and as soon as possible."

Townley looks around him at the faces. No one is responding. "What's he doing now?" asks Alvin Ross, who is sitting off to the side.

"As I understand it, he is trying to set up a government in exile," Townley replies.

"So are we," interjects Juan Pulido, with an edge of bitterness. Pulido is a doctor, a friend of Orlando Bosch, and an elder statesman of the Cuban Nationalist Movement. He is leaning forward in his chair so that his face is less than a yard from Townley's. "We are trying to set up a Cuban government in exile, but we are having trouble getting any support from Chile," Pulido says pointedly.

"I know," Townley says.

"What do you think of that?" asks Pulido.

"I'm sorry about it," says Townley. "But there is nothing I can do about it. And nothing even Colonel Contreras can do about it, because you want things publicly from the government of Chile and we have nothing to do with that. We are the hidden arm of the government. Letelier is a Marxist. He is your enemy as much as he is ours."

"We assume that Colonel Contreras knows Chile's enemies," says Pulido. "But that's not the point. I think we're on the wrong end of the funnel in our alliance. Chile gets from the big end, and we always get from the small end."

Townley answers Pulido's questions politely as long as he can, but he is finally provoked to the offensive. "Look, I cannot be responsible for what the entire government of Chile does," he says sharply. "I am a soldier who can accomplish certain things, and the only guarantees I can make to you are the ones that I can assume personal responsibility for. I can make arrangements for you in Chile all by myself, for example, and that can be important. Had Otero made his arrangements beforehand as he should have done, he would have been deniable and Chile would never have given him up to the United States. I can prevent such foul-ups on my own authority, as some of you know."

Townley pauses to look uncertainly at Guillermo Novo. "Go ahead," says Novo. "Everyone here is all right or they wouldn't be here."

Townley nods. "So you all know that Guillermo was in Chile only three months ago," he says. "It was done properly. I made the arrangements myself, and I can guarantee you that there is no record anywhere that he was in Chile. I can do things like that. I can send you equipment. I can work with you. I can guarantee you refuge in Chile and I can represent your point of view within the service— directly to my Colonel Contreras. Beyond that I cannot go. You have many political ambitions that you will have to pursue on your own with the open parts of the government. All I can say is that I am your best contact to the hidden part."

"We know that, Andrés," says Paz. "If we do this, we do it only because we believe in our movement and we trust you."

The other Cubans speak up over the next hour, alternately hostile and warm, and the meeting ends on a command from Novo. "We will let you know of our decision," he tells Townley. He shakes hands and leads a procession out the door. The others say goodbye to Andrés. Several of them give him the *abrazo*.

Townley has trouble sleeping. He realizes that the ordeal has drained him, leaving him more tired than he has felt in years.

Paz calls early the next morning. "I will pick you up soon," he says. "We have things to do."

Townley dresses hurriedly. He takes Paz's message as a sign that the Cubans have agreed, but he knows better than to ask Paz during the drive to the automobile dealership where Novo works. This is news he should hear directly from the leader himself. Paz keeps giving it away with his bubbly mood, however.

In his relief, Townley cannot keep himself from telling Paz about the nerve compound and the possibility of using it for the mission. The news impresses Paz noticeably, though he makes an effort to conceal his reaction. Paz asks Townley many questions about what the Cubans could accomplish with a portion of Townley's supply.

Novo walks across the street from his office and jumps into the back seat of Paz's car. He looks around vigilantly for spies while maintaining the air of a businessman. "Okay, we'll do it," he tells Townley. "But we have a condition."

"What's that?" asks Townley.

"You have to participate," says Novo. "You have to go down to Washington yourself. We want a signal that this will be a more equal partnership."

Townley feels the bite of Novo's demand. "That is contrary to my orders," he says.

"I thought your orders were to get the job done," says Novo.

"They are," says Townley. "But I'm not supposed to go to Washington."

"That's what we don't like," Novo says pleasantly. "So you better try to get your orders changed. Because if you leave now, it's not going down. It's that simple."

"I can help a lot from here," says Townley.

"That's not good enough," says Novo. "We've already made our decision."

Townley sighs. "Okay, if that's the way it is," he says. "I think it will be all right."

"Virgilio will be working with you," says Novo, nodding to Paz. "But it will have to wait a few days, because we have something else going. And he can spend only a few days on this. I don't have many people to spare."

Townley is already recalculating his plans. "Okay," he says.

"Let me know if there are any problems," says Novo. He gets out of the car and walks briskly away.

It is a warm day, but Townley feels frost in his lungs. The first thing he says when Paz drives away is, "Okay, Virgil, if I have to go down there, it's got to be a bomb."

"Why is that?" says Paz.

"Because that way I can help you follow him and help you build the device," says Townley, "but I can still follow my orders not to be there when you set it off."

Paz shrugs as though it is a matter of indifference to him.

"Do you still have the Fanon-Courier I modified for you?" asks Townley.

"Of course," says Paz.

Over the next few days, Townley tests the beeper equipment in Paz's apartment. The CNM has plans for another operation: a bomb attack on the Russian freighter *Ivan Shepetkov*, which is moored in a berth at Port Elizabeth. This delays Paz, which delays Townley.

He calls Santiago to report Novo's demand to Major Christoph Willeke, the DINA officer in charge of foreign operations. On the second call, Willeke conveys DINA's approval of the change in plans. "What will be, will be," he says. Townley thus learns that it is more important to eliminate Letelier than it is for him to stay out of Washington.

Now his plan is to go to Washington and to leave again as quickly as possible. For security reasons, he does not want to go as a Chilean—especially as an official Chilean. He does not want to go as Hans Petersen. So Townley calls his wife and tells her to send his Kenneth Enyart identity papers to New York by way of a LAN Chile pilot. He asks Cruchaga to keep them for him at his office. He also asks a LAN Chile employee to take a very special perfume bottle back to Santiago. Townley no longers wants to have the substance with him, and he regrets telling Paz about it.

The following Tuesday, September 14, Townley drives to Kennedy Airport and picks up the Enyart papers from Cruchaga. He leaves the Petersen papers there for safekeeping. Then he turns in his rented car, rents another in the name of Enyart, and checks into a different New Jersey motel, the Liberty Motor Inn. It is less expensive than the Château, and Townley is running out of money. He did not expect to be in the United States this long.

At midnight on the fifteenth—just after a bomb blows out part of the *Ivan Shepetkov*'s hull—Townley joins Paz for the long drive to Washington in Paz's car. They have placed the Fanon-Courier and the bomb materials in the trunk. Paz has a pistol strapped inside his shirt. During the early part of the trip, Paz keeps the radio tuned to an all-news station in New York. He shouts in triumph when he hears a bulletin on the damage to the *Shepetkov*. Townley joins in the celebration.

They pass through the Baltimore Harbor Tunnel at four-forty-four in the morning, and they reach Washington itself before sunrise. Townley says that he has drunk too much coffee to sleep and that he doesn't want to pay a motel fee for the wasted night, anyway. So he and Paz take out Fernández's map and begin looking for Letelier's house. It takes them nearly two hours to find it.

Letelier lives on a quiet dead-end street in a neighborhood of relatively expensive homes. Townley and Paz feel a surge of adrenaline when they see the house. Quickly they decide that they cannot initiate their surveillance in that area. It is too quiet. They would stand out too much during the wait.

Townley verifies the license numbers of the two Letelier cars as Paz swings by the house again. "Fernández said they keep the cars out of the garage," says Townley. "That's good." He peers up and down the street, which is only one block long. There are fewer than a dozen houses, meaning that there will be very little traffic. And Townley observes that the streetlights would probably throw very little illumination onto the Letelier cars. "We should come back here and take a look at night," he says.

Using Fernández's map, Townley directs Paz along Letelier's route to work. Shortly after turning onto River Road—one of the main commuter arteries into Washington—they pull into the parking lot of a fast-food restaurant. "We can pick him up here," says Townley.

It is half past eight in the morning. Paz rushes into the restaurant for more coffee and some food, while Townley keeps an eye on the traffic feeding into River Road from the direction of Letelier's house. Neither man says very much after Paz returns. Small talk seems out of place, and they are too keyed up to discuss significant matters. They are working.

Shortly after nine o'clock Townley says, "That's him."

"No," says Paz. "That's *her* car."

They watch the blue Chevelle go by. The driver is alone. "That's him," Townley insists. "That's the license number. Let's go."

Paz pulls into the traffic, still objecting that the car is not the one Fernández said was Letelier's. "I don't care," says Townley. "That must be him. Maybe he took her car today."

They follow Letelier into the city. It is about a twenty-minute drive from Letelier's house to the embassy district near which his office is located. Along the route, they pass a wooded park with no pedestrians or shops on the side of the road. "This would be a good place," says Townley. "Try to pass him."

He wants to get ahead of Letelier just in case the target is suspicious of being followed. Townley knows that it is easier and less conspicuous to keep track of someone from the front, if you know the route in advance. Besides, it would be advantageous to be ahead of Letelier when the bomb went off in order to avoid being trapped in the traffic jam behind the wreck. Townley wants to make this practice run authentic.

Paz finds it impossible to pass Letelier in the traffic. "He's a fast driver," says Townley. "That makes it a little tougher."

They lose Letelier when he makes a left turn onto Q Street just past Sheridan Circle. Paz misses the turn and curses the fact that the next street is one-way to the right. By the time they manage a left turn, Letelier has already passed. They do not see his Chevelle again until they drive slowly past the Institute for Policy Studies. Letelier's car is parked in the alley, just as Fernández said it would be.

"That's still not his car," says Paz.

"Armando must have screwed it up," says Townley. "We'll check it again tomorrow."

He and Paz take a room at the Holiday Inn and sleep most of the day. They eat an Italian meal that night at a restaurant called Luigi's, and they make one late-night sweep past Letelier's house.

They do not follow him to work the next morning, but they do find the Chevelle in the alley again. At Townley's suggestion, the two of them take turns sitting at an outdoor table of the café across the street from the Institute for Policy Studies. Townley decides it would be bad tradecraft for them to sit together. Leaving Paz with the first shift, he takes a long walk through the surrounding streets. He finds almost no security in the area until he reaches the embassy buildings a few blocks away. After passing by the alley several times, he concludes that there is too much pedestrian traffic to allow the Cubans to attach the bomb to the car in the daytime.

Paz leaves the Café Rondo when he sees Townley returning, and Townley, alone, takes a sidewalk table. Wearing blue jeans, a sport shirt, and tennis shoes, he blends well with the patrons of the café. He orders a cup of coffee and waits. Paz thinks this entire exercise is unnecessary, Townley knows, because Paz has already decided that the man in the Chevelle is Letelier. But Townley wants to be sure. He wants to see the man in the flesh and not as the driver of a distant car. For some perverse reason, this strikes him as only fair.

Suddenly he sees the target standing not fifty feet away. He is in a suit. He is carrying a briefcase authoritatively, standing just outside the Institute's front door, talking to a shorter, more rumpled man. Townley is mesmerized. He watches Letelier laugh and slap the smaller man several times on the back. Debonair, Townley thinks. He watches the way Letelier moves, and he can almost see his hand moving in slow motion as it lands on the other man's back. Then Letelier nods goodbye and walks off down the street. Townley has the feel of him already. He decides that Letelier has the presence to make a formidable enemy.

Letelier takes a shuttle flight to New York and meets the woman from Venezuela, who has arrived that day for a visit. He tells her of his struggle to accept her decision to break off their engagement. For months he has been trying to settle his feelings and to draw some peace and wisdom from the experience, but it is not easy. He still suffers fits of anger, and sometimes he finds himself explaining to her why she is wrong and why she did not dare to go ahead. He tells her that he has made some tape recordings for her on these subjects, but he adds with a laugh that he has decided not to give them to her because he wants to spare her all the confusion and self-torture. It is all part of the ordeal of the exile, he says.

The next morning Letelier tells her that it is becoming easier to say goodbye. He is still looking for the complete explanation, but he is learning to take what he has. He has special memories with the Venezuelan of things he cannot share with Isabel, but he also has with Isabel things he could never share with the Venezuelan, such as his family, his political faith, and his "Chilean affairs."

Letelier flies back to Washington that Saturday afternoon, September 18. It is Chilean Independence Day. For the third year since the coup, Chilean exiles observe a day of mourning and political dedication on the eleventh, followed by the traditional day of celebration a week later. Independence Day festivities seem more poignant in exile.

Some fifty Chileans have gathered that afternoon for a party at the Letelier home. He arrives late and finds that the Chilean music has already started. The wine is flowing, and his countrymen are dancing. Letelier greets everyone and laughs, drawing attention to his energy. He and Isabel perform the traditional Chilean *cueca* with such vigor and flair that the guests clear the floor to let the couple dance alone.

For Townley, everything has changed since Dionisio Suárez arrived that Saturday morning with the last necessary component of the bomb, a military blasting cap.* Suárez meets Paz and Townley for late breakfast at McDonald's. As always, Suárez projects an air of business, even when only smiling or reporting on the brand names of the detonators. He promptly leans over the table at the crowded McDonald's and asks, "Have you seen him?"

Townley blinks. "Yes," he replies.

"Do you know where he is?" asks Suárez.

"Not right now," says Townley, looking around at the others in the restaurant. They are paying no attention, but Townley follows Suárez's lead in keeping the conversation vague. "But we know where he lives and how he goes to work," he says. "And we have decided on the best place to work on his car."

"Okay," says Suárez. He thinks for only a second or two. "Is there any reason why we can't go ahead and get this over with?" he asks. "I've got some job problems, and I need to get back as soon as I can."

"I guess not," says Townley.

"Is there anything else we need to know?" asks Suárez.

"No," says Townley.

"Let's go, then," says Suárez.

Townley's heart speeds up, but he retains a bored, languid expression on his face. "Okay," he says.

Paz and Townley have already accomplished a great deal toward the success of the mission, but they have been floating along somehow—as in Mexico and Europe. Suárez has changed their speed. Townley admires his concentration and resolve.

Since breakfast, the three men have spent the day going over the path of the car again for the benefit of Suárez, and they have bought a few extra items at a downtown Radio Shack. Townley needs a soldering kit and a drill for the work he plans.

---

*Guillermo Novo had called a Cuban associate, José Barral, and asked him to provide emergency assistance to Suárez and Alvin Ross. They asked Barral for the blasting cap, which he provided. Barral would later testify about this sequence of events at the Letelier trial.

Suárez is staying in a motel that is decorated garishly in lavender and aqua paint. After supper, he stops briefly at his room and then walks across six lanes of busy traffic in the dingy, industrial part of Washington—not many blocks from the United States Capitol—and knocks at the room of Paz and Townley. Paz pulls him through the door and bolts it from the inside. Townley has his tools and the bomb materials spread out on the motel room dresser. He is already at work on the arduous task of chipping the coarse tar paper off the TNT.

While Paz and Townley flush all the scraps of tar paper down the toilet, Suárez lies on one of the beds. He rises only when Townley says something interesting about the construction of the bomb. The DINA man is lecturing almost constantly on the various elements of the package. He is in his element, and the technical talk soothes his nerves.

Townley has bought three ordinary rectangular cake tins at a Sears store not far from Letelier's house. They fit inside one another. At first he tries to place the TNT in the narrowest of the cake tins, but the largest TNT block is too long. With a screwdriver, Townley tries to chip enough small pieces off the ends so that the block will fit snugly. The TNT is stubborn, however. It is a very hard, nonporous material—like a highly compressed block of tan powdered sugar. Paz helps with the chipping, but he and Townley only wind up bending the cake tin out of shape.

"This is no good," says Townley. "If we were in Santiago, I could melt this down in a heat bath and shape it to fit."

"I'd rather not cook it," says Suárez, from the bed.

"There's nothing to worry about," says Townley. "The fusion point is about 85 degrees Centigrade, and the stuff won't even begin to burn until about 120. There's plenty of margin." He looks forlornly at the mess of fragments on the dresser. "Some of these chips will be wasted," he says.

After rejecting the idea of shopping for a heat bath, Townley picks up the next largest cake tin and starts over. The one-kilo block of TNT fits inside—too easily. It will bounce around when the car goes over bumps. Townley talks out loud to himself about how he might be able to wedge the block into a stable position with other components.

He sweeps the chips off the dresser into the tin. Then he wraps some of the detonating cord around the large TNT block, leaving two feet hanging over the edge for later use. "The whole point of these extra caps is that the TNT will go a thousand different ways, depending on how strong the prime charge is," he explains. "The greater the speed and heat flash we get at the start, the faster the TNT will go up. That means a more complete explosion. The more complete it is, the less chance that anybody will ever find an identifiable fragment."

Paz is sitting in a chair looking on as Townley assembles his own series of boosters. First, he takes two small pieces of TNT, weighing 100 grams each, that he has sent up to Paz from Santiago. Each of them has a small hole bored through the center. This is Townley's own design. In a bomb that is going to rattle around under a car, he wants to make sure that the blasting caps stay near the smaller, more easily detonated chunks of TNT. So he runs the wires of two blasting caps through the holes of the small chunks, "sewing" a blasting cap to each chunk. He wraps the chunks and their blasting caps with more of the detonator cord and secures them to the large block of TNT with tape.

Having already replaced the single-strand wires of the blasting caps with durable seven-strand replacements, Townley now wires the caps to each other in a parallel circuit. The stronger wire, he tells Paz, will guard against the possibility that the movement of the car might jar the bomb enough to dislodge one of the wires and thereby break the circuit.

"But you don't have a circuit yet," says Paz. "What else goes in there?"

"I'm going to try out one of these electric matches," says Townley.

This is enough to make Suárez sit up on the bed. "Try it out?" he says disapprovingly. "What the hell are you going to do that for?"

"I think they're superior to blasting caps," says Townley. "They produce a sharp bolt of intense electric heat, and they're less dangerous to carry around because they look so harmless."

"What do we care about danger now?" asks Suárez. "We are carrying the whole bomb around! I don't think this is the time for any of your experiments, Andrés."

"Don't get excited, Dionisio," says Townley, taking some pride in the fact that he has finally been able to provoke Suárez. "I want to show Virgil how to do this," he says. "It's not easy, but it might be a great improvement in the future. I think it will, anyway. And it won't interfere with those two blasting caps at all, because I've got them wired in parallel. It might help the reaction, and it can't hurt. Any one of these three starters ought to be enough to set it off."

Suárez grumbles that it is a waste of time, but Townley prevails. Giving all but one of the electric matches to Paz as a "present" from DINA, Townley solders two of the seven-strand wires onto the match he is using, thus replacing the wires he had cut off in Santiago. Then he coats the electrical end of the match alternately with the lead azide explosive powder and with thin layers of Vaseline. When finished, he embeds the fully primed electric match in the detonating cord at the bottom of the cake tin and wires the match in parallel to the blasting caps.

Finally, Townley takes the white, puttylike C-4 plastic explosive and molds pieces of it into the crevices between the chunks of TNT, and along the detonating cord on the floor of the cake tin. He smooths it over the way a plumber might caulk a bathtub. The base of the bomb is completed. Townley has used the detonating cord and the small chunks of TNT to wedge the larger one against the walls, and he has covered the components with tape. He leaves about eight inches of detonating cord hanging over the edge of the cake tin, explaining to Paz that he wants to wrap it around the Fanon-Courier receiver to help destroy that instrument in the blast.

He has been working and talking for more than two hours, and now he spends nearly that much time on the triggering system. He makes sure that he has removed the serial number and the identifying panel from the Fanon-Courier beeper. This particular one, he reminds Paz, will respond only to a "0-4" combination from the encoder. Paz writes it down.

In Santiago, Townley has already replaced the beeper's speaker with a transformer that will turn a radio signal into an electric spark. Now he checks his Radio Shack batteries again, and when he is satisfied with them, he puts them into a Radio Shack battery holder and tapes the battery package to the end of the beeper. He has wired a small circuit-breaker safety switch between the receiver and the batteries that will provide the charge to the blasting caps.

Townley tapes the receiver to the outer side of the cake tin. He does not want to put it inside, he explains, for fear that the metal will block the incoming radio signal. And he does not want to put it on the bottom of the cake tin, because it would be more likely to get knocked off if Letelier's car ran over a rock.

"Now comes the fun part," says Townley. It is time to complete the circuit. "Don't worry," he says, "I've got the safety switch engaged." Nevertheless, Suárez stands up and watches with Paz as Townley connects the lead and return wires from the beeper to their exposed counterparts in the first blasting cap, inside the cake tin. He secures the wires to the lip of the cake tin as he covers the entire opening with tape, closing up the package.

"There," he says. He warns Paz and Suárez against flipping the safety switch on and off. "There is the tiniest, most minuscule chance that there is residual current left in the broken circuit," he explains. "Which means she might go when you flip that switch to arm it."

Suárez says nothing. He is studying the finished bomb.

"Which is just the risk you have to take," Paz says woodenly.

"That's right," says Townley. "If it's not all right, you'll never know it."

It is eleven that night by the time Townley finishes washing his hands and cleaning up. Then he sits down and places calls to the bus terminal and the train station. He wants to leave for New York immediately, so that he can be out of town when Paz and Suárez complete the job. But he discovers that all ground transportation is shut down for the night. So are the airlines. He is stuck until morning.

Paz and Suárez have waited patiently through all the calls. Townley teases them for talking softly out of involuntary respect for the awesome creature in the room with them.

"I'm not sleepy," says Suárez. "I think we should go put it on now so we won't have to sit here with it. Are you going to come with us, Andrés? As long as you are stuck here, anyway?"

The question stabs Townley. He looks at Suárez. "Those are not my orders," he says.

Suárez shrugs amiably. "I thought they said it was all right for you to go to Washington," he says. "Did they say you should only go to some parts of the city and not to others?"

"No," says Townley.

"Do they want us to take all the risk?" asks Suárez. "I am just curious, you see."

Townley looks impassively at Suárez and stifles an honest response. He thinks the mission is in jeopardy. The Cubans have shown signs of annoyance with him, especially since he refused to share with them the sarin and his knowledge of its use. He knows that the CNM members yearned to be the first anti-Castro group with a chemical warfare capability. "I'll go with you," he says. "I haven't got anything else to do."

They lock the Fanon-Courier transmitter, encoder, and antenna in the trunk of Suárez's car, and Townley puts the bomb in the trunk of Paz's Volvo.

It is a chilly night for September. Townley changes into some corduroy pants and a sweat shirt he has bought in New York. When he comes outside again, he finds the Cubans standing next to the Volvo. "I'm driving," Paz says jovially. "Who wants to sit in the back seat?"

"I will," Townley volunteers. "That thing's not going off."

On the long drive to Letelier's neighborhood, they talk of little else besides the bomb. It has taken over their minds. Townley describes in great detail the instantaneous chain reaction that will take place when the more volatile substances reach their flash points and in turn set off the more stable ones. It will be a sharp, high-speed explosion, he says, more suited to cutting steel than to moving rock.

As Townley is explaining the equipment he has brought along for Paz and Suárez to use when they attach the bomb to the car, Paz turns to him and says, "Don't bother with that."

Townley stops talking. He knows something is wrong.

"We want you to put the bomb on, my friend," Paz says evenly. "Our movement wants the hand of Chile very close to this act. You put it on. We will set it off. That seems like a fair partnership to us."

No one says anything for the next several minutes. Townley feels that he has been outmaneuvered. He wonders what the Cubans would have done if he had found an available bus to New York that night. "Is this Guillermo's idea?" he asks.

"It is a group idea," says Paz. He is soon driving the Volvo slowly down Ogden Court, Letelier's street, making a circle at the end and easing back up past the house.

"There's the car," says Suárez. He notes that the lights are off inside the house. The Independence Day celebrations have ended.

Townley says nothing. He can hear himself breathing, and he concentrates on doing so more slowly. He knows that the Cubans have the advantage because he wants the bomb placed under the car more than they do. He decides that he must exercise an independent command. He is the only one in position to weigh his ordered objective against the risks, and also to balance the result with a reading of how the Cubans will proceed under the shaky alliance.

"Go around the block," he tells Paz. "And let me off behind the house. I'll go through the woods."

Paz stops the car near the intersection of Cromwell and Devonshire. Seeing no one, he jumps out to unlock the trunk. Suárez stays where he is—having no need to move—but he wishes Townley good luck.

"Do you want a gun?" Paz whispers.

"No," says Townley. "Not while I'm carrying this thing." He is tucking the bomb under the front of his sweat shirt. It is cold against his belly. He taps Paz on the shoulder. "Go on around the block again and meet me at the top of the hill," he says. Then he hesitates.

"And if we hear you yelling, we'll come get you," says Paz.

"Thanks," says Townley. He ducks off quickly before he has to say anything else. He moves from tree to tree through the yards beside Letelier's, and he finds himself stepping gingerly even though he knows the bomb is perfectly stable.

Just as he steps into the street two houses below his objective, he sees headlights turning toward him at the top of the hill, on the other end of the block. They are coming straight down at him. Townley's mind does not function properly. He knows that he should not run, but he must get out of the car's headlight range. He turns and scampers back through the trees. He hears the sounds of a second car behind the first one, and he cannot suppress the fear that the Americans have the whole operation wired. As he runs, he keeps telling himself that the bomb will not go off by concussion if he falls.

Alone on the back street, fearing more cars, Townley runs up Cromwell and finds the Volvo empty. This gives him a jolt until he sees that Paz and Suárez are coming toward him from the shadows of a street lamp. They have been waiting under a big tree.

Townley explains what happened as they drive around the block again. Sweat is pouring off his face, he realizes. "This is harder than building the bomb," he says, trying to lighten the moment.

This time he asks to be let off at the top of the hill. Paz and Suárez will wait near the same spot, but Townley walks down the left side of the street toward the house. He sees no one as he passes it, nor when he quick-steps into the driveway under the night shadow of a tree.

Townley drops to the ground beside the driver's door of the Chevelle, where he realizes to his relief that he is covered on nearly every side by the car, the tree, and the darkness. He puts the bomb on the ground and rests for a few seconds, but his breath is still short when he goes to work. He takes out a pencil-size flashlight and lies on his back—parallel to the car, so that his feet are nearly touching the rear wheels. The first beam of the flashlight frightens him. It is too bright, he decides. He cups his left hand over the bulb and flips the switch with his right. Then he tries to slide his left shoulder under the car.

Townley groans when he discovers that he has less than three inches of clearance for his shoulder. There is no way that he can reach both hands under the car at once, and it is too dark to see a thing under the car. Townley suppresses panic. He flips the flashlight into the "on" position and holds it under the car with his left hand. As he cranes his neck to see the crossbeam underneath, he lets some of the light slip between his fingers. This allows him to see where the bomb should go.

He grabs the black electrician's tape and wraps two or three long strands of it around the crossbeam. By now he knows that he will have to proceed mostly by touch, because he can't possibly hold the tape and the bomb and the flashlight all at once in that cramped space. On a trial run, he wedges the bomb into the angle between the crossbeam and the drive shaft of the car, directly under the driver's seat. He curses when he finds that the cake tin is just a little too deep to sit on top of the crossbeam underneath the floor of the car. Townley reprimands himself for not having used the shallowest of the three cake tins. It would have been a lot easier.

The first strand of tape is by far the most difficult to attach. He flips to his stomach and lifts the bomb from the bottom with his right hand while reaching with his left to touch the tape closest to him. Extending himself as far as possible, he lifts the tape to the bottom of the bomb. Then he holds the bomb and the tape with his left hand, lets go with his right, flips over on his back again, and reaches as far underneath the car as he can to affix the tape to the drive shaft. On the third or fourth try, this single strand of tape holds the bomb up until he can attach a second one.

Then he hears a car. Townley tries to freeze, but his chest keeps heaving from the labor and the tension as he peers down the driveway across the path of the headlights. He almost runs when he sees that it is a police car, but inertia and indecision pin him to the ground. He hears the police car circling quietly at the bottom of the hill, and then, just as quietly, it passes by him again on the way out of Ogden Court. Just a routine patrol, he hopes, but it takes a few seconds for his nerves to calm down so that he can resume work. Now, taping feverishly, he worries that the perspiration from his hands and wrists will foul the tape. He examines the bomb with the pencil flashlight every few minutes to estimate how much it is sagging. He is still not satisfied when he runs out of tape.

Townley is panting as he stops to think. He will not go back for more tape. This will have to do. He thinks it will hold. Now there is only one thing left: the safety switch. He reaches for it quickly so that he will not have time to think, but discovers to his mortification that he has taped over the switch with some of his supporting strands for the bomb. He pounds the driveway once in anger and then tries to control himself. How can he turn the bomb on? How can he be sure that the elasticity of the tape will not turn it off again?

He takes a look with the flashlight, and then he reaches underneath with his screwdriver to loosen the tape. After prying it up from the switch as best he can, he takes a deep breath, reaches under the tape with his fingers, and flips the switch.

Nothing happens. The bomb is live. Townley rejects as foolhardy the thought that he should jiggle the switch to make sure it is free of tape, and within a few seconds he is walking wide-eyed up the street. He jumps into the car and suddenly becomes incandescent with energy, even though he knows he is exhausted. His part is over. He talks about what he did and thought all the way back to the motel.

Paz falls asleep instantly, but Townley keeps thinking. At dawn, he walks to a pay phone on New York Avenue and places a collect call to his wife. "Call Gutiérrez,"* he says. "And tell him that the artifact is in place. And that it is operational."

Suárez drives him to the airport in time to catch the earliest morning flight to Newark.

Propper had been clutching his desk for some time. Townley's soft monotone was making his mind race with a thousand thoughts. Suspects with familiar names were being transformed into killers. The details made the murders feel very near.

Of all the surprises, Townley's announcement that he had actually gone to Washington was the one that put fear into Propper, and the fear had grown with every revelation that took Townley closer to Sheridan Circle: building the bomb, going to Letelier's house, placing the device under the car. "Don't be the one," Propper had been saying to himself. "Please don't let the government's witness be the one who pushed the button." On hearing that Townley had left Washington with the victims still alive, he felt immense relief.

Townley seemed to have lost the drift of his story. He was pacing mutely, as though the memory of placing the bomb had drained him.

"So you left Washington," said Propper, mostly because he wanted to hear it again.

---

*The pseudonym "Gutiérrez" was always reserved in DINA for the officer in charge of foreign operations. In this instance, "Gutiérrez" was Major Christoph Willeke.

"Yes," said Townley.

"Anything else with Suárez?" asked Barcella.

"Not that I can remember," said Townley. "We talked about where the device should be activated and things like that. I told him where I wanted it done. Virgil and I had already gone over it, but I wanted to tell Dionisio. That's about it. Oh, yes, and I borrowed fifty dollars from him at the airport. I was running out of money. I was borrowing money from everybody."

"Go on, Mike," urged Cornick. "Finish it up."

"Let's see," said Townley. "Alvin Ross picked me up at Newark Airport. I was expecting Guillermo, but it was Alvin who showed up. He was completely knowledgeable and he wanted to know what had happened in Washington, so I briefed him. Over breakfast. We had breakfast together. I remember that. And then he took me to Guillermo's apartment, and I went over it again for him. That afternoon I borrowed Guillermo's car and drove up to see my sister in Tarrytown. I didn't really want to do it, since everything had changed so much from the original plan, but I had already told her I was coming and I decided that if the Petersen cover ever broke down, I would say that I had come up to visit her. What I had in mind was that Petersen had never gone to Washington. Enyart had. So I wanted a cover for Petersen in New York. It was some time in the late afternoon when I got up there, I think. You guys probably know better than I do when it was, because you've got my sister's phone records. I called Guillermo from there to tell him I was on my way back and to ask him to give me a ride to the airport."

Townley stopped walking. "Anyway, Guillermo drove to Kennedy, and it took me a little while to solve the Petersen identity problem. I had to get Petersen out of the country." He started to smile.

"How did you do that?" asked Scherrer.

"Well, you know, the airline companies collect the I-94 forms for the INS," he said. "And nobody pays much attention to them. After a flight leaves, somebody just turns all the I-94s over and stamps them, and the INS people come by and pick them up later. So I went over to the Iberia Airlines counter and waited for the right moment. And when nobody was looking I slipped the Hans Petersen I-94 into a big stack they had just collected from passengers on a flight to Madrid. As far as INS records are concerned, Hans Petersen left New York for Madrid on the night of the nineteenth."

"That's pretty slick, Mike," said Scherrer, watching the prisoner's face. It was evident that Townley still got a kick out of being clever.

"From the airport," said Townley, "I mailed the Petersen passport and all my expense vouchers back to Chile so I wouldn't have them with me on my person. But I had a problem. My return ticket to Chile said Petersen on it. So I had to cash it in to buy one for Enyart. That took a lot of arranging.

"And that night I flew to Miami. Got in very late, as I remember. I'm almost certain that I didn't drive up to Fort Lauderdale to stay with my parents. It would have been too late. I think I stayed in the airport motel. And the next day I kind of waited around to hear that something had happened in Washington. I expected them to detonate the device that Monday morning, the twentieth, but nothing happened. I called Iggie Novo that day. He was in Miami. But he hadn't heard anything. And I called a few other people. Nobody knew anything. All I could do was wait. I drove up to Fort Lauderdale that night and had dinner with my parents. I stayed with them that night."

"You stayed with your parents?" asked Barcella.

"Yes," said Townley. "What's wrong with that?"

"Nothing," said Barcella.

After dinner on the night of September 20, Michael Moffitt and Orlando Letelier retire into the den of Letelier's house to work on a paper they have been writing for publication under Letelier's name. Both are trained economists. Recently they have published a magazine article declaring that Pinochet's economic policies have brought ruin to the vast majority of Chile's population, and that such policies can be inflicted only by repression and military force. Moffitt has learned a great deal from Letelier in the previous year. He takes direction well and does not mind doing the bulk of the research to support Letelier's arguments. Moffitt's commitment to the Chilean cause is such that he will happily work until midnight if Letelier is willing.

In the living room, Ronni Moffitt talks with Isabel Letelier. The younger woman is intensely curious about all things Chilean, especially politics. She likes hearing Isabel Letelier's anecdotes so much that she is reluctant to leave when the men call it a night at eleven-thirty.

The Moffitts' car has not been working that day, and Letelier offers them the loan of his Chevelle: they can take it home with them and return the next morning.

They return shortly before nine o'clock on Tuesday, just after the Letelier sons have had breakfast and gone to their jobs or schools.

Isabel is busy in the kitchen when she sees the Moffitts arrive, and she runs upstairs to find her husband still half asleep. She tells him to hurry and she runs out to tell the Moffitts that he will be awhile. Michael Moffitt is already at the door, and his wife soon comes inside to wait. They hear Letelier showering and bustling around upstairs. Finally, he runs downstairs, tying his tie, making fun of himself for laziness, spurning breakfast. He kisses Isabel, promises to call her later in the day, and is off. To her, the morning is rushed, unsatisfying, amusing—completely normal.

Townley, as Kenneth Enyart, has been huddled all morning with AID's chief engineer trying to figure out a stubborn repair problem on a complicated piece of triangularization equipment. He has lost track of time. Shortly after noon he calls Ignacio Novo to find out if he has heard anything.

"Have you heard the news?" asks Novo.

Townley knows from his voice that it has happened. "No, I haven't," he says.

"There was an explosion in Washington," says Novo. "Turn on your radio."

"Have you had lunch?" asks Townley.

"Yeah, but I'll buy you a drink," says Novo.

"I'll be right there," Townley replies. He hears the bulletins on his car radio as he drives to Miami to meet Novo. The disembodied voice of the radio announcer makes him feel the enormity of the event. It seems very distant to him, and at the same time it is his own private creation.

He toasts the outcome with Ignacio Novo that afternoon and satisfies Novo's curiosity about his night under the car. But he swallows his worry about the extra victim and the location of the blast until he calls home. "Have you heard?" he asks his wife.

"It's on the radio already," she says nervously. "Everybody's going crazy. They're saying it was right across the street from the embassy, and some of the people think it was Ambassador Trucco who got killed."

"No," says Townley. "But there was somebody in the car with him. A woman died, too. I don't know who it was. That's what they're saying up here."

"We haven't heard that," she says. "Why did they do it that way?"

"I don't know," he says. "It wasn't supposed to be that way. I left orders. Has Gutiérrez called?"

"He called three times yesterday and twice today already," she says. "He was beside himself. He wanted to know why nothing had happened."

"Well, he doesn't have to worry anymore," says Townley.

"I don't like it," she says. "What makes them do something stupid like that?"

"I don't know," says Townley. "These guys are always looking for a show. Something symbolic. But this may be a very dangerous show."

"You should get out of there," she says.

"I'll be home tomorrow night."

Townley spends another evening with his parents in Fort Lauderdale, and then he packs for the return to Santiago. He makes sure to take the third and flattest of the cake tins (the one he wishes he had used in the bomb) home to his wife for use in the kitchen. He never wants to waste anything.

On hearing his report Espinoza will say, "I would rather have had it another way, but it's all right." He will congratulate Townley, and the legend of Andrés Wilson will flourish among the members of DINA's inner circle. Still, Townley will not receive his military commission. A year later his wife will leave him temporarily in a fury over Contreras's failure to provide even the facilities of the officers' club for their daughter's wedding reception.

"That's about it," Townley said.

"No, it's not," said Propper. "Who pushed the button? We still don't know that."

"Well, there were two buttons, actually," said Townley. "You had to push them in the right combination at the same time."

"But who pushed them, then?" asked Propper.

"I'm not sure myself," said Townley. "I assume it was Suárez, because I was worried on the morning it happened. And I called Paz's house in New Jersey from my parents' house. Virgil answered, which surprised me. He was real gruff, like I'd just waked him up. And he hung up on me. So I guess he couldn't have done it if he was in New Jersey. That leaves Suárez."

"I guess so," said Propper, shuddering to think what might have happened if Suárez had testified under his grant of immunity.

"And I guess you realize, of course, that the guy who probably pushed the buttons is the same guy you let go about four or five days before you got me up here," Townley said wryly.

Propper stood up from his desk. He had a headache. He felt conflicted—simultaneously elated and depressed without bottom—but he was certain that he did not want to listen to Townley's boasts or opinions. "That's enough for now, I guess," he said.*

Outside the conference room they were all subdued. Cornick and Scherrer said they would make another run at pulling details from Townley that evening, but they doubted they could hold up much longer. They shook hands with the prosecutors and went back inside. The four of them knew that there were a million things to say, but they would say them later.

The prosecutors went to Barcella's car in something of a stupor. They did not speak a word to each other. Nor did they speak in the car. Barcella tried the radio to drown out the silence, but he quickly turned it off.

Propper started to speak a dozen times, but nothing seemed right to him. Neither relief nor satisfaction nor sadness seemed to be the response he should make. Not knowing how to express himself, Propper instinctively began to focus his thoughts on the one sure thing he could now count on: the trial. His prosecutor's mind began planning the trial in open court, dividing up the witnesses, assessing the strengths and weaknesses of various bits of evidence. When Barcella spoke the first words between them, some twenty miles down the highway back to Washington, Propper knew he would never forget the demonstration of telepathy between them.

"You take Townley," said Barcella.

"Okay, you take Canete," Propper replied, right on cue.

"You take Isabel," said Barcella. "And I'll take Mike Moffitt."

They went on through the prospective witnesses, and only then did they let out their joy. "Larry, there's going to be a trial," said Propper. "I can't believe it."

---

*As required by law, Suárez had been released routinely at the expiration of the term of the grand jury before which he had refused to testify.

21 ▣ THE CONTINUING AFTERMATH

On May 5, FBI agents heard that Dionisio Suárez was in his new home in San Jose, California, apparently on a clandestine visit to his wife. The agents instantly alerted Cornick in Washington. He called Newark and learned that Ignacio Novo was at his home there. Cornick scheduled simultaneous arrests for that night, taking account of the time difference between the Pacific and Atlantic coasts—seven o'clock in California, ten o'clock in New Jersey.

Five minutes before the FBI struck, Cornick called Propper. "Listen," said Cornick, "we may have a problem. The guys in California say they can't be positive it's Suárez in there."

"What?" said Propper. "I thought they saw him!"

"Take it easy," said Cornick. "They're just trying to get another ID before they go in. They say they know there's a man in there with Suárez's wife. They can see him through the window. But he's standing up, and they can only see him from the knees down."

"Tell them to stop!" said Propper, who was already pacing rapidly with the telephone. "How can they identify Suárez from the knees down? Do they know what his knees look like?"

"They're pretty sure it's him, Gene," said Cornick. "Who the hell else would be in there with his wife?"

"Carter, it could be anybody!" cried Propper. "Don't let them bust him! This is critical! We can wait!"

Propper walked a rut in the floor of his kitchen. He knew that a mistake on Suárez might ruin the entire case. Until now, the arrest warrants had been completely secret and Townley's testimony had been merely rumored about in the press. No one knew what he had told the United States government. An attempted arrest would warn the entire CNM network and send Paz and Suárez farther underground. Moreover, the arrest of Ignacio Novo—the least important of the defendants in the conspiracy case—would start the prosecutors' dreaded clock ticking under the "Speedy Trial" act. They would have only forty days to bring an indictment against all defendants. They needed six months.

A dejected Cornick called back shortly. "It was a neighbor out there," he said. "I tried to stop it, but you've got to defer to the judgment of the man on the scene in a situation like that."

Newark agents did arrest Ignacio Novo, and the warrant against him became public. For the prosecutors, it was the worst possible outcome. Cornick described Propper and Barcella as either "ripshit" or "henshit" for the next few days.

———

May 12, 1978

In Asunción, Scherrer and Ambassador Robert White led an American delegation into a conference with the Paraguayan chief of protocol, Dr. Conrado Pappalardo, who listened impassively as the Americans asked about the two Chileans who had obtained special Paraguayan passports in July 1976. "I don't recall any such incident," said Pappalardo.

After many changes of story and some impressive verbal fireworks, however, Pappalardo acknowledged that he vaguely remembered meeting Townley. He claimed to have intervened to stop the passport fraud.

Scherrer presented the contradictory facts patiently, guiding Pappalardo toward the central conclusion: that the events in Paraguay had been essential parts of the continuing conspiracy to murder Letelier. For that reason, Scherrer declared, the United States would expect Paraguayans to give evidence about how Contreras himself had made the arrangements to have the Paraguayans "cover" Townley with a false passport.

"That will never happen," Pappalardo said heatedly. "You are talking about the actions of intelligence officers and military men. You are asking us to betray the confidences of an intelligence chief of a friendly nation. No country in the world would permit that, including your own. It's impossible!"

———

May 18, 1978

By diplomatic pouch, Propper received an extraordinary letter from Santiago. Addressed to *"Señor Fiscal, Don Eugene Propper,"* it began, "We are relatives of people who were picked up by the National Intelligence Directorate (DINA) whose whereabouts we do not know." There followed an emotional plea that Propper question Townley to find out what had happened to the missing relatives. It concluded: "The high sense of justice that has prevailed in the investigation into the death of Orlando Letelier gives us reason to hope that you will fully understand our request." The letter was signed by 219 petitioners, whose names and signatures filled eight legal-size pages.

For once, Propper was speechless. His pride in the fact that so many foreign citizens had appealed to him personally, as the *fiscal*, collided with the realization that he was helpless. For a moment he saw his own investigation in a new perspective. He saw that no matter how many headlines and sexy international spy details the Letelier case generated, it concerned a crime against two victims whose relatives were grieving and feeling the injustice no more or less than each of the 219 unknown people who had signed the petition in his hands.

May 26, 1978

Cornick accompanied Scherrer to Buenos Aires, where the two agents began to dictate teletypes on the results of an unsuccessful trip to Santiago. During the process, Cornick asked Scherrer to retrieve a document from the legat's CHILBOM files for reference.

Scherrer, looking through his file drawers, asked, "By the way, Carter, when did you stop writing reports on this case, anyway?"

"What do you mean, Bob?" asked Cornick. "I'm *still* writing reports, and I think I'll be writing them when I'm too old to sit up."

"That's funny," said Scherrer. "I only got one."

"Wait just a damned minute," said Cornick, becoming alarmed. "I sent them all to you. There must be a dozen of them." He pulled up a chair and nervously began flipping through Scherrer's CHILBOM files. His jaw dropped. "Bob, where's the fat report?" he asked.

"What fat report?" Scherrer replied.

"The great big one with all the crime-scene stuff in it," said Cornick.

"I never got it," said Scherrer.

"You're kidding," said Cornick, but his panic grew as he flipped through and found only one of the missing reports. "This is an unmitigated disaster," he said. "Those reports have all kinds of stuff in them. That's where I reported all the results of the grand-jury sessions. I didn't put that stuff in teletypes."

"I didn't get any of that," said Scherrer. "That's why I kept pushing you guys to start putting Cubans in the grand jury. I thought you were crazy."

"My God," said Cornick. "I thought you were crazy to keep bugging us about it when we were hauling Cubans into the grand jury almost every day."

Over the next few hours, the two agents combined their knowledge and discovered gaping holes in Scherrer's files. They attributed the gaps to the drones at headquarters, who had no doubt simply ignored Cornick's requests to forward material to Scherrer—either out of mistaken judgment or, more likely, out of a desire to avoid the extra work.

"Bob, it's a miracle we ever got this far," said Cornick.

He and Scherrer felt lucky, but they resolved to entrust as little as possible to chance. To circumvent the rules requiring all communications between FBI agents to be routed through headquarters, they agreed to send sealed letters to each other through ordinary Bureau mail.

———

June 2, 1978

Only legal technicalities were at issue in the procedural hearings, but the New Jersey courtroom was packed because Cornick was to reveal that day the first official account of Townley's testimony on the Letelier assassination.

Reporters scrambled for the doors even before he finished testifying. From Cornick's brief synopsis, they now knew that the United States had a witness who admitted building and placing the bomb that killed Letelier, and that the witness said he had been an operative of the Chilean DINA.

———

June 10–13, 1978

In a strongly worded editorial entitled "On Pinochet's Doorstep," *The Washington Post* called for the resignation of President Pino chet, declaring that, at the very least, Pinochet had failed to control the DINA operatives who reported directly to him. The editorial caused a prolonged, emotional backlash in Chile, where it appeared the next day on the front pages. Pinochet's critics joined his supporters in condemning the editorial as an example of imperialist intervention on the part of the United States. On the night of June 12, fifty Chileans gathered in the streets of Santiago to burn an American flag publicly. Their act was reported favorably.

The next day, the prestigious *El Mercurio* denounced the *Post* for giving evidence that the Letelier investigation was nothing more than a political tool for Chile's enemies, as many Chileans had been saying all along. "We have seldom had a better proof than this about how U.S. newspapers look upon Latin America as a conquered territory . . ." said *El Mercurio*.

At the embassy, Ambassador Landau endured the barrage of criticism. "Pinochet must have a friend inside *The Washington Post*," he told his aides. "He couldn't have asked for anything better."

<hr/>

June 22, 1978

Along with the Chinese ambassador to Chile and a dozen ambassadors from Latin American nations, George Landau attended a formal dinner at the Pinochet home in Santiago. During the toasts, Pinochet shocked his guests by becoming emotional and declaring that even if he and his closest allies in Chile were forced to relinquish power, other members of the Chilean army would continue his policies. There was silence in the dining hall.

Later that evening Pinochet drew Landau aside for a private conversation. Pinochet took another Scotch-and-soda off the tray of a passing servant and looked intently at Landau. He was wearing the full-dress uniform of a Chilean general. His cheeks were flushed, and his eyes showed great feeling. "You are causing me a great deal of trouble," he told Landau, and then passed temporarily to other subjects.

"I must tell you something, Mr. President," said Landau. "I am leaving tomorrow for Washington. My government is recalling me for urgent consultations in regard to the Letelier case. I'm sorry to say that we do not believe we have received the cooperation your government promised us in this matter."

"I'm not surprised you're going," said Pinochet. He said that he had always been a great admirer of the United States but that the crooked American policy was making him bitter. He said the United

States had betrayed him many times, citing examples. He said he knew Chile had many enemies within the United States government, including the officials who induced *The Washington Post* to publish its June 10 editorial. "That kind of thing will not happen here," Pinochet declared. "Tomorrow I shall close *La Segunda* as punishment for publishing an interview with a fool who took the side of *The Washington Post*."

Pinochet began rambling almost incoherently. "I will tell you now and you can tell your superiors if you want," he said. "I don't care. You and your government can meddle in Chilean affairs and bring back political parties. Maybe you can. And if you do, you will cause another bloody revolution. People will die. You might be able to do that. You might be able to cause more grief to the people of Chile. But I am warning you that I will not allow it. I will fight you, and you have no idea of the strength of the Chilean people." Pinochet pointed his finger toward the Chinese ambassador across the room. "You see that man over there?" he asked heatedly. "Do you see him? Well, I can go to him. Believe me, Chile can turn to China. We are not married to the United States. I could even turn to the Soviet Union. They would help. They would do anything to hurt you . . ."

". . . Excuse me, Mr. President," said Landau. "I want to make sure I understand you. Do you really mean that last statement? Do you really mean that you could become an ally of the Soviet Union?"

"Absolutely!" said Pinochet. "I would do it to protect my country. The Soviet Union will always intervene against American interests. It is unfortunate that you Americans always fail to comprehend this."

———

June 23, 1978

Crowds of news reporters tried to interview Ambassador Landau at Pudahuel Airport, without success. His departure was the biggest story in Chile. Rumors flourished. His temporary recall was said to be a permanent one. Radio listeners heard that the United States had broken relations with Chile and that Argentina's army had moved to seal the border.

———

June 26, 1978

From the prisoners' pay phone inside the Manhattan Correctional Center, inmate Antonio Polytarides made his regular call to customs agent Joe King. Polytarides had access to such sought-after weap-

ons that he had been flooded with purchase orders from fellow inmates inside the New York prison. He told King that a new
customer, inmate Guillermo Novo, had approached him with an offer
to buy five MAC-10 submachine guns, with silencers. Novo told Polytarides that he wanted the guns for a couple of hits his group was
planning, and to bolster his credentials as a bona fide recipient of
arms, he told Polytarides that his group had been responsible for the
assassination of a Chilean named Letelier in Washington.

Some time later,* Larry Wack called Propper with the news. "But
don't get too excited," he said. "I doubt if we can use the guy. He's a
customs informant. He doesn't work for the Bureau. That's why I
didn't tell you earlier."

"What do you mean?" shouted Propper. "Screw that stuff. We've
got a double murder trial coming up! What're the customs people using the guy for? It *can't* be as serious as this case."

As it would turn out, customs agent King was uncommonly generous with his informant, Polytarides. When Propper expressed desperation to locate Novo's fugitive colleagues, Paz and Suárez, King
would instruct the informant to attempt to find out where they were.
This ploy backfired, however, as Novo became suspicious and broke
off contact with Polytarides.

Propper still hoped to use his testimony.

———

July 3, 1978

Propper asked Cornick to make another effort to get the FBI to
offer a public reward for the capture of Paz and Suárez. Cornick said
it was hopeless. The Bureau had rejected his proposal a dozen times
already, for the same reasons: it would make martyrs of the Cubans
and would advertise the Bureau's inability to find them. Also, the
FBI was already offering a $10,000 reward to its informants, quietly
and privately. Cornick confided to Propper that agents and informants alike would resent a public reward because it would mean that
the informants would be competing with outsiders for the money.

Propper lost his temper. "But, Carter, you don't have that many
informants!" he shouted. "I want ordinary people everywhere to see
those pictures and know they can pick up twenty or thirty grand for
reporting these murderers! Anybody! Somebody could see them
walking down the street!"

*Shortly after the August 1 indictment of the Letelier case defendants.

"I see your point, Gene," said Cornick. "And I agree with you. But forget it. You're beating your head against a stone wall."

Propper asked caustically how the FBI's attitude could be reconciled with the quotation chiseled into the stone of the mammoth headquarters building, in which J. Edgar Hoover declared that the best weapon against crime is an active, informed citizenry. That night he leaked a story about the private $10,000 reward to Jeremiah O'Leary. Cornick told Propper the Bureau was henshit.

July 10, 1978

As a consequence of Ambassador Robert White's successful diplomatic battle with the Paraguayan authorities, Scherrer's assistant legat received from Colonel Benito Guanes in Asunción a statement about how Contreras had contacted Guanes and his men in Paraguayan intelligence to facilitate the mission of Townley and Fernández. As a bonus, Guanes delivered a copy of one of the cables he had received from DINA. Guanes told the assistant legat about his telephone conversations with Contreras regarding the Townley-Fernández mission.

July 14, 1978

Now that the prosecutors had what they needed from Paraguay, Propper called Jeremiah O'Leary to say that he could go ahead with a story he had agreed to delay. It ran on the front page of the *Star*. The headline in the paper's first edition read: PARAGUAY IMPLICATED IN LETELIER KILLING. After much hysteria, the headline was changed for subsequent editions: PARAGUAY IMPLICATES CHILE IN LETELIER KILLING. Propper teased O'Leary, saying there was quite a difference.

"I don't write the headlines," said O'Leary.

July 20, 1978

About seventy-five FBI agents, U.S. marshals, prosecutors, technicians, and marines crowded into a bunker on an isolated field at the Quantico firing range. It was a very hot day in Virginia. A Chevelle just like Letelier's was parked in the grass about fifty yards from the bunker. Stu Case, the FBI's explosives expert, was underneath the Chevelle, attaching the bomb he had built to Townley's specifications as an exact duplicate of the one that had exploded at Sheridan Circle.

With the special high-speed cameras rolling in the bunker, the FBI's electronics expert, William Koopman, pushed the button on the Fanon-Courier transmitter he and Townley had modified. Nothing happened.

Propper, Barcella, and the other spectators tried to relax, but the tension was too strong. Case, Koopman, and Townley tried to figure out what had gone wrong. They tinkered with the machinery and spoke a technical language none of the others could understand.

Case crawled back under the car to check the bomb, as the spectators watched in disbelief. He soon emerged to say that the bomb was fine. The pressure shifted to Koopman, who, with Townley, checked the electrical systems. Koopman asked someone to bring one of the FBI cars up near the bunker, and Townley wired the transmitter to the cigarette lighter of the car—just as he had for Paz and Suárez.

When Koopman pushed the button again, the ground rocked and the spectators lost their breath from the concussion. A deafening aftershock hit them, and then they heard the soft patter of falling debris. There was an awed silence, as everyone paid involuntary respect to the power of the bomb.

Propper was the first to speak. "My God," he said softly. "I can't believe Michael Moffitt survived inside that car. I can't believe he's alive."

When Case permitted it, the spectators walked numbly toward the car. Cornick took out the crime-scene photographs from Sheridan Circle so that he could compare the damage done by the two explosions. Excitement soon replaced the awe in Cornick, as he passed out photographs for others to see. It was more than uncanny, he kept saying, it was a miracle. The two mangled cars were identical. Every bend, twist, and buckle of metal was the same.

Townley looked only briefly at the car. His normal banter was gone. Propper and Barcella noticed that the blood had drained from Townley's face and neck. He was silent, looking uncomfortably at his shoes and the ground. They had never seen him this way. Finally, Townley turned abruptly to the marshals who were there to guard him. "Let's get out of here," he said.

———

July 23, 1978

The White House press office routinely announced that Assistant Secretary of State Terence Todman was leaving his post to become

American ambassador to Spain. To replace him as Assistant Secretary for Inter-American Affairs, President Carter named Viron P. Vaky, who was currently American ambassador to Venezuela. This news brought a unanimous groan from the Letelier investigators.

———

July 25, 1978

FBI Director William Webster formally notified the Justice Department that the Bureau would offer no public reward for the capture of Paz or Suárez. He declared that the FBI had not offered a reward since November 1937 and that rewards were a nuisance because they often led to "controversy among claimants" and to "spurious allegations."

———

August 1, 1978

At a crowded press conference, Earl Silbert announced the issuance that day of a grand-jury indictment in the Letelier-Moffitt case. Seven men—Manuel Contreras, Pedro Espinoza, Armando Fernández, Guillermo Novo, Alvin Ross, Virgilio Paz, and Dionisio Suárez—were charged with the following violations: conspiracy to murder a foreign official, murder of a foreign official, first-degree murder (Letelier), first-degree murder (Ronni Moffitt), and murder by use of explosives. Also, Guillermo and Ignacio Novo were charged with two counts each of making false declarations before a grand jury, and Ignacio Novo was charged with one count of misprision* of a felony.

That same day, through Ambassador Landau in Santiago, the United States asked the Chilean government to arrest the three indicted Chilean military officers and to hold them in confinement while the American prosecutors prepared a formal request for their extradition to the United States for trial. President Pinochet ordered the arrest of Contreras, Espinoza, and Fernández that night.

By that time, Silbert, Barcella, Propper, Cornick, and Bob Steven were sitting in a Washington bar, celebrating the indictment with extremely strong drink. Congratulatory telegrams were arriving from all over the world. Newspaper stories were stressing the indictment of Contreras, which answered a major betting question of the last three months: would the United States indict the head of an allied intelligence service for murder?

———

*The crime of concealing, or failing to report, a crime.

Through his lawyers, Michael Townley received a letter that had been mailed from somewhere in Peru. "You are a traitor," it said. "You have negotiated with the FBI to save your filthy hide. You will pay with your life. In no part of the world will you ever again live in peace. The long arm of exiled Cuban brothers will overtake you. I have never trusted you, and I trusted you even less when I lived in Chile and Comrade Otero was delivered."

The letter went on to threaten Townley's wife and children. "Don't allow the blood in their veins to stop running because of your treason," it said. The signature was "Virgilio."

———

August 17, 1978

Propper answered a call at his desk. "Is this Mr. Propper?" asked a voice.

"Yeah," said Propper. "Who's this?"

"We're gonna blow off the legs of that fucking judge and then we'll get his family, now or later," growled the voice. "And then if we have time, we'll get you. But you're not a motherfucking black Communist lover."

The phone clicked. Propper reported the threat to the FBI. Barrington Parker, the judge who would preside over the upcoming Letelier trial, had received a similar threat at his home, by mail.

———

August 25, 1978

Robert N. Shwartz, one of the assistant United States attorneys in New York's Southern District, introduced himself to Propper over the telephone and told him that Alvin Ross, a prisoner at the Manhattan Correctional Center, had been bragging to a fellow inmate by the name of Sherman Kaminsky.

Kaminsky, Propper learned, was a rather colorful criminal with an arrest record stretching back to 1945, who had decorated his cell with a photograph of himself proudly wearing the uniform of the Israeli Haganah, the elite commando organization that had used terrorist tactics to help win Israel's battle for existence. It was the photograph that first attracted the attention of fellow inmate Alvin Ross, who had volunteered that his own organization, the Cuban Nationalist Movement, made a conscious effort to emulate the methods of the Haganah.

Shwartz told Propper that Kaminsky had reportedly taken offense at Ross's coarse manner and his political fanaticism. Ross had boasted to Kaminsky that he was a sophisticated electrician who could design systems for detonating explosives under water by means of a radio beam. Also, said Kaminsky, Ross had talked at length about an explosion in Washington, in which the person who was blown up was a "double agent who had been educated at the Espionage College ... by the CIA."

By one of the odd moral standards that criminals often reserve for one another, Kaminsky determined that Ross was a danger to the national security of the United States. And when Ross told him about the CNM's plans to blow up Russian ships in American harbors, Kaminsky was moved to write up a list of Ross's statements to him—and to ask his lawyer to give the statements to the CIA, so that the Agency might take steps to thwart the Cuban Nationalist Movement.

The lawyer had asked prosecutor Shwartz to find out who was handling Ross's case and to transmit the notes to him. Shwartz had located Propper, and now he wanted to know if Propper wanted to see Kaminsky's notes on what Ross had said. Propper pounced on the offer.

———

August 30, 1978

Robert Shwartz enclosed Kaminsky's notes in an August 28 letter to Propper, explaining that he had blacked out several lines "out of an excess of caution to avoid even the suggestion of a 'spy in the defense camp' argument."* Propper had agreed to this precaution in advance. If the notes ever became evidence at a trial, he and Shwartz wanted to make sure that Ross's attorney could not claim that Kaminsky had provided the Letelier case prosecutors with inside information about Ross's line of defense.

A quick perusal of the notes convinced Propper that they were authentic. They contained bits of information about Ross that Kaminsky had no way of inventing. Also, the notes corroborated Canete's portrayal of Ross as an angry braggart. "He is ultra-right wing, and all his conversations generally start with a tirade against the Commies, his total hatred of the Kennedys and the CIA," Kaminsky wrote. "... On August the 3rd, he told me that the 'traitor' in his case will be eliminated one day, if it costs the movement a million

---

*As a further precaution, Kaminsky's lawyer had reviewed and redacted the notes before giving them to Shwartz.

dollars. . . . The traitor he referred to (he mentioned a name quickly that sounded like Tullie) may hurt him, but that he has enough friends in Washington (politicians and lobbying groups) that will come to his aid. . . . He said that if he had had any inkling that the traitor would talk, the sharks would have eaten him. . . . He refers to Chilean generals as good people and says he knows one personally. . . ."

August 28–September 1, 1978

Manuel Contreras telephoned the CIA station chief at the embassy in Santiago with a request for a meeting, which was declined on the ground that Contreras was an undesirable contact.

Subsequently, representatives of Contreras arrived at the embassy and asked for the station chief by name. He received them and was asked to pass a message on to Washington: Sergio Miranda Carrington, Contreras's lawyer, wanted to meet with lawyers from the CIA and the State Department to tell them that Contreras would reveal damaging information about the CIA and the United States government unless the Letelier prosecutors dropped their plans to seek his extradition. The station chief agreed to forward the message.

In Washington, Propper went to see Frank McNeil as soon as he heard of the threat. It was causing quite a stir inside the government. Security officials were wondering in whispers how much damage Contreras could do. Propper asked McNeil the same question.

"I don't care," said McNeil. "The man's accused of murder. We're not going to have any meetings over here, Gene, because I can already answer for the State Department. Fuck him. That's what I say. Let him say anything he wants, but we're going after him."

Propper smiled. "That's great, Frank," he said. "Would you put it in writing?"

"Not in quite that language," said McNeil. "But even diplomats have to be blunt sometimes. If this isn't the time, there will never be one."

"What about the Agency?" asked Propper.

"I don't know," said McNeil. "That's a different story."

To Propper's relief, the CIA's legal department reached the same conclusion as McNeil. A message went back to Contreras's representatives: neither State nor CIA saw any reason to meet with Miranda Carrington, but *Fiscal* Propper would be happy to do so. Contreras did not reply.

September 10, 1978

The enormous "side project" was completed. Six hundred pages of documentary evidence had been written, translated into Spanish, individually notarized, and sealed—according to the prescribed forms for an extradition request. The package was sitting in Barcella's office, surrounded by seals, wax, and ribbons. At Cornick's direction, the "elves" in the FBI lab had drilled a neat hole through all the paper so that a testimentary ribbon could be passed through and sealed as a sign that the documents were intact.

Propper, Barcella, and Cornick experienced a mixture of exhilaration, impatience, and fatigue as they contemplated the last item: the high-speed film of the experimental explosion at Quantico. It was bulky. They could fit it in the box beside the documents, but how could they seal it?

"We can't just put a big glob of wax on the back of that envelope," said Propper. "It wouldn't look good."

"And I refuse to plaster another one of those FBI labels on there," said Barcella. "We need something impressive. We need a real imprint seal." He told a story about how he had once used the buttons of his Dartmouth College blazer to make fancy identity cards so that he could pass for legal age in bars.

Cornick suddenly smiled. "Wait a minute," he said. "I've got just the thing." He began blowing expectantly on his fingers.

"Yeah, right, Carter," snickered Propper, staring at Cornick's ring. "Is that something else from the University of Virginia?"

"It's even better," said Cornick. "It's the Cornick family crest."

After examining the crest, the three men laughed and then stared at each other as the idea became devilishly more attractive. "Why not?" said Propper. "There's no legal reason not to."

Ten minutes later Cornick ceremoniously implanted his family crest into hot wax on the back of the film. "If that doesn't impress them, nothing will," he said, and he would later joke that this act marked the end of a century of Cornick family suffering that had started with the Civil War.

═══

September 20, 1978

In Santiago, Ambassador Landau delivered the extradition package to Foreign Minister Cubillos and requested that it be transmitted to the Chilean Supreme Court, as required by law.

═══

October 31, 1978

Propper flew to New York to meet Kaminsky, Kaminsky's lawyer, and New York prosecutor Shwartz. The three lawyers repeated their instructions to Kaminsky. He was never to seek out Ross in the prison. He should let Ross initiate any conversations, and under no circumstances should Kaminsky ever ask Ross specific questions about the Letelier case. By insisting upon these rules, the prosecutors would remain within the guidelines laid down by the Supreme Court in *Massiah v. United States*. In that landmark case, the Court had ruled that the prosecution had "deliberately elicited" incriminating evidence from an indicted defendant by means of "indirect and surreptitious interrogations" that violated the defendant's Sixth Amendment right to counsel.

Kaminsky said that he had always followed these rules and that it was easy to do so, as Ross was a compulsive talker. Kaminsky said that he spent a lot of time trying to make Ross *stop* talking.

When the informant returned to jail, the three lawyers discussed a new problem. Prison officials at the Manhattan Correctional Center had routinely shifted cell assignments, with the result that Ross and Kaminsky no longer had access to each other. The issue was whether Shwartz should ask the prison officials to put the two inmates back on the same floor. Shwartz was worried about possible "*Massiah* problems." He and Propper decided to seek opinions from the solicitor general's office and from the Appellate Division of the Department of Justice. The prosecutors agreed that they would make no requests of the prison officials unless the appellate lawyers assured them that they would defend such an action as legal under the terms of the Court's *Massiah* decision.

Within a week, Propper would secure the blessing of the solicitor general's office, and shortly thereafter Ross and Kaminsky would be placed on the same floor of the prison.

November 22, 1978

In Santiago, a powerful bomb exploded at the home of Israel Borquez, the Supreme Court judge considering the American extradition request. Borquez announced publicly that he would not be intimidated by such measures. Privately, he asked General Mena about gossip in Santiago that CNI employees might have been involved in the bombing. Mena denied the charge, saying that it was probably the work of former DINA men who remained loyal to Contreras.

———

December 2, 1978

Sherman Kaminsky sat down in his New York cell to make notes on another of his marathon conversations with Alvin Ross. That Saturday morning, Ross had talked with much merriment about how he and Novo had advised Propper, the federal prosecutor, that they would send him a "present" when the trial was over. Ross told Kaminsky that Propper had understood that there would be a bomb in the present, and that Propper had said he didn't need any such gifts. All this had occurred during a break in a pretrial hearing, as Ross told it to Kaminsky.

This report excited Propper and Barcella, because the incident had indeed occurred exactly as Kaminsky said. Only four people—Propper, Barcella, Novo, and Ross—had known of it. Therefore, the prosecutors reasoned, Kaminsky could not have invented the details or read them in a newspaper; he must have heard the story from Ross. This report greatly enhanced Kaminsky's credibility as a witness.

"He raved about 'rats,'" Kaminsky recorded in his notes. "Said that 'the U.S. government had agents and rats everywhere. . . .' He then went into a very emotional tirade about the informer (T) and his wife, using a lot of abusive language and telling me how much he hated them. He said: 'The guy really fooled me and took advantage of my electrical ability—my life is hanging in the balance over two pieces of wire.'"

———

December 3, 1978

A powerful bomb exploded at the home of Sergio Dunlop, the Chilean judge who had been assigned to conduct an inquiry into the bombing at Judge Borquez's home eleven days earlier.

———

December 15, 1978

Isabel Letelier was on the witness stand. Barcella and Dianne Kelly, a third prosecutor recently assigned to the trial team, sat in the jury box, and Propper stood at the attorney's lectern. The four of them were alone in a courtroom, practicing for the upcoming trial.

"I'd like you to get a feel for the courtroom and what it's like to talk from the witness stand," Propper told Isabel Letelier. "So why don't you just try to tell the story in your own way. Tell us what you know firsthand."

"Okay," she said. "I'll try." She began to talk in her soft voice. She talked of her courtship by Letelier in the 1950s, of their marriage, of a few notable scenes in Washington, including several contacts with Secretary of State Kissinger when Orlando Letelier was Allende's ambassador to Washington. She told of returning to Chile as the Allende regime was tottering, and of her own contacts with General Pinochet when that officer worked loyally, almost servilely, for his boss, Defense Minister Letelier. She told of the coup and her husband's disappearance, and of her months under house arrest in Santiago. "When I finally saw him as a prisoner, he was so emaciated," she said. "But he looked very good to me. I remember he gave me this stone then, and I have worn it around my neck ever since. It is made of volcanic rock. Orlando carved these letters in it, *ISA*, for Isabel. He told me he polished the stone by rubbing it in the sand. That's the way he kept his sanity . . ."

She told of Letelier's release after one year, of the family's reunion and its life in exile. She told of their marital separation and their struggle to reconcile, of Orlando Letelier's growing political stature in exile and the threats against his life. Finally, she told of his speech at Madison Square Garden and of his last day. "I received a telephone call from the Institute," she said. "They told me there had been a terrible accident and I must come quickly. They would not say what it was, but I knew it was Orlando. When I got to the Institute, everyone was crying. They told me then that it was Orlando, but I still didn't know what had happened. We went to the hospital. There were many people there. Everything was very confused. I asked them to let me see him, and they told me that would not be a very good idea. I said why not? They told me he looked very bad. By then I knew there had been a bomb. I knew he was not alive. I told them I wanted to say goodbye to him, but they told me it was not a good idea for my own sake because he was very bad. I said I don't care. I said who are you to tell me that? I said I want to say goodbye to something, even if it's only to a hand or a foot. I want to say goodbye to my *compañero* of all these years. He is my *compañero*. I want to say goodbye to him. Finally, someone let me in, and I kissed him and said goodbye. And that is how I came to be here."

Isabel Letelier stopped talking and looked up from the witness stand. She had seemed to be in some kind of trance. Barcella and

Kelly were weeping quietly in the jury box. And Propper was chok-
ing back tears beside the lectern. It was the first time he had ever
cried at the office.

═══

December 19, 1978

At the Manhattan Correctional Center, Guillermo Novo had renewed his acquaintance with Antonio Polytarides after learning that
the latter had been granted parole and would soon be leaving prison.
This meant that Polytarides no longer needed favors from the government and was therefore much less likely to be an informant.

On December 19, Novo and Alvin Ross sought out Polytarides to
finalize a purchase agreement for ten MAC-10 silenced submachine
guns, twenty pounds of C-4 explosive, and two hundred M26A1 grenades—all to be delivered to Cuban Nationalist Movement associates
"on the outside." Novo finally agreed to Polytarides's price of $500
per pound for the C-4. Payment would be in cash.

═══

January 9, 1979

The Letelier trial opened in Judge Barrington Parker's courtroom
under the heaviest security arrangements in the history of Washington, D.C. At the outset, Guillermo Novo's lawyer, Paul Goldberger,
objected that the prosecutors had two water pitchers on their table
while the defense had none. The lawyerly disputes built from there.

═══

January 15, 1979

In his opening statement Goldberger told the jury that the defense
would prove that neither the Cuban defendants nor the Chilean
DINA had been involved in the assassination. "We will prove to
you," he declared, "that . . . this assassination was carried out by Michael Vernon Townley . . . working as an agent for the CIA."

Propper and Barcella wondered why the defense lawyers had assumed the gratuitous burden of defending DINA. They assumed it
was because Contreras was supplying funds to the defendants.

═══

January 18, 1979

The government's star witness, Michael Vernon Townley, took the
stand. Propper and Barcella spent much energy trying to block ef-

forts by the defense lawyers to introduce new defamatory information about Townley. Judge Parker sustained some objections and overruled others. "As far as credibility is concerned," said the judge, "I think that there is enough before the jury right now showing that Mr. Townley is not the person that you would want to sit next to at a Sunday worship service."

January 19, 1979

"If my memory serves me well, it was 31.040 megahertz," Townley testified, referring to the frequency he had used in the Fanon-Courier transmitter to detonate the bomb.

Later that day, Townley refused to acknowledge any remorse about his role in the death of Letelier. "He was a soldier, and I was a soldier," he said.

January 19, 1979

Only *El Mercurio* gave Chilean readers anything like an objective report on Townley's testimony, in a front-page story headlined TOWNLEY: MY MISSION WAS TO ASSASSINATE LETELIER. The story in *Últimas Noticias*—"TRAITOR!" THEY SHOUTED AT TOWNLEY—focused on the spectators who denounced Townley outside the trial for betraying the anti-Castro cause. The afternoon paper, *La Segunda*, ignored Townley's testimony in favor of EXPLOSIVES FOUND IN MOFFITT HOUSE, an error-filled, misleading article about the obscure fact that police dogs had sniffed for secondary bombs at IPS and at the Moffitt home.

The government-owned newspaper, *El Cronista*, put its Letelier story inside the paper under the headline NO TESTIMONY CONFIRMING TOWNLEY'S DECLARATIONS: NEVERTHELESS PERSISTS IN INVOLVING CHILE IN A CRIME.

February 1–6, 1979

Defense lawyers moved to block all testimony by Sherman Kaminsky and Antonio Polytarides on the ground that it would violate the defendants' Sixth Amendment right to counsel. Propper and Barcella argued vehemently against the motions.

After listening to the arguments and to extensive examination of the prospective witnesses outside the presence of the jury for two solid days, Judge Parker ruled that Kaminsky could testify only about what he had heard Alvin Ross say before October 31, the day he first met Propper, at which point Kaminsky might arguably have become a prosecution "agent" conducting "surreptitious interrogations," as prohibited by the *Massiah* decision.

As to Polytarides, Parker disallowed all testimony about his early conversations with Guillermo Novo, including Novo's confession of involvement in the Letelier assassination, on the ground that Polytarides was already a customs agent when he met Novo and that he had been directed to find out information on the location of Paz and Suárez. Parker did allow Polytarides to testify about one statement he had heard Novo make in December of 1978: "We have been betrayed by some people in our case, but we will pay them back." The judge held that Polytarides was no longer a government informant at the time this statement was made and that Novo had initiated the contact with Polytarides. Finally, Parker disallowed any testimony from Polytarides about Novo's efforts to buy explosives and weapons outside the prison, on the ground that these constituted unproven criminal allegations that might prejudice the defendant in the eyes of the jurors.

The complex series of rulings pleased neither side. Propper and Barcella believed they had been deprived unfairly of many critical pieces of corroborative testimony. The defense lawyers expressed disappointment that the "jailhouse witnesses" were allowed to testify at all.

February 13, 1979

To his everlasting regret, Propper was unable to deliver the closing argument he had dreamed about for more than two years. He was too sick, and he had no voice. Barcella was pressed into duty for both the closing argument and the rebuttal, even though he was sick himself. For the past few weeks, Barcella had fought a cold with a constant treatment of nose spray, which, he would soon learn, had deadened his senses of taste and smell.

After Judge Parker's instructions, the jury began deliberating. Propper, Barcella, and Cornick ran into the defense lawyers in the courthouse cafeteria. In the sportsmanlike manner of lawyers, the two sides congratulated each other for a job well done during the grueling five-week trial.

"You know, you guys did an incredible thing," said Goldberger.

"You did something nobody should be able to do. Not only did you get your story into evidence, you got it right. All the way down the line. That's even more amazing than getting as far as you did."

Cornick and the prosecutors stared blankly at one another. "Thanks, Paul," said Propper. "But that'll make it even harder to take if the jury comes back with the wrong verdict."

Goldberger smiled. "You only got one little thing wrong," he said. "Just one."

Barcella almost jumped into Goldberger's suit. "What's that?" he asked.

Goldberger held a thumb up and dropped it through the air. "Who pushed the button," he said, with satisfaction. "You got that wrong." He refused to say any more.

The investigators speculated furiously on the way back upstairs. "I think I know what he means," said Barcella. "It's Paz. It's got to be Paz. That's the one part of Mike's story that's never really made sense to me. Why would Paz go back to New Jersey that Tuesday morning when it was Suárez who had the job? Paz didn't have any reason to get back. And why would Paz hang up on Mike at a time like that without saying anything? It doesn't make sense. I think Mike lied to protect Paz, his buddy and traveling companion. Mike didn't know shit about American law, and I think he figured he could hurt his buddy a little less if he said Paz wasn't there for the murders. He didn't know that Paz would be just as guilty. I'll bet anything that Suárez drove the car and Paz pushed the button."

———

February 14, 1979

After eight hours' deliberation, the jury found the defendants guilty as charged, on all counts. The defendants shouted "*Viva Cuba libre!*" as they were led off to jail.

———

March 23, 1979

Judge Barrington Parker sentenced Alvin Ross and Guillermo Novo to two consecutive life sentences apiece for the murders of Letelier and Moffitt. Each man would serve a minimum of forty years before becoming eligible for parole.

Parker sentenced Ignacio Novo to eight years on the lesser charges of false declarations and misprision.

———

May 14, 1979

In Santiago, Judge Israel Borquez formally denied the request of the United States government for the extradition of Contreras, Espinoza, and Fernández. Furthermore, Borquez declared that all evidence from Michael Townley was inadmissible and of no value, and he ordered a Chilean military tribunal to determine whether the remaining evidence was strong enough to warrant a trial in Chile.

May 16, 1979

Ercilla, a Chilean weekly news magazine, published an interview with Supreme Court Judge Borquez that contained the following exchange:

> *Ercilla:* What did you think about the decision of the U.S. court that sentenced Townley to ten years?
> Borquez: The Americans are very good actors, and they are famous for believing in the credulity of the rest of the people. Imagine! To form the jury of the court of the District of Columbia, they chose—even the judge, Barrington Parker, who presided—only little brown people, maybe so they could not show their blushing when they heard the evidence.

This remark drew widespread condemnation in Europe and in the United States, where commentators charged that its blatant racism only led to further doubt about the wisdom and impartiality of Borquez's decision in the extradition case.

May 24, 1979

Deputy Secretary Warren Christopher chaired a large interdepartmental meeting to discuss how the United States should respond to the Borquez decision. Each participant had been given a copy of proposed instructions for Ambassador Landau on what he should tell the Chilean government when he returned to Santiago. On behalf of the Justice Department, Propper argued that the proposed instructions were far too weak. "We have to do more," he said. "We have to tell the Chileans that we will not back down and that we will not accept such conduct from them."

Undersecretary for Political Affairs David D. Newsom fielded this opening statement diplomatically. "We understand your position, Mr. Propper," he said. "But you must also understand that we have to take this matter in the context of our entire range of bilateral relations with Chile."

"In the *context* of our relations with Chile?" asked Propper, looking surprised. "The Letelier case *is* our relations with Chile!"

"That is certainly a position that can be argued," said Newsom. He called on the next speaker and then turned to Christopher, conferring privately.

Christopher stood up, interrupting the proceedings. "Excuse me," he said. "I can see that this issue still needs to be staffed out some before it can receive full attention." With that, he and Newsom left the conference room.

Without Christopher and Newsom, the meeting broke up quickly. Frank Willis whistled gleefully to himself in the hallway. "I would pay to see that again," he said. "A rinky-dink prosecutor taking on the number-two and number-three guys of the most powerful foreign ministry in the world."

=====

June 2, 1979

On the flight back to Santiago, Ambassador Landau studied his instructions. He would call the Borquez decision legally and morally unacceptable. He would also tell the Chileans that the United States was "equally distressed and offended" by the utter lack of progress in the Letelier investigation Chilean authorities claimed to be conducting on their own. Finally, Landau would warn the Chilean government that if the Borquez decision was affirmed on appeal, the United States, having exhausted its legal remedies, would have no choice but to register its "outrage" through diplomatic sanctions. Landau would mention some of the sanctions under consideration. He would warn the Chilean Foreign Ministry that "the future course of our relations with Chile will depend very heavily on the outcome of that appeal." Although he had argued that his instructions should be even tougher on the Chileans, he felt certain his words would not be lost.

They would be delivered in private, however, and the public aspects of the case bothered Landau greatly. The Chilean media were hailing the Borquez decision as final proof that Chilean entities were innocent of Letelier's murder and that the extradition request had been nothing more than an American conspiracy to intervene in Chilean politics. The righteousness and hypocrisy of the articles enraged Landau, and although he was not supposed to comment on the case publicly, he pulled out his old portable typewriter and began pecking away.

More than fifty reporters greeted him at Pudahuel Airport. Facing them, concealing his anger, Landau read the statement he had just written on the plane:

> As you are aware, I have just returned from Washington. There I participated in a thorough review of all phases of our relations with Chile. Until I have discussed the results with the Foreign Minister, I am obviously not in a position to make any comments.
>
> While in Washington, however, I followed with interest the Chilean press and I found a number of articles highly critical of the United States. In particular, there was much said about how we violated Chilean sovereignty by complaining over the decision handed down by the Supreme Court president. I believe it is quite normal for a plaintiff to complain when in his view he has a good case and is nevertheless turned down. The remedy is at hand: an appeal to a full chamber of the Supreme Court. This we have done.
>
> However, talking about sovereignty, one should not lose sight that in this case U.S. sovereignty has been violated. And not by word but by deed. We should not forget that two persons, a former foreign diplomat and an American citizen, were killed in cold blood right in the heart of our nation's capital. If this terrorist act is not a violation of our sovereignty, then I do not know what is. We cannot allow terrorist acts of this nature to go unpunished. If so, it would be an open invitation to others to commit similar crimes. For that reason, we are determined to see that those who planned and committed the murders are brought to trial. This is the issue at stake and nothing else.

Landau pushed his way through the crowd without saying another word. Two years later, he was still carrying this tattered statement in his coat pocket.

━━━

June 4, 1979

Townley, fearful that the Italian government would seek to question him by Letters Rogatory about the assassination attempt on Bernardo Leighton, sent a message from his prison cell to his CNI superiors in Chile: "I can answer or I can invoke the Fifth," he said. "If I answer, things will remain quiet and hidden—but only for the moment. If I invoke the Fifth, many questions and suspicions will remain. My decision is a dilemma, but it is a dilemma that I have to resolve by taking the Fifth. This could appear wrong at first sight, because many will say, 'See, he's hiding something, he's protecting people, he doesn't dare to talk.' But as I don't have any idea about the current or future position of Alfa or 'Caller'* I can't organize myself to respond and then have someone say something different for whatever dirty reason. Then I would face additional charges for possible perjury...."

Townley went on to say that he was still trying to influence the American authorities to the benefit of Chile, and he promised to keep sending intelligence reports from the prison.

———

July 27, 1979

Propper could help little with the extradition proceedings in Chile, and he found himself utterly incapable of concentration on other cases. He resigned from the Justice Department, after eight years' service.

———

August 9–12, 1979

From his prison cell, Michael Townley replied clandestinely to General Mena's urgent request that he attempt to locate American bank accounts used by Mena's rival, ex-General Contreras. Townley said that he thought he knew where some of the accounts were located, and under what names, and that he had passed the ideas along to the FBI for investigation, as Mena had suggested. At least one of the accounts, said Townley, had been opened years earlier by Contreras to receive payments from the CIA.

Townley was happy to help Mena with this particular request. Since his incarceration, he had been playing a dangerous, complicated game of survival with Mena. Townley knew that Mena wanted to know everything he knew about Contreras's crimes, but Townley also knew that these secrets were his protection: they kept the payments coming to his wife and allowed his family to stay in their DINA home in Santiago. Mena was disappointed that Townley had not cooperated more fully in the clandestine war against Contreras, and Townley believed that Mena had retaliated by falling behind on

---

*Authors' approximation of the name, which is illegible in the handwritten message. The name is assumed to be a pseudonym.

the upkeep of his house and by delaying payments to Mariana. Also, Mena had delayed payments for Townley's legal bills in the United States.

Now, in return for information about Contreras's bank accounts, Townley wanted Mena's guarantee of prompt delivery of $1,500 per month for Mariana Callejas, of $165 to himself in the prison, and of $20,000 for payment to his lawyers. Later he would send a much longer list of repairs that he wanted done on the house—painting of the swimming pool (two coats), maintenance of the washing machine, replanting of the garden, and so on.

———

October 1, 1979

The Chilean Supreme Court formally denied the American request for the extradition of Contreras, Espinoza, and Fernández. Moreover, the Court declared that there was insufficient evidence to warrant even an investigation of the Letelier assassination in Chile, voiding Judge Borquez's order on that issue. There would be no murder trial, and the investigation was limited to allegations of passport fraud.

To reach this blunt decision, the Court was forced to adopt a long series of remarkable declarations. First, the Court reversed a longstanding tenet of international law that bases the standard of admissibility of evidence in extradition requests on the laws of the requesting country (the United States). The Court simply declared that it would evaluate the admissibility of the evidence by Chilean standards. Then the judges proceeded to dismiss all evidence from Michael Townley on the ground that it was the fruit of a plea-bargaining agreement (although many Chilean criminal statutes recognize the validity of plea bargaining). To dismiss Townley's confession to General Orozco at Quantico, which was made before Townley signed the plea-bargaining agreement, the Court ruled that General Orozco had no authority to receive such a statement on American soil and that the statement was therefore invalid. To dismiss all evidence gathered by the American FBI agents and prosecutors in Chile, the Court ruled that foreign officials cannot act validly in Chile. Finally, the Court dismissed the affidavits and documentary evidence from the United States on the ground that it had not been validated by a Chilean judge. From there, it was easy to dispense with the entire American request.

———

October 8, 1979

After a brief meeting with Christopher, Vaky, and Ambassador Landau, Barcella called Propper. "Gene, they're doing a marshmallow on us," he said.

"What do you mean?" asked Propper.

"Well, I can't tell yet, but Vaky's running the show and that's a bad sign," said Barcella. "All our friends at State are gone, and it makes a hell of a difference.* The sanctions they're talking about now are even less than what they were planning before, when everybody thought the Supreme Court would uphold the Borquez decision. There's a lot of backpedaling going on. All Vaky said today was that he wanted to have a big meeting so all the government bureaus with 'Chilean equities' could have their say."

"What's a Chilean equity?" asked Propper.

"I don't know," said Barcella. "He means all the people who have a piece of the action in Chile."

October 15, 1979

All the places around Warren Christopher's enormous conference table were filled, and nearly thirty government officials stood or sat around the periphery of the room. There were representatives of the Pentagon, Agriculture, the Peace Corps, Commerce, Treasury, the Export-Import Bank, the National Security Council, and several other departments, along with officials from half a dozen different branches of the State Department. Barcella represented the Justice Department.

One by one, the officials around the table gave short speeches on their agency's interests in Chile and how they would be affected by the proposed sanctions. Robert Pastor, Zbigniew Brzezinski's Latin America specialist on the National Security Council, talked about Chile's strategic importance as an American ally. "I suppose my question should really be directed to the representative of the Justice Department," he said. "Mr. Barcella, are we *that* confident in the evidence that we presented that we can say with assurance that the decision of the Chilean Supreme Court was in fact in error?"

Barcella had already sensed a strong adverse tide. "Well, I'm a lit-

---

*Vaky had fired Frank McNeil. Bob Steven and Frank Willis had been transferred routinely to other jobs.

tle surprised, frankly, that at this late date we are going back to questions about the strength of the government's evidence," he replied. "Our evidence is overwhelming, and it is certainly far stronger than what Chile normally requires for extradition." He was beginning to show some annoyance. "I think we're forgetting, gentlemen, what it is that brought us here," he said, placing the autopsy photographs on the table before him. "These are pictures of Orlando Letelier and Ronni Moffitt after the Chilean secret police did their work. All of you should feel free to look at these later if you want to. But for right now I simply want to remind you that we have unequivocal proof, including one heavily corroborated confession, of the most heinous act of political terrorism ever committed in the nation's capital. We have proven that it was agents of a foreign power who carried it out. That foreign power has now blatantly rejected our request to see that justice is done, and it's up to the people in this room to respond. If we do not, we will simply be inviting further crimes like this."

"We are all agreed that the crime was reprehensible, Mr. Barcella," said Assistant Secretary Vaky. "But that doesn't tell us what to do, you see. Our problem is how to balance those facts against all other American interests in Chile."

"Well, I don't believe I should comment very much on specific sanctions, Mr. Vaky," Barcella replied. "But since you've asked, I would say that the Chilean Supreme Court has rendered our extradition treaty a legal nullity, and that we should strongly consider canceling the treaty altogether, as is our right. Apart from that, I would only point to the case of Dr. Sheila Cassidy, a British doctor who was tortured by DINA in 1975. DINA did not kill her, but the British government withdrew its ambassador from Chile to protest that brutality against a British subject. As I understand it, the British still don't have an ambassador in Santiago now, four years later. I would suggest that we take sanctions against Chile in proportion to those the British took in the Cassidy case."

"That is true," Vaky replied. "But you ought to know that the British have been trying to get their ambassador back into Chile; they just haven't yet found a good face-saving way to do it."

"That's right," agreed Ambassador Landau. "The British would like very much to send an ambassador back to Santiago. They need an excuse to do it, and they haven't found it yet."

Mark Feldman, chief of the State Department's legal office, agreed with Barcella's legal analysis and formally recommended that the United States renounce the 1902 Extradition Treaty with Chile. He was the only representative in the room who advocated a sanction that would affect his own sphere of interest in Chile. In the end, all other department spokesmen with interests to defend recommended that their own agency's program be excluded from any package of sanctions. Nothing was decided. Vaky announced that Secretary Vance would receive and weigh the various opinions that had been expressed.

Barcella called Propper when it was over. "The marshmallow is getting bigger," he said with a sigh. He said he felt personally hurt by Ambassador Landau's support for Vaky. "I'm telling you, it was a different George Landau in there today," said Barcella.

=====

October 16, 1979

At the State Department, Barcella talked with Frank Willis and learned that Mark Feldman had rescinded his recommendation that the United States renounce the extradition treaty. "It was decided for him," Willis said pointedly.

=====

November 4, 1979

When Iranian militants stormed the American embassy in Tehran and took most of the American employees there hostage, Latin America experts in the State Department informed Barcella that this was a calamity for those who favored strong sanctions against Chile. "The Iranians are upset with us because we won't extradite the Shah," said the new Chile desk officer. "And now we are complaining about the Chileans because they won't extradite Contreras. We can't really talk about sanctions against Chile without appearing to support the Iranian militants."

"Wait a minute," said Barcella. "That's the most skewed analogy I've ever heard. First of all, the Iranians haven't even requested the Shah's extradition. The analogy would only be apt if we hadn't asked for extradition at all, and instead Gene and I and a few hundred of our fanatical FBI friends had stormed the Chilean embassy in Washington and taken everybody hostage."

"That may be, Larry," said the desk officer. "But this puts us in a diplomatically vulnerable position."

=====

November 30, 1979

The United States government announced diplomatic sanctions against Chile that included cancellation of Export-Import Bank loans to Chile and a reduction of U.S. embassy personnel. But Ambassador Landau would remain on duty in Santiago, the treaty would remain in effect, and there would be no trade or commercial sanctions, or restrictions on lending by private banks.

September 15, 1980

Barcella felt slightly sick as his colleague John Terry handed him a printed manuscript. Terry had a stricken look on his face. "Don't tell me," Barcella said softly. "That's the Letelier decision?"

"Yes," said Terry.

"We got reversed?" asked Barcella.

"I'm sorry, Larry," said Terry.

"On Iggie?" asked Barcella. He and Propper had always been prepared for the possibility that Ignacio Novo's conviction might be reversed, on the ground that Novo—not being charged with the murders themselves—should have received a separate trial.

"Yes," said Terry. "And the others, too."

Barcella could hardly speak. "Both of them? Guillermo and Alvin? On the murders?"

"I'm sorry, Larry," said Terry.

Barcella felt nauseated. "Why?" he whispered.

"I haven't read the whole thing," said Terry. "But it looks like it's because of Kaminsky and Polytarides. We won all the other major issues on appeal."

"Kaminsky and Polytarides?" said Barcella. "That's impossible." He looked at Terry's miserable face. "I guess it's not," he said. He started to say a number of things, but none of them seemed important. Barcella felt himself growing numb as well as sick. "Just leave the opinion on the desk," he told Terry. "Thank you."

September 17, 1980

Propper and Barcella met at a bar to console each other. Each of them had forced himself to read the lengthy opinion of the Court of Appeals panel, and as they reviewed the work, they alternated between fury and utter despair.

The judges had based their decision on a new Supreme Court case, *United States v. Henry*, which had been handed down on June 16, 1980. The defendant in that case, Billy Gale Henry, was arrested by FBI agents and later indicted for armed robbery of a bank in Norfolk, Virginia. While Henry was awaiting trial, one of the FBI agents on his case approached a longtime FBI informant who happened to be incarcerated in the Norfolk city jail along with Henry. The agent instructed the informant not to initiate any conversations about the bank robbery but to listen carefully if Henry volunteered any information. The informant later testified at Henry's trial, and the prosecution failed to disclose to the jury that the witness was a paid informant.

By a 6–3 vote, the Supreme Court reversed Henry's conviction in a decision that extended a defendant's Sixth Amendment protections under the *Massiah* case. Chief Justice Warren Burger, writing for himself and four other justices, held that even though the government had not directed its informant to *question* Henry about his case, as in *Massiah*, it had nevertheless violated Henry's right to counsel "by intentionally creating a situation likely to induce the defendant to make incriminating statements without assistance of counsel and having deliberately elicited the incriminating statements." The majority of justices thus objected to the FBI agent's clandestine efforts to intercept incriminating words out of Henry's mouth. In one of the dissenting opinions, Justice William Rehnquist had argued that the government had not coerced either Massiah or Henry into testifying against himself, that both defendants had spoken voluntarily to the informants, according to the agreed-upon facts. The evidence should be admissible as long as it was provided voluntarily, he wrote, and the witnesses' status as government informants should affect the credibility of their testimony rather than its admissibility.

Barcella and Propper agreed with Rehnquist, of course, but that was only the beginning of it. They had taken great pains to comply with the dictates of the *Massiah* decision, they believed, and they also believed that their witnesses fell within the stricter requirements of the *Henry* decision. The more they studied the decision of the three-judge Court of Appeals panel, the angrier they became. How could they, the Letelier case prosecutors, have created a "situation likely to induce" incriminating testimony from the defendants through Kaminsky and Polytarides when they had not even known of the existence of either witness until after Ross and Novo had confessed to them? Both witnesses had first learned about the Letelier assassination from the defendants themselves—not from coaches in the government. The informants had not met anyone working on the Letelier case and knew nothing of its victims or of the accused conspirators when they heard the initial confessions. Indeed, Kaminsky had not even recognized the significance of what Ross told him about the assassination; his purpose in turning over his notes was to warn the CIA about Ross's plans to blow up Russian ships.

To apply *Henry* to the Letelier case, the three Appeals judges* referred to a sentencing transcript from one of Sherman Kaminsky's 1978 cases, in which an aged and cantankerous New York judge had lectured Kaminsky on his criminal habits, and had ordered Kaminsky to assist the authorities everywhere on any criminal activity that came to his attention.

The Appeals judges ruled that the New York judge's speech had transformed Sherman Kaminsky into a government informant and had indirectly created a situation "likely to induce" incriminating statements from Alvin Ross to Kaminsky. Therefore, by the logic of the *Henry* decision, Ross's murder conviction was overturned because *none* of Kaminsky's testimony should have been admitted—including that which was based on conversations with Ross before Kaminsky knew anything about Letelier or the Letelier prosecutors. The judges also held that this error contaminated the conviction of Guillermo Novo, and they added, almost as an aside, that Polytarides should not have been allowed to testify, either.

In the bar with Propper, Barcella bitterly denounced the "Rube Goldberg logic" of the reversal. "*Massiah* and *Henry* were bad enough," said Barcella. "But whatever happened to the idea that they have to show we deliberately elicited information from the defendant? How can a speech by a judge turn somebody into an informant for the executive branch? Whatever happened to the separation of powers?"

Propper and Barcella exercised their best courtroom rhetoric on each other until they attracted looks of worry from their barmates. What incensed them above all else was that the three judges had gone out of their way to express satisfaction with the evidence against Ross and the Novo brothers, stating that the three defendants seemed to be guilty by the weight of the evidence and that the

*Howard F. Corcoran, George E. MacKinnon, and Roger Robb.

reversal had nothing to do with that fundamental question.

"Don't worry, Larry," said Propper. "Anybody can see that this is a terrible decision. We'll get it reversed."

———

September 26–27, 1980

The Venezuelan War Council announced that there was not sufficient evidence to warrant a trial in the case of the Cubana Airlines bombing that had killed seventy-three people in October 1976. The council ordered the immediate, unconditional release of Orlando Bosch, Luis Posada, and the two Venezuelans who had confessed to placing the bomb in the aircraft. All four suspects had been held without trial for nearly four years.

The next day, Cuban Premier Fidel Castro peremptorily withdrew all Cuban diplomats from Venezuela in protest of the War Council's decision.

A few weeks later, as it became clear that the prisoners would remain in jail while the Venezuelan military command "reviewed" the order of the War Council, the Cuban diplomats would begin drifting back into Caracas. Observers would say that the review would take considerable time—perhaps years—and that the Cuban government had stopped a "trial balloon" on the part of the Venezuelans, who wanted to dispense with the Bosch case.

———

February 2, 1981

Propper, Earl Silbert, Carl Rauh, and other former prosecutors joined Barcella in lobbying with Justice Department contacts to make sure the Letelier case would be taken to the Supreme Court on appeal. When the Reagan administration took office in January, Propper called one of the new officials blindly. He advised Propper to present his arguments in writing to the new attorney general, William French Smith.

"In recent days I heard both President Reagan and Secretary of State Haig expound on the problem of terrorism," his letter began. He went on to describe the Letelier murders, the investigation, and the convictions of Ross and the Novo brothers. "The Court of Appeals for the District of Columbia Circuit reversed those convictions based upon actions taken by the Judicial Branch of government, not the Executive Branch," Propper wrote, "and its opinion is one which can be of great harm to law enforcement if not challenged. It is based on an unfortunate and incorrect interpretation of a relatively recent Supreme Court case. . . ."

Propper explained that the U.S. attorney had formally asked the Justice Department to petition the Supreme Court to review the case. "That decision is now before the Office of the Solicitor General," he wrote. "Any decision by the Supreme Court cannot do anything but improve the existing state of the law. . . . There is not much time left to petition the Court. . . . I would ask that you look into this matter and that you authorize a petition to the Supreme Court. The importance of the case merits it; the state of the law merits it; and the deterrent to further terrorism mandates it."

February 20, 1981

The State Department announced that Secretary Haig had officially lifted the two most serious sanctions that had been applied after Chile's Supreme Court denied extradition in the Letelier case. Henceforth, Haig declared, Chile would again be invited to take part in joint exercises with the United States Navy, and Chile would again be eligible for Export-Import Bank credit and for Overseas Private Investment Corporation loan guarantees.

Haig's decision outraged Barcella, who abandoned all bureaucratic caution in comments that would appear on the front page of the next day's *Washington Post*. "The original reason for the sanctions was to protest the Chilean government's total inaction and totally irresponsible investigation over the twenty months preceding the sanctions," he declared. "Today's action could be viewed as rewarding Chile for its continued intransigence and failure to do anything worthwhile in the ensuing fifteen months."

February 24, 1981

Barcella and his new boss, United States Attorney Charles Ruff, presented their case for appeal to Deputy Solicitor General Andrew Frye, Assistant Solicitor General Edwin Kneedler, and William Bryson, chief of the Appellate Section of the Justice Department's criminal division. By prearrangement, Ruff began with a strictly legal argument on why the Court of Appeals decision was faulty and inconsistent with *Henry*. Ruff more than held his own with the three Justice Department officials, all of whom had worked on the *Henry* case in a losing effort for the government. After roughly forty-five minutes of discussion, the five lawyers agreed that the solicitor general could make a powerful argument to the Supreme Court that the Court of Appeals had grossly misapplied *Henry* in overturning the Letelier case convictions.

The appellate lawyers still expressed reservations, however. They stated that it was generally unwise to take a case back up to the Supreme Court soon after losing one on similar issues. *Henry* was only seven months old, they said, and it would be better to wait for a similar case a few years later. Also, they argued that the Letelier case did not offer the ideal set of facts for a legal challenge to *Henry*. Even if the Supreme Court reinstated the Letelier convictions, the decision would have no beneficial effect on the state of the law because the Letelier facts were much *worse*, from the government's point of view, than the facts in *Henry*.

"You could accomplish most of what you want whether we go to the Court or not," said Kneedler. "You can always take this case back to trial and convict these people all over again."

"Now wait a minute," said Barcella. "I'm the one who would have to do that, and I want you to understand that it won't be all that easy. First of all, the three Chileans and the two Cubans most instrumental in the conspiracy won't be there. Second, my star witness is a confessed assassin who made a deal with the government. My next best witness is a con man, Canete, who's been arrested again since the trial two years ago. Frankly, I'm not even sure I could find him. There are about ten factors like that, plus the fact that the defense can present an entirely new theory of the case if they want to. They can surprise us, but we can't surprise them. They get all the advantages the second time around. I think I can convict these guys again, but I'm telling you, it won't be easy."

The appellate lawyers expressed understanding of all the difficulties Barcella would face at a second trial, but they also said that these considerations were irrelevant to the appellate decision. Barcella and Ruff soon rolled out their last argument. "You guys know the Court better than we do," said Ruff. "Let me ask you something. Do you think the Court would accept *cert.** on our case and then affirm the Court of Appeals? That would never happen, would it? If they were going to turn us down, they would simply refuse to hear

---

*For *certiorari*, the writ by which the Supreme Court agrees to accept a case for review.

the case. Right? If they grant *cert.*, we're almost sure to win. Don't you think?"

The appellate lawyers agreed unanimously. "All right," said Ruff. "Then we have nothing to lose by trying. The worst that can happen is that the Court will deny *cert.*, and then Larry will have to take the case back to trial."

"That's right," said Barcella. "The bottom line is that the Justice Department has a lot to gain and absolutely nothing to lose by taking the case to the Supreme Court."

"Well, that's basically true," said Kneedler. "But we do have some possible losses. We have a reputation with the Court to consider. Right now, the Court grants *cert.* on more than eighty percent of the petitions we send up there. Whenever we lose, it hurts our credibility with the Court a little."

"I agree with Barcella," said Frye, the senior man in the room. "I think we ought to go up there and see if we can get this thing reversed. It's a terrible decision."

Frye said he would present his recommendation to the solicitor general that week. There was some urgency, as the deadline for filing a petition of appeal was less than two weeks away.

* * *

February 27, 1981

U.S. Attorney Ruff called Barcella with some bad news. Solicitor General Wade McCree, a holdover from the Carter administration, had unexpectedly reserved judgment on Andrew Frye's recommendation. Instead, McCree had asked for a written presentation of the arguments on both sides of the question. He would consider it over the weekend and make his decision Monday. It was now Friday.

To make things worse, Frye was leaving that night for vacation. This left only Kneedler in the solicitor's office to draft the paper, and Kneedler opposed the appeal. Bryson, of the criminal division, had volunteered to draft the paper that night and to take it to McCree on Saturday. There was nothing anyone else could do.

* * *

March 2, 1981

Barcella could not reach Ruff by telephone all morning. Finally, he walked down to Ruff's office. "The news must be bad," he said, "or you would have called me."

"I'm afraid so," said Ruff. "The SG decided not to appeal. He said he would wait for a more advantageous set of facts."

"I can't believe it," said Barcella. He took a deep breath. "Chuck, we don't have any choice now," he said. "We've got to see the attorney general. We've got to ask him to direct the SG to make the appeal."

Ruff looked pained. "I don't know, Larry," he said. "The attorney general almost never intervenes in decisions like this. You know that. Besides, I don't know this attorney general. If Ben Civiletti were still over there, I wouldn't hesitate a second. In fact, I'd have probably already been there before. I'd just walk in. But it's not so easy with Smith."

"Chuck, I can't think of a better way to introduce yourself to the new attorney general than this," argued Barcella. "You can go over there as the guy with the biggest terrorist case in history, and you're asking the AG to come down on the right side!"

"Yeah, but I don't know how he'd look at it," said Ruff. "He might see it as a can of worms, asking him to overrule the SG. He probably doesn't even know McCree."

"I don't know what to say," Barcella said desperately. "You've got to go! That's all. And if you don't want to go, let me go by myself, okay?"

"I'd rather we went together," said Ruff. "Let me think it over a little. I'll let you know."

Barcella soon went back up to his office and began calling Ruff's closest aides, lobbying with them to point out to Ruff the political advantages of making the appeal to the attorney general.

A reporter from *The Washington Post* looked into Barcella's office during his lobbying campaign and said, "I hear the solicitor general has decided not to appeal the Letelier case to the Supreme Court."

Horrified, Barcella pleaded with the reporter not to write the story. "If you write that, you'll be making the news, not reporting it," he said. "We've got a week to try to turn the SG around, but he'll never change his mind once it's out in public!"

Hysterical arguments followed, along with deals, postponements, and a hundred phone calls. That night, the reporter called Barcella to say that the *Post* would run the story the following morning. Barcella moaned. "I don't have any comment," he said. "But tell me one thing, will you? Who told you?"

"Someone in Justice," said the reporter. "And Chuck Ruff."

April 9, 1981

Exactly three years after Michael Townley landed at Baltimore Airport in handcuffs, Judge Barrington Parker freed Alvin Ross and Guillermo Novo on bail, pending the outcome of their new trial.

———

April 22, 1981

Before the last status call for the upcoming trial, defense attorney Paul Goldberger stepped into Barcella's office to make a plea offer. "Both Novo and Ross will plead guilty to conspiracy," he said, "if you agree that they will serve no more time than they've already served. That's the deal, and if you go for it, Novo's offered to throw in a sweetener. He will guarantee to stop all violence by Cuban exiles in the United States. We assume you guys don't mind violence overseas."

"What?" said Barcella. "How can he guarantee that there will be no more violence in the United States? Who does he think he is?"

"Political violence," said Goldberger. "By the Cuban exiles. He says he can do it."

"Even if he could, how do we enforce it?" asked Barcella. "How can I come lock him up just because somebody gets shot in Miami? There's no way we could do that."

———

May 30, 1981

A federal jury acquitted Alvin Ross and Guillermo Novo of all murder charges, while convicting Novo of false declarations before a grand jury.*

"We accept the jury's verdict," Barcella told reporters, but he went home sick and talked of quitting the government.

Propper tried to console Barcella and himself by pointing out that more had been accomplished than anyone had ever expected. The assassination plot had been exposed to the world, he said. Townley was in prison. Contreras was out of power. No more ex-Chilean officials

---

*As Barcella had predicted, the Cuban defendants completely changed their defense at the second trial. They did not try to absolve DINA of responsibility or to blame the murders on the CIA.

Later, in October 1981, Ignacio Novo would plead guilty to a charge of false declarations.

had been assassinated. Novo stood convicted of lying about the murders. The fugitives, Paz and Suárez, could never lead normal lives underground and might someday be caught and tried for their roles in the bombing. Other potential terrorists would see that the United States would not tolerate political murders in the capital.

"But the system didn't work," said Barcella. "Once the crime was solved, nobody wanted to back us up."

Propper struggled to remain optimistic. He was temporarily out of schemes to improve things, but he predicted that justice would claim more.

INDEX